Love At Bramley Hall

Boxed Set + Bonus Content

Michelle Helen Fritz, E.A. Shanniak

Clear Spring Books LLC

Love At Bramley Hall: Regency Romance Boxed Set by Michelle Helen Fritz

Co-Written with: E.A. Shanniak

Copyright © 2021 Michelle Helen Fritz

All rights reserved.

Cover Design: Wanderlust Ink & Tome LLC

Chapter Heading Art: Samaiya Art

Developmental/Line Editing: Tiffany P.

Proofreading: Megan O. & Cathey N.

Formatting: E.A. Shanniak

Published by Clear Spring Books LLC of Clear Spring, MD

Contents

Love At Rescue

"Good Heavens, sir!" Miss Purcellville exclaimed.

The crowd gasped and threw curious gazes toward the frightening scene that had just occurred. Simon felt heat creep into his cheeks at the unwanted attention. It took him a few moments to untangle their limbs from the lady's cloak. Upon gaining his feet, Simon bent down, helping the beautiful, yet unsettled woman, rise to her feet.

The lady glared at him, holding a crumpled letter in her hands. He paused mid-motion wondering if he should help dust her off or if it would add to their precarious moment. The woman blinked at him, trying to fix her bonnet and auburn ringlets that were in disarray. Her reticule was discarded in the grass near her slippered feet. Simon bent down to retrieve it and offered it back to its owner.

"Are you all right?" he inquired softly.

Simon took a step away for propriety's sake, admiring the pink hue in her cheeks and the curls of her auburn hair peeking out from beneath her bonnet. Long dark lashes batted angrily at him. He spied the pout of her full lips and the chocolate color of her eyes, which were flecked with hints of gold under the glare.

The lady was nearly trampled by a runaway horse and carriage. She was so absorbed in her letter, she didn't hear the bellowing of the carriage driver nor the frightened shrieks of passersby dashing to the side of the road for safety. Forgoing all civility, he dashed to secure her life; only to land on the manicured city garden, becoming covered in stains and flower petals. Unfortunately, by saving her, it put them in quite the scandalous predicament.

"I say, Mr. Morten, thank you for saving my daughter's life," Lord Purcellville boomed, breathing heavily as he came to his daughter's aid. "Dearest Alicia, my sweet girl, are you all right?"

"Yes, Papa," Miss Purcellville replied, removing the glower from her brow. "What was all the fuss over?"

"Do you not recall?"

Miss Purcellville shook her head. "No, I do not. I was completely absorbed in my letter."

Lord Purcellville turned, motioning to the soldier before them. "Mr. Morten saved your life."

Miss Purcellville's cream-colored face paled slightly. She immediately dipped her head and went into a curtsy. Simon bowed in return, feeling the heat return to his cheeks. He was not some green lad, yet he found he could not help but to degenerate within her presence. It was most unmanning and his natural confidence was waning. Miss Purcellville was a magnificent creature with a voice that could put the angels of the heavens to shame.

"Thank you, Mr. Morten, I am forever grateful," she said.

The softness in her voice coupled with the sparkle in her eyes left him entirely speechless. How could he begin to formulate a response when a goddess stood before him?

Simon shook his head and softly cleared his throat. "The pleasure is all mine, I assure you."

Lord Purcellville grasped his daughter's hand, folding it into the crook of his arm. "Simon, could you please accompany me back into my study? There is something which we need to discuss."

"Yes, Lord Purcellville," Simon replied with a bow.

Simon followed in step, slightly behind the lord and his daughter. He swallowed, wondering if he was going to be reprimanded and be given duties for disobedience. Simon pulled at the collar around his neck, watching his booted feet and the ground pass him by.

Glancing up, the marble columns of the Purcellville estate greeted his gaze. Potted plants with evergreen shrubs mingling with golden flowers were placed on either side of the columns, adding elegance and a cozy, welcoming feeling. The butler opened the double polished oaken doors for Miss Purcellville and she entered, calling for her beloved mama.

"Simon," Lord Purcellville called from the cusp of the entryway, "please follow me to the study."

Simon nodded his understanding, feeling this throat become parched at the cold air surrounding him. He followed the distinguished lord into his study. Lord Purcellville took his seat and motioned for Simon to take his. His blood ran hot under his skin, wondering at what kind of reprimand he would receive. Lord Purcellville was an excellent yet strict commander of the King's Armies. To make the situation more precarious, the way he had tumbled in his plight to save the woman made it look to the ton a bit more than just saving a damsel in distress. He wondered briefly if this would be an act of chivalry gone terribly wrong.

"Thank you again, Simon, for saving my daughter's life," Lord Purcellville stated as he leaned back in his desk chair.

Simon forced his hands to stay in his lap instead of rubbing the clammy nerves off on his pressed regiment-issued pants. "'Tis an honor I shall cherish forever."

The man nodded, a grin creeping across his face. Simon slowly closed his eyes, wondering what he would have to do. Certainly mucking stalls or shining boots was a fitting punishment? Surely this good deed wouldn't land him in disbandment from the regiment, dishonoring his family name?

"In appreciation, I would like to bestow you with my finest hunting hound, what say you?" inquired his lordship.

Shocked, Simon replied, "Excuse me, could you repeat that, sir?"

"Of course, if you would rather, you may have my daughter's hand in marriage. Alicia is beautiful, is she not?"

Simon nodded. "Absolutely breathtaking." Simon swallowed. Was this great man jesting with him? The strict face of Lord Purcellville crumbled slightly at the corner of his lips. Simon felt a bead of sweat trickle down his back.

"I have a proposition for you, Mr. Morten," the lord began, leaning back in his chair. "My daughter is quite smitten with you. So, you can either court my daughter or have my finest hound."

Simon blinked, finding himself stuttering for words.

"Your answer, my boy," Lord Purcellville prompted.

"I would be honored to court your daughter as I have no need for a hound."

Love Flames Anew

Before Love At Last Begins...

Tiny winged pixies with pitchforks were stabbing Harrison repeatedly in his eyes and all along his brain. The incessant drumming of his heartbeat in his ears made him nauseous. He groaned in dismay and nearly fell from his leather-backed chair at the sound as it engulfed his entire head in flame. *Nay, 'twas not pixies tormenting me, but little demons with pointy teeth. If only they would tear into my heart and rip it from my body, then mayhap true peace could be found.*

Ever so carefully, Harrison turned his head to the side. From the dark drapes covering his study's windows, the rays of sunlight were attempting to invade his sanctuary. He cringed. *What day is it?*

Harrison reached for the leather-bound diary resting atop his desk at the tips of his long-tapered fingers. Picking up the distasteful book, he opened it and leaned back into his chair. From the embers clinging to the ashes within the fireplace came a soft glow that lit the room. Harrison angled the little book so his eyes could make out his last entry.

Date... I have no conceivable idea.

What a waste this stupid thing is. Why Edmund is so set against me discarding this useless tome is beyond me. Nothing of substance is contained within. I find the idea of keeping an account of my broken heart to be very tiring. For the record, Edmund, I should fire you for your impertinence, but I lack the fortitude to do so. Do not be overly surprised when the day dawns that I chuck this useless thing from the window or mayhap the fireplace would suit as a better resting place.

Harrison ran a hand down his face and his fingers tangled in his beard. Beard? When had that gotten there? His eyes felt gritty and bloodshot and for a moment he wondered when he had last bathed and groomed. Shrugging his shoulders, he reasoned that it didn't signify whatsoever. He had no one to be presentable for. He was the master of this tomb in which he dwelled, and he was all alone. Mr. Lyons, his steward, had been tending to the tenants and his butler was seeing that the staff was being paid. All his responsibilities were being attended to, his presence within the world truly didn't matter. *I could die right here and now, and nothing in this world would change so drastically that it would much matter.*

Staring off into the dying embers, Harrison let his mind wander to kissable lips and golden hair. Hazel had become his favorite color and his ruination. *Where had I blundered,* he wondered for the millionth time. *I paid calls upon her, I took her for rides, I showered the lady with praise and attention, and still... I came up short. I must have done something woeful, said something distasteful, or mayhap it is all of my miserable self-combined; because my failings had me passed by for Michaelton, whom I considered to be my friend. How has this happened? Jilted and left all alone. I am ever left alone.*

The study door opened and in sauntered his valet, Edmund. "Good afternoon, my lord! The birds are singing, and the sky is such a beautiful sight this day." Edmund made his way further into the room and drew the drapes to the sides of the windows as Harrison once again groaned.

"I *should terminate you!*" he bellowed, then winced as the pain flared within his head. *Seems as if the pixies are content tenants.*

"Tsk. Then you would have to miss me, too. We can't have that happen. 'Tis time to begin your day. Shall I ring for tea and breakfast?" Edmund strode to the massive mahogany desk and reached for the waste bin. He began to gather crumpled papers and empty bottles of spirits to discard.

"That one is not yet empty!" Harrison leaned forward and grabbed the brandy from his valet with a sneer marring his handsome face.

"There's not but a drop or two within," scolded Edmund.

"Every drop is a balm to my soul."

"*Every drop is a nail in your coffin,*" muttered Edmund, shaking his head at his employer. He walked to the study door and opened it, placed the waste bin outside of the door, and closed it again. "It reeks in here. We need to air out this room and, I daresay, you as well. You cannot continue along in this manner, my lord. What would your esteemed parents say to all of this?"

"You can have no idea what they would say, you never met them," deadpanned Harrison.

"That matters not. I have heard tales and your confidences. As your friend, I beseech you to turn your thoughts beyond this bitter betrayal."

"How am I meant to set this behind me? I loved her! I love her still, and I shall never have her!" Harrison rubbed his chest and ran his tongue over his teeth. There was an unpleasant taste lingering and he gagged.

Edmund's eyes grew large, and he dashed to a corner table where a porcelain vase rested. He quickly brought it over for his lordship. When his master stopped heaving into the antique family heirloom, Edmund set it outside of the study alongside the waste bin. "Today is a brand new day, my lord. You can begin anew."

"To what purpose? I have no one, Edmund. I am alone in this world and fear I always shall be."

"What a load of rubbish! You have your staff, your tenants, and you have the Mortens. Simon has paid a call every day this week and you have turned him away each time. Yet, he is loyal to you. You have your entire life ahead of you and you are wasting it. You could be doing so much good and yet you are content to rot within this chamber day in and day out. And where are your nights spent? In that same chair! By goodness, I shall not stand by and aid you any longer! You want to molder in that chair, so be it, but I won't stand by and witness this descent for a moment longer." Edmund strode for the study door with his face a mask of outrage.

Harrison wanted to care. He wanted to rise and see to his affairs, but he just wasn't capable of such a feat. His body was weary, and his mind was tired. Sleep eluded him, and those few nights that he fell into slumber were fitful and plagued by nightmares. He had relied on the brandy to douse his thoughts and calm his mind, for only when he was truly in his cups, could he find peace. "Wait, please," he tentatively called out.

Edmund stopped with his hand on the door but didn't turn around.

"Have the London papers arrived yet?" Harrison inquired with hesitancy as if he were attempting to find words to say.

"They have."

"I do not believe my eyes at present will allow me to focus upon the words. Would you read it to me?"

Edmund turned around slowly and raised his brows. "If you recall, I tried to read to you the day before and you demanded I take my leave. I'll be glad to read to you, if you can be civil."

Harrison hung his head and felt horrid. Had he not rescued his valet at university from abuse? *And here I am bellowing at him and mistreating him.* "Forgive me, my friend, I never meant to behave so appallingly."

"I can forgive you anything, my lord, except the ruining of yourself. That I shall no longer accept." Edmund crossed his arms, his stance rigid. His eyes seemed to be focused intently upon the floor under his boots.

"First the paper and perhaps a bath and a shave?" Harrison attempted to sound chipper, but he couldn't keep the glower from his features.

"Very good. I shall ask for some eggs since you haven't consumed anything edible in days." Edmund promptly opened the door and left Harrison to his thoughts.

It had not been easy, this reclaiming of his life and purpose, but he was at least trying. He was reading the newsprint himself and eating what was put before him. He was still drinking here and there, but not to excess. He was riddled with shaking and nausea if he didn't sip from the spirits here and there throughout his day. Harrison was making himself do all manner of things, even though the nightmares persisted. He was far from ready to be entertaining or to be out amongst society, but he was attempting to be a better man, not such a ghost of his former self.

Edmund crept into the study and in his wake trailed Simon. Harrison narrowed his eyes at his valet, who pretended to ignore his irritation as he quickly quit the study. Simon entered further into the room and blinked his eyes. The lighting was dim as Harrison was still in the habit of shying away from the sunlight. The horrid sunbeams beckoned his notice and bid him to venture to the out of doors where life was rife.

Harrison was upset with Edmund for placing him in the position to play host and so he sat as still as a statue. Cold and unmoving. Harrison watched as Simon propped himself into the leather chair before his desk. His friend rested one booted foot upon his knee and jiggled it every so often. For a half hour, they remained locked in the oppressive silence of the room.

When Simon could take no more, he hastily said, "Look here, chap: it can't be *that* bad."

And looking at his young friend who was staring at him with such an honest and open look, Harrison spoke.

"I'd been in Town and met a lady. I believed she was attached to me and courted her with the express purpose of making her my countess. She accepted my pursuit and my gifts. I even traveled back here to fetch mama's ring to make her mine, to give her a token of my affection when I took to bended knee. When I returned to her parent's townhouse, Michaelton was there. He beat me to it. She was all smiles and simpering and he was boastfully proud of his coup of stealing her away. I was dumbstruck there in the sitting room, attempting to offer congratulations and keep my wounded heart from bleeding all of its pieces upon the carpet before the pair. When I was finally able to make my departure, Samantha followed me to the foyer and confessed that she hoped I was not too *upset*. She tittered and remarked that it wasn't as if we were in love. And blast my stupid tongue, for I told her that for me, every moment, every stolen kiss, every lingering caress had meant a great deal." Harrison took a breath and reached for the decanter of brandy. He poured a fingerful and drank it down, savoring the burn. He wished it could burn the words from his mind and the haunting memories from his heart.

Simon sat forward and balked, "Good God, man! The harpy! You are much better off knowing her true character now. The devil take her and Michaelton!" He reached for the brandy decanter and stood. He made his way to the liquor cart and selected a glass. He poured himself a decent amount of the amber liquid and set the decanter back down onto the cart. Then he took a sip and reclaimed his seat.

"Do you know how she greeted my confession?" Harrison quirked a dark brow.

"I am afraid to ask." Simon shook his head.

"She looked at me and replied, 'I do not want *you*! I want what Lord Michaelton can give me! I never wanted *you*! Why, the idea is ridiculous!' She found my feelings so merry that she laughed." Harrison could always count on Simon to take up his cause and share in any joy or indignation. Simon did not disappoint.

"A pox upon her and her entire house! And Lord Michaelton's! May she plague his heart out! Honestly old chap, you dodged a bullet. Who needs women? They are such a nuisance, except for my sister but she does not signify." Simon waved a hand in the air.

Harrison nodded. He both admired and esteemed Simon's sister. They had all been playmates and Harrison, being an only child, delighted in their companionship. The oldest Morten sibling was away with seminary studies, but Matthew had been great fun too. Many of his most cherished memories had been created with the Morten family at its center. And when his loving parents had been unexpectedly taken from him, 'twas Mr. Morten, the parson, who had consoled him and offered him aid and guidance until his uncle could be by his side. *I have been remiss in my sequestering away from them. When they have lifted me and carried me through time and again from despair. What must the youngest of the family think about my poor behavior? And yet... My heart must mourn... Am I to never know joy again? Happiness?*

"She misses you, you know. She all but begged me to bring her along today. Mariah is growing into quite the beauty, and I fear for the hearts of all the local country lads."

"But she would never stoop so low as to break any of their hearts. She certainly wouldn't find entertainment in such a thing." Harrison took another swig from his tumbler.

"Right you are! So, we shall only consign the lady who duped you to Hades. 'Tis time to seek greener pastures, my friend. You must be out and amongst society. There are other ladies who are worth your notice. Let all thoughts of the silly chit flee from your mind. She did not deserve you."

Harrison felt a smile overtake his face. At first it was hesitant, and then it morphed into something more. How long had it been since a sincere smile had formed upon his features? His mood was lightening within Simon's presence. How was it that a visit from an old friend could so alter his mood? Simon could be cavalier in his manners and bordered on the fringe of impolite in certain situations, but his heart always meant well. Harrison was blessed to know him.

The two men were content within each other's company, that they didn't exchange many more words thereafter.

When Simon rose to take his leave, Harrison felt sorrow to see him go.

"I am sorry to see you depart. But I shan't be demanding and require you to stay. But mayhap if you have the time, you would consider returning?" Harrison kept his gaze solidly upon the desk before him. He didn't wish to ascertain what his friend thought of his request, he only desired the knowledge that his friend would be returning.

Before Simon could take another step, he replied, "I give you my word, that I shall come again." He inclined his head toward him.

Simon's declaration did much good to Harrison's mending heart. *True friends are what keeps one going when all seems lost.*

Harrison had spent another sleepless night and his humors were foul. He didn't want company and told Edmund to turn Simon away if he paid a call. His mood was darkening again with feelings of self-doubt and loathing. The words of his parents within his nightmares and their faux disappointment with him stalked him at all hours. No matter how he tried to reason and rationalize their harsh accusations away, they refused to leave him be. He felt their disapproval clean to his soul, no matter that it was all in his mind.

In life, his parents had been warm and loving, not the ghouls who unrelentingly haunted him. They had nurtured him and encouraged him in all he undertook. This unrelenting assault upon him stole the warmth and love that his memories usually granted to him.

With Edmund by his side, he had spent the last few days tackling the mountain of correspondence that accumulated. Slowly, order was being restored to his life. He was thankful that in this at least, he was excelling.

A week had not yet passed by when Billingsley, his butler, walked in and announced that Simon had come to pay a call and was accompanied by his sister. Dread filled his being at the thought of such a bright light as Mariah witnessing his current failed state. He at least looked like the lord of the manor now that he was allowing Edmund to dress and groom him again. Truth be told, he felt immensely better being presentable. His state of disarray and surly attitude had frightened more than one maid. But still, still, he was not the man that he had once been, and he doubted that he could ever be such a cavalier young man again. His makeup had forever been altered.

Harrison took a deep breath and nodded his assent to Billingsley to allow his guests entrance. He should have risen and greeted his guests in the drawing room, but he hoped they would soon take their leave. *No need to be too welcoming...*

Simon entered the study first, followed by Mariah. The man had not overstated his sister's blossoming. Her form had much altered since last they met. *Time marches onward. She is stunning.*

Mariah was now graced with a womanly figure and, while she had always been a beauty, he was knocked for a loop. He would happily plant a facer to any pup who dared look her way. Reigning himself in, he reasoned he felt the surge of protectiveness toward her as he had long ago served as her hero in their childhood antics. *I am nothing more than another of her brothers...*

He quickly gained his feet and closed the distance between himself and his guests. He halted before the siblings and bowed at his waist: Simon bowed in return while Mariah executed a perfect curtsy.

Clearing his throat which had gone mysteriously dry, Harrison spoke, "I trust that you are well?" This statement was directed to the lovely woman as he motioned toward the pair of wingback chairs near the fireplace.

"I have been in excellent health, my lord," she said with a blush infusing her lovely complexion.

Harrison discovered that he had no desire to venture far from her side, which wasn't horribly curious as he had always enjoyed her company... But now, he found that he could not break his gaze away from her own intense stare. *What is this bemusement lingering between us?*

Billingsley re-entered the room and brought in the tea service, which broke the spell betwixt them. Harrison blinked his eyes as Mariah immediately made her way over to the side table and began to prepare tea for the gentlemen. She remained silent as she served the tea but gave Harrison a brilliant smile that did odd things to his heart. Mariah never needed to be told more than once what was one's preferred way to take their tea, she was such an exceptional hostess. When he had his tea in hand, he watched her softly pad over to the tray and lift a small basket. She returned to his side and pulled aside the covering, showing the contents to him.

"I made these this morning, especially for you, my lord. I do hope lemon is still a favorite of yours." Mariah retrieved a biscuit and gingerly held it out to him.

Harrison took the treat and cast her a small grin. "Still a favorite. Thank you for the trouble you undertook." His heart was acting very bizarrely, and he found this interaction was unsettling him in ways he could not name. *By Jove! What is the matter with me?*

Waving her hand in the air she replied, "What trouble? I enjoyed thinking that perhaps my small gift would brighten your day." Then she turned back to the silver tray and picked up her own teacup and saucer.

Simon strode to the drapes and pulled them open with a triumphant, "Huzzah! Now we may pay a proper visit and expel this doom and gloom." Then he took his refreshments to his seat in one of the armchairs before the desk.

Harrison could not spare one word for his friend. His gaze was locked upon Mariah who had taken a seat in the direct sunlight. Her brunette hair was gleaming in the light and her sapphire eyes shone with pleasure. *She still delights in the rays of the sun. And how lovely she is. So like an angel of heaven that has been delivered into that very chair. Why, she is ethereal, otherworldly... A goddess. But she is a sister to you, old boy. Best to cease these errant thoughts at once. But I'm not making my pulse race, no, that is her, and her alone. And just from the sight of her. Surely, she could never see me as more than just a friend. Lord, is this your prompting? Are you in the midst of working your wonders? Though she is young, she will not always be so. Whether or not you have set her in my path, I shall guard her from afar if I must. It shall be my duty and honor to ensure that she never knows the heartbreak that I have clung to for much too long. I cannot bear to see her suffer, not when I may act as a buffer.*

The lady was speaking to him, and he had not heard one word. He cleared his throat, again. "It seems I was woolgathering. What were you saying?"

She beamed at him and said, "I was wondering if you would dine with us tomorrow or perchance, the day after?"

His brows furrowed. He would have to venture out and leave the safety of his estate to do so. While he was unlikely to meet any gossips of the ton, he was hesitant. But when he did not give his acceptance of the invitation within a few moments, he watched her face clear of mirth. She looked at Simon and frowned.

"I would be delighted to join you," he quickly answered. He waited for a sourness to squeeze his insides, but none came. He felt content in his resolve to her well-being and happiness.

"How wonderful! Mama shall be overjoyed. We have all missed you." Her smile was back in place, though she would not meet his eyes. *Does she feel this thing that is lingering between us?*

From now on, he would stop wallowing in his sorrow and be the man God intended. This visit with his childhood friends was a resounding call to find good, to seek out the light, even in his darkest hours. He would endeavor to be a good steward to his tenants and servants, and a better friend to those who welcomed his presence. The Morten family had long taken him under their wings, and he was happy to bask in their warmth in whichever manner he may. If something ever came from this feeling stirring within him toward Mariah, he would rejoice. And if he had to let her go, then so be it. He had always held great affection for her, only now, he wondered if it was morphing into something more. Was he fickle to move on from thoughts of Samantha to Mariah? What did that say about his character? Was it fickleness that was his greatest downfall? Perhaps an attack of pride? His feelings were so complicated. The two women could not be more different. But how was he to ignore the stirrings of his heart when he had thought that the useless organ was never to beat for another? These budding feelings were awakening pieces of himself that his time with Samantha had never touched. It was certainly a quandary, something to ruminate upon at a later date, within the presence of only himself. For now, he would allow God to lead his steps on the path that He desired him to walk and discover the answers as they presented themselves.

"I am sorry to be remiss in my duties upon the family of Morten," he teased. He was feeling as light as a feather.

"I suppose, just this once, you may be forgiven," she allowed with a delightful tease coloring her tone.

Harrison bowed his head at her. "I thank you for your many kindnesses."

He realized that Simon was poking about at his bookshelves and the sight was curious to him. When had Simon ever willingly perused books? Still, he felt grateful that his friend was allowing this playful turn of the conversation. If he could suss out what her feelings were for him, he would know how to proceed. Perhaps there was hope for him after all. Something more to rejoice in. Mayhap this ending of one love could lead him to the grandest of all loves. One that would last. He would wait and bide his time. He would treat the lady with the respect and kindness that she deserved and perchance, in time, his heart would heal. Any favor, any task he could see to for her would be readily undertaken. He would shelter her when she needed, and he would encourage her when she faltered. He would treasure every encounter and see if things would evolve from there. Because no matter what the future held for her, his greatest wish was for a love that lasts. For both of them.

Original Prologue to Love At Last

T he summer sunshine would soon give way to the cool breezes of Autumn in the small town of Bramley. Mariah was enjoying the warmth of the day. She removed her bonnet, but the scolding of her Mama soon had it back in its place.

Mariah rose from the plain brown blanket, which her party was happily spread out upon, and shook out her dress. She had decided to wear her best green day gown as it was one of her favorites. Its floral embroidery and exquisite lace made her feel like a princess. Her cream capped sleeves added a touch of elegance.

Looking toward Bramley Hall, she smiled. She was but one small piece of greenery amidst the rolling hills and vibrant foliage presently on display.

"Where are you off to, Miss Morten?" Inquired the Earl Pembroke as he rose to stand beside her, smiling with his usual good humor and sculpted aristocratic features. His chin had a dip in it that drew the eye to his handsome masculine features.

He was positively breathtaking in his tan buckskins and charcoal colored tailcoat, even his cream-colored cravat was tied to perfection. His ebony hair shone in the sunlight like a raven's wing. He'd set his topper beside him on the blanket, but had not reached for it before he rose.

"For a walk. It's a glorious day to stretch one's limbs and take in the scenic beauty," Mariah answered as she gazed into his teal-colored orbs. It simply was not fair for a gentleman to possess such dark, lustrous eyelashes.

"Capital idea. May I join you?" the Earl inquired with an easy, relaxed smile.

Mariah looked toward her parents and Mama nodded at her.

"I shall enjoy your company." Mariah waited for him to rise.

Harrison groaned as he stood. "I indulged a little too much," he grinned sheepishly. "The pudding was divine."

Mariah grinned, staring down at her slippered feet to hide the blush she felt creep to her cheeks whenever she was around Harrison. "All the better to rise and walk it off."

When they'd walked a fair bit away from their party, Harrison said, "There's no one about to stop you from removing your bonnet at present." He waggled his dark eyebrows at her.

Mariah gave a soft laugh and removed her straw bonnet. She turned her face up to the warm sun and smiled.

"Better?" Harrison asked, unable to remove his eyes from her perfectly shaped face.

Mariah brought her face around to look up at him. "Much. Thank you for the suggestion. "

Harrison inclined his head in acknowledgement. "Will we soon have visitors from Town to call upon you?"

Mariah's brows kissed as she answered, "I have no reason to think so. Whom are you referring to?"

"Why, your score of suitors, of course," he waved his hand about in a circular motion.

"Ohhh," she blushed. "I don't have scores of suitors. I don't even have one," she frowned. "I did have several, then they just seemed to drop off. I've no idea why and Mama was disappointed when we left Town."

"Curious," he stated. Clearing his throat he continued, "I am expected back in Town this week. I'll be away for a fortnight at least, attending to estate business."

"We shall miss your company, greatly." Mariah stopped walking and turned to take in the spectacular view behind her. Bramley Hall rose up in all of its stone glory. The clematis clinging to its walls made for such a beautiful sight, even from afar. She added to its beauty. The sight made his heart swell with unnamed emotions.

Harrison looked upon his home as he joined her side. "And I'll miss you."

Turning to him she asked, "Do you miss our younger days? When we ran and played amongst these towering trees?"

"No, I don't miss them. I rather like being grown and independent." He tugged on a loose brunette curls, twirling his finger in it, then letting it spring back into place.

"Women aren't allowed to seek their independence," she frowned.

"Oh no, will I soon have a bluestocking upon my hands?" Harrison asked with a teasing smile.

"Not quite. I'm simply stating a fact," she shrugged.

"I'd like you anyway you came, Miss Morten. I hope to see Matthew while I'm gone."

"How wonderful! I'm sure he'll be glad of your company. Give him my love, won't you?" Mariah's sapphire eyes were twinkling.

"Certainly. Will you be glad for my company when I return?" Harrison had a thoughtful look upon his face.

Frowning slightly, she answered, "But of course! I don't have one memory you and my brothers haven't influenced. Though they're away. I get to keep you close by." She smiled beautifully up at him.

Smiling Harrison felt his heart clench. Would Mariah's heart ever see him much more than a brotherly figure? He hoped so. He would continue to hold out hope until his very last breath.

Love At Last

Chapter One

Curious News

The September day was clear but cold. A chill made its way down Mariah's spine. She scanned the field before her for signs of people or animals. How she loved riding. When her mount galloped, she felt as if flying was the only freedom she could taste that was of a proper sort for a parson's daughter. Most activities such as dipping her toes into Bramley Lake would cause a rebuke from her mama. How fortunate her neighbor, the Earl of Bramley, allowed her the pleasure of having the use of his stables and property, which were her only means of escaping expectations and reprimands.

Their family horse was needed to convey her father, Mr. Morten, in his daily duties as parson of Bramley. She wouldn't dream of taking the liberty of inquiring whether she could have use of her dear father's horse. Caring for her safety more than his own, her dear papa would happily have her mount up as opposed to his own comfort.

Her father would have gone about visiting the members of his parish on foot if the horse was otherwise engaged. His parish members were happily situated through the town, and traveling without his horse, with many stops, would have taken the entirety of the day. Mariah would not ask such a thing of her father. She was blessed to have him still with her as he had suffered a cardiac episode a few months prior. The episode had affected his sense of balance, so riding atop a horse was quite impossible. Her father mainly traveled by means of horse and pony cart. Therefore, her presence in the stables and fields of Bramley Hall was an ever-fixed engagement, if she desired to continue to traverse the countryside while on horseback.

Taking a deep breath after her gallop, she found herself direct-ly in front of Bramley Hall—the great house the Earls of Bramley had long held in their possession. The story behind Bramley Hall was rather mysterious, and Mariah never knew fact from fiction, as the rumors residing within those grand stone walls were ever changing with wagging tongues.

She smiled, tilting her head to the side as she gazed affec-tionately at the manor. She recalled a tidbit of news that the first Earl of Bramley title came into their family line because, a many great-grandfathers ago, he had completed a most unusual and secret mission for the King. This mission was superbly completed, pleasing the king so well that, ever since, Bramley had been a shining jewel in their family lineage.

Mariah sighed, *Oh, to reside within those high walls!* But of course, silly Mariah would never know the joy of calling such an estate her own. For that privilege would only belong to the next Countess of Bramley, and she was sure whoever she was would be some grand lady indeed. There were few of the fairer sex that the current Earl took interest in that deserved such a husband and glorious home.

There were rumors that some years ago the current Earl was enamored with one such lady, but alas, as these affairs of the heart unfolded, his lady was neither his nor of the mind to give up the pleasures of the society of the ton. She enjoyed being admired and was not ready to choose whom she would wed. Though it was years ago, the chit had gone and wed a most notorious rake. How foolish of her to choose such a man over Harrison.

Mariah shook her head at her musings. She steered her horse at a leisurely canter across another expanse of the Bramley estate, keeping an ever-present eye on the manor. She smiled at the thought of a certain Earl being inside the mansion home, wondering on how he was faring.

I do so desire him to find happiness in this life, she thought.

Harrison was one of the best men Mariah believed she would ever know. Their families had been neighbors and friends all of her life. Harrison's parents had passed away in a tragic carriage accident when he was only five and ten. Such a young age to inherit the responsibilities of an Earlship. Fortunately, his father had a younger brother, who, though he had a family of his own, came and stayed to help Harrison manage the family holdings, which were rumored to be quite extensive.

In no time at all, and with the appointment of an estate manager, Harrison was free to attend university and travel the continents. His parents never employed the use of a private tutor due to their progressive views. Harrison had no need to worry about the estate, as Mr. Lyons was a most excellent man in faith and morality and never neglected the care of the estate. The crops grew abundantly under his watchful gaze, and any repairs the villagers needed for their homes were promptly attended to. Mr. Lyons was surely the best estate manager Bramley Hall had ever known. The whole town prospered because of his exceptional management.

Mariah turned her mount into an open field, galloping the same path she had every day since being allowed on the estate. She smiled at the wanton freedom of the wind rushing through her pinned locks; her riding bonnet had been quickly untied, and its ribbons dangled firmly from one hand. Her mount turned, giving her another view of Bramley Hall—undoubtedly her most favorite, with the manicured garden and clematis archways leading to a gurgling fountain in the middle.

She spied Harrison out walking in the garden, hands clasped behind his back. His long mop of ebony hair fell forward into his face. A servant walked behind him some ways, nodding at orders only to directly scurry off. Harrison had lately been in Town, and his arrival back in Bramley was a surprise.

Mariah's lip curved upward. Mariah was born when Harrison was just six years of age. With no siblings of his own and his father being a great man of faith, the Morten family were often in attendance upon their neighbors at Bramley Hall. Harrison was always in Mariah's most cherished memories since he was so often with her. She took her first steps within the walls of Bramley Hall. She and Harrison told their secrets to each other and were always engaged in games during their childhood adventures. Even after the tragic news came to the parish of the deaths of Harrison's parents, he was the one to offer Mariah comfort as her heart broke. It was through her tears for him that she learned just how strong he truly was. She had shed a few tears over the short course of her life, but none had ever flowed with pain for another as they did in the days after that tragic accident.

Sighing, she turned her mount toward the stables. Her eyes gazed across the estate, landing on an old gnarled oak tree. She smiled tenderly at the tree, her mind reminiscent of times past.

Mariah was the third child of Winston and Amanda Morten. Their first child was a son which greatly pleased both her parents. They bestowed upon him the name of Matthew. Two years following Matthew came another son, Simon, and three years following Simon, the little family was blessed with her.

While it delighted Harrison to enjoy the boyish activities of the brothers, he was certain to include Mariah in their play. When their adventures included climbing trees or fishing, Mariah was always morose to have to miss out. But it was never long before Harrison left the brothers to their mischievous activities and joined her. He was always happy to sit and sip tea with her or read a story. He was even the best of brothers to her dolly. They told jokes together, told tall tales, and shared their many ambitions. It was a wonderful time of childhood joy.

One thing is certain: one grows up, she mused. Nothing stops childhood play more than maturing and accepting one's role in society. One day, Mariah's oldest brother, Matthew, went away to continue his seminary studies. A few months after his departure, the awful carriage accident took place which robbed Harrison of his beloved parents, and soon after, the childhood games and amusements came to an abrupt end. There were ever growing responsibilities for the new Earl of Bramley.

Mariah watched from afar as Harrison became a man, leaving behind all childish things. She got left behind too, in a sense, but she knew this was how the world worked. Harrison was hers no longer. He was "my lord" or the Earl of Bramley. She was no longer Mariah but Miss Morten. Now, when they met, it was with smiles of remembrance and a shared amiable friendship.

She smiled wanly to herself. *At a dinner party last spring, he offered me use of the stables, and we shared a near hour in deep conversation.* She glanced over her right shoulder, watching him stride back inside the manor. Her heart soared with his continued goodwill and camaraderie, showing he had not forgotten about her after all.

Her horse whickered, tossing its mighty head. Mariah spied a deer running through the woods. She despised hunting and was hoping the poor deer would escape to safety. She understood well the importance of having a meal upon the table. She just didn't care to witness the process of beautiful deer being cooked into venison pie. Mariah bore a sensitive nature but also comprised practicality. One needed to eat, and hunting was a part of the process. If only one could live without the harm of another.

Reaching the stables, the lean form of the head groom, Toby, approached her. He waited for Mariah to dismount and offered her a kind smile. Mariah reached up to adjust her riding bonnet, which she had redonned, to make sure none of her brunette curls had escaped its many pins. Feeling all was well, she smiled in return.

"How was your ride, Miss Morten?" Toby inquired with a soft voice.

He was a man of four and forty with silver gray hair. Every careful movement he made showed the years of the position he held with expert care. All the servants the Earl employed were of utmost skill, diligence, and intelligence in their post. A lady need never worry when encountered by a member of the Earl's household.

"It was fabulous, Toby," Mariah replied. "It started out as such dreary gloom, and it seemed as if a great battle raged between the sun and the clouds, but the sun—oh, the sun—it came shining through like a conquering lion! A very excellent morning's ride." Mariah's sapphire eyes twinkled with amusement.

Toby smiled and shook his head. "Ah, Miss Morten, you have indeed been kissed by the fairies to sprout such a tale! Lion indeed. I'd be happy to tell you that his Lordship would indeed be quite the lion if he knew you rode without a groom. His roar is one you'd not soon forget! Plus, he'd make my position here most miserable if I didn't send Tom with you the next time you go out." He replied, his kind brown eyes becoming pinched.

"His Lordship a lion? *Pfft*. I have never encountered his roar. If it is indeed a quality he possesses, I've never known it." Mariah straightened her brown riding habit. She could not dispel the amusement from her countenance.

"You may not have seen it yourself from his Lordship, but I have it on very good authority that your papa would not approve, and neither would your mama. Please take Tom in the future. Had I been here, he would have accompanied you, Miss." Toby waggled his index finger toward Mariah and frowned. Since she liked Toby immensely, no offense was taken from his lecture.

"Yes, sir." Mariah nodded her head as a petulant child would. "I shall endeavor to do better in the future." She turned to walk away and heard a quiet harrumph, making her secret smile increase.

As Mariah walked back toward home, she thought again about the upcoming season. Here she was, at nine and ten, and headed toward spinsterhood. True, she had only celebrated one season and the little season, but here she was, unwed. She did not have an immense fortune. Her mother's brother had willed her a modest dowry since the poor man sired no children of his own. Still, her dowry was enough to draw the attention of the young bucks. Though valiantly they tried, none had yet claimed her affection to win her hand.

And dare I say I compare them all to his Lordship, she thought with a soft smile.

Mariah was quite a beauty, or so her mama assured her. Men stared at her and smiled, but it was as if they knew she was the daughter of a parson. Possessing a fortune makes the world spin, and those who had it could partake in the very great luxury of choosing whom to love. Mariah was not holding out for a love match, just someone she could see herself spending a long time with. Truth be told, she would be the happiest of wives ever if only the love she witnessed between the late earl and his countess could one day be hers.

Mariah glanced over her shoulder and sighed, *I hope Harrison, or rather his Lordship, finds a suitable match. After so much tragedy in his life, he deserves the brilliance of happiness. I hope such a woman exists to bring merriment to Bramley Hall, its residents, and Harrison.* She turned back around to leave, a guarded, soft smile upon her face.

Mariah walked briskly back to her humble home. She stood on the front landing a moment, ensuring her ensemble and hair were correct so her mother wouldn't make a terrible fuss. Satisfied with her quick critique, she padded into the parsonage parlor. It was a cozy room filled with cushions and figurines. Her mother loved being surrounded by pretty things possessing bright color. Currently, Mrs. Morten was bent over a letter and did not seem to hear Mariah enter the room.

Wondering whether she should interrupt her mother's focused attention, Mariah softly said, "Mama, I have returned."

Her mother looked up at her, blinking. "Oh, darling. There you are at last! I hold here in my hands a most surprising letter, penned by my dearest, youngest son. He states he has taken a wife. A wife, and all without our having met her! Can you conceive of the idea? I know marriages take place all the time without parental consent, but this seems so hastily arranged.

"Oh, I do hope it was all innocently conceived. Your father will be very surprised at this. I myself have been sitting here this hour past rereading such content until I am sure I do not know my own thoughts any longer. I have gone through disbelief, shock, anxiety, and now, well—now, I am all consternation. I do not know what we shall do until we are to meet her. For your brother will be here any day to present her," Mrs. Morten said hastily, waving her handkerchief back and forth, her hazel eyes shining.

Not very sure how to arrange her own thoughts on this news, Mariah began with, "Dear Mama. Shocking indeed! How has this come to be? He would not, I feel sure, be introducing us to his new wife if she was not delightful. I'm sure there was a reason behind the hasty match, but let us reserve our concern until after we have become acquainted. You are the very example of Christian generosity, and to think any ill of the proceedings would not do either of them, nor indeed yourself, any good at all," she finished, joining Mrs. Morten upon the small settee.

"I am sure you are right. I know you are right. Mothers never have the ear of their sons. Sons grow and are gone about their adventures much too quickly. They wed where they may and have not a care for a mother's poor nerves. You, my sweet girl, would not behave in such a manner. I take great comfort in knowing you, and your sweet demeanor lightens my heart. We will wait calmly, if possible. Come with me to announce the news to your poor papa," Mrs. Morten requested, standing up and holding out her hand to Mariah.

Mrs. Morten's figure was neither rotund nor slight. She was usually the very vision of health, even though she was touched by age around her firm mouth and large expressive eyes. From time to time, however, she suffered from feelings of maladies and anxiety, and both Mariah and her papa tried their best to help quell those happenings. Their home was never happy nor peaceful when Mrs. Morten was in a dire state, for she was the heart of their family.

The pair briskly walked to the study where Papa was amidst writing Sunday's sermon. Dear Mr. Morten was bent over his desk with a quill in his left hand and his chin resting upon his right fist. His hair was gray and slicked back yet slightly frazzling on the ends. The worries of his parish had long ago turned his hair a most gentlemanly gray. If he had possessed less heart of feeling, he may not have grayed so young, but he was a very remarkable man. Never selfish, always seeking whom he might be of service to, he was the very heart of Bramley.

"Dear Mr. Morten, I do so wish to not disturb you, but I fear it must be attempted if you can spare the time." Mrs. Morten stepped before the desk of her husband, still clutching Mariah's hand.

Mariah stood beside her mother as they both waited patiently for Mr. Morten to finish his thought and look up at them. The brilliant sun was shining across the floor rug, and little bits of dust were floating along the room. Mariah looked to the portrait of the ship being tossed upon the sea that hung on the wall to her left. This painting always made her fearful of sea travel, but her papa said it was a testament to the Lord's protection—that even in the midst of the storm, God still held them within His hands.

Mariah glanced about the room. The bookcases were lined with all the books in their home in this smallish room. Her papa encouraged her to pick out a tome and plumb its depths whenever she entered. Mariah smiled affectionately at the memories of afternoons spent in this room, nose deep within pages and her and Papa discussing the meaning of the book and its significance. She clasped her hands in front of her, turning her smile upon her father.

It took a moment, but Mr. Morten put his quill down and straightened in his leather chair. "My dear Mrs. Morten, to what do I owe the pleasure of your presence? Hello, Mariah. How was your ride? Did you find the land as it should be? Everything right in our little piece of the world?" he smiled warmly at the pair.

Mariah looked at her mother, who nodded her consent to answer her father. "Yes, Papa. Everything was as it should be. "

"Excellent. Now, Mrs. Morten, what is it you are so expectant for me to hear?" Mr. Morten was a gentleman, but he did delight in teasing his wife.

Mrs. Morten turned an excellent shade of pink when she was aggravated, and it clearly marked the exasperation upon her lovely face. Mariah glanced between her parents, noticing the loving twinkle in her father's eyes as he beheld his wife and her mother's slight smirk on her pursed lips. Mariah's heart clenched, wondering if she too was worthy enough to merit such a loving relationship as well and, if so, would it be so enduring, like her parents', with loving longevity.

Mrs. Morten took several steps forward, exposing her son's recent letter. "My dear Mr. Morten, I have in my possession a letter from your youngest son Simon, and 'tis very newsy indeed." She stopped to see what he would say, frowning instead of smiling.

"Indeed, Mrs. Morten? Well, we all like news. Do go on, my dear." Mr. Morten steepled his fingers and nodded.

"Perhaps you would glean more by reading its contents yourself?" Mrs. Morten held the letter out to her husband, not wishing to impart any of her present anxieties upon her spouse.

Mr. Morten took the letter, and his face changed through many expressions as he read. He never stopped in his reading to remark once, and Mariah knew it increased Mrs. Morten's anxiety. Mariah watched him closely and kept silent.

"Well, well, Mrs. Morten," he began, "it's my understanding we are to welcome a new daughter to our family. Simon seems smitten by her, does he not? I wonder at the rush though, as if something forced it along..." Mr. Morten tweaked his enormous nose.

"Oh, Mr. Morten, my fears indeed! Mariah has said we should reserve our judgment until our meeting with them, but it hardly soothes my racing thoughts." Mrs. Morten blew her nose delicately. The tears from earlier threatened to flow again.

Having sensed his wife's impending waterworks, Mr. Morten addressed his two ladies. "Mariah is our jewel, Mrs. Morten. Her heart does us all credit. Yes, yes, we will wait until they arrive. Then, perhaps depending upon hearing how this all came to be, I may box the lad's ears. I feel sure, though, nothing untoward has occurred. Simon has always been impetuous, but he means well. Let us think happy thoughts and wait and see." Mr. Morten refolded the letter and opened his desk drawer, placing the letter securely inside.

Papa looked up at Mama and smiled. He was not a violent man, and the idea of him boxing anyone's ear was fantastically funny to Mariah. She covered the laugh that escaped her mouth through her fingers.

"As you wish, Mr. Morten. You are, as ever, right. We will wait, and if you do not box his ears, I will do so for you, whether this was all brought about respectfully or not. I do hope our new daughter is every ounce meek and mild. Come, Mariah; we will leave your Father to finish the sermon or we will have no words to comfort us come Sunday."

Mariah hid a smile with a handkerchief and a dab to her nose. Mrs. Morten was not given to fits of temper nor rage, but she was excellent at giving a good dressing down when the occasion called upon it. The manner in which the pair disciplined their offspring was vastly different, but one thing was for certain: Mr. Morten was the head of the household, and his decision in all things was final, except, of course, when Mrs. Morten could turn the neck upon which that head rested, and it was often she did so.

Mariah gently closed the door to her father's study and climbed the stairs to her own quaint room. Today was a curious day between the weather and her brother's news, needing to be finished with a quiet moment in her room, a good book, and a view of Bramley Hall's fields.

Chapter Two

Welcoming the Newlyweds

The household was in an absolute tizzy. So many preparations needed to be completed in order to welcome a new daughter-in-law. The windows needed cleaning; the guest room needed a proper cleansing and airing out; all the dinnerware needed to be accounted for, polished, and ready to serve tonight's grand meal. The laundry needed to be attended to, and there was a pig in the process of being butchered.

Such a whirlwind swept through the parsonage. Persons did well to stay clear of Mrs. Morten and do as directed with a prompt: "Yes, ma'am." Mrs. Morten was certain to drive Mr. Trawley, their manservant, quite mad with all of her constant directions, but he bore them well. Mr. Trawley had long been used to the vexatious nature of the parson's wife.

Mariah glided past her ordering mother with a bundle of linen in her arms. In over an hour, she had yet to see Mr. Trawley emerge from her father's study. She lifted the bundle in her arms to hide a ladylike chortle.

It was not uncommon to find Mr. Trawley locked away in the study with Mr. Morten as the pair shared a quick drink and the baffled companionable silence men engaged in. But always, there were none that could say Mr. Trawley did not earn his wages. He was a good man who earned his keep honestly. If he felt the great need, from time to time, to hide away with Mr. Morten, there was nothing one could say to find fault in his actions, even though it was not common practice for a servant to drink with his employer.

Mariah dropped the linens off with another servant, heading back past her father's study. He had spent the entirety of the two days finishing and polishing his sermon. Though he had aged, the time spent creating his sermons had shortened. He knew the vices of his parishioners, and he let his heart lead him in his messages, for giving his heart the reins was surely letting the Lord speak through him.

Mariah sighed, shaking her head lovingly at how her parents ran the household. Her mother had control over the house while her father had control over everything else. Whether her father noticed the odd speck of dirt remained to be seen. As far as Mariah observed, he never did.

With her part in the chores completed, Mariah happily went out the back door and toward the lane leading to and from most everywhere in Bramley. It was an excellent spot to be situated to see any newcomer. A trio of rabbits, who hopped about both from under and out of the bushes, annoyed her, making quite a fuss. So engrossed was she in looking for her brother that it wasn't until a horse was quite near that she heard its clopping hooves.

Giving her best smile, and expecting to see her brother and new sister, she turned back toward the road. Instead, her heart didn't skip a beat; it practically leaped from within her breast. How silly to think the hooves of but one horse were enough to convey her family to her.

"Whoa. Easy, boy," said the Earl of Bramley. He stopped his horse and folded his hands upon the pommel as he looked down upon Mariah. "Good morning to you, Miss Morten!" He beamed at her.

"A good morning to you, my lord." Mariah bobbed her head. She was aware her skin was turning pink; whether it was from the cold or the odd embarrassment she was now feeling was uncertain. There was an odd fluttering within her stomach, and it quite perplexed her to feel such a sensation residing within her. Turning her mind from the matter, she gave her full attention to her friend.

"How did you know to greet me as I came this way?" Harrison teased, his smile warm as his eyes held a look of genuine pleasure.

Mariah was rather curious as to which event gave him more joy: the ride or seeing a friend. "I did not know. But I'm overjoyed I'm among the first to welcome you home. How did you find the roads?" Mariah shielded her eyes from the sun as she continued to gaze up at him.

How wonderful he looked, so tall and dignified and in complete command of his steed. His gray trousers and matching black greatcoat became him in a manner that made him look all the more refined. His long ebony hair came over his eyes a touch, and he gently swept it out of his face with a wide hand. His large, expressive teal eyes the glorious color of a swelling sea were enough to make her heart stutter.

"Very fine, indeed, as was the weather. Why, then, are you out on such a crisp, cool day?" He frowned. "I would hate to see an illness befall you," he said, wrinkling his forehead and bringing his right eyebrow up as he patiently awaited her reply.

"It's not that cool, my lord. We are expecting visitors, and my curiosity could wait no longer. Mama is practically pacing the floors, and I have not seen Papa since breakfast. I suspect he is hiding from us all until he must make his appearance." Mariah continued to smile.

"Who are these guests? Do I know them?" He leaned forward and patted his horse upon the neck. When he looked down at her again, his greenish-blue eyes were twinkling jovially. It was hard for Mariah to decide on the exact color of his eyes, as they seemed to change as often as his mood did. But, oh, those eyes...They were enough to make her forget her words.

Mariah smiled softly, enough to cover up the fact she had been impolitely admiring his countenance. "Indeed. I wonder: have you by chance heard that dear Simon has taken a wife? We are all very surprised and are set to make the introduction to my new sister-in-law today. Papa says it cannot be another day's wait, for they must arrive today." Mariah stepped toward his horse and stroked his velvety nose. She loved how his ebony coat gleamed in the light.

"I am all astonishment! You truly had no idea he was to wed?" Harrison adjusted his seat in his saddle. Again, his facial features drew together.

"None. I do not know if we should rejoice or weep. It seems rather sudden. Papa is determined we should all curb our curiosity and welcome the pair without prejudice."

"Hmm. Well now, I'm curious as to what sort of creature could have affected Simon so. Do you think she is an angel sent from heaven above? Or perhaps a wood sprite? Better yet for her to be Zeus's daughter?" the Earl teased, gazing down and smiling brightly at Mariah.

Harrison's features were no longer drawn together, and this was how she loved to see him: carefree. There were many responsibilities that came with being the Earl. He was much too serious these days and not given to cheer too freely. Life and its events had changed the course of his life, and things had never been quite the same. Mariah felt her heart constrict for him.

How he must be so lonesome, handling all the affairs alone and without companionship. His teal eyes bore into hers softly. The twinkle she remembered from years prior resurfaced, and her heart somersaulted.

Mariah pursed her lips, taking bait to his gentle, teasing tone. "I think not. I hope not. How will the rest of us mere mortals conduct ourselves in the presence of such a deity? Tell me, will you endeavor to ease my mind and join us for dinner tonight? I cannot wait to hear how you've been passing the time, and if the evening should prove dull, you can regale us with tales of your travels." Mariah hoped he would accept her invitation. She really had missed him. She gave him what she hoped was her most convincing smile.

"What a splendid idea! I believe I shall. Perhaps we can get a close enough look at her ears. Pray they not be pointed! Promise you'll head inside now, as you'll freeze otherwise, and I do not wish to dine without you, should you catch a cold," he said, casting her a severe frown.

Mariah could not help but to find it endearing. "I do believe I shall, for my fingers are rather cold. Promise me you'll arrive early?" she asked, cocking her head to the side.

"You have my word." With that, the Earl raised his hat and led his horse, Brutus, toward Bramley Hall.

Mariah watched him ride away for a few moments, and when it was apparent he would not look back toward her, she turned to head indoors. She entered through the parlor door and found her mother sitting while sewing sat upon her lap. Mariah picked up her sketchbook and said not a word to her mother. She found it odd Mama did not address her but supposed her mind was likely engaged in thoughts upon the coming meeting.

Mariah let her mind wander to Harrison. She measured all men who showed an interest in her against his character. He was what every titled man should be, graceful both on the dance floor and in the parlor. He was gentle and knowledgeable. He had ideas to impart in all conversations that added more amusement and understanding to all. His simple dexterity of manners put everyone at ease.

How long she had loved him she did not know. Where she had thought of him as a brother at first, the familial affection had now grown into more of a romantic notion. Since they were so vastly different in station, she aptly cast those thoughts aside on more than one occasion, though her heart and mind were readily there to allow her to dream of him once more.

Mariah sighed softly to herself. *If only such dreams could be fortuitous, though I greatly fear they would not be victorious.*

Mariah glanced at her mother, remembering that she hadn't told her about Harrison. "Mama," she began, "I have just seen Lord Bramley and have invited him to dine with us tonight. He will arrive early, and we can all visit together." Mariah thumbed through her sketchbook, not looking at her mother.

"Is he back? I wonder if, by chance, he met Simon and his wife while coming down from Town?" Mrs. Morten replied, seeming intrigued by her question. Her hazel eyes showed the excited state she was currently residing in.

"He came by way of horseback, Mama, and I cannot imagine Simon would expect his wife to ride such a long distance upon a horse." Mariah put her sketchbook back upon the side table by the window. "Besides, I gave him the news of Simon having wed, and he was just as surprised as we were. When asked, he gave no indication he had come across them." Mariah shrugged her shoulders.

Mrs. Morten harrumphed as her face pulled down into a moue. "Bother. I wish we had some information about my daughter-in-law. I cannot believe Simon wrote not a word regarding her! Not even to impart a name! Oh, the uselessness of men when it comes to letter writing. They never get it right. Sheets and sheets can be written about their activities regarding horseflesh without giving precious details as to who else was in attendance and what they wore!" Mrs. Morten put her sewing into her basket and sighed.

"I believe you are right. It is an eternal flaw." Mariah sighed, too, to cover her amusement.

Mr. Morten entered the room, looking from wife to daughter. "Oh, the waiting when one is all a-twitter with curiosity. It does us no good. But wait we must and let the happy couple arrive when they shall," he chuckled lightly at the teasing of his wife as he sat down in his favorite cushioned chair. He stretched out his long legs and crossed his ankles, shining boot over shining boot.

Mrs. Morten turned her nose up at his humorous tone. "I am half agony and half dismay. I do hope they arrive before we dine this evening." Mrs. Morten pushed her basket under the side table. "If the roasted hens are tough when we dine, so be it, but I shall let it be known it was not due to either my fault nor the cooks.'"

Mariah glanced out the window to hide a wide grin and a soft chortle. Her eyes were drawn to the clouds and the light wind pushing them past the window before she got a proper look at them. She laid her head softly on the arm of her cushioned settee, trying her best not to smile at the constant thoughts of Harrison.

Her heart fluttered. *Even after all this time, he makes my heart stutter, and I have to remind myself to breathe. But oh, the follies of daydreaming over someone I could never hope to behold as mine.*

She frowned, pushing her wanton thoughts to the side. Harrison was meant to be someone else's, and pining such as she was would bring her further heartache and dismay. Their stations were much too different to permit such an affair.

"Why the frown, daughter?" Mr. Morten asked.

Mariah lifted her head up, smiling. "I was thinking since autumn is upon us, I do not wish it to rain so soon. But the Lord will do as He pleases, and if it's rain, then rain it shall be."

Mr. Morten glanced outside, wriggling his nose, and sniffed. "Rain will be good for the fall crops getting ready for harvest."

Mariah nodded, not in the mood to talk further about crops. She picked up her embroidery, feigning interest in making a flowered handkerchief to appear busy while her heart ached.

She made slow progress, hoping no one noticed. Try as she might to push Harrison from her thoughts, he was an ever-present figure. She smiled, remembering when she was first learning how to embroider and he commented that her pink flower resembled a sorry sow. Her cheeks had turned an embarrassing shade of red while he smirked. Right then, she knew he was teasing. Harrison corrected himself about her poor flower once finished and said it was the most beautiful pink carnation of sorts he'd ever seen.

Mariah anxiously raised her head up from her embroidery. The noise upon the lane excited her with the clopping of many horses' hooves. Such excitement the noise created! Mrs. Morten rose to her feet and clapped her hands. Mr. Morten also rose and cleared his throat. Mariah stayed in her seat and tried to not seem too eager. Mr. Morten's hunting dog, Solomon, barked and jumped around outside, making a terrible racket.

Mr. and Mrs. Morten flew to the front door when the carriage came to a stop. The pair gave no time for Amy, the maid, to open the door. Mr. Morten opened the door himself with such gusto, it banged against the wall beside it. Mariah grinned at her father's lack of care.

Mariah stepped up to the window, smiling at the carriage. Quietly, she opened the window to hear the conversation and to get a clearer picture of the scene outside. She was not one for gossip, and it was rather chilly outside, but oh, my, what a splendid carriage with its burgundy curtains and new wheels! The craftsmanship and care spoke volumes to someone of importance

or of great wealth with a dark mahogany frame and silver door handles. *The woman my dear brother married must be well off,* Mariah thought.

Simon turned back toward the carriage and stretched out his hand to his wife, helping her descend the wooden steps. So dainty were the tan colored gloves that held her hands! She seemed to be the epitome of grace and ease as she straightened her brown traveling overcoat and dusted off her husband's scarlet uniform coat. From the window, Mariah could make out wisps of auburn hair just peeking from under the lady's elegant bonnet that boasted two feathers and sumptuous lace.

Rushing out to the newly arrived couple, Mrs. Morten flew by the dog with a sharp, "Hush now!" followed up by a victorious cooing noise at her son and new daughter-in-law. Mariah pressed the back of her hand to her mouth, stemming the giggle.

Reaching the couple, Mr. Morten greeted them excitedly. "Welcome, welcome!" He smiled warmly first at his son and then at his daughter-in-law.

What a beauty the lady was! All smiles and poise. And her brother had appeared to grow taller since she last remembered. He had broadened out since joining the military, and now, with his new wife on his arm, Simon seemed to radiate with joy.

"Thank you, Papa! Allow me the very great pleasure of introducing you to my wife, Alicia. Is she not the prettiest woman you have ever seen?" Simon wore a look of sheer adoration upon his face.

"Oh, stop now, my dear! They will think you are conceited." Alicia swatted her husband's gloved hand.

Mariah squinted, trying to catch what her sister-in-law looked like. Even from this distance, she could make out Alicia's playful lashes lowering over her rather large tawny eyes. Her skin was pale but turning a hue of pink. She took the arm of her husband and smiled broadly.

"Indeed, my son is correct; you are very pretty, my dear," answered Mrs. Morten. She reached up on tiptoe and kissed her son upon his cheek. Drawing back, she encircled the free arm of Alicia and gave her a peck upon her cheek since the bonnet prohibited a kiss upon her forehead. "You must tell me of your journey. Was it pleasant? You must have passed through some pleasing country."

"It was beautiful. I remarked so to Simon, did I not, my love?" Alicia replied, looking at her husband.

"Yes, I do recall our conversation. Let's go inside! It's been ages since I've been home. Hello, Solomon, you daft fool, barking at my bride." Simon reached down and patted the offensive pet who had not quieted down at all. Solomon tried to pull his rope from the tree but gave up. Mariah smiled at the scene. Almost abashedly, she hurried to shut the window and stand in front of the fireplace as the front door opened, permitting her mother's shrill, scolding tone.

"You have grown so brown, Simon!" chided Mrs. Morten. "I really fear that your insides would cook completely! English men should not grow so dark!"

Laughing, Simon replied, "'Tis from marching under the blistering sun, Mama!"

The couples came into the parlor, and Mariah curtsied when they entered.

Alicia began, "My, what a room, and it's so cozy! I can just picture you here, Simon, as a boy, playing." She took the seat she was offered upon the settee next to her husband. Her gown was brown, and on others, it may have looked dowdy and dull, but Alicia's coloring in both her hair and pale complexion went decidedly perfect with it.

"Alicia, you must be introduced to another pretty young miss: my very own sister, Mariah." Simon nodded over at the fireplace where Mariah remained standing. He tugged on an auburn curl that hung over his wife's shoulder.

Not noticing her husband's attention, Alicia rose at once and went to Mariah. Putting her arms out to Mariah and taking her hands, she leaned in and kissed Mariah's cheek. "My, but you are divine, are you not? We are going to get along famously! I've never had a sister, and I am happy we meet at last."

Mariah smiled and said, "You are most kind. I too am thrilled at the prospect of having a sister now. The change in conversation will be enthralling," Mariah returned the hug she was given.

"Well, here we all are. May we know how this all came to be, if you please, Simon? Because Mrs. Morten and myself were considering boxing your ears," asked Mr. Morten when the two ladies returned to their seats.

"Ah, Papa. I cannot tell you the hour nor the look that tied me forever to my sweet wife. We often met in the society of the regiment, as Alicia is the only child of Lord and Lady Purcellville. As you know, Lord Purcellville is in command of us all and does quite a grand job of it. We all agree he is a most diligent commander and quite amusing when off duty too. So, as fate would have it, I was waiting upon orders. I had a note of importance which I had handed over to his Lordship. I was standing in the road which courses through town when a carriage was rampaging its way toward the very spot in which I stood. I quickly gathered my wits and got out of the way when I saw Alicia unaware of what was happening. She was reading a letter from her cousin, and she said with all the usual noise in town, she took no notice of what was transpiring around her. So concerned for her welfare was I that I ran to where she sat perched upon a stool beside the road near a pretty spot of a city garden. She never noticed me, for if she had, I'm certain I would have been dealt a blow. I lifted her up into my arms and dove into the grass toward the house. I was thankful we landed well and she was not under me." Simon paused, smirking with merriment while his eyes gazed fondly at Alicia, then went to the edge of his seat, continuing, "It took a moment for me to extricate myself from her cloak which had become entangled with my own person. So calm was she that I remember being extremely glad she had not fainted. Her papa came to us as we were struggling to rise. I had slightly twisted my left knee in our rough landing, though I should gladly have suffered much more for the knowledge that Alicia was completely unharmed. Lord Purcellville was quite relieved I had the sense to rescue his daughter. He offered me his best hunting hound as a reward."

Alicia put a delicate hand over Simon's and leaned forward, "But instead, he ended up with me!" She giggled, all merry in manner.

There were none in the room who were not smiling and in a general jolly mood.

"Oh, my. To think he traded a hound for a wife! How very extraordinary! But how did you end up with this lovely young lady after all?" inquired Papa.

"I think it was later that same evening, as I had been invited to dine with the Purcellvilles and my fellows, that an idea was hatched. You see, I kept stealing glances at Alicia to ensure myself she suffered no harm. She kept stealing glances at me to make sure my knee was not paining me overmuch. The whole table noticed our behavior. Well, by the time the men left for their port, I was approached by Lord Purcellville, and he gave me the surprising information that such a man that could put himself in harm's way to secure a member of his family would make an excellent addition to his family. And despite my having no real connections in society nor title nor land, he would be pleased to welcome me into his home. But then he said, in a very serious tone, if I'd rather have the hound, I may still, but he could not bear to dispose of both his only daughter and his favorite hound all at once! Ha!" Simon finished, laughing uproariously.

"One must wonder how you felt about this transaction?" asked Mr. Morten of his new daughter-in-law, to which Mrs. Morten nodded.

Alicia smiled demurely. "Oh, to be sure I was surprised. To think my hero asked for my hand was something from a dream. Of course, I agreed to the match. How could I deprive my father of his best hound?" Alicia giggled, regarding the entire room.

"We have traveled at great speeds to get here as soon as possible. I trust you are not angry at me for my lapse in communicating the whole of this to you sooner? 'Twas much to impart using ink and paper, and we did so want to see your faces as we told you. My regiment is soon to move on, so we wanted to meet you before we left. We shan't stay but three days time. Though my father-in-law seems to like me now, he may not were I to make the whole regiment slow in maneuvers and training timetables," Simon relayed, gazing upon his wife.

Mariah watched them look at each other; how they were so full of love and contentment. She wished to soon find such happiness with another. She wanted marital bliss, absolute love. She would hold out for such affection, though her mother would box her ears for it instead!

Mrs. Morten smiled broadly as she rose from her seat. "I believe luncheon will soon be on the table. You must be famished! Oh, dear, have I not mentioned that Lord Bramley dines with us tonight? No matter. You must be longing to refresh yourselves from the journey. I believe Amy is set to see to your needs." Mrs. Morten left her husband and opened the parlor door. She then led the way, ascending the staircase to the room the new couple would be using. "I hope roasted hens appeal to your appetites!"

Mariah could not keep the grin off her face. She was indeed happy. Her brother was settled down, and so well at that! Alicia was a very welcomed and pleasant sister. She longed for her own intended to share in the same intimacies her brother and his wife so clearly experienced. That was what she would wait for. Nothing but the deepest love would ever induce her to say yes to leaving her family, even at the expense of becoming a spinster. After Simon and his bride returned to the parlor, the party retired to the dining room.

Mariah quietly sat in her chair and waited for a chance to learn more about her new sister. According to Alicia, her family was well-placed in society; they were well-off with connections to many families that had a likeness to the Earl of Bramley. Mariah smiled, knowing such grand connections would make her mother's heart overjoyed.

Mariah wriggled in her seat as her mother continued to pry information from Alicia regarding her dowry. Mariah wasn't one to delve into fiscal accruements. Although she understood money, she found it at times impolite to discuss, especially when the conversation then turned to her and her intentions to marry.

Mariah politely directed the conversation toward other familial ties and shared acquaintances. At once, her mother and Alicia began discussing news of cousins, weddings, and babes. It was a most pleasant afternoon. After luncheon, they retired back to the parlor, where the conversation continued to flow effortlessly.

After some time, Simon came to his feet and said, "My wife is very tired, Mama. I would not have us out of sorts when Lord Bramley arrives." Helping his wife to stand, he smiled at his mama.

"Oh, but of course, we should all rest! What a day this has been. I shall accompany you to your room on my way up the stairs," Mrs. Morten said, leaning down and kissing her husband upon his cheek.

Mr. Morten smiled. "Are we then done with the notion to box the boy's ears?"

Mrs. Morten chuckled, "Oh, my dear Mr. Morten, perhaps we can overlook his one indiscretion."

"Thank you, Mama," Simon chortled.

Mariah smiled fondly, watching her brother, his wife, and her mother leave the small parlor to retire and freshen up. She let out a contented breath to hide her own jealousy and longing for what her brother and new sister-in-law had.

Mr. Morten turned his attention to his daughter. "What have you to say, Mariah? Does your new sister please you?"

"Oh, Papa," answered Mariah. "I find that I like her very much. I believe she and Simon are well-suited. Though is it not surprising that a titled man would not seek out a peer to wed his only daughter to?" She furrowed her brows.

"So it would seem. We can only praise the Lord that He has worked it all out in their favor. I will not question the situation further. Tell me, my dear, when will we be parting from you?" Mr. Morten inquired, imparting a look of fondness to his daughter.

"I have no answer for you, Papa, to give at present." Mariah shrugged and smiled.

"Oh, well. These things happen all on their own timetable. I do hope whoever he is, he settles you near us. For heaven's sake, try not to love a soldier." He laughed.

"I shall do my best." Mariah shrugged again.

"Forgive me," Mr. Morten stated, stemming a yawn. "How did our Lord Bramley seem to you when you met?"

"How do you mean?"

"Was he well?"

"It appeared he was in grand spirits."

"Poor boy. I hope he soon takes a wife and takes care of his heart in the process. We could use a countess around these parts. Bramley Hall used to have grand balls many years ago. The Earl doesn't entertain much since taking up the title," Mr. Morten replied with a thoughtful look as he gazed out the window.

"Well, he entertains us when in residence, and he's always here attending upon us," Mariah replied, wondering why her father seemed worried for Harrison.

Her father worried about all his friends. Mariah thought it was very sincere of her father to be troubled over someone else, though she attributed his gray hair to the needless worry. Mariah smiled fondly, also thinking of Harrison and hoping he too found a suitable match at some point. All were deserving of love.

Once, long ago, she had dreams of marrying Harrison. Then when she got older and realized what her station was as compared to his, she realized such dreams were folly, and she disregarded them. Yet whenever he was around her, she couldn't help, even now, to entertain the idea for just a moment longer. Her heart loved Harrison despite having warned it numerous times of their differences. It was like her heart did not care to heed her warning.

"Perhaps he may start entertaining again once a countess is in residence. Though I do hope he is not hasty in settling on one. I would rather it take some time being attended to than her being a cretin," Mariah replied, gazing into the fire.

"Indeed. We would not be all comfortable if she were a complete cretin. You're as pretty as any girl; perhaps you'll catch his notice," Mr. Morten teased.

"Dear Papa," she sighed. "The Earl would, I feel sure, never take notice of me being more than his neighbor now that we are grown."

"You were close once..." He trailed off, gazing into the hearth.

"Indeed, but time and broken hearts tend to alter things and certainly one's perspective," Mariah sighed.

"Yes, that is true, my dear. Well, I'm off to my study. I have a few letters that need attending to. What shall you do now? Rest as well?" He got up and waited for her answer.

"I think I am feeling a little rest would do me a world of good." Mariah rose and proceeded him out of the parlor door, which he held open for her. She turned toward him and kissed his cheek.

"What was that for?" Mr. Morten asked.

"For just being you, dear Papa. You worry and attend to us all." Mariah smiled beautifully at him.

"'Tis part of my calling, my sweet girl. Now off with you, then. We cannot all be drowsy when Lord Bramley arrives." Squeezing her hand briefly, he took off toward his study.

Chapter Three

Entertaining Indeed

Harrison was absolutely thrilled at the notion of dining with the Mortens. It had been a few years since he had last seen Simon, and to meet the woman who had marched him down the aisle was sure to be a most rewarding event. He felt at peace within the walls of the Mortens' cozy home. Mr. Morten had given him sound advice many times before, and he felt it was in line with that which his own father would have imparted. Mrs. Morten was graceful, if a little anxious. She was a genteel hostess and a wonderful mother. But Mariah, ah, Mariah...What were his feelings to be seeing Mariah again in such an intimate yet familiar setting?

It seemed as if his life was in constant change. He delighted in Mariah's smiles and confidences when they were children. He still felt at ease with her, and teasing her seemed to be second nature. She was now of a marriageable age, and that put a great distance between them. He struggled sometimes to restrain his manners toward her. He took pains to be sure he was every inch the gentleman and that his manners were impeccable and irreproachable.

Watching her during the season gave him little comfort, so dismayed was he with her dancing partners and the young fools who seemed to flock to her. On more than one occasion, he had sought out one of those bucks to give them a severe dressing down as to how they should conduct themselves with her, or any young woman for that matter. He guessed if he were one of those dandies, he too would have been drawn to her and acted a fool.

Everyone was drawn to Mariah. She was sweet, even-tempered, intelligent on most topics, and quick-witted. Her accomplishments in domestic hospitality were exactly what her mother had instilled in her from such an early age. But to him? To him, she was everything, and no one could catch his eye more so than Mariah Morten.

He sighed, running a hand over his face. Since they had known each other as children, he had long since been like an adopted elder brother. It was hard to draw the line with her for propriety's sake. Draw the line he must, though, so as to not get in her way where suitors were concerned. *Suitors.* The word made him cringe.

He had been torn before whether or not to call on her, whether to see if she saw him as anything more than a brother or a neighbor. Oftentimes, he hoped so. Other times, he was scared to rightly find out. How could he live through another heartbreak?

Harrison sighed, hanging his head as his horse trotted down the road. *Maybe I should let all of it go...After all, there is much between us now, including social stations.*

The Mortens' house came into view, and he smiled at the room he knew to be hers. *I'll see her before long,* he reminded himself. *And then I will get another memory to tuck away if I cannot have her.*

He trotted up near the front door and dismounted his horse. Harrison straightened his formal dinner attire after handing his horse, Brutus, off to the servant. He removed his dark riding gloves and tucked them into his leather pouch affixed to Brutus. He then took his formal white dinner gloves from his leather pouch before nodding to the servant to lead his mount away. His valet had tied an especially clever knot with his cravat. If he wanted his boots polished in the morning, he had better not make a mess of the artwork.

Harrison rapped upon the door and was greeted by a manservant who also served as their butler. Mr. Trawley bid him welcome and stepped aside so Harrison could enter. He handed over his topper and outerwear once he entered.

Harrison caught sight of Mariah descending the stairs until she was almost to where he stood. *My, when had she ever looked lovelier?* Her hair gave her another inch of height, and the blue gown did something peculiar to her extraordinary blue eyes, or maybe her eyes had always been so fine. Mentally shaking himself, he smiled down to where she stood before him.

"Good evening, Miss Morten." He greeted her with a bow, and she returned his gesture with a curtsy. Taking her hand, he placed it upon his right arm, and they walked toward the sitting room.

Addressing Mr. Trawley over her shoulder, Mariah said, "I shall announce Lord Bramley's presence. Thank you, Mr. Trawley."

Mr. Trawley nodded his assent and walked away.

Leaning slightly to whisper into Mariah's ear, Harrison inquired, "Do you like your new relation? Has she normal ears?"

Laughing discreetly, Mariah returned his whisper. "She is delightful and graceful; you will like her as we all do. Come to think of it, though, no, I have not seen the complete shape of her ears since her curls covered them. Perhaps her hair will be caught up differently this evening, and we may ascertain the answer together?"

Smiling brightly at her, Harrison threw open the door to the sitting room and waited for her to enter the grand room. This was indeed a stately room—the best in the whole parsonage. It was reserved for when guests were in attendance and lacked the coziness of the parlor. There was a large settee in the middle of the Aubusson rug, and two rocking chairs were carved with rosettes by the roaring fireplace.

There were also four armchairs with paw-shaped feet placed at various points of the room, which ensured all who sat within the room could take part in the general conversation if they chose. This room was located in the back of the house, where the parlor was situated in the front and the windows gave sight to where one could easily spy the comings and goings of the lane. The room also contained a pianoforte by the window, and a desk with a small chair occupied a corner.

Upon entering the room, all stood to greet him. Mr. Morten gave his arm to his wife, and they approached him at once. Mr. Morten clapped him upon the back and bid him enter and have a seat. Mrs. Morten offered him a warm, maternal smile and a quick curtsy and said how delighted she was to receive him.

Further into the room stood Simon next to his new wife. Harrison strode to Simon, smiling at his longtime friend.

Simon reached for his friend, grabbing him into a hug and exclaiming, "There you are, old boy! 'Tis good to see you! Allow me the very grand pleasure of introducing you to my new bride. My dear Alicia, this fine fellow is Harrison Pembroke, the seventh Earl of Bramley, and if there ever existed a better man, I do not know him."

Harrison bowed deeply toward the new lady and caught her gloved hand into his, kissing the air above her knuckles after she curtsied to him. "How do you do, Mrs. Morten? I cannot wait to hear how all of this business came about. I see he looks none the worse for wear and can only guess at your steadying influence upon him. My very sincere thanks for claiming him, ma'am."

"The pleasure is all mine, I'm sure. Thank you so much for your hearty welcome, my lord." Alicia turned a pretty shade of pink, which delighted her husband to no end.

Simon promptly relayed how he came to be the husband of his beautiful wife. Harrison nodded accordingly, though his thoughts were elsewhere. *If I could be so fortunate like Simon...* He dashed the thought from his head, focusing on his lifelong friend's thrilling marriage tale.

Harrison beamed, thrilled to be at the most welcoming home he had ever been in. Even though Bramley Hall was his home, here in the Morten household, it felt more so. He glanced quickly out of his peripheral vision, catching the shy smile of Mariah. His heart thudded within his chest.

After a few minutes of general conversation and pleasantry, dinner was announced by Mr. Trawley. Mr. Morten took his wife's arm, and Simon took Alicia to his side. Had manners been of the utmost importance, Mrs. Morten should have taken her guest into dinner, but they never stood on ceremony with him unless there were others to grace their table. So naturally, Harrison offered his arm to Mariah, and she shyly took it.

"Thank you, my lord," Mariah whispered to him. "My sister-in-law's hair is arranged very beautifully tonight, which gives one the clear view of her ears. Indeed, they are as normal a pair as I have ever seen. Do you not agree with my assessment?"

Amused, Harrison answered, "Undeniably. She is mortal. We may all breathe easier now. And how fortunate it is that she is not a daughter of Zeus either." Harrison mused, heaving an exaggerated sigh as Mariah laughed. My, but he did love her laugh. It was musically appealing to his mind and soul.

His heart tumbled again, pulled at wanting to be in her presence longer than propriety deemed polite. He wanted a forever with her, though it was unfortunate it could not be had. It was vain to hope. He could not help it. She was delightful, effervescent, and thrilling to be around. Though their stations deemed a match insufficient, he did not care. He would happily have her, but alas, she viewed him as a brother, and that therein laid the problem for his misery.

Harrison held in a sigh. *Hopefully, I shall find a lady as charming as Mariah*, he thought, peeking at her affectionately. *And if not, I shall wait until I can find one or until I may, perchance, gain Mariah's affection in a more intimate way.*

He helped Mariah to her seat before taking his own across from her. She smiled at him. Her eyes held a subtle mischievousness in them he had long admired.

Dinner was served to him on the Mortens' best dining ware. He grinned at it, feeling special to receive such a hearty welcome.

"Lord Bramley," Mr. Morten addressed him, "pray tell us how you have been faring, along with any adventures you care to delight us in."

Harrison grinned, nodding, and began one of his tales, his sole focus on Mariah and how she received his news. He entertained the party with talk of how he met with some friends that he had attended Eton with and proceeded to catch up with at a dinner party.

After some time, Alicia tilted her head to the side. "My lord, I believe I know a cousin through marriage that claims acquaintance with you."

Giving his whole attention to Alicia, Harrison put down his fork. "Is that so? Who is this acquaintance?" He smiled at her.

"A Lady Michaelton. She is older than I, but I believe you knew her during her first season. My mama has a sister, and she is her daughter." Alicia beamed at him.

All were silent around the table waiting for his reply. He refrained from narrowing his brows or the ticking in his jaw when it came to that particular woman. He made eye contact with Mariah and swore she intimately knew his feelings.

He refrained from sighing, though the inside of his body bubbled with emotions that battled between anger and sorrow. Lady Michaelton had broken his heart. That wicked creature had nearly ruined his reputation and much else, for that matter. Harrison dipped his head, remembering his manners.

Before he could form his answer, Simon said, "My dear, I thought we would remain silent on your relations. One does not wish to bore Lord Bramley." He smiled fondly at his wife, then turned to nod at Harrison, with an anxious look upon his face.

Lest any unpleasantries arise, Harrison spoke when he saw confusion cross Alicia's face. "We did meet ages ago. How fares your cousin?"

His face remained the practiced form he used when socializing within society. He would not end this dinner poorly due to his displeasure. He slowed his breathing and looked at Alicia. He did his best to completely ignore Simon and the concerned look he gave him.

It had been many years since he had seen Lady Samantha Michaelton, and he intended to keep it that way. Though she was married now, last he heard, his heart was still sore from her, still pained. He gave his all to that woman, and she ruined him and near everything he held dear.

"Oh, very well indeed. She has just borne her second child, a daughter. I'm told all are well. She was overjoyed with a girl since her first was a son." Alicia beamed at him again.

"What a pleasure for her. I am glad she is well," Harrison said, offering no more, and the silence in the room was a curious thing to behold when each had been so vigorously engaged before. In vain, he struggled for more to say—something of interest—but he could not make his mind obey him. He was unprepared for discomfort within this home.

Mr. Morten soon began the topic of his stable, and there were none at the table who had much to offer on the subject. Harrison listened aptly, offering a word here or there. However, the dourness in the room due to his reply was not to be mistaken as all lapsed into silence as they ate. It was a curious thing, as even the ever-talkative hostess could not revive the conversation through no fault of her own.

Chapter Four

Adventure Must Begin

M ariah had time to consider that which had just taken place. How odd that all should fall silent and the mood should be so altered. Who was this Lady Michaelton, and how did Harrison know her? She supposed they had often been in society together. Perhaps they had danced? Had they courted? Her lips pursed in a sour manner as she looked down at her plate. She dared a glance at Harrison. Watching the seemingly serene expression on Harrison's face, a thought occurred to her.

Could this meeting have taken place four years ago? Was Lady Michaelton the same lady who had turned Harrison away? Was she the one who had chosen another, and if so, was that choice Lord Michaelton? Simon would have asked Alicia to keep silent on this topic if he had known the subject would cause their dear friend pain. Did the memories of Lady Michaelton cause him pain still?

She frowned at the thought. She stabbed the pear upon her plate with her fork, mulling the matter over.

Feeling eyes upon her, she looked up from her pear and caught Harrison looking toward her. He was frowning. She smiled at him, and it was several seconds until he smiled in return. He did look pained, and it left Mariah feeling uneasy. There was something that led his look to be pinched around his eyes; no doubt something was weighing heavily within his mind. Mariah wished it were proper to question him, wished it were proper to be alone with him, to lend her confidence once again to him and bask in his presence while she could selfishly have it.

If only I could be the one to ease his suffering heart, she thought, watching his intelligent and warm teal eyes. *Surely, whoever this woman was, she must have been something to bring dear Harrison to his knees in agony.*

When every gentleman had eaten his fill, Mrs. Morten rose from the table. Each of the men rose as well to help each lady from her seat and then watched as the ladies followed her to the sitting room to leave the men to their port. Mariah took one last fleeting glance at Harrison, hoping he was all right as she followed her mother and Alicia out, but she was unable to catch his eye for her own reassurance.

Taking her seat upon the floral padded settee, her mother and Alicia spoke animatedly about Brighton, where Simon was to be stationed next. According to her sister-in-law, she had relatives in Brighton—particularly her parents—who would be most pleased to have Mariah stay with them if she so chose.

Mariah smiled, feeling uneasy about adventuring far from her dear parents. After the season she had had, she wasn't ready to head back into society yet. She liked the quiet life around her, her daily rides surrounding Bramley Hall and the still countryside. The life of the ton was a bit much, and here Alicia was, already conveying her dearest request for her to come to Brighton.

Alicia strode across the quaint room to take Mariah's hands in her own, her beautiful eyes begging for her to agree to accompany her.

"For you see, you really must say yes." Alicia awaited an answer from Mariah, expectant and hopeful.

"What do you think, Mama?" Mariah asked, turning toward her mother.

"It is only early October. I do not see why you shouldn't go. Of course, we shall have to ask your father. But oh, Brighton at this time of the year should be very busy, and you'll have lots of events to attend. I rather like the idea of expanding your social circle. Plus, this will introduce you to a whole new crop of suitors!" Mrs. Morten clasped her hands together.

Alicia nodded vigorously. "I brought the carriage just so you could return with us. Both Mama and Papa are eager to make your acquaintance. We'll all be staying at the Brighton house, so you needn't feel any lack of privacy. There is a splendid library, and we can shop when it doesn't rain. There will be balls and soirees to attend throughout the week. Of course, there will be scores of officers to keep you entertained as well." Alicia's smile was bright, and her eyes crinkled at the corners.

The idea of declining was utmost in Mariah's mind, but with her mother looking so pleased and Alicia pleading, she felt the choice was made unless her father put a stop to the adventure. Mariah doubted Papa would object, so she might as well become used to the idea of going. She rather liked the security and routine she enjoyed here at home.

Mariah refrained from looking beyond their little sitting area to where Harrison would be. He had just returned back to Bramley Hall, the thought of leaving tugged at her heart. She swallowed it down, knowing harboring any feelings wouldn't do her any good.

She nodded, smiling demurely at Alicia. "Sounds delightful. I would indeed enjoy seeing Brighton."

The sitting room door opened, and in walked the gentlemen. Mariah blew out a breath she was unaware she was holding, thrilled that the subject would change with the men arriving. Now, the females would be content to pay attention to their spouses' needs.

After Mr. Morten had settled down, his lady addressed him at once. "Dear Mr. Morten! Had you any idea Simon and Alicia were to invite your own daughter to Brighton when they depart?" Mrs. Morten inquired excitedly. She clasped and unclasped her folded hands to her chest and waited hopefully for his agreeable reply. Mariah's heart thundered in her chest. She knew her father would not decline, though part of her wished he would. She stole a peripheral glance at Harrison, his brow raised a touch while he slightly leaned forward in his seat.

"Mariah?" inquired Mr. Morten, turning his attention to his only daughter.

"But of course, Mariah," Mrs. Morten said, not appreciating his teasing tone. "We have not another daughter—at least I have not—and if you have one somewhere else, she has been a great secret these past twenty-seven odd years, and your marital bliss is about to be revoked." Mrs. Morten drew her brows together and regarded her husband impatiently.

Chuckling at his wife, Mr. Morten asked Mariah, "What are your feelings on this, dearest *only* daughter?"

Feeling the entire room waiting for her reply, Mariah spoke. "I do not want to disappoint since it seems to be most carefully planned out."

Simon clapped his hands. "Indeed. My wife needs a companion, and you would suit nicely! Harrison is to travel with us to Brighton. He has business to see to, and we agreed how wonderful a joint venture would be."

"I did not know you had interest in Brighton, my lord." Mrs. Morten smiled at Harrison.

"Rather, it's a favor for a friend. He asked me to inquire after a property that is to be up for sale. He would have made the visit himself, but his first child is soon due. Seeing as I had no other obligations, I offered to attend to the errand myself," Harrison informed the party.

He smiled broadly at them, displaying a mouth full of perfect white teeth. Mariah smiled back, hoping it conveyed friendliness and not the desire she felt. She had to constantly check herself around him. It was most taxing emotionally, as all she wanted was to be his.

Stop it this instant, she scolded herself. *You know better, Mariah Morten. All this hopeless dreaming will only make yourself depressed.*

Even though the self-scolding should have kept her in line, she couldn't help but admire Harrison, every bit the handsome, aristocratic, benevolent man he was. She tried her best to be friendly as the friend she had tried hard to portray, though more often than not, she caught herself slipping past that friend-only, self-given line. Their differences in station would not permit anything beyond cordiality.

Mayhap some gentleman in Brighton will be like Harrison and suitable for me, she thought, resolving herself yet again to let the notion of Harrison Pembroke go.

"What wonderful news! Our circle would much be influenced by an earl. I do hope you will stay at least a fortnight with us, for you must stay where we all will be! The matter is nicely settled. My, how lovely things are turning out!" Alicia exclaimed, smiling beautifully.

"Lord Bramley and I will ride our mounts while you ladies enjoy the carriage. A better way to quickly acquaint a person I never knew!" Simon said cheerfully, taking his wife's hand in his. "You will say yes, Mariah?" Simon asked, turning his head to look at her.

Mariah nodded. "I will say yes. Will I not be a bother staying so long as a fortnight?" Mariah inquired of her brother.

"Nonsense. If you truly miss home, perhaps we can arrange for you to return with his Lordship and your maid, should he extend his stay?" Simon looked at Harrison.

"Let us consider the matter all tied together. We shall remain for a fortnight, and not a touch longer if Mariah is agreeable," Harrison stated, inclining his head.

Mariah let out a breath that Harrison was coming with her. It took immense pressure she didn't know was there off her shoulders.

Simon then insisted his wife play the pianoforte and moved an armchair close to the instrument. Mariah relaxed against the settee, watching her sister-in-law's fingers glide across the instrument. Not only could she play really well, but she sang in a lovely manner too.

Harrison came and sat beside Mariah on the settee, and thanks to the music and singing, as Simon had a lovely baritone, they could talk in whispers. Mr. And Mrs. Morten were so enthralled with the performance, she and Harrison were aptly ignored.

Harrison began, "Are you looking forward to your travels?" smiling at her.

"I should say yes with fervent enthusiasm. I will admit to feeling better now that you too will be there. I hardly know what schemes my sister-in-law has swirling in her head. Promise you'll try to remain my entire stay?" Mariah practically begged him, wanting to know she would have the possibility of returning home, should the mood strike her.

She knew that his presence would truly make her comfortable. Having known Alicia for only a few hours, she found the woman was direct and a tidbit pushy, although it seemed that she meant well. Mariah was terrified the woman might try to get her to wed the first man she came across. Mariah wouldn't have it, of course, but she didn't want it to escalate to a point where there were hard feelings. She wanted the freedom to choose whom she might and not have a husband chosen for her. And, by her standards, if any man did not measure up to Harrison Pembroke, then she might not ever marry.

"I feel certain you will enjoy Brighton. As for any scheming, there will be moments where I will be absent. But I can promise: you only have to express your desire to return, if you so wish, and it shall come to be. I shall endeavor to do my best to stay by your side and protect you accordingly," Harrison promised, gazing at her seriously. Mariah wondered if his mood was affected by the conversation at the dinner table regarding a certain Lady Michaelton.

"How fortunate I am to have such a champion in you," Mariah replied, smiling warmly at him.

How he made her heart flutter erratically. However was she going to find a husband now with the presence of the Earl? Or mayhap her luck was changing? She pushed the notion from her head, opting to instead bask in his presence while she could.

Chapter Five

Splendid Company

Harrison feared that there was not much he would not slay down in order to see her well-being intact. This truth was not new to him; he'd always felt protective of Mariah. But this time, he was sensing something odd about his mood, and it had nothing to do with anything he cared to explore. Their stations were just too different, but he found that the more he thought about it, the more he started not to care. What would such a matter be if they could surmount social status? He couldn't give a fig what society thought if it meant that Mariah could be his.

He shook his head slightly. *She views me as a familial brother, nothing of the sort of a romantic intention.* He fixed his look to be an open and protective one, to assure Mariah he would remain by her side.

"I'll do my best to watch over you while you are away from home, Miss Morten. Certainly, I shall ensure that your well-being is my sole concern. Since we shall be under the same roof, I expect we will be partners to all your brother's wife's plans. Please remember: should you wish to return home, we certainly may," he stated, smiling genuinely at her.

"How did you find things upon your return?" Mariah inquired, changing the topic.

"All was in order as they ever are. I am of a mind that should I ever disappear, my steward could manage for ages without my input," Harrison chuckled, giving Mariah a lopsided smile.

"What a perfectly dreadful thought, my lord. Say you would never attempt a disappearance!" Mariah exclaimed with a cute pout on her pink lips.

Harrison smiled at her impish expression. "Would you miss me, then?"

He was teasing her but deep down sought an honest answer. Would she miss him? He felt sure looking down upon her that were she to disappear, he would feel most bereaved. And if she missed him, then surely, her feelings for him were changing? Part of him hoped she saw him otherwise.

"You should know my answer upon that! Of course I would miss you. What a dull-witted question." She rolled her eyes and shook her head.

"Pfft. Forgive my lapse of wits. I am glad to know there are those that would mourn me."

Harrison realized that a discussion such as this was not ap-propriate, especially with their bodies facing each other so closely together. He would not for the world risk her reputation, even amongst her family; no lapse in censure should befall her by his hand. He leaned away from her, still smiling but more reserved now.

Reaching inside his coat pocket, he located a letter and hand-ed it over to Mariah. "Some delightful information for you," he said, perking a teasing brow.

Harrison watched her delicate brows draw together as she opened the letter to peruse it. Her intelligent blue eyes scanned the missive faster, gaining more excitement as she read it. She finished it quickly and passed it back to him.

"How wonderful indeed! When should this happy event take place?" Mariah excitedly replied, her sapphire eyes sparkling.

"Perhaps during Twelfth Night. I am happy to host the festivities. You will, of course, help in the preparations?" Harrison asked, looking most earnest that she should be so inclined to help plan it.

"Of course! Your aunt, I think, will be too occupied with her new little one to hostess overmuch, and I cannot think of a more splendid way to bring us all together. Shall you invite all of the neighborhood?" Mariah inquired.

"I had thought of it, but it's been such a long time since anything this large has been attempted at Bramley Hall—since my parents' passing," he finished, feeling his face turning pensive at the reflection.

"They are always much missed and in our hearts. You do such a credit to them, my lord. You are exactly what they would have wanted in a son and as the Earl of Bramley."

Harrison felt his heart pang at such a soft and sincere expression. Mariah was always one to express what she was feeling through the vibrancy of her heavenly eyes. Most would not know what to make of her intelligence and quick tongue, but he knew they were just words; to gain her true emotions, all one had to do was get lost in her gorgeous sapphire eyes.

"Excellently done, my dear!" Simon suddenly exclaimed to his wife.

Alicia smiled sweetly as the room clapped their approval over the end of her perfectly performed piece.

"Have you had a pleasant exchange?" Simon asked Harrison as he settled his wife into a chair near the settee where Mariah and Harrison were seated.

"Of course. I enjoy myself whenever I am in attendance upon Bramley Parsonage. The food is splendid and the company exceptional," Harrison replied, smiling warmly at the party.

The rest of the evening was spent in communal chatter about the estate, the weather, and all things Brighton. Harrison was fine with the topics, listening most intently when Mariah had something to say on the subject.

Upon the stroke of midnight, Harrison got up to take his leave of the Morten parsonage. He bent gallantly over each lady's hand with a kiss and bid each one a restful night's sleep. He lingered over Mariah's hand, and as he straightened, he gave her a wink. Mariah turned a lovely shade of pink. Her reaction was more than her words could ever say in regards to him.

Mayhap there is a chance after all, he thought. His heart thundered in his chest over the thought of renewed hope once again.

"Good night, all," Harrison said once more, taking his leave from the Morten household.

The ride home was moonlit and quick. His horse knew the way despite his eyes having trouble adjusting when a cloud covered the soft moonlight. The tall structure of Bramley Hall came into view, and he smiled.

How lovely it would be to have a wife within these walls—someone alike to Mariah, if not the fair lady herself, he mused. He reined in his horse near the stables, dismounted, and walked Brutus inside. His stable master, Toby, came out with a grin; despite trying to stifle the fact, he yawned.

"Thank you, Toby," Harrison replied, taking off for his home some hundred feet from the stables.

Once Harrison reached the safety of his study, he could give way to venting his feelings. How unfortunate he should be greeted with news of Lady Michaelton. He had hoped to never hear of her again after that horrific day of being abysmally rejected. He hoped the heavens were merciful and he never encountered her again.

He sat upon his great leather chair, threw his legs upon his desk, and crossed one booted foot over the other. Continuing on with his musings of the night he believed he recovered himself quite nicely. He had hoped neither Mariah nor Simon's wife noticed anything was amiss with the mention of that dastardly woman.

Having observed Mariah, though, he knew she sensed his unease. How like her to pick up on his altered mood. Of course, Simon knew the particulars of his dealings with Samantha, now Lady Michaelton, and had done his best to steer his wife to a different topic. Harrison had confided his broken pride and heart to both Simon and Mr. Morten, granted, though, at different times. He thought he would never get over Samantha. The one woman who had toppled his whole world and brought him to his knees.

His faith in himself had been greatly shaken, and for a time, he had forgotten how to pray.

He was a dunderhead to have ever believed Samantha cared for him. He had been a pawn in her scheme, and that fact still rankled. To have been duped by such a calculating female, to have lost his heart to her was an unforgivable action upon his part. No one person had ever brought him to his knees before. He still bore the stain of humiliation. And the proof was, he was still a bachelor, even now.

He thought about the possibility of encountering Samantha in Brighton. Should a meeting take place, would he be able to stay remote and distant? Surely, she was another man's wife, and she had jolly well made her bed, so she might as well lie in it. How would he feel if she was happy, truly happy? A tiny part of him wanted to see her wallow in misery and be in utter despair at having spurned him at the last second. She who had so willingly sought his attention and led him along as one leads a hound. He was no one's pet and he vowed that never would he behave in such a way again and let another person lord over him.

He knew it did him no good to let his thoughts contain her, for hearing her name, hearing any small detail of her, felt like a thousand pricks to his heart. Was it pride or did he still burn for her? Love is to burn, to be on fire. Well, he had been burnt at the stake!

He slammed a fist on the table. "I must forget her," he said out loud. "Bully to her. I shall endeavor to not ever think of her again."

Searching his thoughts, he concluded it was only his pride that suffered still. If he were to ever meet her again, he was sure he could do so without much pain. He desperately hoped that was the case. Harrison said a quick prayer for guidance and wisdom.

He got up and headed toward his bedchamber. His valet, Edmund, followed to help him out of his dinner attire and into his nightshirt. Harrison kept replaying the night's events in his head with his notions also constantly turning to Mariah.

He climbed under the cool sheets, reached to extinguish the light, and sighed. Precious Mariah. She was dear to him, and he could not deny it. Alas, she only knew him as a brother, though when he kissed her hand, he did notice the pink in her cheeks. Did she wish to be more than that? Did he? His heart told him he could not suffer another unrequited love. His pride would forever suffer were he to declare himself to her and Mariah not return his regard. Women—why did one have to put up with them? They were troublesome creatures to be sure, but they certainly enhanced the human journey. It was amazing what a pair of lovely eyes in an expressive face could do to the pace of his heart.

Yawning, he came to the conclusion that Brighton would be good for him. He would be under the same roof as Mariah and much thrown into her company. He would watch her closely to see if she could ever return his admiration for her. He was settled on being a bachelor forever if he could not claim the love-likeness which burned between his parents and which was so steady in consideration between Mr. and Mrs. Morten.

How did one begin as friends when society observed men and women being friends as ludicrous? Harrison knew he meant to marry his best friend, but how much work would be involved in making her fall in love in return? He knew he would be there to catch her whenever she did fall. He did not in the least mind the idea of having to earn her heart. A lifetime of happiness was worth the diligent work it just might require.

Chapter Six

Come On, Old Chap!

S imon sat in his father's study while the women hopped about like hens in a coop. Such a busy place was the Morten household! He couldn't even walk down the hall without running into someone hustling or hearing his mother's shrill bellowing of orders. He opted for the safety of his father's study to remain out of the way until at least luncheon.

Gloves, fans, bonnets, gowns, stockings, shoes, pelisses, and all the rest had to be accounted for to ensure there were enough outfits for any occasion Mariah might attend. Simon refrained from rolling his eyes at the busyness the women put themselves through. Although he appreciated his wife's effort in looking her best, it was still much at times.

Per her usual, his mother, Mrs. Morten, watched the maid Amy ensure all was packed appropriately. Since Amy was to depart with Mariah, they would be employing Sarah to take care of Amy's duties in the parsonage. While Amy saw to the packing needs, Sarah was busy elsewhere dusting and helping the cook, Mrs. Kurly.

The whole morning passed by very quickly to his utter astonishment, and soon all the house was seated around the dining table for a delicious luncheon. Unfortunately, much of the talk was concerning packing and what was still needing to be accomplished prior to the departure and even after their arrival in Brighton—thoughts about how his dear sister Mariah was to instruct Amy in the unpacking and setting things to rights.

Simon was mind-boggled at how any woman could care so much for their raiment. It was one of the reasons he joined the military with provided uniforms and being instructed how to dress. It was simple, really. And while out of uniform he still wanted to look his best, he did not care about the manner in which his wardrobe was packed, only that he had clean undergarments.

He glanced about the room, hiding a small smirk at his father's complete disinterest in the conversation. His sister nodded politely, almost obediently, though he could see by her blue eyes that her head was about to explode like gunpowder. Simon leaned a touch toward the table, catching the sweet gaze of his lovely wife and smiled.

His wife smiled at him, getting up from her seat. "Dearest husband," she began sweetly, batting her long black lashes, "would you mind running a short errand for me, please?"

Simon nodded, thrilled at the prospects of being out of doors. "More than happy to, my dearest wife."

Simon glided from his chair and gave his wife a peck on the cheek. Since luncheon was finished, Alicia gave him a short list of essentials to acquire in town. Happy was he to escape the activities and get some fresh air. He rode his most favorite horse, Damascus, who was also happy to be out and had a most excellent pep in his gait today. His chestnut bay was a sight to behold with a magnificent, shiny bronze coat! Damascus tossed his head, very proud in his gait and eager to show off.

Simon loved his horse and took great care of him. Never too many oats, and never underbrushed. The horse somehow knew its importance to him. Being in the regiment only increased his regard for his beast. He had won his stead from a fellow officer in a game of whist and kept that information to himself. It would never do to let it slip that he was gambling within earshot of either of his parents. Better to let them guess, if interested, as to how he had acquired the magnificent horse.

The ride to town was uneventful, and getting his wife's essentials took less time than he anticipated. Upon leaving the required shops, Simon let out a breath. It was cool outside but, thankfully, his greatcoat was sufficient to keep him warm. He started on his journey home when he spied the Earl of Bramley and called out to him with a wave and a "What, ho!"

Lord Bramley was not but a few yards ahead of Simon and broke his speed to meet his friend. "Hello. Sent out upon errands?"

"Aye. The females are overrunning the place with their tittering and packing. Papa is brushing up on some philosophy in his study, but I have not the mind to concentrate on a book. I'd much rather be out of doors." Simon turned his horse to walk back toward Bramley Hall with his neighbor.

"I have it easier. Edmund, my valet, is busy preparing for travel, and here I am, enjoying my estate," Lord Bramley stated with a shrug of his shoulders. "And you always used to be out of doors in our youth, oftentimes engaged in some mischief or another."

"Yes, well...we can't all be paragons of virtue. I seem to recall you being a willing partner in many of my adventures," Simon winked at him.

"Someone had to take charge and rein you in," the Earl chuckled. "But now, those days are long gone, and we're grown. I wonder, has your behavior changed since you've found wedded bliss?"

"Indeed, it has. My father-in-law happens to be a strict lord. He wouldn't hesitate to take me to task, and I admit, it's time to be responsible. How dull that sounds." He chuckled, ending with a crooked smile.

"I have no doubt that you'll survive. Are you ready to return or would you like to race down the lane in remembrance of past youthful follies?" his Lordship inquired, quirking his eyebrow.

"I'd much rather join you than immediately head back to my wife. She frightens me with questions and plans."

Lord Bramley laughed. "Is that so? Blessed man are you to have such a wife to keep you upon your toes. You would be bored to tears with a quiet, complacent wife."

"Of a certainty, 'tis true."

"How do you find the other aspects of married life? Is staying with your in-laws cramping your ways?"

"No, I find it very diverting. You know I never shy away from others, and my in-laws provide endless entertainment. I do not feel shy at all taking my wife here and there and leaving them to their own devices. As Alicia is an only child, her parents are rather fond of her. It would break hearts all around if we lived apart from them. But, old man, what of you? When will we see a countess upon your arm?" Simon asked, shooting him a pointed look.

"One cannot say." Lord Bramley answered quietly as he stared straight ahead of himself.

"You cannot hide away from the world forever. Besides, marriage is such fun. You may wink at a gorgeous lady that is your wife with no fear of reprimand nor an unwanted marriage forced upon you." Simon smiled roguishly and wiggled his eyebrows, then watched as the Earl's face passed between several emotions: sadness, envy, and longing. Simon's own face morphed into concern.

"Is your sister still hesitant to go, do you think?" Lord Bramley asked without looking at him.

Simon acquiesced to the subject change and fixed his face so as to not alarm his Lordship with his concern. "Perhaps. But she'll be very comfortable, and I shall do my best to rein in Alicia. You will be an ally and see that my fellow officers won't press upon her too much? I fear, around my wife, I seem to lose my focus."

"Count on my chaperoning Miss Morten. I shall see nothing untoward occurs. I know she is skittish to leave her mama and papa. I shall do my best to spend the whole fortnight, if not longer, in your company. With Mariah and her maid in the carriage, and I on my horse, nothing amiss could be said of our journey home," the Earl assured, steering his horse away from a rut in the road.

"Good man! I knew I could count on you. Perhaps you will do us all the very great favor and relief and marry my sister yourself. She is pretty, and her temperament suits you." Simon teased in part but did love the idea of it all. Having an earl in the family would be a great boon to his social activities. Plus, he liked the man more than most of his acquaintances, and Mariah was always fond of the earl even if she played well at hiding it. Simon knew better. Furthermore, it would be beneficial to Mariah, as he could not stand the thought of some impish goon having his sister's hand.

"I am looked at as another brother. I do not believe she shares your enthusiasm on the subject," Lord Bramley replied, not meeting his eyes.

"Ah, but there, perhaps you make your mistake. I see how she looks at me and at Matthew, and there is *much* difference with how she studies you with mindful fondness and adoration. Her eyes practically alight from their sockets," Simon assured.

He was certain his sister carried a tender heart for Lord Bramley. He saw it more so last night when they thought they were all alone while he was singing with his wife. His dear sister was smitten with the man, her face often changing to reflect the hard battle of remaining in propriety's grace.

He watched as Lord Bramley shook his head, and when he would say not a thing, Simon felt forced to go on.

"You will have to see for yourself, then. Perhaps this time away shall bring you back a changed man. Four years is too long to mourn that hoyden of a woman. Had you married and shared your life intimately, then you could have had as much time as would be needed to overcome her. But it did not happen; rather, she devoured you, and what she left was a hollowed-out man. The she-wolf had better plague her husband now. I have asked Alicia to *not* invite her cousin while you and my sister reside with us," Simon relayed, nodding his head over at his friend.

"I thank you on my part, but I do not wish to make your lady uneasy. She may invite whomever she pleases, and I shall act the gentleman. Perhaps seeing Samantha again would let me know I am free of her. I could not in good manners seek another when I do not know if I may be completely comfortable should she appear." The Earl smiled slightly.

"Is that it?" inquired Simon. "It might be like playing with fire. Burnt once, stay away."

"I must be able to see her again and know I am free. As much as I would like to build a life with another, I must be certain she no longer holds my interest. I had thought if I should ever see her again, I should run as if the hounds of hell were after me. But I think my future wife deserves all of me and all of my mind and heart. Do you not agree? Would you be happy to see your sister shackled to a man who cannot give the whole of his heart to her?" Lord Bramley asked, looking utterly miserable.

"You are wise in this, I see. If you must be in her company to gaze upon her, so be it. I shall ask Alicia to invite her after a week or so of our arrival. Be prepared, my friend. I am exceedingly troubled in this," Simon replied, frowning in displeasure.

With that, Simon and his friend parted ways. Simon prayed the Lord would give Lord Bramley the strength and guidance that he would need to take on this monumental scheme. He prayed for his sister's heart and well-being as well, hoping she would hold out for the Earl to come around.

Chapter Seven

Away to Brighton

A my woke Mariah early the next morning. Mariah heard that the others were already awake by the thumping and banging of trunks and doors, the hollering of orders, and the hitching of horses to the carriage. Rubbing the sleep from her eyes, she pulled the coverlet from around her. Her traveling dress was hanging up, and she needed only to quickly bathe and have Amy arrange her hair, and she would be set for her day.

Mariah hurried to accomplish her tasks, not wanting to keep anyone lingering. It took her no time at all, and she was impressed with herself. Mariah stood back to critique herself in the full-length rosewood mirror and saw that everything was right. She took a moment to admire her traveling attire; it was such a lovely shade of midnight blue, making her sapphire eyes more vibrant, her skin appear a light cream, and her hair even darker.

Mariah walked to the door, then turned around to look at her room. She would miss it. She would miss the comfort and security, the late nights delved in a good book and daydreaming about planning her future life. Now, a new adventure was set before her, and she was excited to see what it had in store—if perchance, it brought her closer to Harrison. Sighing, she closed the door while Amy tidied up. Her parents met her at the top of the landing, smiling fondly, as they descended the stairs together.

Mr. Morten turned to her with an affectionate smile. "How will you fare in Brighton? Remember you have given your word to not fall in love with a single officer!" He waggled a finger at her.

"I will do my best!" Mariah laughed.

"What?" queried Mrs. Morten. "Whatever do you mean? What is wrong with an officer? Your own dear son is an officer, and he married extremely well!" she huffed.

"Forgive me, madam," Mr. Morten started. "I meant no disrespect. You know how treasured our Mariah is. To have her settled so far away would never do. I rather believe you would never be happy, should she choose such a mate."

Mrs. Morten deflated at her husband's explanation. "Perhaps Mariah should stay here after all," she replied, studying her daughter. "Mariah is dear and would be such a comfort in our old age. She is very attentive in the sick room."

"May I speak?" asked Mariah of her mama. When Mrs. Morten nodded her assent, Mariah continued, "I do believe I shall be able to leave Brighton quite unaffected, dear Mama. However, if your fear is too great, I would gladly stay at home."

Mariah felt a measure of hope the whole idea of her ever venturing to Brighton would be laid to rest. She was excited yet extremely nervous. To be around wealthy people akin to Harrison had her nerves on edge. She did not know how to handle situations should they arise. Mariah would do her best to avoid them but knew that God tended to throw one into a muddle as a test. She could only pray to pass through unscathed, leaving her honor, her parents' honor, and that of Harrison intact.

Her father shook his head. "No, Mariah, for you shall go. Your new sister is greatly set that you should go. I think you would do well to see how one lives in Brighton. Besides, our own dear Lord Bramley will be in attendance, and I have his word you shall be happy and safe or you'll not stay in residence." Mr. Morten stepped forward and kissed her forehead.

"Thank you, Papa," Mariah replied, smiling wanly.

"Come, food is readied downstairs," Mrs. Morten announced.

Mariah followed her parents at a leisurely pace, being the last to come from above and entering the dining room as the rest were happily enjoying eggs, toast, ham, and hot chocolate or tea. It was a hearty breakfast for a long journey. Hot chocolate was a favorite, and it was not often offered. She did not doubt that it was a gift sent over from Harrison's kitchen, as he well knew her love of it. She smiled at his kind gesture. Mariah ate as much as she could without feeling too full and dabbed her mouth. She wasn't adding much to the conversation; her nerves were wound too tightly.

Mariah understood the gentlemen easily could have made this journey to Brighton within a day, arriving maybe a little later at night. They would be stopping and resting here and there for Alicia and herself. The horses would require a few moments of rest as well from pulling the cumbersome carriage.

Thankfully, the day was quite clear with no threat of rain, though no one ever could say whether the rain might fall or not; sometimes, even guessing how the next town was faring was a tricky business.

In no time at all, Solomon, the crazed dolt of a hound, was barking, and servants were exiting and entering to prepare for the trip. It seemed one had to pack so much for a fortnight's sojourn, if not longer, should it be suggested. Harrison's trunk had arrived earlier and was added to the growing pile.

Turning from the sitting room window, Mariah heard Harrison's deep voice greet her brother. She stayed where she was, for she did not wish to see her mother cry as she had been doing all morning since she had risen. One simple glance at Mariah sent her mother into a fit of waterworks. To lose three children was nigh impossible for Mrs. Morten to bear. At the very least, she took comfort that Mariah would be returning, as she was set to hostess the Earl's Twelfth Night celebrations, and that was something she could not send her apologies about. Mr. Morten assured his wife that Mariah would have no chance of falling in love with a soldier, as the good girl had given her word not to—a promise she intended to keep. All would be well.

It was not long before Mariah's mama entered the room. "Make haste and fetch your bonnet, gloves, and reticule. You are set to depart within five minutes, and you know how Simon is a stickler for promptness," she directed, wiping her eyes with her handkerchief. She smiled tearily at Mariah.

"Yes, Mama," Mariah replied, passing by her mother to do as she was bid.

Coming down the steps, she saw Alicia and Simon just walk out to the carriage. Mariah followed and was greeted by Harrison. He looked so handsome in his tan breeches and bronze tailcoat. His ebony hair was tousled from the breeze, and his eyes appeared more green than blue in the early morning light. His strong jaw was set, his face freshly shaven.

"It's a fine morning for travel, Miss Morten," he said, bowing deeply.

Curtsying, she nodded her agreement. "It's a fine day, indeed."

Mr. Morten clapped Simon upon his back and said, "Now, be sure to consider your sister in your plans. We cannot have her missing her mama and papa."

"You have my word." Simon nodded at his father.

Mariah watched as her sister-in-law and brother embraced her parents and bid their goodbyes, offering to visit again soon. Simon passed Alicia up into the carriage. Mariah stepped forth, having awaited her turn to tell her family goodbye.

Mr. Morten turned to Mariah. "We will anxiously await your return, my dear. That being said, enjoy Brighton. Remember to write. Sheets, if you can. I would love to hear you describe all the details." He kissed her upon her cheek and stepped away so his wife could have a turn.

Grabbing Mariah to her bosom and holding her there, Mrs. Morten began, "Be considerate to your hosts. Don't dance with the same man more than twice in one evening, and avoid too many sweets. Do write sheets and sheets to us, for your poor papa will miss you so." Unable to say more as her tears came again, Mrs. Morten let go of her daughter.

Harrison came forward, taking Mariah's hand. He held onto it as she ascended the wooden carriage steps. He squeezed her fingers and let go. Mariah withheld the heat creeping to her cheeks from his touch. So long was he had allowed it to linger, and dare she say, she loved it so and was remiss when it ended. Mariah was sad when the groom closed the door.

From the back window, she watched Harrison climb onto his horse and give the command for the carriage to be on its way. Mariah and Alicia waved and watched Mr. and Mrs. Morten until they grew too small to see. Mariah's heart clenched, knowing this was going to be hard on her parents. A fortnight or more away was sure to make her mother frantic with worry and her dear papa a touch melancholy.

Amy, Mariah's maid, sat across from the two ladies. She looked excited to be traveling. She kept her eyes alert and her mouth silent, staring out the window at the passing scenery.

"La, but you will have so much fun, dear sister!" Alicia began. "There will be scores of suitors for you. We'll be sure you are never left alone. Have I told you how much I love dancing? Of course, married women may dance and dance and dance. I cannot tell you how pleased I am that my papa was so willing to let us marry! I had thought Papa aspired for me to gain a title, but I'm awfully glad with how it all turned out. Simon is so handsome, is he not?" Without waiting for a response, Alicia continued on. "I have been remiss. Have I not told you of my very dear friend, Cora? You will certainly adore her, and I've no doubt she'll adore you. Cora is the wife of Mr. Liftgrove who serves in my papa's regiment. I met Mr. Liftgrove before he met Cora. They are a charming pair and have not long been married. You must meet my very good friend, Leticia, as well. She is the daughter of an officer, and though she is not much to look at, she has the sweetest temperament that ever existed. Her brother is also an officer, though not in my father's regiment."

Alicia went on and on; when one travels, what else is there to do? Mariah made sure to nod and click her tongue at the appropriate times. Her mind was elsewhere as Alicia droned. Mariah brought out her embroidery, something she wasn't even quite fond of, just for something to do while Alicia hardly took a breath, going on about all the officers and their wives.

"And you must be sure to—" Alicia continued.

Mariah nodded, hoping there would be a bit of silence somewhere.

Chapter Eight

Oh, No, My Sweet

Harrison strode into the hotel ahead of their party to secure accommodations. The Tiger and Rose Inn was one of his favorites to stop at if he felt the need to rest, as it marked the halfway point to Brighton.

He held open the door, permitting the ladies to enter. Alicia was talking about some officer and his wife while Mariah looked to be faring poorly. His brows furrowed low over his eyes.

"Mariah," Harrison began, "are you all right?"

She nodded. "Just fine. Nothing a good night's sleep will not be able to cure."

Harrison nodded, giving her a concerned look to which she smiled wanly, more for his reassurance of her predicament. He hurriedly got the accommodations made. The proprietor of the inn hustled servants to make certain the upstairs lodging was fit and well.

He happily paid for the rooms, urging for one to be readied immediately, as he did not wish to see Mariah tax herself more. How she was still standing on her feet, smiling and conversing with Alicia, he knew not.

Seeing Mariah unwell made him fidget. Never in all his days had he seen her so pale and quiet. She hid it well from her brother. And blast the man for not noticing his sister's health, but in the same twist of the tongue, Simon was a married man now. Still, he thought it would be pertinent to note Mariah's well-being.

How Mariah had not made a fuss about her state was beyond him. Any other lady he knew would have made them stop for her to recover. He smiled wearily at the door on his right. Mariah was not all women; she was sharp, kind, and above all else, the most tender person he ever knew.

"All the rooms have been prepared," the proprietor lady announced. "Follow me, if you please."

Harrison offered Mariah his arm. She took it, her grip a touch feeble. The lady stopped at the first room after ascending a staircase, and Harrison got the door for her. Mariah thanked him with a smile and curtsy, heading inside with Amy on her heels.

The lady took them down to their other rooms, but Harrison could not go in. His heart would not allow him to have reprieve of himself until he knew Mariah was taken care of.

Harrison sighed, standing outside her door. At last, the door opened, and he met Amy in the hallway.

"All is well?" He drew his brows together.

"Of course, my lord. Miss Morten is sound asleep. I took rose water and bathed her forehead," she explained, curtsying to him.

"Excellent. Thank you, Amy."

Harrison's bedroom was situated beside Mariah's, and he took comfort in knowing that should she need anything, he would be within easy reach. He watched her maid scurry away down the stairs before he entered his own room.

Harrison's valet, Edmund, was waiting patiently in his room to attend him. Edmund turned from the window when Harrison came through the door. Helping him with his coat, he placed a chair in front of Harrison. Harrison sat and let his man servant remove his boots.

Edmund had been employed with him for a long time. The man had been more like a confidant and friend, permitted to speak more freely than he knew others allowed their servants to. Edmund was a kind man with alert and observant brown eyes. Harrison appreciated the care Edmund took and also the companionship.

"How is Miss Morten?" Edmund asked, tugging one boot off and then the other.

"I hope faring much better. Her maid said she was asleep," Harrison replied, rising from the chair.

"Ah, but that is good. I noticed you paid her quite an amount of attention today." Edmund smiled knowingly.

"How is that so? We were separated by a carriage," Harrison countered, allowing Edmund to remove his clothing.

"There were times she was not in the carriage. You watched her every chance you had." Edmund smiled smugly, dropping his head in hopes of hiding it.

"Are you keeping such close tabs on me, then?"

"The whole of Bramley Hall would welcome her into the household," Edmund stated truthfully.

"Is that so? Was there ever a time she was turned away?" Harrison wondered.

"No. You misunderstand my meaning. She is all that is gracious, thoughtful, and kind. We all like her immensely." Edmund helped Harrison into his sleeping attire.

"Is that the turn the servants' conversation takes? Deciding upon who will be the next countess?" Harrison grinned, shaking his head.

"It's only that we all wish you happiness, and a countess would be a wonderful addition to the household, especially if it's a woman akin to Miss Mariah Morten. I do not mean to speak in such a way as to offend," Edmund added quickly, gathering up the clothing as he tidied up.

"Hmm, are you sure about that? My valet, of all people, giving me marriage advice?" Harrison remarked, knowing Edmund meant kindness instead of cruelty. "Perhaps I shall leave you stranded here to learn a lesson."

Edmund dipped his head, hiding the smirk Harrison knew was there. "Perhaps 'tis what I deserve for speaking out of turn, my lord. Though you should know: no one owes you more than I, and there is no one who wishes to see you happier than I. Well, good night, then." Edmund walked to the door and bowed before he closed it behind him.

Harrison chuckled. "Impish man," he said to the air. He knew what his valet was speaking of. They had been together since Oxford, though Edmund had not been a student. He was the servant of another classmate, and when Harrison had spied that man abusing Edmund, he had stepped in. Harrison had angered his classmate due to his interference and dismissed Edmund from employment. Harrison promptly hired him on the spot and sent Edmund to Bramley Hall to learn his duties. Harrison could still see his classmate with a bloodied nose and a blackened eye.

He sighed, staring at the door his friend and servant walked out of. It was Edmund who saw him through the rough days after Samantha's rejection. Edmund made Harrison live and go on with the things that needed to be done. By goodness, if that man hadn't earned the right to tell Harrison like it was, then there was no one who could. Harrison remembered how badly he had let himself behave in those days. Rejection had stung, and he feared he would never love another again. He simply had ceased to care about his responsibilities as an earl; he'd stopped eating and not allowed anyone to pay a call upon him. He had holed up in his vast estate and became quite the hermit.

Edmund would bring him the paper, and when Harrison took no notice of it, Edmund would read it aloud. It was the same with his letters of business. When Harrison would wander the halls at night while the house slept, Edmund would walk with him. Whether the kindly servant feared he would end his life or whether he walked with him just to keep him company, Harrison was grateful for the man. They'd talk about women they had known and then would wish the devil took them all.

Harrison smiled at the memory, heading for his bed. Then one day, Simon came to see him. Edmund let him into the study, disobeying his order for complete privacy. Simon plopped himself into the leather chair and said not a thing for half an hour until he could hardly stand it and said, "Look here, chap; it can't be that bad."

For some reason, Harrison told Simon all that had transpired between himself and Samantha. Simon was not one to sit back and listen, though Harrison was grateful that day for his being there. Simon was very vocal as he listened. Simon went on to urge him to be about and socializing again, as the silly chit was simply not worth the time nor the effort of another single thought. 'Twas past time to put the whole of the matter out to pasture and to seek greener fields. There were other ladies in the world who were far above Samantha in station and grace. Truly, she did not deserve either his heart or his title. Four years was a long time to mourn a woman and an even longer time to love one without hope of her returning his regard.

The next day, Simon had brought Mariah to call upon him. Shy and as sweet as ever, Mariah served them tea and biscuits she had personally made for him. Simon purposefully drew the curtains open, and he remembered how brightly the sunshine had poured into the room, but it was not nearly as bright or as lovely as when he had glanced at Mariah; her brunette hair was gleaming in the sunlight and her blue eyes were steady and kind. She looked as if heaven had opened up and delivered her into the very chair in which she sat. She smiled glowingly at him, offering him kind words that were lost to him as he stared at her radiant beauty. It was then that he experienced the first time that he took notice of her as a man notices a woman.

Harrison sighed, *By Jove, that was four years ago. And I swear to God Himself, Mariah grows more beautiful and gracious by the hour,* he thought as he shook his head. *Why did I ever waste so long in admiring another when there was such excellence in Mariah before me?*

He had hoped from that day when he took real notice of Mariah that he would prove to be worthy of her gentle heart. She was still too young to make an offer of marriage for, and the last thing he could let himself entertain was the thought that she might scorn his interest. He reminded himself she was an innocent, gentle lady, and while the world had not yet touched her kind spirit, she ought to have the chance to spread her wings.

Harrison hoped things would fall into place in Brighton. He hoped to win the hand of his lady, and he hoped that seeing Samantha again would not leave a pain within his heart. More importantly, he hoped he could exist in the same room as Samantha and not mourn her. Instead, he could gaze upon her, feel free from her influence, and start his new life courting another.

He sighed, turning over. There was a very small part of his brain warning him against letting another into his heart. *The risk will be entirely worth it if one day I may be so fortunate to call Mariah my wife,* he concluded.

Chapter Nine

Darting Glances & Flirtation

Harrison arose early the next day. Peering through his window, he spied the inn yard that was bustling with activity and the orders that were being given from the ostler to his men. He yawned and awaited his valet. It was not long before Edmund arrived and they began the morning preparations and the breaking of his fast.

Stepping outside into the hallway, Harrison stopped in front of Mariah's room where he heard the lady in conversation with her maid. He hoped that Mariah was feeling better. Though they did not have very far to travel today, any complaints were sure to make the journey most difficult.

Anxiously, he made his way to the stables to check upon the processes of readying the horses and carriage. He discerned this was an excellent way in which to spend his time. He always felt better when he took action, even one as menial as checking on his horse when he could not do more in a situation. The grooms were already addressing the animals and were awaiting further instruction.

After petting his favorite animal, Harrison walked into the sitting room where his entire party had met and were exchanging pleasantries. He was very relieved to see Mariah looking the picture of perfect health. He greeted Mariah with a bow. She smiled broadly in the way he had come to love and curtsied.

"You are looking much improved from yesterday. I trust all is well again? For if not, we can stay a day behind, and I can escort you and your maid tomorrow. It would be of no trouble to accommodate you," Harrison offered.

Mariah smiled, inching a touch closer beyond what was proper. "That is most kind of you, my lord. I am indeed faring much better, and we won't be in the carriage for as long today. I'm determined all shall go well," Mariah replied. She smiled up at him, and he caught his breath. Taking her hand in his arm, they thanked the lady of the inn and departed for the stable yard.

Harrison escorted Mariah outside to the awaiting carriage that had yet to pull around. The sun was shining brightly today, giving way to clear roads and a promising day. Birds chirped merrily, fluttering in the light breeze. Mariah smiled at the sky, putting a hand beside her bonnet to block the glare.

He watched her out of the corner of his eye as she promptly moved her bonnet off her head, letting loose her brown curled hair in some manner of upswept hairdo. She stuck her face toward the sun, a soft smile graced her gorgeous face, and a calming sigh passed her pink, full lips. He smiled, admiring her joyful spirit and enthusiasm for the out of doors and the world. It panged his heart and furthered his resolve to allow her to spread her wings a little without his interference nor baggage of a broken heart.

Harrison watched her fully before he ever realized he was. Mariah was beginning to blush, her cheeks flushing to a beautiful pink hue. She dipped her head, her long, dark lashes fluttering in such a manner, it made his heart palpitate with her charm and beauty. Harrison caught his breath, looking toward his horse trotting ahead beside Simon's mount.

Recovering himself, Harrison smiled. *My, what a minx, and wherever did she learn to do that? Her look would have put to shame the finest courtesans of the ton. Did every woman have this innate ability to steal a man's breath and make all coherent thoughts flee from the brain?*

He would never have guessed Mariah capable of a look so...well, he couldn't say exactly what it was since he was still addle-minded. He knew of only one other woman with whom he had ever felt his senses go begging when she looked at him.

The thought finally occurred to him that perhaps she was not flirting with him, but he could not stop the pleasure he had gained from the look she had given him. Pleasure, because it gave him hope that perhaps she too felt something deeper for him. He really was becoming a doddering old man to be so disconcerted by a mere look. Mayhap it wasn't so much the action as the lady executing it.

The two stood in unsettled silence for the span of a minute or two until Simon and his wife joined them. At Simon's instruction, the carriage was brought before them, and he conveyed his wife into it, by giving her a hand up as he made a great show of winking at her. Giggling demurely, Alicia flushed finely, adding to his merriment. Simon turned toward his horse and mounted, leaving Harrison to assist Mariah into the conveyance.

After completing this task and closing the door, Harrison ascended his stallion, Brutus. He heard Simon laugh in his direction and turned to raise an inquiring eyebrow at him.

Simon said, "You see what very good fun a wife is? I highly recommend marriage, old man. Get thee a wife and the sooner, the better!" Simon then gave the order to the coachman and away they went.

Harrison thought of his friend's words. Would marriage be fun? Could it be as joyful as what he observed with Simon and Alicia? Harrison's lips twisted and pursed at the side of his face. *Mayhap it could be with someone like Mariah. Mayhap I could be so fortunate as to have a woman such as her.* He leaned in the saddle, taking a fleeting glance back at the carriage, and grinned. *I could be happy with someone such as her. I just need to get the gumption to ask her how she feels.*

Mariah returned her bonnet to the appropriate position once she was situated, hoping it helped to hide the blush upon her cheeks. Feeling Harrison's eye upon her and feeling a tad ridiculous for her behavior, for what lady wants the sun to shine upon her features, she turned to him with lowered lashes. When she slowly brought her eyes up to meet his, she heard him gasp or cough, making some sort of strangled noise. She hadn't meant to seem as if she was attempting to flirt with him.

Mariah was not a seasoned flirt, and heaven help her, she hoped she did not have to use such skills upon any gentlemen. Still, even though Harrison had winked at her just a few nights before, it did not mean she should have taken up flirting with him in return. Perhaps he still saw her as he ever had: a young girl who tried in vain to follow in the footsteps of her older brothers. She knew it was more possible than not; he would never look upon her as a young lady worthy of his gentlemanly notice. Not that he was anything but a gentleman. She knew better than to hope one day he might be *her* gentleman...but how her heart achingly wished it would be so.

The carriage rolled on, turning a sharp right up the road to Brighton. Alicia immediately began prattling about the state of her room and how she hoped Mariah's was just as equal.

Mariah felt guilty when she realized she was ignoring Alicia's words. How long had she been so engrossed within her own thoughts? No more than a moment or two? She tried to quiet her mind, but it was of no use. She had to give the whole of her attention to herself. She kept thinking about the odd sound Harrison had made at her when she had looked up at him. She was aware she had seemed to be flirting with him, and Mama would be ashamed of her for having given him such improper attention.

Her cousin, Emily, had practiced flirting in front of a mirror before her first season had concluded. She had been quite proud of herself and had tried to instruct Mariah in the fine art of fan fluttering and flirting. Mariah had thought it was a terrible waste of her time, but when pressed upon by Emily, she too had practiced a touch.

Mariah pursed her lips and frowned. *Would he now be ashamed of me? Or was that just the sound a man makes when he is flirted with?* Though she had practiced the look, she had never dared to use it before, and, come to think upon it, she had not even practiced since that day Emily had been so insistent. It had been amusing to watch Emily perform her husband-catching tactics, and Mariah had Emily clapping when she mastered the same actions. Well, there was only one way to discern Harrison's thoughts about the matter: she would just have to use the look again and gauge his reaction.

Her heart pounded at the thought. *And if he looks upon me as before again, mayhap there will be a modicum of a chance for me? Dearest heavens, I hope so!*

Chapter Ten

A Purcellville Welcoming

B righton at last! It was almost five o'clock, but they had finally arrived, and in good time, at that. The carriage had barely stopped when Lord and Lady Purcellville stood in the street, gleefully calling out welcomes. Mariah could understand Alicia's lively manner at first glance of the lady waving her handkerchief so spastically. Lady Purcellville was a short, rotund lady with auburn hair and smallish eyes. Mariah could not make out the color of her eyes, and so she directed her attention to Lord Purcellville as the man himself threw open the carriage door. He was tall, lean, and held quite a commanding presence. He was neither gracious nor rude, more alert than anything, and anxious to be acquainted with his guests.

Simon first introduced the Earl of Bramley and then turned to his left to introduce Mariah. Mariah curtsied and was drawn into the ample bosom of Lady Purcellville upon gaining her footing. She thought she would soon die of squeezing and lack of air, and to her relief, she was soon let go. Smiling at the lady, she turned her attention to Lord Purcellville. He bent over her hand and helped her rise from her curtsy. His keen eyes were gray and looked as if nothing escaped his attention. He assured the party they were indeed most welcome and he very much wanted to get them all happily situated within the house.

Mariah smiled demurely at the interactions, finding it very endearing and almost alarming in manner, given the station of Alicia. Either way, Mariah was delighted to be in Brighton at last.

"This way to the parlor, if you please," Lord Purcellville declared. "I will have refreshments prepared here shortly. I believe a brief respite prior to adjourning until dinner would be delightful. Do you not agree?"

"Indeed," Harrison's voice boomed his agreement.

Mariah smiled as Alicia attempted to refrain from spilling all the details at once. She was like an ocean swelling and trying to calm itself at the same time. Mariah hid an amused smirk, falling in behind Simon while Harrison spoke with Lady Purcellville. Mariah was grateful for the lack of attention so she could observe those around her. With Alicia talking nigh the entire time in the carriage, this was a nice break in conversation.

Mariah admired the tall, glistening white marble columns and the broad foyer entering the estate home. Potted plants in various stages of fall bloom were set on either side of the columns while evergreens stood by the large double oak door. Large bay windows decorated with rosette moldings let in the precious sunshine that sometimes hid amongst the clouds.

She held in her breath as she took in the white marble floors bespeaking the wealth of the hosts. Giant oil paintings decorated the walls with splendid colors of garden scenes. A painting of a man in full regalia hung on the wall giving entry to a different section of the large home. Lord Purcellville led them down the hallway to a separate room on the left, bidding them all entry.

Mariah floated inside, taking a seat on the very far left of the settee so as to watch the whole room. Shortly after arriving inside the parlor, two servants bustled inside, bearing trays of drinks and small finger sandwiches. Mariah graciously took a drink, and accepted the offered sandwich even though she had no appetite. She would courteously attempt to nibble at it. She didn't want her first impression to be that of a rude and ungrateful guest.

The room was filled with conversation about Simon and Alicia's stay as well as how traveling such a great distance happened to be. Mariah observed Harrison's mannerisms, how he was polite in his smiles and replies yet his countenance was a touch reserved and hanging back and his eyes were narrowed a trace. She knew him so well, like the back of her hand.

Her mind reeled with the thought of testing him again, to see if he liked her beyond the childhood gaze he once held her in. Her stomach was in knots, though not from feeling ill. *I have to see for myself tonight what comes about when I flutter my lashes at Harrison. I would surely love for something to blossom between us. Though if he doesn't at least give me an inclination he fancies me as well, then I must be diligent and separate myself.*

Mariah excused herself to get ready for the evening meal, wanting to not only impress her hosts but also Harrison. Upon reaching her room, she let out a deep breath. Lady Purcellville spoke just as animatedly and quickly as her daughter.

Mariah smiled, heading to where Amy was unpacking her dresses and chose her favorite gown. After Mariah dressed and freshened up, it took Amy no time at all to have her hair styled in a simple and elegant fashion on top of her head, her brunette curls framing her oval face. She wished that she had seed pearls or flowers with which to decorate her hair; even a comb for an accent would have been most welcome.

Taking a deep breath in the hallway, she rounded the corner leading into the salon. Entering the large room, she felt Harrison's eyes upon her. She had dressed in a modest sky blue evening gown with dark blue ribbon trim around the collar and empire waist. In all, it was a plain dress, not quite like the other ladies wore in elegance, but it was one she felt elegant in.

When dinner was announced and the party had entered the formal dining room, they walked to their places with each lady upon a gentleman's arm. Since it was a family affair, they did not stand upon ceremony and sit in accordance to their rank.

Harrison pulled out her seat and scooted her in while whispering in her ear, "I am sure we will never know a moment's boredom while in residence. What a charming couple our hosts are." He smiled at her.

"Indeed. I cannot wait to get to know them better," Mariah replied.

Once the party was seated, Lord Purcellville began, "My, what a celebration this is most certainly! We have two new friends under our roof! I trust all your needs have been seen to?" He turned toward Harrison with one fuzzy gray eyebrow raised.

"Of a certainty, Lord Purcellville! You are most kind to invite me so warmly into your home. I am exceedingly grateful to have been included. This meal is manna from heaven, and the table is set as prettily as ever I have seen. What talent your dear lady possesses, to make one and all welcome." Harrison complimented, grinning as Lady Purcellville blushed, inclining her head toward him.

Mariah internally beamed at Harrison and the way he addressed people. Not many men openly praised women in any manner of tidings, yet he did so with exquisite grace and eloquence. A *gentleman and champion if there ever was one*, she mused. She held in her beaming smile, hoping he caught her expression in her eyes.

"None of this *my lording* back and forth upon my part. You must, of course, address me as Purcey as one and all do here!" Lord Purcellville waved his hand to gesture to the whole space of the room.

"I thank you. Please freely address me as Bramley," Harrison offered.

Turning toward Mariah, Lord Purcellville said, "My dear Miss Morten, have you any tales to regale us with about the hijinks young Simon partook in?" His merry voice matched the twinkle in his warm gray eyes.

Mariah smiled bashfully. "I have several, my lord." She would not address him without his title since he addressed her properly. She knew she should not allow such an action to make her heart quicken as it did, but she was nervous. Even though Lord and Lady Purcellville were kind and gracious to allow her to stay, they were well above her in station, and she did not wish to offend.

"Now, dearest sister, do not give way to all my terrors," Simon teased.

"Dearest brother, I could not speak of all tales; it would take years perhaps."

The room laughed while Simon chortled, dipping his head and shaking it. Mariah looked at her brother to scc what he thought of such a question. He seemed to have a neutral look upon his face while she wondered what would be proper and welcomed to relate. With Simon's affirmative small nod, Mariah decided the safest course was to reminisce upon the occasion in which her brother went fishing at the break of dawn. The memory brought a grin to her face.

Hesitantly, Mariah began, "I recall it was early spring. The lake had just thawed, and Simon was *adamant* to fish," she paused, wriggling in her seat. "I was in Mama's quaint little room off the dining room, sewing, when I heard dishes clatter something fierce. Mama screamed terribly as if a great terror had come upon her. I dashed to the dining room to see what the fuss happened to be. My heart was pounding so; however, it was only Simon. He stood triumphantly on Papa's left, beaming proudly despite his dripping clothes and a dirty face. He victoriously swung this huge fish right onto the table, clattering dishes and ruining Mama's best tablecloth. Mama was beside herself. Simon was quite unrepentant then, and I can observe that by the twinkle in his eyes, he is still so." Mariah laughed.

"Yes, I'm afraid I am still unrepentant, dear sister. Allow me now to relate the whole matter entirely! For you see, it was not my idea to fish that morning. It was Lord Bramley's! He planned the activity and I went innocently along with it. We traversed to the large pond upon his estate after he woke me up by throwing stones at the window. I dragged upon my clothing and made my way out of doors to inquire why ever he disturbed me at such an hour. Why, the sky had barely gained any color! Well, the pair of us went right off and fished in the pond. Since neither of us had a proper pole, we found sticks." Simon paused, glancing at his cohort.

Mariah glanced at Harrison too and shook her head. Here were facts she had never yet heard. Harrison waved his hand at Simon to continue.

"It took what seemed like forever for two boys to catch something as simple as a fish, but catch a fish we did. I speared the ugly creature, and it was his Lordship who helped me lift its squirming body out of the pond, which I can assure you was not an easy task! Why, I do believe the fish was half of our size and possessed the strength of at least a dozen other fishes. Lord Bramley and I slipped through the mud, getting aptly soiled, but we did claim the prize in the end. I hadn't realized how much mud covered me until Mama was screeching at me. Anyway, once the fish was dead and we two lay exhausted next to it, Lord Bramley suggested I take it home for Mrs. Kurly, our cook, to prepare. Seemed like the proper end for the fish, so I returned home with it and proudly displayed it for Mama and Papa, though they were not as delighted as I." Simon threw back his head and gave a hearty laugh. So infectious was his laugh that all joined in.

"I cannot to this day believe you flung it at your poor bewildered parents!" Harrison smiled brightly.

"Well, I did. Mama promised a swift and severe punishment and bade me meet Papa in his study once I was properly bathed and attired. You cannot imagine the dread I suffered! I thought for certain I was to become an angel that day!

"I knocked upon the study door and entered once I was given permission. Shaking in my boots, I approached Papa, and he inquired as to my actions. Once I related the events, Papa looked back at me and smiled warmly; he even laughed softly. Then he said he thought the whole matter was rather humorous, but he bid me approach him behind his desk. I did not know a prayer could be uttered so quickly!

"Once I reached the armrest of his chair, he took my hand and brought me over his knees. One swift swat broke the silence, and then I was righted again. Smiling, Papa told me to go forth into the world again but to take great care to not aggravate my mama and to not dare to soil another tablecloth. Promising reformation, I quickly escaped the study and am alive today!"

Mariah smirked, glancing from Simon to Harrison. Simon took a huge sip of his wine, smacking his lips from the approving taste. Lord Purcellville dissolved into loud laughter as his wife laughed faintly. Alicia smiled affectionately at her husband, shaking her head softly.

Mariah perked a teasing brow at Harrison. "I cannot believe I have never heard the entire relating of the tale before! You, certainly older than I, must have known Simon would get himself into trouble, yet you let him. Friend indeed, my lord." Mariah clucked her tongue and shook her head at Harrison.

Feigning distress, Harrison clutched at his heart and addressed Mariah. "I am deeply affected, my dear Miss Morten. I should have taken my blame in the matter. If I had thought Simon to be in any real trouble, I would have come forth from my hiding spot in the bushes outside of the breakfast room. Upon my honor, never once did I spy any real trouble for him," Harrison replied, looking so sincerely at her that she broke into a brilliant smile. He quickly added, "I'll never forget the look upon Simon's face as he plunked that dead fish upon the table! He was beaming! Your dear father's eyes grew larger than the tea saucer, and your mama turned an alarming shade of red and was waving her arms here and there." Harrison chuckled.

"You watched my disgrace, my lord?" boomed Simon from across the table.

"Indeed, I now confess that is so," Harrison admitted, chuckling.

"Hmm. I never knew that in particular. Would you have rushed in and pleaded my case, Earl of Bramley?" Simon asked, mocking his friend.

"Upon my honor!" Harrison bowed as best he could over the table toward his friend.

"I shall have no choice but to believe you, old man!"

"Well, with that, I do believe it's time for the gentlemen to have their port while we ladies retire to discuss our plans for your visit, Miss Morten," announced Lady Purcellville, rising from her seat and nodding at her husband.

The gentlemen all rose and turned toward the ladies who were easing onto their feet, helping to pull their chairs away from the table. Mariah followed Lady Purcellville out of the room with Alicia clamped on her arm. Alicia had already started chattering gaily away. *My, but the courses all passed by so quickly as the dinner conversation progressed.* Mariah wondered how anyone present at the table had taken their fill, but eaten they all had. She glanced over her shoulder, wondering when the opportune moment would happen to test Harrison. *I am so eager to know, yet I must insist upon myself to use patience.*

Not even in the room yet, and Lady Purcellville began regaling her with tales of who was around in Brighton. Mariah did not think so many titled peers would be in attendance for this season, but it appeared she was misinformed. Her stomach clenched slightly from nerves. So many people! Lady Purcellville promised not to leave her on her own or without a proper introduction to most.

"You are all kindness, my lady," Mariah addressed her hostess, who had just finished relating all of the comings and goings of the inhabitants of Brighton. There certainly would be many entertainments while she resided with the Purcellvilles. Balls, dinners, walks, calls, and even a play would give her enough to fill several sheets of paper, to her parents' delight.

"Cora shall call upon us tomorrow, I am sure, Mariah, and then you may meet each other!" Alicia announced, clapping her hands together. "She and you, I feel sure, will get along fabulously!"

Mariah smiled and said, "I shall be most pleased to know her."

The gentlemen came through the doorway and into the large sitting room. The room silenced, waiting for the men to take their seats. Simon took the chair next to his wife as Lord Purcellville took the corner chair by the fire. Harrison chose to sit on the settee next to Mariah.

"My, I do say, we shall never be bored here in Brighton, shall we, Mariah?" Simon commented to the whole of the room.

"Most certainly not! I cannot wait to meet several of your friends of whom you have been endlessly speaking," Mariah replied, setting a smile on her face.

She was nervous about meeting so many people from lords and ladies to those who held station similar to Harrison and above. It was more than she imagined. She could only hope and pray that she did not embarrass herself nor her family in any way. With Harrison's promise to remain by her side, she relaxed a little though the nerves still tried to prick at the edges of her lips to pull into a frown.

"Alicia, my dear, would you please play my favorite piece? I feel as if it's been ages since you were on the pianoforte!" Lady Purcellville addressed her daughter.

Obeying, Alicia directly sat down and began to play. The music was slow and quite beautiful, reminding Mariah of a play which she had once seen put on in Bramley Hall. That was, of course, before the death of Harrison's parents, when the Hall had many entertainments. She frowned, and she let herself think upon the past. It had been years since Bramley Hall had seen any sort of merriment. She hoped this year while helping with the Twelfth Night celebrations, it would remedy the long spell of melancholy on the beautiful home.

"Whatever are you thinking which has you so unhappy?" Harrison inquired, his dark brows furrowed.

Taking a moment to decide upon how much to share with him, as she didn't really want to alter his mood, she fidgeted in her seat, pondering how best to proceed with his query. "Do you remember how bustling and loud Bramley Hall used to be? There was always laughter, and everyone was always so busy! It will be good for us all to see Bramley Hall festive again this Twelfth Night." Mariah said softly, hoping she had not said anything to upset him.

Smiling at Mariah warmly, Harrison nodded. "It will be a wonderful holiday for us all. Time to break the silence and peace the great hall has endured for far too long."

"I hope your aunt and uncle will be pleased when they arrive. I promise to make the preparations go smoothly, and I cannot wait to begin decorating!" Mariah gushed with delight.

"I am your servant! I shall do exactly as you direct me. No task shall be too much, and no chore shall be left undone," Harrison said, looking into Mariah's eyes.

Mariah felt her cheeks growing warm. He was such a handsome man to gaze upon. She appreciated his thoughtfulness and care when it came to her—how he always took a moment to ask if she was all right. And now, preparing Bramley Hall for a celebration after a decade would be such a treat and a feat to pull off. With Harrison helping and his gentle care to detail, she was certain that between the two of them, it would be an accomplishment with which to be truly pleased.

Mariah stared into his gorgeous teal eyes. How the color morphed between blue and green she knew not, but she got lost in them with each passing moment. When the music stopped, it was as if a spell had broken. Harrison's lip upturned slightly, and her cheeks heated. Harrison was the first to blink and make himself move.

Mariah sat and blinked her eyes for a second or two, looking over at her hosts. The lord and his lady were speaking in hushed tones by the fire, much like how Mama and Papa always did.

Dear Mama and Papa. She had not thought to miss them, not until this moment, and she could feel her eyes mist. How could she miss them though little time had passed since she had seen them? Mariah was certain they missed her. For so long, it had been their happy trio dwelling in the parsonage and partaking in one another's company.

Mariah swiped at an errant tear upon her reminiscent thoughts of her family.

Harrison gazed at her concerningly, "My dear, what has upset you so? Tell me so I may correct the slight at once!"

Turning her head toward him, she felt acutely embarrassed. "Oh, 'tis nothing, my lord. I fear the hour grows late and I am tired. I let myself wonder about home—what Mama and Papa are doing, how they might be missing me, as I am quite certain they are because I am missing *them*. What a great comfort to know they are so well-suited to each other and have a great love. It seems Simon and Alicia enjoy a love match as well. I looked at our hosts, and I have come to the conclusion that most I know have the pleasure of being wed to someone they love. Such a comfort. I know this is not the way of our society with people marrying for various reasons, but it gives me hope to know such love does exist," Mariah replied.

Fearing she was rambling, she felt herself heat and knew her cheeks were a bright rosy hue. What would Harrison think of her with her unabashed thoughts? She was beginning to wonder if her skin would forevermore be tinged pink.

Instead of censuring her over the topic she discussed, Harrison's look softened. "I know your feelings perfectly. I suppose I have remained a bachelor because I would rather let the estate fall to pieces than suffer a wife I find I cannot stand, though it seems selfish upon my part. I long to have a comfortable home where my devotion to my wife is a shared entity. I love Bramley Hall and would hate to wed a shrew and feel forced to spend most of my time elsewhere."

"Promise you shall choose wisely, my lord, for I would be very grieved to see Bramley Hall without you." Mariah smiled sweetly at him. Bramley Hall without Harrison would be such a dreary place to reside.

"I shall endeavor to do my best...my wife shall have to have great character but also more sweetness than ever I have seen. She shall have to be well-informed so we have something to discuss on rainy days. She shall have to be pretty, as I couldn't stand a plain female; her countenance should match mine so when we are in my curricle, all who see us shall be in wonder at the glorious pair we present. She shall have to have such grace, all my bad tempers greeted with a *tut-tut* and an affectionate kiss. She shall have to bear my children, and they should all be perfect little specimens, beholding the fine qualities of us both. In our old age, she shall never be allowed out of my sight so any little need of mine will be promptly addressed. She shall never be permitted ill tempers or outbursts, and she shall always, always be a lady of the first water in every situation." Harrison stopped, drawing a serious brow at Mariah's giggling outburst.

Mariah put a hand over her mouth in an attempt to stem the giggling but could not. Harrison waggled an eyebrow at her. She chortled, gazing at her lap to calm herself.

Finally reposing herself, she began, "Such a paragon I never knew! No wonder you yet retain your bachelorhood! I wish you well on your search for her," she said merrily, laughing so much, her eyes were welling up with tears as she sat next to him.

"Aye, I may need your well wishes indeed," Harrison delightedly grinned. "At least for a moment, I was able to entertain your thoughts with my ready wit."

"What have you two been discussing that has Miss Morten in such a merry state?" inquired the loud, booming voice of Lord Purcellville from across the room.

Rising to address the whole room and striding the length of it, Harrison stopped and turned toward his observers. "We were deeply engrossed upon the subject of my doom as a husband. It seems I may have too high of expectations," he relayed, taking a walk about the room.

"You cannot be serious!" called out Simon. Turning to his bride, who still sat at the piano but before silent keys, he continued, "He cannot be serious."

"'Tis true, Simon." Mariah added, looking very seriously at her brother. "My lord has very high expectations indeed for his future bride. She, whoever she may be if such a saint exists, will have her hands very full in dealing with all the wishes and whims of your friend. I am sorry to tell you, but it must be said."

"Truly well, from one married man to one that is not, I can tell you with great certainty that once your heart is affixed, it matters not what expectations you formerly held. You will view your beloved with eyes clouded by adamant love. I shall like to see you walking around in a mooncalf state!"

"Oh, no," sighed Mariah. "That shall not happen to our Earl of Bramley. Never shall we see him in such a state. It would not be befitting to his stature in the least. No, if ever he falls in love, he shall retain his clear thinking and good judgment. No woman in her right mind would have an earl who appears to be addle-brained, and if she didn't care for his lack of wits, then she is no friend of Bramley Hall. Better we remain without a lady than to have one who allows her husband to worship at her feet, for I could never respect a man who placed the whole of his worth upon such a woman," Mariah chortled, ending her speech.

Again, she felt her cheeks coloring. Afterall, she knew nothing about marital bliss or its concerns, and she was teasing the Earl in front of the entire party. Harrison smiled, his eyes twinkling with amusement, though Mariah could not say the same of the others in the room.

No one spoke for the span of a few seconds until Alicia announced how tired she was with the wish to retire so any who called the next morning would not see her looking ill or old. Alicia expressed how much fun it was to have a husband and her wish that Mariah should not linger too long before retiring as she bid goodnight.

As the door closed behind Alicia, Mariah rose and wished the others a good night. She smiled at her hosts, ignoring the heavy gaze of Harrison. Curtsying, she promptly took her leave.

Chapter Eleven

Introductions to Brighton

The next morning was very busy indeed. After partaking of breaking the fast, the ladies of the house had a steady stream of visitors. Mariah was overwhelmed, to say the least. And who knew word of her and Alicia's arrival traveled so quickly as to have all of their society pay calls of introduction?

Harrison had dismissed himself to handle the business which had brought him to Brighton, declaring that once he completed the favor, he would have his time free and be at ease with all the planning his hostess had undertaken for them. And since his departure to handle his affairs, Mariah had missed his calming presence greatly. Having Harrison with her was a huge asset for her nerves.

Carter, the ancient butler, announced the arrival of yet another new guest. "Mrs. Liftgrove." The butler stepped to the side, allowing the woman entry before he bowed and closed the door.

"Dearest Cora!" Alicia exclaimed, standing at once and greeting her dearest friend. "Please allow me to introduce you to my new sister, Mariah Morten. She's ever so pretty, is she not?"

The two ladies curtsied to each other.

Cora stepped forward, embracing Mariah as she said, "So very pleased to meet you at long last, Miss Morten. We have heard Simon mention you for quite some time. He adores you, and now, standing before you, I can understand his sentiments."

Cora was not a beauty, but there was such intelligence in her gray eyes and such easy grace in her manner of speech that Mariah knew she was going to like Cora immediately. Cora silently curtsied to her ladyship after realizing she had not yet properly greeted her. Lady Purcellville inclined her head, indicating the slight led by Alicia had not caused offense to her elegant hostess.

"You are much too kind in your praise, Mrs. Liftgrove. I'm ever so pleased to make your introduction, as I've heard much of you and your husband," Mariah replied, taking her seat as Lady Purcellville indicated they should all do.

"Oh, dear, you poor creature," began Cora, "enclosed in a carriage with our dear Alicia for hours on end! How you managed to reach us here at Brighton with your hearing intact is a mercy!" Cora smiled sympathetically at Mariah.

Alicia rolled her eyes. "La, you make my presence seem like torture, and if I did not know you better, I would believe you quite mean-spirited. Thankfully, we've known each other for so long, I know you jest. She is not serious, dear Mariah."

Mariah smiled demurely, hoping the kind facial gesture was enough to ally Alicia without giving way to the fact Cora was exceedingly correct.

The rest of their conversation ranged from news about their many acquaintances to the weather and finally to the ball that was to be held in three nights' time at the home of Lord and Lady Whittby. They would be opening the ball up to the officers, which was a grand event indeed. The regiment had been readily accepted within the social circle.

Mariah listened intently while Cora, Alicia, and Lady Purcellville spoke of the regiment and the available men that would try to vie for her hand. She nodded politely at certain cues, though mainly her attention to listening was because of all the possible dancers she could be stuck with. She was not sure if the idea was thrilling or dreadful.

Carter came into the room, announcing luncheon. Mariah held in a sigh, hoping for a quiet reprieve. Much to her great satisfaction, luncheon was a quiet affair with the three ladies since the gentlemen were all engaged in their businesses. Mariah found she need not exert herself with conversing as Alicia and Lady Purcellville had much to say in all matters. It was a mercy to relax in their company, and it gave Mariah ample time to take in her surroundings. The house was beautiful, and so were all of its lavish furnishings, from the oil paintings, to the large crystal and candle-laden chandeliers, to the marble statues on pedestals of dark mahogany.

Seeing Mariah glance around the room, Lady Purcellville addressed her. "Is not this house divine? If I were allowed, I would not change even one chair nor the carpet. We have been here off and on for five seasons and find it very much suited to our purposes."

"You do not own this then?" inquired Mariah.

"Oh, indeed, no. Should it ever come up to be bought, I shall press Lord Purcellville to offer for it. Our landlord, who is a friend going back far with my own dear husband, had no occasion in which to travel here after the death of his wife. She died of consumption—though not here in this house—some seven years back. Having never met her, I cannot speak for her prior health, but I do know she was much beloved by her dear husband. When Lord Purcellville took the lease, we were very pleased, as we disliked the idea of living somewhere we could not properly entertain, for entertaining the officers and their wives is paramount in our circle," Lady Purcellville explained, looking at Mariah thoughtfully.

"How very considerate of you to take such great exertions on behalf of the regiment's sake," Alicia added, smiling serenely upon her mother.

"Indeed. Mind you, there have been times I thought another soiree would be the death of me, but it's my duty to see our men engage in social activities that may curb any waywardness. It's only natural, and if these men were my own sons, I should take great comfort in knowing there was a lady such as I keeping them in the right," Lady Purcellville imparted, taking a delicate bite of her pudding and smiling. "Oh, and we are to dine this evening with Lord and Lady Ramsgate."

Alicia clapped her hands. "How thrilling. Mariah, we must adjourn to our rooms to get ready for this treat!"

Lady Purcellville wasted no time in speaking of the Ramsgates, though she spoke so animatedly, Mariah only caught maybe half of what was being said. With arrangements to retire and rest, Mariah politely excused herself, and with a relieving sigh she made it back to her bedchamber and shut the door. The silence was blessedly relieving.

Chapter Twelve

Fine Dining

Mariah woke sometime in the late afternoon and promptly began getting freshened and dressed. She had not an inkling as to who the Ramsgates were, though according to a quick missive from Alicia that was dropped off at her door, they were very influential with the Crown. One of the most sought-after invitations came with the Ramsgate insignia sealed in wax.

Mariah directed Amy to style her hair as elegantly as possible. Amy's deft hands had her dark tresses exquisitely curled and swept up in the classic Greek style, with curls close to her head but with the mass of her hair drawn back, dangling along her delicate neck. Mariah put on her best cream satin gown with a round train. The dress was low-cut, making her feel that it was rather revealing though it came well above her bosom. She did so love the Greek and Roman influences that inspired the current fashion, even if it seemed a bit improper.

"You look divine, mistress," Amy said, taking a step back.

Mariah smiled. "Thank you Amy. Please take the evening to yourself. I will take care of myself when we return."

"Thank you," Amy replied.

Mariah sighed, rising from the mahogany dressing table where Amy had arranged her hair. She took the cream elbow-length gloves Amy held out for her. She then took her reticule and lace fan and smiled and nodded at Amy.

She exited her room, heading directly down the grand curved staircase. She paused once she reached the front door and donned the burgundy cloak Carter held out for her.

Harrison approached her, bowing grandly. Mariah smiled up at him as she curtsied in return. She held in a blush trying to sneak its way to her cheeks. He held out his right arm, which she happily accepted. He looked magnificent in his topper and cloak. His left hand carried his gold-handled walking cane, an absolute statement to his wealth and position within society. She smiled up at him, catching herself admiring how the gray and cream of his waistcoat added to the breathtaking allure of his sea green eyes.

"You're a vision this evening, Miss Morten," Harrison complimented her as he guided her out of doors.

"Thank you, my lord. You're rather dashing as well," Mariah replied, descending the marble steps to the street.

Magnificent gray horses in a team of four pawed at the ground, greeting them. A grand carriage Mariah couldn't even describe made of dark wood flecked with gold accents awaited them.

No one was jesting in regards to the Ramsgates' wealth, she thought, swallowing though her mouth was already dry. *They must be most influential to the Crown to obtain such a magnificent carriage and matching team of horses.* Lord and Lady Ramsgate had sent their carriage to gather their friends for the evening's event.

So talked about and bragged upon were the Ramsgates that Mariah began to discover her nerves to be quite on edge. How silly, yet she feared if she were not careful to make the best of impressions upon the lord and lady, all would not be well, and her visit to Brighton might as well be over. Not only was this her worry, but any mishap would soil her name and possibly those in connection with her.

I shall endeavor to not disgrace myself nor my family. Oh, Lord, please, if you may, lend me guidance, grace, and your strength to make it through this event, for I cannot do this alone.

Upon entering the carriage, they were greeted by the rest of their party, which led to merry conversation, making the time fly by. It seemed all had passed in such relative quickness. Mariah lost track of time, as it had not taken long to reach Marine Parade, where their invitation took them this evening. Brighton was a relatively small town, and Marine Parade boasted the most sought-after addresses. The boulevard ran parallel to the sea, giving way to the glorious sights of the sea and landscape and the scents of the ocean and vendors but most importantly giving way to the grand views of the magnificent houses. It was an ideal area in which to truly take in the scenery.

Mariah kept her seat in the carriage until the last occupant had departed from it. She let out the breath she had been holding and rose to take the hand of Harrison that greeted her once she reached the carriage door. Gripping his hand a bit tightly, Mariah climbed down the steps to join him. Harrison took her hand and placed it upon his arm as they climbed the great steps to the house.

Whether or not Harrison deduced her unease, he leaned down and whispered in her ear, "My, such a grand house! I do hope I do not end up making a cake of myself. Pray, dear Miss Morten; please keep me in check!"

"Only if you endeavor to repeat the favor, my lord," she whispered back.

"Of that, I have very much doubt that you of all people would paint yourself in a poor light."

Mariah smiled at the compliment. The image of Harrison ever not at ease was humorous. Some of her nerves began to lift knowing she had such a friend as Harrison to think of her comfort and well-being.

Mariah handed off her burgundy cloak, a smile still on her face. She stood beside Harrison, waiting in line to be introduced to their hosts. She looked around the great hall, and opulence dripped from every corner. There was no question as to the affluent wealth the Ramsgate name held. There were Greek statues every six feet, oil paintings hanging upon the wall, and various sizes of vases depicting scenes from nature in between.

Lord Purcellville was speaking to Lord Ramsgate as Mariah gazed around, admiring the home. Mariah's head snapped to attention when she heard her name being mentioned. Turning her thoughts toward the room the men were entering, Mariah observed Lord Purcellville standing before a squat man with the most outrageous cravat she had ever seen. With it all puff and lace, she could barely notice the man's double chin. His squinty dark eyes examined her person before affixing upon her face, and then he gave a slight nod. Next to this dandy was his lady, and she was a foot taller than her husband, bearing a regal look that left no doubt as to her superiority within the ton. Her hair was adorned with feathers and pearls weaved throughout it. She held her chin tilted slightly upward.

Bowing before Lord and Lady Ramsgate, Mariah felt gloved fingers reach beneath her chin and bid her rise. She looked into the very large eyes of Lady Ramsgate and waited for the lady to speak.

After a moment of scrutiny, Lady Ramsgate said, "Such a pretty thing you are indeed. My, how they do grow beauties in the country. How fortunate you must feel to be in such a polished society as you now find before you." Lady Ramsgate sniffed delicately, dropping her large green eyes a touch.

"Indeed, my lady Ramsgate, I am very fortunate," Mariah managed to reply from her dry throat.

Before any more words could be passed, Mariah was gallantly saved from further attention as Harrison led her to the corner where a pretty little velvet chair was situated. Sitting down upon the plush blue velvet, Mariah smoothed the wrinkles from her lap. She looked up at Harrison and watched him take in the society before him. Numerous people were in attendance at this gathering. She hadn't a clue who they all were beyond those she already knew of. But Harrison watched them observantly, his keen teal eyes not missing a thing.

She sighed softly to herself, feeling relief he was here with her. Mariah turned her head, pretending to admire the oil painting of the ocean which hung on the wall, though she was actually watching Harrison from her peripheral vision. Harrison had a slight smile upon his lips. His head swiveled as if looking for the people he wished to speak with. His handsome face was freshly shaven, removing the stubble that she liked from his jaw.

Returning her gaze to the room, Mariah took several deep breaths, hoping to still her nerves after a most insulting introduction with the Ramsgates. *The nerve,* Mariah pouted in her head but was sure to keep the displeasure from her face. *Just because I was born in the country doesn't make me the slightest dolt.*

Harrison glanced down, perking a dark brow. "Are you all right?"

Mariah nodded. "Attempting to think without appearing that I'm lost in thought."

"Ah, well, I know all too well what has your beautiful face bedraggled, so let me allow myself to put your mind at ease: that woman is an old worn hat."

Mariah put a polite hand to her face to cover the snorting laugh. Harrison's bright teal eyes shone at her with such warmth and mirth, she caught her breath.

"Come with me, my dear lady," he announced, offering her his broad gloved hand.

Harrison led Mariah through the room toward a rather old man and his lady. "Lord Halifax, Lady Halifax." Harrison bowed before the pair with a grand smile. "Please allow me the very grand pleasure of introducing Miss Morten to you."

Mariah curtsied. She smiled at the pair as they bent toward her.

"A pleasure, my dear." Lord Halifax smiled warmly at her. Turning toward Harrison, he stated, "She is a pretty one, my young friend. You should take care introducing her, as you never know what young buck may swoop in and take her from your side forever." Lord Halifax gave Harrison a serious look and then went on. "Unless, of course, you have settled your sights upon her. Eh? Is that the way of it?"

His hazel eyes were twinkling within his wrinkled face. Mariah smiled at him. He reminded her of her dear grandpapa, long passed to be with the Lord. He was just as outspoken, with a twinkle of glee in his gaze.

"My dear! You speak much too freely!" Lady Halifax chastised, seemingly mortified at her husband's speech. The lady was his junior by at least thirty years. The feathers woven into her pale hair waved upon her head as she looked from Harrison to her husband to Mariah. The plethora of feathers made Mariah think of a grand turkey instead of a beautiful woman.

"*Pah*." Lord Halifax waved at his wife. "Long have I known the lad, and what can age permit an old man such as myself if not the great good fun of making assumptions where I may? He'd do very well with a wife, and such a pretty one she is! Why, it's time a nursery was started at Bramley Hall!" Lord Halifax exclaimed, slapping Harrison on the back.

Mariah turned her head to the side, pretending to look at a vase to keep from blushing greatly. To speak so candidly was something she had not observed yet in society, and here Lord Halifax was, gushing to Harrison about her! True, her family had alluded to wishes such as these, but never were they so plainly stated. Mariah took a deep breath, looked back to the group, and smiled wanly at Lady Halifax.

Smiling and seeming completely at ease, which surprised Mariah, Harrison replied. "Old man indeed! I have seen many an old man, and never was a man said to be old who retained such an eternal spark and possessed such amusing humor. Ah, there is the dinner bell. I believe lobster is on the menu tonight, and I know how you rave about Brighton fare."

They parted from each other. Harrison once again offered his arm to lead Mariah toward the line to go into dinner. It seemed that of the entire party, only she and Harrison were not yet wed. What a curious thing! The thought was enough to cause her to blush. Though promptly, she yielded herself from the full extent of it.

Mariah was escorted into dinner by a Mr. Michaels to whom she was quickly introduced and who took her to her chair. Then Mariah stared at the portrait across from her as if she were admiring it. *Does Harrison truly think that the thought of marrying me is humorous? Is the idea such a great joke?* She felt herself fall into a melancholia. *I don't find it at all humorous.* He was certainly attentive to her needs and wishes, a true testament to the fact he quite looked upon her as an obligation and nothing more. Here in the midst of strangers, she was quite in fear of having her heart break into many pieces, yet she was forced for the rest of the evening to pretend otherwise. It would serve her well to distance herself from his attention, not only to stave off rumors but to spare her heart as well.

Mariah hardly tasted the lobster bisque when it was put before her. When called upon for her opinion of it, she answered it was exquisitely delicious. With such a simple answer, the topic of the conversation turned toward other matters, and with no information to add nor anything of importance to impart, Mariah kept silent. She felt out of place in this grand dining room, surrounded by the cream of Brighton society and their discussions which she knew nothing about. The chandelier was the grandest she had ever seen, with crystals and pearls adorning it, and she was sure the paintings upon the walls must be by van Dyck, they were so rich in color and subject.

Mariah sat between the thin Mr. Michaels who had a permanent scowl and a Lord Neamly who was rather handsome with a strong jaw and gray eyes. When each gentleman learned that Mariah was not well-versed in conversation regarding the horse races nor knew the elites within the ton, they each turned their attention to their partners on the other sides of themselves and didn't bother to address her again.

Having observed all the paintings within eyesight and the chandelier, Mariah gazed down at her empty plate and wondered when the night was going to conclude.

Once dinner was over and the men and women dispersed to different parts of the mansion home, Mariah plastered a polite smile to her face. She sat on a chaise facing the group of women and tried to regain her composure, though in truth, all she wanted was to return home into the arms of her beloved parents. She realized she was once again not paying attendance to the inhabitants of the room and was not doing her utmost to make new introductions. She was not behaving well at all.

My mind is a murky mess from what Harrison said, she thought, *and not only from that, but also from not being so well-versed in all matters political or otherwise. I am so out of sorts here.* She glanced about the room. *I need to do better and make some introductions, lest my actions cause my mother to scold me when I return home.*

She took in a deep breath and paid the whole of her attention to the lively game of whist the ladies were enjoying. Lady Ramsgate gave an excited cry and presented her winning hand. The ladies joined in her good humor and made hearty congratulations.

The door opened as the tables used for playing their games were put away. Getting up to take a turn about the room, Mariah decided to place herself on the settee beside Alicia.

Simon came forth, bowed before his wife's hand, and said, "My dear, darling wife. I trust you've enjoyed the evening?"

"Of a certainty, dear husband," returned Alicia, smiling up at Simon.

Mariah looked away and happened to lock eyes with Harrison, who was conversing with Lord Halifax and Lord Ramsgate. Why his eyes were not directed to those whom he was talking to Mariah did not know, but she could not bring herself to look away. So intent were his teal eyes that she seemed to be drowning within them. Mariah would not return his smile, and either her lack of one or a turn of his conversation soon saw his smile fade.

She intently watched him while her heart somersaulted with decisions to either let him go his merry way or to try to turn their friendship turn romantic. Even her poor heart could not guide her in the choice, however, and her brain was not being a cooperative party either. She was filled to her brim with indecision. Harrison turned further, giving her a view of his entire person, and she sighed. He was so regal, so handsome, so out of her circle for her to even desire having him, yet she could not bear to think of him with someone else.

Mariah tilted her head to the side now, though, believing she heard her name being spoken by Harrison. It was not his voice, however. Then, hearing her name again, she turned toward her brother.

"I say, Mariah, have you not heard one detail we've been discussing?" Simon shook his head at his sister with a sly smirk.

"Indeed, I confess not." Mariah smiled, realizing he had sat down next to his wife.

"She rather does that, you know!" Alicia pealed with laughter while Mariah blushed and pressed her hand against her gown to smooth out unseen wrinkles.

When Mariah looked up, she found that Simon was staring at her. "Why ever have I captivated your interest, Simon?"

"Perhaps it is your lack of interest or your blatant boredom that has made you my chief observation." He waggled his index finger at her. "Though if you give over to me now, I may not have to repeat myself yet again."

Mariah nodded her assent for him to go on.

"It seems the regiment is to practice its exercises for the whole of tomorrow, and Lord Bramley has offered to see you and Alicia escorted to some of the local shops. I do know how you ladies love to choose ribbons for hour upon hour."

"Oh, I shall find it hard to be without you, but I shall be glad to shop with my new sister," Alicia gushed with excitement. "You'll soon see that Brighton has much to offer in the way of materials. I'm quite a favorite patron, you know."

"My dear, there is a pianoforte," Simon now announced. "Let us have a turn when the others are finished. Will you not have a turn too, dear sister?"

Mariah nodded. "I shall since you have asked. I would not wish to disappoint you further this evening."

The rest of the evening saw each lady take a turn upon either the harp or the pianoforte. Mariah took comfort in knowing there was nothing lacking in her accomplishments on either instrument. She was made slightly nervous when Harrison ceased his conversation to place his whole attention upon her. Mariah simply ignored him and watched her sheet music. She felt that when she had completed her piece upon the pianoforte, she had performed really well. At least, in this attempt, she had not failed nor caused embarrassment to her brother, nor those in her party.

Once she rose from the instrument, it was Harrison who came forth, offering his arm to lead her to a quieter corner of the room. There were two chairs that sat facing each other, and he chose them for their occupation. After Mariah sat and he took his seat, he smiled at her, but she remained silent, racking her brain for a topic of conversation.

"I do hope you will not be wishing you were at Bramley Hall once our shopping trip has ended tomorrow," Mariah said, plastering on a smile for Harrison.

"Never fear. If I had had a sister, perhaps such errands would tax my patience. However, I am quite ready to accompany you into all the throes of shopping in Brighton upon the morrow." Harrison bowed slightly before her, causing Mariah to laugh, as he was bowing from his seated position. His movement should have looked awkward, but Harrison rarely possessed any awkward manners. Mariah could think of nothing else of value to say, so she looked down at her folded hands and remained silent.

Harrison cleared his throat and began, "I know you are not quite yourself. I have been trying to see if any slight has occurred but cannot seem to have caught any. Has there been a person or a situation that is making you feel poorly?" The frown upon his handsome face was very sincere, and he waited for Mariah to form her words.

"You mistake the matter entirely, my lord." Mariah looked up from her gloved hands toward him and smiled her brightest smile. She would rather stick her spoon into the wall right here and now than give Harrison any inkling that he was the source of her melancholia.

"Truth now, young miss. I will have the whole of the truth," he pressed.

"Indeed, my lord. Do not trouble yourself over the moods of any young miss whom you may meet. Far be it for me to say I am fickle or ill of humor. I'm indeed well, and you must not think otherwise, though, in truth, I'm rather exhausted. I'm not used to such traveling as we have undertaken." Mariah looked into his eyes and smiled, hoping he would not see anything that would make him question her more.

"Hmm," Harrison huffed as he again frowned.

Thank the heavens above, Lady Purcellville arrived, standing beside Mariah and making it known that she desired to return home. Mariah sighed internally, putting her and Harrison's conversation to an end as all rose to bid their acquaintances adieu.

Chapter Thirteen

Tortured Hearts

Mariah woke exhausted. Her night was entirely fitful, with vivid dreams of Harrison. They disturbed her, as she was in danger of him understanding her very deep feelings for him. In her dreams, he had laughed at her with malice when she told him how dearly she loved him, and he then told her how he regarded her as a mere child and had always seen her as his sister. The dreams twisted until she was indeed his sister and his parents were also her parents, laughing at her as well. So disturbed was she that by the time Amy came into her room with the tray to break her fast, Mariah had been awake for hours. She grimaced when Amy drew the drapes open and the bright sunlight streamed into the room.

With no real hunger to speak of, Mariah drank her hot chocolate and sampled her ham. She was in very real danger of a headache, and that would not do. Alicia was so excited for their little shopping trip that Mariah knew she must not disappoint her. Simon would be put out if his wife was made unhappy. She would never hear the end of it. Knowing her brother, Simon would make her feel shameful for her behavior.

Having eaten, Mariah dressed simply in a pale yellow day-gown with gray kid gloves, not wanting to put on her best clothes for a shopping trip. Making her way toward the ladies' parlor, Mariah watched as Amy flitted about the room in ex-citement, announcing that the carriage was just about readied.

Mariah made her way to the front of the beautiful mansion home, wanting to bask in the sunshine and silence before Alicia reached her side. She collected her cloak and ensured that her bonnet was tied correctly.

Harrison soon came from the direction of the library and donned his cloak and topper. Once he held his walking cane in his grasp, he held out his right arm to her, bowing and grasping her hand to his lips for a kiss upon her knuckles. Mariah's knees wobbled as she rose from her curtsy and took his proffered arm. They didn't speak, as Alicia had made her way down the staircase and now accepted her cloak from Carter. Alicia was in such a merry mood that she had not stopped remarking upon how fine a day it was nor about how she could hardly contain her excitement for their first shopping trip together.

Once in the carriage, Alicia still had not broken from her oration. She conversed about one and all things; whether she had the full attention of Mariah or Harrison, it seemed it mattered not to Alicia. Mariah had not known a woman could speak so animatedly first thing in the morning until her in-troduction to Alicia. Harrison's eyes grew big at one opinion Alicia expressed regarding the cut of the gown she was to wear when they attended the next ball. Mariah had to bring her gloved hand to her lips to soften the laugh that escaped. Alicia wriggled in her seat, grinning profusely. "Well, I for one am glad to see you in very good spirits today! Simon thought you were ill last night, and I assured him you were not. I am glad to be right!" she laughed.

"I am well. I think I shall, erelong, feel quite at home, dear Alicia. I apologize if I've seemed out of sorts. I have resolved to do better," Mariah explained, smiling at her.

Feeling she now had the truth, Alicia launched into talking about the latest fashions yet again, and she wanted to know Mariah's feeling on each article of clothing. But each time Mariah started to express an opinion, Alicia went on to a new tangent of conversation. She never was silent long enough to glean any understanding of Mariah's taste.

When the carriage stopped in front of the desired shop, Harrison climbed down first. After handing Alicia down, he proceeded to reach for Mariah's hand. She took his hand and climbed down gracefully, but instead of taking his arm, she attached herself to Alicia's, and the two walked into the shop together. Since last night, she did not wish to give him any false hope. Marriage to her would not be a joke, at least not in her eyes. Her heart ached, but she would not give herself nor him any false sense of something more.

The bell upon the door jingled, announcing their arrival to their first stop. Alicia addressed an older woman with raisin-like eyes and a hawkish nose who sat behind a counter. "Yes, Mrs. Hopewell. I have come for your superb ribbons and maybe a few other items. I am so glad to see more colors this visit!"

Alicia dragged Mariah all around the shop and proceeded to quiz her on which ribbon would suit this dress or look best upon this bonnet. It took a few hours to pick out the best ribbons. Alicia had a plethora in her basket while Mariah only had a few.

Having chosen the best selections, it was on to reticules, and off Alicia went in that direction as Mariah picked up a pretty blue ribbon and studied it. She had just reached Brighton and did not wish to spend the whole of her pin money at one shop.

"A most becoming shade, Miss Morten," Harrison complimented, coming up behind her. Mariah startled. He had been with them the entire course of the visit but had hung back, perhaps in awe of Alicia's shopping exultation or the fact she was never at a loss for words. For whatever reason, he had taken advantage of their respective aloneness before now joining her at her side.

"Oh, yes, I do like it, as well as that lavender and white one too." Mariah turned toward him with a smile.

"Hmm, quite the dilemma, but why not have them all?"

"I cannot think of an immediate use for the white, though I know exactly what I shall do with the blue. As for the lavender, I do so love its shade. I cannot make myself comfortable purchasing them all if I cannot reason a use for each one," Mariah explained, glancing toward Alicia, who was addressing Mrs. Hopewell again in raptures over various bolts of lace.

"I can understand your reasoning. Let's purchase the three and rescue Mrs. Hopewell from Alicia's great praise," Harrison offered. Taking her hand, he wrapped it around his arm and led them off to purchase her goods. When she made to retrieve her coins from her reticule, Harrison stopped her and instead drew the amount needed from his own coin purse. Mariah tried to tell him it was unnecessary, but he would not be swayed.

Mariah thanked him and then joined Alicia. They stood together arm in arm as Alicia chose the last of her purchases. Mariah could not help but think of how bankrupt her poor brother would soon be; hopefully, Alicia's dowry had been substantial. At least he only really had to appear dressed in his scarlet regimental uniform; otherwise, he might soon be made nude with how Alicia shopped.

The pair watched as Alicia paid for her purchases. As Mrs. Hopewell was wrapping up her bundles in brown paper, Harrison said, "If there is anywhere else you wish to go, you simply need only ask. If there is something you are eyeing, please inform me straight away."

Mariah looked up from her place beside him and wrinkled her forehead. "Indeed; pray tell, why should I do that?"

"I promised to escort you, and it's my duty to see that you have all you need and wish for," he replied, reaching up and directing an errant dark curl back into her straw bonnet.

Mariah felt her embarrassment grow from her unease. The nightmares from earlier were still with her, and she feared to show any discomfort. Any affected manner would not do. She felt his eyes upon her again, and she slowly looked up from the floor to meet his gaze. She made sure to squint her eyes for the span of several seconds. The look upon Harrison's face made her breath catch. Her intention was to show a slight flirtation so he would not sense her unease, but perhaps what she had done was unwise. How wise was it to flirt and carry on as they ever had in the best of humors? Was it now unseemly?

Harrison stared at her with a mixture of adoration and confusion. Mariah quickly righted her look, tucking in her lips with the hope that she had not offended. *Oh, goodness gracious me,* she thought. *I have lost my mind. I should not be carrying on this way, but my heart hopes too great that he will come to adore me as I do him.*

Alicia moved toward them with her purchases, and it was settled that they should pay a call upon Mrs. Liftgrove. Once settled back in the carriage, it was a mere matter of minutes until the trio stood, greeting their hostess in her cozy cottage. Her home was smaller than the parsonage, but it was lovely. The added touches of feminine appeal were visible in almost every corner, with embroidered pillows and lace doilies. Mrs. Liftgrove sought to have her dearest friend all to herself for a few minutes, so she suggested his Lordship accompany Miss Morten for a walk along the coast.

Harrison offered his arm to Mariah, and they were soon out of doors. Carefully, they made their way toward the sandy beach. Neither spoke, only taking in the sights of the crashing waves, the scent of the refreshing breeze, and the chilling allurement of the cold, crisp breeze. The music of waves crashing was peaceful to her ears. Neat rows of bathhouses were not far from where they were walking, and Harrison made a point to turn around. Mariah could not imagine taking the waters in such cold weather. How others seem to frolic in the water she couldn't understand.

Lord Purcellville always drank a tiny amount of the salt water after he broke his fast each morning. Mariah had tried the salt water one morning but felt excessively thirsty after and just a little nauseous. She vowed to avoid the awful stuff as much as could be done without causing offense.

In tandem, they walked along the beach. The walk was refreshing and calmed her mind from thoughts of him for a time. Upon leaving, however, she couldn't help but return her thoughts to him.

I must endeavor to distance myself, she thought. *For his and my sake,* she decided, staring at the seabirds rising and falling in the sky.

Harrison scarcely knew what to do! He could not think of anything to say while walking on the beach, after her look in the ribbon shop. In fact, all his mind replayed now was that moment. It was certainly committed to his memory. He was utterly caught in her gaze and could not look away. His mouth was running dry, and he feared at any moment, he would have an unfortunate amount of spittle run down from his open mouth.

That minx! That pretty little parson's daughter has given me a flirtatious look again! Any man would follow her for miles just to quench his thirst by drinking in her presence. How she did that by just a look made his blood run hot and his skin shiver for more. He had been in the society of the ton for years now, and never once had any woman addled his mind and caused his heart to race. How did she manage to turn his world upside down? It was most befuddling yet wholly welcome.

Surely, she had to know by now that he saw her otherwise? By that look, she had to have seen him in a different light now? His heart and brain battled for words—thoughts, even—that could string together enough coherent syllables for him to decide whether or not he should call on her or they should remain as they were. Harrison could not properly think. Even now, by her side, walking along the sandy beach, he couldn't decide what to do.

The soft lilt of her voice pulled him from his deep musings. She must have noticed, as she stopped mid-sentence and began again.

"Pray, do you think there will be time enough to begin a letter home? I have neglected my dear mama and papa so," asked Mariah.

Clearing his throat and gaining his power of speech back, Harrison answered. "Indeed. We shall see to the matter upon our return."

Harrison guided Mariah around the shore, conscientious that they had no chaperone. He was glad that he had embarked upon this trip. If Alicia could not be entrusted with the proprieties of chaperoning, he would gladly step in. In truth, he was pleased to be useful in this manner. It certainly gave him ample time in Mariah's presence.

"Shall you venture into the waters?" Harrison asked, a teasing note in his deep voice.

Smiling and shaking her head, Mariah answered. "Nay. I would sooner muck out the regiment's stable than so much as set one toe into that frigid water. I cannot see the benefit of such cold waters. I cannot think you mean to venture forth?"

"Much too cold for me too. I would rather muck out stalls beside you." Harrison laughed, his baritone vibrato ringing out against the crashing of the ocean waves.

Releasing her hand from his arm, he bent down to retrieve a tiny shell from the sand. It was pink and shiny and smaller than his palm. He turned it over in his large gloved hand and then held it out to Mariah.

"So very pretty," Mariah murmured, gazing upon it lovingly in her gloved hand.

"So you shall always remember Brighton," Harrison stated, handing it over into her hand. He gazed into the bright and vivid blue eyes of hers that held his raptured soul. How long had her eyes been so blue, calling to him like a sailor to the sea? How long had she been so beautiful that the sun hid in shame? Her gracious nature, witty charm, and bright, captivating soul put all to shame in his eyes. Mariah Morten was beauty incarnate inside and out, and he was happily drowning in her presence.

Breaking the spell, Harrison looked toward the sky and said, "The wind is picking up. We should make our way back to Alicia. Luncheon should be served soon, and I promised Lady Purcellville we would not be late." Without waiting for a reply, he took her hand and placed it upon his arm as they started forward. He remained silent, not knowing what else to say to Mariah that would be anything short of spilling his love for her.

Mariah too was silent, opting for gazing at the scenery to her direct right as they made their way back to Mrs. Liftgrove's sitting area. Harrison wished that he could lay his heart bare before her. It was agonizing, wondering whether she might return his ardor, but pride and a fair bit of caution held him in check, though he did not know for how much longer.

Chapter Fourteen

A Flawed View

L uncheon passed by calmly, as the regiment was engaged in its business. Lord Purcellville was not in attendance, so it was just Lady Purcellville, Alicia, Harrison, and Mariah that shared in their meal of cold sandwiches, fruit, and a creamy pudding.

Mariah set about to write her letter to her Mama and Papa. She found paper and a quill in Lord Purcellville's library. As she wrote, Harrison was also busy writing, though his letters were directed to his man of business. Mariah strived to include all of the activities she had taken part in thus far. When she was finished, she had covered both sides of her paper. Feeling she had accomplished her mission, she rose from the little round mahogany desk that faced the busy street outside, which was framed by a large bay window.

Mariah went about the room reading the titles of the books. While the selection was nothing as grand as Bramley Hall's library's, this library held enough titles to make it very enjoyable. Mariah knew that if she had nothing more to do in Brighton, she could at least enjoy being cooped up to read. There were little nooks with cushioned bay window seats giving privacy to the reader throughout the large room's corners.

She heard Harrison rise behind her, having sealed his letter as well as hers too with wax and his signet ring. He rang the bell and waited for the footman to answer. Harrison gave the man prompt instructions to have the letters sent out.

Lady Purcellville and Alicia had been conversing in one of the corners, as neither had seemed to have the wit to entertain a novel that afternoon. With most of their close circle residing in Brighton, letters were not necessary to stay well-informed or to keep up on current affairs elsewhere. All Mariah had to do was ask Alicia or Lady Purcellville, and all the latest gossip would enter her ears.

Glancing up at the little terrace leading to the landing outside of the library, Mariah spied a telescope. Seeing her interest from across the room, Alicia rose and came toward her.

"Come, let us make use of the telescope to spy who is taking 'the cure,' as the locals call it. It's rather stupefying if you ask me—to take a plunge in icy water and call it a cure. It's always good fun to see whom one can make out, though," Alicia announced, clamping her hand around Mariah's arm. They climbed the steps which led them out of doors.

Alicia looked through the telescope and said, "La, but there is Mrs. Manning. She rather looks as if the frigid water disagrees with her. Ooh, and there is Mr. Riley! He is swimming rather close to the ladies' side! Upon my word, naughty, naughty man. Here, have a look, Mariah!"

Not really wanting to spy upon those she either knew or did not, she peered through the telescope hesitantly. Would Papa be pleased? No, she thought not. She saw a man that must have been the scoundrel in question and quickly stepped away from the telescope. Why, she thought: if someone decided to swim, would they think kindly upon being of interest to one and all? As she and Alicia journeyed through Brighton, there were a great number of telescopes wherein one could view the sea, the ships, and the bathers.

Harrison joined the two women and said, "My dear ladies, it is rather cold. You should come away from that instrument or else you're likely to catch colds and then to miss out on all of the soirees, card parties, and balls, as well as the library and the theater. Simon would not forgive me for not caring for his ladies."

Harrison was very serious, and all of his earlier good humor seemed to have vanished. Whether it was because of her being out here with Alicia or because of his letters Mariah knew not. She slightly turned pink, then lightly shook her head, hoping the movement would absolve her of any allegations Harrison might have for her. Mariah could not ascertain his thoughts, though. She bowed her head as she entered the house and came to rest on the settee. She could hear Alicia talking, and her embarrassment grew.

"La, my lord, we were only spying on the beach and water. I know Brighton so well and should never be thought to lead our fair Mariah into anything amiss. As I'm a married woman and you are an experienced man of the ton, I know that we both understand propriety. So never fear; I shall not lead Mariah into ruinous sights. We shall save her into being as docile as a dove for the day you wish to make your claim!"

Alicia did not wait for Harrison to reply. She made her way inside and sat beside Mariah on the settee, flattening the creases from her pale green dress.

Mariah pretended to pick lint from her own dress. How mortified she was! That Alicia should make such statements in regards to anything happening between her and Harrison was scandalous. How could she be comfortable now if members of her own family were making such statements? Why was everyone settled on the fact that she should one day be Harrison's wife when the man himself wasn't set on the notion? Would everyone be disappointed if the day never came? Maybe Mariah should test the waters and try to gain the attention of others. She was in Brighton, after all, and was she not here to meet new people and possibly, if by God's graces, find a suitable match?

Harrison closed the terrace door with a crisp snap and came back into the room. Remembering some business he had to see to in town, he excused himself, promising his return for supper and then his escorting of the ladies to an evening card party at

Donaldson's Library. Harrison looked not once at Mariah, and she wanted to sink through the floor or fall into the sea.

Mariah excused herself to her room, stating she wanted to rest before tonight's dinner and entertainment when, in fact, she wanted to be alone. Alicia's voice lilted behind her, describing how much fun she would have and what she should wear. Mariah only half listened, scurrying to her chamber and shutting the door.

She tried her best to rest, but it was of no use. She was mortified. How her brother's wife could do such a thing to her was beyond her ability to comprehend. It was also just Alicia's nature to be so outward, outspoken, and brash. Still, an observant person could attest to the differences in personalities and make a proper judgment. It appeared Alicia lacked that forethought, and it cost her the embarrassment of all.

I try to be accommodating to all parties, yet it always seems to backlash on me somehow. I can only pray that Harrison believes me innocent of Alicia's whims. For I surely did not look but for a moment, she grumbled. She rose from her bed and sat by the window, watching the scenery pass her by until it was time to get ready for the night's entertainments.

Mariah tried to nap after dinner, as she knew the evening would be long and she had not slept well the night prior. She was still very embarrassed. What must Harrison think of her? She should have not gone with Alicia and certainly should not have looked through the telescope, but how was she to refuse the request? Harrison had not even looked at her when taking his leave. And it hurt her heart more than she would ever let on.

What would she face when, one day soon, he took a wife? They could not be friends as they now were, should one or even both of them take a spouse. True, she had heard rumors that once a lady had produced an heir, she was free to pursue any relationship she pleased. She could not fathom taking a spouse only to turn away from him after starting their family. What sheer and utter nonsense. When she married, for she knew she must not forever be a burden upon her family, she wanted to wed a man she could trust with her well-being as well as her heart, and she knew that the Lord would never be pleased by scandalous behavior. She could not understand what would entice a marriage to become a sham.

She certainly made a mess of her heart, giving over her thoughts to Harrison. She was unworthy of such a great man as he. She must make use of her time in Brighton. She must allow herself the opportunity to see if another could esteem her. Her station in society was so very much beneath his. No titled man had ever looked in her direction for a wife, or if one had, she was certain it had been for more of a mistress. Her dowry was not significant enough to gain attention.

Mariah pursed her lips. *Does Harrison view me as I see myself? Oh, Lord; at the same time that I wish it so, I wish it were not. Harrison deserves better, deserves the world. I can appease myself with an amicable marriage so long as he is happy.*

Mariah sat up on the bed, staring out the open window. *Evening is drawing close,* she thought with a sigh. *I had best get ready. I do hope Alicia doesn't make any more comments regarding myself and Harrison.* There was only so much teasing that Mariah could stand, even if it was in good faith.

Mariah set about, putting herself to rights and stepping into a plum evening gown. She called for Amy, who arranged her hair in the same style as the night before. Mariah wanted to make her request as easy as possible on Amy. Already, her maid was a dear for not only coming with her but also for making herself available at all hours. Though, Mariah supposed, no one but she would give that fact a second thought. Mariah viewed Amy differently than most would a maid. All were people and children of God in her humble opinion, so all should be given the same courtesy regardless of station. Mariah dared not speak this opinion aloud, however. Most would heartily disagree, save for Harrison.

"Come, Mariah," Alicia said, knocking but once upon the door before allowing herself entry. "Come; let us away to the fun!"

"One moment, please," Mariah replied, feeling herself heat from embarrassment about being walked in on, with a slight twinge of annoyance.

"You're all readied, miss," Amy announced.

Mariah rose from her stool at her dressing table. "Thank you, Amy. Please enjoy the evening to yourself. I would like you to also have some enjoyment while here in Brighton."

"Mighty kind of you, mistress," Amy replied, beaming.

She desired that Amy could be experiencing Brighton and not spending all of her time within the house. She wanted her to venture forth. And with the bright smile that Mariah received from Amy at the notion of enjoying herself, Mariah certainly hoped Amy would take her up on it so she could hear about it on the morrow.

Mariah allowed Alicia to link her arm in hers and take her down to Carter, who assisted them in donning their evening cloaks. Then they ventured down to the awaiting carriage.

The ride to wherever they were headed was a surprisingly quiet affair, which was much appreciated by Mariah. Mariah kept her eyes on her lap, not wanting to look Harrison in the eye or speak. The embarrassment she felt from earlier still fluttered to the surface every once in a while.

Upon their arrival, Harrison, ever the gentleman, helped her down from the carriage, not speaking a word either. Her heart hurt. Surely, he did not still think her addle-brained for not really glancing through the telescope. Whatever he thought, it mattered not now. It was said and done. She should do her best to forget the situation—and the man too—and move on.

Mariah walked unaccompanied into the library. Seating herself between two elderly matrons, she watched the games of cards taking place. She felt safe to dwell in her thoughts, as neither lady seated beside her seemed interested in conversation.

She thought back to dinner and how, all through the four courses, Harrison had not addressed her once. In truth, he had only addressed anyone when answering a direct question. Mariah felt small and unhappy. Why should her mood depend upon the notice and attention of his Lordship? When had she become such a petulant being? She should stop this thinking about her whole happiness being dependent upon Harrison. That was too great a burden for either of them to carry. Where was the kindness she so readily relied upon within herself?

Rising, she made her way to the refreshment table. Once arrived, she reached for a cup of watered-down lemonade. Before she could secure the cup, however, another larger hand grasped it. Frowning, she looked up at the offending person. He was dressed in his scarlet regimental best and turned a surprised expression upon her.

He held out the refreshment for her to take, but Mariah did not make a move for it.

"Excuse me," the officer began, "I'm deeply mortified to have been so unchivalrous. Please accept my humblest apologies." Here, he made a precise and pretty bow to her.

Mariah curtsied in return. "I hold no grudges, sir," she began. "No need for apologies nor ill feelings." She smiled brightly and accepted the proffered cup.

"That is very good news. We have not been introduced, but I am your servant, Major George Wallis. I know our meeting is unconventional. I also apologize for that as well." His chocolate brown eyes were a perfect fit for his curly dark brown locks, which he wore styled short.

"'Tis quite all right, Major Wallis. I am Mariah Morten," she replied, inclining her head, her sapphire eyes sparkling. She was aware introductions such as these without a joint acquaintance were not appropriate, but she took an instant liking to the man standing before her.

"Ah, yes, Simon's sister! I had heard you had come back to keep Mrs. Morten company. How are you liking Brighton?"

His smile was resplendent, and Mariah felt this was a man that had easily stolen female hearts from simply walking into a room, but she still felt that her heart rested securely within her breast. "So far, it has been full of comings and goings. Any who could claim boredom here certainly is not trying hard enough." She searched the room for signs of any of her chaperones. She wasn't attempting to be rude or discourteous. This position she found herself in would have society's tongues wagging as fast as Alicia's normal speaking tone.

"Can I not see you safely returned to your party?"

"Oh, please, do not trouble yourself. I see them there in the corner, Lord and Lady Purcellville."

Mariah smiled and made to turn toward them. She felt her gloved hand become clasped. Turning back toward the man, she met Major Wallis' warm brown eyes.

"'Tis no trouble. I'm quite honored to be of service."

He set her delicate hand safely onto his arm. Then he led the way to her destination.

"Ah, Major Wallis, I do believe you have captured one of the handsomest women in the room!" Lord Purcellville roared.

"It's my pleasure to see her safely by your side. You are perhaps retiring to home?" Major Wallis' brown eyes darted from the lord to the lady.

"Aye, 'tis true. I'm well worn out from today's marches. Even overseeing the maneuvers seems to drain me. I am not a young man any longer, I fear. If I were, I would certainly stay and enjoy the society. Alas, I'm an old man and not given to be made to stay where I'm not wanting to be." Lord Purcellville beamed upon his audience.

"You are many things, my lord, but I should never venture to think you old! He is in perfect form, my lady; do not think he is not!" Major Wallis' attention was claimed by a loud shouting of cheers from a table at which sat a few officers. "Ah, I see Mallory is in his glory." The man who must have been Mallory was drinking from a glass and was an alarming shade of red. He was surrounded by other men who were also wearing their scarlet uniforms. Mallory put his glass down with a resounding thud and drew his winnings toward his person.

Turning from the scene, Mariah smiled at Lady Purcellville and inquired, "Have you seen the Earl of Bramley? He seems to have vanished."

"No, but he may yet be in the gentlemen's quarters. It was rather busy this evening, and I saw him conversing with a gentleman he seemed to know. Perhaps they have gone off together?" Lady Purcellville took her fan and flicked it open elegantly.

"How strange; I cannot think he would have left without informing one of us. 'Tis not like him." Mariah frowned.

"Oh, now, no need to fret, Miss Morten. I'm sure you're missing your good Earl, though I declare he has not abandoned you," Lord Purcellville stated.

Mariah could feel her cheeks pinkening and shook her head. "He is not my anything…"

"Let us leave this place, my dear. Miss Morten, my daughter and her husband have not left yet. Should you wish to stay, Major Wallis can see you to Alicia's side. I am sure the Earl will reappear at any moment. I shall send the carriage back once we reach home," Lord Purcellville remarked, offering his arm to his lady.

"I do not wish to inconvenience Major Wallis. I shall accompany you," Mariah said, taking her hand from Major Wallis' arm.

"'Tis no hardship upon my part, Miss Morten. Have no fear. I shall rather be glad to have the eyes of the room upon me as I see to your every wish." Major Wallis smiled brightly, and Mariah blushed even more deeply.

He made no mention of wanting to partake in any of the card games, so they found a settee close to the table Alicia sat at. Major Wallis seated first her and then himself. Mariah caught Alicia staring at her and Major Wallis several times. Their conversation contained accounts of the life of a country parson's daughter and the early life of Major Wallis.

"So being the youngest son, I decided upon the regiment as my trade as I thought I could do no worse, and traveling seemed like a grand idea," he stated.

"How adventurous!" Mariah decided now was a very good time to practice her flirting. She looked down at the floor, then up into his warm brown eyes, making sure she took her time in gaining his attention. She saw his eyes narrow and become darker than she had seen them before. He was about to say something when they both heard a cough toward their side. They broke eye contact and looked up.

Harrison was frowning; indeed, he wore a scowl upon his face, and it only seemed to make him look more glorious. Mariah wondered if he knew how magnificent he truly was when he was aggravated. She smiled at him, and when he did not return her smile, her own smile fell from her face. Her brows drew together, and she cast her eyes toward his polished boots.

"I believe it is late and the carriage has returned for us. I think it a very good idea that we take our leave. Should Simon and his wife wish to stay, we'll send the carriage back again." Harrison leaned down and held out his arm to Mariah, and once she held it, he pulled her to a standing position. Mariah gazed back at him, watching his gaze become intense. The hardening of his jaw and his rigid posture spoke of his severe displeasure.

Major Wallis reached his feet as well and bowed before Mariah, saying very quietly, "My pleasure to have made your acquaintance. May I pay a call to inquire how you fare tomorrow?" His brown eyes were hopeful, and Mariah did not have an answer as she rose from her curtsy.

"I trust you have good reason for asking. I will thank you for respecting *my* wishes that you do not press yourself upon Miss Morten," Harrison all but growled.

Harrison's teal eyes were stormy and challenging. Mariah was stunned. Never had she heard him talk in such a cold and aggressive manner. Never had she seen him so enraged as he seemed to be now. Harrison took her hand again, setting it firmly upon his arm with his other hand over top.

Major Wallis cast a softened look at Mariah, then spoke directly to Harrison. "I offer my apologies, my lord. I was not given the information that Miss Morten was matched. It would be better to stay by her side, as she is not known in our circle here and there are none who would wish to cause offense." With that, Major Wallis bowed, backed away, and left them.

Mariah dared a glance at Harrison. His jaw was still hard-set and ticking. Mariah did not say anything. She was deeply mortified. They said not a word to Alicia nor Simon as they went toward the entrance of the library. She simply allowed Harrison to lead her to the front door for their outerwear and then to the awaiting carriage.

Chapter Fifteen

Much Too Close

Harrison was beyond rageful. He had nearly lost his sight when he came upon Mariah and the cad. Blind, black rage had almost suffocated him. What an idiot he had been to have left her side, and he did not need to hear another man tell him such. He quite understood the matter.

Mariah—*his* Mariah—had given the pup the look she had given him twice. Did she not understand the ideas and sensations that look caused to come upon a fellow? Nay, she would not know, having grown up in the sheltered way she had. How she could even give such an alluring look in the first place was beyond him. But, by the graces of God, how it undid him.

Harrison ran a hand over his face. All the events of today were almost too much to bear. Earlier, when Alicia, the well-meaning but bacon-brained woman, tried to get Mariah to peer through the telescope, it was such a terrible thing to entertain. He knew Mariah hadn't looked for more than the briefest of moments, and even though it angered him, it wasn't much like this moment currently. But now, the rage he felt within his chest was more dominant. Mariah was his!

And how could anyone in the room have been so unobservant as to not know she was alone, he seethed. Blast Simon and his bird-witted wife. They should not even be allowed to chaperone a cat!

He was more than slightly annoyed that Alicia and Simon had seen her partake in a private conversation with a man not known to her and neither had stepped in. His talk with Simon earlier in the day about better chaperoning Mariah had accomplished nothing.

He was a fool. He was a fool to think a familial member to Mariah could do an adequate job at being a better chaperone.

Blast Simon, he cursed again. To do this to his sister is an outrage! How dare he be such a moonling! And poor Mariah is the subject to woeful tidings imparted by the lack of care.

Harrison dared a glance out of his peripheral vision at her. She held her charming face stoically though her shimmering sapphire eyes were on the verge of tears. Her lips were slightly pursed, holding back more emotion. Harrison sighed, looking away from the hurt she felt.

I am such a fool to have left her alone...

Mariah was beautiful and innocent, sweet and intelligent. He had given his word that no harm would come to her. He had promised that neither her heart nor her person would come into contact with pain. And yet, in pain she was.

He'd seen men like that regiment officer stare at women before, and no good could come of their intentions. Yes, he was a fool. No reason was excusable enough to leave her unattended to, not even for a mere moment. He had been overjoyed to have met up with his old friend. He had not known how long they had reminisced, but he had come to realize he should end their conversation and check on Mariah.

When he had taken out his pocket watch to learn the time, he had had a foreboding that would not leave him. Indeed, the anxiety proved to be real as he came upon the scene. His heart felt like it had been seized from his chest at the sight of Mariah so intent upon another man. He felt his heart lying at her feet and could only think of Samantha and how she had treated him. The two women were nothing alike and should never have been given cause to be compared. But the emotion of losing his heart to the floor was the same. His body felt both squashed beyond reason and like it had fallen off a cliff at the same instant.

Harrison raked his fingers through his hair. He opened his mouth to speak, then promptly shut it. He couldn't say anything. Not yet. His words would be venomous, and his dear Mariah did not need to hear his ireful declarations. She needed to hear about how much she meant to him. And at this moment, he wasn't capable.

He helped her into the carriage and shut the door behind him. She took the seat opposite him and dared not to glance in his direction. She sighed very heavily and also did not speak. Through the light of the swaying lantern on the outside of the carriage, he swore he could see tears lining her dark lashes. As quickly as he thought he saw them, Mariah raised her head, though, looking poised yet bleak.

They reached the house quickly enough, so she rose just as the carriage came to a stop, exiting the conveyance before he could assist her. She entered the house, gave her cloak to Carter, and, without saying a word, climbed the stairs to her room.

Harrison followed behind her and watched her ascend the stairs. He wanted to call out to her, to keep her near him, but he knew he could not speak yet. He needed to settle his feelings before he attempted to converse. He walked off to the library and closed the door with a quick thud.

Pacing for a moment, he took another turn before he sat down on the chaise. This wasn't going how he had hoped it would. The event was much too close a call for him.

Harrison shook his head and sighed, *How am I to tell her?*

Chapter Sixteen

Rain & Resolve

The next morning was bleak and raining. It fit Mariah's mood perfectly. She ate her morning meal from a tray in her bed. She could not bear the thought of facing Harrison this morning. She wasn't ready to face him nor his words. She wasn't ready to face the world and plaster on a fake smile to cover the damage of her breaking heart.

Tonight was the first ball she would attend since coming into Brighton. Her excitement vanished, as she had no hope of dancing with Harrison. Maybe Major Wallis would be in attendance, but she was mortified of her behavior with him, and, if she was honest, Harrison's as well. She would try her best to avoid the man.

After dressing, she found Lady Purcellville, Alicia, and Harrison in the parlor. She said not a word but simply slipped into the room and sat in a chair near the fire. Harrison was reading the paper, and she was aware he did not look up at her entering the room. Alicia and her mama were engaged in some sordid gossip. Today, they were to stay home and receive visitors. Thankfully, she wouldn't be forced into the confinement of a carriage with Harrison—at least, not until it was time for the ball. Sitting beside him would be unsettling, and sitting across from him would be absolute torture.

"La, but both of you are in a terrible mood!" Alicia exclaimed, standing and crossing her arms. Neither Harrison nor Mariah acknowledged her, and so with a humph, she took her seat again.

Mariah felt like hiding, although it would be rude of her to do so. So she forced herself to sit there and wait for him to say something. She felt as if she did not owe it to him to be the one to break their separation. At each turn of events while being with him, he had made no inclination that he liked her as a man does his intended. All of his kind considerations seemed to be born of the desire to see her safe and well-chaperoned as he was tasked to do. That, perhaps, would be the only reason driving his attention her way.

She sighed heavily, keeping the noise quiet to herself. *I must resolve to put away these childish notions of us being together. I have to endeavor to feel confident without his presence...but God's graces, how am I to land myself a match? Am I destined to be a spinster?* She crossed her arms over herself and stared at the fire. If only her heart and mind would cease to war with each other, she could put her past dreams to rest.

It was not long before the visitors came. To Mariah, the whole process could not have been concluded quickly enough. Mrs. Liftgrove came, and several other regiment wives came as well, alongside Lord and Lady Halifax. Mariah spoke only when necessary. She did not raise her eyes to look at Harrison, and she felt her head begin to thump in time with her heartbeat.

It wasn't long before the ache found its way behind her eyes. She was very relieved when no rumors of an engagement between herself and Harrison were brought up. She owed a great deal to Major Wallis for remaining silent upon the subject.

When luncheon was announced, Mariah made her excuses and quickly fled to her room. She did not bother to eat her meal when Amy brought it up; she only wanted to be still and have the headache cease. She sent Amy away and did her best to fall asleep to ease the ache in her head.

The pounding in her head in tandem with her heart did not relent. She opted to stare out the window at the dismal and dreary day, admiring the fall of the rain upon the lead-framed window. It gave her a moment to rest her head upon the glass and not worry about who would see her since her room faced the gardens out back.

The cool glass eased the pounding in her head slightly, though it did nothing to alleviate the ache in her heart. How dare Harrison make such a bold claim and then speak not of it.

Mariah sighed. *How I wish to return home. Coming here was such a terrible idea. It would be best to leave and find someone around my own home to marry. It would leave me close to Mama and Papa and put an end to this endless longing and torture.*

The door to her room opened, permitting Amy inside. "Mistress, it is time for dinner."

Mariah shook her head. "Please inform our hosts I am not coming. I will be in attendance at the ball once I curb this headache. If you could please come back to arrange my hair for the evening, it would be appreciated."

"Yes, mistress," Amy said. Then she left.

Mariah sighed, crossing her arms over herself. Her stomach rumbled, and she ignored it. Getting off the window seat, she dressed in one of her other best evening gowns of a dark cobalt blue. She smiled softly to herself, admiring her reflection and how the dress complemented her skin tone. Soon, Amy came in as requested, standing behind the stool at the dressing table where Mariah was to sit to have her hair arranged.

Alicia let herself into the room too, standing behind Mariah and watching as Amy arranged curl after curl atop Mariah's head. Mariah knew the weight of her hair might bring back her headache, but she did not care. She knew her hair was at its best with many curls adorning it.

Amy had even woven a shimmering cobalt ribbon through the curls; the result really was stunning. When Amy finished, Mariah expressed her gratitude and dismissed her again to enjoy her evening.

When they were alone, Alicia approached Mariah who was still seated at the dressing table. Alicia's dress was pale green, with ribbons intertwined just under her bosom. Her auburn curls were arranged up in a knot upon the crown of her head, which cascaded down the length of her peaches-and-cream–colored neck. Alicia placed her gloved hands upon Mariah's shoulders.

"You will be the envy of all the unwed misses! I love your hair arranged like that. The Earl of Bramley is sure to notice you and fall at your feet. Perhaps Major Wallis will be in attendance upon you as well tonight. Mama bade me to see how you are. Papa and Mama would both be happy to sit at home with you. Now that I am married, they need not attend every function." Alicia giggled, taking her hands away from Mariah's shoulders.

"I am well and determined to conquer it, should my headache return," Mariah replied, rising from her seat and reaching for her fan and gloves.

"La, but the Earl of Bramley sure was in a state last night, was he not? I feared for poor Major Wallis; you might not know it, but he was quite a favorite of mine. There was a time I thought I would die if he did not offer for me. Then Simon came along, and all paled in comparison to him."

Alicia was smiling, and it did Mariah good to know that no matter what Alicia lacked in propriety, she truly did love Simon.

"There, I am all ready," Mariah said as she twirled in front of her full-length mirror. Her sapphire eyes were brimming with excitement, and she was determined to dance tonight and forget about teal-colored eyes.

The ladies linked arms and left Mariah's bedchamber, heading down to Carter to don their cloaks and then to the awaiting carriage which would transport them to the Old Ship where tonight's ball was to be held. Mariah got herself into the carriage with the assistance of the footman, sitting on the far side. She dared not look at who else entered after her. She was ready to make the most of this night. The chatter around her was made in polite tones, and she felt all eyes rest upon her at some point or another, though none spoke to her directly.

Mariah took in the scenery of the night around her, with lit oil lanterns casting beautiful shadows on gardens and homes. The journey to the Old Ship was a quick affair. She was still reeling from the travel between Bramley and Brighton, comparing every-thing to it, though she felt most of the comparison had to do with the level of chatter.

Once she stood outside of the carriage, she smiled, taking in the famous home. The Old Ship was famous for its decadent balls. With more room than most residences, it was an easy location for the various local members of the ton to host their assemblies and balls. The only other leading hotel was the Castle Inn. It was common to see the Regent and his friends frequent those locations, and none who were deemed suitable for his company passed through its entrance without his being made aware of their presence. Lord and Lady Halifax were prominent members of the ton, so they were frequent visitors upon the Regent in the Pavilion. Lord and Lady Purcellville could claim an acquaintance with the Regent, but it was not a strong connection, as Lord Purcellville commanded the reg-iment.

There was a huge chandelier brilliantly lit with dozens of candles. It was absolutely mesmerizing. Mariah took notice of it as she handed over her burgundy cloak. She wanted to be sure her next letter to Mama and Papa held the details of this evening since they had never been to Brighton. This evening was more for them than it was for herself.

She was surprised when Harrison came up beside her and offered her his arm. She hesitated for a few seconds, then placed her hand upon his ebony evening coat. She still avoided his gaze. Her heart fluttered, and for a moment, she allowed herself to gush about how right they felt together! She matched his pace as they strode to the staircase to be announced.

They waited in the receiving line for a few minutes, and still, neither spoke. Looking about herself, Mariah spotted Ma-jor Wallis and quickly looked away before he caught her gaze.

Harrison soon gave his and Mariah's names to the crier, who announced them. They walked down the staircase togeth-er, and Mariah held her head high just in case any rumor had started circulating regarding her. She felt that since Alicia was a wagging tongue, most here would be similar, if not a dash worse. And despite her tumultuous feelings regarding Harri-son, the last thing she wanted to do was embarrass him.

Harrison noticed her movement, and, bending his head to reach her ear, he whispered, "Good girl."

Mariah did not respond vocally, but she did squeeze his arm under her hand. If he had not been so bold, she wouldn't have had cause to be concerned. And she felt his words to be a touch callous too, though they were not meant as such. It bothered her nonetheless. They were not engaged, and his constant attention would only fuel rumors. There were those who would not be satisfied with the claim that he was a dear family friend.

Mariah and Harrison came before their hosts for the evening and exchanged greetings. He bowed, and she curtsied. They barely spoke to Lord and Lady Struthers.

Immediately after the greeting, Harrison led Mariah to the dance floor where the soothing music of a waltz was playing. She curtsied before him as he bowed to her and then his strong arms pulled her toward him. Harrison placed one arm around her waist, and Mariah placed her hand in his free one. He smiled down upon her, and she smiled back weakly. He shook his head, then smiled again at her with his eyebrows arched. This time, she returned his smile wholeheartedly as they glided gracefully upon the floor, fully aware people were watching and she had to keep up appearances. If this was to be done, she would do her part exceptionally.

They did not speak but looked deeply into each other's eyes. Mariah felt as if she were floating. She had never been so breathless and so completely happy. She felt the eyes of others upon them, but neither broke their eye contact. His teal-colored eyes seemed to convey his feelings which she did not yet understand; how could he care for her in such a manner? He was far above her in every aspect. Her confusion upon his actions left her feeling cautious, but still, the hope that this was a beginning and not an ending between them made her euphoric.

Around and around they danced, and Harrison brought her closer to him possessively. Surely, society would be speaking now. Mariah knew she should try to put distance between them, but she could not bring herself to perform the action. Even looking away from his eyes was a chore she was not capable of. She knew that she, or even he, should look away. Not breaking eye contact was a sure sign they were meant to be engaged, and soon.

Good graces, what am I doing?

Chapter Seventeen

A Declaration at Long Last

Harrison drank her in. He couldn't get enough of her. She was lovely. She was beyond lovely; she was the most gorgeous creature he had ever beheld. Her dark hair was perfection, though he longed to take the pins from it and let it fall gloriously down her back. Why was it fashionable to hide such beauty? The way she fit perfectly within his arms was blissful torture. He could easily bring her against him with no space between them, and he knew he would be able to rest his chin upon the top of her head. He swore in this moment that God Himself had created her perfectly for him, for there was none else he could imagine being with in all his life. Internally shaking himself now, Harrison reined in his rampant thoughts.

Mariah's sapphire eyes were sparkling, and her smile was a prize he sought. He only wanted to see her happy; it had almost killed him to see her suffer from the megrims earlier. He wanted more than anything to wrap her in his arms and keep her safe from all heartache, headaches, or otherwise and all eyes that might view her disparagingly. He felt it all the way into his bones that he could search the world and never find her equal. He was well aware he should be looking about him, at the room, or at the other dancers around him, but he could not make his eyes obey. He should make his mouth address her—talk of the weather or some such mundane topic—but there was still a separation between them, and he needed to repair that gulf before it further enlarged.

How her dazzling eyes shine with such sparkle and warmth that could bring me to my knees in such a welcoming way, I shall never know.

The minutes ticked by, and the waltz came to an end. Harrison walked her back to where Lady Purcellville was perched. He had to be reasonable; he knew many would want to dance with his Mariah. *His Mariah.* He liked the idea of her being his in a more permanent fashion. Some medieval maleness made a smug look cross his face; thankfully, he banished it before anyone seemed to notice.

Mariah smiled demurely at the members of their party, and her attention focused upon a man in the regimental colors who approached her, wishing to dance with her.

Harrison took a step toward the man. "You may have one dance," he said, his eyes and voice darkening to a level that he hoped would convey the seriousness of the only one dance. Mariah met his steadfast gaze and smiled shyly up at him.

Harrison took a step back and allowed Mariah to go forth and dance with the young regiment soldier. The man appeared to not even be out of his early teens; Harrison could have scoffed at the thought of Mariah liking the young man. Nay, dear Mariah was his, and he was bound to make it known tonight. As of right now, he would be keen to keep a watchful eye on her. She was the belle of the ball. And the belle was going to be his completely by the end of the night.

Mariah was breathless with laughter as her partner, Lord Remford, brought her back to stand beside Harrison. He bowed over her hand as she curtsied to him and he backed away, thanking her for a delightful dance and winking at Harrison. Mariah wondered what that look meant but became even more curious over the intense sharpness in Harrison's eyes. "You must be in need of refreshment after all those dances?" Harrison inquired, perking a dark brow.

Mariah smiled and nodded. She had danced with four different men besides Harrison and was thankful to take a small respite. She took his arm and allowed him to fend their way through the crowd.

They were before the refreshment table in less than five minutes, and Harrison handed her a cup. Mariah took a sip, barely knowing what she was drinking. Harrison watched her so intently, it was almost unnerving. Staring at her cup of bubbling liquid, she downed the entirety.

When she had finished her cup, she gave it to a passing footman, who placed it upon his tray.

"How did you find the champagne?" Harrison asked.

"Oh, is that what it was? 'Twas delicious."

Mariah felt bubbly from the inside out, but surely, she had not consumed enough to make her feel this way. Her feelings came from the way he looked at her. She'd tasted the bubbly drink before, but this evening was utterly magical.

She glanced outside, noticing how even the rain and storm did not mar the gaiety of the room. With the weather changing to colder temperatures, the room was not overly hot despite all the bodies in the residence either dancing or talking.

Harrison led Mariah away from the refreshment table, and they made their way toward Lord and Lady Halifax. Lord Halifax greeted them, then quickly bowing and curtsying, they all fell into conversation.

"'Tis quite crowded tonight! I hate a crowd—makes an old man feel his age," Lord Halifax remarked and shook his head.

His left eye was clouded over, and Mariah felt a twinge of sadness for him. Lady Halifax had her hand upon his arm, smiling warmly and proudly at him. They were quite the lovely couple, with his sharp masculine features and her soft feminine grace. Even though they were at least a score difference in age, if not more, it was delightful to see them still so deeply in love.

"What is one to do?" inquired Harrison.

Then Mariah felt a tap upon her shoulder and turned. Major Crawley, she believed was his name, had requested a dance with her, so here he was to claim his turn. Smiling, she took his arm. He led her amidst the dancers, and they took their places. They talked of the weather and the regiment. When they had concluded the dance, he walked her over to Alicia, who was chatting away with Mrs. Liftgrove. Alicia smiled at her but continued on with her conversation.

From Mariah's right, she spied Major Wallis approaching her. Feeling uneasy, she waited in place for him to pass.

Major Wallis stopped before her and smiled. "Here you are, at long last. I hope the evening has not tired you out excessively?"

"Indeed not. I am well. I owe you an apology and a thank you. By now, I think it is safe to say you know an engagement is not in place between the Earl of Bramley and myself. Thank you for not repeating his Lordship's words," Mariah addressed him, and she only stopped to see what he was thinking. She gazed into his brown eyes and saw nothing amiss.

"No need to apologize. It would dishonor us to spread such rumors. I have no taste for salacious gossip. You may count on me being discreet. I would never seek to wound you, my dear lady."

"I thank you, sir," Mariah smiled sincerely.

"Would you allow me to call upon you on the morrow?" His warm chocolate eyes were so intent and earnest. She disliked the thought of rejecting him, but the thought of encouraging him seemed cruel: if she allowed him to call, there would be rumors or a seed of an idea for him to believe she wanted his advances...but did she?

No, she decided firmly. *I do not want him to believe in anything other than my friendship.*

Forming her words carefully, she began, "What I said was correct. There is no understanding between myself and his Lordship at present. I have no idea if such an understanding may ever take place. I do not wish to injure a dear friend. I would not wish to encourage you with false hope for the world either. If you seek a friend, for that is all I can offer you at present, I am most happy to oblige. If you wish otherwise, however, you may not call."

"Ah, I see," Major Wallis stated. The poor man turned a slight shade of pink, which, given his tanned appearance, wounded Mariah to witness. Never had she sought to embarrass such an amiable man as Major Wallis.

"Here comes your hero. He looks a tad more civil this evening than last. I shall bid you adieu before I am challenged to a duel at sunrise." Major Wallis bowed over her hand and pressed a kiss upon her gloved knuckles. He turned and left just before Harrison reached her.

"Whatever was he sniffing around about?" Harrison asked, looking annoyed.

"That is unkind, my lord," Mariah began. "He was a gentleman through and through. I think if you gave him time, you would meet as friends."

"Bah," Harrison waved his hand through the air. "I repeat: what did he want?"

"If you must know, he wanted what the other gentlemen have sought after this evening: my approval for them to call upon me. I rather like him too...," Mariah said, looking up at him to gauge his reaction. She thought if Harrison's mouth grew any tauter, it would crack at its sides and start to bleed. His eyes became so narrowed, she wondered how he could even see through the thick scowl and long lashes.

"What answer did you give him?"

"The same which I have given them all, my lord: that I would never give a man false hope of my affection. If they wished for my society in a friendly manner, then I would most welcome them. Otherwise, they might not call upon me," she replied, her face firm as she concentrated upon his handsome face. The slight cleft in his chin always invited her gaze, and sometimes, she caught herself wanting to touch it.

The strains of another waltz began, and Harrison started to lead her toward the floor. She did not readily follow, so he turned toward her with a patient look. He smiled, and this time when he moved, she went along with him. There were words of caution screaming in her head that another waltz with him would ruin her reputation or be the source of wild rumors as to them being soon to wed. It was only proper to have two dances with any one partner during the night, and never were those two to be both the waltz. Three were sure to earn her censure and to make the tongues of the ton waggle. Mariah and Harrison would be well within the ton's right to expect banns to be read.

Mariah frowned slightly but corrected it promptly. She would dare not ruin her association with Harrison due to her conflicting mind.

"Have I offended you?" he asked, a scowl of his own upon his handsome face. "Have I done something wrong? If you like, we can take some fresh air instead."

Mariah knew this was dangerous, but still, she went on. "It's only that I do not seek to be the source of unwanted rumors. Two waltzes in the same evening may make a statement you do not wish to declare." Mariah broke her eye contact and instead focused her gaze on his cravat.

"Is that so? Would it be so disastrous if the ton thought we were betrothed?"

Mariah could hardly meet his gaze. She forced her eyes upward, seeing the soft smile upon his lips and the twinkle in his eye gleaming. She worried her bottom lip a moment. "Why would you wish to be the source of scandal? I do not wish to provide gossip for the whole ton to delight in; never where it pertains to you."

"Scandal, no. I do not wish that upon anyone. Would the idea of being my wife repulse you?"

Looking up into his eyes, Mariah saw sincerity and something else. Dare she hope it was love? Dare she hope that her wildest dream would come true? She felt her eyes begin to sting with the threat of tears.

"I could never be repulsed by you. I would rather see you happy, content, and truly in love than to be leg-shackled to someone who is undeserving. I want only your happiness."

"You make me happy. My whole world is tied upon your needs and wishes; your gentle words and radiant smiles light me up inside my heart. I can think of no other who I adore as I do you. Say the word, and I will fly to your father and ask his blessing. You are all I want, all I desire. I would spend the whole of my life counting your smiles and sighs and would consider myself to be the richest of men. It only you would say that you, in return, care for me."

Harrison had both her hands in his and was patiently waiting for her response. Mariah blinked back tears. Could this truly be happening, and in such a public place? She searched the depths of Harrison's gaze, hoping to see a dream, but she found the reality she had always desired with Harrison. She felt people's eyes upon them both but refused to break their beautiful moment by looking away from his beloved face.

"I would be honored to be your wife. I can think of no other purpose for me. A thousand times will I say yes to you and love you until the end of time."

She was so happy, she was giddy and could not stop smiling. At long last, her very dear and beloved Harrison was and always would be *her Harrison.*

"Then I happily say unto you, my dearest Mariah Morten, would you do me the greatest honor of becoming *my* Countess of Bramley whom I shall love and cherish above all else?"

Mariah nodded, finding it hard to breathe. "Yes, my dearest, beloved Harrison."

Harrison took her hand, quickly departing the ball shortly thereafter to numerous stares and unanswered questions. Mariah felt as if she were existing in a dream state. She could not believe her heart could hold such happiness and still beat.

Chapter Eighteen

Welcomed Relations

T he next morning, Mariah was humming as Amy helped her to dress. She could not wait to see her betrothed again. Would he be just as excited to see her? Did he miss her as she missed him? Silly though it was, she found it hard to be without his company for long.

Finally, she found that she had achieved her first good night's sleep since she had left the parsonage. Her dreams had been filled with happy laughter and endless love within the stone walls of Bramley Hall. She had dreamt of having tea and coffee out in the garden while she watched their children get into mischief as they had used to. It was an enjoyable dream, one she knew would be a reality soon enough.

Mariah sighed, fidgeting in her seat while Amy styled her hair.

"You seem very happy this morning, mistress. Are things going well now?" inquired Amy.

"They certainly are! I am so happy, I am close to bursting." Mariah smiled at her image as she gazed into the gilded glass mirror affixed to the dressing table.

"Wonderful news, mistress," Amy replied.

Mariah could not keep from grinning. "How are you finding Brighton, dearest Amy?"

The maid grinned, "I am finding my time here very enjoyable, thank you."

With her hair done and there being no correctable flaw in it, Mariah thanked Amy and headed toward the dining room.

She was smiling as she came through the door where Simon and Harrison were howling with laughter at something Lord Purcellville was saying. The men rose and then seated themselves again after Mariah took her seat.

"And so, my dear boys, never ask your wife to hand you an apple after you have said something like that to them. Delicate creatures they may be, but they sure know how to bruise." Lord Purcellville boomed this out amid the hearty laughter of Simon and Harrison.

Mariah smiled, thinking it best to remain silent. She felt as if she were happiness itself just sitting beside Harrison.

Turning toward her, Simon told her, "Our aunt and uncle have arrived. They mean to pay a call this very morning. I will not be here, but you shall be, and that is why they are coming."

"To see me? Surely, they are paying a call to meet your Alicia. Mama and Papa said they would be coming to Brighton." Mariah forked a piece of her egg and brought it to her mouth. The lightness of her eggs was divine. The cook here was magnificent.

"I shall be delighted to see them again; I never heard better sense than from Mr. Hughley," Harrison added, a beaming smile on his handsome face.

"Indeed? Come on now, old man; he is a complete bore, and I have no idea how my aunt puts up with him," Simon said between bites of his toast.

"Simon, you are being unkind. Our uncle is a gentleman and takes great care to make our aunt happy," Mariah scolded.

Simon pretended to pout and Harrison laughed at him. Simon scowled. Harrison held up his hands palms out in a sign for peace and said, laughing, "You know, you do pout; your wife was correct."

Seeing Harrison laugh so merrily made Mariah giggle and hold her hand over her mouth. Even Lord Purcellville nodded his head in agreement to Harrison's statement and joined in with the laughter.

Rising now, Simon bowed before his sister and said, "Since you are all against me, I shall take my leave! Never let it be said that I readily accepted being laughed at." With that, he strode out of the room.

Lord Purcellville bellowed after him, "Now, now, young man. Shall I call my daughter down to straighten you out?"

No one could quite make out the reply Simon gave, but that was probably for the best.

"Ah, but he is quite the thing needed for an old man like myself. I know my daughter can be a handful, but they do keep each other amused. It's time I was on my way as well. Enjoy breaking your fasts," Lord Purcellville chortled, rising and waving his hand at them.

Once Lord Purcellville was through the door, Harrison wiped his mouth with his napkin and placed it upon his plate. "Now, my dear Mariah, how shall we entertain ourselves this day?"

Mariah withheld a shiver that desired to creep down her spine at the mention of her given name upon his lips. How the pronunciation had changed over the years from a youthful lad to a grown, magnificent man, and it made her heart stutter to hear it from him. Now that they were engaged, the propriety in addressing her could be dropped.

Drinking her hot chocolate, Mariah thought about what to do for the day. She returned her cup to the table and said, "I shall like to see my aunt and uncle. I would love to include them in our plans if they have no prior engagements. It's been ages since we last met."

"Of course; perhaps we can attend a soiree. I believe the Castle Inn is hosting one this afternoon. Most, I imagine, will be at the races this morning. Would you like to attend a race while we are here?" Harrison questioned.

"I do not care where we go; as long as I am by your side, my happiness is secure." Mariah replied, setting her napkin upon her plate.

"Well, if you have no idea, perhaps we shall become bathers today!" Harrison teased while he waggled his eyebrows at her.

"Oh, please, no! Even if the water is warm, I would fear the spies with all of the telescopes so visible at every house! How anybody can so freely embark on such an adventure I cannot say. I'm just pleased I barely glimpsed it." Mariah shyly smiled, thinking of the man Alicia had bade her look upon. She wondered if Harrison still bore annoyance about the incident.

"Perhaps you are right. I would fear for my virtue should I spy a lady peering at me through the instrument!" Harrison chuckled.

"You are not being serious. Men—or women, for that matter—spying on other persons while they're in such a state of undress is reprehensible. I cannot think you would spend your time in such a manner." Mariah seemed certain he would not, at the very least, and she hoped she was correct in her supposition.

"Indeed, no good could come of that activity," Harrison began, his voice quieting as he leaned in. "Lady Purcellville and Alicia should still be abed. I cannot imagine any caller to arrive before half past eleven, if not later. We could venture to the library, if you wish."

Slightly blushing, Mariah said, "My aunt has a great sweet tooth. I remember her favoring licorice. May we find some this morning?"

"Let us be off!" Harrison rose from his chair and helped Mariah to stand. "While we are about, let us purchase a token for Lady Purcellville," he said, leading Mariah out to the staircase. "We shall take your maid with us. So make ready, and I will see that the carriage awaits."

Harrison brought her hand to his lips, and he kissed the back of her hand with a feathery touch. Mariah stopped breathing. When Harrison straightened, he wore a look of complete seriousness.

"I await your return. Pray do not keep me waiting too long," he said, giving her a handsome smirk.

Mariah nodded and ascended the stairs as she released her breath. To be soon married to such a man as he! She did not understand what she had done to earn his favor, but she was awfully glad she had.

As promised, she did not keep him waiting long. She did not change her dress but made certain her hair was still proper and grabbed her reticule. Luckily, Amy was in her chamber making the bed and bringing in fresh laundry. Mariah hastened Amy to grab her items for town.

Mariah practically beat Amy down the stairs and to her cloak that Carter laid out for her and helped her don. It seemed she reached the front door before Harrison. She grinned, wanting to tease him about his keeping her waiting.

Harrison strode down the steps, taking her out to the carriage and helping her and Amy inside. The ride to town was quick enough and quite enjoyable on a crisp fall morning. The sun glared through the darkening clouds, but in all, it seemed to her that at least it wouldn't rain.

The carriage stopped outside of a cute little shop. The coach-man made a comment of it being a favorite of most ladies in Brighton. Mariah beamed, thrilled to spend the morning with Harrison and shop together.

Mariah was happy to procure the licorice for her aunt and found a very pretty lace fan for their hostess as well. She felt Harrison's eyes intently upon her as she browsed the fine goods before her. She grinned, feeling a creeping heat to her cheeks from his close proximity and doting attention.

She passed the token lace fan to Harrison to hold on to. She held another lace fan in her hand, pondering on if she should get it for herself or not. Her lips pursed, and she made a motion to set it down.

"You only have to ask, and it shall be yours. I would not see you without when it is in my power to provide it," Harrison whispered, taking her hand in his.

"You are most kind; however, I was thinking of a gift for Alicia. She may find it unfair to not be gifted as well, though I admit, I do not see anything of notice for her." Mariah frowned.

"Hmm, how about a pretty comb for her hair?" Harrison offered, pointing to a table where the combs laid.

"It is not my wish to bankrupt you in the space of a day," Mariah teased.

"It would take many days of heavy spending to bankrupt me. I think we shall find it near impossible to ever go through my fortune. It would be exhausting."

Mariah nodded, not wanting to say another word on such an improper subject. What Harrison had in his holdings were none of her concern.

Mariah approached the table and looked upon the combs. They had a splendid variety. There was one comb that had a pearl set in the right corner, and filigree in silver covered it. It was so lovely. Mariah touched it.

"Is this the one?" Harrison asked, picking it up.

Mariah shook her head. "I rather think one with more color should suit Alicia's hair better. I would not want it to lose its appeal once it was placed within her tresses."

Mariah considered a comb of black with tiny perfect seashells upon it. She thought it would suit her sister-in-law perfectly. It was flamboyant like Alicia. Mariah believed the color would complement her hair and style well. She held it up for Harrison's approval.

"Lovely." Harrison smiled deeply at her.

They stood, looking at each other for the space of a few seconds longer than would be considered proper until Amy coughed. Then Mariah hid a smirk on her lips, tipping her head down to browse more combs. She swore she could feel Harrison smiling as well. Turning to look at her maid, Mariah smiled at her too. Then she took Harrison's arm, and they all made their way to the counter to purchase their goods. Mariah was truly happy, thinking of the joy the treasures would bring their intended persons.

With their shopping done, they promptly returned to the Purcellvilles' manor. Making her way to the parlor, Mariah paused in front of the mirror, ensuring her hair and gown were not soiled from their quick trip to town. Satisfied with her appearance, she continued on her way to the parlor, seating herself between Lady Purcellville and Alicia.

"My, what have you been up to?" inquired Alicia.

"Shopping," answered Mariah.

"Oh, how wonderful! What did you bring back?" Alicia giddily asked, her bright eyes shining with curiosity.

"You shall have to wait to see, as it was the Earl of Bramley who actually made the purchases," Mariah teased her sister-in-law.

"Oh, bah, I hate to wait!"

Laughing, Mariah said, "Oh, very well! I should not like to wait either. I am just as anxious to see how they are liked." Mariah rose. "I shall fetch them now."

The parlor door opened, admitting Harrison. Mariah smiled at him. Harrison opened his mouth to say something, but Alicia cut him off.

"Do not distract her!" Alicia hollered. "She is on a mission."

Laughing softly, Mariah left the room. It was not long that she returned to the parlor with her gifts in hand. She again took her place between the two females and caught Harrison's eye. He smiled, so she first handed Lady Purcellville her present.

Lady Purcellville seemed surprised as she unwrapped the brown paper to see the fan created from very fine cream lace. The lady had been mentioning her intent to purchase another, as she'd left her finest one behind at their London townhouse.

With a delighted gasp, she now said, "Oh, my dear girl! And you as well, dear, sweet man! I cannot believe my eyes! I am all astonishment! I thank you both very sincerely!" Rising, she pulled Mariah to her feet and gave her a hug. Then, after she crossed the short distance of the room to Harrison, the good man rose to her approach as well. Lady Purcellville held out her hand to him and said, "Thank you. I am most touched."

"It was my pleasure, my lady," Harrison replied, squeezing her hand.

"Now, it's my turn!" Alicia playfully demanded.

Lady Purcellville retook her seat and lovingly fingered her new fan.

All eyes were on Alicia as Mariah handed her the little package. When Alicia finally saw the comb, she gasped. "'Tis lovely! It must have cost a fortune! Thank you, my lord." Alicia nodded at him. "I thank you too, dearest Mariah! I cannot wait to show Simon!" Alicia reached over and hugged her.

"I am so pleased you like it," Mariah told her.

"I'm quite in love with it!" Alicia exclaimed.

Harrison dipped his head and smiled at the women. Mariah beamed back, allowing her eyes to linger a touch on him and admire the way the sunlight through the window played with his masculine features and strong jaw.

Carter opened the door and announced Mr. and Mrs. Hughley. Her relatives came into the parlor. Mariah rose and went straight into her aunt's arms. Harrison was at her side, shaking her uncle's hand.

Harrison cleared his throat. "Lady Purcellville, Mrs. Morten, might I introduce to you Mr. and Mrs. Hughley."

"You are lovely, dear niece," Mrs. Hughley told Alicia, which brought a tinge of pink to Alicia's cheeks.

"Thank you, ma'am," Alicia answered.

"How were your mama and papa when you left?" inquired Mr. Hughley, his attention on Mariah.

"Enjoying good health, dear uncle. I am so pleased you have come to join us!" Mariah smiled at him. "How have you been?"

"Doing well, as has my wife. We had a lovely trip here and did not find the roads too bumpy," Mr. Hughley said merrily.

"Fantastic news indeed," smiled Harrison.

The party took their seats as directed by Lady Purcellville, and tea was rung for. Light conversation was made as to the events they had attended. Of course, the conversation was led to the topic of fans, decorating bonnets, upcoming holidays, and who was marrying whom.

Mariah was happy to keep silent upon her engagement. She was aching to tell all and sundry the exciting news, but she knew she would not forgive herself if she did not allow her papa the first joy of accepting Harrison into the family.

Harrison came and sat beside Mariah. He smiled at her and said very quietly, "I have an errand to see to later, but you shall not miss me, as I'll leave once you are resting for the ball tonight."

"Oh? Can you not divulge what your mission is?" Mariah asked seriously.

"No, for 'tis a secret." He took her hand and squeezed it.

Hearing his answer made her suspicious. She furrowed her brows but said not a thing. She looked up at him and knew she would never tire of his handsome face. He still held her hand clasped in his, and she looked around at the others in the room. They risked censure in possibly being caught holding hands. Sensing her unease, Harrison replaced her hand in her lap, and she smiled again at him. She was relieved he had let her hand go, for when he touched her, it took her breath away. He was so near that she was sure he could hear her heart beating erratically.

"I can go now, as to return to your side all the sooner," Harrison offered, his teal eyes watching her intently. Mariah often heard other women talk of practically swooning when a man took their hand. If that was what this feeling would be like each time he was near her, touching her hand, then swooning she was indeed.

Mariah lifted her eyes, batting them at Harrison. "It would be much appreciated. I hate any moments without your company."

Harrison lifted her hand to his lips, laying a gentle kiss upon the back of it. "Then I shall see you soon, my sweet Mariah."

Mariah felt her cheeks turn crimson. Luckily for her, the rush of emotion passed quickly, with neither Lady Purcellville nor Alicia the wiser.

Chapter Nineteen

Gifts & Kisses

Mariah sat on the stool while Amy styled her hair in the Greek fashion again where her hair would be tightly curled and put up with tendrils framing her face and a few curls falling down her back. She picked a light, soft pink gown for her evening that was sure to complement her skin tone, or at least, Amy remarked it would.

She stared at the door through the mirror, wondering when Harrison would be back. He had left shortly after her aunt and uncle arrived, missing luncheon, and now, it was time to get ready for the ball tonight. Mayhap it was silly to send him on his way; she should have devised a reason to keep him situated at her side.

Mariah got out of her seat, going to the darkened window to see if she could spy any inkling of rain upon the glass. With a relieved sigh, she turned back to her dressing table. A knock sounded at her door, and for a moment, she held her breath, thinking it happened to be Alicia. She loved the woman dearly, but she needed a reprieve from her chatter.

"Mistress," Amy said, stepping to the side.

But the Earl of Bramley stood before her, holding a small brown wrapped parcel. He strode to her with his teal eyes looking her over with adoration and a brilliant smile brightening his face.

It was not customary nor proper for gifts to be exchanged between those not already wed, though she was uncertain if she should decline such a favor from Harrison. She opened the brown paper, and inside it sat the black comb with the silver filigree and the pearl. She gasped when she lifted it from the paper. Looking up at Harrison through the mirror, she saw he was watching her intently.

Mariah smiled at him. "It is so very lovely. Truly, I have never owned such a piece before. I thank you very much, dear Harrison."

He was towering over her, this man that she loved. He looked so pleased that her heart was near to bursting.

"I am exceedingly glad you like it. I thought it should be directly placed into your hair. I could scarcely contain myself and almost marched up the stairs upon arrival." He leaned over her, kissing the top of her head. Mariah felt his lips linger, hearing a soft inhale. She felt herself blush at the tender gesture. He was so gentle with her. She could imagine a lifetime of his gentle attention, and she released her breath in a sigh. Harrison—her Harrison—smiled back at her. Their eyes held each other, and Mariah wondered if the butterflies inhabiting her stomach would carry her away.

Amy coughed from her spot by the bed, and Mariah broke her eye contact with Harrison to look at her. That Harrison should be in her bedchamber even while Amy stood in their presence was most improper, bordering on scandalous. What would the servants, or even worse, the lord or lady of the house, think?

Harrison seemed to gather his thoughts, and he straightened to his full height. At just over six feet, he bore an imposing stature. Mariah thought he looked elegant with a lace cravat and black breeches. His coat was a dark blue, making his eyes seem darker than usual, or mayhap it was just the same darkening color that she was seeing when he looked at her.

Harrison retreated but did not leave. Amy came behind Mariah and took the comb from her. Selecting a place upon the back of Mariah's head, Amy secured the gift where it was sure to be admired. It was a lovely addition to her person. Amy held the hand mirror to the back of Mariah's head at an angle so she could see the comb. Mariah smiled sweetly, radiating her joy. Mariah pulled on her white gloves and gathered her reticule and rose.

Mariah walked to her full-length mirror and quickly looked over her person, turning around by the mirror to make certain all was right. She did not want to linger excessively, as she did not want Harrison to think she was conceited. She walked toward him and took his proffered arm. The happy couple walked from the bedchamber and down the stairs.

Mariah felt safe and secure as she always had been when in the presence of Harrison. His body radiated strength and warmth that she could feel through her gloves and his coat. He had broad shoulders, and Mariah wondered which of her brothers in build he most resembled. She settled upon Simon. Simon had muscles from his career in the regiment, and she knew Harrison was an avid sportsman, preferring fencing, which she attributed to his stature. They reached the butler at the bottom of the staircase, who held out their cloaks.

Harrison was helping her into her cloak when Simon and Alicia came down the stairs next. Alicia was beaming at them both and bade them look upon her hair. Mariah had been correct that the black comb with tiny seashells would look perfect in her auburn tresses.

"It's stunning! Thank you both again! Simon was quite jealous of the trinket, and I had such fun at his expense, telling him it was a gift from another!" Alicia laughed.

"Oh, dear," stated Mariah, looking from the wife to the husband.

Simon smiled at his sister and said, "Have no fear; all is well."

The couples would be attending the ball alone, as Lord Purcellville had another engagement and Lady Purcellville had a headache. Heading out to the carriage, Harrison helped Mariah inside first, with Alicia quickly following out of the biting wind. They sat in the carriage, with Simon seated next to his wife and Harrison beside her. They conversed about their day with Mr. and

Mrs. Hughley. Simon was overpleased they showed such warmth toward his wife.

The carriage soon pulled into the line to await its turn to empty its occupants, who were a merry four and were in no haste to enter the Castle Inn. When their turn came, it was Simon and Alicia who alighted first.

Harrison was next and took Mariah's hand to bring her toward the steps. He let go of her hand and grabbed her around her waist and lifted her up from the ground. My, but he lifted her as if she weighed nothing more than a feather! She placed her arms onto his shoulders, and she felt his hard muscles working as they moved beneath her fingertips. Her breath caught, and she met his eyes as he lowered her. His gaze held that dark look again, a stormy sea, and instead of feeling wary of the color, Mariah rather felt lost in his eyes. Harrison let go her waist and offered his arm to her. She set her gloved hand upon his arm. She would have very much enjoyed spending the whole evening locked within his arms.

"The horses have been through. I thought it better to see you through the muck. I hope you are not overset," Harrison quickly explained.

"Not at all. I thank you instead, my lord." She looked straight ahead and not at him, as there was a great number of people in attendance. *What a crush*, she thought. Conversation was useless, as everyone seemed to be speaking all at once.

They waited along with Simon and Alicia in the receiving line. It was not long before they had progressed into the ballroom and were all looking for Mr. and Mrs. Hughley. It was Harrison—who stood an inch over Simon—that located them. Harrison led the others toward them.

After genial greetings, Mrs. Hughley linked arms with Mariah, and they walked a few steps away. In a lowered tone, Mrs. Hughley said, "My, but you look lovely this evening! I've been watching you and his Lordship every opportunity I have had. He pays you a great compliment in singling you out with his attention. Tell me, my dear, as your aunt who loves you dearly, is there an understanding between you two? It goes no further than us, whatever your answer may be," Mrs. Hughley asked. Her dear aunt looked radiant in a dark green gown that complemented her pale skin.

Not wanting to be coy or to flat out fib, Mariah was at a loss for how to proceed. She knew her aunt was not one given to wild flights of "fancy", or gossip, for that matter. She began, after a moment's hesitation, "How astute you are, dear aunt. I cannot say much on this delicate subject, but rest assured that soon enough, all will be settled." Mariah hoped her answer was sufficient.

With a nod of her head and a wink of her eye, Mrs. Hughley patted her cheek and told her, "I understand you perfectly. Your father is not here, and it would not be right to enter into an agreement without his consent, at least publicly. I shall stay mum on the subject here after."

Relieved, Mariah smiled brilliantly. Feeling Harrison's presence rather than seeing him, she was not surprised when he touched her elbow.

"I believe this is our dance, fair lady," Harrison stated, bowing to her.

"Is it?" smiled Mariah as Harrison straightened. He gave the back of her hand a kiss, and Mariah knew her cheeks had pinkened. Would she ever learn to control such responses brought about by him?

Harrison led her to the floor, and after their brief exchanges of courtesy, they started the country dance. They turned and walked and skipped this way and that with their fellow partners. Conversation was not to be had due to the exertion of the dance, and that was fine.

When the dance had ended, they each found themselves with new partners, and so the night took off. They danced again several times, and there were many matronly ladies who delighted in presumptuous rumors about them. It seemed as if the gentlemen sought out where Harrison stood after each dance concluded, because Mariah was always presented with a parting bow back at his side. She rather thought it to be a humorous situation.

Her eyes locked on Harrison, and he beamed at her.

"Miss Morten, how well you look this evening!" Major Wallis stated.

Mariah's head whipped so fast in Major Wallis' direction, she was certain she heard her neck pop. From her peripheral vision, she watched Harrison's eyes narrow on the intruder.

"I wonder, may I claim a dance dear lady? Or is your schedule full?" Major Wallis clutched at his heart, and Mariah laughed at him.

Being very serious, Mariah answered him. "I shall, of course, make room for you! I thank you for your gallantry," she answered, taking his hand. She glanced at Harrison, who nodded at her.

Major Wallis was a very graceful man, which one hoped for in a dance partner but was not always blessed to have. They glided across the floor and talked of all manner of things.

"May I inquire when you will be making for home?" Major Wallis asked after a complicated turn.

"I believe a little more than a fortnight. We have been here for five days; I can scarcely understand where the time has flown to," Mariah smiled.

"Indeed, a great many things can happen in just five short days. I shall be saddened to see you depart." He frowned.

"Why should you be sad at my leaving?" Mariah furrowed her brows.

"It is rare indeed to find a creature with such beauty, sweetness, and sense." Major Wallis heaved a sigh, which was difficult, considering they were both breathing heavily from the exertions.

"You certainly do not give my sex the proper credit at all. Not all women are silly and empty-headed," Mariah informed him.

"Not very many I have had the pleasure to know have been sensible. No, the women of my acquaintance have all been fickle and vain. They see a second son, a military man, and no more. I'm fine to enjoy during a ball or to make a fourth at cards. When it comes to invoking more sincere feelings other than excitement, I am at a loss." Major Wallis seemed deep in thought as Mariah watched him. He suddenly gathered his thoughts and smiled again.

"May I ask a question of you?" Mariah bit her bottom lip. She wished to not cause him offense.

"You have but to ask away, Miss Morten."

"Alicia has mentioned you were among her favorites before her marriage. Did her marriage cause your poor heart to suffer?"

"I cannot say I was not left unaffected. I wish the couple well, so please do not think I am brooding about the match. Mrs. Morten is suited to her new husband, and all can see the happiness they have found. I confess, though, there was a time when I thought she would choose me, but it was before your brother. And I must confess further that after a brief acquaintance, it became apparent that our personalities were vastly different," Major Wallis solemnly said.

"You poor, dear man. You have my sympathy!" Mariah smiled sadly up at him.

"Yes, I am to be pitied. Not once but twice has my happiness escaped me." He sighed, shaking his head as he looked away from her.

"Twice?" prompted Mariah.

"Unfortunately. You see, before me dances the latest doomed object of my affection."

He looked so serious, Mariah almost misstepped, but he put her back to the steps without falter while Mariah held in a chortle.

"Major Wallis! How can you flirt so openly with me! I do not like being teased."

Mariah would not look up at him; instead, she searched the room for Harrison. She found his eyes. It seemed to her as if he suddenly felt her gaze upon him, as his head turned like an owl and he immediately locked eyes with her. She watched his left hand clench as well as his masculine jaw tighten. Feeling relieved he was still there, ever vigilant, Mariah returned her attention back to Major Wallis.

"I am sorry to have acted so brashly. I have found that if one sits back and never adventures, there are many missed opportunities. I could not look back upon this time and know I never spoke to you. I am sorry to have flustered you, and I promise from here on in to act the perfect gentleman. Never again will I press upon you my wishes or sentiments. May we part as friends? I only wish to see you happy," he asked as the music about them came to an end and their dance was concluded.

"I assure you, I am honored, and I thank you very highly for your compliments. I hope I have never made you feel as if I was pressing for you to declare yourself?" Mariah replied, taking his offered arm.

"No. You have never led me to believe that you returned my regard. 'Twas only my own sentiments that dared to hope."

Major Wallis led her through the throng of bodies toward the Earl of Bramley.

"Friends." Mariah smiled at him.

Harrison met them at the edge of the dance floor. Major Wallis bowed before Mariah once they reached Harrison and kissed her hand. She let out a breath she hadn't known she was holding, ever happy to be within the presence of Harrison once more.

Major Wallis looked at Harrison and said, "She is indeed to be treasured. Pray take care to make her happy." With that, he turned and fled to the other side of the room.

Harrison wore a puzzled look as he gazed at Major Wallis' retreating back. Mariah quietly explained the exchange between them, and Harrison nodded. She saw the beginnings of a smirk upon his lip, though he held it back.

"Shall we rest for a bit? There is a lovely garden view, and it's open for all who pass by to see. It would not be improper to repair there," Harrison told her, though there was a frown on the edge of his lips.

"What a wonderful idea; yes, please," Mariah replied, needing the cool night so she could breathe fresh air into her lungs and not the humid air of the inside.

The garden was lit with torches, casting a depthless glow upon the manicured garden right out of an oil painting. A small white marbled bench was not far from the inn that he led her to be seated there. After Mariah sat, he paced before her, and she waited for him to speak.

"Do I need to call the cad out, Mariah?" Harrison's face was set in stone and his voice was harsh.

Mariah laughed. She knew she was acting horribly in the face of this question, but he really was the dark, stoic lord seeking who he might devour for offending his lady. Harrison had managed to cease his pacing and now stopped before Mariah, staring at her incredulously.

Mariah gathered herself together and finally managed to say, "I am so sorry to have caused you pain! I could not help laughing at the figure you made. Your countenance was something which I have only ever read about and never had occasion to witness. No, please; you need not call out Major Wallis."

"He upset you," Harrison stated.

"Yes, but that passed, and we have now parted as friends. You must not think of him as a complete coxcomb. He paid me a very great compliment, and though you and I are intended to each other, no one knows of it yet," Mariah replied, gazing up at him

Harrison's ebony hair was shining in the moonlight, and he looked rather fierce still, reminding her of an etching she had seen once at Bramley Hall. He was so handsome. His lips pursed, working back and forth, adding an amusing light to the stoic man.

"The insolent pup!" roared Harrison, which caused a young couple to stop midstride and look at them.

"Shhh, if you please, my lord!" Mariah cautioned.

Harrison began to pace again, and the couple moved on.

"I do rather like the man..." began Mariah, to which Harrison stopped and looked at her, bewildered, with a mixture of anger. Mariah smiled bashfully, "He is really very sweet. Did you know he had thought that at one time he and Alicia would suit? Poor man. It was not meant to be."

"You take his cause to your heart readily enough," Harrison scoffed.

"Is that so?"

"Perhaps I should leave and pay a call directly upon your father," Harrison said, and ran his hands through his ebony hair.

"Only if I may go too, please?"

"I shall endeavor to wait. Could you please at least avoid Major Wallis?" Harrison requested, coming to sit beside Mariah on the bench.

"I cannot see how, my lord..." Mariah said quietly. "We are in the same town and frequent the same events."

Harrison blinked, staring blankly at her. A multitude of emotions crossed his handsome face in a space of mere seconds, yet not one eluded her observant gaze. He knelt down on the cold stone ground. In one fluid motion, his hands delicately came around the side of her face to cup her cheek as his warm lips claimed hers.

How wonderous his lips felt against hers! He was hard and strong in some places, and then in others, like his lips, he was velvet soft. Somewhere deep inside her brain was a very small voice telling her she should stop this at once. Oh, my, but she could not. The euphoria of his kiss had her senses claimed.

Harrison pressed his lips to hers more vigorously, and his arms came around her waist to pull her more tightly against him. Mariah instinctively leaned into his kiss and brought her arms up over his shoulders. Her hands encircled his neck, then sought out his hair and clasped the back of his head. She felt a million tiny little jolts of lightning all over her body.

As quickly as he claimed her lips, he now parted from them. It felt so long to have kissed, yet not long enough. Mariah brought her fingers up to her mouth, and when she caught Harrison's eyes, she knew she blushed furiously. She was hot all over and caught in a daze.

Sighing and mentally shaking herself, Mariah looked up at the stars.

Harrison looked up as well and softly said to her, "They shine for you."

Mariah smiled. "Do they?"

"Indeed. How can they not when such beauty is before them?" Harrison rose and straightened his clothing. His tailcoat was askew, and he ran his fingers through his ebony mane.

He held out his hand for Mariah to rise. When she did, she shook her dress and asked, "How has my hair fared?"

"It's lovely. You should see the moon sparkle on your new comb. It's as if a million tiny moonbeams are nestled upon your tresses. You should always be shown in moonlight; you glow under its radiance." Harrison took her hand and placed it in the crook of his elbow.

"You speak like a poet. 'Tis not a side I have known of you before."

"You have never seen me besotted before, my dear. The moonlight always makes romance more apparent." Harrison led her back into the ballroom, certain that no one had seen him lose his wits.

Upon going back inside, Simon and Alicia immediately came to them, speaking upon how they had had their fill of the night. Gaining their cloaks, and Harrison his topper and walking cane, they stood waiting upon their carriage. Once secured within it, they all departed from the Castle Inn while the festivities were still happening.

From the plush, dark, velvet-seated bench of the carriage, Simon addressed one and all. "Lord, I am done in! How I will ever rise in just a few short hours I do not know. Papa would not forgive me if we kept dear Mariah from the Sunday services. I pray the message is meaningful and quickly approached upon," he finished, ending with a yawn.

Alicia smiled. "I always think I shall never tire once I am dancing, as if I could dance forever! Then when I am in the carriage after the fun, I find myself so terribly exhausted!" Alicia yawned as well.

"I saw Major Wallis after your dance with him, Mariah. I must say, he was in quite an agitated state," Simon told her.

"Oh, la! Do take care, Mariah. You will soon have a constant companion in Major Wallis, and then he will have to fight with your Earl for your honor. Sounds romantic, but I rather like them as they are. Each is without any holes in their person at present," Alicia merrily said.

"Harrison would not fight anyone. He would not have to. Mariah knows where she is best situated. They need only inquire as to where her heart lies, and the victor may claim his spoils," Simon laughed at his own humor.

Mariah smiled embarrassedly but did not comment. At such times, it was best to ignore her brother and his wife lest she fuel their teasing. They were perfect for each other: pleasant, childish, and lacking propriety.

As if sensing her unease, Harrison spoke. "Mariah is no more guilty of luring anyone in than a flower could be. She cannot help anyone taking notice of her. It's a compliment to her that so many admire her."

"A great compliment to you soon, you mean. Confess—you are on the path to the altar!" Simon beamed at them.

"Simon, please!" begged Mariah as she began to rub at her temple.

"When there is an announcement to be made, you will be in our closest circle to hear it," Harrison told his friend.

Upon arriving back, Mariah took the stairs to her room. She tried to make her mind quiet down. She kept reliving the kiss which Harrison had bestowed upon her. It was her very first kiss, and she could not imagine it happening in any other manner or at any other time. True, her body was very tired, but her mind would just not obey her command to sleep. She tossed and turned, soon giving up on the idea of slumbering.

She hummed to herself and thought of the life ahead of her and Harrison. How wondrous to be his wife, to share in all of his happiest moments and to comfort him in his sorrows. She would be an exceptional wife. She wanted to bring him the happiness he so readily gifted her. She wanted nothing more from this new day forward than to be a blessing and a joy to him. She knew that she truly had his heart now, and she meant to forever treasure it.

Chapter Twenty

The Euphoria

Mariah was so awfully tired, but she would not live to tell her papa that she had not attended church while in Brighton. So there she sat, trying desperately to hold in her yawn and pay attention to the sermon. She suddenly felt a wave of homesickness. Thinking about her mama and papa was enough to render a few tears the permission to course down her cheeks. Vainly trying to locate a handkerchief in her reticule, one was passed to her via Harrison, who looked ardently alarmed at her present state. She took the handkerchief and dabbed at her face.

"If you are ill, we may make our way back to the house," Harrison quietly said, his face pained at the distressed sight of her.

Hearing him, Simon hurriedly said, "Yes, please. Let's make haste, and at once!"

Mariah smiled into the handkerchief. Simon looked awful, but his wife had lectured him until she was blue in the face during the carriage ride home in the early hours this morning about his drinking. And, not wanting to admit Alicia was right, Simon did the only thing he could do and went to church.

They sat toward the back of the church. It seemed most of the inhabitants and visitors of Brighton were packed within the holy dwelling. They had entered when the church was cool, though now, it was quite stuffy. It would be a great offense, should they depart early.

Harrison still looked at Mariah with a pained expression, inquiring about the state of her well-being and distress. Turning her head, Mariah gave him a bright smile. She hoped that that one action had allayed his fears.

"Let us be off. I cannot make my mind understand any of the proceedings," Simon whined.

"Do stuff it, young man!" commanded Lord Purcellville in a harsh whisper. "'Tis your punishment for imbibing too much. Now, sit there, and keep quiet."

No one dared to utter another word for the remaining hour that the service lasted. Mariah tried to recall what the parson had been trying to enlighten them on but failed. They were too far back to hear anything, and there was more than one snore issuing forth from the parishioners. How unlike the Sundays that she was used to.

Mariah's mind was occupied with reminiscences of Harrison during the summer when they were children, catching butterflies and having tea parties with all her dolls. He was so attentive to her then, and even now, years later, his kindness had never faltered. Though now, they could imagine having tea parties with their own children.

Once outside, though the day was overcast and gray, Mariah felt immeasurably better. The wind was just beginning to blow when they all climbed into the Purcellvilles' carriage, and Mariah felt the crispness give her newfound awareness. It was a wonder what fresh air could do for one's spirits.

For once, Simon looked too ill to speak, and Alicia said not a word, tired as she was. Lord Purcellville was relaxed and enjoyed the silence, for it was a rare occurrence. Lady Purcellville sat silently beside her husband.

Harrison cast Mariah another worried look with his brow furrowed, and she informed him that she was well, merely suffering from being overtired. She was still trying to assure herself that her engagement to this wondrous man was not a dream. *Turns out that even being in a euphoric state can exhaust one*, she thought. *But I do miss my parents terribly and even the stables of Bramley. I miss taking meals at the parsonage table and conversing about the day's events with Mama and Papa. While Brighton has been filled with new discoveries, I am homesick, and I don't think anything can cure that.*

She sighed, promising herself to send yet another letter when she got back to the Purcellvilles' home. Mariah was content and so full of happiness, she wanted to share her feelings and joy with her parents.

She took her hand from her lap and set it beside Harrison's fist on the bench. He smirked at her, watching her from the corner of his eye. She loved him wholeheartedly. Her Harrison would soon be hers forevermore, and that was something to rejoice in.

Chapter Twenty-One

The Consent

Mariah yawned and stretched. She was feeling much better. Looking toward her window, she noted that the sky looked dark, and she wondered what the time was. She was not quite so used to constant balls and soirees. Brighton was full of amusements that she was not used to taking part in every day, and after experiencing the excitement, she felt she had had her fill.

Amy came through the door with a tray.

"Goodness, what time is it, Amy?" Mariah asked.

"'Tis after nine. Here is a dinner tray for you. I believe the Earl of Bramley has asked after you every half hour since four," the kindly maid smiled at her. "If you like, after you eat, we can make you presentable enough to venture downstairs." Amy placed the tray before her and lifted the lid from the plates.

Mariah nodded her thanks and set about eating her roast beef, Yorkshire pudding, and greens and sipping her wine. She was famished after missing her midday meal.

Shortly after eating and setting herself to rights, Mariah found Harrison in the library with Simon. Alicia and Lord and Lady Purcellville attended a dinner party at some lord's residence or another. Simon and Harrison ceased their prattle once Mariah came into the room. They were both looking at her, and she wondered if she had better take her leave. Before she could back out of the door, Harrison spoke.

"How are you faring now? You've slept for the whole day," Harrison asked, coming toward her and, taking her hand in his, bringing her further into the library. He settled her upon the settee.

"I am much better; I think I was overtired," Mariah replied, glancing at both men.

No one spoke. Simon sat in a chair with his legs stretched out and his ankles crossed. Harrison perched on the padded edge of a chair, not sitting next to Mariah.

"If I am interrupting, I shall be happy to leave," Mariah hesitated.

Harrison shook himself and said, "You need never worry about interrupting. Simon and I have just had a disagreement is all."

"Truly? What about?" Mariah looked at Simon, but he would not meet her eyes.

"It seems that Simon had a caller today. Or rather *you* had a caller," Harrison told her. He smiled with half of his face, which did not at all diminish his handsome features.

"Indeed. Who, pray tell, came to call?" Mariah looked at Simon.

"Can you not guess?" inquired Harrison softly.

"In truth, I cannot." Mariah furrowed her brows and felt the stirring of another headache.

"'Twas Major Wallis," Simon told her.

"Oh. Why?" Mariah was puzzled as to why he would call. She had informed him several times, as well as discussed the matter with those around her, that they would remain friends. This greatly alarmed her.

"He came to see if you would be willing to allow him to court you," Simon said, and took a drink from his glass. He swirled the amber contents around the glittering glass.

"I am sorry—I think I misunderstand you?"

"No, you heard correctly. Seems he is smitten and cannot think of scarce else but you." Harrison looked into her eyes. Mariah hoped the distress in her countenance helped portray the answer he seemed to be seeking.

"Well, I cannot make sense of his coming here. I told him there was an understanding between the Earl and myself that Major Wallis and I were nothing more than friends." Mariah hoped she made sense.

"Seems that until such a time as an announcement is made, all is fair in love and war," Simon said.

"You refused him for me, of course dear brother?" Mariah squinted at him.

"Do not squint; it causes wrinkles, and you will soon look like a nag, and then we will never marry you off. Of course, I said no... but I hated to say it," Simon admitted.

"You do not approve of your friend?" Mariah asked, her voice rising at the incredulity.

"Of course I do. Harrison has always been a part of our family, and it's only proper that we have a connection. I hated to say no only because I looked into Major Wallis' eyes, and I believed him to be sincere." Simon looked pointedly at her.

"Oh, dear. What a muddle. I do wish we were soon traveling home," Mariah sighed.

When no one again spoke, Mariah was still confused. "Why were you disagreeing?"

"We were only plotting the best course of action required," Harrison confessed.

"Need we take any action?" Mariah frowned.

"Do you wish for him to court you?" It was Simon's turn to look incredulous.

"Oh, for heaven's sake, no! But why must we handle him? Did you not say no?" Mariah was puzzled.

"There are some men who do not give up once a *no* has been issued. Major Wallis is one of 'em," Simon acknowledged.

"Well, then, I shall do my best to never be alone while there is the possibility he is within the same space as I," Mariah replied, believing it to be a sensible idea.

"Can you not see the irrational train of thought that is?" Simon bellowed.

Mariah sat pensively. Harrison shook his head. "Take care with your tone, Simon," he directed at him in a low, menacing tone.

"We should take action and announce an engagement," Simon decided, more sedately.

"No!" Both Mariah and Harrison spoke.

"Why ever not?" Simon ran his free hand through his dark hair.

"Papa has not consented. That is all the reason I need." Mariah looked pointedly at her brother.

"Bah!" Simon said into his drink. "Do not think for one moment that Papa would object to you marrying Harrison. Anyone else, perhaps yes. But not Harrison. There is no reason to ask."

"There is little choice, then. I shall leave on the morrow to see your father." Harrison nodded, satisfied in his decision. Then he frowned. "But what of the time I'm to be missing? How will you chaperone her, Simon?"

"Whatever can you mean, old boy?" Simon pressed the bridge of his nose.

"I think his Lordship needs encouragement that you'll stick close by my side in his absence, though I am not sure what good it will do, as you both were present during each encounter I had with Major Wallis. Can I not go home, please?" Mariah looked hopefully up at her brother.

"No," both men stated.

Mariah pouted and looked down at her hands clasped together in her lap. "Why not?"

"I will reach the parsonage much quicker on horseback than by carriage. I can be there and back within the span of two days," Harrison told her.

"I think it the best course of action," Simon agreed.

Mariah looked pointedly at Simon. "Surely, for two days, we can avoid places Major Wallis might frequent."

But now, Mariah gave up. She knew that Simon wished her to stay so Alicia would be made happy, and she could not fault him for wanting to ensure his wife had a companion, though she was frustrated at not being able to return home. She has been promised that should she desire to be returned home, it would come to pass. Though, she understood that leaving now would be more like running away. The gentlemen before her desired that she enjoy Brighton and not be made to leave it prematurely. Mariah was content to do as they wished.

Harrison nodded at Mariah, then rose from his perch and came and sat beside her. "Two days is nothing when compared to a lifetime's happiness." He took her hand in his larger one and rubbed the back of her knuckles. The action made her shiver. It was their first intimate touch since their childhood. They had kissed, yet this touch meant so much more than their past touches. Looking up into his stormy eyes, Mariah could see a deep burning, and she feared it was mirrored in her own.

Clearing his throat, Simon glibly stated, "They say absence makes the heart grow stronger...poor Major Wallis."

Mariah frowned and looked at Simon, but Simon only shrugged his shoulders.

"I shall send a missive to my aunt and uncle!" Simon sat forward. "On the morrow, they shall take over as your chaperones!" He set his empty glass down on the side table and steepled his fingers together.

"Capital idea!" Harrison nodded. "I wonder why we did not think of it before..."

Mariah nodded her head, thinking that now, surely, all would be well. She loved her brother and Alicia, but those two were terrible chaperones. She would not even entrust an animal to their care.

Simon rose and looked at Harrison. "I shall directly write to my uncle. Pray behave yourself, Harrison. I should hate to meet you at dawn with pistols." Though it was a threat, it was given with much good humor. Harrison only smiled at Simon as Simon opened and then closed the door behind his departing form. Mariah sighed.

Turning toward Mariah, Harrison reclaimed her hand and said, "Alone at last, my dear!" to which he waggled his eyebrows at her.

He was trying to dispel the dreary mood hanging over them both. Mariah wrinkled her nose and giggled as she made to put some distance between them.

"Oh, no..." Harrison scolded her. He put his arm around her shoulder and pressed her against his side. "I shall be gone soon, and then you will miss me dreadfully." He clasped his heart and gave her a wounded look.

"You are being overly naughty, my lord! If you do not reform, I shall be forced to seek out Mrs. Higgins," Mariah told him solemnly.

"Now, you leave my old nanny out of it, you little minx!" He brought her hand up to his mouth and proceeded to place a kiss on each perfect finger.

Mariah could feel her pulse racing and hoped he did not notice. "Nanny is just the chaperone I require," Mariah replied, attempting to valiantly keep her face expressionless lest she blush at his actions.

"What a tyrant! Not a chance! You know, I never knew a fiercer woman in the whole of my existence. She could make a saint quake in his boots. Poor Nanny. I have not thought of her in ages." Harrison reached over to place a kiss upon Mariah's forehead.

"Men never think of a woman unless they need her."

"That is not so."

"Is it not? Tell me, then: when is the last time you thought of a woman, the last time a woman flitted through your mind, and it was not prompted by a need?" Mariah smirked up at him.

"Hmm. I am stumped. Very well. I concede because I find myself in need of having you in my home as my wife forevermore."

Mariah laughed at him. He looked at her all astonishment, and then his eyes narrowed. Mariah knew she should flee. But flee she could not. Harrison was so much larger and faster. She squared her shoulders and instead decided to face her fate.

He got ever closer to her. She waited to see what he would do next. He took her hands in his and gently tugged her closer to him. Once they were face-to-face, he brought one hand up to carefully cup her cheek.

He then ran his thumb over her lips, and she kissed it. She meant it as a teasing gesture but felt alarm when his eyes widened. She became absolutely still watching him. She had not meant to be so improper. Her gesture of affection was innocently given. She was mortified, just thinking her playful action was so crass and beneath her, for surely, it must be to cause him such alarm. *What must he be thinking?* she wondered as she waited for him to speak. She only thought to turn his wayward thoughts toward another direction. Another kiss shared between them might lead to somewhere that neither of them would quickly recover from.

Harrison looked at her for a very long time and then sighed. He released her and rose to his full height. He walked to the fireplace and stood before it with his back to her. He clasped his hands behind his back.

Fearing all manner of things but especially fearing being the first to speak, Mariah sat still as a statue. She felt color stain her cheeks, and a little shame plagued her heart. Would he beg off calling upon her father? Had she ruined her chance with him? Utter confusion mired about within her mind. Had she been too forward? Too wayward?

Like a church mouse, she fled. Mariah gained the steps and fled up them in utter mortification. Her mind was warring with her heart, but they were both screaming at her for her improper behavior. What would Papa say?

It was a tiring day, so she rang for her maid. Amy came quickly. Once she was lying in her bed, Mariah bid Amy goodnight.

Stupid, foolish, wanton, willful idiot, Mariah kept chanting in her head. Harrison had been taken aback; he could not even face her! She cried herself to sleep.

Chapter Twenty-Two

The Despair of Love

M ariah's head ached, and her nose was stuffy. How wonderful to feel as if she had a cold. Well, if this was the Lord's punishment for her behavior, she would suffer through it. She thought it would be a miracle if indeed Harrison had set out this morning. Perhaps he had changed his mind...

Amy entered the bedchamber with a breakfast tray and gave her mistress a smile. "Good morning," Amy greeted her, placing the tray upon the bed.

"Good morning, Amy," Mariah returned, and then she noticed the three red roses that sat upon her tray. She looked up at Amy with a questioning frown.

"Perhaps the note would help..." Amy directed, pointing to a neatly penned piece of paper under the roses. "Do you have a preference as to your dress this morning?"

Mariah shook her head as she picked up the roses and brought them to her nose. She was amazed she could detect their fragrance, as stuffy as she was. But, it was there, and she smiled beautifully. She then reached for the letter:

My Dearest Sweetheart,

I shall run with the speed of your affection; it shall guide my steed. Enjoy the roses, as they reminded me of you. I hope to be soon returned to you with the blessing of your parents. Please know you have my heart now and forever; you are holding my whole happiness in your hands. I shall endeavor to deserve you each day of my life.

Yours, and only yours,

Harrison

He had forgiven her! Dear sweet, wonderful, adorable man! He still wished to marry her. Mariah felt tears spill down her cheeks, but they were tears of happiness; she was so very happy. She sniffed, delicately wiping her face clear of waterworks.

Such a wonderful day, she thought. *I shall endear this day to my heart forevermore.*

As Mariah's tears stopped, she gazed around the bedchamber. It was decorated in a lovely manner, and she knew she would miss this space that was all her own, this space that saw her dreams come true. This is where her heart had become full and fixed and where a missing piece, which was Harrison, had aligned itself to her and endeared itself to her heart for eternity.

Mariah was enjoying the day immensely. The sun was shining, and though it was cold out, the lack of wind made it acceptable.

She spent the majority of the day with her aunt and uncle, taking a stroll beside the shops and making small purchases. Mariah bought her mother a lovely shawl, and for her father, she found a nice leather-bound tome for his lectures.

After shopping, Mariah went back to the Purcellvilles' along with her aunt and uncle to drop off her purchased items. The trio reached the house in time for tea. Carter announced their arrival and let them pass into the parlor.

Mariah spied a very beautiful woman who, though she was a few years older than herself, was striking indeed. Mariah was introduced with great excitement by Alicia.

"My dear, this is our cousin, Lady Michaelton. Samantha, this is Mariah, Simon's sister." The ladies curtsied to each other.

After Alicia introduced Mr. and Mrs. Hughley, they all took their seats.

Lady Purcellville was bouncing a baby in her arms and cooing at it. The baby smiled and squealed excitedly.

Lady Michaelton informed Mariah, "That is my newest addition, Matilda. She is three months old and quite has her father wrapped around her little chubby fingers. My son is three years old and is napping at our house with his nanny." She reached a hand up to push a piece of her golden hair back into place at the base of her neck.

"How precious. Has Lord Michaelton come to Brighton with you?" Mariah inquired.

"Oh yes, indeed. He had an elderly uncle here, so once we reached our house, he departed for the gentleman's residence at once," Lady Michaelton explained, and gave Mariah a cool look which made Mariah withdraw her questions. Lady Michaelton's hazel eyes were focused intently upon Mariah.

The conversation flowed along as tea was drunk and cakes were consumed. Mariah watched Lady Michaelton with quiet reserve. She could see something not quite right in the lady's manners. She was not crude, but sometimes, her statements bordered on the uncivil side. Perhaps she was of French descent. That could very well explain her curt behavior. Her complexion was a bit darker and gave her a regal, exotic look.

Alicia came to Mariah, sitting down with a sigh. "The Michael-tons are to dine with us this evening," she stated, her eyes widening a touch.

Mariah felt her blood heat with embarrassment. Of course she would dress up for dinner. Why ever would she not with someone as beautiful and regal as Samantha? Mariah rose and excused herself, stating she was going to pen a letter to her mother and ready herself for the later engagements.

After penning her mother a two-and-a-half-page letter about all that had transpired, Mariah made sure she looked exquisite for dinner that evening. She had felt rather dull next to Lady Michaelton whose extravagant attire and jewels were a clear indication of her station within society. Mariah chose her favorite blue dress and bade Amy to take extra time arranging her hair. Amy threaded a blue ribbon through her curls—the new ribbon Harrison had purchased for her. For added elegance, the comb he had given her was set onto the right side of the crown of her head.

Mariah felt beautiful as she met the others in the parlor. The ladies were all chattering while they waited for Lord Purcellville and Lord Michaelton to finish their port and join them. Everyone chatted about relations near and far. Mariah listened intently, trying to get a feel for those around her.

Lady Michaelton rose, approached Mariah, and said, "I wonder if you would take a turn about the room with me?"

Nodding her head and feeling uneasy, Mariah rose and linked arms with the lady. She waited for Lady Michaelton to speak.

It was not long before, in a hushed tone, the lady began, "I am sure you have seen my husband's desertion toward me. It almost broke me some years ago. I have striven to rise above his disdain." She paused and looked at Mariah.

"I have noticed a distance..." Mariah hesitated.

"Indeed. Who could not notice? You see, I acted rashly some years ago, and I lost the best man I have ever known. I fear he loathes me now too." Lady Michaelton brushed at a tear that threatened to course down her delicate cheek. She looked around the room to learn if they were being observed. Alicia was on the pianoforte, and it seemed the other ladies gave her their attention.

"Oh, dear, Lady Michaelton," Mariah was interrupted.

"Oh, but you must address me as Samantha, for we are as good as cousins, are we not?" Lady Michaelton replied, giving her a dazzling smile.

"Of course, Samantha, and you must call me Mariah," Mariah stated, smiling back.

There was something Mariah distrusted about this whole business, though. Why should a married lady single Mariah out in order to express her marital woes? Perhaps Lady Michaelton feared darkening Alicia's mood? Something in Mariah's gut churned on a sour note, hinting to her of something that contained malevolence. Never had she encountered such a feeling before. She became certain to take into consideration her ill feelings and to proceed with caution in her manner and choice of words.

"You are such a dear, sweet thing! You remind me so very much of myself. Tell me: do you have a favorite beau? You must have many, for you are quite the beauty!" Samantha stated, shooting her a sly look, which made her hazel eyes look very dark.

"I must confess, there is a gentleman. He is all that is good and kind, and we have known each other the whole of my life," Mariah confessed carefully. She did not wish to divulge much to this woman. She withheld the prickles of her skin and the shiver that attempted to course up her arms.

"You must do all you can to secure his affection, then." Lady Michaelton nodded.

"He is traveling to ask for my hand this very minute."

"Oh, what wonderful, happy news!" Samantha smiled and squeezed her arm.

"I thank you."

"To be sure, though, my husband does not care for me, I can express my good wishes to all you young ladies upon hearing of your love matches. For he has declared his love, has he not?" Samantha inquired, looking pointedly at her.

Mariah thought. Well, what had he said? That he adored her...

Well, that was the same as love. Was it not? He had not ever said the actual word, but his eyes conveyed his feelings, so she felt that he loved her...

Warring with herself, Mariah nodded at her companion.

"Very good news; you should always have the sentiment expressed. My favorite beau, indeed the one I let slip away, told me at almost every meeting of his burning love for me..." Samantha sniffed.

"I am so sorry you are so affected," Mariah frowned.

"As am I, for you see, there was a time, brief as it was, that I thought William hung the moon and the stars just for me. I still bear him some affection, for I have borne his children. But he does not pay me addresses any longer; he ignores me largely." Samantha stopped and turned their course as she had been doing the entirety of their walk.

Mariah shook her head. She felt out of her element and did not know which words would soothe the lady.

"I should stop my whining. I must be stealing your joy. I caution that love is a very fickle thing! Do take care of your heart."

With that being said, the door burst open and the gentlemen came through.

Separating herself and Mariah, Samantha walked the length of the room and sat beside Lady Purcellville. Mariah sat in a chair by the fire, and seeing her thus situated, Lord Michaelton took the chair opposite her after he caught her gaze. Alicia was still at the instrument, playing beautifully while Mariah watched the emotions of the room turn.

Watching her to a degree that made Mariah squirm in her chair, Lord Michaelton leaned forward to be sure his words were for her only. "You must take care with what opinions my dear wife leads you to form. She can be quite adept at turning a story to fit herself as the heroine."

"Indeed?" Mariah met his gaze.

He nodded and continued, "Pity her not, Miss Morten. She has made a mess of her happy domain, and try as I might to have pleased her, it would seem I have failed. Domestic felicity between spouses is a chance one takes. I always thought it would be enough to seek a beautiful wife and that my happiness would runneth over. I was wrong. Pray do not make the same mistake. Love is a fickle thing." He straightened and said no more.

Mariah angled her head and looked away. *Oh, dear, what a conundrum of a couple.*

Chapter Twenty-Three

Blessings Bestowed

It was very dark when Harrison reached Bramley Hall. The stars were hidden by gray clouds. There was hardly a moon to light his path. He dismounted and handed the reins to his stable boy. It was much too late to pay a call on the Mortens, so he would instead attend to the matters of his estate.

Muddy and odorous, Harrison ordered a bath first, and once he was under the warm water, he began to relax. His muscles were tight from his constant seat upon Brutus. He had stopped only to let his horse rest here and there and had found an inn in which he had taken his midday meal. Harrison knew his horse was the finest specimen to be found, so he did not fear exhausting him. Harrison was of the mind to board Brutus at once if he found him lagging, and then the beast was indeed happy to perform. Harrison would give him rest tomorrow, however, and take another horse with him when he set out again for Brighton.

Harrison sighed, throwing his arms over the edge of the tub and leaning his head back. His thoughts moved to Mariah and how he heated so when she kissed his thumb. She meant to be affectionate, but it sent his blood boiling with how tender and sweet it was. Knowing her for so long, he knew she was embarrassed. Later, when she became his wife, he would be sure to tell her and show her just how much he liked it. He thought about her sudden disappearance after that enticing action and wondered how lost in his own thoughts he must have been to not hear her exiting the room. It wasn't until Simon had returned that he was able to focus upon his surroundings.

He glanced outside, seeing the moon hanging high. Harrison wondered what his lady was doing at this very moment. Did she miss him? He longed for her greatly. It gave him joy to know that soon she would be established within his home, and he would never need to miss her again. Well, almost never.

His valet had made the long journey with him, and since they were both tired, Harrison told him to attend to himself once they had arrived home. Edmund was just as dirty as he was, so there was no sense in his attending to him.

John, a footman, poured the hot water over his head instead and held up the towel for him. Once he had wrapped the towel about himself, Harrison dismissed John. He walked toward the fireplace where the heat was flowing from the glowing fire. The firelight cast shadows upon the ceiling and walls. Harrison dried his ebony locks and proceeded to dry his body.

Harrison pulled out a shirt and a pair of trousers. He needed to dress slightly in order to go about his house. He was not given to rambling about his estate in his dressing gown. He would, however, dismiss donning his cravat, which was a general nuisance to tie anyway and, without the assistance of Edmund, nearly an impossible task which wasted his patience. He didn't bother with stockings or shoes. Instead, he reached for his slippers and encased his feet in them.

Once he was dressed and had let his hair dry a bit more, Harrison treaded down the stairs and into his study. He went to his desk and retrieved a key. Once he was at his mahogany side wall, he reached behind a portrait of Bramley Hall that had been painted by his grandmother and felt for a switch. He flipped it, and the painting beside his grandmother's swung away from the wall and turned on its side. Harrison now used the key to unlock the door that appeared. Inside the small room, he felt for the solid wooden box and retrieved it. He used the special combination on the lockbox and opened it. It contained many precious jewels, family heirlooms, and a token from the King himself. Harrison remembered his mother had worn a few of them. He could not wait to see them gracing Mariah. He took necklaces, bracelets, and other items out as well and looked for the blue velvet pouch that contained the one particular treasure he sought.

Harrison finally came across the pouch and checked inside to be sure it was the jewel he intended to gift to his beloved. Soon satisfied, he returned the other pieces to their resting places and replaced the box in its hiding space. Harrison relocked the secret door and straightened the picture that belonged over it. It was amazing that not much had changed about Bramley Hall since his grandmother's time. A few of the trees had grown taller, and the flowers in the flower beds had changed in color, but hardly any other changes were noticeable nonetheless.

Harrison now sat at his hulking mahogany desk to attend to his letters of business before he would become completely exhausted. His footman, John, opened the door to allow a footman to proceed to the desk with a tray of foodstuff. Harrison thanked the man and hungrily ate.

Checking the clock against the wall and the predawn of the sky, Harrison sighed and set his quill down. He hadn't meant to take so long. But since this business was now concluded, he could get started on the other business which had brought him back to Bramley Hall.

Wiping his hands free of ink, Harrison smiled at himself, thinking about what Mr. Morten might say. He was giddy, eager to head on over there, and he would go right now; a botheration, however, was that his house shoes were still on, and he was missing his other clothing which would make him presentable. Harrison strode out of his study and up the steps to his bedchamber, calling for John as he went. He dared not wake Edmund to tend him. His friend and valet needed the much-deserved rest.

Properly dressed, and forsaking his annoying cravat altogether, Harrison practically raced out of the Hall and to the stables. He ordered the stable master, Toby, to ready his other mount, Percy, while he checked on Brutus. All the while, it seemed as if his pocket watch was ticking by slowly, and the sun rose higher in the sky. Harrison could hardly contain himself from just running to the parson's home himself.

"My lord, your mount, sir," Toby said with a bow.

Harrison thanked him, mounting deftly and speeding off toward his intended's home. Everything sped by in a blur, and before he knew it, he was waiting on the front steps of the parsonage home after having knocked.

"Well, my dear boy! What a surprise this is! Come in, come in. Where is my daughter? Not with you, I see?" Mr. Morten blew his rather large nose into his handkerchief. Mr. Morten stepped aside so Harrison could enter, then closed the door after him.

"Come, come," Winston Morten said with a smile. "To the study, where we will be ignored," he chortled.

"Mariah is not with me. She was happily ensconced in Brighton when I left it," Harrison explained, removing his topper.

"Good, good. Has she missed her home much?" Mr. Morten sneezed.

"Very much," Harrison offered.

"Well, good. She is much better off there than here, however, I am certain, for we all have colds. Mrs. Morten has taken to her bed, and our maid is quite busy attending to her." Mr. Morten opened his study door and let Harrison follow him into the room.

"Oh, dear. I am sorry for the illness. I'll make my business here brief, then, so you can rest." Harrison sat.

Mr. Morten held up a finger and mightily sneezed again. He was in his chair behind his desk. "No, no. You, my dear boy, are always welcome in our home. We received Mariah's letter but have been remiss in answering it. Let me see...here is the one Mrs. Morten has started. Well, you might as well carry it back with you. You are returning to Brighton?"

"This very day, I shall depart as soon as I leave here," Harrison assured him.

"Well, let us have it, then. What could have brought you here?" Mr. Morten gazed at him through his spectacles.

"I came only to ask for your daughter's hand in marriage," Harrison explained, growing suddenly nervous. He sat forward in his chair, then sat back into it again.

"Have you any notion that Mariah means to accept?" Mr. Morten blew his nose.

"I have every reason to believe it. In truth, I have asked her, and she has said yes. I am uneasy that I did not address you first, but events were unfolding so quickly." Harrison brought his leg up and placed his booted ankle over his other knee. Then he undid them and sat straight.

"Hmm. Could you not wait until your return to inquire?" Mr. Morten coughed.

"Mariah," Harrison began, "or Miss Morten, has many admirers, and one that is rather persistent. Simon and I thought it would be prudent that I come here and settle matters."

"I see. Well, you know we are all in love with you, and so I welcome you into our family in a more permanent manner. I cannot wait to relate these events to Mrs. Morten. Happy shall we be to see you and our daughter meet at the altar. This is very wonderful news, my boy! You have my blessing a thousandfold. Were it anyone else asking, I would take more care," Mr. Morten chortled, rising and coming from behind his desk to clap Harrison upon the back.

"I thank you, sir. I promise she will be happy and well cared for, and everything I do will be to increase her happiness," Harrison assured. He stood and looked at the man who was most like a father to him. He had not thought the man would answer negatively, but sitting in his study brought about a severe case of nerves.

"Yes, yes, see to it, my boy." Mr. Morten sneezed.

"I will take my leave, then. I traveled swiftly yesterday but wish to be swifter today and reach Brighton before she retires." Harrison smiled.

"Yes, take flight at once! Give my daughter all my love." Mr. Morten ushered him out of the study after handing over his wife's letter.

"We shall see you soon. I do not think Miss Morten will seek to stay the whole month. I shall have the banns read once we return home but feel safe to say that the gossip will travel long before the first reading."

Harrison put his topper back upon his head as the men reached the front door.

"Very good. We shall be on the lookout, then. Godspeed, my son." Mr. Morten once again sneezed. "Pray you will not catch this horrible cold. It's dreadful business."

Nodding to him, Harrison turned and walked to Percy. Edmund had arrived, waiting outside with both of their horses, and they each mounted, ready to begin the arduous task of returning to Brighton.

Chapter Twenty-Four

Wishes for Happiness

Mariah was seated between her aunt and uncle at another soiree. She was very anxious for Harrison's return, but her aunt assured her that the quickest way to pass the time was to keep busy.

The grandfather clock in the room tolled four in the early evening. Much to Mariah's great relief, it was time to depart. Now, at the conclusion of this little party, Mariah was standing off to the side of her aunt and uncle when she felt someone stop next to her. She turned to find Major Wallis smiling most animatedly at her.

Raising her eyebrows, Mariah looked about herself. Her relations were deeply engrossed in conversations with others away from her. There was nothing for it; she had to address him.

Bowing before her, the Major began, "You look marvelous this evening." His gaze swept down and then up her person again, coming to rest upon her eyes.

Smiling timidly, Mariah returned his bow and said, "I thank you, but you are too excessive in your praise."

"Indeed not! Upon my honor, 'tis the truth. And where is your champion this evening?" he asked her from very close to her ear.

"He had other business to attend to. I believe he shall soon be returning, perhaps later this evening." Mariah addressed him as coolly as she knew how to, which wasn't much at all.

Drawing his eyebrows together, Major Wallis said, "I wonder at his ability to leave you."

"You are much too harsh upon him," Mariah stated.

"I think not. Has your brother spoken to you?" His warm eyes studied hers.

"We converse every day, Major Wallis."

Mariah was trying desperately to be vague and to appear disinterested by glancing about the room. Her eyes couldn't help but remain fixed on her aunt in hopes that the woman would look for her and realize her distress.

"Yes, but that is not what I meant," the Major sighed.

"Pray, what did you mean?" Mariah asked, not meeting his eyes. She tried her best to give him no inkling that she was going to speak with him. Surely, he knew she was not interested. She had made it all perfectly clear many times before.

How can a man be so persistent? she groused. He got in front of her to gain her full attention, and she was forced to look at him.

"I meant, I spoke to your brother, asking if I might court you."

"Oh. Major Wallis, it is not proper to announce it, but the Earl of Bramley's errand took him to my papa. He seeks my hand in marriage, truly, and I have no reason to believe he will receive anything less than a positive and most welcomed response. I am sorry to wound you, if indeed that is the case, but so it is." Mariah frowned.

"I see..." the Major said as the muscles in his jaw worked.

"I am sorry. I had made my intentions known regarding our friendship only."

"Indeed, you had. May I inquire if the Earl has laid out the full force of his feelings to you? In short, has he declared his love for you? Has he said the word love?" the Major demanded, being very adamant in his words.

Mariah frowned and looked at the floor. *That question again*, she huffed. She looked back up to meet the Major's brown eyes and said, "No, he has not used the word love, but rest assured, he shows me his devotion in other ways. Is it not customary for gentlemen to stay mum upon the word? Is it not fashionable to only say such a sentiment to one's wife?"

"If that is the fashion for how titled gentlemen should conduct themselves, then they are all fools," the Major said forcefully.

"That may be so. People marry for all sorts of reasons, do they not? For money, connections, appearances. I would rather have a spouse I can depend upon that I truly admire and esteem. I feel secure in his affections. It is enough for me," Mariah stated firmly, hoping her words brokered no room for further argument, though she felt there were still words to be had.

Her head pinched, and she felt another stirring of a headache. She also felt a blush creeping up her cheeks. This was not a proper subject to be discussing, and she wished the discussion were not taking place, especially in such a public place where anyone might listen in.

"Were I in his place, the first thing I should do is tell you I love you, immeasurably, wholeheartedly. I would never leave you in doubt of my sincerest affection or devotion. I would say the words!" Major Wallis boldly announced. His handsome features became animated in his speech.

Mariah felt trapped; she did like him, but he was pressing her so. "Major Wallis!" Mariah took a breath, and it was almost a sob, her anxiety was rising so much.

"It is not my wish to upset you, Miss Morten. That is not my intention." The Major gently touched her shoulder.

"Pray, what is your intention?" Harrison practically growled his words, coming to stand at Mariah's side, his voice low and lethal.

Mariah looked up at Harrison and let out a huge breath, her nerves on end. She was in very real danger of becoming over-wrought. She had never felt more relieved about his sudden appearances. She put a hand to her chest and willed her heart to stop its erratic beating.

"To let the lady decide her future knowing all of the facts. I wish her to understand my very sincere feelings and wishes for her happiness," Major Wallis declared, standing his ground.

"Well, you may make free with your good wishes and congratulations, as we are engaged with her father's full blessing now," Harrison stated, reaching for Mariah's hand and bringing her gloved digits to his mouth for a kiss, staring into her eyes.

Mariah's emotions were all over the place. She felt tears gathering in her gaze. She glanced at Harrison, smiling broadly. A tear full of happiness tracked down her cheek.

"Oh, I see," the Major said, swallowing, his face falling to sadness. "I wish you the very best, Miss Morten, and I am forever your servant."

He bowed at her, and she was sure that it was despair that was simmering within his expressive chocolate-colored eyes. Without another word, he turned around and left them.

Harrison offered his arm to Mariah, and she took it gratefully, smiling up at him with both much sadness and great joy. She did not like that her immeasurable happiness had caused another person anguish. Her heart felt adrift at the thought of causing true pain.

"I believe it would be the proper time to make our way back to the house," Harrison softly said close to her ear.

He was a coil of pent-up rage. He had done his best not to knock the bloke's head off of his shoulders. The sight that greeted him when he had first found Mariah made his blood boil. There she was, practically trapped up against the wall by that insolent pup, and Harrison had seen by her face that she was close to tears. Harrison was all set to call Major Wallis out with swords and seconds at dawn. He thought better of it, though, as he could not very well stay by her side if he were incarcerated in Newgate. Oh, how he wanted to draw blood. At the very least, the cad deserved a blackened eye or two.

Harrison guided Mariah through the crowd and, catching the eye of Mr. Hughley, inclined his head toward the door. Mr. Hughley nodded his understanding and called a halt to his own conversation In order to locate his wife, who stood not too distantly from himself.

It was not long until both couples sat in the carriage. It was a quiet ride back to the house. Harrison kept catching Mr. Hughley looking between himself and Mariah. Harrison seethed. He couldn't help it. He wanted to wallop the man who had made his beloved shed tears. It was apparent to all that dear Mariah was endeavoring not to shed more tears that were sparkling in her blue eyes.

Harrison sighed as the carriage came to a halt and they descended. He took Mariah's hand in his, squeezing it affectionately. By Jove, how he wanted to do more! To take her in his arms and kiss her tears, her fears, and all maladies away.

He led her into the foyer where Carter took their cloaks and outerwear as they repaired to the parlor. Lord and Lady Purcellville were in attendance upon the Pavilion while Simon and his wife were dining out with the other officers and their wives at one of the hotels.

Mariah went straight to the settee and threw herself down, to which she bounced back up. She looked into the fire and said nothing. Harrison placed himself next to her on the settee, and her aunt and uncle took to the chairs by the fire.

No one spoke for a quarter of an hour until Mrs. Hughley spoke, "Dearest, will you not disclose the source of your anguish? Can I not tempt you with anything? Offer any solace?"

Shaking her head, Mariah continued to look into the fire.

Gaining his feet, Mr. Hughley spoke. "I believe the hour is late. Come, my dear. Let us leave this couple to themselves."

Mrs. Hughley allowed her husband to help her rise but looked conflicted. Afterall, it was her duty to chaperone.

Seeing her difficulty, Harrison spoke. "I can assure you: nothing untoward shall occur. I only wish to see Mariah in better spirits."

"We shall see you both on the morrow, then. Feel better, dearest," Mrs. Hughley said as she let her husband lead her from the room.

"I have a letter for you from home." Harrison produced the cream stationery. He held it out to Mariah.

Mariah looked from the fire to his hand and sadly smiled. "I thank you. I wondered why I had not received one yet. Was all well?" Mariah looked up at him. She had conquered the tears within her brilliant eyes.

With much relief, Harrison smiled. His Mariah was far from unaffected, but she was finally giving her attention to him. He touched her soft, creamy cheek, allowing his hand to linger. Mariah closed her eyes as his hand stroked her skin, and by the Lord above, Harrison couldn't wait to call her his permanently.

"All was not well, as your parents have colds. Your mother was abed, though I did speak to your father. He heard my knock and answered the door."

"Oh, dear. Perhaps I should leave to nurse my poor mama." Mariah furrowed her brows.

"If you wish it, we shall leave."

"I do not wish to disappoint Simon either. I shall write on the morrow and insist that if they should become worse, they shall send for me directly." Mariah nodded resolutely.

"Excellent. You look better." Harrison smiled softly at her.

"I feel better now that you are present once again. I had no idea we would find Major Wallis at the soiree. Rather, he should have been at the regimental gathering that Simon and Alicia attended. I give you my word that I did not seek him out," Mariah earnestly spoke.

"I have no fear upon that, my dear." Harrison looked seriously at her. "I have a token that I now wish to present to you." He slid from his seat beside her and knelt down in front of her. He produced the blue velvet pouch from his pocket and opened it.

Mariah's mouth made a silent oval shape as Harrison withdrew a blue sapphire on a golden base.

"You may remember this resting upon my mother's hand? 'Twas the same ring my father presented to her, and it has gone through many generations. It is now yours and shall be passed down one day to our son." He took her smaller gloved hand in his own and placed the ring on her left hand upon the fourth finger.

Mariah sucked in a breath. "It is lovely, and I do remember it upon your mama's hand. I used to love watching it shimmer in the light. I can hardly credit it as belonging to me now."

"It looks perfect upon your hand. Like it was created just for you. I cannot wait to begin our life together," Harrison said, kissing her hand.

"Begin it? We have lived our lives together from my first breaths, have we not?" Mariah laughed.

"Indeed. We certainly have. I cannot wait to grow old and see how our family grows. I mean to have a house filled with the sounds of our children. I always dreaded Bramley Hall when no one was there—no happy laughter, no shouting. I mean to have it be boisterous and brimming with life once again." Harrison smiled at her.

"Sounds like a dream," Mariah sighed.

"I promise to make you happy. I shall do all in my power to see you happy. I will never cease in my adoration of you."

"Adoration?"

"Yes, I adore you."

Her light brown brows furrowed. "But do you not feel more than only adoration for me?"

"Yes, I do feel more, and I am sorry if I have not expressed it before. There was a time when I overused the words and they became hollow and worthless to the hearer. I am grateful for all that has passed on before, however, for if things had gone in any other direction, we would not be here together now. I am so utterly in love with you and only you, dearest Mariah." Harrison rose from before her and sat down next to her.

And she wept right there in front of him, mumbling how much she loved him in return. For his part, Harrison was content to offer her his handkerchief and his chest as she gave way to her emotion. He knew a lot had taken place in the span of one evening. He felt safe in the knowledge that these were happy tears she was shedding. He meant to produce many more of the same good tears from her for the rest of his life.

Chapter Twenty-Five

The Inconvenience of Snoring

Mariah knew that before she could be truly happy, she needed to sit down the next morning with a quill and paper. She wrote, beseeching her parents to send for her, should they worsen. She told them of all of the things she had been engaging in, and she told them of the great love she bore for Harrison. After she had finished, she handed her letter over to the footman, feeling carefree and very happy.

Mariah found Harrison in the study with Lord Purcellville. She was bidden to enter as Lord Purcellville came toward her.

"I understand congratulations are in order, my dear!" Lord Purcellville boomed at her. He took her much smaller hands in his and shook them both.

With absolute radiance, Mariah answered him, "I thank you!"

Letting her hands go, Lord Purcellville made his way to seat himself back into his chair behind the desk. Harrison came toward Mariah and promptly winked at her while seating her into the chair beside his. Then he took his seat.

"I think it shall not be long until we are seeing your marriage take place." Lord Purcellville nodded and smiled at them both.

"I hope we can say our vows before December reaches us," Harrison spoke.

"Yes, yes. All would be very well if they were seen to by then!" Lord Purcellville waved his hand. "Bramley tells me that your parents are ill, Miss Morten. 'Tis better to stay with us, for catching a cold so soon before your nuptials would not be the thing at all."

"I have written to Mama and Papa with my sincere wishes that, should they need me, they are to write immediately. I could not be made easy if they were in need of me and I were not there to attend to them," Mariah spoke clearly.

"You are to have no fear; I have also written to my household, and should any there hear of the illness not ceasing within a few days, Billingsley is to let me know." Harrison gave her a sincere smile.

Mariah looked into his eyes and nodded. Hearing familiar voices in the hallway, Mariah rose as did the gentlemen. Mariah smiled at Lord Purcellville, and he nodded his assent to let her leave the study.

"My dear, you do look much recovered today!" Mrs. Hughley wrapped her niece in a hug.

"I am well." Mariah smiled, stepping away from her aunt. She looked at her uncle and smiled at him. Harrison was beside her, and she took his arm as the four of them retired to the drawing room.

Mariah was seated beside Harrison on the settee. She reached up to make sure her comb, the gift from her beloved, was situated where it had been before. Amy had secured it perfectly.

Arising from her seat, Mrs. Hughley gasped as she grabbed Mariah's hand and seated herself on Mariah's other side. She brought Mariah's hand up to her face. Mariah's eyes grew large at her aunt's behavior.

"What is this jewel upon your finger? Can this be the errand that both carried away and brought back his Lordship to you?"

Mrs. Hughley brought her eyes away from the sapphire and looked into Mariah's eyes.

Blushing slightly but meeting her aunt's eyes, Mariah nodded as she bit her bottom lip. "Indeed. Is it not lovely?"

"It's stunning! But then—this means you are engaged?" Mrs. Hughley looked from Mariah to Harrison.

Harrison answered, "Yes, you do not mistake the matter. We are to wed. I am the happiest of men and so richly blessed by my future wife." Harrison took her hand and brought it to his mouth with a kiss. The look they exchanged couldn't leave Mr. and Mrs. Hughley in doubt of their affections.

"Well, love is lovely, is it not?" Mr. Hughley said with a small chuckle.

The plans were arranged for the party to attend a luncheon at Mrs. Liftgrove's, with Alicia joining them. They arrived when they had been expected to, and all celebrated the wonderful news of the engagement. Mrs. Liftgrove was all politeness in manner and dress. She made each feel completely at ease, and the food was divine.

With full stomachs, the party sat in companionable merriment in Mrs. Liftgrove's parlor.

"La, if only our cook could do that with our fish courses, I'd never tire of it!" exclaimed Alicia.

"I thank you, dear, for the compliment!" Mrs. Liftgrove beamed at her.

"Such a day this has been!" Alicia bounced upon her chair. "I can think of no other joy than that of a couple about to be wed. Nothing gives the families more entertainment than watching the couple watch each other."

Mariah felt her cheeks grow pink, and she looked down at the ring upon her finger. She turned it from side to side, observing it glitter in the fire's bright glow.

"To be sure, it is amusing," mused Mrs. Hughley. "I remember when Mr. Hughley and I were not yet wed and the excitement that I felt whenever he came to call. Papa would fire all manners of questions upon him, and it made me feel sure that he would break off the whole thing and I would never see him again."

Chuckling, Mr. Hughley looked at his wife. "As if he could have kept me away! I was intimidated as to his intentions, but nothing and no one could keep me away from your door. I shook in my boots at his stern looks but stood my ground, I did."

"Well, after all these years, do you regret not breaking our engagement?" Mrs. Hughley looked at her husband and fluttered her lashes.

"Not once!" Mr. Hughley sat forward in his chair and frowned. "Do you regret my pressing on?"

"I must confess...that there was a time I was most unhappy with my choice. But thankfully, that has passed and all is, and has been, well ever since." Mrs. Hughley looked down upon her hands that were folded in her lap. There was a hint of a secret smile about her lips, but with her head bent, her husband missed it.

"Upon my word, woman! Whatever can the meaning of this be? When did you regret me?" Mr. Hughley was turning purple in his face.

"Now, now, my dear, do calm yourself! You will suffer an apoplexy," Mrs. Hughley said once she had looked up again at her husband.

Mariah looked around herself at each person. Alicia was staring at the scene with her mouth drawn into a perfect O. Mrs. Liftgrove was looking out the window in an attempt to not observe what was being said. Harrison was sitting perfectly still in his chair, with a frown upon his handsome features that gave the whole of this attention to what was taking place.

"Well, keep me in suspense no longer, madam!" Mr. Hughley demanded.

"It was on our wedding night, actually, if you must know," Mrs. Hughley said to the whole room.

Mr. Hughley looked at his wife as if his wits had gone begging. Mariah felt her own eyes grow large while she heard Alicia give a giggle. Mrs. Liftgrove was still staring out her window. Harrison moved in his chair and coughed.

Mrs. Hughley elaborated, "It was after such a long day, you see. So many wonderful memories had been made. You were holding me, and then you fell asleep. Then the most dreadful noise I have ever heard made me jump up! I looked around the room, waiting for elephants or whatever the source of the impending stampede was, and I found the noise came from beside me in the bed. From you, to be specific. I almost fainted dead away. There you were, looking so boyish and still, yet you were creating such awful noises as would wake the dead!" Mrs. Hughley told him solemnly.

"Well..." Mr. Hughley was so astounded, he sat blinking at his wife.

"There, there, my dear. That was the only time I sought to leave your side forever. The second night of our marriage was no better, but one sleepless night had quite tired me out. So I found that if I was very tired, I could block out your noises easily enough, and do you know that when we are separated, I cannot fall asleep?" Mrs. Hughley shook her head.

"Indeed." Mr. Hughley took his hand and rubbed his face.

"Simon snores too, and it's quite rude of you men to force us women to endure you. La, Mariah, what joy you will soon have to face." Alicia laughed.

"Well, it must be true love for you dear creatures to remain by our sides," Mr. Hughley gathered his mind together.

"For my part, I must own that my dear husband never snores. He never has, but if he did, I feel sure I could bear my part as you ladies have. After all, that's what separate chambers are for," Mrs. Liftgrove stated, looking away from the window.

Mariah had never considered separate bedchambers before. Her mama and papa shared a room, as did Simon and Alicia. But she'd played hide-and-seek within Bramley Hall before, and so she knew that there were separate bedchambers for the lord and lady of the house. She wondered how she'd feel, all alone in such a great space.

"Let us take a walk outside in the garden before the weather turns and keeps us inside," Alicia requested.

"Splendid idea," Mr. Hughley agreed.

Donning their outerwear, the party went outside into the massive garden that led to a path that wound its way down to the beach. Alicia had her arm looped in with her friend's, as did each respective pair. Mariah and Harrison remained at the back of the party, walking slowly behind everyone else.

"You are enchanting. Do you know how much I love you?" Harrison cooed into her ear. The wind was whipping about, and she had to strain to catch his words before the wind carried them away.

Before them, Alicia and Mrs. Liftgrove braved the wind with their arms entwined together.

"How much, my lord?" Mariah inquired with joy upon her lips. Harrison's side was pressed against hers, and she matched her movements to his. They took step after step as one.

"There are a million words that could be used, though they fly out of my head in your presence. I forget myself entirely, as I only live for you. Know this, nothing shall keep me from your side. I shall brave wind, rain—oceans, even—to be always at your side. You are my future, and where you are is my home. I shall always make you smile, and sadness will not be a part of our lives from this moment on." Harrison looked at Mariah earnestly.

Mariah smiled at him, and her heart felt full. Oh, dear, she very much hoped she would not turn to blubbering as she had last night. Would she always sob at his declarations? That simply would not do.

"I am so happy. I did not know such happiness was in the world. I never dreamed I would feel such happiness with you. I hoped for it and have dreamed of it for such a long time. I thought it was all some childish thing that would never come to be. Do confess, though: as blissful as we are now, there was a time where you only thought of me as a child." Her wide sapphire eyes looked up at him.

"Hmm, perhaps so. But come to think of it, you were always dear to me. I cannot remember a time in your presence where I did not seek to entertain you or simply see you smile. I have always been fond of you," Harrison trailed off.

"Yes, but something had to have changed. When and how did that change come about?" Mariah was pressing him, but her curiosity could not be silenced.

"I cannot exactly pin the moment down. I only know that there was one moment which led to another and another. Then all the moments that came after were filled with my longing to make you mine. I hoped before that I had reasonable hope and that you could come to care for me more than you would a mere brother. We grew up together yet were not related. I watched you to see if there would be a chance between us, no matter how small it might be, so that I could ascertain your feelings. It was not until we reached Brighton that my self-doubt fled, and I felt certain I could court you. But what of you? When did you begin to care for me?" Harrison waited for her answer as they walked along the coast. The waves were splashing against the shore.

"I am embarrassed to admit it, but I cannot recall a time when I did not hope you would someday be mine. I suppose it is due to women being of a more romantic nature? I knew I loved you for certain when I was but two and ten. I knew that I would die of despair at five and ten when you did not seem to like me overly much. So long have I sought your notice that I grew used to the idea that you would marry another and I would never be made content. I am happy the years have shaped us together and apart, for now, I stand by your side and declare to the world that you are mine at last."

Mariah was surprised at the honest truth of her words. True, she had had plenty of time to dwell upon her feelings through the years, but she found she was neither ashamed nor embarrassed, after all, to admit the truth to him.

"We have waited a lifetime to come together. It would seem we are now brought together by God's perfect timing and I am content at long last." Harrison gave a heavy sigh.

Mariah matched his sigh, and though they may have looked like besotted fools, she couldn't care less. All was exactly as she could ever wish it to be.

Chapter Twenty-Six

Cruel Intentions

Mariah wore a lavender gown with tiny cream flowers upon it that suited her alabaster skin perfectly. She gave herself one last look in the full-length mirror, certain that there was nothing more to be attended to. She had not seen Harrison since their return from Mrs. Liftgrove's. She patted her curls that were piled atop her head and that still wore the comb he had given her, as she could not bear to part with it.

Mariah made her way to the drawing room, and Carter, the ever-attendant butler, opened the door for her. She nodded at him and moved into the room. Harrison stood up and came toward her at once.

"You look divine, darling," he told her and led her to a chair.

Mariah smiled at him. "Thank you. You always say something along those opinions."

"'Tis the truth, fair lady!" Harrison clutched his heart and then took the chair opposite her.

Mariah looked at Alicia and Simon, who were conversing with Lord and Lady Purcellville. Her aunt and uncle were not in attendance tonight, as they had plans with a friend of Mr. Hughley's.

Again, the door opened, and Carter announced Lord and Lady Michaelton. From the corner of her eye, Mariah could see Harrison stiffen. Why he should have cause to do that made her uneasy.

Lord and Lady Michaelton greeted everyone in turn, and Samantha rested her eyes upon Harrison, who seemed to be visibly shaken. She gave him a hesitant smile, and the smile vanished from Mariah's face. Samantha...Harrison's reaction to her...

Alicia had claimed at dinner when Mariah had first met her that her cousin claimed an acquaintance with Harrison. Samantha and her Harrison...years ago...

Oh, no. The pieces began to fall into place. She was the woman that Harrison had loved before Mariah. She was the woman who had nearly broken her beloved Harrison. Anxiety came at Mariah like a runaway carriage as she wondered what manner this night might turn out to.

Mariah rose and waited in place beside Harrison to greet the couple. Lord Michaelton brought himself and his lady to stand before them. After bows and curtsies, Lord Michaelton inclined his head toward Harrison and addressed him. "It's been ages, Bramley. I trust that things have been well for you." He looked pointedly at Mariah.

Showcasing a mouth full of straight, perfect teeth in a smile, Harrison answered, "Very well indeed. Thank you for your kind consideration."

Lady Michaelton smirked but said not a word. She looked radiant in a cream gown that had tiny seed pearls sewn into it. Her golden hair was swept up, with half cascading down her neck. Her hazel eyes were affixed to Harrison. In all, she was a vision of glorious beauty, and try as she might to help it, Mariah felt small in comparison.

Dinner was announced, so the gentlemen joined together to escort the ladies to the table. Harrison was rigid and stiff beside Mariah. She could barely breathe. Harrison seemed to be deep in thought. *Mayhap thinking of Samantha? No, I believe he wouldn't.*

As Mariah sat down, she blushed, feeling as if her heart and mind were one in their racing cadence.

Biting her bottom lip, Mariah thought back to her first meeting with Samantha and how the woman must have known that she would be meeting with Harrison again. She had gone so far as to tell Mariah how very unhappy she was in her marriage. Did Samantha wish to resume a relationship with Harrison? It was not unheard of for married ladies to enjoy the attention of unmarried men after they had seen to heirs for their husbands. And it also wasn't uncommon for married men to have mistresses.

Mariah looked at Lord Michaelton to see if she could ascertain what he was thinking, if anything. But he was watching his wife. Mariah told herself to breathe. Harrison loved her. She was his choice...

But perhaps she was only his choice since Samantha had rejected him?

Mariah could not concentrate on the conversation flowing along around her. She felt Harrison's eyes on her almost constantly but would not meet them. That she could not do, not here and not with concern brimming within his stormy eyes. Mariah's emotions were so turbulent, she felt she might burst forth in tears.

Her heart was near to shattering, and she could not pick up the pieces of cutlery. She did the only thing she could do: she smiled and forced herself to eat what was put before her. She could not taste a single bite; all of her senses were focused on keeping her mask of calm and the comments she made. She wondered if she ever would be able to embody the training and the grace of indifference the ton seemed to possess. Mayhap she wasn't meant to live amongst them. She felt ill about continuing on with this falseness of feeling, but what was she to do? She kept avoiding Harrison's blatant stare; it was the only sure way to keep herself together. Too many conclusions and subjections were swirling around within her mind.

Before she knew it, the dinner was over, and she rose with the ladies, letting the footman pull her chair out. She did not look at Harrison as she walked straight out of the room, telling herself that nothing ill had yet occurred. There was no reason to heap all of her emotions upon Harrison's shoulders when he had not been given the chance to speak with her. All must be well. She would do her best to trust in her feelings and that his would remain true.

Once Mariah took her seat by the window, she hoped for peace, but that hope was dashed once Samantha took a seat beside her. That she would stay her distance; China would not be far enough away.

"My, it is chilly tonight, is it not?" queried Samantha, smoothing her dress out.

Mariah nodded but could not bring herself to speak. Nothing she thought of would be the correct answer. She was burning with questions which she dared not pose to this woman. She would give her intended the opportunity to speak first on the matter of the past.

From across the room, Alicia was beside her mother, who was directing the footmen on the placement for the table games that would commence once the gentlemen had arrived.

"I must congratulate you on your upcoming nuptials! You sly creature. The Earl of Bramley is quite a catch. You could search the world for another man of his ilk and never find one," Samantha said, giving Mariah a blinding smile.

Mariah shifted in her chair and knew she must say something. "He is quite remarkable. Thank you for your good wishes."

"Certainly. Do not take him for granted, my dear. A man such as he has large appetites that must be sated or else he'll look to others to meet his needs." Samantha smirked.

"Is that so?" Mariah furrowed her brows.

"Of a certainty, he is a man, and they are fickle things. They simper and coo and promise you the world. Heed my word: do not be disappointed when he looks elsewhere for comfort," Samantha disclosed, looking Mariah in the eyes and never wavering to bear the intimate contact. Mariah felt her stomach churn at the venom behind Samantha's gaze.

"You have met him before?"

"Oh, yes. Why, that was ages ago. We were both different people then." Samantha clasped her gloved hands in her lap.

"Is he much changed from your memories?" Mariah forced herself to look at the lady. She felt ever-growing disdain for this creature before her, but her curiosity could not be put to rest quite yet, though this door opening was one that she knew she could not close once it had been opened.

"He is exactly the same. Men never age as we women do, though he pays you a great deal of attention. I noticed him trying to meet your eyes at dinner, yet you would not look at him. Do not make the mistake of dismissing him; there are those who will stop at nothing to have such a man lavish his attention upon them. Our circle is full of many unhappily married women."

Mariah could not help but think Samantha's words held a hidden warning. Mariah was gaining a headache from this conversation which she knew was full of malice. Would Lady Michaelton bring Harrison back into her life? Would she seek him out for her own purposes? Mariah's stomach rumbled with apprehension that Samantha was indeed devious enough to attempt it.

So deep in thought was Mariah that she hardly noticed that Samantha had risen until she heard her speak.

"'Tis a pleasure to see you again, Harrison." Samantha's dulcet voice lilted at his appearance.

"A pleasure." Harrison bowed over her hand but did not kiss it.

Samantha pouted and took her hand back. "I am sorry we never meet anymore. Can we not lay the past to rest?"

"All is forgiven upon my part," Harrison coldly stated.

Mariah watched their exchange and wanted to escape to the security of her room, yet if she went now, how could she ascertain the situation and what Harrison's true feelings really were?

"Excellent news!" Samantha gave a seductive smile to Harrison, and Mariah realized how practiced the look really was. Everything the lady did seemed to be done with precise movements.

Harrison nodded at Samantha and turned from her toward Mariah. He bowed over her, reached for her gloved hand, and placed a gentle kiss upon the back of her knuckles. His eyes were warm now where they had been cold and guarded when he was looking at Samantha. He dismissed Samantha with his lack of attention, and Mariah heard her silently retreat.

"It is you I love," Harrison whispered. Smiling deeply and sincerely at Mariah, he placed himself in the chair opposite her. Mariah smiled, though it was filled with fear and insecurity. She so wanted to believe that all was in the past. Even though Harrison's exclamation moments ago should be enough to alleviate her fears, there was a darkness to Samantha she didn't trust, and it made her nervous.

They sat in heavy silence for the span of about five minutes time until they were called upon to make couples for a game of whist. Mariah's headache only increased, and it was a full hour before she could make an excuse to retire. Mariah did not want to seem rude in retiring; she only knew she had to leave the room for a few moments to gather herself. If she were to see Samantha trying to gain Harrison's attention one more time, then she would be sure to say something quite direct to her, or worse, she would be sick all over the carpet. So sick of head and heart was she now that she longed for a rest from all of the uncertainty and tension that wracked her body lest she act in a manner that was unbecoming.

What Mariah really wanted to do was give the shrew, Samantha, a severe dressing down in front of the entire room, but Mariah didn't relish the idea of what such an action might cost her. Mariah did not want to lose face with any in her immediate residence nor bring censure to her parents. There was also the matter of not understanding Harrison's feelings. If he truly felt something for the lady, then how would he react to Mariah's acting upon her feelings? What Mariah wouldn't give to march over to the ladyship who would not cease with her direct gaze following each of their movements and smack the smugness from her beautiful face. And while Mariah needed to ascertain what it was that Harrison truly felt for Lady Michaelton, it was not a topic that could be broached just now. Mariah said a quick prayer for forbearance, yet the longer that she sat, the longer her mind had to engage its wild imagination.

Mariah quietly told Lady Purcellville she was feeling ill, and after a few whispered exchanges with the lady, wishing her well, Mariah was free to leave the room. She just barely stopped herself from running. She looked to see Harrison's attention on Simon and felt safe in quitting the room.

In her bedchamber, she sat at the dressing table. She sat there for a quarter hour without ringing for Amy. She needed to be alone. She was torn between staying put or making her way back to the drawing room. She was so unhappy and did not know what to do. She wished she were under her parents' roof and could at any moment seek one of them out. How she missed them. Life had been far less complicated when she had never ventured forth into Brighton.

She finally gave into her feelings which were closing in on her with such force. Mariah let her tears fall, and they only added to the pain in her head. Love was a wondrous thing, but would she always be so unhappy? Would there always be something or someone to make her cry? Were the few minutes of joy worth a lifetime of uncertainty? Would she always question her place in Harrison's world if she chose him forevermore? And more importantly, was there a force already set in motion against them?

Chapter Twenty-Seven

The Missing

Harrison felt anxiety grip his heart; where was Mariah? Why was she not returning? He looked around the room, trying not to catch Samantha's eye. *Idiot*, he chided himself. Looking at Samantha, the only feeling he felt was a very deep loathing. He was surprised that was the feeling he could claim the most. Where once he had worshiped her, he now loathed her. How had he been so blinded by her?

The realization came quickly that he had never been in love with her. He had idolized her, admired her, hung on her every word, and, yes, worshiped her. So it was his pride that was affected the most, it seemed. Harrison knew love now. Love was what flowed like the very blood in his veins for Mariah. Mariah he loved; Mariah gave him purpose and a future. Mariah would give him children and make his house a home. Mariah. Where was she?

Leaving the room, he directly proceeded to ascend the staircase until he stood before her bedchamber door. He rapped upon the door, and when no answer came, he did so again.

"Mariah, are you in there?" shouted Harrison. It wasn't his intention to cause a scene, but hang it all. If that was the action he needed to take, he would do just that, and the devil take anyone who might dare to question him upon the matter.

"I am fine. You will scandalize the whole neighborhood with your shouting." Mariah spoke loudly through the heavy door.

"Let me in!" Harrison commanded.

"No, 'tis a very improper thing to do!"

"I repeat, let me in. You are to open this door at once!" Harrison bellowed.

"Be reasonable! You cannot stay out there all night. Can we not talk in the morning?" Mariah pleaded.

"Mariah. My dearest love. Open this door now or I will kick it in!"

Harrison was astounded by the truth of his statement. He *would* kick the door in, or do himself very real injury in trying to do so. This was madness; why would she not open the door? Why was she hiding away? He would lose his mind if he did not speak to her face-to-face.

Harrison pressed his forehead to the door and simply said her name. He was not certain if she could hear it.

He heard Mariah turn the lock on the door. He backed up as she pulled it open just enough to peek around it. She was in her nightgown and dressing gown, for goodness' sake!

Harrison looked at her with eyes starved for the sight of her. He said nothing but simply drank in the sight of her. As Mariah stood there, her hair came from behind her back to curl over her shoulder. Harrison exhaled a long breath. He almost groaned with the desire to reach his hand out and grab a handful of her dark, luscious tresses. He loved her brunette curls that were glowing with sun-kissed highlights.

"What do you want?" Mariah asked. Then she added, in a hushed, harsh tone, "Go away! This will cause a scandal!"

"I wish to speak with you," Harrison simply and reasonably said.

"Speak, my lord. I am listening." Mariah would not budge from her stance half hidden behind the door.

Annoyance coated his voice as he spoke. "I will not speak out here in the hallway. If, by some miracle, my being out here is not known, I will not risk what I wish to say to you being more fodder for the house. Please?"

Mariah sighed, then stepped away into the room to allow him to push the door open wider and enter through it. She walked to stand before the fire and stood with her arms across her chest, waiting for him to speak. He came to a stop a few inches from her.

Seeing Amy from her place beside the bed, he said to her, "That will be all."

Mariah's eyes grew large as she said, "She most certainly will not leave!"

"With what I would say, I would rather not have an audience," Harrison told her quietly.

Mariah seemed to hesitate before she finally nodded that Amy should follow the order. Mariah watched Amy withdraw with a grim set to her mouth.

"I am sorry—truly sorry—if I have added to your unease this evening," Harrison began. When Mariah made no answer, he continued. "Are you ill? You look unwell."

"I have a headache." Mariah bowed her head.

Harrison took a step toward her but stopped when she unfolded her arms and held her hands out to ward him off. Harrison, seeing her behave thusly, stopped and said, "I am sorry. Can I offer you any comfort?"

Mariah shook her head but spoke. "If we could continue this exchange on the morrow, I would be most grateful."

Harrison opened his mouth and then closed it again. Seeing Mariah firmly set against unburdening her heart to him crushed his own heart. They were working on being one, of being husband and wife, and he wanted no secrets between them. So, he held her sapphire gaze and simply said, "Please."

Mariah seemed to waver for a moment before she blurted out with, "What does Lady Michaelton mean to you?"

"Nothing," he quickly replied and then swallowed. His mouth suddenly became dry.

Mariah made a sound of disbelief and turned away from him.

Closing his eyes and praying for strength, he knew that he needed to be an honorable man of his word. So he began, "At present, she means nothing to me."

"But she did? At one time?"

"Yes. You only need to know that my heart resides with you. You are, I will confess, the only woman that I have ever loved. My greatest regret in my life was being blinded by her and especially now because it is causing you pain. I would walk through fire for you, dearest, loveliest Mariah." He tried to convey what his heart felt for her through his voice.

Mariah turned around and faced him again. Taking a deep breath, she squared her shoulders and told him, "You have no idea about the unkind things I wanted to do to her tonight. To say to her. To wound her. That is not in my nature. I have been raised to show grace in every trying situation. I am completely out of my element here, in this society and in this house. But I feel sure that that woman is enough to cause even a saint a moment's doubt of Christian charity. I still want to march down those stairs and pull her hair out." Mariah's countenance showed her vexation. It reminded him of the frustrations he bore toward Major Wallis.

Harrison could not help but chuckle as he said, "We are so well-matched. My dearest sweetheart, I appreciate your restraint. I cannot imagine a more demonstrative display of possessive love. You do me a great honor with the strength of the depth of your sentiments. Let us put this behind us. I can assure you, I am only tempted by a set of vivid blue eyes. They are the ones that call to my heart and no others."

Taking a deep breath, Mariah only nodded at him. He hoped and prayed that she understood how much she meant to him. It was hard to convey what she meant to him when he only wanted to embrace her and show her the depth of his vast love for her.

They stared at each other for a few more moments. Then finally, he said, "Very well. We can drive out so that we may talk more on the morrow privately. We are engaged and can, therefore, I believe, go out in a curricle alone. Perhaps Lord Purcellville will allow me the use of his." Harrison raked his hands through his ebony locks.

Mariah nodded at him. "As you wish."

Harrison closed the distance between them, and despite her objections, he gathered her into his arms. He held her there and waited until the tension left her body; when it did, he felt his tension exit him as well.

"I love you, sweetheart. I am torn apart by your unhappiness; never doubt it," Harrison whispered into her hair.

He brought his mouth down and gently whispered a kiss against her mouth. Mariah grew still as he kissed her. She neither demanded he stop nor pushed him away, so he felt free to continue to woo her. Harrison moved to kiss her eyes and her nose, her chin and the soft flesh behind each of her ears. Mariah sighed as her arms encircled his neck and pulled him closer to her.

Harrison breathed her in. She was so soft and warm and sweet—very sweet. He could not stop kissing her and exploring the planes of her face with his fingertips. He had never found kissing another woman to be so exquisite before. None had ever melted into his senses in this way before. His pulse was racing, and his temperature was rising. Harrison was fully in control of himself, though. It was of the utmost importance that he did not give way to his desires. He would be selfish and take his moment with her. He didn't know when another occasion alone would present itself. He ran a hand through her dark loose tresses as he had long wished to do. Her hair was thick and felt like silk as it slipped between his fingers to fall against her tiny waist.

Mariah opened her eyes and looked deeply into Harrison's. She bit her bottom lip and tilted her head to the side. Her eyes were heavy with desire, and he knew this could not go too much farther. He only meant to assure her that she was indeed his everything, his treasure.

Harrison brought his lips down upon hers again, and this time, they both sighed. Mariah opened her mouth in surprise, and Harrison instantly moved his velvety tongue along the opening. Mariah gasped in shock. He slid his tongue into her mouth and swirled it about. She tasted of wine and honey, and all of his best dreams. Her tongue began to duel with his and it was sheer madness and heaven at the same time. After a few moments of bliss, Harrison pulled away, because if he did not cease his attention to her, they would be wed by the next eve, and that would not do. She deserved so much better from him. Her innocence was not a gift that he would waste.

Regretfully, Harrison pulled himself from Mariah's arms as she pouted. He shook his head at her when she again tried to move into his arms. He held her at arm's length, then let his hands fall to his sides. He took a few strides toward the door.

Mariah stayed in the same spot, moving her fingers across her mouth and looking very dazed. She had a dreamy expression, and he delighted in the knowledge that he alone had created such feelings stirring within her.

"I shall discuss the curricle with Lord Purcellville," Harrison said, still laboring to breathe properly.

"Wait," Mariah called out to him when he opened the door.

Harrison turned and closed the door again but did not take a step toward her; instead, he ran his hand across his face. Despite his very great need to quickly and quietly remove himself from her bedchamber, he would hear her out.

"Are you displeased with me?" Mariah inquired in a small voice, not looking at him. She was staring at the color pattern upon the rug.

"Hear me now," Harrison began, then stopped, waiting for her to look up at him. He stepped toward her again and lifted her chin with a finger. It took Mariah a few moments to gain enough courage to finally meet his eyes.

"I could never be displeased with you. I am sensible of the lateness of the hour and the impropriety of the situation. I would not for the world tarnish your character or have your actions be called into question by another. I love you too much to cause you censure. I was remiss to insist that you let me enter your room. Sleep well, my dearest sweetheart. I shall see you soon." Harrison looked at her for a moment longer, then exited the bedchamber.

He strode down the hallway until he reached the very end of it, then entered into his bedchamber. He sat upon his bed to regain his composure. What an evening! Samantha and his Mariah both claimed center stage within his mind. The two bore no resemblance to each other. Thanking his decent common sense, Harrison was indeed pleased he had summoned enough strength to stop kissing Mariah. It had taken every part of his being to appease his conscience and set her out of his reach. He wondered if he would ever be able to extinguish the fire that ran in his blood, which she, and only she, was the cause of. He doubted that even one night, let alone all of the nights of his love, would ever cause that fire to die.

For now, though, Harrison doused the boiling fire that Mariah caused in his blood because his mind turned toward how Samantha had caused his beloved to suffer. Had that witch always borne such hardness? What had transpired while he was away that had caused Mariah to flee from the room? What had Samantha said to her? Harrison had never witnessed such animation toward violence from his beloved before.

Rising, he straightened his tailcoat and cravat. He gazed into his full-length mirror and saw that only his eyes betrayed his earlier actions. Taking several deep breaths, Harrison soon had his eyes clear of any remaining desire for his woman.

Returning back to the drawing room, he entered and sought out Lord Purcellville. The curricle was arranged for the ride, and all was well. Harrison took a chair by the fire and looked into the hot flames. Suddenly, though, the movement of an occupant into the chair opposite him caught his attention.

Samantha took the seat and placed her most sensuous smile upon her mouth. "That is quite the little parson's daughter you have there, Harrison. I am sure she will suit your purposes perfectly."

Looking at her as if seeing her for the very first time ever, Harrison saw a woman he had never met. She was trying to dazzle him, to goad him, and there in her eyes lay such deep sadness. Harrison had known such sadness before, after the death of his parents and then again after she jilted him. He wasn't sure what his own feelings were, to be seeing that upon her face, and truthfully, he wasn't sure he even really cared.

Instead of voicing the warnings that rose to his lips, Harrison said, "Miss Morten will be the perfect countess for not only myself but for all of Bramley Hall. Her generosity knows no end. There is such a sweetness about her—a real heart that one can witness at work in all that she does."

"Yes, well—that is all very well and good. I know the passions that flow in your body. I'll wager that you will be bored out of your mind within a fortnight! Come, now; you must admit you'll soon be seeking a mistress," Samantha's dulcet voice cooed. Her hazel eyes were studying him, and she still wore that seductive smirk upon her face.

Harrison snorted derisively. "How very droll of you to think so. Really, I thank you for your concern for my well-being, especially since that has never been your object before. So please, put any concern you feel for me away and place it elsewhere. Your husband is looking at us, and I would not, for the world, upset his humors." Harrison watched her as she patted her golden locks.

"My husband need not feel such curiosity. We are old friends, are we not?" she purred at him.

Harrison's lips twitched. "Friends? No, I can truthfully answer that that is not something we have *ever* been."

"*Pfft.* You are being obtuse." Samantha looked over at her husband and narrowed her eyes at him. Then she looked back to her main attraction and brought tears into her eyes. Harrison became alarmed at the sight of them.

"You have no idea what I have suffered at the hands and whims of my brutish husband," she delicately sniffed.

"Have you truly suffered, Lady Michaelton? 'Tis not a matter of my concern. You made your choice, and whether it was wise or not at the time, *you are his*. I would not cause one moment of grief for your husband no matter what your plans might be. If you think to seek some manner of revenge, leave me out of it. Better to find an inexperienced puppy to help you with those means, for it shall *not* be me." Harrison folded his arms across his broad chest and looked at her.

Huffing and wiping at her tears with her gloved hand, Lady Michaelton started to say something, but Harrison's abrupt rising from his seat cut her off. He bowed to her, then exited the room. He would not allow that venomous woman to try and goad him into pity.

Chapter Twenty-Eight

Sweet Rides

T he next morning, Mariah was seated in the curricle next to Harrison, and while it was again windy, she did not feel cold. She loved being next to him, and her spirits were soaring high. She was still reeling from last night's glorious kiss.

Harrison was an excellent horseman, and he drove the pair of dappled grays with such ease and grace. Mariah would gladly have risked the censure of the ton to be permanently at his side. Thankfully, they were engaged, so the rigid rules were able to be relaxed just a bit.

"There is Mrs. Tiggins, waving at us." Harrison pointed to their left, and they both waved back at her.

"I wonder at her always and forever being out of doors," Mariah mused.

"I have heard that she dislikes the confines of darkened rooms and she has an excellent skill at growing things." Harrison slowed to let a couple pass by.

"Can one grow many things in this climate?" Mariah inquired.

"I suppose that may be half of the thrill, yes?" Harrison smiled down at her.

Mariah smiled and did not feel a need to say more. Just being in his presence was enough to make her heart swell with happiness. Harrison spoke to fill the silence of what he wanted to attempt to grow himself at Bramley Hall.

They arrived at the hotel in time for luncheon with Mr. and Mrs. Hughley. They ate in the dining room and were greeted by so many others that by the time the dishes were cleared away, Mariah still felt hunger. *Oh, well; tea will come at some point.* It seemed the news of their engagement must be congratulated by one and all. It seemed that their engagement was no longer a secret.

The party repaired in the sitting room that was the Hughleys'. This was where they would visit with one another instead of with half of Brighton, Mariah was sure.

"Has any word come from your mama or papa yet?" Mr. Hughley asked.

"No, not yet. I must confess to feeling uneasy. I do wish I were there." Mariah frowned.

"Well, 'tis better you are here so your own health does not suffer. People rarely expire from colds." Mrs. Hughley patted her hand, for they were sitting beside each other on the settee.

"We can set out for home, should you wish for it," Harrison told her.

He had been telling her this at least three times a day whenever she would grow quiet. He knew her so well as to guess what her thoughts were. Mariah shook her head at him.

"Well, another ball tonight. What shall you wear for it?" Mrs. Hughley sighed.

"I had not thought about it. I am sure Amy will choose for me. She has quite the eye, and I really only have a few dresses with me. What shall you wear, dear aunt?" Mariah smiled at her.

"I do not know. I love society, but balls can grow tiring for one who is aged such as I. If not for your being here, I believe we would be off visiting with my sister," Mrs. Hughley answered.

"Please do not make yourself uncomfortable on my behalf!" Mariah told her.

"Oh, no; here, I feel useful to your parents. I know that our being here is a comfort to them, and while they are ill, we must ease their minds upon that score." Her aunt again patted her hand.

The gentlemen each sat in a chair and watched their ladies converse. Mr. Hughley patted his portly stomach and said, "My, but with so many congratulations flowing to you from all around us, I feel as if I had not a bite to eat."

Laughing at her uncle, Mariah said, "It was rather a busy meal. Aunt Agatha, do you perhaps have anything sweet about? My uncle looks in rather low spirits."

"No, I confess I do not. Now that it is mentioned, however, I do feel a rumbling within my own stomach." Mrs. Hughley looked at her with a gentle half-smile.

"Well, this will simply not do." Rising, Mariah made her way to the rope and pulled the bell. She returned to her seat beside her aunt. "We shall all perish and then be ill. I am happy to know I am not alone in my hunger. I rose from the table most confused at my own feelings of hunger but thought I must be the only one!"

"Thank the Lord!" laughed Mr. Hughley as he clapped his hands and rubbed his bulging stomach. "I am famished!"

Harrison laughed too and said, "One learns how to shovel food in at a ball or other social gathering, as all are likewise engaged. I would often barely catch a mouthful before we were interrupted. So amusing that we should all be suffering in the same manner but afraid to venture upon the subject!"

"I promise: as your wife, I will ensure that you are always properly fed, no matter the length of time we are at the table," Mariah merrily vowed.

A quick rap upon the door announced a servant. Mr. Hughley ordered him to make haste in fetching sandwiches and lemonade for everyone. Once the servant left, Mariah cheered happily and was met with giggles over the excitement for food.

The servant was quick and was back in a matter of moments, it seemed. Mariah helped her aunt situate the table, which was covered in delicate silk dyed a rich forest green and was set with cut-glass goblets and china that gleamed in the firelight. Silence reigned as they all began to dine blessedly without interruption.

Mariah beamed, with a satisfied full stomach and a contented sigh. Then Mr. Hughley rose from his seat and announced a means for them all to repair before the ball that night. He helped Mariah's aunt to rise. Harrison then helped Mariah, and each person said their farewell.

Mariah and Harrison once again sat in Lord Purcellville's curricle. This time, they were headed back to the house. Mariah was tired, and she rather looked forward to a rest before they would all spend the evening dancing. Mariah wondered how many dances she could get away with now that she was engaged. Surely, she could have more than two.

She perked a brow at Harrison, wondering how many dances he could endure in one evening.

"Shall you miss the balls and soirees once we are home?" Harrison asked as he maneuvered the grays.

"No. They have been wonderfully entertaining, but I also dearly love being at home. I think there will be much to attend to once we find ourselves returned," Mariah replied, pulling a curl back from the side of her face and tucking it into her bonnet.

"Indeed. I suppose you will have a new trousseau and then the planning of the special day to see to."

"Yes," Mariah trailed off.

"What has you worried?" Harrison asked, grabbing her hand in his. He was able to steer the horses with only one hand.

Smiling down at their intertwined hands, she sighed. It was foolish to worry about matters she could do nothing about. "I suppose my trousseau will be costly? The differences in dress between a countess and a parson's daughter are vastly different."

She was embarrassed, but not of the fact that she was a parson's daughter. She was embarrassed to wonder whether or not she could be truly comfortable as his countess? Would she belong in that sphere? She, unlike daughters of the peerage, had no training in how to handle the daily affairs of an estate. She was not ignorant in household duties, but she did not feel herself sufficiently capable of managing such a grand house with several servants, as she was not used to really entertaining the upper elite class like Harrison was. Mariah wanted to do him and their station proud.

"My dearest darling," Harrison began, "you have no need to worry at the expense, nor does your papa. I shall cover the expenses of whatever you may need."

"Do you not wonder how your household affairs shall proceed once I am in residence?" Mariah drew her delicate brows together.

"Why should that concern me? You will set yourself up to the task of learning all you need to in very short order. You will be surrounded by help that will gladly guide you, and you need only to converse with my aunt to learn all you need to know. I feel sure that, after a while, you will excel and feel confident. I have every faith in you." Harrison smiled down upon her.

Catching his eye for a moment calmed the roiling sea inside of Mariah. She knew that Harrison would see that everything went smoothly, and as her father was a practical man, Mariah knew that her father would see the sense in Harrison funding her new wardrobe. Her dowry would not even make a dent in the costs of her new wardrobe. As for the rest of her troubles, she would take her days one at a time.

Mariah sighed. *Everything will work out. God has brought us together, and I need to rest my worries upon Him and use His strength to see me through.*

Chapter Twenty-Nine

Burning Betrayal

Feeling slightly embarrassed, Mariah gazed into her full-length mirror and felt her cheeks warm. She had worn this ball gown before while in Brighton. She was not yet a countess, and there was nothing she could do now, for wishing with all she had for a new gown would never make the gown appear. Still, she looked the best that she could, and despite her gown, she knew she wore nothing that would make herself an embarrassment to herself nor Harrison. She might be lacking in lavish attire, but if he was not bothered why should she be?

Her blue ball gown was stunning and matched her eyes perfectly. Her brunette hair was piled atop her head, with just a few curls left to cascade down her neck and rest upon her alabaster back.

The effect, she knew, was quite stunning. She was not a vain creature, but she was not blind either. She knew her facial features were neither bold nor lacking. Her lips were generous, and her brows were formed in a becoming arch above her eyes. Her nose was quite acceptable, with just the hint of an upturn at its point, which was the only flaw it had, if indeed a flaw must be found. Her hair was colored with highlights of varying shades of browns and was far from mousey. Her figure was well-rounded, and she was in no doubt that when she walked or stood, she was well-admired.

Nodding to Amy and dismissing her for the rest of the night, Mariah took her reticule and made her way down the stairs. She was greeted by Simon and Alicia.

"La, but I do love you best in blue!" enthused Alicia. Simon nodded his opinion.

"Thank you, dear sister. I think that shade of green most becomes you," Mariah returned the compliment.

"I am as proud as a peacock to be in the company of the prettiest ladies that have ever graced the earth. Indeed, I feel sure there are angels in heaven that could not match either of you in grace nor look." Simon adjusted his cloak. He plopped his topper onto his head.

"You are too much, dear husband! I should never tire of your sentiments, though, so I won't scold you too severely." Alicia beamed up at him.

Lord and Lady Purcellville joined them and began dressing themselves in their outerwear. Carter carefully handed off each piece they donned.

Harrison stopped to replace his gold pocket watch into his pocket, then strode forth. It was not like him to be the last to join them. Mariah caught his gaze as he approached and reached for his cloak, walking cane, and topper from Carter. Harrison winked at her, which gave her the sudden blush upon her cheeks that he knew would appear.

Offering her his arm once he was properly attired in his outerwear, Harrison led the party out of doors to the carriage.

Once all were seated and the coach was off, Lady Purcellville stated, "I do hope Lady Everly does not wear that obtuse feather in her hair! It waves about as she moves, and I have seen a great many gentlemen choke upon it. One would think that receiving looks for a fortnight would be enough to scare that dreadful feather off. Why, the Regent even remarked at how odd she looked," she scoffed and clucked her tongue.

"Indeed. Well, not all can be as fastidious as you," Lord Purcellville stated.

"I do think she likes the attention. Why else would she keep adorning that horrid piece?" Alicia sniffed.

"Do you know: I was standing behind her two nights ago, and that feather was weaving, waving, and bowing upon her head. I almost plucked it and ran away," chuckled Simon. "I daresay it would have been a mercy to one and all."

Turning to Mariah, Alicia raised her eyebrows. "Have you given any thought to your trousseau? We could start shopping for it now, while you are here in Brighton."

"Oh. Well, I have given it some consideration. I would not slight Mama for the world and feel that she might feel out of sorts if she were not a part of choosing it," Mariah said earnestly. She did not want to injure Alicia's feelings either.

"You have the right of it. Mama has never shopped for a countess before and would feel robbed to not share in the excitement." Simon inclined his head.

The carriage pulled up into the line which was fast forming. Alicia would not stop remarking about how excited she was for the ball.

Once their time arrived to disembark from the carriage, all let Simon and Alicia depart first, with Lord and Lady Purcellville quickly following.

Lady Ferguson's ballroom was quite impressive. It was situated with a perfect view of the ocean, and with its balcony doors being held open, it let in the wind from the sea as a welcome addition to the press of bodies. The air was heavy with perfume from ladies. There were many candelabras that gave a soft glow so that there were no dark corners that might give the matrons the feeling of impending doom.

After Harrison and Mariah had greeted Lady and Lord Ferguson, they stepped onto the dance floor, as the ball was well under way. Harrison twirled and parlayed his lady about with such grace and ease of manner, there were none who could say they were not enchanting together.

Mariah looked deeply into Harrison's eyes and knew she would always feel such joy. He would deny her nothing, and she in turn would bow to him in all matters. Their life together would be blissful and elegant. Poor Harrison had to relinquish her hand many times throughout the night. She was certain to keep him in eyesight; his eyes, she swore, held a mixture of loss and pride.

When the dinner hour came, Harrison sought her out, and they seated themselves next to Alicia and Simon. Mariah hardly heard the rapturous joys Alicia related to them. She only wished to offer her full attention to Harrison, and he in turn seemed to address only her.

Quickly after dinner, the amazing accompaniment began a dazzling cotillion. It was after a dance with Mr. Farner that Mariah caught sight of Major Wallis. He was making his way expediently toward her, and Mr. Farner seemed oblivious to her anxiety.

Major Wallis stood in front of Mariah, and she curtsied to him when he bowed. What a pity that she could not seem to locate Harrison.

"May I partner you next?" The Major was looking at her most adamantly.

Knowing she could not refuse, for to do so would be reprehensibly rude and would cause her to have to sit out from the rest of the dances that night, and with no other partner to claim her, Mariah answered, "Of course."

Claiming her hand, Major Wallis led her to the floor. They turned toward each other, and a waltz began. Mariah liked to save her waltzes for Harrison, but he was not to be seen, and here she was, already engaged.

After the dance ended and they exchanged bows, Major Wallis encircled Mariah's waist with one hand and brought his right hand up for her to hold on to. He gave her a serious, considering look.

"Major Wallis, what can have you so enthralled?" Mariah asked him.

"Do not pretend you do not know my thoughts," he softly said.

"How can I claim to know what you could be thinking? We have not often been in each other's company enough to ascertain the other's feelings on subjects like literature, plays, favorite meals—the general things which acquaintances discuss." Mariah broke off their eye contact. She forced herself to stare at his perfectly tied cravat.

With amusement in his voice, he said, "True, but I have not made my sincere regard for you silent. I have sought at every opportunity to present my sentiments to you."

"But I am engaged. You know that it is so now. Why must you keep hoping?" Mariah posed this question to his left shoulder, for her sight was now directed there.

"Hope is often all one has. Though many trials and sorrows we may face, hope is the divining force that guides us. Until you are truly the Countess of Bramley, hope will reside within my heart." His richly warm brown eyes were brimming with sincerity.

Looking up to meet his gaze and seeing the measure of his words, Mariah almost slowed her pace and just missed stepping upon his toes. Major Wallis was looking into her eyes too but was able to get her and himself back to the same tempo as before with very little difficulty.

Mariah needed to say something to tell him it was foolish to hope. But she found she could no more dash his hope than she could swim the Channel. So boyish, so handsome he was that any woman would gladly welcome the attention of him, yet she could not. She loved Harrison and knew she always would, come what may.

The music concluded their dance, and Mariah felt broken and brittle. Never had she been one to cause pain to another, and it was not a feeling she wished to ever court again.

The Major led her to the side of Lady Purcellville, and as he bowed over her hand, he looked at her again one last time, then backed away into the crowd.

"Are you quite all right, my dear? You look peaked," Lady Purcellville inquired.

Pulling all of her strength together, Mariah found her voice. "I am well. I think I should find the retiring room, though."

When Lady Purcellville nodded, Mariah moved away toward the ballroom's doors. She needed a moment to regain her composure, and she hoped she could find a quiet corner though it was considered improper. She really should have had a chaperone, but she didn't dwell upon that thought for long.

She turned a corner and found her steps to be faltering. Before her, she saw Major Wallis's back rigidly straight. His arms were folded across his broad chest. She wondered what could have captured his attention right in the middle of the hallway. She really didn't want to have to pass by him. She needed quiet to process her time with him.

Peering around him as quietly as she could, she was able to see the source of his interest, and it brought tears to her eyes.

Chapter Thirty

Swallowed by the Sea

H arrison had been attentive to every man who had held Mariah in his arms and had danced with several passably pretty females. He did as much as was required so that he would not look like a coxcomb pup. But truth be told, he was jealous. Mariah was his, and he had to fight the feeling of hauling her off to Bramley Hall at once. Oh, he knew she would happily set out with him, but her reputation would suffer, and he was above injuring her so. Some things could not be overlooked simply because one held a title. He would recover, but his lady would be the topic of rumor within the ton which had long, fickle memories.

Heaving a sigh, Harrison decided it was better to walk around the edge of the ballroom and keep his eyes off his betrothed. He did this for two or three dances before he felt like a madman and sought to exit the ballroom. He had only one more dance available to him with his lady. Why, oh, why, were more than two dances forbidden?

Harrison left the ballroom and was striding along the corridor when he felt a hand reach out to him. He stopped his gait and looked at Samantha. A feeling of unease prickled his spine and raised the hairs upon his neck and arms.

"Darling, I have been hoping to catch you! I am so very glad that at long last, I have," Samantha purred, letting go of his arm to encircle his neck with her slender arms.

Harrison stood stock still looking down at her with dismay. What a tricky situation. He looked up and down the hallway and knew that at any moment, they could be discovered. He reached for her hands to unclasp them, but she was holding on very tightly, and he did not wish to injure her. If he were to leave a mark, not only would rumors fly, but Lord Michaelton might call him to draw swords at dawn.

"Samantha, you must stop this! 'Tis madness. Think of your husband!" Harrison shook her thin shoulders in an attempt to wriggle her off.

"Why ever should I want to think of him when you stand before me? You loved me once! Can you not still feel love for me?" She leaned up to place a kiss upon his lips but missed her goal and instead reached his cleft chin.

"Your husband is a good man, Samantha. He is a highly thought-of member of the realm. His politics are spot-on, and I have never seen him lose his calm. Why do you seek to wound him so profoundly?" Harrison reasoned with her.

"He has wounded *me*! Only let us not discuss him. All I want is to be yours. I think about you constantly. How wrong I was to ever choose him over you. I regret my folly greatly. Darling, can we not be together?"

Samantha was pressing her body against his and had yet to release her hold upon him. He attempted again to disentangle himself, turning his shoulders and keeping his head away from her, but she was like a loathsome leech.

"No, we cannot. I have had a long time to consider our former relationship and can firmly tell you, things are as they are meant to be. You made your choice. I am sorry if it pains you now. I cannot—not now nor *ever*—come back to you. My heart lies elsewhere, and I would not, for the world, cause your husband anger. This will not happen; know that now. I was never in love with you. I am in love with Mariah, and now that I understand the nature of love—how it feels, the joy it holds—I know it was not the feeling I bore for you," Harrison resoundingly told her, his voice firm and brash so that it echoed in the empty corridor.

Shaking her head, Samantha let her arms slip from his neck, and he used the moment to untangle her arms from his person. "But you loved me. *You* love me still," she stuttered. Her hazel gaze demanded his agreement.

Harrison crossed his arms over his chest and took a step back. "I tell you, I do not. Not ever." Harrison did not relish the look of hurt in her eyes or the defiant posture she bore, but it could not be avoided.

In one last desperate attempt to make him see reason, Samantha flung herself at him and again clasped her hands around his neck. She used her full weight and hung on him so that he stooped his shoulder a little to support her. Seeing his change in stance, she finally found his lips and hungrily pressed hers upon his. He knew that she was not going to stop her ministrations, as she was narcissistic and manipulative. In a bizarre thought, he felt the only way in which to show her he held no feeling for her was to simply let her kiss him. He did not return her kiss, only stood still and let her kiss him. He felt absolutely nothing other than repulsion to have to suffer through this forced action.

Finally, Harrison pulled himself away from Samantha, giving her a glare full of malice. Samantha took a step back, her left hand going to her lips. She dropped her hand and smiled sadly at him.

Harrison simply turned and walked into the ballroom. He knew that her little obsession with him was over. He felt a great weight lifted from his shoulders as he reentered the ballroom. He had faced her and had even let her kiss him, and he felt nothing. Nothing but relief; he was free. Now, to find his sweetheart. He sorely needed to be near her and erase the stain of Samantha from his mind.

Chapter Thirty-One

Broken Faith

Mariah gasped. She was trying to stop the sob that wanted to tear her apart. How could this be? How could her Harrison be kissing that vile woman? She felt her lungs constricting for air and could not make herself breathe. She wanted to make her body move away from this scene, this terrible betrayal. She felt Major Wallis looking at her but could not meet his eyes. He must think her the biggest simpleton that ever was. Here, she had remained firm in her devotion to a man who did not return her regard, who did not love her, and who had lied to her face time and again.

Major Wallis came to her and took her arm in his. He made her move with him as they moved along the corridor and entered the library. Mariah felt numb. What could she do? What should she do? She would not marry Harrison, not now, not ever. She would not let him tread upon her heart. How she had loved him! She stood inside of the library while the Major paced back and forth.

Stopping to look at her, he said, "Tell me: what I can do? How can I be of service to you?" His jaw ticked as his warm eyes implored her.

Mariah fought for control of her thoughts. She finally found a coherent thought and said, "My aunt and uncle. Can you locate them? They are here tonight."

"Yes, yes, immediately. Only please, do sit down. You are pale, and I cannot leave you now to find you soon upon the floor when we return."

Major Wallis took her elbow and led her to a chair. She sat and watched her hands shake. Major Wallis opened the door and exited.

Mariah waited, and her thoughts kept churning. Home—she must leave for home at once. She could not bear to look at Harrison, not now, not tomorrow, not ever. What a fool she had been. A plain parson's daughter to wed an earl. How ridiculous she was! She found that her tears would not fall, and she was grateful. She could not be found blubbering to anyone who might happen upon her. She and her heart were a farce.

The library door swung open, and Mrs. Hughley took one look at Mariah and bade the two gentlemen to wait outside the door. Mrs. Hughley approached her niece and thought her heart would break from the sight of her.

"My dear, what has occurred?" Mrs. Hughley asked as she knelt in front of her, not caring if she crushed her pale blue dress.

"I wish to go home. Can we not leave at once?" Mariah implored her.

"Of course. I shall have Mr. Hughley find Lord Bramley and—"

Mariah interrupted her aunt. "No. I do not wish to see him." Mariah looked away. "I meant to ask if we could depart for the parsonage?"

"It is late, and we would have to pack and ready the horses and carriage. It would be better to start our journey on the morrow. Only tell me: why do you not wish to see his Lordship? Whatever can he have done? Couples sometimes have spats, but that's easily overcome. You must converse with him to sort out this little spat," Mrs. Hughley consoled, patting her arm.

"No, I cannot recover from this. He has acted abominably, and I do not wish to see him. Can we not leave upon first light tomorrow?" Mariah begged her aunt.

"Of course we can. Let us get you home."

Rising, Mrs. Hughley walked to the door and spoke with her husband. When she returned to Mariah, a few minutes had passed, and she was holding Mariah's burgundy cloak.

Mariah rose too and let her aunt help her put the cloak on. Then Mrs. Hughley led her through the door. She and Mariah's uncle remained positioned on either side of Mariah as they walked with her to the door and then into the carriage. Mariah climbed into the carriage and saw that Major Wallis sat inside as well. Mr. and Mrs. Hughley followed her. They all traveled in silence, giving Mariah and each other anxious looks.

Finally, Mr. Hughley could stand the silence no longer and said, "Please tell me what has occurred. I am fine in leaving on the morrow, but please tell me why we are to keep it secret and why Lord Bramley is not accompanying us," he implored.

Clearing his throat, Major Wallis answered him. "Mariah has had a great shock. I do believe her engagement with the Earl of Bramley has ended."

Gasping, Mrs. Hughley asked, "But why? How came this to be? Mariah?"

Looking up, Mariah said, "He has shown himself to be unequal to my measure of affection. He sought the arms and attention of another, and I cannot forgive him for it. Please, do not say a thing to him. I shall leave a letter behind. I would not be so cruel as to leave without an explanation. Please believe me when I say that I have no wish to be his wife."

Mrs. and Mr. Hughley exchanged a look.

"Say no more now, dearest." Mrs. Hughley frowned.

"How shall we leave without his knowing?" Mr. Hughley scratched his chin.

"There is a gathering early tomorrow, and both Simon and his wife are to attend. I had heard a conversation of Lord Purcellville's that had asked the Earl to join him. I am certain that he will attend.

You look unwell, and your attendance would not be expected, at any rate," the Major stated, nodding at Mariah.

Mariah wrung her hands in her lap, but what else could she do? She had to get away.

"It is deceitful, but our duty is to you. We shall have your letter delivered after luncheon to Lord Bramley, and that should give us a good head start on him. We shall have to make haste so we can arrive before he sets out. Unless I am much mistaken, I have every reason to believe he will give chase." Mrs. Hughley rubbed her gloved hands together.

"'Tis the way in which we shall proceed. Major Wallis, if his plans differ, I rely on your letting us know." Mr. Hughley looked at him pointedly.

"Upon my honor, it will be done," Major Wallis replied, dipping his head.

Nothing was said as Mariah left the safety of the carriage and entered the house. She went straight to her room and threw herself onto her bed, finally letting her tears flow. Her every happiness had vanished in a moment. Now, she would never be the same again. Half of herself would forever be missing. And the other half—the former happy self—would remain here in Brighton where it had begun itself and ended.

Chapter Thirty-Two

Miserable Travels

Mariah had not slept well at all. She was tired and felt very ill. She understood how characters in books could perish from a broken heart. She ached from head to toe. Her heart hurt her the most. How could Harrison do that? How could the man she thought she knew above all others seek attention from another? Has she disappointed him? What defect in her makeup could he see that she could not?

She arose from her bed before dawn, as there was only torture and a wondering mind to be found lying in her bed. She considered the blank sheet of stationery in front of her. What should she reveal to him? She had to give his family ring back; she had to end her dreams. She did not worry about wounding his heart. Did he possess a beating, feeling heart such as she did? She thought it was his pride that would suffer the most. Refused by the parson's daughter; how extraordinary.

Mariah took a deep breath and began. It was the easiest way to break off their engagement. She could not face him for, if she did, she knew she could forgive him of anything, and it was not what she intended to do just at present. She longed to be in his arms and to be his only love. If she went to him now, though, she would live through years of agony in wondering about his mistresses. She wanted to be the only one to claim his affection.

Dear Earl of Bramley,

I am returning your ring. I have accompanied my aunt and uncle to the parsonage. Please do not cut your visit short. Stay and enjoy Brighton. I have no wish to see you just now. I'm sorry to break off our engagement but really feel it is the only option available. Please know this was not an easy decision. I shall not see you if you come to call, so please stay away. I think it speaks to good judgement that I have left now. I would not settle either of us to the other with doubting minds or hearts not fully joined.

Respectfully,

Mariah Morten

Mariah would not let herself think about what his thoughts and emotions would be as he read the missive. It was better to never wonder at all. She sat at her dressing table, brushing out her hair. Her headache, she knew, would not vanish for days to come, so she might as well let it rage away.

Amy appeared with her morning tray just a few minutes later. Mariah had informed her of her plans to depart today and had bade Amy to keep the news quiet. She did not want anyone to know before they were all safely on the road. Of course, Carter and the footmen would know once they departed, and so would the other servants. Mayhap she could beg Carter to deliver the letter which contained the ring after luncheon? She feared to leave it in her room, as it might be delivered much too soon to the recipient. It was imperative that she depart as quickly and as silently as possible.

Mariah dressed in a pale pink traveling gown and had Amy pin her curls up with no elaborate detail.

"Shall I secure the comb?" Amy asked, holding the comb Harrison had given her just a few days ago.

Bringing her hands up to her cheeks, Mariah shook her head. She could not, would not, let her tears fall again. Not until they were on their way.

"Leave it upon the dressing table. Someone may find a use for it," she replied.

A quick rap upon her door announced her beloved aunt and uncle. Mariah sighed, relieved that they came so promptly. Mariah refused her breakfast tray and alighted straight for the carriage, not caring if it was readied yet or not.

Mariah stared out the carriage window as the world passed her by. Dawn was beginning to break the sky into a dreary gray when the carriage finally rolled away from the Purcellvilles'. Mariah hardly noticed it or how much time had passed. She was miserable. Her headache was raging, and the silence in the carriage was enough to make her scream. Every time a look was cast her way, she felt as if it were breaking her into more pieces. She wanted to dissolve without an audience. She was so desperately trying to hold on to all of her pieces tightly so that she could then scatter them in the safety of her own room and patiently collect them for later.

Mayhap one day, she would be able to put herself back together. Her mind reeled, trying to understand what her eyes had seen. She tried to reason the events to make sense and to make herself indifferent to them but could not. Everywhere she looked, her mind brought the image of Harrison kissing and embracing another. Mariah turned her thoughts to that direction. She seemed to remember golden hair and felt for sure it had been Lady Michaelton.

Mariah sighed and closed her eyes. *How could it not be her when she practically flung herself at Harrison? Harrison knew Samantha before; he said so. Long ago, he suffered at her doing. Yet he returned to her.* Mariah inhaled deeply, willing her tears to stay behind her eyes. *Even when he said he loved me.*

Darkness was falling, and the clouds broke loose with rain. The air was chilly, and the wet and cold seemed to seep into her bones. Would they never arrive home? The clouds and rain only grew darker and refused to relent. Mariah's eyes seemed to see the passing scenery, yet she did not recall ever really seeing it. She was in a daze, in complete utter shock. Her heart ached fiercely—as did her head—in replaying the scene which she had witnessed, and at each remembrance of what she had seen. Mariah tried to make sense of why Harrison would hurt her so, and what if anything, she had done to deserve it.

The horses whinnied, and the coachman stopped the carriage. Mariah alighted immediately, heading for the security of her home and room.

Mariah saw her papa waiting at the door for them and quickened her pace. She reached the threshold of the door and flung herself into his awaiting arms. He embraced her back, kissing the side of her face. She heard the footsteps of her traveling companions enter after her.

Her mother stood in the entryway, her face full of concern and questions.

"Welcome! What a surprise this is! How came you all to be traveling at such an hour?" inquired Mr. Morten, still hugging Mariah to his side.

Mr. Hughley spoke to him. "It was agreed upon we should make haste and return your daughter to you, as nothing could make her peaceful except the thought of home."

"What has happened?" Mr. Morten looked at him. Mrs. and Mr. Hughley looked at each other and then at Mariah.

Mariah turned to her papa. "We had to depart under a shroud of secrecy. I have broken my engagement with the Earl of Bramley and did not wish to encounter him. My aunt and uncle have been so gracious in accompanying me home. It was a miserable trip with the constant rain, and we are all overtired."

"Broken your engagement? Are you run mad? A countess! You would not break off being a countess?" Mrs. Morten was horrified.

"My dear, it is late. We can discuss the particulars in a few hours once daylight has appeared and some rest has been achieved. Go to bed, Mariah. My dear, see to your relations. I am sure this will all resolve itself. There are puddles collecting upon our floor," Mr. Morten stated.

Without another word but with a huff at her daughter, Mrs. Morten led her sister and brother-in-law to their room. Mariah reached up to kiss her father upon the cheek.

He smiled down at her and said, "You are not given to flights of fancy. I will not press you now, but has Lord Bramley placed you in a difficult position in some manner that was not gentle?"

Shaking her head, Mariah admitted, "Please know I have not been harmed. Only my heart suffers. I do not wish to see him if he should appear. Please send him away, or if you must meet with him, do not send for me. He has abused my trust, and I cannot so easily recover from that."

Nodding his head and looking at her, Mr. Morten kissed her brow. Mariah hurried up the stairs to the comfort of her room to finally let her pent-up emotions out of their tightly closed trunks.

Mariah woke up with a start realizing that a new day was greeting her. 'Twas not a surprise as exhausted as she had been. She looked around and saw all of the beloved furnishings around her. Her sketches and watercolor paintings were hung upon the wallpapered walls, and her beloved sketchbooks were resting upon her oak desk. Her favorite lavender curtains hid the view of the outside from her.

She was home, but she felt no joy. Her eyes were gritty from her tears, and her head still ached. She felt very old, but she was dry and warm and did not give a fig if she were to take ill. She doubted illness would overtake her and carry her away forevermore, though.

Mrs. Morten breezed into her room at midday and tsked her tongue at her. "Now, please; an explanation is needed. Why have you come home without the Earl?"

"I have told you that we are no longer engaged. I thought I knew him, but I do not," Mariah sadly said.

"Nonsense! I have been married these twenty odd years to your own dear papa, and still, I feel there are times that I do not know him!" Mrs. Morten stood by the bed.

"I believe the Earl's heart is fixed on another." Mariah wiped away a tear.

"How can this be? He has asked your father for your hand, and we have all watched you together. There has never been a doubt there that he bears much affection for you." Mrs. Morten dabbed at her nose.

"I believe he does care for me. He did when he gave me his mama's ring—the same ring that many other countesses of Bramley have worn. It fit perfectly. He did look at me with such love that it was like a waterfall, all of his feelings, and emotions overflowing from his expressive gaze." Mariah pulled the pale lavender coverlet up to her chin.

"And so he does care for you! Men, whatever they say about it, are indeed fickle. How came you to know he had slighted you?" Mrs. Morten came to sit beside her.

"I saw him in the arms of another—kissing, to be exact," Mariah answered her quietly.

"No, I cannot fathom that. Unless...Mariah there are men who can never contain their passions to just one female. They seek others. He may still adore you, but like most men of title, he may leave your side from time to time. But you still would be his wife; he would always return to you." Mrs. Morten touched her arm.

Mariah's mouth hung open. Anger knitted her brow. "And that is said to comfort me? The thought of me always waiting for his passions to be satisfied? I am not a proud person, but I cannot wait at home for him to return to me each time he strays. I cannot live with the constant breaking of my heart. You would still have me wed him?" Mariah could scarcely hold her tears in.

"If you love him above all others, if you think your place is beside him, if you can esteem him enough to take him into your arms each time he returns to you, then you are his equal. Think of all the good that can be done for your family. Matthew may yet find a more suitable living situation. Simon and Alicia will have an elevation in their circles. Your papa and I would need never worry about old age," Mrs. Morten desperately told her daughter.

Mariah shook her head incredulously, "These are reasons enough for you to settle your daughter to an unhappy state—for the comfort of all besides myself? Mama, I do love him, but he has broken his faith with me. He has broken his faith with all of us! Can you not see it?" Mariah said, her voice rising higher and angrier with each finished sentence.

"Yet he is a man." Mrs. Morten smiled slightly at her, but the sentiment did not reach her eyes.

Mariah snorted, shaking her head at her mother. Looking around her room, Mariah did not know how to go on. Did all men court more than the one they were to wed? Did Simon have another lady besides Alicia? No, she was sure he could not. Why, then, could Harrison? Simply having a title meant more than one of everything?

She wanted to hide under the coverlet to will the world away. How could her mother be so callous with her and her feelings? How could she have the audacity to ask this of Mariah and not offer any maternal solace? Mariah sniffed, tears tracking down her face.

If one loved another wholeheartedly, then this was the biggest slight Mariah could imagine such a person performing. And they were not even wed yet. To just have announced their engagement to the ton and then have this happen, it seemed to prove Mariah as a most egregious fool. Her reputation would never recover from this breaking of such a momentous promise.

Mrs. Morten patted her shoulder, offering minimal comfort. "You do not have any other offers, Mariah. If you did—if there was a possibility of another...but we cannot afford another season for you. Your papa does not enjoy Town, and we are needed here." Mrs. Morten rose from the bed.

"If I had another option, you would consider him?" Mariah inquired.

"I do not think your father is unreasonable. He would not let you wed the Earl if he thought you would be unhappy. Have no fear, Mariah. We will not cast you away." Mrs. Morten gave her one last long look before closing the door behind her.

Mariah sniffed, feeling more than miserable. Her heart was a jumble of emotions only made worse by the uncomforting and harshly accurate words of her mother. Mariah was beginning to think she would never know any other feeling. Was she keeping her family in dire straits by not marrying Harrison? Were they in desperate states? Surely, they were not. Her brothers had left in search of their own futures, and she knew nothing had changed in the living situation of her father.

Mariah crept from her bed. Outside her window, the sun was shining, and the birds were chirping. All was right in her place in the world; only everything inside her revolted at the idea that she might be unharmed. She *was* harmed! She was broken, and the one person who usually mended her was the very one who had betrayed her.

Taking a deep sigh, Mariah set herself to rights with the help of Amy who Mrs. Morten had called for. Not wanting to earn even more displeasure from her mama she hurriedly scrubbed her skin and redressed. Amy quickly arranged her hair, and for a brief moment, Mariah mourned the beautiful comb which she had become accustomed to using.

Mariah made her way downstairs. She stood on the threshold of the parlor, watching the room. Rude as it were, she was uncertain if she should enter. Her heart was a jumbled mess even though all other aspects of her were seemingly put together—her hair and her dress.

Mr. and Mrs. Hughley sat with Mr. and Mrs. Morten in the parlor. Mariah saw that they all watched for signs of anyone's approach upon the lane from the window, but no one had yet come.

There was not much for the Hughleys to impart upon the Mortens in the way of what had driven Mariah from Brighton and caused her to break the engagement. All that could be shared was the news that in some manner, the Earl of Bramley had broken Mariah's faith in him. The couples sat and drank tea.

"'Tis a mistake—a misjudgment, to be sure," Mr. Hughley assured his listeners. He patted his knee and blindly inspected his brown trousers.

"I cannot credit his Lordship with any ill use of Mariah, though Mrs. Morten has said that Mariah will not have him back. What is to be done?" Mr. Morten scratched his head.

Mariah felt she should enter now, not wanting to hear more of how, mayhap, it was *she* who had misunderstood. She knew what she had seen, and she would not allow herself to be slighted. Out of all the distress that had been brought upon her, having her family question her should not have been one of them.

"Why should anything be done, Papa?" Mariah softly inquired as she slipped into the parlor and stood beside the fire.

"I cannot bring myself to think ill of him, dearest. 'Tis some muddle that bears explanation." Mr. Morten looked back at her.

"He does not care for me as he led me to believe. I am a fool and am weak to have ever thought I was enough for him," Mariah replied, not turning away from the fireplace.

"Mariah, you must agree to hear him out when he calls. You must do this!" Mrs. Morten railed at her.

"I mean to hear him out, just not today," Mariah trailed off brokenly.

Changing the topic, Mr. Morten beckoned her over. "You have received a letter. A Major Wallis writes to you. Tell me: have you left a few broken hearts behind in Brighton after all?"

Mariah shook her head. "Rest assured, I have not. Major Wallis is a man who tried to gain my affection, yet I refused him for the Earl."

Frowning, she reached for the letter. It was indeed from Major Wallis. She felt embarrassed as to her last encounter with the man. He must be writing to see how she was faring. She was not faring well at all.

Mariah took the letter over to the window and broke the wax seal. She withdrew the vanilla parchment and read.

Dear Miss Morten,

Please forgive my forwardness in writing to you. I have not been able to expel you from my thoughts. I cannot tell you the

great anxiety I bear for your well-being, such a shock as you have received. It is my hope that returning to the bosom of your family has given you immersible comfort. I would very much like to see you again, if only for a few minutes so I may be made comfortable again. I have some business that may see me passing near your home. Please know I will not press my feelings upon you; you may be perfectly at ease upon that account.

I am, as ever, your servant,

G.W.

Mariah blinked, stunned Major Wallis had written to her. She wondered whether she should write to alleviate his feelings. Was it proper? He had indeed rendered her a great service with his secrecy and speed in bringing her aunt and uncle to her that night at the ball. He at least had proven she could trust him. A niggling thought that perhaps no man should be trusted weighed on her mind.

"Who is Major Wallis?" Mr. Morten stared at her. He took off his spectacles and then put them back on.

"He serves with Simon. We attended many of the same events while in Brighton, and he has proven himself most reliable," Mariah told him.

"I believe he is rather smitten with Mariah and was one of the reasons the Earl of Bramley returned here to ask for her hand. Everywhere we went, Mariah met with him." Mrs. Hughley smiled sadly and placed her hands into her lap.

"Ah, I see. Do you return his regards, Mariah?" Mr. Morten asked.

"Not in the same manner, not with the same feelings he has made clear to me. I respect him—I like him in friendship—but that is all." Mariah slipped the letter back into its envelope. She ran her hand down her side. She had chosen a dress of lavender in the hopes that she would not look quite so pale.

Rising, Mrs. Morten rang for more tea.

Squeaking in alarm, Mariah bolted for the parlor door. One look out of the window confirmed that the rider approaching was Harrison. Her heart almost exploded upon his arrival. How she longed to throw herself into his arms, but she could not. She still felt betrayed, and her wound was very deep. She wanted to make amends and continue on with their wedding preparations, but could she do as her mother had advised and overlook his indiscretions? Was she strong enough to endure the other women whom he chose to spend his time with? Could she ever be enough for him?

Mariah closed the parlor door behind her and ran up the stairs to the safety of her bedchamber. She closed the door and turned to lean herself against it. She looked at her bed, at her dressing table, and at the desk that sat before the window.

The dreaded knock sounded upon the door.

Chapter Thirty-Three

Hoofbeats & Heartbreak

Harrison paced the drawing room floor. He had not seen Mariah all morning nor during the afternoon. Everyone he had come across knew not of her whereabouts. It irked him terribly.

"Ho, now. You must stop with these exercises; you will wear yourself out, old boy!" Simon called out to him.

Harrison waved his hand in the air. He had asked Alicia, at long last, to check upon Mariah. He knew she must be at death's door to be abed all day. Stupid man to have not barged in last night!

The drawing room door opened, and Alicia returned. She came toward him, holding out two objects. One was the comb he had given Mariah; the other was a letter. A *letter*? He took them both, slipping the comb into his pocket. He looked at Simon, who shrugged his shoulders. Alicia took her seat next to her husband.

Breaking the seal, Harrison retrieved the single sheet of cream paper. His ring—the ring he had given Mariah—fell out into his hand. He looked at it and frowned. What could this mean? A terror that was real clawed its way into his stomach, and he almost wretched.

Seeing the object in his hand was a ring, Simon called to him, "What can this mean? *Where* is my sister?" His once-friendly tone turned sinister.

Harrison unfolded the cream sheet of paper and read it quickly. What did she mean, she did not wish to see him? She was *gone*, and their engagement was *broken*? Harrison's whole world was spinning. He groaned and almost fell to his knees.

Simon was beside him in an instant and led him to a chair. He snatched the letter from Harrison and began to read. Simon swore an oath. Alicia, for once, said not a word.

Harrison could feel the blood in his veins freezing over. Suddenly, a realization came over him. She knew, though he did not know how she knew, the ordeal with Samantha. He held his head in his hands and groaned again.

"What is the meaning of this? My sister flees from my side, and the blame seems to reside with you. What has happened?" Simon fumed.

Harrison could not raise his head; he could not look at his friend. He had failed with his most important duty: keeping his beloved's heart safe. He had wounded her, and she wanted not a thing to do with him, never wanting to see him again.

"Answer me, man!" Simon bellowed at him, grabbing him by the knot of his perfectly tied cravat. "I shall get to the bottom of this at once! You shall answer my questions; I know you know why she has fled!"

Harrison set a hand upon Simon's shoulder. "I do not know for certain, but this leaves little doubt. I believe she saw me in the arms of another and therefore has broken our engagement."

"*What*? Very badly done! I should call you out," Simon seethed. "How I desire to rearrange the nose upon your face. But I shall not." Harrison nodded, completely understanding Simon's anger toward him. He felt like a cad, only even worse. His heart felt as if it had been wrenched from his body and trampled upon. How could he have done this to the one woman he loved? How could he break her heart so miserably?

He heaved a great sigh, willing the tears to retract. *By God above, I need to make this right and claim my beloved woman.* He sat down in a chair before the fire, raking his hands through his hair.

"You will not because she would never forgive either of you," Alicia softly said from her perch upon the settee.

"I deserve your worst, Simon; have at it," Harrison said and rose. His eyes felt haunted, sunken into his face. He felt as if the clothes upon his person were sagging as he died a thousand deaths.

Simon stepped before him, glaring daggers. He raised his fist and then lowered his arm to his side. "You are not worth it, my lord," Simon spat.

"What shall we do? Is she with your aunt and uncle?" Alicia inquired.

Simon turned to his wife and nodded. "Yes, they have accompanied her. She is safe with them, I have no doubt. They may even arrive tonight if they stop but a little." Simon walked away from Harrison. "Though I would feel much relieved if someone would follow them."

"I shall set out at once," Harrison announced.

"No. *You* have done enough. Tell me, was the tart worth it?" Simon sneered at him.

"No, she was not worth it then or now," Harrison stated quietly.

"You cannot mean...what madness, my lord." Simon dragged his hand across his face.

"I came upon Samantha, and I should have walked away. I did not. I stayed and listened to her complaints, and when she threw herself at me, I should have made her let me go. Instead, I allowed her to kiss me. Though you must know, I did not engage her in the least. Some part of me thought that if she saw that I held no interest for her, she would give up. I know it was foolish, it was stupid, so I hope we can recover from this. We *must* recover from this. My heart is Mariah's." Harrison brought his fisted hand up to his mouth.

"Mariah will forgive you; 'tis not in her nature to do otherwise. Whether she will take you back is entirely another matter. Did you ever discuss Samantha with her?" Simon asked.

Harrison looked at the pair and admitted, "No. At least not in great detail. How does one discuss a former betrothed?"

Simon looked at his wife and pointed his finger at her. "Alicia, you will forget the lady's name. You are never to discuss this with another soul."

Alicia nodded her head and gave her husband a wide-eyed look of seriousness. Satisfied by his wife's response, Simon turned back to Harrison. The room felt colder. Life felt colder without Mariah, and now, Harrison was ever the dolt for losing the only woman who had ever held his heart. He was finding it difficult to hold on to his anger. Simon knew this, as he had witnessed first-hand the damage that Samantha had wrought against him the first time around. Still, this thought did little to ease the tremendous ache in Harrison's hollowed heart. He was a simpleton, only even worse.

"You shall leave tonight. I know better than to think you would not. You will be traveling by dark, which is neither safe for you nor your beast. Consider setting out tomorrow instead? You will not be able to reach your destination until the early hours and would not be able to call upon her then. You can reach Bramley Hall by evening next, so set out on the morrow. 'Tis best to leave her alone for a day or two anyhow, old boy."

"She will not see me; I know she will not. But I aim to have her know I sought her out at once. I will camp outside of the parsonage if need be. She must see me. I have to explain everything," Harrison said animatedly.

"Poor man. You'll catch your death so she may know your sincerity," Simon mused.

"You would behave differently?" Harrison questioned him.

"I would not." Simon came toward him. "Let us get you on your way. You can stop once it gets darker and rest for the night. If you set out early again, you should reach them at a proper hour to call," Simon said, holding out his hand.

When Harrison clasped his hand in his, Simon brought his other arm around Harrison and thumped him upon his back. Harrison let out a breath.

"Blast the hour. I'm leaving immediately," he said, and strode out of the room.

After traveling into the night, stopping at the inn, and leaving before dawn, Harrison saw himself back at Bramley Hall before luncheon. He cared not what state of dress he was in, though Edmund made a fuss about it as Harrison stood before him to be dressed. Harrison only cared to see Mariah. Edmund would not let him out of doors without looking his best, though. One had to look their best when groveling.

Harrison's breeches were as black as his Hessians. His cravat was snow white; so too was his shirt. The buttons upon his shirt gleamed, and gold was the only accent Harrison liked upon his person to state his position in the world. His great coat was dark blue. The color was striking, and his ebony hair was combed to lie just right. He was in top form to plead his case to Mariah. Come quaking grounds or bursting mountains, he would see Mariah.

Harrison steered his steed, Brutus, toward the parsonage. He felt as if his shoulders carried the weight of the world. He certainly did carry much upon his frame as the Earl, but it was nothing compared to surmounting this. Harrison was never one to brood over his estate. He sought to always take notice of things that needed to be attended to. His tenants had few complaints that went without his notice. All agreed he was a very good man. But he did not feel like a good man at present.

Today, his shoulders sagged because his very great hope—the desire of his heart—

might yet be put off. He hoped that Mariah would see him. What would he do if she did not? In the light of day, he knew he could not camp out under her window; it would be absurd, and he did not wish to occasion more grief upon his beloved nor her household.

He took a moment to breathe deeply. He still felt the gaping hole that had etched itself into his soul when he had received Mariah's letter. He had known instantly that word of his behavior must have reached her ears. Alicia and Simon had been very put out to find her missing and were right to lay the blame upon him. This was his doing. His poor decisions and lack of self-control. If only he had been able to shelf his jealousy, he never would have left the ballroom. Now, he carried Simon's threat to call him out if he did not make this right, and truthfully, if he could not repair this rift, then he would gladly stand before Simon and let him run him through with his sword. Death was preferable to an existence without his one true love.

Harrison was greeted by Amy, who would not meet his eyes upon answering his insistent knocking. Harrison handed over his topper, his walking cane, and his dark cloak. The sky today was hidden behind clouds, so there was very little light in the hallway. It seemed to Harrison as if even the sun had decided to withdraw its favor from him. Harrison internally had known nothing but rain and despair since his light had decided to flee from him.

Harrison's eyes soon grew used to the dimmed light, though, as he followed Amy to the parlor door. Once he was announced, he passed through the door and scanned the room. He frowned when Mr. Morten came toward him.

Mr. Morten bowed to him and said, "Welcome, my lord. Gloomy weather we are experiencing."

Harrison nodded at him and warred within himself to find something to say. Mariah was not with them, and he hoped she was not ill. He felt slightly ill, though whether it was from his sense of loss or the fact that he had been soaked through during the endless travel home he didn't care to discover. "I wonder if we may speak privately?"

"My study awaits." Mr. Morten held his hand up toward the door. He waited for Harrison to proceed. Once Harrison exited the parlor, Mr. Morten followed and closed the door behind them.

Harrison opened the study door and let Mr. Morten pass through. He watched the older man seat himself behind his desk as he closed the door and took his own seat. Harrison began, "I do not know what you have learned. But I am here to make everything as it should be. Has Mariah talked with you?"

"She has, but I feel as if I do not know it all. Mrs. Morten spoke briefly with her earlier, and from that conversation, it was gathered that you were found in a rather delicate position with a member of the opposite sex. Is that true, Harrison? Because I can scarcely believe it," Mr. Morten stated, leaning forward in his seat.

"I have not talked with Mariah, so I do not know what she has seen, but it's more than reasonable for me to say I have an idea of what drove her from Brighton. I wish to see her so that I may relate the event to her. It is not as it seemed," Harrison assured Mr. Morten, bringing his fist to his mouth. He was almost overcome by his very great feeling of despair.

"I thought there was an explanation. I would like to hear it before you present it to my daughter. As much as I love you, dear son, I must protect her as best I can." Mr. Morten's eyes were kind but firm.

Harrison nodded and folded his hands across his middle. "I have behaved very badly indeed, though not as poorly as she may think. We were at a ball. I came across Samantha. You must remember what our past has been?"

"Ah, I see," was all the reply Mr. Morten made.

"She pressed herself against me and was insistent I kiss her. I told her I had no wish to and no wish to hurt her husband nor the one I was engaged to. She would not hear my words, and fool that I am, I did not force her to let me go. I let her hang on because I thought if I forced her to let me go, I might injure her, and I feared bruising her person as well as the explanation she might later give. So I left her as she was. She clung to me. I felt nothing for her. You cannot imagine the immense relief I had that I feel nothing for her. Because I love Mariah, I can understand that the feelings I once bore for Samantha were not true, honest, or virtuous. And these were the feelings that Samantha fought to bring back to me. Before I could react, she was kissing me, though I did not kiss her back." Harrison sighed, hanging his head in his hands and hunching over.

"And this is what my daughter came upon? Poor Mariah. Poor you as well. How unfortunate that this indiscretion was witnessed. I can say I know she will not see you this day. You have wounded her deeply. Mariah has a kind heart, a gentle spirit. I think in due time, she will come to forgive you. Are you willing to wait her out?" Mr. Morten asked, steepling his fingers together and resting his elbows upon his desk.

"I would wait forever for her. I will wait and do everything in my power to gain her trust again. I am not whole without her. You do not know how I have grieved my actions."

"Very well. I shall plead your case for you. Mariah will listen to me. But do not think this road will be easy. She has another suitor," Mr. Morten said pointedly, looking Harrison in the eyes.

Drawing his brows together, Harrison asked, "To whom do you refer?"

"Can you not guess? Did you not seek my blessing so that you could secure her away from him?"

"Major Wallis? Has he called?" Harrison sat back in his chair and took a deep breath.

"No, he has not called, though he has sent a letter in his stead." Mr. Morten regarded Harrison with a serious look. "Depend upon me to see my daughter happily situated whether it is with you or without. I should rather it be *with* you, but I will not force her."

"I understand. I still have your blessing to try to earn her again, do I not?"

"Of course. Try to find some matter to content your mind with. All will be as it should be. With Mrs. Morten constantly pressing your match, Mariah may need time. That is all you can give her now, is time," Mr. Morten replied, sitting very still.

Harrison nodded, feeling his heart bleed upon the floor. How would he win his heart back?

Chapter Thirty-Four

Deep Sorrow

Why *was he not leaving?* Mariah was all despair and nerves as she paced the floor in her bedchamber. Why was Papa not making excuses and sending Harrison upon his way? Oh, the suspense of what was happening was almost too much to bear!

Harrison was so very close, yet she could not make herself seek him out. She was half afraid that a summons would be given at any moment. Back and forth across the length of the room, she paced.

Finally, to attend to something which might occupy her mind, Mariah sat at her desk and withdrew her letter from Major Wallis. She might as well write to him. She felt he deserved a reply. Taking a deep breath, she settled a piece of the cream stationary upon her desktop and reached for her inkwell and quill.

Dear Major Wallis,

I am forever in your debt for the kind service which you have rendered me. Please be sure that I am well. Though I am far from carefree, I know I shall be all right. You honor me, sir, with your care and attention. I feel it is most unfair to you to give you false hope, yet I can perfectly remember your sentiments which you so eloquently expressed to me about this very subject. I should like to see you again, if you can manage it, as friends, for you are my very good friend. I hope you are well. I shall await word or shall visit with you soon, whichever may come to pass first.

In friendship,

Mariah

Was she too forward in signing her name simply as Mariah? She did not know. She was not satisfied with her letter. It was staid and impersonal, yet she could do no better. Sighing, she sealed the letter and waited to have it be sent out.

With the letter written she began pacing her room again. The biggest question upon Mariah's mind was when would Harrison leave? She had been hiding in her room for a solid two hours, and still, he did not take his leave! What impertinence! What glib satisfaction was he taking in keeping her hostage within her bedchamber? For she would not leave her room until he took his leave. *Oh, go away,* she thought.

Harrison's horse whinnied. Hesitantly, and with great caution so he would not see her, Mariah peeked out the window, watching him leave with great relief. She was starving, having been cooped up in her room for hours.

Mariah went down to dine with her family. They were all a very grim group, but so be it. There was nothing she could say or do to change the gloom and doom. She was not ready to hand her heart over to Harrison so that he might do with it as he pleased again. She loved him, but whether he loved her was another matter, and she feared to learn his true feelings. It had been rather difficult for him to say that he did love her in the first place in Brighton. Had she pressed him too hard so that he felt honor-bound to say such words? Mariah huffed out a sigh.

"Mariah, I would speak with you after dinner, if you please," said Mr. Morten as he took a bite of his venison pie.

Only by nodding did Mariah give her answer. She was too deep in thought to hear any of the dinner conversation around her. She removed herself from the table directly after the meal and headed to her father's study. Seeing her rise, her papa followed her there.

Settling herself into the chair before his desk opposite her father's in his study, Mariah remained in her pensive mood.

"Now, now, my child, you must hear the details of my conversation with Harrison this afternoon. Perhaps it may shift your views of him. But first, let me hear from you what has caused your change of heart where he is concerned. Tell me, without reservations, what brought you home," Mr. Morten asked, sitting patiently in his chair.

"Must I, Papa? I feel like such an idiot. A complete fool." Mariah bowed her head.

"Yes, I would have the truth, my dear." Mr. Morten ran his forefinger down his large nose.

"I came upon him with another woman in his arms, and they were engaged in a kiss. He just stood there, Papa, and held her, and I could not even bear to breathe!" Mariah sucked in a breath and steeled herself against more tears with crossed arms over her chest.

"That is not quite the whole of the matter. Yes, he was in an embrace with a lady, but it was *she* who pressed her attention upon *him*. He had previously been engaged to her, and while she now has a husband, it seems she thought it a great sport to chase after Lord Bramley. He feared harming her by extracting himself from her person, and he did not know what, mayhap, she would later say of such an indiscretion."

"That is what he told you? Who was this lady?" Mariah fur-rowed her delicate brows. For a brief moment, she feared that perhaps it was not Samantha at all as she had originally surmised.

"That I will leave the telling of to his Lordship. It concerns his past, and it is not for me to relate those things if he has not. Talk with him, Mariah. Spare yourselves this heartache. He cares very deeply for you. If only you could have seen his despair today, you would have heard his explanation."

Mariah nodded. Her papa was a sensible man and not given to flights of fancy; if he believed what Harrison had told him, Mariah knew she should allow Harrison to call upon her, no matter the damage her heart might yet suffer.

Chapter Thirty-Five

No Swords at Dawn

T he next morning, the sun was shining. It made a huge difference in the whole household. Mariah had not cried herself
to sleep, and it was something she was heartily thankful for. She
found she needed another day to gather her thoughts together
before she faced Harrison. Her whole future and happiness depended upon how she proceeded with him. It was not a light
endeavor to embark upon.

Mr. Hughley and Mrs. Hughley decided to take a walk. They
invited Mariah to accompany them. She readily did, needing some
fresh air.

The trio set out after breaking their fasts and while the air was
crisp. There was just enough sunshine to not feel the deep cold
through their clothing. Thankfully, the rain had abated. Each was
bundled up and quite ready to enjoy the autumn day. The route

they took saw them through the forest and kept them away from the lane. If Harrison was about, they should be able to avoid him altogether. While it gave Mariah a pain in her chest to not see him, it did her mind much good. She thought it considerate to have a clear head when she heard him out.

She used the fresh air to gather her thoughts. Could she forgive Harrison? If her father believed his words to be true, and she knew that her papa was a great judge of character and morals, should she lean on his understanding and trust that what Harrison had said was correct: that it was she who was being the tart and not Harrison, playing a devious game?

Mariah glanced around herself, taking in the sight of the beautiful maple leaves that were turning colors and the smell of the soil. Today, Mariah would hear Harrison out and cast her own judgement. Granted, she would take into consideration her father's words, but in the end, it was *her* decision.

The long walk had her out of doors for well over an hour, by her estimation. When she returned home, she realized it had been well over two hours. Mariah's cheeks were all pinkened from the exertion, and she felt better for the exercise. Mr. Hughley was rather winded, so he repaired with a cup of tea in the study with Mr. Morten. Mrs. Hughley and Mariah took to their bedchambers to put their hair in order and then found Mrs. Morten in the parlor.

The rest of the day was quiet. Mariah felt saddened she had missed Harrison's call, but time would be good for her heart to continue sorting through it all. Mayhap the morrow would be best. Right now, the numbness was lessening considerably.

Harrison was busy with Mr. Lyons, his steward, for the rest of Saturday. There was much to be done before the winter came. He looked over the list Mr. Lyons had completed and added a few of his own notes. He kept himself occupied in this manner for hours.

Toward nightfall, Harrison was surprised to see his butler enter into the study and announce Lord Michaelton. He stood from behind his desk and regarded the man warily.

"I hope you will excuse this intrusion. I have just left Brighton," Lord Michaelton stated, sitting down in one of the wingback chairs in front of Harrison's mahogany desk.

From his own chair, Harrison spoke. "I hope you have left Brighton with all being well?"

"Indeed. I will get right to my reason for being here, Bramley." Lord Michaelton sat forward in his chair. His hair was mussed, and his clothing was wrinkled from hours in the saddle.

Harrison gestured his consent for the man to continue with his hand.

"I know the history which you have with my wife. It was no secret that, while in Brighton, she sought out your company. I witnessed her display the night Miss Morten left, and I want to thank you." Lord Michaelton inclined his head.

"Why should you thank me?" Harrison was bemused by his words.

"I saw with my own two eyes the way in which you restrained yourself. My wife was most insistent, yet you did not court her attention. I saw you try to send her away from yourself, and I heard your words. I had wondered if, were you to face her again, you would be able to resist her charms. So I thank you for not honoring her wishes. I am sorry that your Miss Morten was a witness to my wife's terrible display. How goes it with your reconciliation?" Lord Michaelton asked, bringing his leg over his knee.

"Slow. But I am persistent. You must know that at no point did I kiss your wife back," Harrison stated, feeling the great need to clarify this point.

"I did see that as well." Lord Michaelton sighed, looking off into the fire.

"I was wondering if you would seek me out with the promise of swords at dawn. I am relieved that you mean no such thing." Harrison got up and went to his sideboard. He filled two glasses with his finest brandy and walked to Lord Michaelton, offering him one.

Lord Michaelton took the glass and saluted him. "I do not believe that, in the future, my wife will not cause me to uphold her honor. She is most unhappy with me. Try as I have, I cannot bring her joy nor contentment. Why does the ton give permission for our wives to take lovers after they produce our heirs? It's most unsettling." He took a large drink from his glass and then swirled the liquid around, watching the light play on it. Harrison frowned at the despair of his former friend. He had known Lord Michaelton for years and was relieved to hear their friendship would remain intact after this visitation. It was neither one's fault, the way Samantha had treated them.

"Do you still have feelings for Samantha?" Harrison inquired, taking his own sip. *This conversation is most bizarre to be having,* he thought to himself. *I will put the whole of the matter readily behind me once he leaves. Good graces, what a wrecked week. Lesser men than me might have given up and stuck their spoon in the wall.* He also stared into the fire, conjuring Mariah to his mind, and imagining how she would look before it, with just the two of them as a married couple. His heart constricted, praying he wasn't too late in winning his beloved back.

"I do. I tried to let them wither away, but they would not cease. It's torture to know that the one you love cannot stand you. True, she chose me, but the fact offers little comfort." He cleared this throat and began again. "I would speak with Miss Morten on your behalf, should you wish it. The actions of my wife are my own fault. Too long have I allowed her free rein, and I mean to put a stop to her machinations," Lord Michaelton stated, growing very serious.

"Though I thank you for the offer, I shall take my own actions upon myself. I was remiss in my behavior, and it is up to me alone to mend Mariah's heart," Harrison replied, sitting forward in his chair and leaning his forearms upon his desk.

"Does she truly care for you?"

"She does, or she did." Harrison frowned and stared into the amber liquid from his glass.

"It is a blessing when one's wife likes oneself, and it's a piece of heaven itself when she loves him. If you can ever hope to reclaim her affection, do all that you can, man. Women who are not after one's title or wealth are rare indeed. I wish you all the best, my friend," Lord Michaelton said, finishing his drink.

"I am sorry for your present pain. I do hope things turn to your favor." Harrison truly wished he could offer some advice which the man could benefit from. He did not relish in the knowledge that Samantha plagued him.

"I shall fare one way or another."

Lord Michaelton rose from his chair. Harrison stood as well, and the two nodded at each other. Lord Michaelton turned and left the study. Harrison took his chair again and heaved a heavy sigh. He had dodged a bullet when Samantha had jilted him. Thank the Lord for that!

Chapter Thirty-Six

Sad Farewells

C hurch would have been torture to sit through beside Harrison, so it was a reprieve that Mariah's father allowed her to stay home, though it left her open to callers. Particularly the one who stood before her now.

After Major Wallis bowed and Mariah in return curtsied, Major Wallis spoke. "I hope you are not being kept home from church because you are ill?" he asked, sitting across from her at the settee.

"I am well. I thank you again for your kindness shown to me. I would not have gotten through the ordeal without your generosity," Mariah replied, smiling at him.

"'Twas most ardently done. You have spoken with the Earl?" The Major's brown eyes showed his concern as he inquired.

"I have not." Mariah frowned. "He has called, but I have not seen him. He has instead visited with my family."

"Ah, I see. Do you wish to see him?"

"I do. If only to say goodbye, if that is how this will end between us. Harrison had related the event to my papa, who in turn told me Harrison's view. Before, I thought I would show great weakness of mind and heart when I saw him, but I have reconciled myself to a meeting. But...that is not what you wish to hear?" Mariah gave him a sad smile.

"I confess: if you should resolutely say you should never again see him, I would be the happiest of men. I said I would not press my suit, though, and I am nothing, if not a man of my word. Did you know that I am a second son? My brother has been married for nigh ten years, and his union has produced no heirs. He has given up hope. It may come to pass that myself or my own son shall inherit an earldom. So you see, I may not be wholly without prospects." He rose and walked to the fire, his back to her.

"Oh, Major Wallis. Do not think a change such as one in your circumstances would change my opinion of you. You are worthy of my highest regard whatever your name or connections. I hope you do not believe me to be only seeking a title?" Mariah said, with a little distress in her voice.

"I have never thought that your preference for the Earl of Bramley to be situated because of his title. Perhaps I misspoke." The Major turned around and looked at her. "I only intended to arrive and ask after your health. You must think me the biggest cad."

Mariah could feel his eyes burning a hole straight through her person. She was at a loss as to how to proceed from here. "Major Wallis..."

He interrupted her. "Can you address me as George?"

"Very well. George, you must know that I like you very much. You are all that is honorable and good."

George broke in again, "But I hold no interest for you." He smiled sadly and came to sit beside her.

"You hold my sincerest friendship. I wish you with all of heart, contentment, and happiness," Mariah told him. She tried to smile but failed.

George took her hand in his and said, "You must know that I only came to see for myself that you are well. I came here with the purest intentions. Will you only consider myself as an alternative to him? I know it is the way of elegant females to refuse a man at first presentation, though I know you would never act in that manner. If you tell me all hope is gone, I shall remove myself at once."

The look he gave her tugged at her heart. Mariah wondered at that feeling and waited for the feeling of guilt to overtake it. Taking a moment to pause and reflect upon her feelings, she was surprised that she did not feel guilt in considering him. That caused her to frown, and George replaced her hand to her lap.

"I could make you very happy; I know I could. But if you love him still, we shall never be content. My watching you mourn for a man that you could have had will not content me. You are too good-hearted to marry me and long for another, so a marriage then would not be prudent. I think about you when we are separate, and I do not see things as they are; I see them as I wish them to be." He chuckled at himself and looked down at his boots.

"I wish I could say yes to you, for there are not many men like you. You are a treasure, and I wish I could call you my own. Some woman will make you an excellent wife, and I shall be happy for her and you as well. If I cannot wed Harrison, I should not marry anyone, at least not until I can mend my heart. What use would I be to you if I cannot give the whole of my heart away? I would not see you miserable for my entire world. I know asking for friendship is much too cruel a thing to do. But I have deep affection for you, as my dearest friend, George." Mariah began crying and could not say another word.

George came before her on his knees. He kept his hands at his sides but withdrew his handkerchief from his pocket and presented it to her. She accepted it. "I would not see you shed a single tear over me. I am a blaggard for making you weep." He smiled and had tears in his own eyes which had yet to spill.

Reaching to clasp his hands in hers, Mariah smiled at him through her tears. She wished she could love him with all of her heart, but her heart belonged to Harrison. It would be unfair and cruel to love him instead. What she had to do was listen to Harrison before making her decision. It was only fair to the Earl.

"I shall take my leave, fair Mariah," George said as he rose, drawing her up before him. Mariah reached up and kissed him upon his cheek. She still had tears, but they were no longer rushing down her face. He took her hand and kissed the back of it.

"I shall walk with you to your horse," Mariah said, leading him from the parlor.

They walked in silence to the front door and to the tree he had tied his mount to. He followed her the whole way. She offered his handkerchief back to him, but he stayed her hand. He smiled sadly down at her.

Mariah watched him place himself into his saddle and tip his hat at her. She waved at him as he started moving his horse. He did not look back at her but kept his gaze forward. Mariah watched him for a few moments; then her tears gained momentum again. How could she treat such an honorable man in this way? She felt a little bitter part of her heart start to wish she'd never met the Earl, and though the thought was impossible in every way, it gave her comfort.

Mariah continued to watch George ride away and then heard a sneeze. Turning, she saw that her uncle, aunt, mother and father all stood next to Harrison. Surely, they must have been witnesses to George's departure. Mariah stood rooted to the spot even though she had told herself that she would talk with Harrison when next she saw him. She found now that her spirit could not undertake the task.

She met Harrison's eyes with her own through watery vision. He started to come toward her when, suddenly, she threw up her arms, and he halted immediately. Mariah shook her head at him and ran into the parsonage.

Inside her bedchamber, Mariah heaved heavy sobs, and neither her mama nor her aunt could calm her. She cried so much, Mrs. Morten was certain she would do permanent damage to herself. Mrs. Morten threatened to call the doctor to attend to Mariah, but even the threat, idle as it was, did not make her stop.

Mariah was trying in vain to stop her tears. She could not breathe; her corset was restricting her lungs. She felt that if she were to faint, she would at least find peace in her heart. She would welcome the darkness.

When she had seen Harrison before her, the last thing she had wanted to do was to take comfort from him. How odd it was, but it was the truth. Had he not kissed that vile woman, she would not have been so reliant upon George. It was Harrison's own doing that had once again sprung the hope in George's heart that he might yet claim Mariah's hand, yet she refused him a third time; her heart still tenaciously leaned toward Harrison. She hated her heart and herself for those emotions.

So much did Mariah weep that it was not until she was exhausted and fell into a deep sleep that her tears ceased.

Chapter Thirty-Seven

This Ends Now

Monday was another gloomy day, as was the day prior. The sun could not seem to peek its way beyond the clouds. It matched Mariah's dour mood, though not as much as yesterday had.

After finishing her hot chocolate, sausages, and peaches from the tray that she used as she reclined within her bed, she took a bath. The bath did her a world of good, and she soaked in the warm water. Mariah leaned her head back against the tub and sighed. Somehow, the water had made her mind go blissfully blank. Instead of her heart aching terribly, it now became warm and numbed by the water.

She cleaned her face clear of tear stains and their track marks upon her cheeks. Mariah put a warm cloth over her face to soothe her taut skin. Yesterday was the cry she had not realized she'd needed, yet at the same time, today, it made her feel a little better to get it all out.

Mariah sighed, staring out the lead, glass-paned window. A breeze tousled the treetops and removed the turning leaves with it.

Out of doors matches the turbulence in my heart, she surmised. *Just when I think the wind will tamper, just like my heart, a new torrent rips through and causes me great pain.* She scrubbed her arms and legs, pursing her lips as she did so. *But I needed yesterday to cry and get it all out. For so long, I let the shock rule my heart, and so I had not allowed myself to grieve properly. Now that my cry is done, I believe I can see the Earl of Bramley and hear him out. It is the least kindness I can bestow upon him.*

Finished now, Mariah stepped out of the tub and dried herself off. She slipped into a plain gown of blue, hoping that the complementary dress would bring color back to her skin and life to her eyes. Mariah let Amy arrange her hair atop her head. The curls cascaded down her neck and tickled her shoulders. She made her way to the parlor where her aunt and mama were busy sewing. She sat in a chair near the fire and said not a word. Being out of her bedchamber was a huge celebration nonetheless.

The clock struck ten and chimed, and Mariah almost missed the sound of horse's hooves pounding upon the lane. She moved to the window and was just looking out when Harrison caught sight of her. She quickly drew away from the window and clutched her chest. Panic seemed to be her chief feeling.

When she heard the rap upon the door, she fled from the parlor. All bravado to hear him out fled again. She just couldn't.

As she was rushing up the stairs to the safety of her bedchamber, Harrison came through the front door. It seemed, inevitably, that each time she saw him, she couldn't help but picture the other woman in his arms and become sick.

Harrison watched her flee from himself and stopped his stride at once. The color leached from his face. His heart was close to dropping from his chest, and it seemed to be lying dead upon his own feet. The actions he had permitted of another had destroyed his lady's fair heart. Harrison collected himself and allowed Mr. Trawley to announce him to the ladies of the parlor.

After exchanging greetings, all sat. As soon as Harrison sat and looked at Mrs. Morten's and Mrs. Hughley's distraught gazes, he abruptly rose again and said, "Forgive me." He then walked from the parlor and out into the lane. He stood looking at his horse and then at the window he knew was Mariah's. His heart pounded, aching in his chest.

If she would only speak with me, just once, then we could go our separate ways if we must.

The clouds gave way, and great big raindrops fell upon him. Harrison stood there in the rain, not moving. He was torn between returning to his home and barging back into the parsonage, demanding Mariah see him. He fumed as the cold rain pelted him. He saw movement from her window and knew she was watching him.

In a moment, his mind was made up. He walked the short distance to her window. He called her name. A few seconds passed, and he heard no return call. He grabbed ahold of the ivy that clung to the side of the parsonage and gave it a great tug, thinking it might just hold his weight. He pulled himself up and found footholds in the grooves of the stones made on the wall. He looked up at his destination and kept blinking as the rain continued to fall onto his face and into his eyes. Since he only needed to climb to the second story, his work was quickly accomplished.

Harrison looked into her bedchamber and rapped upon the window. Her desk was below her window, and he frowned. He would have to wait for her to move her items before he might enter.

He spied Mariah upon her bed with arms crossed over her chest. Her eyes grew large, but she made no movement. Suddenly, she was up, shoving papers into her desk. He clung on tenaciously for her to finish. Upon shutting the desk's door, Mariah threw the window's lock and opened it for him.

Harrison pulled it further open, and hope and love flooded his heart. He motioned for Mariah to stand back. She backed herself a few feet away from her desk and watched as he entered her room. Harrison brought his legs in to rest upon her desk, then hauled his frame in as well. He slid from her desk and smiled at her lopsidedly. His hair fell onto his forehead and dripped into his teal eyes.

Mariah handed him a blanket, keeping several steps' distance between them. Her eyes looked anywhere but him.

"Open your door and call for your mama, your aunt—anyone," Harrison directed her with desperation in his voice.

Nodding, Mariah went to her door and opened it. "Mama? Papa? Aunt? Uncle? Is there anyone who may come up the stairs at once?"

It panged his heart to see her keeping her distance from him, but given what had transpired between them and the intimacy of the entire situation, he understood it perfectly. Her eyes shone brightly, whether from more tears ready to brim and burst forth or from the deep ache in her heart he knew not.

"I would speak with you. Please, please, dearest, darling Mariah, do not send me away. I have been in woeful agony since I discovered your leaving Brighton." Harrison stood before her with hope and love burning from his eyes.

"What is happening here?" inquired Mr. Morten as he adjusted his spectacles. Mrs. Morten gasped, her eyes going from anger to confusion.

Finally, Mariah's aunt and uncle stood in the doorway too with surprised glances. Mr. Hughley turned around, leading his wife away from the scene.

"Forgive me. I am not myself. I have not been myself..." Harrison addressed Mr. Morten.

"Yes, yes. Well, my boy, say what you came to say." Mr. Morten gestured toward Mariah.

Harrison watched Mariah shift uncomfortably. The blue dress she wore complemented her alluring eyes and her softened complexion. His mouth went dry, and for a moment, he forgot how to speak. With a quick shake of his head, his eyes pleadingly met Mariah's.

"I have longed to see you and speak to you, yet I wonder if I may ever earn your respect again. I love you still, and I shall always. I felt as if my heart had been torn asunder when your absence was discovered. You cannot know how I have hated myself since." Harrison stopped to look deeply into Mariah's eyes.

They were wide—fearful, even. He had torn her heart apart, and he wondered if he had the love and strength to piece it back together or whether she would permit the actions. He would spend his lifetime making her happy if she allowed him to.

"I rode through the rain all night. I would ride through worse if only I could see you smiling at me and giving me hope that what I have done can be forgiven." Harrison took a small step toward her and sneezed. He pulled his handkerchief from his pocket but found it to be dripping, so he restuffed it away.

"Perhaps it would be well done, should you relate the whole of the situation to Mariah and inform her as to who you were with at the ball." Mr. Morten offered Harrison his handkerchief, coming forward with it.

"Thank you," Harrison said, both to the advice and for the handkerchief. His head was aching, and he shivered. Well, he had gone and gotten himself a cold, and it was wholly deserved.

"You came upon a most unfortunate scene, and I was an idiot to not have put a stop to it. The woman I was with was Lady Samantha Michaelton, the woman of whom we have partially spoken about before. Samantha sought to take up her and my former relationship despite my continued refusal of her. Do you remember a few years ago when I returned from Town and would see no one?" he frowned, waiting for Mariah to speak. She nodded and closed her eyes. She furrowed her delicate brows and tilted her head to the side before opening her eyes again. Watching the action made his heart momentarily stop.

"I was to be married to her, and in truth, I thought I would never find love again. Samantha jilted me, and with Lord Michaelton, and at the time, I was distraught. I thought I had lost the most wonderful woman, and I did not know how or if I should ever recover from the heartbreak. I had long been a fool, as I now have come to understand." Harrison paused, sneezing into the handkerchief. Mariah made a move toward him but caught herself.

Seeing her motions, Harrison continued. "I have only ever loved one woman. I never knew love until she looked into my eyes. I thought I loved Samantha, but what I felt for her pales in any comparison with you, Mariah. I think my pride suffered where Samantha was concerned. I never loved her; it was always you. It always has been and always will be, my dearest, sweetest, loveliest Mariah."

Tears coursed down her cheeks. She crossed her arms over herself, taking a step back from him.

"Do not cry, my love, not anymore. I cannot bear to see your tears fall." Harrison's voice grew low and grave.

"You love me? But I found you locked within her arms, and you were kissing her. How can this be if you hold no affection for her?" Mariah sniffed with bitterness in her voice, swiping at her cheeks.

"I did try to disengage her from my person. She kept holding on, and I feared to leave bruises upon her. Do you remember when Alicia mentioned my acquaintance with Samantha the night I dined with all of you here?" Harrison cleared his throat. She nodded at him.

"Simon had said he would do his best to encourage Alicia to keep her away while we stayed with them. I expressed the stupid thought that it would do me good to face her and know I felt nothing for her. So come she did, though *not* on my personal request. That night at the ball, after many a man had requested a dance with you, I had paced the room to cool my hot-blooded anger from tearing each man asunder in my jealousy, and there, Samantha found me; there, I adamantly refused her. I was right in my thinking that I would feel nothing for her, but she was not content with such feelings.

"She came upon me at the ball when I sought to take some air. I am grieved you witnessed my folly. I let her kiss me, but nothing came from the kiss. It served to show that I felt nothing for her, that she could not invoke anything in me. She is a prideful woman, and now, I know she will never attempt to trap me again. You were not the only person who witnessed it. Lord Michaelton saw it as well," Harrison explained, then blew his nose loudly. Mariah gasped at the news. "He came here to see me. He is a sad man in that he does still love his wife while she does not seem to return his regards."

"Did he call you out?" Mariah inquired, worrying her bottom lip between her teeth.

"No, he came to thank me for not engaging his wife in an in-discretion. He witnessed my rigid posture and heard my constant refusals. He knew I had no plans for her. Lord Michaelton even offered to speak with you on my behalf, and I refused. I alone had to do this. Dear Mariah, my future is for you alone. I will do anything to please you. You are my heart. You have it entirely. Only say that we may begin to repair what is between us," Harrison asked, closing the distance between them and taking her hands in his.

Mariah's brows furrowed as she gazed at her hands tucked in his. "I have more questions. I do love you, but I need to feel secure in that love."

"I will give you all of my time to ensure that you know me and my heart is and always will be yours." Harrison sneezed again, and this one shook his whole body. He let her hands go, and he groped the chair for support.

"I know you will." Mariah smiled at him. Then she looked at her papa. "Can we make Simon's bedchamber ready for his Lordship? He needs a change of clothes from the wardrobe, and tea, I think, would be good for him as well. 'Twould not do to send him out in the rain again."

Mrs. Morten answered, "At once," then left the room to do just that.

Turning back to Harrison, her eyes pensive yet thoughtful, Mariah continued, "I cannot spend time with you in your house, as you are with a cold now, so I shall keep you here where I can watch over you." Mariah took her hand and pressed the back of it to Harrison's forehead. Harrison closed his eyes as this bit of heaven floated before him. He felt Mariah kiss his hand, and he wondered if his fever could rise any more. He was burning up and knew that some of the cause was an illness, but he also knew that some of it was because his love had touched him and allowed him to touch her.

Harrison would gladly lay ill at her feet if only she would shower affection upon him. Her cold hands felt wonderful against his feverish flesh. His heart found heaven in her love.

Chapter Thirty-Eight

Love at Last

Mariah barely left the sickroom. They had installed Harrison in Simon's old room. Mariah had constant companions, never left alone with Harrison. Amy would take a turn, as would Mrs. Hughley and Mrs. Morten. Even Mr. Morten sat beside Harrison's bedside with Mariah sometimes. It was Harrison's valet, Edmund, who really helped with his care, though.

Dr. Abrams was called, as they really feared for Harrison's health. His fever was high, but he had not given into delirium yet. Dr. Abrams decided it was not a good idea to bleed him, so that option was cast aside to much relief of the residents of the manor. Leeches were such vulgar creatures.

The doctor thought his ailment stemmed from the fever and an acute cold; therefore, bleeding him would not let a blood infection out and was useless. However, if Harrison did not improve within three days, the doctor said that bleeding out would be the only way in which to proceed with treatment.

Harrison slept a great deal, and it gave Mariah ample time to consider her heart. She still had some reservations about their match and meant to have answers once he was well again. And upon receiving those answers, she would then be able to determine her course of action, whether it was to continue on and marry the Earl of Bramley or call back Major Wallis to encourage their friendship.

Mariah watched Harrison sleep, putting another cool cloth to his head. Her mind constantly reflected upon his words of rebuke toward Lady Michaelton, though they did not ease the ache in her heart of what he had done.

On the morning of the third day, before Dr. Abrams came to see him, his fever broke. Mariah held great anxiety as she watched over Harrison, though once his fever was extinguished, he really looked much better. He was able to take nourishment, and Mariah fed him and helped him to drink. She mopped his forehead and neck all through his sickness with a cool cloth. She loved touching him and knew that when he looked at her even through fevered eyes, he enjoyed her caresses.

"Well, your fever has left," Dr. Abrams said as he examined Harrison. "You should be up and about in no time. But I caution you to not tire yourself overmuch. You still need rest." He sat on the edge of the bed.

"I shall do as I am told. I do not wish to anger my future wife," Harrison replied, smiling at Mariah.

"Excellent. I shall come again this evening. Mrs. Watkins is near her time to deliver, so I expect to be busy with welcoming her new babe." Dr. Abrams stroked his clean-shaven face. He was a man of three and fifty, but he was very competent in his care. He was reed thin, but he seemed, even at his advanced age, to be constantly in motion. He liked to be busy and useful, and the residents of Bramley counted themselves very blessed to have him amongst them.

"Please send our well wishes to Mrs. Watkins. I shall call upon her in a few days. I thank you, Dr. Abrams, for your very good care of our dear Earl," Mariah added, rising from her chair to lead the doctor to the door.

"Yes, yes. Good day my lord; Miss Morten," Dr. Abrams said as he bowed before them and grabbed his medical bag. He turned and left the room.

Amy sat in the corner by the window and sewed.

"You heard the doctor," Mariah said, tucking Harrison into bed. "Rest. I shall be in the parlor for a few moments."

"I shall do as I am bidden, my lady," Harrison said, turning on his side.

Mariah halted the wan smile that came to her face. With Harrison on the mend, they would have to speak soon, and she had more questions burning in her mind to ask. She left his room, going down to the parlor for a rest and some tea. She sat on the settee, making herself a cup.

"Well, I for one am glad he is on the mend, for now we shall be able to begin the wedding preparations." Mrs. Morten nodded her head.

"Mama, please. I have not settled everything yet, and I cannot take part in preparing for a wedding when it may be futile," Mariah said over a cup of tea.

"Pah! Oh, you *will* marry him, my dear! He climbed into your window, and we do not know who was around to see him. You will have each other! Or Mr. Morten will scold you both unmercifully, and I shall not see you again until you wed the Earl!" Mrs. Morten huffed.

"Mama!" Mariah exclaimed.

"I will keep my word," Mrs. Morten rebutted.

Knowing it was useless to argue her point, Mariah took a sip of her tea. She wanted to marry Harrison, but did no one understand that she had to converse with him first? She needed assurance that a marriage between them would not lead them to despise each other. She doubted whether she could ever despise him, but he was a man, so he may well come to regret his choice of bride and take another.

"I feel sure that once they are able to discuss their future, all will be set to rights. Worry not, my dear." Mr. Morten smiled.

Amy came into the parlor with a note from Harrison. He had bathed and was situated back in bed with fresh clothes and sheets. Mariah left with Amy in tow, surmising that if Harrison felt good enough to bathe, then she would have her questions answered now too. Her answer about whether to continue their engagement or not was dependent upon his responses.

"May we talk? Are you feeling well enough?" Mariah asked, studying Harrison with concern.

"I should like to discuss whatever pleases you," Harrison replied.

Whether he gave any indication of knowing what she wanted to discuss or not she didn't know. She felt secure, having his undivided attention.

Glancing over at Amy who sat in the corner sewing, Mariah lowered her voice. "I should love nothing more than to be your wife. I have discovered I could never find contentment, should you choose to find affection with another. I can bear many things, my lord, but having you seek out a mistress, I could not overlook it. I am aware I am only a woman and have no right to dictate my wishes to you, but please know a marriage that is not of shared thought in this matter will only serve to cause grief later." Mariah looked at him but ended up with her gaze upon her folded hands in her lap. She was mortified to have brought up this topic, yet how could she continue to gift him with her heart if she could not have assurances he would reciprocate?

"Mariah, look upon me now, please?" pleaded Harrison. Mariah looked up at Harrison and waited for him to continue. She felt as if her whole world hung upon his next words.

"Be safe and secure in this matter. I want no other but you. You are my heart's desire. I should like to build my memories with you. I promise you, no other will ever find my favor. It is you and you alone I will spend my days and nights loving," Harrison assured her, reaching for her face and cupping her cheek. "I shall spend every moment I have proving my affection to you. Everything I do will be to prove myself worthy of you, for you alone have given me the greatest of gifts. You have made me feel truly loved at last." He looked at her face, willing her to believe his words and to see into his heart and mind, for nothing he had ever done or would ever undertake was as monumentally important as this moment between them.

Mariah searched his face and smiled. She believed him, heaven help her, but she believed him, with the whole of her heart. It was the assurance she needed to see in his eyes that went beyond the suffering they both had endured. Her father had once called her a strong judge of character, and she believed it now. And if her father believed in Harrison too, then she could also take peace in his assurances.

"I feel foolish for even having doubted you, but I had to know that you were all mine. Our talk in Brighton and my confessions of difficulty regarding Samantha made the sting of rejection all the harder to bear. I could not bear to share you." Mariah leaned toward him, and their foreheads rested against each other.

"You never need share me. I am yours; every last bit of me is yours, my sweetheart. I cannot state how deeply apologetic I am for causing this separation between us." Harrison brought his head away from hers and brought his lips to hers.

It was a chaste kiss, as Amy was in the room, and while Mariah knew Harrison longed to deepen the kiss, as did she, he was sensible about propriety.

Mariah held on to his hand, and neither spoke a word for a quarter of an hour, for they were happy merely to be near each other.

It was Mrs. Hughley who came into the room and separated them. She came toward the bed to hold out a letter to Mariah. Puzzled, Mariah took the envelope and drew her elegant brows together.

The letter was from George, or should she not continue to address him as such? Mariah chewed upon her bottom lip, thinking upon the matter. Then she smiled at Harrison and walked toward the window so that she might read. Breaking the red wax seal, Mariah unfolded the letter.

My dear Mariah,

I know we did not part on the best of terms. I confess I was upset at our parting. I was not a gentleman, and I beg for your forgiveness. No matter your choice, it is my deepest wish

that we shall remain friends, but I bow to your wishes in this affair. I long for a letter telling me how you are faring.

I shall now share my news. My elder brother has departed the earth for a better place. It seems I am to inherit the title, and I can scarce believe it. I have left the regiment with the well wishes and sorrows of Lord Purcellville. I write this as I am awaiting a meal at an inn. I could not travel any farther away from you without wishing you well. I hope that when we meet again, it will still be as friends.

Yours as ever,

George

Mariah smiled at the letter sorrowfully. Her heart was aching for George and the loss of his brother. How he must shoulder the weight of a position he was not born to. She rather shared that burden with him—their being neither born nor bred for their impending positions.

"What was the news in your letter?" inquired Harrison.

Mariah smiled brightly at Harrison and then came back to her chair beside his bed. "It was from a friend. He has lost his elder brother and is traveling to say his goodbyes."

"Which friend is he?" Harrison raised his eyebrows.

Smiling with a small laugh, Mariah spoke, "'Tis George. He writes me sheets and sheets as to his devotion for me," she teased Harrison. Then she frowned and very seriously said, "I do not recall ever having received sheets from you."

Harrison growled from the bed. "That is because I prefer to shower you with praise in person. I do not hide behind stationery and prose." Harrison pouted, folding his arms across his chest and frowning.

Laughing again, Mariah leaned toward him and kissed his cheek. "I suppose that it is better to have you here in person. One cannot gaze lovingly at a letter, as one's relations would think they were mad."

"*Humpfft.*" Harrison nodded at her.

"I only tease. I refused him most adamantly. I made my intentions to be friends clear from the beginning, as you well know," Mariah said, a smirk hiding upon her lips. "So, what does one have to do to obtain praise?"

Harrison rolled his eyes, and Mariah laughed.

Epilogue

T he wedding was the most joyous occasion that could be recalled by anyone for quite some time. The flowers chosen
came from the hothouse. Roses and lilies gave the parish the scent
of spring on the frigid winter's day.

No expense was spared, and everyone agreed that the dress
Mariah wore was stunning—she looked like a princess. None could
say she lacked enough satin, lace, or roses in her hair, which was
curled high upon the crown of her head. Mr. Morten cried as
much as was proper, and Mrs. Morten smiled and gave her new
son-in-law much praise as was due an earl.

All attended the wedding who had received an invitation. No
one dared to miss the exciting event. Major Wallis came. He truly
wished much happiness to the bride and groom. Lord and Lady
Purcellville were exalted in the presence of the best of society
within the ton. Simon, who was accustomed to much smiling
anyway, could not be seen without much joviality. Long had he
predicted such a day as this! Alicia wore a very pretty brown

muslin gown, and the comb which the couple had gifted her while they were in Brighton made its appearance upon her locks. Even Harrison's uncle and aunt were in attendance with their offspring. Since it was late November, they were to extend their stay at Bramley Hall to help in the celebrations of Twelfth Night.

The wedding breakfast was held at Bramley Hall, and everyone was invited to attend. It was quite a feast, and the first of many to be held. Bramley Hall would no longer resemble a tomb. Harrison would not hear of anyone not staying there with himself and his new bride. He loved that so many were able to witness his greatest joy.

With everyone now returned to their homes or abed, Harrison stood on the balcony with Mariah enfolded within his arms. Harrison sighed. Yes, he was a very blessed man. All he could wish for was before him. He had his bride locked within his arms, and all in his world was as it should be. Soon, he would hold her in his bed, and there would be none of that "sleeping in separate beds" nonsense some of his peers seemed to prefer. He meant to never spend his nights without his beloved again.

Turning in his embrace, Mariah stood on tippy-toes and kissed him.

Sighing—which Mariah was given to do very regularly these days—she said, "Now, I am yours. Forever. I do hope you will not regret me, my lord. I shall never tire of you. All that I am is yours now." Mariah smiled with full sincerity up at him.

Harrison snuggled his nose into her neck and deeply breathed her scent in. She was his forever. Tonight, he was blessed to have so much beauty before him. He drew his wife back into their bedchamber where he became even more enamored of her.

Bonus Content

Alicia's Point of View

A licia was startled awake from her nap by the ardent attentions of her husband. Simon was kissing her ear which
caused a giggle to escape her at the warm sensations of his
breath against her skin. My, how married life was so much fun!
She had yet to tire of Simon's kisses and all the intimacies a
married couple enjoyed together.

"You must awaken if you are to be presentable to the Earl.
You shall pout later if your hair is not perfectly arranged, my
love." Simon sat on the edge of the canopied bed.

"I never pout, rather that is your lot when things do not go
as you wish!" She climbed out from under the coverlet and sat
next to her husband.

Simon raised her hand to his lips and pressed a delicate kiss
upon it. "What an absurd notion you have of me. I never pout."

"Did you not pout this morning at the inn when your tea was cold?" She smiled sweetly up at him.

"I was not pouting. I was tossed into a dismal malady when I thought to present that cold offering to my new wife. My discomfort was all born for you, my dearest wife." Simon returned with his most charming smile.

"Is that so? Well if I remember correctly, it was your fault if the tea was cold." Alicia turned her head away from him to hide her smile.

"Hmmmmmm, I suppose it was," Simon recalled.

"Now will you please call your family maid to help me dress? I shall want to look my best for you. We could not have you ashamed of me when your titled friend arrives." Rising, she pulled her dressing gown around her shoulders and walked toward the wall mirror.

"As if I could ever be ashamed of you. You are all that delights me. I will ring the maid and leave you to your preparations. Only promise me one thing?" Simon gave her a look that very much resembled one of her father's best hound's litter of puppies.

"Anything you wish," replied Alicia, turning from the mirror to look at her spouse.

"Wear the pale green gown? I don't know the reason, but it seems to hang rather nicely upon your figure." He smiled again, this time winking at her.

"If you insist, though to be honest, I had rather chosen the brown with the lace. I will need the maid quickly then in order to press the green, so please make haste in your errand." She turned back toward the mirror and heard him close the door behind him.

Alicia smiled broadly as she waited patiently for the maid to arrive.

Bonus Content

Mariah's Return

Mrs. Morten gingerly rose from her bed. She felt slightly better and was eager to be gone from her bedchamber. Mr. Morten was well again; he never seemed to stay ill for long, which was such a blessing for him. Mayhap she got his share of sickness as he rarely was ever ill. Rarely had she ever seen her husband out of sorts, either. He was a man of even temperament. She was more than thankful that he was never harsh with her. There were times when she felt she had expressed herself too strongly on some matter and, though he was not pleased, he never scolded her.

Pulling her dressing gown tightly against her and tying the sash, she peered out her window. The hour was late and Mr. Morten had not yet come to bed, but that was his way some-times...to retire late. They certainly did not need the rain that was pouring from the heavens in bucketfuls. She heard the drip drop of its presence in a pot by her bed. They would need to repair that patch of roof immediately. Such a pity that things were always and forever falling apart. Dear Harrison, he was so attentive to the needs of his residents. They all depended upon him so, and their needs were never neglected.

What was that noise? Why, 'twas close to midnight and she could distinctly hear the rattle of a coach. *Oh dear*, she thought, with the palms of her hands resting upon each cheek. *Are we to be murdered in our beds? Were some midnight bandits come to call?*

Mrs. Morten quietly tiptoed down the stairs and met her husband as he came out of his study.

"There are callers at this hour, my dear Mr. Morten! Could they mean to do us harm? Steal what little we have?" Mrs. Morten looked at him with horrified eyes.

"In a carriage, with it making such a noise, no, I think not my dear. Persons usually do not attempt to get away with their ill-gotten gain in a carriage when a horse and rider can so easily and effectively halt them. Have no fear Mrs. Morten, we are very blessed." Mr. Morten was still dressed and he ran his hands over his brown breeches.

They stood still waiting to see if the rumble upon the road would cease. Mrs. Morten thought of her mother's locket with much dread and anxiety. She couldn't bare to lose such a treasure.

The coach did halt just before the gate that led to their door. What surprise and wonder this brought to the parsonage.

At the sound of the racket, Mr. Trawley, their manservant, came blinking and stumbling toward them.

Mr. Morten was at the door and peering out when he spied his own Mariah alighting from the carriage. She was followed by the maid and his wife's sister and husband. The party was hurrying toward the door and he was anxious that they should come inside to escape the raindrops.

Bonus Content

Harrison & Edmund Travelling

Dawn had come and still Harry and Edmund rode forth. They were sore from the saddle and absolutely soaked. The rain had changed from downpour to drizzle, but that made little difference to their dishevelment. Ignoring their shivers, they pressed on. Harry thought a fever was the least he deserved, but certainly winced at the thought of becoming delirious. He needed his wits intact so that he may repair the breach of trust that his actions had brought about. They had seen no sign of trouble and knew that, by now, the carriage containing his precious cargo was safely home. They had inquired at the inn to see whether the carriage had stopped for the night, but it had only stopped for a quick respite and to change horses. So on they rode.

When Harry finally caught sight of the lane which led to Bramley Hall and the parsonage was located upon, he allowed himself to feel some measure of relief. Soon, he would begin to make amends. Mariah had to see him, she simply had to.

They rode to his stable and as Harry climbed down from his saddle, his legs almost buckled; he had to hang onto the pommel to let the blood flow through his numb limbs. His head groom, Toby, looked at him with growing concern, but Harry could not address him. He took a step and knew that walking to the Hall would be difficult as exhaustion threatened to pull him under its punishing force. He began the walk, looking at nothing in particular. His estate meant nothing to him if he could not have Mariah.

Harry nearly fell asleep in the bath, but urged himself to continue his bathing. He needed to sleep and gave instructions that he should not be disturbed. He needed to sleep to ward off the cold that was threatening. He hoped his man, Edmund, would be able to stave off any illness as well. It would not do him very much credit to send his valet to Heaven's Gates.

Love Lingers on for Lord Michaelton

L ord Michaelton's estimation of the Earl of Bramley rose to a higher degree. He had sat in his wingback chair, watching the exchange between his wife and her former beau. He saw all the machinations his wife tried to use upon the man, from the flaunting of her eyelashes to the casual leaning forward to expose her full breasts, but the man would not be baited. The Earl just sat with a slight curve of his lips and a loathing in his eyes while he let her run through her practiced exercises. No matter. The Earl of Bramley rebuffed the woman's words, and Lord Michaelton felt a great debt owed to the man.

Samantha was a handful and had daily proven that fact. Lord Michaelton knew she would make his life interesting when he offered for her, he just had not given her enough credit for how entertaining she could be. Despite all of her many flaws, and he had categorized each and every one, he still loved her deeply. He suspected she still bore love for him somewhere within that frozen heart of hers.

How they had gotten to the place where they hardly conversed, or enjoyed each other, he did not know. Samantha had quite a wicked tongue, and could dress a man down quicker than the matrons of Almack's. He had failed her though; he had failed them both and the worst part was he did not know how to win her back. He had never been rebuffed and neglected by a female before and did not know where to turn. He needed to rein his wife in and show her who was the leader in their marriage, or so his mistress had said.

Ahhh, Mrs. Haversham, his mistress, knew how to treat him. He had never thought he would be a man who sought out affection from another once wed, but yet there he was, upon her doorstep a few months ago. Mrs. Haversham had taken one look at him and not refused her services. But even though he could rely upon her ample charms to soothe him, he still missed his wife.

Samantha could be an entertaining companion; from her humorous wit to her adventurous side in wanting to run through the cold ocean waters. It pained him to watch her employ her claws upon him so viciously. She was merciless in her words. She would become so incensed that she would use her fists upon him and what else could a gentleman do but quietly allow her abuse? He could never bring himself to strike his own wife.

He knew they could not go on in this manner for too much longer. He was a man and a member of the realm; he would not play the fool happily while his wife sought out lovers. Nor would he relish the idea of calling out his friends.

How to woo her back? What would secure her affections again? So deep in thought did Lord Michaelton employ himself that he was surprised at the lateness of the hour.

It was time to retire to his residence and take his wife away with him. He rose and went over to her chair and held his hand out for her to take. Rise she did, but with daggers in her eyes for him alone. It hurt. She knew it would, but still she kept her frosty gaze upon him the whole of the carriage ride home.

"I love you," he whispered quietly to her.

He still loved her. He always would. Samantha snorted, shaking her head, and stared at the closed velvet curtain covering the carriage window.

He followed her into their house and up the stairs. Mrs. Haversham was in London and that was too far for him to ride to seek any comfort tonight. It was time for his wife to act like a wife and there was no time like the present. He would take her in hand tonight and put a stop to this endless torture.

Love That Lasts

Chapter One

Excuse Me, What?

S pring was preparing to pay a call upon the town of Hathwell. The snow was melting, making a muddy mess upon the fields and roads. Birds and animals were beginning to explore the newness of the earth. But within Hathwell House, the earl was in despairing spirits and in mourning for those he had lost to either death or another. It had been a harrowing year for the man, with many changes both monumental and minuscule.

George Wallis, the Fifth Earl of Hathwell, raked his fingers through his mop of chocolate brown hair. Outside the lead-framed windows of his study was a dreary world in which love and family did not exist. He was all alone now - no parents, nor siblings, not even a lovely wife. The world lacked all color, despite the sun shining brightly at midday over his vast estate.

He thought he had found the vivacity of life in the accompaniment of Miss Mariah Morten. She was a lovely creature, articulate, adventurous yet kindly. Alas, she was in love with another and married him a few months ago in a lovely wedding just before Twelfth Night.

And the world is colder still, he mused, pushing the stubborn hair from his face. He had accepted the invitation to their nuptials, wanting to show his happiness for the couple and with the intention of putting it all behind himself. Then why did his heart and mind still fixate upon the loss?

He pressed a tired hand to his head, sighing heavily. It felt like years, though it was only a few months ago, he lost his dear older brother Robert to a wasting sickness. Prior to that, his poor brother had lost his wife to childbirth, where not even the babe survived. In the muddled twist of it all, George became the Fifth Earl of Hathwell.

He was not prepared for this role and truthfully did not desire it. It was Robert's duty being the eldest to take over the Earldom. Being a second son, his father had not thought it necessary to include earlship duties in his studies. George was perfectly content serving in the regiment under the esteemed Lord Purcellville. But now, with this new duty, it released him from service honorably and here he was, struggling to fulfill the duties and title that now graced his name. His days were long and the nights longer still.

Leaning back in his cushioned leather chair, he kicked his booted feet up upon the mahogany desk. All tasks, questions, and letters were handled for the time being. Spring was a time of rebirth and renewal, a time to gather and be grateful for the coming bountiful harvests and nuptials. Preparations were made for the coming spring weather with the births of animals and flowers blooming. It was also time for making repairs to his tenants' homes. His land steward, Mr. Barlow, had presented quite the list earlier that morning. They had prioritized that list within an hour.

George groaned, stamping his feet brusquely upon the floor. He pulled his tailcoat straight and brushed off the non-existent dust from his brown sleeves. Striding out of the study, he made his way up the polished wood staircase to his bedchamber. Being inside Hathwell House for days made him feel anxious to get out and breathe a taste of the world. Granted he walked his estate almost thrice daily, yet he desired to be out for a respite and some socializing at White's Club.

Thank the Lord the miserable weather had passed, he mused, entering his bedchamber. George shucked the plain brown tailcoat and simply knotted cravat as he rummaged for something more befitting his new title. He rang for his valet Seth to tie his cravat and have their horses readied for Town.

To his grateful delight, Hathwell House was not far from Town. A ride would take him a few hours to complete at a brisk trot and nothing more. His brother had a residency in Town, with an address that the cream of the ton also shared. George packed his own bag, not yet used to being served by a valet, and having been on his own for years.

Satisfied with his appearance, and donning a beaver skin top hat, he happily left his bedchamber, and practically sprinted down the stairs to the out of doors. The crisp air struck his nose with the scent of freshly tilled soil and rain. It was a pleasant scent, something he'd forgotten he missed about Hathwell House.

George took a moment, gazing around his land. The fields, green and bright from the previous week of rain, were verdant and plentiful. Off to the east side in the afar distance, laborers began planting vegetables that come summer would be filling the air with the scent of garlic, onions, and other leafy greens.

His horse, London, was brought to the front of the house where he was standing, not too far outside the manor doors. The groomsman stood to the side, hand flat out offering the reins for his steed. George took them, dipping his head and offering his gratitude. The title of Earl and everything that came with it felt uneasy to him. If comparable to anything, it was like wearing a burlap sack underneath the finest attire - itchy, uncomfortable. An earl should always be a gentleman and ought not to complain, but offer gracious smiles and gentle company.

Seth tied his bag to the saddle while George checked the coin purse he had stashed for some late-night gambling. Tying it all snug, he mounted deftly onto his favorite animal. He quickly gave directions, detailing his return within a few days time, if not sooner, to his butler before spurring his horse down the lane. His valet followed behind upon his own equine.

The biting wind rushing past his face made all thoughts and worries dissipate like sugar in tea. The thoughts of loneliness, the emptiness he felt at being at Hathwell House solely, went out of his head. George closed his eyes, allowing the hollowness of the moment to overcome him. It was satisfying to feel as if he were flying over the landscape where it felt like not even God could touch him. London whinnied, bringing him back to the present.

Opening his eyes, he found himself down the road toward Town quicker than he realized. London, he figured, knew the way by heart since he traveled often enough in the regiment. A few more hours would see him at his residence where he could be readied for the evening's entertainment.

The sun waned overhead, announcing the evening sky would be coming forth soon, and with it, a curtailed breeze. The road to Town was clear and uneventful. He passed a carriage headed in the same direction as him. He scowled, figuring he might recognize it but being so reclusive as of late, he couldn't properly recall, nor could he view, the insignia gracing its side.

"Lord Hathwell!"

He stopped his horse, glancing over his shoulder to see the smiling face of Harrison Pembroke, the Seventh Earl of Bramley. The man popped his head from the curtained carriage window. He smiled wanly at his friend, and as of late, business partner in a bit of horse breeding.

"Good afternoon, Lord Bramley," George greeted. "How do you fare on such a lovely day?" The carriage caught up to George and he trotted his horse beside it.

"I'm doing quite well, thank you. I thought that was you. I'm on my way to Town to see my uncle, Mr. Pembroke, you may recall?"

George nodded. Of course, he remembered the man. He had been unable to forget Mr. Pembroke's lovely daughter with beautiful strawberry blonde hair and the most intense blue eyes he'd ever beheld. They had shared a pleasant dance together at his lordship's wedding. Isabelle, if he recalled her name correctly, had fit perfectly within his arms. She was beautiful, radiant, and not at all waspish in the manner that he found some women to be. When she had offered her condolences regarding his brother and family, it grieved his heart greatly. He had come to the wedding to forget, mayhap for a moment, the loneliness of Hathwell House.

Her comments were by no accounts crude nor improper. Nay, it just reminded him of the sorrowful ache ever-present within his chest, not only at losing the last remaining bit of family but also, in a roundabout way, the loss of a love to another man. A man who was currently beside him.

"I do recall," George finally answered, disconnected.

Lord Bramley nodded. "Care to join me and Mr. Pembroke for some dinner later this evening?"

George dipped his head. "I would be delighted. Thank you, Lord Bramley, you are much too kind."

"Please call me, Harrison. We are friends and business partners, are we not?"

George offered a tired yet polite smile. They were business partners. George had an impeccable line of horses that his brother established and he wasn't about to discontinue it. And Mariah's love of animals merged their business dealings together after he was telling Harrison about a new colt his broodmare sired. The colt was now weaned and in Mariah's tender care.

"Absolutely. 'Tis a good thing we have almost reached Town. I shall change and call upon you shortly," George nodded his dark head.

Upon saying their farewells, George galloped London the rest of the way to Town, only trotting briskly through it on his way to the townhouse. He loved the fact that the townhouse was situated on the outskirts of Mayfair on the west end. He rather disliked large crowds since being in the war. He dismounted, taking London inside the mews behind the townhouse.

His brother, always floating from Town to the stately home, had a butler, cook, and stable hand always at the ready. What George didn't happen to have here yet were any of his own clothes. Directing his valet to ready his attire for a night out, George entered his townhouse and readied his coin purse of spending money. Then he made his way to his bedchamber to change and prepare himself for Lord Bramley's dinner. Knowing the earl, it would be a quiet and quick affair in which he could retire to White's Club on St. James's Street, which was the premier place to be, promptly afterward.

George washed his face free of the grit and dirt that he had gained upon the road, quickly dressing to meet the earl. His brother's valet fixed his cravat, tying it in the newest fashion of the ton. George hardly cared. He once took great care in his appearance, but that was before his brother passed and Mariah had broken his heart. He swore he would be a bachelor indelibly. He was raised to give the utmost care and attention to the opposite sex, to be attentive, an active listener, and cater to their feminine needs.

And look where it has me now, he grouched, pulling on his fitted tailcoat. George sighed, looking at himself in the polished mirror.

"This came for you, sir," the butler, Fredrek, said with a bow.

George scowled at the missive. It was in Lord Bramley's quick yet precise hand, detailing his sorrow of having to reschedule dinner as something of great importance had arisen. George left the missive atop his bed. He would send a reply later, inquiring whether everything was all right with the earl and his household.

He sighed, adjusting the fitted tailcoat on his shoulders, tucking his coin purse and flask inside his waistcoat. George strode from the townhouse, heading down the lane on foot. He wanted the fresh oceanic air to clear his mind. He missed it. When in Brighton with the regiment, he always took a reprieve for a seaside walk no matter the time of day. The crisp salty air had always prickled his skin, making him feel fresh and invigorated. Alas, he would have to settle for Hyde Park.

He headed up the road, going straight for the gentleman's club several blocks away. Whether it was proper or not, walking was preferable to him instead of having to handle and navigate a horse; especially after having been drinking. He was not set upon impressing anyone and did not care if his appearance was lackluster once he arrived. He cared not if dirt marred his attire.

George pulled a silver flask from within his waistcoat, taking a swig of some Irish whiskey. The tangy oak mixed in with the savory caramel flavor of the liquor went down smooth, leaving him feeling warm and relaxed.

Upon arriving at White's, an attendant opened the door for him. George walked in, spying several tables already with gentlemen he knew, deep into their card games as well as their cups. Banknotes and shillings were at one prominent table to the far west side of the room. George didn't dare go to that particular table. Not only was there a notable rake there betting, but he didn't plan to meet anyone at dawn with pistols for any reason whatsoever. *Trouble shall not be my companion this eve.*

George ambled his way to the back of the gambling den, away from the crowds and the noise, spying Mr. Pembroke at a table with two other gentlemen. The man was as friendly and sincere as they came. He had a sternness about him when need be, but the twinkle in his blue eyes often spoke otherwise. At his approach, Mr. Pembroke smiled, waving him forward and grinning broadly.

"Lo my friends," Mr. Pembroke stated, "this here is Lord Hathwell, a friend of my dear nephew Lord Bramley."

"Pah, you old codger," another man grumbled, his hair white and combed over excessively. His jowls and scowl scrunched his face up more than a hound dog. "You're using this introduction to throw me off my game. Why, I tell you, it shan't work!"

"Lord Taggart," Mr. Pembroke harrumphed, "do not blame your cognitive inability on me, old friend."

"Wouldn't dream of it, Mr. Pembroke," Lord Taggert replied, chuckling. "Even with my *cognitive inability*, you've yet to best me!" He laughed uproariously as did the rest of the table.

"Pull up a chair, chap," the other gentleman instructed. "We'll keep you away from that old dustpan. He bites."

The three men chuckled.

"Lord Farthington," Mr. Pembroke guffawed. "It's your draw."

"Wagers?" Lord Farthington asked.

George placed his, modest as it was. A uniformed waiter came around, requesting drink orders. George ordered a scotch and to keep them coming as he happily finished off his flask of whiskey.

Smiling and leaning back in his chair, he listened intently to what these men had to say. He discovered his elder brother had relations with both Lord Farthington and Lord Taggart, and had dabbled in a touch of business with Mr. Pembroke. It was heartwarming to hear the niceties they had to say regarding Robert; bringing forth warm memories of his own about times had and now long gone with his dear brother. It made him slightly rueful he hadn't been there when Robert first wrote to him about his sickness. There was naught to be done now.

The waiter brought back an ample glass of scotch. George studied the liquid, taking a sniff of the smoke and apple flavor. He drank it down in one go, ordering another. He placed his bet. Lord

Farthington groaned and folded, declaring he was headed home now that his wife was asleep. They had been playing their hands for hours.

The card game changed to a German one that Lord Taggart knew, calling it skat. George was still unclear about how it all worked. To him, it sounded like bluffing but he couldn't be certain. He drank down another glass of scotch, feeling it swirl in his empty stomach and blur his vision a touch. He was not one to drink excessively, but this evening seemed like a good time to drink.

"Lord Hathwell," Lord Taggart addressed, "forgive my crudeness of the question, but are you unattached?"

"Please, call me George. And yes, sadly I am a confirmed bachelor."

George downed another glass of the lovely light amber liquid. It aided in helping him forget his duties, his brother, and the fact, it seemed, he was meant to exist and die alone. No matter how pleasant he was, attentive, kind, it was never enough to capture the heart of a beautiful lady.

He had many visitors come to his estate. Even the gentry appeared emboldened as of late to have their daughters come by the farmlands when he was out of doors. It seemed everyone wanted to saddle him with their daughters. One such maiden had attempted to paw at him in a most unseemly manner with the approval of her mama. George had had to call in his butler and a footman for reinforcements to assist the ladies into their awaiting carriage. That was not how he envisioned getting a wife.

George wriggled in his seat. *Once anyone gets to know me, they will leave. Just like Alicia. Just like Mariah. Giving a lady my heart will not be permitted by me. Third time is definitely not the charm. Burned twice by fire should be lesson enough.*

He adjusted the cards in his hands, keeping a straight face at his winning hand. He lay it down triumphantly, taking the bet from the center of the table.

Lord Taggart nodded, "My sweet granddaughter, Emerald, would make you a suitable match."

George refrained from shaking his head. Not from the fizzing effects of the alcohol, but from the sly matchmaking Lord Taggart was attempting to make.

"I appreciate the concerns regarding my marital appeal, but I must politely decline," George replied.

Mr. Pembroke laughed, "His lordship would be much better matched with my Isabelle."

Lord Taggart scowled, looking even more similar to a hound. "Listen here spoony, Emerald is a beautiful woman who would compliment Lord Hathwell pleasantly."

"I'm sure she would," Mr. Pembroke placated. "However, how about a wager, shall we?"

The room seemed to spin a touch. His stomach grumbled. George glanced down, unable to discern if from hunger or imbibing too much liquor. Lord Taggart shuffled the cards, dealing them out for what appeared to be the final hand.

"Fine," George replied, picking up his hand. It wasn't a terrible hand and he was certain he could win. "If I lose this hand, I will marry the winner's daughter or granddaughter respectfully. If I win, I want your finest horses."

"Pah!" Lord Taggart grumped. "Do you not know how much my horses cost?"

George grinned. "If those specimens were outside when I first came in, then you better hope you don't lose this round, my friend."

Lord Taggart grinned, chuckling softly. "I accept this wager."

Mr. Pembroke beamed. "As do I," he leaned back in his chair and sighed. "So I am pleased to inform you both, I have won."

Mr. Pembroke laid down his hand atop the table. Lord Taggart threw down his own hand of cards and bid everyone a pleasant evening, wishing to call upon George tomorrow to discuss horse flesh. George acknowledged the statement, even believing he replied to it. However the disaster that had just befallen him made his mind blank. How could he have lost? Was this a trick? Now he was set to be married?

"You remember Isabelle, do you not?" Mr. Pembroke questioned quietly.

George nodded. "Of course I do. She is hard to forget." He raised his brows at that statement, wondering if the drinks had loosened his sense of judgment and tongue. Isabelle was beautiful, kindly it seemed to him, but now to be his wife? It was incredulous!

Rumors circulated that the beautiful half-French daughter was as direct as they came, speaking her mind as if none mattered.

While he didn't mind a well-spoken and educated woman, to be so blunt would be disagreeable and more than a bit embarrassing.

Mr. Pembroke clapped his hands together. "Wonderful. I will have a special license issued tomorrow. Come, my future son-in-law, I will drive you home."

With that, Mr. Pembroke rose from the table and tucked in his chair. George sat stone-still, trying to wrap his head around how he could lose. He had been winning all night. He went to stand and the room swam. Taking one step brought darkness to his vision.

Chapter Two

The Trouble of Boredom

Miss Isabelle Pembroke scanned the manicured lawn outside for any indication that her father, The Right and Honorable, Mr. William Pembroke, had returned from his trip to Town. He had left his family to attend his man of business in London and because his newest addition was yet an infant, his wife and daughter remained upon his country estate. Mr. Pembroke had been gone a fortnight and his family were eagerly awaiting his presence. The halls of the manor house always seemed empty without the patriarch in residence. And the winter roads made his journey all the more anxiety provoking for his family.

Isabelle was the second daughter of William and Beatrice Pembroke. Her elder sister was Annabelle who was born three years prior to Isabelle's birth. They shared a younger brother who was only an infant. Mr. Pembroke had been overjoyed that after so many years his loving wife had produced a son. Having been the second son of an earl, Mr. Pembroke held family ties above all else. Her parents' union had been a love match and they had never regretted choosing each other and delighted in recounting their love affair.

Taking a sip from her rose patterned teacup, Isabelle quickly made a face of disgust. The liquid was tepid, so she placed it back upon the tea service tray that she rang for hours ago. Shaking her head, she walked back to stand before the easel. The portrait was not terrible, in truth it was one of her best. But she was growing weary of painting her French poodle FiFi. *And really how many portraits do I require lining my bedchamber walls of the exact same poodle*, she wondered. Mayhap it was time to broaden her horizons and seek other subjects to showcase her vastly improving artistic skills. However, she happened to like dogs, they were so easy to manage and did exactly as they were directed to do. Unless, of course, a squirrel happened to pass by and you were situated out of doors. But one did not make that mistake more than a handful of times.

People, she thought, *were such troublesome creatures and forever wanting to make conversation about the weather or state other inane comments.* That thinking was precisely the reason why at one and twenty she was on her way to forever being set upon the shelf and deemed unmarriageable. It wasn't her fault that the English gentlemen thrown her way were boorish, staid, and lacked spirit. She could no more tame her tongue than they could direct the seasons. And her words had occasionally come back to haunt her, but what could one do when they lived life with such effervescent joy.

Isabelle recalled Mr. Quincy who had courted her for the span of a month and then had cried off when she stated that she should like to take a cooling dip in the pond. He did not deem such a desire as befitting his future bride. He had an odd gait when he walked, so he really wasn't someone that she regretted losing. Isabelle shrugged her shoulders as she thought about him, choosing to find fault in him and not herself. The manner of his stride had never been a complaint until he severed their acquaintance.

Lord Remington had lasted a month longer and she really began to esteem him until she learned of his gambling habit.

When she voiced her opinion concerning the gaming dens that he frequently attended, he had turned an alarming shade of crimson before storming away from their picnic. His horse had nearly thrown him into the pond when she screeched in protest of being abandoned in such a rude manner. He too, was no great loss.

Mr. Jackson was nice enough, but really had very unruly hair and sweated profusely. When Isabelle suggested that mayhap he needed a different soap that would enhance his complexion, he had risen from his seat and left the drawing room never to return. That was a blessing and she had thanked the Lord abundantly for withdrawing him from her life.

Of course, there were a few others and it seemed as if word of her unsuitability had spread within their social circle. She had been labeled everything from an ape leader to a bluestocking. And truthfully, all the rumors had injured her heart and mortified her parents.

Was she to constantly bite her tongue and hold in her thoughts even when the situation was truly ridiculous? There was a lot to notice amongst the fashionable ton and she could not help but to sometimes point out the vices and nonsense that ran so amuck within their social circle. She prayed for forbearance, a guiding force to nudge her into a more refined state of being, but the good Lord had yet to answer that prayer. She did not doubt that the fervent prayers of her doting parents went amiss as well when the topic of them was herself.

Isabelle had not been raised to stay silent and stuff down her personality. Her *Maman* had taught her to voice her emotions and feelings and give her heart the room it needed to thrive. She was part French and proud of her heritage that *Maman*'s parents had brought with them from their home country when they had been forced to immigrate to England. Her *Maman* assured them both that being of French descent would soon be fashionable again amongst the lower classes. Certain prejudices could not be contained by those below their social standing. The French, and all things pertaining to their culture, were beloved by the cream of the ton. The fashions, furnishings, art, and language had become a breath of fresh air for the peerage who continued to court the love affair.

The suitors were fewer and farther between now and that suited Isabelle just fine. *Besides,* she thought, *I don't relish the idea of leaving behind Maman and Papa for some stranger who will put me into a box.* What she desired was to find a love like that of her parents or even that which shined so brilliantly between her newly married cousin Harrison and his wife Mariah. They had transcended social class and joined together. It was all so very romantic. Did she want a man who would sweep her off of her feet? Would she even let one try? She did not know. However, she was certain that she did not want to reside upon a pedestal nor be held away at arm's length. If she were to marry, she wanted to have a place within her new household that was precious and unique wholly unto her. She trusted that the Lord would supply her perfect match or nothing would induce her to the matrimonial state. For surely it would be nothing short of divine intervention that placed a husband into her path.

Isabelle walked over to the cream cushioned settee which FiFi was happily ensconced upon. She reached out and patted the poodle upon its strawberry blonde head and sighed. Today FiFi had a delicate periwinkle bow tied to the mound of fluff upon his head. He was quite dashing, in his own furry way. Isabelle sighed again as she was bored. She needed to find a new interest. Most of her friends were now installed within their own households and busy raising families. They just did not have the time to gossip and meet her for day-long shopping trips and that greatly saddened her.

She could sew and embroider and all the other domestic traits young ladies must master but she especially enjoyed flower arranging. Flowers were bursting with color and texture and even the scent was enough to send her creativity full to bursting. Her *Maman* was nothing short of a taskmaster when it came to the domestic arts. Happily could she entertain either a duke or a farmer and make them feel comfortable. But she found that while painting she was completely taken from this world and transported to another one, rich in color and texture. Her happiness rested in each brushstroke and play of the light. When attending to anything, Isabelle could find the shadow and light, and she felt as if these observations only heightened her love for viewing the world through art. Art did not just exist on the canvas, it was in every aspect of life. It was found in the beauty of a smile or the way a flower opened its petals. Even a perfectly arranged table set for guests had elements of beauty and she grew impatient with those who could not appreciate the beauty of everyday life. *Which is why I must banish this boredom. If only I had an adventure to embark upon*, she wished.

Looking at the mantle clock that rested upon the marble mantlepiece, Isabelle knew it was time to dress for dinner. She set about cleaning her brushes. She was fortunate to have her own gallery where no one bothered her. This room was her personal haven and she always kept it neat and tidy. There was a small end table to the right of the settee. The Aubusson rug was patterned in burgundies and creams and gave luxurious warmth to the room. Windows lined the room and courted the sunlight to shine its rays upon each corner and crevice. At night, the shine of the stars was visible and no matter the hour of the day or night, it was this room that held Isabelle's heart.

Removing her gray painting overcoat, she hung it on its peg and walked to the full-length rose gold mirror in the corner of the room. Peering into the glass, she studied her features. Her icy blue eyes were large and expressive and always let others know exactly what she was thinking. Her lips were plump with the top one being just a slight bit larger, while her nose was adequate and perfectly pert. There was a smallish beauty mark just to the right of her nose. Isabelle's hair was her favorite attribute about herself. It was strawberry blonde and long, falling to her tiny waist, and had a natural curl to it. It was simple to style and she was thankful of that fact daily for if it became unruly, she could easily repin it. She had long delicate fingers that were blessedly paint-free today. Her figure, which was neither too thin nor too thick, was pleasing. She had never been one to eat large portions, but it was the sweets that were her downfall. She owed her stunning looks to her family, as the Pembroke line was composed of handsome members whose portraits hung in the gallery for all to view. She took pride in her carriage and enjoyed long walks across the estate to retain her shape.

Once she was sure that she looked perfectly presentable and would not cause offense to her proper minded English staff, she called for FiFi to accompany her as she exited the room. Her companion dutifully followed. FiFi was her best friend and partner in all of her endeavors. She would have been heartbroken if her Papa had decreed that dogs had no place within the manor. After her elder sister, Annabelle, had married three years ago, Isabelle had been left feeling adrift and Papa had gifted her with FiFi. While FiFi could never replace her sister within her heart, she did come to adore the furry animal. And if occasionally FiFi wet upon the carpets, she need not fear the master's wrath as Papa was an animal lover himself.

After ascending the staircase and padding to her room, she entered her bedchamber. It was decorated in pale yellows and blues and the walls were covered in framed artwork, mostly of FiFi, but there were some floral scenes as well. The four-poster bed with its pale blue coverlet was the focal point of the room with the small tables located at its head on either side. There was a small mahogany armchair with clawed feet that sat before her fireplace which had rosettes carved into the moldings. It was an elegant room that was welcoming and pleasing to behold. Even FiFi had a little haven that he happily curled into at the side of her bed. Isabelle rang for her maid and sat down upon the armchair to await her presence.

When Emma, her lady's maid, entered into Isabelle's bedchamber, she greeted her with a slight curtsy and purposefully strode to the wardrobe to gather a dress for dinner. Isabelle softly stepped to her rosewood dressing table and sat upon the cream-colored bench to watch her maid pick out the various articles that Isabelle would be donning for the evening. No matter who was in residence, dinner was a lavish affair and her *Maman* insisted that they keep up the mode of dress.

Emma assisted her mistress with a quick scrub of her skin before helping her dress. Isabelle again sat upon her padded bench and watched Emma's deft hands manage her strawberry blonde tresses as elegantly as possible. The finished look was enchanting with her hair curled and swept up in the classic Greek style, with curls close to her head but with the mass of her hair drawn back, dangling along her delicate nape.

Isabelle felt beautiful in her best dinner dress which was a pale blue satin with silver flowers and a thick silver ribbon under her bosom. Isabelle thanked Emma and then made her way to the drawing room where her mother and father awaited her presence.

With a brilliant smile, she raced to Mr. Pembroke and threw her arms around his lean middle in an embrace which he happily returned. He was her first love and would always be the one that she measured the merit of all gentlemen against.

"When did you return?" Isabelle inquired breathlessly.

"Just a short while ago. Enough time to bid your *Maman* hello and to get ready for dinner," stated Mr. Pembroke with a beaming smile upon his face. He looked well with his gray hair parted to one side and the wrinkles lining his face making him appear as one who enjoyed life. He was still so handsome even at the age of eight and forty.

"That's wonderful! We were missing you dreadfully. Especially little Bernard. He is growing so much, I am sure you will hardly know him," Isabelle commented as she stepped away from her father. She had visited with her infant brother daily since his birth and it was a miracle that for such a late in life birth for her *Maman*, that all were as happy and hearty as they were.

"Indeed. I shall have to see for myself after we dine."

Randolph, their aging butler, announced that dinner was served. Mr. Pembroke offered an arm to each of his ladies and escorted them into the dining room which was aglow with the many lit candles shining from the chandelier. The burgundy tablecloth and sparkling tableware were especially inviting this evening. Mr. Pembroke stopped before Isabelle's chair which a footman pulled out and he kissed her cheek before guiding Mrs. Pembroke to her place on his other side.

Feeling overcome with happiness, Isabelle could not keep the smile from her face. "How was your time in Town? Did you meet with anyone with whom we share an acquaintance?"

Nodding at the butler to signal the start of the meal and leaning back to receive his soup, Mr. Pembroke said, "Indeed. You do remember George Wallis, the Fifth Earl of Hathwell, do you not? I believe you danced with him at Harrison's wedding?"

Did she remember him? Of course, she did. He was worth remembering. Their dance had been perfection itself. She had fit so effortlessly within his strong masculine arms as he led them as if they were one being. Their conversation had not been about the weather but about the happy newlywed couple and with many well wishes for their future. It had all been like existing in a dream until she had commented that she was sorry for the loss of his elder brother and inquired how he was settling into his new role as the heir. Everything had gone downhill from there and though they had seen each other the remaining fortnight of his stay at Bramley Hall, he did not single her out again after that dance. She was eternally flawed and this was another example of her doom on the marriage market. She didn't have aspirations of gaining a titled husband. But mayhap that was the idea she had given to the man. Internally shrugging, she brought herself back to the present.

"Yes, I did. He was such a flawless partner," Isabelle said softly, dabbing her lips with a cloth napkin.

Mrs. Pembroke's expression softened over the top of her soup spoon at her daughter. "And you looked so well matched on the dance floor. He is handsome, is he not, *ma petite?*" Isabelle smiled broadly at her *Maman's* use of the familiar term for her, of dear little one. Mrs. Pembroke's hair was styled to sit upon the crown of her hair with golden tendrils hanging down alongside her face. Her beautiful blue-gray eyes were twinkling with mischief. Her dinner gown was a pale rose that brought a lovely hue to her dusky skin. Isabelle was fortunate to possess so many of her mother's finest qualities.

Isabelle nodded. "Of course, I found him very pleasing. If his manners were only a bit more polished he would be quite the catch." She sipped from her wine.

"Perhaps he just needs a wife, the right one, to smooth all of his rough edges," Mr. Pembroke remarked.

The young woman put her hands in her lap, giving her father her undivided attention. "She would need to be exemplary. He would, I fear, be quite the task and any woman would have her hands full with him. He has a quiet nature but a will of iron underneath it." Isabelle recalled still being able to see the hidden depths lurking within his chocolate gaze. They were eyes that she had wanted to lose herself in, but it was not to be. She also noticed how he had gazed intently upon Mariah and wondered if his heart was intact or residing with another. That had decided her upon not seeking out his company; she did not need to break her heart pining after one that was lost in another. It also helped that he did not seek her out.

Mr. Pembroke nodded. "Yes, well, as luck would have it, he is in need of a wife and I think that he and you would complement each other very well, Isabelle. I've decided that a long courtship would be pointless as he really needs to attend to his estate and the business of getting an heir. And really, Isabelle, the offers for your hand have increasingly slowed. You have frightened off all other suitors." Mr. Pembroke rubbed his hand over his face.

"*Papa!* We hardly know each other. You cannot just decide that I am to marry him."

"Actually, I can. I know that this must seem hurried and unfair, but given time, I think that you will come to discover how well suited you are to each other." Mr. Pembroke threw out a hand when Isabelle made to speak and then continued on, "You will thank me. He is not one to easily scare off and he is up to the task that being your husband would set for him. You are my dearest daughter, but I know your faults. Give this time. I will not revoke my decision."

With eyes wide, Mrs. Pembroke addressed her husband, "Surely there is time for an attachment to form?"

"No need. The contracts are being drawn up even now and this will soon be set to rights," Mr. Pembroke remarked with a wave of his large hand.

Isabelle could not take another bite. She was in shock. Never before had Papa made such a ludicrous decree. This was her future happiness and he was just gifting it away. True, she could have been given to another who was undeserving and of a lower class. The fact that this would elevate her family only made this sting all the more. Surely, the man did not want her. How could his feelings be so altered?

"But dear Papa, how did this come to be? How did you address this with him?"

Shifting in his chair, Mr. Pembroke finally answered with, "It was innocently achieved. Have no fear. Lord Hathwell saw the merit in the match and is ready to finish the business at once. You will soon be receiving his lordship to pay his addresses."

Feeling ill, Isabelle soon left the table. Even the rich chocolate mousse was not enough to tempt her appetite to return. Hearing her *Maman* begin to dress down her Papa did nothing to amuse her either as she climbed the stairs. She did not want her parents arguing over her. *Maman* was quite the fierce warrior where the happiness and safety of her children were at stake. If there was a way out of this, she would trust her *Maman* to uncover it.

She retired to her bedchamber and wondered how it was that everything had changed so drastically, so quickly. Could a marriage with Lord Hathwell be her truest chance for happiness? Or were they doomed before they ever said their vows? The last thing she wanted was for any man to be leg shackled to her and not desire her company. Clinging to the hope that in this her father knew better, she tried to slow her racing thoughts as she prayed that somewhere within this plan the Lord was in the midst of working a miracle.

Chapter Three

Congratulations?

The sunlight poked through the drapes in his brother's town-house, waking him from a rueful slumber. George groaned, glancing around in surprise that he had the capacity to make it home. He recalled imbibing quite a plentiful amount of scotch and whiskey, gambling with a few friends, and reminiscing about Robert. There was something else on the threadbare of his mind, eluding him each time he called upon that thread to remind him of what he missed.

George sat up slowly. The churning in his stomach threatened to give way from his mouth. Setting a hand to his head did little to stop the swaying of the room and the churning in his innards. George lunged for an empty bucket that was mysteriously placed on the floor, vomiting into the unlucky container.

A knock resounded from the bedchamber door.

"Yes?" George questioned.

"Your morning meal sir," Seth his valet announced through the closed door. "And several missives."

"Enter please," George called, running a hand over his face. After his wartime activities, he did not like sudden interruptions. His servants knew better than to enter his chambers without announcing themselves. His fist had met the unfortunate face of Seth and he had felt like the worst scourge of society that ever was.

Seth set the silver tray down on the bedside table, handing him his correspondence. George held them loftily in his hands, not quite ready to read them. His eyes were still swimming with black dots coming in and out of his double vision.

"Would you like a cure, sir?" Seth asked, standing in attention by the door.

George shook his head. "No thank you," he winced at the sound of his own voice.

Seth bowed and left the chamber.

He believed any and all 'cure alls' were just a hoax to get the miserable person's coin. A bath, food, and lots of water were the cure, or so he had learned from his brother. He sighed, raising himself from the bed since the spots in his vision cleared. Last eve was a diverting time. He was certain that Lord Taggart mentioned calling upon him today though he was loath to admit that he couldn't quite remember the particulars.

George settled himself on the bed beside the silver tray left for him and set his letters aside to read later. His stomach roiled at the thought of food, but he ate the ham, eggs, and potatoes. He was fairly certain the ache in his heart and the one in his stomach were pulsating in tandem. George swiped a hand over his face, hoping to rub the miserable sensations off. It was of no use.

Rising from the bed, he went to check his appearance in the long mahogany polished mirror in the corner of the room. He looked haggard. And if haggard could look worse, it would be death. George shucked his clothes and gave himself a quick scrubbing with the cold water from the basin located in his dressing area. Then he grabbed the days' attire that Seth had left out for him. He rang for Seth to tie his cravat since the blasted thing never laid quite right for him. Once suitable, he grabbed his top hat and walking cane to head out of the door for a morning stroll, figuring the crisp air would aid in his cure. Looking proper, as if nothing was amiss, would keep the Town gossip at bay.

He checked the pockets of his previous night's attire, seeing a wad of banknotes and shillings. He recalled doing quite well at gambling. But there was something else lingering, something more his brain was attempting to repress from recollection. George shook his head. *A brisk walk shall clear it all up*, he decided.

Striding from his townhouse, George proceeded to Hyde Park. At this time of the morning, it was yet to be crowded. The early morning equestrians were trotting in full view to be seen by their peers. The weather was too unpredictable this time of the year, so open carriages were not yet in season. *Society was all just a grand showing off but the air and brisk pace would do me good.* The warm sun and light breeze made for a most agreeable day.

"Ah, Lord Hathwell," Lord Farthington said cheerfully. His wife hung upon his arm, complete with a kindly gaze and a parasol. "I believe congratulations are in order. Well done. Miss Isabelle Pembroke is a charming lady. Wouldn't you agree, my dear?"

"Yes," Lady Farthington replied though her simple answer was laced in opinion.

"Thank you," George replied, attempting to keep the question from his voice.

"We must be off," Lord Farthington said. "It was a pleasure to see you as always, Lord Hathwell. Pray, would you accept an invitation to dine?"

"Absolutely. Thank you Lord Farthington for your generosity and graciousness."

The stalwart man beamed proudly. "Have a splendid day, chap."

George turned around to gaze at the pathway as a means to hide the bewildered look on his face. What had happened last eve? Why was he meant with the smile, the happiness, and the well-wishes? There had to be something more. Everyone he passed nodded merrily at him. *Dear Lord, what have I forgotten?*

"Lord Hathwell!"

He spun around slowly, upon hearing the high-pitched voice of Mrs. Alicia Morten, formerly Miss Purcellville.

"See dear, I told you it was our friend," she chastised, swatting her husband on the arm and reaching up to tuck an errant auburn curl back into her bonnet.

"Good to see you again, old chap," Mr. Simon Morten greeted, shaking his hand.

George smiled. "It's always a pleasure to see you both."

"Congratulations, George," Alicia said. "Miss Pembroke has ties to the Earl of Bramley as I'm sure you know. She is a charming woman."

"Absolutely," Simon added. "What a catch for you! She will make you a wonderful wife." His eyes were twinkling merrily as he contemplated George.

He couldn't formulate proper words. It was a terrible position to be in since Alicia was known to spread tidings, ill-begotten or not. She simply could not be relied upon to hold her tongue nor censure her wild imaginings.

"Thank you very much," George said, snapping out of his daze. "I find myself quite flabbergasted at the prospect of it all."

"Ah yes, the idea of marriage is difficult to understand. But when love calls, 'tis truly blissful. I hope you find love that lasts through the times, dear friend," Simon replied, smiling broadly and clapping him on the shoulder.

"Indeed. Thank you both for your kind, well wishes. I'm truly grateful."

"La, I hope to reserve a seat at the nuptials," Alicia said at last. "I'm so very thrilled for you, my lord."

"Come along, Dear," Simon directed, "Let us make our way to the candy shop. Have a splendid day my lord!" he called.

Splendid indeed, he mused. George hung his head, pleading with his brain to recollect exactly whatever had transpired yet any inclination alluded him. Clearly, for some reason, people assumed he was getting married. But how could that be? He bet money last night, not marital ties. Could answers be in the notes he left upon the bed?

George hurried home, striving with great care to remain proper for society's sake lest they rip him through mud and a scandal. He took the small stairs two at a time, rounded the banister to the right, and barged into his bedchamber. Three letters remained sealed upon the bed with an assortment of different wax insignias.

He opened the one from Harrison Pembroke, the Earl of Bramley, inviting him to dine with him this evening at Steven's Hotel on Bond Street here in Town. Steven's held a welcoming atmosphere no matter if you were an officer or a gentleman. George nodded, mentally acquiescing to accept the invitation and write back after having read the other letters. The next letter came from Lord Taggart, imploring him to come to his residency to discuss the breeding of horses and possible business. George nodded. Lord Taggart prided himself on his horse flesh. It would be prudent of him to do business with such a knowledgeable man.

The last letter still lay upon his bed with the seal unbroken. George swallowed, his eyes becoming spotty again and he hadn't even read the first line of the letter yet. The missive came from Mr. William Pembroke, uncle to the Earl of Bramley. He broke the wax seal and began to read the contents. The letter dropped from his hands.

"*Married!*" He bellowed. "Married! And Mr. Pembroke has obtained the special license from the Archbishop of Canterbury!"

He picked up the letter again from the bed, reading it thrice and still struggling to grasp the notion with his battered mind. A week hence, Isabelle would be his wife. *By Jove, why did I even gamble?*

Chapter Four

Oh, Dear Me!

Isabelle tried to comprehend the fact that her betrothal was posted in The Times. It was printed in black and white, and still, Isabelle felt numb. How could her Papa have been so unfeeling and completely lacking in regard for her feelings in the matter? She was torn in half. She loathed the idea of marrying a man of whom she did not yet have a clear understanding. A man who she had seemingly injured at her cousin Harrison's wedding. Half of her mind and heart were fixated upon his chocolate-colored eyes and the feelings that had taken flight within her stomach when she had been encircled within his muscular arms. He was tall and... *Oh bother, this will never do. I will not allow myself to become a simpering fool.* Isabelle stomped her slippered foot upon the carpet and tossed the offending paper upon a mahogany side table.

Her actions had alarmed FiFi who had jumped down from his spot upon the settee in the drawing room. He barked at her and she shushed him. Isabelle padded over to the large bay window that overlooked the lane leading to her father's estate. She did not really see what was before her as she was still lost in thought.

"*Ma petit*! You will wear yourself out. Please come away from the window and take tea with me. That is one English custom that I am always ready to partake in." Mrs. Pembroke entered the room so quietly that Isabelle jumped when she had been addressed. When her mother had seated herself in a wingback chair near the roaring marbled fireplace, she waved her hand to indicate the chair opposite her.

Acquiescing, Isabelle silently sat down. When she had arranged her skirts around her feet appropriately, she looked up at her mother. Fifi came to sit down before her slippered feet.

"This will turn out very well. I trust, and you should as well, your Papa to have made an excellent match for you. His sound judgment has never neglected us before." Mrs. Pembroke smiled encouragingly at her with her blue-gray eyes sparkling.

The butler, Randolph, entered the room pushing a silver cart that held their tea set upon it. Since the man was aging, Mr. Pembroke had insisted that he deliver their tea upon the cart and not a tray. It was a kindness that Randolph readily accepted. Stopping the cart before his mistress, he bowed his head to both of the ladies and took his leave.

Once Mrs. Pembroke had served her daughter and herself with tea and a small piece of lemon cake each, she addressed the topic again. "Your father will step in should anything untoward occur. I have made him promise me."

Frowning, Isabelle took a sip of her tea. She had given the matter over to the Lord in the aftermath of receiving the life-altering news. But sometime between then and seeing the article, she had revived her immediate misgivings.

Isabelle gazed at the drawing room around her. The Aubusson carpet was a dark blue that perfectly matched the drapes. The settee and wingback chairs were padded in a cream pattern. *Maman* disliked clutter, instead choosing to surround herself with floral arrangements throughout the house. In wintertime, the offerings were scarce, but no one seemed to mind.

Toward the bay window were two Louis XV upholstered chairs in the rococo style and that was where her parents spent a great deal of their time together. *Papa and Maman were so well matched it sometimes injures my heart to witness their deep affection when I do not know if I shall ever share in that sacred bond with another.*

Randolph stood in the doorway and announced, "Mrs. Hurley to see you, Madam." He bowed and then stepped aside as Isabelle's older sister Annabelle passed into the room.

Mrs. Pembroke immediately rose to her feet and closed the distance between them, enfolding Annabelle within her delicate arms. "*Ma chérie!* How my heart has missed your beautiful face." Mrs. Pembroke had always addressed her oldest daughter with the endearment of *my darling.*

Returning the embrace, Annabelle softly spoke, "It has only been a few months apart *Maman.*"

When they separated Isabelle was struck by how very much alike they both were. They had the same build with golden hair that was quite becoming with their dusky skin tone. Only, Annabelle shared the same icy blue eyes that Isabelle had and that, coupled with their differences in ages, set them apart.

Annabelle turned to Isabelle who had reached them and held out her arms for an embrace. Once they parted, Annabelle told her, "Congratulations upon your upcoming nuptials! Why the rush? I daresay you have not visited Bond Street for your trousseau and how can you become a countess without the proper trimmings?"

FiFi chose that moment to make his presence known by flopping onto his back upon Annabelle's booted feet to have his underside petted. Annabelle reached down to do as bidded, then adjusted his pale pink hair bow.

Before Isabelle could form her answering reply, Mrs. Pembroke directed her children to sit down, then she rang for another pot of tea. Once she seated herself she looked at her daughters. "We have not yet made plans, but I was hoping to set out on the morrow for that very chore. Isabelle will need the best that your Papa can afford. Shall you join us, Annabelle?"

Nodding her head decisively, Annabelle agreed. "I set out this morning with that very idea. I shall spend the night here and we may get an early start. If the roads are clear, we may even reach Bond Street at an agreeable time in the afternoon. This is all possible even though we have less than a week to prepare so we had best get started."

"Indeed *ma chérie!*" Mrs. Pembroke smiled at her brilliantly. "Excuse me, while I make the arrangements with the staff for the carriage and the packing of our trunks. I suppose I shall inform your Papa that we are bound for Town. He may desire to accompany us. I shan't be gone long." Mrs. Pembroke left the room hurriedly with the door closing behind her animated form.

Things were moving very quickly and Isabelle brought her delicate hand to her forehead to rub at it.

"Are you excited by the match?" Annabelle softly inquired as she looked at her sister expectantly.

"Not at all. I hardly know the man. And Papa refuses to change his mind and lengthen the engagement. Plus, there is the fact that I have not received the proper addresses from my betrothed. I fear we will not cross paths until the altar." Isabelle knew her face bore a look of disgust, but she could not make herself hide it away.

"Many couples begin their lives together as perfect strangers. You have the advantage that you have met and have even danced together. Be thankful that he is a *titled gentleman* and that you will not want for anything." Annabelle gave her a look reeking of censure.

"I shall want for *love!*" Isabelle gave her a pleading look that she hoped would assist her in an attempt to understand her hesitation.

Annabelle sighed and then straightened her shoulders. "Happiness, even love, is never a guarantee. Even couples who have formed an attachment can easily fall out of love. Love in marriage is a complete variable. You could spend a lifetime and never form such an attachment, and still your world will go on. You learn to go on despite the losses you suffer."

Isabelle gazed intently at her sister. "That sounds horrid."

Shrugging her delicate shoulders, Annabelle countered with, "Come what may, you still have me, you still have your family. We will be there to support you. Besides, the idea of a loveless marriage for you is unfathomable."

"You are teasing me. I know what you are saying makes sense to you. My heart is ardently against such wisdom. You would not want to endure a marriage not built upon love." Isabelle looked down at her clasped hands in her lap.

Randolph entered the drawing room with a fresh pot of tea and bowed out again.

After serving her sister, Isabelle remained silent.

They sat keeping each other company as they thought about different subjects.

"Isabelle, when I said that not all marriages are built upon love, I meant it. You must endeavor to get your husband to fall under your charms. If he does not, you will have your own interest to keep you busy. Many married couples separate after the gaining of heirs. There is no shame in making separate lives. I myself have gained my independence now that James and I have added two sons to our family. James is free to seek his happiness as am I. We are gloriously happy apart." Annabelle gazed into the fire.

"That sounds ghastly. You have my apologies. I had no idea that your situation was so altered. You did love him, I know you did. Everyone who looked upon you two saw the devotion and care you had one for another." Isabelle wanted to rail at the world for the injustice occurring within her sister's marriage.

"'Tis just as well. I have heard rumors that James has taken up with a doxy. They have been seen in Covent Garden together. If he has found contentment with another, who am I to stand in his way?"

"You are his *wife*! The mother of his children! You do not deserve to be cast aside as he makes his life elsewhere."

Anabelle looked up at her and wistfully replied, "If only he felt the same as you do. I do not tell you these things to gain sympathy. In truth, I wish you well in your marriage. My circumstances do not reflect yours."

The sisters sat in silence and waited for their mother to return to them. Isabelle mourned for her sister's plight. She did not want to ever share in the situation that her sister suffered. And even though she had stated that she was happy apart from her husband, Isabelle did not believe her. For her sister looked unhappy, and she suspected that she was, in fact, still very much in love with James.

Isabelle said a prayer to her heavenly father that she would find a way into her husband's heart. She resolved that nothing would deter her from marital happiness, not even her own spouse.

Chapter Five

So Soon?

George paced the study in his brother's townhouse early in the morning. He had spent all day yesterday reeling that the particulars of his betrothal had been printed in The Times. *Such events were usually kept secret, were they not?* But with the special license obtained by the Archbishop, it gave him less time to become accustomed to the idea of his future bride. He desired more time to perchance woo the woman who was to take his name and settle under his protection. The wedding was not too long out, mayhap four days at most. Part of him was dumbfounded at the prospect of marriage. The other contented himself with a wife of his own drunken making. At least he had the pleasure of seeing her before, so they were not complete strangers. Though he found her to be both beautiful and keen, the pleasant outwardness of their entire one conversation could not merit enough prospect to lend insight to their marriage.

He ran a hand over his face. *She will need clothes befitting the new title she is about to obtain,* he thought. *I am a man of my word. I will not abscond this marital arrangement no matter how quickly 'tis coming about.* George sat down, penning a quick letter to Mr. Pembroke, sending with the missive enough currency for his future bride to obtain the proper attire befitting her new station.

He rang for Fredrek to have his valet, Seth, deliver the communication with haste. He sat back in his chair and sighed deeply. More than anything he wanted a loving marriage where he and his wife would sit fireside together, each content in their own armchairs, yet he had not ever found it for himself. Supposedly having found it with Alicia, he went about doing all he could to lock in her favor - favorite treats, favorite gifts, practically running himself ragged and out of coin to secure a modicum of her affection. Then with Mariah, it was as if the stars were aglow and dimmed all at once from her beauty, grace, and kindness. Granted she had politely informed him she was in love with another, but, yet again, he tried in vain to secure her affection.

I shan't try again, he thought for a moment, though it 'twasn't fair to Isabelle that he at least not try to make an effort in their marriage. *I am just so heartbroken, scorched, and ruined by women, why must I make an effort unless she reciprocates my efforts?*

Issuing forth from his chair, he paced the study floor once more. He opened a window, allowing the fresh breeze in, hoping to stir new thoughts. Another servant, whose name he had forgotten, served him tea and a late meal to break his fast. George continued pacing, stopping only to take a cup of tea.

It's not fair to her that I make no effort, he decided. He was not raised to be a cad, a spiteful rake of a man. He was raised to show kindness, attentiveness. He wasn't about to shame his poor mother's memory. *I shall make an effort,* he decided, *until she proves otherwise.*

Sighing at having the matter settled, he sent word to Harrison, detailing that he would meet him for dinner wherever and however was most convenient to him. Both gentlemen were completely absorbed yesterday in business that they had forgotten to schedule dinner with each other. He wrote another missive to Lord Taggart, desiring to see his horses and make a notion for business to be had between them. Having a foal of Lord Taggart's impeccable lineage would give a great boost to his name and legacy.

George exhaled, having business of the day happily settled, or perhaps, settled for the most part. He ate his meal, pondering what to do next, and decided shopping must be done. He needed to acquire a respectable marital ensemble and ask permission from Mariah and Harrison to hold the wedding breakfast at their country estate, Bramley Hall. It seemed fitting that since his acquaintanceship with his intended began there amongst family and friends, it should therefore be celebrated within the great Hall. He would also inquire whether Mariah's father would marry them. The man was the only parson he particularly liked. All of the other men of the cloth he had ever encountered were of the practice that all things pleasurable must be burned from their souls and that one was to strive for a more pious lifestyle. Bacchanalians in the vices of liquor, or spending their funds on other salacious behaviors would rob the poorer classes of funds that were so sorely needed. Though George had not seen that threats of an afterlife spent in ruin and constant agony aided their cause in any manner. Threats of fire and brimstone in his humble opinion were not the way to entice parishioners to do better nor part from their coffers. Mr. Morten led with a loving and generous heart, he was the perfect embodiment of true Christian charity.

Earlier, he'd ordered a bath to be drawn for him so he could look and definitely smell more presentable while attending to the business of his attire. He left the study, heading downstairs to a separate bathing area where the water could be easily accessed and drained. He shucked his clothes, hopping in the thankfully tepid water, and washed hurriedly. He despised lingering in a copper bathtub to soak unless he was completely run through from regimental practices with sore muscles, but those were no longer applicable to him.

Within moments, he was out, towel drying himself and making his way to the bedchamber to dress, garbed in his dressing robe. The door opened, admitting his valet Seth. George scowled, wondering why he was back so suddenly when the humble estate where Mr. Pembroke resided happened to be a few hours away by steed. He continued to his room, nodding with his head for his valet to follow.

"Sir," Seth said, shutting the door behind him. "The letter and parcel have been delivered."

"How have you managed this so quickly?" George asked curiously.

"Mr. Pembroke and his family were on their way to Town to shop for her trousseau. I happened to intercept them."

He nodded, "Thank you, Seth. Could you please have Fredrek direct the carriage to be readied for me? I, too, need to procure attire."

"Yes, sir."

"And before you leave to see to that task, could you please tie this blasted thing," George said after putting on his shirt and waistcoat, handing Seth the cravat.

Seth smiled. "May I please speak plainly?"

George perked a curious brow, but dipped his head in permission to the request. "Certainly."

"The staff and I thank you for keeping us on. We were fond of your brother and are equally fond of you as well. You treat us like people. It's a kindly service you do for us all."

George smiled wanly, clapping Seth upon the shoulders. "We are all human, are we not? I appreciate the loyalty, dedication, and fortitude of service you provide to this household. It shan't be forgotten."

He paused for a moment, recollecting what he had gone through in terms of figures. These employees had been loyal to Hathwell House and his brother for years, retaining their posts with quiet efficiency.

"I would like to reward you all with an extra three shillings in your pay from this moment hence. My brother had long spoken about what an ally he'd seen in you."

Seth nodded. "He was a remarkable man, sir."

"In private, such as this, please address me plainly as you would a friend and by George," he said, clapping his valet upon the shoulder once again. He did not care to carry on the airs that his fellow members of the peerage did. He was no better than anyone else.

The man looked ready to burst into tears. Seth spun on his heel, heading out the door while George finished dressing and pulling on black trousers and his high tanned leather boots. In all, it was a very simple yet fashionable outfit. He wanted to be back home before he happened to run into Mr. Pembroke or his daughter. Part of him desired to call off the wedding, longing for an extended engagement, but it would look distasteful of him. His family worked tirelessly to obtain and keep the reputation they had. He dared not soil it, he would not disappoint his proud ancestry with muddied waters.

Still, he wanted to shop and hoped to be done before he ran into the Pembroke's. With his luck, it was bound to happen, but one could hope for better fortune. He wasn't quite certain what he would say. When he had first met Isabelle at Harrison's wedding, he was struck by her beauty and lacked the ability to formulate words. It was she who began the conversation. And while pleasantly dancing with her, holding her supple form within his arms, it was perfection. He nearly ruined everything as his eyes tracked Mariah with his pining for a relationship and a deep love like she had found with Harrison. Isabelle had offered her condolences which struck a chord deep within him. It was given in a thoughtful and heartfelt manner from her. He had promptly strode away, not wanting to remember all that he had lost. It was badly done of him and he hoped that interaction did not present him in a negative manner to his intended.

George ran a hand over his face. Heaving a great sigh, he fixed his hair and adorned his topper. Movement outside the window caught his eye. The carriage was readied. The trip to Bond Street would be a quick affair.

Striding down to the awaiting conveyance, he clambered in, motioning for Seth to join him as the man had a discerning eye for what was currently in fashion that George cared not to possess. His wife could dress him for all he cared after their marriage. It was a luxury to have the regiment deem clothes for him. He never had to ponder coordination.

The stable master, also driver of said carriage, took off down the road at a brisk trot as they made their way toward Bond Street. The Town came alive as they rounded a corner. Shops and people milled about. George had the driver stop in front of a well-known tailor, parking behind a carriage he swore he recognized but could never place distinctly. He had seen it at the wedding. Mayhap Pembroke borrowed one of Harrison's conveyances since Mr. Pembroke was Harrison's uncle.

George pursed his lips, then fixed his face. *It couldn't be her*, he decided, alighting from the carriage and heading to the tailor door with Seth in toe. As he reached for the handle of the shop, it opened, admitting Mr. Pembroke and his wife.

"Lord Hathwell," Mr. Pembroke began, "so good to see you and so soon indeed. You remember my lovely wife, Beatrice?"

"*Belle comme toujours madame*," George said, picking up Mrs. Pembroke's hand and kissing the back of it.

"She is beautiful as always," Mr. Pembroke replied, preening. "Isabelle and my eldest Annabelle are dress shopping at the modiste," he said, shutting the door behind him.

"Thank you for the trousseau, my lord," Mrs. Pembroke's soft voice spoke as she inclined her head.

"My greatest pleasure. If you do not have any plans, would you care to dine this evening at my residence?"

"We would be honored," Mr. Pembroke replied, smiling unfeigned. "I know Isabelle would look forward to this greatly."

George swallowed, feeling his voice constrict and become thick. "We shall meet again this evening. I shall send my carriage to collect you."

Mr. Pembroke dipped his head, wishing him a pleasant pilgrimage. George felt fastened to the entrance of the shop. Seeing Isabelle tonight would be a welcomed sight. Perhaps he could speak to her about their impending marriage and gauge her reaction. He hoped to make a good impression.

George straightened his greatcoat, blowing out all the nerves in a breath though it still lingered in his chest. Shaking his left hand free of the remaining torment, he opened the door to the tailor. Four more days and he would have a wife.

Chapter Six

What A Night, Indeed!

I sabelle was both elated and exhausted as she surveyed all of the trimmings lining her bedchamber in the townhouse. There were various bags and boxes stacked up precariously. She watched her mother and sister direct her maid Emma on how best to store and pack the items. Isabelle was heartily relieved that she did not need to be bothered with the chore that her attire was proving to be. She was more than happy to let Emma deal with it. While she loved clothing herself in beautiful attire and even enjoyed the procuring of said items, she was just done in. She sighed, running her hand over an exquisite piece of lace trim upon the neckline of the gown she was to wear this evening to Lord Hathwell's townhouse. Isabelle had been confused when the money had been handed over to her Papa. Was not her dowry sufficient to state the case that her father was well enough off to purchase her trousseau himself? After careful consideration, she decided it was a thoughtful gesture not meant to offend. Her father had not seemed the slightest bit put out, so why should she be? *It is a splendid beginning to our marriage as it demonstrates that George possesses a great capacity to be thoughtful and kind,* she mused.

Not everything was going to be ready in time for the wedding day as it took time for new clothing to be sewn. Isabelle had been measured and poked for what had seemed forever, but it would all be worth the wait and time it had taken. The modiste and her seamstresses were set to work around the clock to ensure that her wedding gown would arrive on time. She had fallen in love with the satin that perfectly matched her icy blue eyes and made her dusky skin practically glow. It was to be adorned with silver flowers and tiny seed pearls. It would be the most decadent gown she had ever worn. As to the rest of the dresses and gowns, they were also a work in progress. With a few pieces that had already been created that needed slight alterations, she was to have a wardrobe befitting a countess.

Now she was mere hours away from dining with her betrothed. Isabelle had butterflies fluttering around her stomach. She almost felt lightheaded, but that could be attributed to the lack of sleep the prior evening. Her nerves were a jumbled mess. *Would I please my intended? Would he find fault with me? Would he be brutish and offended easily?* She was no stranger to causing offense and knew that she was flawed when it came to the sensitivity of others. Her Papa possessed a no-nonsense personality and she had inherited shades of his manner, which for a woman was not a virtue.

Isabelle glanced around her bedchamber as she petted FiFi upon his strawberry blonde head. She retied his red ribbon and rubbed his stomach and she thought of how much she would miss the decorations of her suite. It was decorated in a pale yellow and cream and the window faced the street upon which they resided. It was a beautiful room in a spectacular house in Westminster. Her grandfather had left this townhouse in his will to her Papa. It was easy to upkeep and the staff was on the smaller scale. The only dissatisfaction that Isabelle could fault the townhouse with was that it lacked a room for her to create her art, and so she much preferred the country house.

Once the bustle had quieted within her bedchamber, Isabelle had asked Emma to help her disrobe so that she could have a proper nap. She desired to be the best version of herself while meeting with her betrothed and a face drawn from lack of sleep simply would not do. Normally a few hours of missed sleep was not a cause for an utter disaster, but then it was not every evening that she was to dine with her intended. Sleep soon claimed Isabelle.

Isabelle awoke with the gentle voice of Emma calling her name. She blinked blurry eyes and sat up to inquire about the time. Learning that she had slept so long, she leapt from the four-poster bed to step into her awaiting bath. Feeling some of her anxiety wane, she smiled sincerely for the first time in what seemed like days.

When Isabelle stood in front of her rosewood mirror she was very pleased with her reflection. Her eyes were bright and her upswept hair, with curled tresses hanging alongside her face and loosely knotted in the back, bolstered her spirits. The cobalt-colored empire dinner dress was a sumptuous satin with cream lace trim along its neckline and hem. There were tiny powder blue flowers sewn along the fabric. Her cream-colored elbow gloves made the blues striking. Emma held out her reticule and she took it with a smile from her lady's maid.

Her slipper encased feet carried her from her chamber and down the staircase to her awaiting family members who had already donned their outerwear. Randolph handed her the burgundy cloak which she accepted with gratitude: it would be a chilly evening. The promised coach was waiting for them so they exited the townhouse and made their way to the stately carriage.

Once seated within the conveyance Annabelle remarked, "What a lovely carriage! The upholstery is well padded and comfortable. His lordship is set to spoil us all."

With a chuckle, Mr. Pembroke said, "He is a very thoughtful host."

Mrs. Pembroke smiled at her. "He has certainly begun to woo you *ma petite*."

Isabelle smiled and tried to soothe the sudden onslaught of nerves that assaulted her. How was she to eat in his presence?

She let the others chatter on while she lost herself in her own thoughts. Would she be permitted to continue with her painting, or would Lord Hathwell deem it inappropriate for his countess? Would he welcome FiFi into his life, for the idea of parting from her beloved pet grieved her excessively.

Before long, the carriage halted and the footman opened the door to assist them in descending. The wooden steps that were placed before the carriage were polished to a shine and reflected the bright moonlight. A butler stood with the door open and Isabelle followed her family up the few steps and into the townhouse.

A glittering chandelier with candles burning hung from the high raised ceiling and made the crystals shimmer in a rainbow effect upon the walls, floor, and ceiling. There were two Greek statues on either side of the entryway and a painting of an estate with fields of flowers adorned one wall. It was breathtaking the way all of the shadows and light created its own kind of beauty. This townhouse was enchanting and Isabelle had only viewed very little of it. A grand mahogany staircase was the focal point, set in the middle of the townhouse, with rooms on either side of it. There was a burgundy runner that lay upon the entire stairway.

"This way please," the butler requested, leading them to a room. He paused before the door and opened it, addressing their presence to the occupants of the drawing room as he read their names from the engraved calling cards he had been presented with. Stepping aside, he allowed them to enter.

Isabelle took a deep breath and grasped Annabelle's arm so that they could enter the room together succeeding their parents. She did not bother to take in the room's furnishings nor decor as her sight went directly to Lord Hathwell. He was welcoming her parents as he bent over her *Maman's* gloved hand to place a kiss upon it.

When his lordship rose, Mr. and Mrs. Pembroke moved further into the room but Isabelle did not notice with whom they conversed. Lord Hathwell greeted Annabelle first and then he turned his full chocolate gaze upon her. He was easily the most handsome man she had ever met. He was tall and well built with a narrow waist and long muscular legs. He was dressed in black trousers and a forest green tailcoat. Her gaze alighted to the starched white cravat he wore that caressed his strong jawline. It had been tied in a complicated knot which she decided was pleasing. His black Hessian boots shone and his silk waistcoat had an embroidered golden design upon it. He was donned to the heights of fashion, yet he was no dandy, that was absolutely certain. His rugged physique was a testament to the fact that he was not a man given to an excess of leisure.

When Lord Hathwell bowed before her, she remembered to curtsy but forgot how to breathe. He reached for her hand, helping her to rise, and then he placed a gentle kiss upon her gloved knuckles as he stared directly into her eyes.

"I am honored that you are here this evening. I trust you have been in good health?" His lordship released her hand to place it upon his arm as he escorted her further into the drawing room.

"Yes. And you I trust are well, my lord?"

"I am made better by your presence." Lord Hathwell smiled down at her. "Please address me as George; distance between husband and wife has never been my preference. May I address you as Isabelle?"

Isabelle beamed up at him. "As you wish, George."

"'Tis so wonderful to see you," Mariah sweetly said as she pulled Isabelle to her for a warm embrace. Isabelle had missed this demur creature that her cousin Harrison had finally convinced to marry him. Theirs had been a love match that had not easily been secured. The happiness that radiated from both her cousin and his beautiful wife struck a chord of jealousy within her. Mariah practically glowed. Could she find that with Lord Hathwell?

"What a wonderful surprise! I had no idea we would be meeting with each other this evening. How have you been?" Isabelle inquired as they were directed to take their seats. She sat beside her sister on a settee as she felt her betrothed's eyes upon her. She stole a glance at him and saw him smirk at her. She quickly looked at Mariah who was situated across from her in a wingback chair with clawed feet. She felt a slight blush infuse her.

"I am extremely well. Since you are all so dear to us, Harrison has news to share with you," Mariah held onto Harrison's hand, giving it a squeeze before letting it go. She folded her hands into her lap. Her gown was a cream-colored confection with the empire waist that was the height of fashion. Her dark hair was upswept in the current Greek style, much like her own was arranged. Her sapphire eyes shone brilliantly with suppressed excitement.

"We all so do like news, my boy, what is this that you have to impart upon us?" Mr. Pembroke spoke from the chair situated beside his wife.

Clearing his throat, Harrison smiled brilliantly at his audience. "I should like to inform you that there will soon be a new member of the family. We are set to welcome our babe late this summer."

With a sound of glee, Mrs. Pembroke flew from her seat and threw herself at Harrison who caught her in a heartfelt embrace. "Congratulations!"

Mr. Pembroke was on his wife's heels, and when his wife gently enfolded a laughing Mariah who had risen to her feet, he clapped Harrison upon his back as he shook his hand.

Annabelle rose next to offer her congratulations in a quieter manner.

The smile was wiped from Isabelle's face when she looked over to Lord Hathwell who was scowling at the couple receiving all the attention. Was his heart injured by this news? He looked stricken and much like he was about to be ill. This was not the reaction of a man who was free to give his affections to another. Isabelle felt her own heart splinter. She felt as if her own happiness was forever fleeing and there was not a thing she could do about it. If his heart remained with another, she had no room for him in her own. What a ghastly discovery. She would bite her tongue as much as she needed to tonight in order to get through this dismal ordeal. *One thing is certain, I shall guard my heart from this moment forward.*

Isabelle made herself rise from the settee and close the distance between herself and the happy couple. First, she reached up on tiptoe to kiss Harrison's cheek, then she embraced Mariah saying, "I am delighted for you. Such an exciting time for us all. I trust when you are naming godparents my name shall top them all." She was proud of herself for keeping her voice steady for, despite how Lord Hathwell felt for her or for the woman standing before her, she was happy for her family. A babe was always something to celebrate.

It was then that the butler informed them that dinner was served.

Chapter Seven

Not Smitten...

W hen Isabelle had first entered the townhouse, he was struck in place. He swore his heart stopped beating, his lungs gave out and fell to the floor, for his eyes had never before taken in anything so radiant. Isabelle was a goddess, far surpassing the Greek goddesses of lore. But beautiful women were fickle, or so he reminded himself. Alicia scorched him for another, and so had Mariah, even after her intended was caught in a rather compromising situation. Could this walking moonbeam be of the same cut of cloth?

Once his guests were comfortably situated in the drawing room, he watched her with burning intensity. She was poised though the tightness in her plump lips gave way to her true masked feelings. He could not fault her in that accord. They were meeting for the first time in months and their wedding was but a few days hence.

When Mariah and Harrison had announced their good news, near to bursting with love they had for each other, it had struck a jealous chord within him. He wanted that same happiness. He desired that same love, adoration, and affection. He wanted love everlasting to the point it bound their souls together for eternity. But could he have that with Isabelle?

George raked his fingers through his hair, catching her stare at him with a peculiar look upon her face, as if she were judging what she saw, yet did not seem to know what to do with her conclusions. Should he discuss his desires with her? Would it even be possible to have a familiarity between them?

He found upon closer inspection he did not find fault in the fact that Mariah was with child, but still, it was not something he had given much thought to. It had nothing whatsoever to do with him. This was between the couple and his heart wished them joy.

Sighing softly to himself, he brought his intended back to his thoughts as his guests conversed. He had heard rumors regarding the beautiful half-French goddess of Mr. Pembroke. She was blunt, with a sharp tongue-a no-nonsense woman, same as her father. Even if honesty was a virtue he liked to have in a wife, would she be receptive and listen? Would she then care? He had practically bled his heart to Alicia, yet held back with Mariah. He wasn't ashamed to say he was more of a soft-hearted man, but to be married to a hot-tempered, troll of a wife was a different matter. He wasn't sure he had the constitution to bear it.

Fredrek announced dinner was served and directed the party to the table. Since this was a more intimate and familial setting, none really cared about society's determination of proper. Harrison and Mariah were the first to proceed to the dining table, followed by Mr. and Mrs. Pembroke and Annabelle. George stood back, waiting to see if Isabelle would wait for him or take her sister's hand. Isabelle turned toward him, offering a small smile.

George approached, smiling softly at his beautiful intended. "I hope you were able to acquire all that you need," he offered. "If there is anything more I can do, please do not hesitate to ask it of me."

Isabelle heated slightly, the light pink creeping across her cheeks added to her ethereal beauty. She paused, batting her long lashes that kissed the tops of her cheek. Her icy blue-hued eyes turned toward him.

"In the manner of my trousseau, I must say I am astounded by your kindness and generosity toward me."

George couldn't help the grin. "I shall never want you to lack for anything."

Isabelle opened her mouth to say something and stopped herself, before turning toward him, a slight scowl on her delicate brow. "George?"

"Yes?"

"Might I ask you something?"

"But of course," he assured, trying to prove it through his calm tone.

"Would it be possible for me to continue with painting and to have my poodle FiFi with me once we are wed?"

He nodded, patting the top of her gloved hand in the crook of his arm. "I would not dream of asking you to leave behind or to cease that which makes you happy. If you require a room to create your art, then it shall be so. And FiFi is most welcome. I am entirely relieved that FiFi is not a cat."

"And what would have become of it if so?"

George sighed, a smirk edging its way to his lips. "Welcomed the animal still because it made you happy."

Isabelle laughed delicately, the soft, smooth noise was like nectar to his ears. He was easily finding himself becoming smitten, wanting to woo her and make her comfortable. He moved toward the dining hall, all the while chastising himself. *I cannot allow my heart to fall for someone I hardly know*, he scolded himself. Caution was his best course of action.

He assisted Isabelle to take her seat, waving away the footman, scooting her in himself. He aptly remembered the strict lessons of his mother and the sharp tone of his father when it came to women and making them the apple of his eye - to forever hold in esteemed regard and to always show the utmost care and courtesy.

George seated himself and indicated to Fredrek to begin serving. The staff brought out a silver tureen filled with a delectable white soup. He took a moment to observe his guests being served.

Mrs. Pembroke grinned over her glass of wine, casting glances between George and Isabelle. "Thank you ever so kindly, my lord, for entreating us to such an evening."

"'Tis, as always, my pleasure," George replied. "I hope Town is finding you well?"

"Absolutely, the change of atmosphere is always refreshing. Though, I already pine for home."

"As do I," Mariah added. "I cannot aptly describe the sensations of home. There is no other feeling quite like it."

"I wholeheartedly agree," Mrs. Pembroke said after swallowing a delicate portion of white soup.

"What makes a splendid home are the people within it, and that feeling is what I think cannot be adequately described," Harrison offered, staring adoringly at Mariah.

All George could do was nod. His parents had died when he was younger. His lovely, caring mother died of female-related issues. Heartbroken, his father died of consumption months later. Home was never the same thereafter. 'Twas as if there was a dark cloud hovering over Hathwell House. What made Hathwell home was gone and it was irreplaceable.

Since Robert was eldest, and the heir, he took over the estate. For a while, George felt as if he was reeling from a terrible dream over the sudden and tragic loss of his family. His parents were married in their teens and very much in love. Their deaths weighed heavily upon his heart. He attended Oxford, attempting to piece his life back together, though he shortly left thereafter and joined the regiment. The structure and camaraderie gave him some semblance of that familial longing he desired.

"George," Mariah addressed.

George quickly gave Mariah his full attention.

"I've told my Papa about your upcoming nuptials," she continued, "and he declared he would be most put out if he did not officiate over your wedding. He offered the church-"

"Though if you'd rather," Harrison said, taking over for his wife, "you're welcome to make use of Bramley Hall."

George glanced at his intended over a focused bite of salmon which had just been served. He had desired to ask Mr. Morten to marry him and Isabelle. He was fond of the man after having spoken with him intimately over the course of Harrison and Mariah's wedding celebrations. There were no other level-headed and astute men quite like Mr. Morten.

George ate and swallowed, appearing focused on what he was doing when he was precisely watching Isabelle. She maneuvered her hands in her lap, taking several sips of wine while her gaze fixated upon Mariah. It seemed Isabelle would be comfortable there. He wanted her to be content, surrounded by a familiar setting.

"I think that's a splendid idea," George finally said. "I appreciate the offer most kindly and accept it. I must confess that the idea had entered my mind. What better way in which to begin our lives together as husband and wife, than to do so where we first met?"

The relief of Isabelle's face struck him. He tried not to take it to heart that she wasn't trying to be discourteous. After all, they hardly knew each other outside of these two simple conversations. George enjoyed his meal while the women sprang into detailed action, guided by Mariah's thoughtfulness about how best to decorate given the timing.

"And what endeavors are you wrapping up here in Town?" Harrison asked.

George patted his mouth with a cloth napkin, having finished his dessert salad. "A new business deal that I find will aptly benefit my estate."

"I wish you the very best in that endeavor," Harrison offered. "Are you returning to Hathwell House on the morrow?"

"Indeed," George nodded, sitting back in his chair while the plates were cleared. "Are you and Mariah headed back as well?"

"Nay. We are headed back the following day. Since we are expecting, Mariah wants to ensure the little darling will have all the latest essentials."

Seeing his fellow men were finished, he offered to retire to his study for brandy. Lord knows, he should have one, but he was considering having several. He went around, assisting Isabelle to rise from her seat. The dress became her in a manner he had not yet taken into consideration. At first, he was struck by her beauty. Now, it was the entirety of her. She was elegant and graceful. A true lady and diamond of the first water.

He escorted Isabelle to the drawing room, not finding any words to say. He tried to convince his mind that he was not smitten. He was intrigued by her but wouldn't allow himself to be anything other than that for now. Burned twice, he dared not be scorched a third.

George left Isabelle on the settee, placing a gentle kiss upon the back of her hand. He instructed Fredrek to get tea and cake for the ladies while he and the men retired to the study.

I am not smitten, he thought, pouring himself an ample glass once his male guests were tucked within his study and had drinks of their own in hand.

Chapter Eight

A Chivalrous Man?

When there was a lull in the conversation, Isabelle looked at the furnishings around her in the drawing room. It held a very masculine presence with dark drapes, carpets, and furniture. *It needs more color and a woman's gentle touch,* Isabelle observed. She wondered how she may improve it and then wondered if she would be allowed to. Would George consider it foolish to redecorate a room that was far from shabby just to please her? The room held so much possibility to be warm and inviting. She wanted to provide a home to those she loved, not just a place in which to reside.

When the gentlemen returned to the drawing room, Isabelle was pleased that George took the chair beside hers near the fireplace. He bowed his head toward her and smiled. Isabelle returned his greeting, trying to think of a topic that might interest him. "Does your estate have many tenants upon it?"

George stroked his chin with his index finger. "We have nigh to thirty. There are farmers and a few families that hail from business and others in between. I hope you find the society pleasing."

"I am sure I shall. *Maman* organizes an annual bazaar event in which the whole town participates. The proceeds for the tickets benefit her charity for widows. I always enjoy helping to attend the stalls and watch the games be played. Does Hathwell have anything like that?" She smiled up at him and was very happy to see that she had his whole attention.

George leaned toward her and spoke, "I believe we have an annual church function during the springtime. I have not attended it in years. I believe this year it would be fitting to attend, with you by my side."

Isabelle smelled the brandy that lingered upon his breath. She was not against the drink, but did not desire to have a husband who was constantly three sheets to the wind. She peered into his chocolate eyes to discern whether he was indeed drunk. Uncertainty was her answer. "I shall be honored to, my lord."

They each sat in the silence of the moment lost to the gaze they shared, filled with secret longings and promises of what could be. Isabelle had never found herself so attracted to a man before and wondered what their first kiss would be like. *Would he be a gentle or a fierce lover?* She had been kissed before, and there was one that stood out, but that was years ago, when she was an untried miss, new to society. Now she was a woman, with not only a woman's heart but a woman's body as well. And she felt the odd urge to reach out and run her ungloved fingers through his dark mop of hair. On another gentleman, she suspected she would have thought that he was in desperate need of a trim, but George looked rugged and manly and made her heart pitter-patter.

Harrison rose from the wingback chair he had been residing in and announced, "'Tis time for me to retire my wife to our own townhouse. The hour grows late and she tires easily these days." He held his hand out to assist Mariah to her slippered feet.

George rose as did Mr. Pembroke, which was the thing to do when a lady stood within a gentleman's presence. It marked

George's character that he behaved with such refined manners. She should not like to be saddled with a beast of a man.

"I thank you for your company tonight, Harrison." George said coming to stand next to him, then he turned to Mariah and addressed her. "Thank you for all of your thoughtful planning of the wedding. I am exceedingly grateful to you." He nodded his head at her.

Mr. and Mrs. Pembroke said their farewells to their nephew and niece. Annabelle and Isabelle each embraced the couple and expressed again their joy and well wishes for the babe to be. Lord and Lady Bramley withdrew from the drawing room.

When Isabelle had observed the parting, she found no discernable attraction between George and Mariah. In truth, she had never seen anyone catch Mariah's eye but Harrison. And to his credit, her betrothed did not seem to pay his cousin's wife any special attention. True, she had not been taken into confidence about the events of Brighton that had secured their mutual affection but she had learned that George had played a significant role in how things came to be. Still, she caught no indication that any lingering desire remained for either party.

Mayhap his heart was not entrenched within another. There was hope in her own heart of a happily ever after.

Isabelle tried and failed to hide her yawn behind her gloved hand and was struck with embarrassment. A lady was never to show her tiredness as it was a poor indication to her host that her attention was waning.

Seeing the slight blush rise to her skin, George turned to her. "It has been a very busy past few days. I shall release you to the carriage so that you may rest."

Mr. Pembroke clapped George upon the back. "What a pleasant evening, my son. I shall look forward to many more."

Isabelle noticed the slight flush that appeared upon her intended's skin and smiled. He was humble. That was a wonderful discovery to make.

"I am pleased that you enjoyed yourself, Mr. Pembroke." George ran his large hand through his hair.

Stepping forward, Mrs. Pembroke reached up to place a soft kiss upon George's cheek. "Good night, my lord. We shall see you in just a few days time."

George nodded and then bowed.

The party walked from the drawing room and to the entryway. When the butler began to pass out their cloaks, George reached for hers and helped to secure it upon Isabelle's delicate shoulders. Feeling very warm and cared for, Isabelle gave him a dazzling smile. When Mr. Pembroke held his walking cane and had his topper atop his graying head, the party gave a final farewell and he led his wife and eldest daughter from the townhouse. Before Isabelle could reach the threshold to the out of doors, George reached for Isabelle's hand and brought it to his mouth for a warm kiss upon her gloved palm. Then he placed her arm along his and guided her from the townhouse and to the awaiting carriage. Isabelle felt her heart race and her blood sizzle with excitement. Mayhap she had found her perfect match after all.

She was the last to ascend into the carriage with George's hand firmly gripping hers. Isabelle was dismayed when he released her but realized the foolishness of her feelings. When she was seated forward-facing next to her sister, George popped his head in through the door and smiled at her, and then at her family. He closed the door and called out to the driver to commence the ride back to the Pembroke townhouse.

Isabelle leaned back against the plush fabric of the bench and sighed.

Isabelle was filled with joy for the wedding preparations. All of her favorite people were in attendance and each was pitching in with floral arranging and last-minute details directed by Mariah. The Countess of Bramley Hall had taken great care to ensure that all was in order for the ceremony and that Isabelle was not overtaxed.

Mariah had burst through Isabelle's bedchamber door at first light and had issued forth an army of commands to both ladies maids who were also present. She had brought Annabelle with her and the two hurried Isabelle from her bed. Within a few hours time, they had eaten and had the unwanted hair stripped from their bodies, their nails buffed and all manner of female grooming habits had been undertaken. Isabelle had never felt so pampered before. She absolutely adored all of the lotions and waxes that left her skin feeling soft. Their chatter was wonderfully entertaining and she suspected that for Mariah, who has been the only daughter within the family, this experience of companionship was a first for her.

Isabelle had fallen to sleep the prior evening despite her wedding day jitters. Today had been beautiful and the expectation of the ceremony and the celebration dinner to follow it was forefront in her mind. Mr. and Mrs. Pembroke along with herself and Annabelle had traveled yesterday to Bramley Hall to begin preparing for the day. Since Mariah had requested that they move the wedding to the early evening, it gave her more time to ponder upon her intended. An evening wedding was not fashionable and she had felt a slight hitch in her heart at the change. *However, 'tis just a small matter and I shall not dwell upon the lateness of the hour.*

Now, given the pampering that Mariah had treated her to, she could understand why her cousin-in-law had wanted to push the wedding back by a few hours. She was grateful.

When everything had been attended to and Isabelle stood before the full-length mirror, her nerves came out in full force. What if George came to regret her? What would she do then?

Mrs. Pembroke approached her and kissed her cheek. "You are the vision of loveliness, *ma petite*! The wedding gown looks just as beautiful now as if you had worn it this morning, it's suitable for any time of day with its extravagant decoration."

"Thank you, *Maman*. I think it does look stunning." Isabelle smiled at her mother through the glass' reflection.

The bedchamber door opened and in sauntered Mr. Pembroke saying, "A more perfect bride, I have never seen, excepting for your own dear *Maman* of course." He turned to smile at his wife. "I wonder if I might have a moment alone with our darling daughter before the ceremony?"

"But of course, you may." Mrs. Pembroke inclined her head to them both before she departed the chamber.

"You will remember this day for the rest of your life. I hope it is a fond memory that you shall treasure," Mr. Pembroke told her as he reached her side. He clasped her elbow and turned her toward him. Then he placed a kiss upon her forehead. "He had better treat you right, or he will have the Devil to pay."

Isabelle tried to smile but it faltered.

"All will be well, daughter of mine, never you fear."

Isabelle nodded her agreement and allowed her father to entwine their arms together. For better or worse, she was about to join her life with the Earl of Hathwell and become his countess.

Chapter Nine

Marriage For The Times

George sat in his bedchamber at Bramley Hall, dressed in his wedding finery and slightly buzzing from the whiskey in his flask. None had yet to arrive so he didn't make his way down to where the vows would be exchanged. To say he was nervous was an understatement. He had brought the liquor for courage and vowed to not have another sip after today. After seeing Isabelle slightly recoil from the brandy upon his lips while at the townhouse, he dared not begin their marriage with stumbling blocks placed before them. He had Fredrek remove all traces of alcohol, instructed him to not tell him where it was, and to bring out a bottle for special occasions and company only. If their marriage was set to flourish, then it must be done with having removed this difficulty.

He wrung his hands together, wiping them off on the clothes he changed out of to don his wedding attire. Seth has been by his side as any valet worth their weight would be, but George had sent him away as he preferred the solitude of his own company. He was nervous, scared even. He wanted his soon-to-be-wife to like him, to not find fault in him like the previous women had. He did not desire to have children with her just to procreate and then sever ties. He wanted marriage to last forever. He hoped he could find his forever with Isabelle.

George sighed, raking his fingers through his hair. *Only a few more hours perhaps and we'll be married. Then tonight, we shall begin our joint lives as a married couple at Hathwell House*, he shook his shoulders free of nerves. *I hope she likes me*, he thought, taking another swig of whiskey.

It had been decided to forgo a morning wedding in favor of an early evening one. There simply had not been enough time to decorate the Hall as the ladies had envisioned. With the sound advice of Harrison, he readily agreed to the change; he wanted the ladies to be satisfied in every way.

A horse whinnied, pulling him from his thoughts. Guests were arriving via carriage at Bramley Hall, granted they numbered few. George peered out the window, spying Mr. and Mrs. Simon Morten descending from a carriage. The elder Mr. and Mrs. Morten were behind them in another conveyance and two more stood in the line just shortly behind, awaiting their turn. Harrison and Mariah were out of doors, greeting guests into their home. George had invited his sole remaining uncle though the fellow replied he wouldn't be in attendance since he had gout.

George inspected himself again in the polished mirror. His dark hair was long and swept out of his eyes. The cut of his dark blue fitted tailcoat accentuated his muscular arms and the black trousers made his legs appear long and solid. He brushed a hand down his waistcoat which was decorated with silver threaded flowers. The cravat was tied, mayhap not the most elaborate of designs but it would suffice. He went over to the washbasin and brushed his teeth twice to be certain there would not be any liquor lingering upon his breath. And to be more certain, he emptied his silver flask out of the window. He was done with the stuff forevermore. He set the flask down on a side table and left it there.

With a groan from nerves, he strode to the door, heading out and down the hallway to where everyone was to be gathered. It appeared not many had come, which suited him fine. He was not one to crave attention and being at its center did not help settle his nerves.

Mr. Pembroke approached him, smiling broadly. "A fine day, is it not?"

George smiled back, shaking the man's hand. For a soon to be father-in-law, he was kindly, honest, and George greatly esteemed the pleasant man. His wife made her way over, her gray-blue eyes shimmering with unshed tears.

"Good afternoon, my lord," Mrs. Pembroke greeted. "You look dashing."

"I am pleased you think so. I do believe my future wife and yourself will have to dress me if I am ever to look as picturesque as Mr. Pembroke," he said, kissing the back of Mrs. Pembroke's gloved hand. "And please, both of you, hereafter call me George. We are family."

The couple nodded their agreement and directed him to use their Christian names when addressing them as well.

"Once Mr. Morten is readied, I think the ceremony shall begin. I heard he is not well as of late. I shan't think he would be staying long," William, his soon-to-be father-in-law, said.

"I hope he recovers," George replied.

He had always admired the great Mr. Morten. Ever since their lengthy conversation at the last wedding George had attended here, it was one he would always treasure and reflect back on. The man practically seeped wisdom and thoughtful responses. He was learned in Biblical truths but also made up of sincere practicality: the man had a wonderful way of making those around him feel appreciated.

The elder Mr. Morten entered the house with a cane clacking rhythmically against the marble floor. His wife, looking concerned but proud, helped him along. Mr. Morten ambled his way to where the wedding would take place. George followed, offering his arm to the man and expressed his greatest gratitude and highest honor of having him officiate.

Mr. Morten patted his hand, smiling wanly. "My boy, I wouldn't dream of missing out upon witnessing you find wedded bliss."

George smiled, hoping the merriment, instead of the worry that shrouded him, reached his eyes. He wasn't sure he would have wedded bliss. He wanted amicability, he desired companionship, at least. He hoped for more. But given his success rate, he would settle for less, vowing to always remain faithful and not take a lover as so often he found his peers doing. The practice was distasteful. Did no one honor their wedding vows any longer?

Mr. Morten patted his hand, taking the seat that had been placed down for his comfort. "My boy," he began fondly, "bliss is what you make it. God says love is the most powerful thing in the world. Put from your mind everything that previously injured you, because your future awaits."

George nodded, leaving the man to rest before the ceremony was set to commence. He strode to the back of the room where he could greet people prior to taking their seats for the indoor wedding. Given the nature of springtime, indoors was always best. The altar Mariah and Mrs. Pembroke had erected was elegant and beautiful with the remaining white winter lilies complemented by the vibrancy of the early spring tulips. The rows of chairs set up made an aisle with a vibrant burgundy runner laying the path to the altar.

He took the time to greet every guest, thanking them adamantly for coming to his nuptials. George knew the majority of them, yet there were a few he had not yet made introductions to, so Harrison had stepped in to perform the kindness. In all, he figured they were friends of Harrison's or Mr. Pembroke's; and the ladies in attendance were most certainly friends of his bride's.

He straightened his fitted tailcoat and proceeded down the aisle once everyone had been seated. Though he seemed to be stooped over quite a bit Mr. Morten stood at the front of the room with his walking cane held firmly within his grasp. The man certainly looked his age though his eyes were bright and merry. George took his place on the right, looking at where Isabelle would come in through the closed doors. Liveried footmen stood on either side at the ready.

George shook his hands free of nerves at the side of his body. The doors opened wide, admitting the evening light and the most exquisite woman that he had ever beheld. Her light blue satin wedding gown was dotted with tiny pearls and embroidered silver flowers that looked like stars upon her body. Her dusky skin looked vibrant, glowing, and complemented her icy blue eyes, that even from a distance pierced his very soul.

"Close your mouth, son," Mr. Morten whispered, chuckling.

George mechanically did so, not realizing he was ogling her in that unbecoming fashion. Heat crept to his cheeks, and he found himself doing it again as she neared closer still. She was the complete embodiment of celestial, looking more graceful, more stunning than the heavens of God himself. He was a blessed man to have the honor of taking her to be his wife.

Mr. Morten began speaking, yet George heard not a word. Everything sounded muddled, and he could not bring his eyes to part from Isabelle. She had yet to make eye contact with him, she was instead intently focused upon Mr. Morten and his words.

"George."

He heard his name. He swore he responded. Mayhap he did not. He couldn't truly tell. All he knew was he was awestruck, simply too far gone from his head by her heart arresting beauty.

"George?"

"Hmmm?" he finally replied.

Those in attendance chortled.

"Do you have a symbol of your affection for Miss Pembroke?" Mr. Morten's kind eyes regarded him with humor glinting within them.

George felt his cheeks heat, pulling from his pocket a lovely silver circlet with three sapphires intertwined. It was a simple ring, a beautiful ring, and one his father had bestowed upon his mother. It was special to him. He could only hope, once he told Isabelle the story behind the ring, she would find it lovely as well.

He slipped it onto her finger as he repeated his vows, not wanting to meet her observant gaze, but he simply could not help himself. Isabelle held his gaze for a moment. Her eyes were clear, a hint of a tear lingered at the edge of her lashes. He attributed the tears to the emotions that she must be feeling given that she was now married, and was leaving her familial home behind. *These are no small changes for her.*

"You may now kiss your bride," Mr. Morten announced.

George inched closer, tilting her chin up toward him with his one long index finger. The feel of her soft flesh against his skin set his entire body alight. He kissed her softly, not wanting to scare her with his ardor but to be as delicate as possible since, to him, she was petite and therefore delicate.

Those gathered in the room clapped loudly for them. George pulled away from their kiss, seeing her eyes change to a darker shade. His heart fluttered at the fact she enjoyed his kiss. Though a rosy hue pinked at her cheeks, she did not shy away from him. His enchantment grew even more.

"Thank you," he whispered to her.

Isabelle dipped her head, carefully biting her lower lip. George grinned, folding her smaller hand into the crook of his arm to lead her into dinner. They stood by the doors leading into the dining hall where gilded silver plates and glass wine goblets on burgundy tablecloths awaited the party. Side by side, he and Isabelle greeted and thanked everyone who attended their wedding. They did not exchange a single word with each other, only sincere smiles.

Since the wedding dinner was to be a more intimate affair, it was on a smaller scale, mayhap numbering in the teens in total, it felt more relaxed and informal. Larger guest lists were not in fashion and he much preferred having those closest to them in attendance. Harrison took a seat at the head with Mariah on his right. George took a seat to Harrison's left with his wife taking the other side of him, and her parents on that side of her. All were cheerful and merry. The wine flowed, though as per his earlier vow to himself, he did not touch it. Whether or not Isabelle noticed, he could not say.

He had a difficult time keeping his eyes elsewhere but upon his breathtaking bride. He was dumbstruck by her incredible beauty, though he desired to be captivated by her intellect and charm as well. Their prior meetings had left him wanting more. Whether anything happened tonight was of little importance. He wanted to get to know her beyond this smitten blushing they both seemed to be engaging in. If and when their marriage was a success, he hoped that she would eagerly welcome his addresses.

Dinner began with soup, followed by a savory beef. George happily took his share and then served his bride as was the custom when meat was set upon the table. He grinned at the dish, knowing it was a well-loved staple at Bramley Hall.

"Cheers to the lovely couple," Simon announced, raising his glass to them.

Everyone raised a glass and toasted them. Isabelle blushed yet again. He found that he was coming to love the rosy hue to her glowing dusky skin. In the future he would do all he could to ensure she blushed at least thrice daily.

"Your marriage is beginning much like ours," Alicia said, brimming from ear to ear with her smile.

George scowled slightly, "How so?" unable to recall how they had exactly met, though he knew it was due to her father overseeing the regiment.

Simon, too, gleefully grinned, leaning toward his wife. George swallowed, knowing his friend was going to give an excellent story. "So I saved my lovely, most glorious wife from a runaway carriage. It was all very heroic and made a slight scandal. For, you see, neither of us could keep our eyes from each other. And I must say, her blushes gave me great satisfaction. Seeing our exchanges, her Papa took me aside. To my very great surprise, in exchange for my gallantry, Lord Purcellville offered me either Alicia or his finest hunting hound. Of course, I chose the loveliest option over the quietness of a hound," he laughed as Alicia swatted his arm. "It appears to me you have had the same effect, George, taking a beautiful bride over horseflesh. Well done, old chap!"

George internally cringed. While he loved Simon and his loyalty, the man was a daft board. He simply did not know when it was best that he kept his mouth shut.

He turned to see the reaction upon his wife's face. Isabelle gazed at him incredulously. Her blue eyes so fiercely shone with hurt, she looked as if she was close to shedding tears. He felt utter mortification and regret for having caused these feelings to take root.

"My hand was gained through honest means, was it not?" she silently questioned her father though the entire room heard.

"Isabelle," Mr. Pembroke began.

George hung his head. His marriage was already off to a swell start.

Chapter Ten

Absolute Bliss

T he shock Isabelle felt left her insides reeling. She did not want a scene to arise at her own wedding celebration. But the look her father was casting her way left no doubt that he had withheld vital information from her. She felt betrayed even though he had yet to explain what Simon was on about.

"Isabelle, 'tis nothing you need to concern yourself with. You, and I must say, George, seem to be smitten with each other and all is exactly as it should be." Mr. Pembroke tried to smile, but it was not reassuring.

"You did not answer my question. I deserve to know the truth since it is being bandied about. Do you not owe me that much?" Her voice was barely above a whisper.

"Isabelle," George began.

"Nay, do not speak. I want to hear the details from the man who has forever changed my life by giving me away."

"It was time for you to wed. An opportunity presented itself and I acted upon it with not only your best interest involved but that of George's as well." Mr. Pembroke spoke stiffly, but concisely.

"What opportunity was that and where were you both?" Isabelle was proud of the fact that she kept the shaking to only her hands, which were gripped firmly together in her lap under the table.

"At White's, actually. We were playing a hand of cards and the idea came to mind. I kept looking at the man and thinking of how perfectly suited you were one for the other."

"There must be more. I implore you to reveal all."

George stood and pushed his chair back. He then leaned over to Isabelle and offered his hand for her to take. When she refused to acknowledge him, he simply waited. Taking a steadying breath and not meeting gazes with any other gathered that were intently focused upon her, she rose. She allowed her husband to pull her chair back and calmly walked at his side down the hallway until they reached the safety of the conservatory. When George softly closed the door behind them she turned to meet his stare.

"If you respect our marriage at all, you will tell me exactly how my father coerced you into agreeing to wed me." Her tone was civil and she promised herself that she would not shed her tears in front of this man. He was a stranger to her and, if it was not his desire to wed her, she would not allow herself to show him the depth of her feelings for him.

George swallowed audibly and ran his large hand through his hair. "I cannot exactly recall."

"Why ever not?"

"I had been drinking. My judgment was not what it should have been."

Isabelle's eyes grew large and she felt herself flush with anger. "So let me make it perfectly clear what you mean, my lord. You were drunk. So much so that you cannot remember how you became saddled with me. Though, from what Simon said, you must have lost a wager against my father. Horseflesh was mentioned. I assume you meant to win a horse and ended up leg shackled to me.

I do not know which to be more horrified by. That you frequently drink to excess or that you gamble for high stakes."

"Isabelle, I..." George's face was twisted with regret.

He must regret many things, including me, she thought.

Before he could finish speaking Isabelle, cut his words off. "There is nothing you could say to me to make this better. Have you any idea what it's like to be embarrassed so thoroughly in front of your family and friends? They knew! They knew why this marriage was taking place and I seem to be the only one without the vital information. Congratulations, my lord. You've just lost a bride. This dinner is over. I wish to leave at once. Have the carriage readied."

"Not everyone knew. You mustn't blame anyone else. This was my doing. No matter what words you throw at me, you are my wife. I will make this right. I swear this to you." The man looked like he simultaneously wanted to break something and weep. What did she care about his misery when she was so completely lost to her own?

Isabelle made her heart further harden itself against him. He could not injure her if she ceased to care about him entirely.

"May we depart?" She refused to meet his gaze.

She saw him nod his head, "Aye." Then she heard his booted steps cross to the door. He silently slipped from the conservatory and closed the door behind him.

Isabelle gave herself a moment to feel her heart break. She doubled over as she let her tears fall. It was no wonder why he had been so kind to her, he simply could not care less what she did, nor what happened to her. He only sought to make the match and nothing more. He didn't want *her*. Great, wracking sobs tore through her. She collapsed to the hard floor. She was to have a marriage just as miserable as her sisters.

She did not know how long she cried upon her knees. It could have been minutes or it could have been days. It mattered not to her. Resolutely she gathered herself together enough to stand. Then she reached down for the hem of her dress and used it to wipe away the tear streaks.

Spying a mirror along one wall, she hurriedly made her way to it. There would be no mistaking that she had shed tears. Her eyes were glassy and red-rimmed. Her face was flushed. Her hair faired well enough, so she did not bother it. She looked down at her dress. She had ruined it with her tears. Her gown bore a stain from her fall to the floor when her legs had crumbled beneath her. Her appearance was appalling.

In the glass' reflection, she saw Mr. and Mrs. Pembroke enter the room. She could see that her mother was furious by the way in which her mother and father were standing apart.

Mrs. Pembroke glided to her and enfolded her into loving arms. "*Ma petite*, I promise you, I knew nothing about this. Your Papa kept it from both of us."

Isabelle was in fear of letting more tears fall so she moved away from her mother and looked at her father. His face was a mask of remorse. She would not forgive him so easily. He needed to hear what she had to say, to understand her feelings upon the entire affair.

"You have betrayed my faith in you, my trust. You've made me the source of amusement and folly. I do not know that I will ever come to terms with the lies. You have wedded me to a drunkard and a gambler, a poor gambler at that. What will become of me if he drinks himself to death or loses everything to cards? That is the man you have chosen for me? I was under the misunderstanding that you cared for me."

Mr. Pembroke moved toward her, but she flung her hand out to stay him. He spoke to her from across the room. "My darling daughter. I have not failed nor forsaken you. George is a good man, I stand by that statement. He has lost his way and I knew the best thing for him was a woman who could speak her mind and stand up to his bad behaviors. You are his match. Given time you will come to see reason."

Isabelle laughed at him. "You, of all people, think me unreasonable?"

"You have been so before and are being so now. This is but a bump in the road to your happiness. Take this and make something beautiful out of it. For this is one thing that I am absolutely certain about. It's your determination to take the bad and bring the injustices to light. You can create a wondrous marriage if only you would try."

Shaking her head she bitterly remarked, "I shall see what miracles I can accomplish, if only I can keep my husband from the gambling dens and the bottle. Happy thoughts indeed." Did no one understand that one could not save another if they did not desire to change? "And the conversation we had earlier? It proves your intentions of pulling the wool over my eyes. How could you be so callous?"

The conservatory door opened again. A footman entered and informed them that the carriage was readied. Isabelle thanked him and turned to her mother. She placed a kiss upon her cheek and they silently embraced. She did not so much as glance at her father as she passed him by.

Isabelle followed the footman out into the hallway and then out of doors to the awaiting carriage. He helped her to arise and once she found her seat she released her breath. She was thankful that she had not encountered a soul on the way.

Sitting across from her was George. She scoffed at his presence. The coward had hidden away instead of returning for her. Well, she'd just add it to the ever-increasing tally within her head. She could tell he wanted to address her but she wasn't ready to deal with him yet. She crossed her arms and looked out the window. This was going to be quite a long journey.

Chapter Eleven

Long Ride Home

The five-hour journey home felt like an eternity. Isabelle dared not to look at him, all the while tears tracked down her face like a river. George had not known for certain whether or not she knew about the wager that led to their union. It was now apparent that she had not known the details prior to Simon's thoughtless comments. He liked Simon save for his lack of tact and sensitivity. George's attempts to woo Isabelle and win her heart by being considerate and courteous were just crushed by a blabbermouth seal of a man. Every hope of having a splendid start to their marriage was dashed. He had prayed that they could quickly grow fond of each other, and eventually, find a lasting love together. Now their marriage would either wither or thrive, and he had little doubt that at the moment he held no sway in which direction it would take.

What am I to do to correct this slight? I never would have wished to cause Isabelle pain...

George raked his fingers through his hair. Before settling into the carriage, he had overheard her shrill voice abhorrently stating that she was now saddled with a poor gambler and a drunk. She was correct to a point. However, he had vowed to give up the drink upon their marriage. He still meant it. He would also abstain from gambling this point forward just to show her that he wasn't truly a ruined man.

After he left her weeping and conversing with her parents, he had the carriages readied as she requested, loaded with her handmaid Emma and the little fluffy dog she was so very fond of. The second carriage practically brimmed with painting supplies and all of her belongings.

He had sighed, softly shutting the second carriage door after helping Emma into the carriage. Harrison came out to bid him well wishes and to evoke a lot of patience in their newly married state. In return, George thanked him and gifted the colt to Mariah to keep. He no longer cared about the profit of horseflesh at the moment. Hands shaken and fare thee well's made, he went to the carriage, assuming Isabelle cared not to see him. He was not disappointed. She came into the carriage, sat quietly, and that was the end of it for these unending hours as their carriage rolled down the bumpy road.

George glanced at her again. The tears had ceased trailing down her cheeks and leaving stains upon them; those same tears had fallen and marred her wedding gown. His heart lurched for her. He desired this marriage to succeed more than anything. He longed for what his parents had, what Harrison had with Mariah. He wanted a love that lasted through decades, that would be spoken about by their great-grandchildren. The love his parents shared together had always remained an example of what he most sought. Though it seemed to him that love was forever to elude him. *My wife cannot even bear to look at me.*

"Isabelle," he said softly.

She didn't meet his gaze.

"Whatever you think of me, I understand your mind will not be easily dissuaded," he paused. Isabelle gave no indication of acknowledging him. He sighed, continuing, "Before our wedding,

I vowed to give up drinking, having my butler Fredrek dispose of it all. I did not wish to start this marriage vilely."

She rounded on him, icy blue eyes glaring fiercely like swords piercing his heart. "No, you just began it that way. How dare you!"

George glowered. "Our marriage can begin however it may, though it doesn't have to end before it even begins."

"I don't care!" she seethed. "I'm bound to have a marriage just as *miserable* as my sister's now. I cannot bear that."

The words struck deeply within his chest. Was he such a horrid man? Was he such a rake, a terrible libertine, that no woman would ever want him or see that he wasn't deplorable? He shook his head. Alicia refused him. As did Mariah. And now his own wife. George bit his lower lip, nodding his head to speak his mind before the night was spent.

"Whatever you decide to do, I understand," he choked out. "I will not forsake this marriage for the company of another. I will not enter another gambling house nor take another sip of liquor. If anything, I do want my wife to be somewhat pleased with me."

"Truly?" she hissed. "I do not take promises lightly. My father implored that you are, at the *very* least, a man of your word. I hope he is not incorrect."

George lowered his brow, trying to mask his hurt. He could not understand how a woman such as she could have already determined a sharp judgment against his character. There were worse men, of worse character, that obtained wives in the most degrading of ways. This wasn't so for them, but then again, it was not ideal either. They had only spoken thricely. It stung his heart that women, and now his wife, found him so shameful. What was lacking within his makeup to inspire such rancor?

He took a moment to reflect inwardly, trying to find fault within himself that would suffice the sharpness he kept receiving. Perchance he was too pushy? To forward with his feelings? He had learned his lesson with Alicia that items and doting could not bear her affection. Neither could offering all the love he had in his heart to Mariah. And in his current situation, Isabelle would not receive his time nor company. He was at an utter loss.

He sighed woefully, hardly able to meet her scrutinizing gaze. "I do not break my word. I may be a lot of things, a terrible cad in your eyes, but I am a man of my word above all else."

Dare he see it, that her gaze slightly softened? He blinked, witnessing it return to the quick, judging gaze he was becoming accustomed to receiving from her. She stared at the ring on her finger, biting at her lower lip as she adjusted it. She twirled it around, clenching her fists at her sides, and removed her stare abruptly from it.

"It was my mother's ring," he offered. "My parents married in their teens against my grandfather's explicit wishes," he peered at her over a hooded brow, seeing he had gained her attention. "My mother was the daughter of a laundress. My grandfather revoked my father's earlship due to my mother's low birth, but being that my grandfather had only one son, Hathwell House was kept in our name. Neither my grandfather nor my father spoke to each other hence. However, no matter what my parents endured, they remained blissfully in love."

"What happened to your parents?"

"My mother died from a feminine illness when I was six and ten. My father, in his sorrow, died of consumption shortly thereafter. Theirs was a love bound forever... even in death."

They rounded the lane toward Hathwell House, heading down the paved driveway. The house was illuminated beautifully with candles, ready to greet him and his wife. His staff was lined up in front of the manor waiting to greet their new mistress. He found the scene absolutely dismal.

The carriages stopped in front of the steps leading up to the manor. Isabelle absconded before he could assist her down. He felt his heart crack further that she would do anything to be removed from his presence. He nodded to his staff who he was sure had witnessed the state his wife had arrived in. They all averted their eyes from his gaze with their heads now bowed low. What a sorry introduction, it was badly done, but there was nothing to be done about it. George went to the second carriage and indicated which of her trunks to have the footmen immediately bring in, and then led her inside the manor home. His butler opened the doors wide.

He entered and continued up the flight of stairs, with Isabelle on his heels remaining silent as ever. He paused in front of his bedchamber door, wanting to set her trunks in the room he longed to share with her. The icy glare she gave him said more than she would. Hanging his head and pinching the bridge of his nose, he went to the next chamber down from his which was the proper room for the Countess of Hathwell. At least they would share the same private sitting room, if only she would deign to make use of it.

Isabelle opened the door, going inside to stand by the four-poster bed with white gossamer curtains shrouding the bedroom in feminine elegance. This room, the one his parents shared, was exactly as he remembered - mahogany furnishings, white and dusky pink trimmings and decorations, everything that a lady of refinement would adore.

"I hope this room finds you well," he offered, not wanting to risk more censure.

"Good night, my lord," she said, turning around to face the window.

George pulled at the skin on the back of his neck. He opened his mouth to offer something, then snapped it shut. Taking a deep breath, and willing his heart not to shatter, he began, "Go down the staircase and turn left. Follow that short hallway. The first door on your left has been made into your painting room. It possesses a pretty view with adequate light. I furnished it completely with everything I could think of which you might require," he paused, feeling his throat constrict and softly cleared it. "I bid you a pleasant slumber."

He walked out of the room, shutting the door softly. The grandfather clock chimed twice. Sleep was going to elude him tonight. Instead, he went to his study, shutting the door behind with a snap. Having vowed to remove liquor from his life completely, it was going to be a long night with nothing to keep him company but his own self-destructive thoughts. What a banger year it had been and it was only the beginning of springtime.

Chapter Twelve

Making Introductions

Isabelle spent a miserable night with only FiFi to keep her company. What a horrid wedding eve. Her waking hours were torn between regret and something deeper that nudged her to truly consider her future happiness. In truth, there were moments when George had shown such consideration for her, such as the room just for her art. He still took her breath away much to her dismay. *How can I be attracted to him after all of this?* But for heaven's sake, it was the principal of the underhandedness of how the match was made. They were all very blessed that the scandal sheets had not written the particulars, something of more interest must have been discovered. Isabelle would praise the Lord for that just as soon as she could keep the hurt from cutting her so deeply. She would not pray with such bitterness coating her heart, even if it took her days or weeks to calm herself. It would be fantastic good luck, if, in her whining, the Lord decided to smite her even more.

Emma crept into the room later on in the morning. Rubbing the sleep from her eyes, Isabelle saw that it was after ten o'clock and that made her irate with herself. She was not one to lounge around, nay, she was one who accomplished things while others lazed about.

If only she could return to the happiness of yesterday! Mariah had surprised her with a bathing party. It had been such fun and was a wonderful memory to tuck away. She would need those memories in the coming days. Annabelle had also enjoyed their time and that gladdened Isabelle's heart further. In her female relationships, all was indeed well. It was the males closest to her that had caused her the most strife; her father and her new husband topped that list.

Isabelle sat up in the four-poster bed and waited as Emma set down a silver tray to break her fast. Placed upon the plate were sausages, eggs, and toast. The tea was just what she needed. Isabelle broke pieces of sausage apart and fed them to FiFi. She thanked Emma who was straightening up the room and choosing the dress and undergarments that she would be wearing for the morning.

It was difficult to silence her conscience, which was railing at her for her horrible manners in leaving the wedding without farewells and expressing appreciation. What must the guests think of the new countess? She had given them all the cut direct. When she thought of writing letters to express her thankfulness, her mind quieted down. She would write to Mariah first and then to her sister. After that, she would slowly seek to restore any tarnishment her poor actions had earned.

Emma opened the drapes to let in the sunshine. The cheerful day did not match Isabelle's dour mood at all. Where were the dark clouds, the booming thunder, or the sheets of pelting rain? Mayhap her imagination was borrowing from a gothic novel that she had read just a few months ago. If only the weather matched her dismal mood, she would not be left feeling so adrift.

Here Isabelle was, established within a new household far removed from her familiar residences, and with no accustomed things in which to comfort her. Everything and every person she was to meet with were all new to her. She worried that she had made a complete cake of herself in her arrival, avoiding each servant and demanding to be left undisturbed. But the matter of her bruised heart was not open knowledge and it was truly no one's business. Still, she must take great care from this moment further.

After she had eaten the last bite, she signaled to Emma to remove the tray; it was time to ready herself for the day. There were servants that she needed to woo if she ever hoped to reign over a well-stationed household. She needed their allegiance if she was to entertain and take up the mantle of the Countess of Hathwell. She could restore their faith in her.

Emma helped her to don a pale pink morning gown with lace trim and a lace ribbon along her empire waist. The beautiful matching slippers were comfortable and suitable as she had no intention of venturing out of doors. She was thankful that the last of her trousseau had been sent to Bramley Hall to be taken with them once the wedding vows were exchanged. Emma arranged her hair in the Greek fashion with it caught up and pinned in the back in a loose knot with tendrils trickling down either side of her face and neck. Her eyes were still puffy, but she did not look worse for wear. Another blessing to count. Isabelle stared into the mirror of the rosewood dressing table as she sat upon the padded bench. She twisted the ring upon her finger as her thoughts flew to her husband.

She had not been disappointed by the ring he had placed onto her finger. It was simple, yes, and usually jewelry was to reflect the station in which one was properly titled. Isabelle suspected that it was a family heirloom and that had pleased her. She was not so hard-hearted as to sneer at a gift. When George had told her of its significance, she had nearly turned into a watering pot once again. She had had to fight against the threatening tears. It was such a touching gift to bestow upon her. But she had guarded her heart at the moment and was not sorry for her reaction to his tale.

While she was not nearly ready to face her husband, she was ready to tackle the day. She hoped not to encounter him. She did not know that her heart could handle the pain. Isabelle rose from the dressing table and thanked Emma. She pulled a peach ribbon from her dressing table and bent down to tie it into FiFi's strawberry blonde fluff. Straightening up, she asked Emma to see that FiFi was let out of doors onto the rope. Then she promptly and with purpose followed the trail George had led her upon just a few hours ago. Once she had descended the staircase, she looked for another one off to the side in which to enter into the staff quarters and kitchen area.

A maid caught sight of her when she rounded a corner. Curtsying she inquired, "May I be of service to you, my lady?"

"I am searching for the housekeeper or the kitchen, whichever I locate first," Isabelle told the pretty girl who had stunning green eyes and auburn hair.

"I can take you to Mrs. Howell, who has newly come to Hathwell House as our housekeeper. Her office is this way."

Isabelle indicated that she should lead the way, "What is your name?"

"Marney, my lady." She looked over her shoulder with a kind smile.

"Pleasure to meet you, Marney."

They continued on in silence. *Maman* has always insisted that being too friendly with one's staff made them lax in their duties and they would not respect your station. Her relationship with Emma was thusly modeled. They were not close. One did not treat the servants as friends. The distinction was essential in running a proper household. Still, that did not mean that you were unkind toward them.

They stopped before a closed door and Marney knocked upon it. When a female voice bid they enter, Marney opened the door and stood aside so that her mistress could enter. Marney closed the door as the lady behind the desk looked up. Her mouth hinged open in shock and she quickly rose to curtsy to her.

"Your ladyship! I apologize for not meeting with you in your chambers. Shall we adjourn to a more comfortable setting?"

"This shall do quite nicely. May I sit?" Isabelle waved to the vacant chair that stood before the desk. The lady nodded and waited for further instruction. "You are Mrs. Howell?"

"Indeed, my lady." Mrs. Howell inclined her brunette head. She was mayhap in her forties with set features and while she was no great beauty, she was comely. Her hair was touched with a great deal of gray.

"Very good. Shall you sit?" Isabelle smiled at her.

"Indeed, my lady." Mrs. Howell sat and arranged the papers upon her desk in a busy manner, seemingly trying to bring them to order.

"Shall we discuss the running of the household?"

"As you wish, my lady. I am new to Hathwell House and am just learning the accounts myself." Mrs. Hathwell informed her with a nervous hitch within her voice.

"Mayhap we can learn them together. May I see the stack you have there?" Isabelle reached for the papers which were quickly handed to her.

Within an hour they had gone over all the accounts and posts within the household. New staff would need to be brought on to handle the increased needs. Isabelle left the housekeeper in her office and made her way down to the kitchen.

Mr. Williams was busy directing the kitchen staff as they diligently attended to their duties. The man was lean and muscular and she found it an odd contrast for a chef. Her breakfast was superb. She had nothing to complain about. When the man looked up at her, he smiled and strode to her. The kitchen staff noticed as they all curtsied to her.

"'Tis a right pleasure to meet the woman that George brought home!" Mr. Williams greeted her with a flourish to his bow.

"George?" She questioned, being taken by surprise by the lack of propriety.

Nodding his head he told her, "Indeed, my lady. George is as best as they come. We go way back. We served together in the regiment. I was forced to find other employment when a bullet met my flesh."

"Oh, dear me," Isabelle said as she touched her heart.

"'Twas a few years ago, when the eldest brother was alive. He was a right nice chap, too. Must run in the family."

"Where did you learn to cook?" She tried to mask her growing surprise.

"At my mum's feet. She was a baker in a village not too far from here. I met George and we hit it off." He rubbed his large hands together and said, "Shall we discuss the menu? I have a little cove around the back that we can tuck ourselves away into." He winked at her.

Isabelle was completely and utterly at a loss for words. She smiled again and let him lead the way. She was half bemused and half astounded, finding this interaction very odd. *What would Maman say?*

"Here we are. Do make yourself comfortable, my lady." Mr. Williams directed her to a chair, the only chair in the room she noted. He perched himself upon the window sill and his long legs were only a hair's breadth away from her own. This was almost improper.

"Thank you," she said. They spent a quick half hour planning the menu. Isabelle did find it helpful that he had knowledge of all of George's favorite meals. She was tempted to remove them all from the menu, but persuaded the errant thought to the back of her mind. While it was enticing, she would rise above. *I shall not be that spiteful!*

When she ascended the staff staircase she thought that now was the time to have a word with the butler. He had not been in his office and she was afraid that he must be sequestered away with her husband, so she decided it was an opportune time to begin her correspondence. Since Mrs. Howell was new to Hathwell House, she suggested that the butler could mayhap give her a tour. He would have much more knowledge to impart upon her about the history of the house. That would have to wait for another day.

Isabelle made her way up the grand staircase and padded to her bedchamber. When she opened the door, FiFi greeted her with a wagging of his puffed strawberry blonde tail. His little body was shaking with excitement at her having returned to him. The poor dear must be as discombobulated as she. This was all new to him and she did not know where he would be welcome. She reached down and patted his head and then let him follow her.

Opening the adjoining sitting room door, she peeked inside. George was absent from the room and she sighed in relief. She was learning more of his cavalier attitude toward the staff and wondered at the peculiarity of it. Did he not understand that he best helped them by allowing them to serve as they were meant to? Employing friends- who would have ever thought that was a brilliant idea? Wondering how the House had fared without her, she resolved to set all to rights, even if it meant that she would have to discuss the matter with her husband. She supposed that it was natural for second sons to be more *laissez-faire*, more lax in manners, but this was bordering on the uncivil side; it just was not done within polite *society*.

Pulling out the chair to the rosewood writing desk, she seated herself. FiFi promptly settled himself onto the settee near the fireplace. Isabelle searched the desk until she came across cream stationery with the family crest of antlers and a rose between them. Though it bore the name and title of her husband at the top, she would use it anyway. Locating the writing instruments, she crossed out his information and began her letter to Mariah. One to Annabelle followed. She expressed her gratitude to both and her sorrow for such poor behavior in leaving so suddenly. She told them how the wager came to be and how she was still stunned by the news. She begged them for hasty replies as she dreadfully missed them. Once she had sealed them with the wax seal, she gathered them up and departed the cozy room. Isabelle would ask Emma to see that they were handed to the butler for posting.

It was time for luncheon and that meant she must make her way to the dining room. How she hoped for a further reprieve from George, but she suspected that it was not to be.

Chapter Thirteen

Keeping The Peace

George kept to his study. He hadn't even changed out of his wedding attire. Sleep was a hopeless cause as he was sure to be plagued by nightmares of former horrors. He did not want to add night terrors to his list of faults that his wife was accumulating so he busied his mind as the long hours passed by. George was accustomed to staying awake and he much preferred that state than to wake in a confusing manner not understanding where he was, nor how he came to be there. Drinking had been his one certain way of a dreamless slumber.

He sat in his padded leather desk chair, curtains drawn, wondering if he should pen a letter to Mr. Pembroke asking for advice regarding his daughter or if he should leave everything well enough alone. He opted for the latter. Isabelle was already upset.

He didn't want to make it worse. Involving her father was certain to further earn her ire.

Linden came to inform him that luncheon was ready and served. Isabelle was there. He shook his head, dismissing the man. Linden had already given him a report on her, practically sprinting through the manor and checking both ways for him before she crossed the space to the next task. It made his heart lurch. There was also the matter of his aging butler's heart giving out with such exercises. This could not continue.

He ran a hand over his face, wondering how to make it right for her. He figured space and time might do it, or it might deepen the rift between them. He couldn't decide what direction he wanted to go, whether to force her to spend time with him or to give her adequate space.

George walked out of the study, hands in his pockets. Ambling up the staircase, he went into his bedchamber to change out of his wedding shirt and waistcoat at last, and remove the blasted cravat. Opening the door, he found his bed still made, all of his items undisturbed. That was normal for him, to avoid slumber at night, so he was accustomed to a tidy room. His troubled dreams would only be made worse by the situation he found himself to be in with his wife. He threw his cravat on the floor and quickly changed his shirt. He was sans a new waistcoat and cravat and he was immensely comfortable for it.

Choking hazards those things are, he grumbled, stepping over it.

Going to the door on the right-hand side of the room, he opened it a crack, hoping to catch a glimpse of his wife. What he saw instead was her little dog, perking its head up at him. George smiled, heading inside her room to pet the fluffy little thing.

The dog sniffed his hand, licked it, and immediately flopped onto its back. George smiled, petting the sweet small dog, giving it the belly rub the spry thing desired. He raised his eyebrows, discovering that what he assumed was a female given the name was in fact a male. The colored hair ribbons had only aided in his confusion.

"FiFi, huh," he said to the little dog. "You sure are quite an adorable little thing."

"What are you doing here? And what do you mean traipsing about the house in this undressed manner?" Isabelle demanded from inside the door.

George didn't startle nor look up. He didn't say a thing either. He hadn't a spectacular enough reason to give as to why he was spying upon his wife. And he didn't care to give her any ammunition against him. Whatever he did would be plenty enough, words or otherwise.

"I hope the staff are meeting your needs," he offered.

"They are lackadaisical," she replied, crossing her arms over herself. "You do not give them enough tasks, and they are taking advantage. And your cook is far too familiar with how he addresses you."

George continued to pet FiFi as he replied, "How Brandon addresses me is just fine. We served in the regiment and I shan't have him address me in any other way. Though I will give you credit that the other staff are all yours to govern how you see fit, and whether to keep them employed or otherwise."

Her jaw worked back and forth a smidgeon. He wasn't about to let her get away with too sharp a tongue. He didn't mind a direct response, but to be callous toward him when he was being gracious, hurt him. Granted, last night was an embarrassment to them both. However, the day was anew. He had given her ample space to cool down, though it appeared to him, she still desired space, and she hadn't cooled down nearly enough.

He rose from his squatted position, turning to face his wife head-on. She had her arms crossed over herself. The rosy pink dress and ribbon under her bosom accentuated her petite figure. Her blue eyes, so soft yet so fierce, continued to glare into his. Aside from the manner in how their marriage came about, there was, in his mind, no excuse for her glare. *Other marriages have started out worse and with worse men.* If anything, she benefited from the arrangement entirely. He had given her a title and enough funds to do as she pleased. *She could at the very least be civil.*

He pulled at the skin on the back of his neck. "Will there ever be a day when I may see a smile grace your beautiful face?" he softly asked, hoping to keep the wounded tone from his voice.

She scoffed. "'Tis not this day."

George nodded. "Will there ever come a moment in which I can procure your time to get better acquainted?"

She blinked, not offering a response. Again, he nodded, heading for the door.

"You weren't in your bedchamber this morning. Why?"

He refrained from a wan smile that edged its way to his lips. The fact that she checked on him made him dare to hope things might become amicable. Even if he was never able to procure her love, he wanted something of a companionship, an easiness in friendship.

"I was in my study, sending correspondence to those who attended the wedding and apologizing for our abrupt departure."

She nodded, recrossing her arms. The little dog yipped from the bed, scuttling over to his master where she picked him up in her arms.

"Thank you," she began, "for the painting room."

"'Tis my pleasure," he said, hand on the knob that allowed him entry back into their shared sitting room. "Again, I only want your happiness."

He left her then. The tense interactions were weighing upon his heart. He spent all night and most of this morning recounting every interaction with the women he pursued trying to deduce where he went wrong. Why did women loathe him so? He found he was a trite pushy with Mariah, even apologized profusely for it all. Harrison accepted him readily as a friend and business colleague after their wedding. And truth be told, it was rather a blessing he hadn't married Alicia; she was a gossipmonger whereas he didn't care in the slightest about another person's private dealings.

He ambled down the staircase to the out of doors. The sun was shining merrily though a darkness weighed upon him. He couldn't think of anything to do about their current marriage situation. He was torn asunder between speaking with her and giving her ample space. He felt in his heart, however, that giving Isabelle space would further divide them. George sighed, raking his fingers through his bushy locks. His father used to say - *when lost, pray to the Lord for guidance.*

He paused along the pathway around the gardens, glancing to the sky, and prayed. Taking a seat on the stone bench, he prayed some more for guidance, acceptance, yet constantly reverted back to - would love ever happen for him, or was he that terrible of a man. Was fighting in the war punishment? He felt as if it were so. He had never been insensitive to the lives he had taken, mayhap this was his penance, then. *And here I believed that my nightmares were my damnation.*

The sun shifted through the trees, illuminating the garden in a pre-dusk picture of bright golden oranges mixed in with hints of pink. He forgot what time it was, losing himself in reflection and prayer. He wanted, more than anything, to come to an understanding with his wife. He wanted friendship. And if something were to blossom into more, then that would be superb but, for now, friendship was his ultimate desire with her.

Glancing up, he spied Isabelle, staring at him from a window above. Instead of her scowl, it was wounded curiosity that he discerned. George got up, ambling around to a different side of the manor and in through the back. Since she was in her painting room, he would head there first, hoping to converse with her again. Time must have flown by him.

The scent of dinner wafted under his nose and his stomach growled. Having missed meals since yesterday, he was ravenous. His feet carried him to her room, even though his heart and brain cautioned against the idea.

The door was slightly ajar. Tea steamed from out of the spout of the kettle. He watched her clean her hands off on her painting apron, putting all the cleaned brushes aside for the evening. The room was the brightest in the manor with its many windows. He thought it would be perfect for her.

"Do you find the room to your satisfaction?" he asked.

Isabelle jumped, putting a startled hand to her breast. "Have not you heard of knocking?"

FiFi leapt off the cushioned chair, trotting toward him. George bent down and petted the lovely dog.

"I hope the paints purchased are ones you are familiar with."

She looked him up and down, a mixture of caution and anger still hanging upon her slender frame. Clearly, she wasn't one to forgive easily, and it further scorched his heart. Mayhap he was praying for the wrong thing? He prayed for guidance, forgiveness, and all manner of things. Perhaps this was the Lord's way of saying she wouldn't ever forgive him.

"Would you care to join me for dinner? I would appreciate the opportunity to get to know you and to discover your penchant for painting."

She opened her mouth to reply but snapped it shut, wringing her hands together. Her gaze darted from him. Without her having to say anything, he left. He would take dinner in his study from a tray. *Dear Lord, give me the forbearance to let her be.*

Chapter Fourteen

A Stolen Memento

What was the point in dressing for dinner if she was to dine alone? All her careful attention to her person had gone to waste. Isabelle could have at least brought FiFi down with her. She ate in the oppressive silence of the large dining room. Looking about her, she took notice of the portraits that hung upon the walls. If she was not in the wrong, that was a Van Dyke in the center. Being an artist she had studied the master's work. His attention to detail and use of color had always intrigued her. And to have a painting of his in her own home was a dream realized that she had never known. There were colorful vases waiting to be filled with fresh spring flowers. She would make up arrangements as soon as the garden was in season, mayhap that would gift her with a little piece of *Maman* as well as make her mark upon

Hathwell House. How she enjoyed the artistry of a perfect floral arrangement!

Isabelle took a few bites of her dessert salad and signaled to the butler that she was finished. He came toward her and pulled her chair out. He had informed her before the meal that she would be dining alone, as his lordship was indisposed. When she sat down, it had been with great satisfaction that her horrid husband was keeping his distance. But as the courses were consumed, she felt herself descend into a touch of melancholia. She missed her parents. She even missed the idea of the man she thought she had wed.

"Linden," Isabelle turned to address him.

"Yes, my lady?"

"Would you mind showing me the house mayhap even now?" She looked at him hopefully.

"Of course, my lady. If you would follow me." He walked over to pick up a candelabra and led the way down the corridor. They stopped when they reached the portrait gallery. He lit the few candles in the wall sconces that were arranged throughout the room.

Isabelle padded over to the first portrait. It was darker than her taste, but she fell more than a little in love with the subject. Before her was a scene set in a drawing room. There was a man and a woman who sat down in separate chairs in relaxed poses. Two young sons stood before the couple to either side of them. They all wore smiles and the joy upon their faces seemed to reach out and touch her heart. "Who is this, Linden?"

Coming to stand beside her, he looked up. "That was the former earl and countess. Those young lads are Robert and your George. What a beautiful family. If you look along the wall you will notice that most of the Wallis line were very fine in appearance."

Isabelle desired a family where love was evident to all. When it was time for a painting to be commissioned for her and George, would there be any happy children to paint? Would there be a smile upon her face? Would George's face reflect joy?

"What was young George like?" Isabelle inquired as she followed the butler to another portrait, one which she really was not focused upon.

A smile alit upon the man's face. "Precocious, intelligent, and always by his brother's side. Being close in age, they had a bond that many never get to experience. It nigh broke the new earl in those first weeks, nay, even months after losing him. He grieves even now. When their mother the countess left this world, a light was extinguished within the household. She had been beloved and we all grieved for her. Their father's grief was insurmountable. When he passed on, the brothers remained close, though once George joined the regiment, the distance kept them apart."

"Was George an honest young man?"

"Of course, my lady. There are not many young men of sense and heart enough to think of others before themselves. I am pleased to learn that even after his wartime activities, he remains the same sweet boy, only grown."

Isabelle felt close to tears. If he was such an honorable man, then the fault of their predicament lay with her. She was the one irrevocably flawed. Unless he had altered so much from that personality of his youth. *Though even Papa recommends him.*

"Thank you for your time," Isabelle thanked him and walked away. Her feet carried her into another room that was filled with statues and glass-encased treasures. There were miniature portraits in one display cabinet and she was certain that she had located one of a younger George. He was in full regimental uniform and the genuine smile upon his face called to her heart. She looked out into the corridor and spied not a soul. As quietly as she could, she opened the cabinet and retrieved the miniature portrait. *Mayhap no one would notice my theft, and if I am the mistress of the House, it was not really stealing, was it?* She shrugged her shoulders and tucked the portrait into her hand. She turned and walked out of the room as silently as she could.

It was growing late, or mayhap the lack of sleep was once again catching up to her. Isabelle found herself in front of her bedchamber door and entered. FiFi was curled up by the fire and immediately rose to greet her. She walked over to the mahogany side table by her massive four-poster bed and placed the miniature down. It would be safe there. She greeted the jumping FiFi as she sank onto the floor. FiFi gave her hands licks as he yipped excitedly. She briefly wondered if George could hear the noise.

Rising, she made her way to the bellpull and rang for Emma. It was time to dress for bed. Once Emma entered, she helped Isabelle to disrobe and braided her hair. The actions of Emma's deft hands were soothing to her. It was not long before Emma was pulling the coverlet up around Isabelle.

Isabelle tried to fall to sleep, but she could not. She wondered what George was doing and she acknowledged that she could think about him, wish him well, while still being upset. She was not ready to forgive him, nor the situation, but mayhap she could grant his request to spend time in his company. She would have to school her features carefully.

After another half hour, she angrily sat up in bed. FiFi's ears pricked and he made an inquiring noise. She threw the coverlet aside and let her legs dangle from the bed. Locating her slippers and slipping into them, she took a few steps to the chair which her dressing robe was hanging upon. She pulled her robe around herself and patted her leg for FiFi to accompany her.

It was difficult to get used to a new house. It had new sounds and a completely different atmosphere. Softly, she padded on tip-toe to open the joint sitting room door. Peeking into the room, she did not spy George. So, she entered and closed the door behind her. To her delight, there was a fire roaring in the fireplace. In a few steps, she was before the settee that was situated in front of the fireplace. She seated herself onto the settee and reached for the cobalt-colored wool blanket that hung along the back of it. She shook it open and laid it upon her. Once her knees were bent and her arm was under her head, she called for FiFi to lay behind her bent knees. She was neither too near nor too far from where her husband was resting his head. Within the whole household, he was the one she had the most interactions with. She knew in her heart that, no matter what, he would not let physical harm befall her and so she closed her eyes.

Chapter Fifteen

A Chance Given

George ate his meal in oppressive silence within his study. His heart was bruised. So far, he had tried to lure the bitter woman from her cocoon of anger with no success. What else was he to do? Should he write to Mr. Pembroke and hang the consequences of an already rueful wife? Should he make one last attempt to conjure a conversation from her? *I just cannot deduce the answers.*

He hung his head so far it rested against the cool polished mahogany desktop. What was he to do? He'd done as she asked - given up alcohol and gambling. He let her keep the sweet little dog with a horrible name. George scoffed. *His name needs to be Francois, not FiFi,* he surmised. *All of the bows are completely unmanning.* But still, he'd given in to her desires of keeping the animal as well as encouraging her painting.

George raised his head and groaned. *One last time,* he decided, *rising from his desk chair. I shall try one last time to see if I am to be well received by her and if not, then I will keep my distance. I would never want a woman to loathe me so. If she won't have me, even in friendship, then I will keep to one side of the manor home while she has the other. For I do not think I can bear seeing her glare at me for the rest of my miserable life.*

He moved out of the study and ascended the staircase toward his bedchamber. His feet dragged. His body felt lethargic. Still, it seemed sleep may elude him again. Heaving a woeful sigh, he entered his room. Peering to the right, he thought; *just beyond that little door and through a sitting room, would be my wife.* He bit his bottom lip, wondering if he should enter, just to catch a glimpse of an absolute sleeping beauty. Did she despise him even during her sleeping moments?

Carefully, George tiptoed toward the sitting room. He opened the door a crack, seeing the fire dimly illuminate the space. On the cushioned divan, snuggled in a blue woolen blanket, was his wife. George pursed his lips, curious as to what had lured her to the sitting room and not her bed. Certainly, this was less comfortable?

He strode softly toward her, taking a seat opposite her lovely sleeping form on the settee, watching her sleep. *Does she dream of me?* he wondered. The light rise and fall of her chest gave him comfort that even though she despised him, she felt secure enough in his manor home to gain a modicum of sleep. It was an indication that he had at least accomplished something right.

George raked his fingers through his hair, sitting back in his seat. He debated whether or not to wake her, just to say his piece and be done with it. He wanted to leave his words at her feet so she could decide what she desired to do with them. He knew naught else to do but this. Yet he could not find it in his heart to awaken her. She looked so peaceful, so beautiful curled up on the settee in their joint room. It made his heart swell a touch to know she desired to be closer to him in a sense.

George sighed softly, deciding against awakening her. Quietly, he added wood to the fire to help keep the chill from reaching her. He rose, ready to return to his bedchamber, when Isabelle stirred upon the settee. George reached over, tucking the blanket under her and over her feet. He leaned in to kiss the top of her head and was greeted with strawberry blonde fur instead of strawberry blonde hair.

"Bleargh!" George grumbled at having kissed the dog's fur.

The noise awoke Isabelle. Startling, she grabbed the blanket and pulled it up further over herself.

"I went to kiss you good night upon your head, and instead I kissed your dog!" George explained, wiping his tongue off on his sleeve.

Isabelle laughed, erupting with it. FiFi began barking at her melodious laughter. She threw her head back, exposing the long graceful column of her neck. The merriment in the moment made his heart tumble over. *How can this goddess be the same one who refuses my presence at every opportunity?* Could this be the moment he needed to persuade her to converse? Would she be persuaded to hear him out? If kissing the dog was all it took, he would have done it yesterday.

His wife sobered, smiling slightly at him. "I appreciate the sentiment," she said, softly.

George regained his seat while he still possessed the courage within himself, and since she appeared amicable to his presence. "There is something I wish to discuss with you, if you would not mind."

"I'm listening," she offered.

George grinned, feeling emboldened by her words. 'Twas all he ever desired was for her to simply listen. He bit his bottom lip, chewing on it a moment as he endeavored to find the words he wanted to say.

"I know it greatly bothers you how this marriage began. To me, it doesn't matter one bit. I was smitten by you the day we shared a dance at Harrison and Mariah's wedding. I stayed away though, believing a woman such as yourself wouldn't dare to be seen on my arm," he sighed, thrumming his fingers on the arm of the chair.

His heart constricted. He felt his resolve waning, but he would persevere. He must. This was his chance. Closing his eyes to the tumultuous feelings of fear, abandonment, and loneliness, he pressed on, telling his wife all he thought she needed to know regarding him. From when he first tried to woo Alicia Purcellville to Mariah Morten, how he found great fault within himself; that mayhap he was too bold or too honest with how he felt, and it pushed people away. George told her he desired her friendship, and if she wasn't desiring the same, then he would not force his presence upon her. All he sought was her happiness in the end. His father taught him that a woman's happiness is a man's responsibility.

He gazed into her icy blue eyes, getting lost within the vivacity of them in the soft glow of the firelight. Her eyes shimmered with unshed tears. Taking a linen cloth from his pocket, he gently dabbed under her eyes. His heart clenched tightly at causing her tears on his behalf.

"I'm sorry," he said softly, rising to leave.

Isabelle caught his hand, "Wait," she replied, sniffing. "Is that truly how you feel?"

George nodded, regaining his seat across from her. "Aye."

She fidgeted upon the settee briefly and set FiFi to the side of her. She readjusted herself, giving him her undivided attention.

"I would wish to spend time with you," Isabelle said, looking at her hands in her lap. "I appreciate the thoughtfulness and care you have given me. I apologize for my curt behavior. It was a shock to discover the means to our nuptials. I felt as if my father had betrayed me, and I worried that we would become folly for the gossip rags."

He tenderly smiled. "I understand, which is why I promise to give up those vices. I want to make you proud of me. I also needed to give them up," he looked down at his feet. "It's been hard. I lost my parents when I was a teen. I loved them dearly. Everyone here loved them too. Then when Robert took over the earldom, he became much too busy. We hardly had time to share a meal together. I went to college at Oxford for a period of time. It didn't work out well for me so I joined the regiment and fought in the war. I was on my way home for a visit when I heard of my brother's passing."

George felt immense relief at revealing all to his wife which weighed heavily upon his heart. He wanted to give her the whole of him, even the broken pieces. If she cast him aside because of it, then so be it. In the end, he would always be fond of only her, desiring only her, and hope for this marriage to work. *In my heart, she is becoming my everything.*

It appeared to be progressing in a satisfactory direction. He softly offered a prayer to the Lord in gratitude. George leaned forward, petting the small dog upon the head.

"I'm so sorry for you," she offered. "Once my sister Annabelle was married, it felt much the same for me. I only see her every few months."

"I can take you to visit with her whenever you would like. The same goes for your family. I wouldn't dream of keeping you from them."

"Truly?"

"Aye."

"Thank you, George."

Hearing his name upon her lips in such a soft dulcet voice was honey to his ears. It was superb, divine, all the words that eluded him. He felt the rush come back to him, when he had hosted the dinner at the townhouse, how he knew he was becoming smitten with her. This amiable moment meant everything to him.

Together, they stayed up late, talking about all manner of things from favorite colors to meals, from adventures they wanted to take together, to a life they hoped to have, and surprisingly her answers included him as well. He joined her on the settee, sharing the blue woolen blanket. FiFi took up residence on the chair he had previously occupied. It was a night of communication and understanding, a night George would never forget when his heart fully opened and allowed Isabelle in.

She fell asleep, nestled in the crook of the settee. He smiled at the sleeping beauty, falling asleep beside her in contented bliss, certain that there would be no troubling dreams to disturb their slumber.

Chapter Sixteen

Good Morning

T he sunshine was entirely too bright. Isabelle groaned as she brought her hand up to shield her eyes. When had her bed been located so close to the window before? Emma usually woke her before drawing the drapes. That was the moment that she suddenly sat up and opened her eyes to see George's smiling face. She nearly shrieked. Memories of the last eve flashed before her and she began to relax, until she noticed that the woolen blanket had fallen to her lap. True, she was wearing her dressing robe, but still, this was a new experience for her, and she felt color infuse her cheeks. Reaching down, she yanked the blanket back up to her neck.

"Good morning, lady wife," her husband greeted her, wiggling his dark brows.

"George…" she began.

He held up a hand to stop her, much as she had done to him before. He smiled ruefully at her. "Hear me out, Isabelle. You are my wife and it is not a sentimental endearment, unless you choose to make it so."

Isabelle gazed into his eyes. In the light of day, she only saw warmth reflected back at her. She nodded her head. "Good morning, my lord." She gave him a teasing smile to which he rolled his chocolate brown eyes.

"You delight in contradicting me," he said as he stroked his jaw. Isabelle noted that he was in need of a shave, but seeing him like this gave an intimacy to the moment that she was loath to part from. Mayhap they could continue on in the manner as they had last evening, with an open understanding.

Reaching for her braid, she inspected to see whether she looked like a complete hoyden. She deduced that all was well. It would not do for George to view her in disarray.

When a rumbling sound occurred between them, she jolted back. "Dear me! Is that noise issuing forth from your stomach?"

Chuckling, he nodded his head once. "Forgive me, lady wife."

"You had best see to that immediately, my lord." She refused to address him as lord husband. It was an endearment and she well knew that his addresses to her were as well.

George rose to his feet and stretched. He reached a hand out for her and she hesitated. Then he dropped his hand with a crestfallen look that he had failed to hide.

"I am not decent. I do not mean to rebuke you." She smiled gently at him.

He nodded his head and then said, "Then I shall leave you. Would you care to meet me in the breakfast room once you are properly attired?"

"Of course, my lord."

Isabelle watched him turn and stride from the sitting room. He looked back at her and grinned before shutting the door firmly behind him. Throwing the blanket from her, she hurriedly rose and threw it back down upon the settee. Calling for FiFi, who was still curled up on the chair but rose at her bidding, she glided to her bedchamber and closed the door behind them. She had to look her best for their first-ever meal together unchaperoned.

Half an hour later she was dressed in a lavender morning dress with tiny delicate ivory flowers and slippers to match. How she adored the latest fashion. Her hair was in its usual style and her eyes were bright. She was not blissful, but she felt more comfortable and that was quite the feat.

Emma tied a matching lavender ribbon into FiFi's fluffy hair and then took the dog with her when she exited the room.

Taking a deep breath to settle her nerves, Isabelle opened the door and walked through it. The staircase was lovely, she noticed, with its engraved roses upon its banister. It was a work of art as was so much of the House. When she reached the last step, George looked up from the wall which he had been leaning back against with his arms crossed. He smiled at her. *He has a dangerous smile. It calls to my heart and all the objections beg to flee from my mind. What strange magic he possesses.*

George walked to her and offered his arm, which she took, smiling up at him. His smile was bright, conveying his happiness that she had not rebuffed him. They glided to the breakfast room, which was lovely. Isabelle had yet to visit this room. It was decorated in pale yellows that invited the sunshine that lit up the room from the large bay windows. A polished mahogany table sat in the middle of the room atop a golden-colored carpet that was one of the prettiest designs she had ever viewed. George led her to one side of the circular table and pulled out the matching chair which was padded in the same gold color as the carpet. Isabelle felt bemused by the beauty in this one room, not excluding the man who was pushing her chair in.

Linden entered after them and two footmen began to load the side table with covered dishes. Within a few minutes, all was set.

"Mayhap a brief warning in the future, my lord, before you are ready to sit at the table?" Linden raised a graying eyebrow at him. Isabelle did not take exception to the request, it was given in the hopes of training the lord of the manor on proper protocol. Clearly, he had had no set routine for the breaking of his fast.

George nodded his head with an apologetic smile.

"Will you require anything else, my lord?"

"No, thank you, Linden." George rose from the table and picked up her plate. Isabelle frowned up at him.

"I am perfectly capable of serving myself, my lord." She told him.

"I have no doubt of that, lady wife. But think of my own comfort. For if you are constantly up and down from the table, so am I. As decorum states, a gentleman must rise when a lady does. And we must strictly adhere to all the rules, mustn't we?" His brown eyes were twinkling with his amusement.

"How will you know which dishes to choose from?" She gave him a very somber look.

"Well, that is easily settled, I shall choose them all."

"George," she shook her head at him.

He took the few steps to the sideboard and began to place various foodstuffs upon her plate. Before he returned, he spoke too lowly to Linden for her to hear, and then the butler gave a nod and departed the room. They were alone.

George placed the plate before her and bent down to place a chaste kiss upon the top of her hair. "Much more pleasing than fur," he stated.

Isabelle laughed again over the mention of the past night. She supposed she would always think on the moment fondly. At least he had taken it with grace and was not too terribly offended. Imagining the alternative made her laugh trail off. She watched him choose his own selection from the sideboard and when he sat back across from her he looked at her seriously.

"Have I done something wrong?" He looked like a man awaiting the gallows.

"Nay. You have not. But I think we should discuss something, if you will allow me to introduce a topic?"

He swallowed and nodded his assent.

Isabelle smiled at him and inquired, "Where may FiFi accompany me? Are there rooms off-limits to him?"

George rubbed a hand over his face and sighed. "Is that all?"

She furrowed her brows. "'Tis important to me. I do not wish to cause you unhappiness upon this matter. Should you tire of him, it would break my heart. I cannot stand to part from him. So I ask again, where is his presence barred?"

In the next moment, there came an excited yipping and loud footfalls, as if a person was running, that rang through the hall. A boy who wore the stable livery ran after the dog and into the breakfast room. The boy's green eyes grew large as he tried to still his panting breaths. He came to a halt before them, bowing low.

"Forgive me, my lord, my lady." The boy addressed them both. His face was heating to an alarming shade of red.

George raised his hand to stop his speech. Isabelle jumped up from her chair and her husband instantly rose. FiFi jumped onto her empty chair and looked expectantly at the table as he sat down. Isabelle felt her eyes grow round. Never had her Papa allowed the pets into the rooms reserved for the taking of meals. She awaited the judgment that would certainly follow.

George took one look at her, the dog, the boy, and covered his face with his hands. His shoulders began to shake and Isabelle worried that he was suffering some sort of fit. When she heard his deep laughter she slumped in relief. He was not livid.

Removing his hands from his face, he addressed the stable boy, "You are dismissed Jonathan, all is well," giving the boy's shoulder a comforting squeeze. When the boy did not move, he waved his hand at the doorway and said, "All is well. Return to the stables. Your post is safe."

Jonathan muttered, "Yessir!" and ran from the room.

Isabelle could contain her laughter no longer. She bent forward and clutched her stomach, this was quite the breakfast.

George walked over to her chair with a smile full of amusement. He picked up FiFi and placed the dog on the floor, then assisted Isabelle to sit. "In all my years, I have never witnessed such a scene. I can foresee a lot of laughter in our future, lady wife." Then he rounded the table and seated himself. With gusto, he dug into his meal.

Isabelle picked up a fork and considered her sausage. She forked a small piece and let it fall into her linen napkin, she then let the sausage drop to the carpet. FiFi rushed past her leg to devour the morsel.

"Why do we not give him his own plate so that my lady wife does not need to share her breakfast, or try to pull one over upon her husband," George said as he dabbed his mouth with his napkin and rose from his seat. He retrieved a small saucer and placed two sausages upon it, then made his way back to his chair. He delicately cut the sausage with his fork. Isabelle felt her heart flutter within her breast.

Leaning over from the side of his chair, he called to the dog and placed the saucer before it. When he straightened back up, his smile was dazzling, it took her breath away. "While we have this beastie in our presence, I have a topic to address."

Isabelle inclined her head for him to go on.

"This FiFi business will not do. It's emasculating to the poor fellow. Cannot you call him *Francois*? The bows are one thing but his name is not befitting his station."

"His station?" Isabelle inquired with bemusement in her tone.

"He is now an earl's dog. His peers will poke fun at him. So I suggest we call him *Francois* and then I suppose the bows will not much matter."

"Why *Francois*, my lord?" She arched a brow at him.

"It means one who has been liberated. We are freeing him from persecution and a terrible name." He smiled at her teasingly.

"Is that what it means? Why, speaking fluent French, I had no idea. Am I so horrible to him that he needs saving?"

He hesitated, and lowered his fork from his mouth. "Lady wife, I meant no disrespect. The fellow adores you. Dogs are an excellent judge of character, you know. You can keep his name as is, but when the other titled doggies make him cry, do not say that you were not advised to change the name."

"You are rotten to the core, my lord. I suppose that since you now have claim to him, I shall allow you to address him in whichever manner you so desire."

He bowed his head to her and finally shoved the fluffy eggs into his mouth. Isabelle smirked over the rim of her teacup. This new amiability between them was pleasing. She liked the friendliness, the teasing, the way his chocolate eyes lit up with mirth. She smiled softly to herself, realizing that she was becoming smitten with her own husband. And to think, all it took was for him to kiss her dog!

Chapter Seventeen

Let Us Away

G eorge spent the rest of the morning in his wife's painting room, watching her petite hand swirl colors on a large canvas. He had yet to deduce what her mind's eye was seeing but he was enchanted by just the sight of her. He finally made his gaze take in the painting, which was of the gardenscape out the window. She spoke softly of what colors were best blended together and which ones were more for shadowing. He had absolutely no inkling for color and was thrilled to hear her voice speaking to him regarding something that she loved. George hoped to one day hear words spoken with such tenderness with respect to himself. Until such a time, he would bide his time and show that he was attentive to her.

He watched her paint the bench he had sat upon yesterday with two large potted plants on either side. Behind the bench, the large willow that swept over the garden was beautifully crafted. When she had completed the painting, he would inquire whether or not she would allow him to hang it in his study, so that he may see it every day and admire her artistic ability. He could always be near to her, come what may.

"Lady wife," he began, setting down a letter he was perusing.

"Yes, my lord?"

"For luncheon, would you care to join me in one of my favorite places?"

Isabelle set down her brush, turning to face him fully. "And where would this place be?"

"To be sure, it will be here in England."

"Rogue!" she laughed.

"Never you worry," he grinned, "I shall come fetch you shortly. Then I would like to entreat you to something I think you would find delightful."

"Sir, you are spoiling me."

"Am I not allowed to dote upon my wife?"

She acquiesced. "Very well. How am I to dote upon you?"

George swept his mop of hair from his face. "Spend time with me."

He honestly answered, his fear of driving her away was vanishing with each moment spent by her side. Indeed, they were both growing bolder with each other. He strode toward the door, standing on the threshold. A lovely blush crept to her cheeks though it was more pronounced given the color of her dress. She was a stunning woman, one he was coming to find himself entranced by. Her charm, her sweet melodic laughter at his silly jests, was having him smitten by the passing moment.

Last eve, and their long talk about what each of them wanted, seemed to do the best of good for them. The air was clear. The new beginning was well underway and everything was mending perfectly. He knew she still held her reservations toward him. He couldn't blame her. They were just becoming companions. He hoped to woo her, and if he was lucky, gain her heart that he knew he would never destroy. They were making progress and he was immensely thankful.

He stared at her a moment longer before clearing his throat as he looked down at his boots. "I shall return shortly. You needn't change your attire."

He strode off toward the kitchen where Brandon, his former brother in arms turned chef, was probably beginning to prepare their luncheon. Brandon took a bullet to the leg for him, as he saved another comrade in arms who had never made it back home. They had been friends since childhood and now into adulthood. Brandon was as good a man as they came. And before marrying his wife, often they would share drinks and break bread together. He found his friend preparing to plate the luncheon and setting it onto a serving cart.

Brandon glanced up at him and grinned. "How are you faring now my friend? And how is the *Lady* Hathwell?"

"Better now," George replied, clapping the man on the shoulder. "Would you mind taking this out of doors to my favorite spot?"

"The one by the pond on the southside?"

"Aye, that's the one."

"Yessir," Brandon said gleefully. "Anything special?"

"If you could set up a table, chairs, and candles, that would be most appreciated."

"Consider it done."

"Much appreciated, my friend."

George strode out of the kitchen toward his study feeling merry and lighthearted. FiFi trotted down the hallway toward him, the matching purple ribbon bouncing with his walk. He truly did not care where the animal roamed. Even sat before the breakfast table, it had been well mannered. Dogs were predisposed to run, so the incident this morning was not a slight against him. George beckoned the animal to him, devising a plan that he thought would make his wife pleased.

He shut the door once he entered his study, going to a hidden lockbox on the bookshelf that was situated behind some of his father's favorite tomes. His mother was not one for jewelry but something that she did have, that she wore considerably, was a pearl necklace on a small silver chain. It was her most favorite piece, the first gift his father had given her after their wedding. He thought it would be a perfect gift for his wife. She had seemed to value the ring he had bestowed upon her at their wedding.

George put the box back onto the shelf, locked it, and hid it away. He tied the necklace around the dog's neck, holding him in his arms so he wouldn't get away. George strode out of the study toward his wife's painting room. He spied her, fixing her strawberry blonde hair in a small mirror that hung upon a wall. Paint dotted her forearms. He smiled. She had never looked more radiant.

George cleared his throat. "Lady wife, care to accompany me?"

"Where in England are we venturing off to?" she teased, a warm smile gracing her face.

"To my most favorite place in all of England. It's called around."

"Around?"

"Aye, around the back of the manor and to the south," he chuckled, watching from out of his peripheral vision to see how she gauged what he said.

Isabelle rolled her lovely blue eyes. "You, lord husband, are something else entirely."

George took her hand in his arm and held the dog with the other. She had not returned his endearment before. He was stunned. Was this a sign that she was coming to care for him? He did not wish to point out how she had addressed him, in case it was unintentional. He would tuck this memory away into his heart to savor for later. Now, the goddess stood before him and it was time to woo her.

"What is around FiFi's neck?"

George grinned. "*Francois*, is wearing something special, and I will tell you in a bit," he said, leading her out of doors and down a pathway that would take them the long way to the pond.

He felt like such a special man, having her on his arm. He led her through the same garden she was painting earlier, pointing out his favorite flowers that were just blooming while inquiring which ones she favored. So entranced was he by her soft dulcet voice and womanly charm, he set FiFi down on the ground to ardently admire her better.

Fifi yipped, chasing the birds on the manicured lawn. The barking caught George's attention. Realizing what he had done, he left his wife to chase the small dog.

"*Francois!*" George cried, as the small dog ran through a lingering puddle.

"FiFi!" Isabelle yelled.

George chased the small dog all over the lawn, calling out for the canine to halt, heel, or some manner of ceasing. The little sprite didn't stop running. He was quicker than George gave him credit for. FiFi ran circles around him, barking merrily while his tongue was hanging out. The soft giggling of his wife sounded from behind him. George glanced over his shoulder, seeing Isabelle on the gravel pathway, looking a cross between worried and amused.

He put his lovely wife from his mind, concentrating on the spry little dog that was causing a ruckus. Seizing his opportunity, George leapt at the dog, flew through the air, and skidded across the dewy lawn, catching FiFi by the nub of his tail. *I am immensely pleased that I didn't slip in this muck.*

"Don't hurt him!" Isabelle cried.

"Never fear, lady wife, I would not hurt a hair upon *Francois's* head."

George grinned triumphantly, seeking his prize. He removed the necklace from the dog and set the soiled creature back down. Dismayed, he went back to his wife. He felt dour that his thoughtfully planned gift had gone astray.

"I had something planned," he began approaching his wife. "I wanted to give you this as a present," he said, handing his wife the pearl necklace with the two unsoiled fingers he had. "It was my mother's most prized possession - the first gift my father gave to her after they wed. I want you to have this as a sign of my growing affection."

Isabelle gasped. "Oh, George! 'Tis so lovely. I shall treasure it always."

"I would offer to put it on your person, but I am currently quite the mess."

"You may put it on me," she said, handing it back to him.

George grinned as he rubbed his soiled hands upon his fitted tailcoat. Towering over his petite wife, he opened the clasp and put the beautiful pearl necklace around his wife's delicate nape. She was enchanting. He took a moment to appreciate the gift that was resting against his wife's creamy skin. He inhaled her sweet scent and breathed it deeply into his lungs. He then led her toward the luncheon area, figuring it had now been well over ten minutes as Brandon had requested. George removed his soiled tailcoat, wishing to have Isabelle on his arm once more. He was coming to find he quite liked her comforting warmth.

The path narrowed, going in between a long row of willow trees, sweeping the ground with their long tendrils of lovely foliage, creating a mystical feel as if fae were indeed real. The willows ended, opening up to a fountain in the middle of a pond where wild blue iris and cardinal flowers surrounded the pond in a beautiful array of vibrant blues and reds. On the outskirts of the pond, white winter lilies flourished.

Isabelle gasped, putting a hand to her face. "Oh, George!"

"This is my favorite place. My brother and I would practically live here in the summer while my mother observed from her favorite spot under that willow there," he pointed. A lonely chair with a weathered and beaten cushion looked out of place in such a picturesque place. "She would sit right there for hours."

Isabelle bit her bottom lip, turning toward him. Her soft hands trailed up to his shoulders resting there for a moment, before coming down and swooping around his middle. This was the first time they had embraced and it was the sweetest experience that he had ever felt.

"I am deeply grieved for you," she offered.

George closed his eyes to her gentle touch, embracing her back, savoring this moment. "Come," he eventually beckoned. "I have luncheon prepared for us." He was loath to end this tender interaction between them, but he was in fear of reaching down and kissing her. That, he understood, would be disastrous. He would not ruin all the progress they had made.

Tucking her arm in his once again, he led her around to the back of the small pond where a quaint dock and a single-person boat moored itself at the pond's edge. As requested, a table and two chairs, complete with glowing candles, awaited them. Linden smiled, standing off to the side. George helped Isabelle to sit first before he seated himself. Linden served them both their covered meals. A nice cut of beef served with potatoes, gravy, and green beans; one of George's favorite meals, and he was certain Isabelle knew.

"Thank you for this day, lord husband," she said with a glowing smile.

He could preen, if he were a bird! He knew that in that moment, it was a statement of intentional endearment upon her part. He was certain that the words 'lord husband' had never meant more to anyone else. FiFi yipped, coming into the garden area, and leaped into the pond. The dog quickly got back out, eliciting a laugh from Isabelle.

"Linden," she beckoned, "could you please have him bathed?"

The butler made a face of horror which he quickly masked as he stared at the muddied and soaked animal. "Right away, your ladyship." Linden picked up the ruined animal, holding him out directly in front of him. Isabelle laughed.

George could only stare and smile at Isabelle as he ate. It appeared they both were ravenous, hardly speaking as they enjoyed their luncheon, though smiles and blushes were had between them. This was the happiest he had been in a long while, owing to Isabelle and her charming pup. He would happily chase the animal through the muddied estate if this was to be his reward.

What he thought would be a terrible thing to be married, turned out to be the best drunken, poor excuse for a gambler moment of his life. Though he dared not tell Isabelle that. Some things were best to remain silent about.

"Lady wife," he began amused. "If we were to head to Town, what are some things you would like to accomplish there?"

"Is there a reason to head to Town so soon?"

George nodded. "I have business with Lord Taggart. He and his wife invited us to dine with them tomorrow evening seeing as we were not engaging in a honeymoon. I was hoping to leave after tea once things were made ready, but seeing as how *Francois* is a mess, we can leave early on the morrow if that would be more agreeable."

"I would love very much to accompany you. May I inquire if I am able to procure a gift to bestow upon *Maman*?"

George nodded. "Absolutely. We must shop for a gift for your *Maman* and Papa."

Isabelle beamed. "Thank you."

"My deepest pleasure," he said, sighing and leaning back in the chair. "Wife, earlier you mentioned that your mother does charity work. If the business I have with Lord Taggart goes well, would continuing to do a charity interest you?"

Isabelle immediately nodded, patting the corner of her mouth with a napkin. "Absolutely. What is it you have in mind?"

"To be perfectly honest, and please do not take this as a slight of insult," he paused, seeing her open and alert attention focused upon him, "but with horses. The profit from the sales can, in part, go to us, but also to the men hired to help run the stables. I was hoping to hire former servicemen in my regiment who became displaced due to the wounds received while serving. The revenue from the sales would bolster their families all the while, a portion of the income would go to widows and their families."

Her eyes shone with tears. George internally kicked himself for having been too honest. *What an idiot!* Their marriage began as a bet for her hand or horseflesh and it seemed to have brought it up again, deeply wounding his delicate wife. He was a callow cad. He lowered his head in misery.

"I'm sorry," he apologized. "I shouldn't-"

"'Tis a lovely idea," Isabelle interrupted. "How noble and gracious of you, lord husband." Her smile was lit with joy that gladdened his heart.

George beamed. The frantic fluttering of his heart from his supposed blunder settled. He sighed, setting his napkin upon his plate.

"If you are finished, *mon lys*, would you care to take a stroll with me?"

"My lily?" Isabelle asked, her blonde brows furrowing.

George felt his cheeks heat. He rose from his seat, his nape heating with embarrassment

"I'm smitten by you," he said softly, offering his hand to her. She took it, rising from her chair. "You are as beautiful, wild, and gentle as is the rarest lily. But I am fortunate to call you *mine.*"

Her beautiful blue eyes shimmered. "Oh George," she sniffed, wiping a tear from her long lashes.

He brought her hand up to his lips and kissed it, feeling like the luckiest man in the world.

Chapter Eighteen

Magic In The Air

Dinner was about to be announced and this time Isabelle would enter the dining room upon the arm of her handsome husband; the smile would not leave her face. They had spent the day with each other, getting to understand the little things about one another that only time could allow. He was kind, thoughtful, and admittedly smitten with her. He was close to falling in love with her, there was no doubt. That was all she had ever wished for. If only she could completely erase the manner of the match. With time, she suspected that healing and forgiveness would take place.

A large part of her desired to converse with her Papa. This time she meant to hear him out and attempt to understand what his feelings had been. Being distanced from Papa was difficult, she missed him, but being so far apart with miles of hurt between them was unbearable. When George suggested a trip to London, she knew she would not waste this opportunity to call upon her parents.

"Lady wife, you look radiant this evening," George said with appreciation in his warm voice.

Isabelle was glad he noticed her appearance. She had taken great care in choosing her pale blue dinner dress and had Emma thread tiny seed pearls through her tresses before loosely knotting them, as was the fashion. Her curls hanging either side of her face were soft and shone in the candlelight, and that was exactly how she had planned to appear before him.

"Thank you, lord husband. You look quite dashing." She had noted that he dressed regally for dinner. He was lackadaisical with his clothing and preferred to wander around in various states of undress such as foregoing his fitted tailcoat or cravat, even once not bothering with his waistcoat. It had scandalized her at first. But she was coming to realize that he thumbed his nose at the proper state of dress. Tonight was a complete opposite and this made him rise even more in her esteem for him. He was being considerate of her sensibilities.

Linden indicated that they should take their seats, and so they walked into the grand dining room. George guided her to her place, assisting her with the chair. He sauntered to his own and settled in. They removed their gloves and placed them upon their laps, then allowed Fredrek to place the napkins upon those. The footmen followed with the first course of soup and the meal began.

Isabelle dipped her spoon into her soup and looked over at George. He had his own spoon dipped into his bowl. His hand was shaking ever so slightly. He caught her stare and smiled at her, then brought the spoon up to his mouth. He managed to not spill a drop even with the tremors.

"My lord husband, are you well?" She waited to hear his reply, not bothering to eat.

"I am well, lady wife."

"But your hand was shaking and I know you are neither too cold nor nervous to be in my presence. Will you not confide in me?"

"'Tis a mild effect of giving up the drink; it will pass. Pray, take my mind from it, tell me what you wish to purchase in Town." His smile was genuine.

Isabelle frowned. She had heard of the effects of abstaining from alcohol and feared that he might become very ill. His color was fine and no sweat glistened upon his brow, but how long had it been since he had given up the drink? Was his body in pain?

"I am well. Do not worry yourself," he said adamantly.

She nodded at him and resolved that this was a necessary change for him and their marriage. She would observe him carefully. "I wish to purchase gifts for my parents. I know that there is a book that has recently been published, and it is my hope that we can gift it to Papa before he purchases it himself. As for *Maman*, perhaps a lovely brooch?"

"Wonderful ideas. And for you? What shall we shop for?" George asked after he spooned more soup.

"I lack for nothing, lord husband."

George winked at her. Once the soup had been eaten, they were presented with the venison pie. Then the dessert salad and cheese spread had been set before them. They ate in a comfortable silence. They were both famished as the business of building their lives together took a great deal of stamina.

George rose from his chair and came around to stand behind her. He bent over her shoulder and placed a gentle kiss upon her cheek, taking her hand to help her rise. Isabelle clutched her elbow gloves in her hand, not bothering to don them again. They were home after all and not entertaining. She let her husband lead her from the room.

"Would you object to a quiet evening in our private sitting room? I think the solitude would be welcoming," George inquired, looking down at her.

"No, I would not mind in the slightest. Mayhap you could read to me?" Isabelle smiled up at him as they crossed to the staircase.

"What reading would you prefer? Philosophy? Poetry? Shall I read from the Bible? Oh, we could see what the peerage is up to. It's been ages since I have looked at The Times." He wiggled his eyebrows at her. She had not bothered to so much as glance at the newsprint since their engagement had been printed.

Isabelle laughed at him as they ascended the staircase and made their way into his bedchamber, which they came upon first. He led her through it to the sitting room. She walked to her chamber door and opened it, allowing FiFi to join them. He excitedly ran to George who was finished lighting the fire. George reached down and picked him up as he turned and sat down upon the settee.

"I think he prefers you to me," she pouted at them both.

"'Tis only because I gave him a new name," George teased as he patted the spot beside him.

Sighing, Isabelle made her way to join the pair upon the settee. It was arguably the most comfortable piece of furniture within the room. She sat and FiFi placed himself between them both.

"Now, how about poetry for my lady wife?" George leaned to the side and procured a small brown leather book from the side table that Isabelle had completely overlooked before. She was curious as to what his tastes were and was more than a little excited to be read to. He had a firm masculine voice and she could not deny that when he said certain words such as lady wife, it sent shivers down her spine. *What would words of love sound like issuing forth from this enticing mouth?*

George opened the book and began to read Shakespear's sonnets to her. She was utterly mesmerized, not only by the words, but by the onslaught of feelings those words evoked within herself. If only her husband could pen such words of desire and adoration for her. She was being a silly gel, but there was a delight in dreaming that it was George's own heart that was speaking to hers. She was in very real danger of falling in love with her husband. *Mayhap that would not be such a terrible thing after all.*

After an hour of poetry reading they sat silently before the fire. When she looked over at him, she noticed that the hand tremors had returned and now there was a sheen of sweat upon his brow. Her heart lurched. This could be no easy feat upon him. She rose and made her way into her bedchamber, padded over to her washbasin, and dipped the cloth resting to the side of it into the cool water. Isabelle wrung it out and then returned to stand before George. She smiled sadly down at him, and he met her smile with a half-hearted grin. Isabelle placed the cool cloth against his forehead for a moment, and then gently bathed his face and ears. She reached for his cravat, and when he did not complain, she untied it, discarding it onto the settee. Then she bathed the back of his neck.

"I am stronger than this, you have no need to fear. It pains me much more to see unhappiness upon your beautiful face." He touched her hand and stayed its movements.

"I am your wife, I believe that it is understood that I should attend to you in sickness and health."

He chuckled. "Indeed, you may be right. However, a man does not wish to ever show weakness to his wife."

"What weakness are you referring to? What you are undertaking makes you my hero." She leaned forward and placed a kiss upon the end of his nose.

George sighed, still holding onto her hand. She found that she did not mind the contact and contrast of their skin molding together.

"The hour grows late and we are to set off early. I think we should retire, lady wife." He let go her hand.

"Of course. I shall let you seek your rest."

He rose and kissed her forehead, lingering for just a moment. Then taking her hand in his much larger one, he directed her to the door of her room. He called for FiFi to follow. Walking over to the bellpull, he kept his gaze locked onto hers. She felt butterflies within her stomach and a warmth spread over her. It was disconcerting to have a man in her bedchamber, but it was not unwelcomed when the man was her handsome husband. He returned to her side.

"Sleep well, my lady wife. Dream of fairies and fluffy clouds and whatever else bemuses you. And if perchance you find me in your dreams, I shall consider myself truly a blessed man." George took her hand and turned it over, placing a warm kiss upon the skin of her palm. Isabelle shivered and goosebumps alighted from her skin. George smiled with a touch of wickedness in his chocolate eyes and a saucy wink.

Isabelle watched him walk away from her and close the door after himself. She stood rooted to the floor as she brought her hands up to cup either side of her face. What was she to do with such a man as he? She was certain he would have a prominent place within her dreams. She could only hope that she was in his as well.

Chapter Nineteen

Purchases & Business

George sat in the study of his townhouse, resting after a splendid morning of shopping. His lady wife was pleased as a summer peach to pick out gifts for her family and a few wares for herself. It warmed his heart to see her so elated, especially after her worried looks regarding last night. He felt like an absolute cad for causing her to worry, but there was nothing to be done about it. Her tender care of him had soothed something within him and had made him feel treasured. He would always look back at this building up of their marriage and feel grateful that she had given it a chance.

Before leaving for Town, they had begun their day with a stop to visit with the parson, Mr. Ridley, who was a jolly man with a lean frame and curly graying hair. Isabelle had expressed her interest in meeting the man who George had informed his wife was the organizer of the Hathwell Bazaar. While it was early, the man of God had already begun his daily duties, and when he heard the knock upon his door, he was eager to welcome them in. His housekeeper, who was also his elder sister, had offered tea, but they declined, with the promise to return within a few days to stay for a longer call. George had made his wishes known that both he and his lovely wife would love to be included in the planning as well as performing the needed tasks. Mr. Ridley had been very enthusiastic in his ideas on how the lord and lady could both best be of service, and promised to produce a detailed itinerary upon their next visit with him. The whole conversation was concluded within the span of twenty minutes time. They departed from the parsonage and spent the next passing hours in conversation about anything that came to mind with the gentle swaying of the carriage to keep them company.

They had reached the townhouse a little after luncheon. George had sent a rider earlier that morning to prepare Fredrek for their impending arrival. While they waited to dine, they repaired to the drawing room together to wrap the presents for her parents. It was amusing and lovely to learn how to properly wrap a gift. Isabelle, the dear woman, took over for him because he was no good at it whatsoever. And if he was being honest, he rather liked watching her delicate hands handle the task. It gave him joy to observe her in all she undertook.

After luncheon, she retired to rest. He went to his study to conduct business and prepare himself on the topics of tonight's business dealings with Lord Taggart. He knew horseflesh to a point, not as much as his dear brother Robert, but enough to suffice. He studied, jotting down notes upon which he thought certain details were more important to remember. George listed the amounts of his endeavors in separate columns and then totaled them. The orderly process brought purpose to his thoughts for a time.

Reflecting on his brother brought to mind the melancholia of the eve before. He sighed, hanging his head upon reflection of Isabelle's perturbed face and worried eyes. He decided he must tell her the reasons behind his excessive drinking- he was plagued by his years in the regiment, seeing war, death, and destruction, and his immense regret of not seeing his brother. Death was senseless.

Drinking in excess proved to be a useful temporary solution as he had no others prior to marrying Isabelle. Being married to her, wanting to do and be better for her, to be the husband she deserved, was what he needed to give it all up. He had absolutely no regrets or the desire to drink. He was perfectly content. His lady wife had given him purpose and ended up rescuing him from his vices.

Chills crawled up his spine.

"Lord husband?"

George nearly leapt from his skin. He smiled, seeing his wife enter the doorway, though her brows were furrowed.

"Is something the matter, darling?"

"You're shaking again." She came into the room and took a seat in the padded chair before the desk. Her hands were clasped in front of her. "Please tell me why? Why would you imbibe in excess to damage yourself in this manner?"

George hung his head and rubbed his tired eyes. They had just reached amicable terms. Would telling her the entire truth dour the mood? Would she then come to loathe him, to believe he was a terrible man?

"George?" she softly prompted.

He sighed, struggling to meet her steady gaze. "I drank to forget what happened in the war, and what happened to my comrades," he began woefully. It was a sore subject for him and he winced at the pain it caused him but more so at what it was more likely doing to her heart. "I tried to help those I could, save those I could, but alas, my efforts could not save them all. My mind still flashes with memories, screams, and those that perished around me. Sometimes a certain sound or a phrase will bring a memory to the forefront of my mind, and I am lost in myself. I even have night terrors some nights. It was all so much to handle that I let brandy, or whatever else was nearby, soothe the ache and drive away the despicable memories. I discovered that if I was foxed enough, I slept more soundly. When I returned, I was ready to travel home to see my brother when I got a missive stating he had passed. It was too much for me to bear."

Warm arms encircled him, holding his head tightly. He closed his eyes, refusing to allow the tears of the tormented past trail down his cheeks. He allowed Isabelle to hold him, to soothe him in a way a woman believed they should; and in a sense, her quiet attention worked.

"I vowed to myself that once I was a married man I would quit the liquor. I owe it to my wife to be a wonderful, attentive husband, one she deserves to have, for all I want is a wife to be proud of me. I shall be fine in a few days' time. I am regretful to have worried you so."

Isabelle sniffed. "I am so sorry you had to go through all that you have. My heart aches for yours. Thank you for stopping the drinking. You are a hero, mine especially, and forevermore."

George grinned, wrapping his arms around her midsection, head against her abdomen, and squeezed her. Having the softness of her touch against him sobered him quicker than he dared to think. She was his vice now, his reason for living and committing to this marriage with all he had in him. And to hear she was not in the slightest angered by his reasoning, but understanding, and compassionate meant more to him than he could ever express. It was more than he thought he deserved.

He let her go, rising to his feet to tower over her by at least a head. He swept the curls off her face just to feel the light brush of her angelic skin and softness of her strawberry blonde hair.

"Thank you," he began softly, "for giving me a chance. I cannot express how much gratitude I have for you," he finished, placing a kiss upon the back of her ungloved hand.

Isabelle heated beautifully. "I am pleased as well. I am finding myself becoming more enchanted by you with each passing moment."

George could not suppress his beaming smile nor control his heart that dared to skip a few erratic beats. Could he possibly dare to hope that this lovely creature could return his affection? Would he finally have a love that lasts through the times like his parents'? He hoped so. He would pray for it to be so.

Isabelle disengaged herself from him, regaining her seat across from him at his desk. "Regarding the business tonight, I have several thoughts if I may?"

"Absolutely. Since this pertains to our family, as we are one now, I would love your insight on such matters. What is on your mind, my lady wife?"

Isabelle wriggled in her seat. "I believe Lord Taggart will oblige to do business with you given the exemplary and famous line of Hathwell Horses. In which case, how many men need to be hired to manage the stables?"

George grinned, appreciating how she took an interest in what he enjoyed. He loved animals, horses especially. He would love to do more breeding, perhaps of dogs later, but his brother was already well known for the horses Hathwell House bred. He would endeavor to continue the highly successful line Robert began. George intended to do so, complemented with the impeccable line from Lord Taggart.

"As it stands, there are three stablehands that manage the twenty horse barn. I was considering bringing on six more, not only to broaden the stables to accommodate the addition of another twenty horses, but to alleviate the pressure on the three hands we already have employed."

Isabelle nodded. "Why not hire eight for that matter then? And we can start with interviewing those of your previous regiment?"

George grinned broadly, feeling his heart swell in his chest. "I would love that. We can begin tomorrow once business is concluded with Lord Taggart." He paused, appreciating his wife and her involvement. "You would have the final say, of course."

Isabelle smirked. "I know. Speaking of, I believe we should begin a line of dogs. FiFi would produce an impeccable litter."

"I see," he nodded. "And how many females should we purchase for *Francois*? They would need to have the proper documentation."

"I believe two would suffice for now to see how all goes. That way, if there is naught money to be had, we are not too far into the pit."

"I agree with you, my industrious lady wife. I shall forever be your advisor since you clearly have a penchant for business."

George rose from his seat, leaning against the front of his desk, standing before his beautiful wife. He could see her perfectly from where he was, however, being closer to soak in all her goodness and charm made him feel wonderful. He loved seeing her smile, the way her icy-hued blue eyes twinkled with warmth and merriment, the way the apple of her cheeks heated to a breathtaking rose color and added to her flawless beauty. Indeed, he was lucky to have such a wife as she.

Isabelle laughed melodically. "You jest."

"I do believe I am quite hilarious, though I'm being perfectly frank. I would love to do this business venture with you by my side."

George offered her his hand and bid her to rise. He was quickly becoming addicted to the feel of her soft skin against his. He'd nearly forgotten the time. They were to have dinner with Lord Taggart in but an hour and the carriage still needed to be readied for the trip. George placed a chaste kiss on her forehead. "Do you need a moment to prepare yourself for Lord Taggart's dinner?"

"I only need to fetch my gloves, reticule, and cloak. I already dressed before coming to see you."

"Ah," George grinned, leading her down the hallway, and up the stairs to their chambers. "Always a step ahead of me, I see. That is good to know for future reference," he teased. He should have noticed her change of dress, but he often found his gaze locked onto her expressive face.

"Absolutely, lord husband."

"You look stunning. I can hardly take my eyes off you."

"You flatter me too much."

"Honesty should not be flattering, lady wife," he teased again, wriggling his brows.

George departed from his wife, heading into his bedchamber to get out of his attire. He rang for his valet Seth and for Fredrek to get the carriage readied. Seth assisted him with a quick bath and then dressed him accordingly for dinner. He figured while still in Town, Isabelle should purchase him attire since she might be up for the task of sprucing him up. 'Twas time he had the appropriate wardrobe befitting his station, even if the idea chafed his heart.

Donning his beaver skin hat, gold-handled walking cane, and his coin purse in preparation for purchasing a few horses, he waited for his wife at the front door. Isabelle descended the stairs like the earthly goddess she was. George beamed proudly. Her dark plum gown enhanced her otherworldly blue eyes and her French dusky skin tone. It was entirely hard to breathe. *Keep the salivating to a minimum, old boy.*

"I'm sorry to keep you waiting," she said softly.

"I will happily wait an eternity for you," he replied. He bowed before her with a flourish and a teasing grin.

Fredrek handed them their cloaks and once they were ready, he opened the door for them. George straightened and tucked Isabelle's hand inside the crook of his arm, moving toward the awaiting carriage. Once seated inside, the carriage took off for the Taggart residency.

It would be their first societal dinner as a married couple. He was thrilled and nervous at the same time. He knew Lord Taggart would ask him to have a respite and he would happily decline. He wanted this business deal to go well. In the long run, it would be very beneficial for Hathwell. He greatly desired to impress his wife that even though he was not groomed for this position, he would do honorably by her and their name. *I also mean to show my lady wife that while in the company of other gentlemen I can abstain from social drinking.*

Isabelle peeled the curtain back, smiling softly at the scenery passing by. He was utterly entranced by her.

"I must tell you something of great import," he whispered, leaning forward.

Isabelle's beautiful brows scrunched together, blue eyes narrowing. She leaned forward to partake in his coercion.

"Yes?"

"Lord Taggart may surprise you, though I must insist you stare at his eyes and not lower."

Isabelle leaned back in her seat, a hand covering her mouth. "Is there something that is the matter with him?"

"Indeed," he said in all seriousness. "He has the tendency to look akin to a hound."

Isabelle closed her eyes and laughed. "How crass of you! How could someone appear like a hound?"

"You, my lady wife, shall have to wait and see. We are almost there."

Isabelle chortled. He couldn't keep the smirk from his face at the sound of her laughter. It was his new favorite melody. The carriage pulled into the driveway of the Taggart household. George descended the carriage first, helping down his wife. She looked absolutely radiant and he would endeavor to keep her at home; for he feared if they were about in Town, and even though she was now a married woman, he would still have to draw pistols and fight off all the men who would stare at her. *She is all mine.*

George kissed the back of her hand. Having her on his arm was the most incredible feeling as he strode up the steps. The Taggart butler opened the door, and after George handed him their calling cards, announced them. Lord Taggart and his wife stood ready to greet them just outside of the foyer and near the hallway. Having passed off their outerwear to the butler, George introduced his wife to their hosts.

Lord Taggart, though not as drunk as that night gambling, still resembled that of a hound with his head bowed toward his chest. His long hair tufted at the sides, creating the illusionment of ears. George ensured to always meet Lord Taggart's steady, even gaze, and not look elsewhere. He could not keep a stab of sympathy from pricking his heart. While it was true of his marked likeness, the man was also one fine gentleman.

Lady Taggart was a slight woman. Grandmotherly wrinkles gave away her age yet the keenness of her sharp brown eyes and small smile gave credence to her wisdom. Her long brown hair, flecked with white, was piled in a poof atop her head like a cherry on a cupcake.

"As luck would have it for you, my boy," Lord Taggart began, "it seems you fare far better now," he chuckled.

Lady Taggart smacked his arm. "Harold!" she admonished. Turning kindly eyes on George and his wife, "Congratulations on your nuptials, Lord Hathwell."

"Thank you gracious Lady Taggart," George replied, bending over her hand to kiss it. "My wife and I are pleased to be in your company this fine evening."

"We are most pleased to have you," she replied.

"How is the married life treating you, chap?" Lord Taggart asked, motioning to the dining hall.

"Splendidly."

"I"m enjoying it immensely," Isabelle added softly.

"Wonderful, let's spice it up shall we?" Lord Taggart chuckled.

George and Isabelle glanced at each other worriedly as their hosts led them through the house. They entered the dining room after Lord Taggart took Isabelle from his arm and proceeded to guide her in to dine. George smiled at Lady Taggart as she placed her hand onto his arm to allow him to escort her. George led her to the chair at the end of the table where the footman waited to assist her to sit. Isabelle was seated next to their host and George took his place beside their hostess. Thankfully the table was not long, so that a more intimate dinner could take place.

Isabelle inclined her head toward Lord Taggart and smiled softly in a way which allowed George to know what she was thinking. George grinned as Isabelle tucked in her lips, mirth radiating from her eyes. He couldn't wait for the carriage ride home. She shared in the humor from earlier.

"Don't mind him," Lady Taggart began, addressing the earlier comment. "He's a fickle man."

"Tell the truth dear," her husband teased.

"Oh, pardon me," she grinned bemusedly. "My dear husband is daft."

Lord Taggart boomed with laughter. "And what does that make you dear?"

"A caring, loving, doting wife who cares for her husband in his advanced age."

"I'll concede your point, dear wife," Lord Taggart grinned. "Now tell the truth to this young man."

George grinned at the teasing between the married couple. The joy and mirth within their eyes shone even through the candlelight. He desired to have the same effects later in life with his own wife once the intimacy of marriage took root.

"Tell the truth," Lady Taggart guffawed. "You tell the truth, you hound."

George choked on his sip of water, setting it down and announcing it went down the wrong pipe. Isabelle gazed at him with wide eyes and a sly knowing smile upon her face.

"Fine, I regretfully shall," he said, dabbing his lips, "Lord Hathwell, my wife runs the business. 'Tis she you will be discussing it with. Though deemed improper by society to discuss business over dinner, there is naught else here but us, so pah to that!"

The butler and servants flowed in with servings of the first course. The creamy white soup called to his stomach.

Once the servants dispersed, Lady Taggart added, "Agreed, dear husband. I find business more agreeable over dinner when food warms the soul." She turned her attention to him and smiled.

"And I readily accept the proposal of which my husband has informed me," Lady Taggart said pointedly, after eating a bite of soup. "I shall sell you my stud for a fraction of what I bought him for, however, I desire the first two horses my stud sires in return."

George swallowed. It wasn't a bad proposal yet it benefited the Taggart's immensely, not so much him and his estate. He also wasn't one to discuss business at the dinner table yet it seemed the Taggart household said posh to the cultural norm and did as they desired. It didn't bother him in the slightest but he knew it bothered Isabelle by the way her lips went taught and her eyes narrowly focused on her soup. Still, George admired how the Taggart's did what gave them joy. When one was so high up within the peerage certain things could be overlooked. George didn't care for society, dressing how he wanted and lackadaisical in manner, but knowing Isabelle, she cared greatly, so he would endeavor to do better for her.

George cleared his throat and said, "I propose a different solution. I will pay you triple what you paid for your stud, and if you desire a foal, I shall offer a reasonable price."

"Triple?" Lady Taggart's eyes widened. Wisdom pinched knowingly at her face. "I suggest double price and a foal. And if you're concerned about my breeding, I assure you, I do not care. I'm too old and toward the grave to care," she giggled softly.

George grinned. "I accept this deal."

"Wonderful, enough of this," she waved her hand, as if flicking the conversation away. "We can discuss monetary arrangements later. For now, tell me how you two were matched."

George ate several bites of his ham, trying to find how to go about replying without hurting his wife's feelings. The dishes had been changed as the conversation went along. He figured this question would arise. He had racked his brain all afternoon, trying to deduce a keen way to answer the query without injuring Isabelle.

"We danced together at a wedding," Isabelle said, "I was enchanted from that moment on. So when my Papa mentioned I was to wed Lord Hathwell, I readily accepted."

"How lovely," Lady Taggart awed. "It's so difficult these days to discover wedded bliss in young couples with all of the arranging and indifference," she said with a roll of her eyes. "I am pleased to hear there is mutual affection between you both. I wish you many years of bliss."

"Thank you, Lady Taggart, you are much too kind," Isabelle replied.

George smiled at his wife. His adoration for her grew tenfold. This night was turning out splendidly.

Chapter Twenty

A Gentleman Among Men

The ride home was filled with merry laughter as the two discussed what had transpired while dining with Lord and Lady Taggart. The food had been divine and the company had been surprising and thoroughly entertaining. It had not taken long to reach their townhouse as the Taggart residence was only a few streets removed from their own home.

George assisted his wife to alight from the carriage and escorted her up the steps and through their front door. Fredrek greeted them and took their outerwear.

"Shall we repair to the drawing room, lady wife?" George asked.

"Of course, lord husband." Isabelle placed her palm upon his muscular forearm and let him lead her down the hallway and into the drawing room. She sat before the fire in one of the wingback chairs and waited for George to take his seat across from her. Isabelle began to ponder over the evening and how her husband noted that Lord Taggart resembled that of a hound. She threw her head back and laughed merrily. He was correct. And while she endeavored to do as he had suggested, and only look at Lord Taggart's eyes, hers, however, kept being beckoned to stare at the fluffy tufts of hair beside his ears.

George turned his head to gaze upon her and she covered her mouth with her gloved hands.

"How horrid of you to put the idea of Lord Taggart's being a hound into my mind! I nearly burst out laughing when his wife called him that very name. For shame upon you both! That poor man!" Isabelle contained her laughter. It was not right to condone such amusement at another's expenses, but he really did resemble the animal.

Chuckling, George replied, "I am sorry, my love, but really, one cannot help making the comparison."

Isabelle's face lost its mirth as she avoided his gaze. "Your endearments are growing bolder, my lord."

She stared into the fire that had been lit before they had entered the room. She supposed that George had given the order for it to be attended to. She was not sure if she was comfortable with the word *love* being laid before her in such a way. *Do I return his regard? Was it a slip of the tongue? Oh, these questions will torture me*, she thought.

George rose from his chair and paced the length of the room before turning back to face her. "I cannot help how I feel. My feelings are honest and true. I do not say this to force a confession from your own lips. If you ever feel as I do, I cannot imagine you being able to keep it locked away. You have such a vivacity, a love for life, and for expressing your thoughts. I did not mean to let my feelings be known. 'Tis as much a surprise to me as it is to you. Mayhap we should retire."

He strode to her side, offering his hand to help her rise. She hesitated and then complied with his wishes.

His speech had touched her, but she was not certain what to do with his confession. She was neither rejecting nor praising him. She was miserable not knowing what to say to him. She wanted to ease the situation but dared not attempt it. *What words would make us both comfortable?*

She looked up at him, worry brimming within her eyes. Isabelle made to speak, but he brought his index finger up to her mouth to silence her.

"No words right now, my lady wife," George said quietly to her. Then he was silent as he led her up the staircase and to her bedchamber door. He opened it and waited for her to enter through. "Rest well." Then he kissed her forehead and walked away, not proceeding in the direction of his own chamber, but back down the staircase. His proud shoulders were drooping.

Dash it all, she thought. *I never meant to cause such pain in him, not this time.* Isabelle closed the door and leaned back against it, half of her longing to chase after him and the other part stubbornly wanting to stay put. She had met many men in her life, none so brave with his feelings as her husband. *I am a terrible wife and after he laid his heart at my feet, confessing why he turned to vices.* Isabelle stamped her foot.

Isabelle made her way to the bellpull to summon Emma. She wanted to be rid of these clothes, she might even give them away. She never wanted to be reminded that she had so injured her husband's heart. Was she so irrevocably flawed in her makeup that she could not understand her own heart where her husband was concerned? Yes, she cared for him deeply. She suspected that she was falling in love. There was a part of her guarding her heart in case he decided to scorn her, but that was the complete opposite of his feelings. *Why then, can I not confess that I love him in return?*

Emma disrobed her and sat her before the dressing table to brush and braid her hair. Isabelle was lost in thought and let Emma do as she pleased with her.

"Is something ailing you, my lady?" Emma's expressive eyes held worry within them.

"Hmm," Isabelle blinked and then looked at her through the glass. "What was that?"

"Are you all right?"

"I am perfectly fine, thank you for your assistance, Emma. All shall be well. You may go." Isabelle rose from the padded bench and took the few steps to reach her four-poster bed. She climbed into the bed and laid down, pulling the coverlet over her. Noticing Emma stationed by the door she asked, "Yes?"

"'Tis only I have never seen you in such a state before, my lady. His lordship is a most kind master and if he has been mistreating you, I shall assist you in getting away." Emma chewed her lip instead of meeting her gaze.

"Nay, no, he is the best that ever was. He is honorable and trustworthy and... my *hero*." Isabelle began to softly cry, letting the tears course down either side of her face as they fell onto the pillow beneath her head.

Emma curtsied to her and left the room. That was possibly the most Isabelle had ever said to her ladies maid before. She sat back up, brushing the tears from her face, and reached over to blow out the bedside candle.

She tossed and she turned until dawn began to peek its way through the edges of the dark drapes. Without her beloved FiFi to comfort her, she was miserable. They had agreed to let him rusticate at the country manor despite leaving later than desired to see him set to rights. Isabelle missed his warmth and devotion. Sleep finally claimed her.

When Emma woke her up later in the morning, she brought a tray with her. Isabelle felt marginally better. It was a new day and she could face it and do better, better for herself and for her husband. She did not think she was ready to say that she loved him, but mayhap she could be attentive enough to let him understand that he was of supreme importance to her. In time, she would be able to say the words he so desired.

Isabelle looked at the folded slip of paper upon her tray and frowned. She reached for it and unfolded it. It was from George.

My lady wife,

I have left early to settle financial matters with my solicitor. I shall return before luncheon and after our meal I am hoping that you will accompany me on our errand to hire more stablehands. Your advice and guidance is greatly appreciated.

Yours,

G.W.

Isabelle sighed. It was hardly a love letter and yet, she was touched that he had taken the time to write to her at all. The tone of the missive did not seem angry, so he was not irate this morning. She blew out a breath. *I do not deserve him.* He was a gentleman in every way. She would tuck this away in her reticule to always have with her.

After dressing in a pink morning dress with cream lace trimming and pulling on her gloves, she picked up her reticule and bonnet. Isabelle made her way down the staircase and to George's study. Spying Fredrek turning the corner, she requested that he have the carriage readied for her.

Once she entered the study, she padded to her husband's mahogany desk that was free from clutter and sat down in his leather chair. She located fresh paper in his top drawer and wrote her own note, letting him know that she was on her way to pay a call upon her parents. She hoped that he would join her there with the gifts that they had purchased for the couple. She signed it as "Isabelle, your wife" and blotted the paper. Folding it, she then donned her bonnet and found Fredrek in the hallway.

"Please see that his lordship receives this immediately upon his return."

The butler bowed and said, "Of course, my lady." Then he handed her cloak to her and when it was situated he walked to the door to open it. She smiled and thanked him again.

In the carriage, she prepared to meet her Papa. He would see her, she knew it to be so, but her nerves were unsettled. She felt as if an apology might be due to him. Given the circumstances she felt justified in her response to him at Bramley Hall. He should have been honest with her. But as her parent, he had earned her respect. She was ready to listen to him without prejudice.

The carriage soon stopped and Isabelle found herself standing in the foyer waiting to be received. She had purposely asked Randolph to inquire if her father would see her in his study.

When the butler returned to her, he escorted her directly to the study where Mr. Pembroke stood waiting before his desk. Isabelle walked into the room and stopped before her father. He arched a brow at her with his blue eyes twinkling.

"Papa," she began. "You look well."

"I am experiencing wonderfully good health. Is that why you have called upon me? Shall we discuss the weather next?" Mr. Pembroke teased her.

Smiling at him she said, "It is a glorious day. Have you ventured out yet?"

He wagged his index finger at her and bid her to sit. Walking around the desk, he took his own seat and waited for her to speak.

Isabelle worried her bottom lip between her teeth for a moment. She had to know. Taking a deep breath, she asked, "Will you please relay what went through your head when you agreed to the wager?"

"I was thinking that I had a winning hand. I have known the young man for quite some time. Since his brother's passing, in fact. He is very well suited to you, and you to him. I thought it was beneficial to you both. He is certainly wealthy enough for you to do just as you please. And you can give him credence to his endeavors. He needed a reason to go on, Isabelle. He was drowning himself in vices. He needed *you.*" Mr. Pembroke sat back in his chair and looked at her.

Isabelle blinked. "And did it not cross your mind that a great scandal could have been created alongside your wager? You could have done damage to us all."

"Nothing that a marriage could not correct. Furthermore, George isn't the type of man who would create such an ordeal. If it makes you happy, I never meant to upset you, but I would do the whole thing again. He needed you and you needed someone who wouldn't flinch at your candor. Am I forgiven? Is George treating you well?"

Isabelle nodded. The logic was sound even if she still wasn't thrilled about how the arrangement came to pass. Still, she was happy to be married to George. He was an excellent man with a generous heart. "He is, and you are forgiven. But I shall always wish that you had told me the entire truth. Poor George bore the brunt of my anger and humiliation. I am not worthy of him." She bowed her head.

Mr. Pembroke rose from his chair and walked around the side of his desk to stand before her. He reached down and lifted her chin with his index finger. "Oh, my darling daughter. You are worthy, as is he. A more perfect match I have never known."

Isabelle smiled softly at him as she gained her feet. She leaned toward him and embraced him. He heartily returned her affection and she felt her eyes tear up. Her father bore her no resentment and her heart in this regard was lightened.

Having the great burdensome weight lifted from her shoulders gave her heart the courage it needed to soar straight to George. Tonight, she would tell him of her affection for him.

Chapter Twenty-One

Adoration

George flipped through his coins and handed the accruement to Lord Taggart. He did his best to remain the chipper man these fine people had seen in him last evening, but inside his heart was drowning.

"Always a pleasure seeing you, George," Harold said, squeezing his shoulder fondly. "I'll have your horse delivered to Hathwell immediately."

"Thank you kindly," he replied. "I shall write and let you know how he does with the mares."

Harold laughed. "Just write to my wife," he said, walking away and into the mews.

George grinned, mounting his steed to head back to the townhouse. He felt heavy. While he was enamored with his wife, she wasn't of the same regard. Try as he might to convince himself that it did not matter to him, it did. He wanted a loving marriage, where perchance the woman he called his wife would adore him as well. But so far, it was all one-sided. *Will it forever remain so?*

George took off his top hat, grasping it and the reins in his left hand while the right hand's fingers glided through his hair. He sighed miserably. What was it about him that women found so unappealing? Was he too direct with her last eve? Should he not tell her he was falling in love with her? *I suppose I should let the topic die,* he thought. *Clearly, she isn't ready for affection. I should withhold my regard. I do not want to give our marriage unintended strain.* Putting it from his mind, he put the topper back atop his head.

His townhouse came into view faster than he had intended as his thoughts had been heavy. Fredrek met him at the steps, carrying a note on a silver tray, which he handed up to his master. Staying mounted, he read it quickly. He tried not to read too much into the missive but couldn't help it.

"Fredrek, could you please fetch me the parcels from my study?"

"The two upon the settee, my lord?"

George nodded. "The very same."

"Right away, my lord."

"Thank you, Fredrek."

George dismounted, heading toward the stable to fetch the saddlebag to put the gifts into it. He ran a hand over his face. He would endeavor to put on a cheerful facade in front of her parents.

Having finished attaching the saddlebag, Fredrek handed him the parcels for his lady wife's parents. He instructed Fredrek they would be late for dinner and if it would be any later than he imagined, he would send word to inform the staff not to trouble themselves in preparing anything. They could simply dine out.

George mounted, taking off in the direction of his wife's familial residence. They were not far from his home, just several streets over in the opposite direction from the Taggart residency. Having arrived quickly enough, he dismounted, taking the parcels from the saddlebag. He passed his mount off to a stable hand and climbed the stairs to the front door.

The butler let him in and announced him. Isabelle was the first to greet him, a pale pink dress upon her frame and her blue eyes merry.

"Lord husband," she greeted.

George smiled wearily, handing the parcels to her. "As requested, lady wife," he said, concealing the sting from his voice.

She stared at him with concern. George smiled wanly, hoping his soft smile would allay any concerns she bore for him. He did not wish to make her uncomfortable at the thought that either he was plagued by his lack of imbibing or that he was injured after their last interaction.

Glancing around, he tenderly kissed her forehead. "I'm fine," he assured. "'Twas a brisk ride here, nothing more."

She nodded, leading him into the sitting room where her parents waited. Upon his entering, both William and Beatrice rose to greet him. Tea and finger sandwiches were served. His wife served him a cup first, instructing him to drink to warm his body.

"Dear boy," William began, concerned. "Are you ill?"

George shook his head. "It was a brisk ride here but one I will happily commit to again to see my lovely wife."

Isabelle blushed. "You flatter me."

"'Tis only the truth."

"I'm pleased to hear you are well," Beatrice said over her tea once they were comfortably situated.

"Thank you. I hope you are faring well."

"I am." Beatrice pointed to the packages upon Isabelle's lap. "Ma petite, what are those?"

"Oh," Isabelle said. "They are just a little something George and I procured for each of you."

Isabelle rose, dispersing the gifts. George sipped his tea and helped himself to another sandwich. While the day was clear and the sun was shining beautifully, the breeze held a distinct chill. Beatrice cooed at her gift, immediately rising to put the dark wood and pearl comb in her long blonde upswept tresses. William slapped the book, grinning from ear to ear.

"My dear boy!" William exclaimed. "You and my daughter picked out such splendid and surprising gifts."

"We wanted to show our gratitude regarding our marriage," Isabelle said, taking her seat beside him.

George nodded, smiling yet not saying a word. He couldn't. His tongue was tied in a mixture between hope that his wife was now coming to like him, and fear that it was a ploy to deceive her parents. Though he did not think she would do so, however, the concern flitted through his mind.

He observed Isabelle and her parents thoughtfully as they discussed all manner of things from her new painting room to *Francois*. George smiled gracefully to mask his true attitude, poor as it was. He remained silent, offering his opinion only when directly asked. It seemed no one truly noticed, to his immense relief.

When the youngest Pembroke was presented to the room, Isabelle leapt from her seat to take him from the nanny. She brought Bernard back to her seat where she began to cuddle and whisper into his ear. He was a babbling mass of curls and laughs as the two siblings reunited. George had a peculiar pain in his heart wondering if she would ever hold their child in her arms with such delight.

Together, they visited with Isabelle's parents through luncheon, and then departed in search of stable hands. The newspaper would be printing a second batch of papers and selling them shortly to all the others who still desired a copy. All the members of the peerage had received their copy early this morning.

At William's instance, he walked his daughter to the carriage. George tied his mount to the back of the carriage as William helped his daughter ascend into the conveyance. Whatever had transpired between daughter and father was now mended. It made his heart glad. He knew the disconnection had weighed heavily upon her.

Kissing Beatrice on the cheek and shaking William's hand, he scaled the carriage steps and seated himself across from his wife. The driver moved the carriage forward, taking them to the part of town where help could be acquired. There were those who checked in with the newspaper daily to see if there was work to be found. It would be prudent to begin there to see if anyone lingered. He thought to see who Lord Purcellville knew but he opted against it, not wanting to see Simon nor Alicia as they had taken up residence within Town again. He didn't think he would be very kind since it was Simon who had disclosed in a terrible manner the particulars of the union at their wedding day.

The driver pulled up in front of the newspaper building. Men from his former regiment were waiting outside to grab their copy of the paper. George alighted from the carriage. He beckoned them over to the side of the carriage where his wife could view the potential hires from the safety of its window. 'Twas not that he figured they would harm her but a lady surrounded by men was sure to cause an issue. Her safety was paramount in all things.

"Edgar Smithy," George greeted happily. "'Tis good to see you chap!"

"Same to you old friend. Sorry to hear the news in regards to your brother," the tall dark-haired man answered.

"I appreciate the thought," George began, "Edgar, are you in search of employment, perchance?"

"Indeed. I was unable to reenlist due to receiving a bullet in the arm. Pray tell, do you know of work?"

George nodded, "Hathwell House Stables is in search of hands. Will you accept employment?"

Edgar readily nodded. "My missus and-"

"Bring them too," George said, clapping him on the shoulder. "Come to Hathwell when you're readied." He handed the man some coins for the travel expenses.

Edgar beamed, striding off up the street. George smiled sincerely. Edgar was a good man, helping in the war far more than he was given credit for.

George peeked inside the carriage, seeing the taut face of Isabelle. He assumed the pointed look was for his title not being addressed. It was hard for him to have a man he fought beside address him in another manner. He saw them as equals.

"He's a good man," George began.

"Why do you not have them address you as befitting your title?" she inquired, tilting her head, with curiosity alight within her eyes.

George rolled his shoulders back, facing his wife through the curtained carriage door. "When in war, the man beside you is not your better nor your lesser but your brother in arms. I saved his life as he did mine. I was fortunate to not succumb to wounds.

Edgar has. 'Tis the same reason Brandon and I address each other as we do. I apologize if it upsets you."

Isabelle nodded. "I... I am coming to understand your reasoning," she offered, smiling demurely. "It is one of the reasons I adore you so, lord husband. You have the most giving heart."

George had been taking in their surroundings while they conversed, but he whipped his head in her direction and smiled brightly. His heart skipped several beats at her proclamation. He reached through the window for her hand, placing a soft kiss upon the back of it.

"Dear wife, you are too good to me," he said earnestly.

A light blush crept to her cheeks and he grinned. Out of the corner of his eye, Caleb Matthews strode by toward the newspaper building. George hired him as well. In a matter of approximately a half hour, all positions were filled for the eight openings at Hathwell House. Isabelle turned away several when the men stammered in answering a direct question. Even though he understood her logic that a man who stutters at a direct question is hiding something, it pricked his heart a bit. He wanted to help all he could. He was glad that in the end, all the men hired were all former soldiers who happened to serve with him under Lord Purcellville and some under Lord Taylor.

George climbed into the carriage, taking a seat opposite his wife for the ride back to the townhouse.

"Lady wife," he began, leaning forward in his seat. He took her hand in his, rubbing over the back of her knuckles with his thumb. "I do not want you to feel as if I am forcing your affection in any manner. I want to let you know that I adore you."

"You are not forcing me," Isabelle said.

George smiled gently. "While you were still abed, I took the liberty of sending a letter to Lord Bramley inquiring if we may impose for a brief visit. I know in our conversations you have mentioned missing Mariah."

Isabelle grinned broadly. "How thoughtful of you. I have indeed missed her."

He nodded. "Wonderful, then tomorrow we shall set out for Bramley Hall. I hope that suits you?"

"It certainly does."

Again he nodded. He didn't know what else to converse about. Even though he showed her endearment and tried his best to make her comfortable with him, in their marriage and in her new surroundings, he didn't want to repeat the same mistakes. So he decided to maintain somewhat of a distance and let her get settled, hopefully becoming more comfortable with him. If their marriage was to bloom, it would do so. Either way, he was committed to her, regardless.

The carriage pulled up to their townhouse. George helped her down and inside where he instructed Fredrek to have an early dinner prepared. He retired to his study to send more missives in regards to builders for the addition to the stables. The task took his mind off the lovely woman in the next room over. It was a gentle reprieve from the ache that tried to swell in his heart.

Chapter Twenty-Two

Alone Among Friends

After an intimate dinner, Isabelle and George retired to the drawing room to discuss all that they had accomplished. Isabelle was satisfied with their new employees and glad that her husband had turned those away who were not suited to the task. *It seems as if many a soldier had turned to drink.* It was a shame, and while her heart felt for them, she did not desire their company for her husband. His tremors had vanished, she had noticed. He still bore sweat upon his brow from time to time, though he had yet to ever complain. The stables were set for their future endeavors and the estate was set to prosper even more. George had been pleased with the idea of fattening up the coffers and adding to their holdings.

There was a noticeable distance between them that left a chill in Isabelle's blood. After how things had concluded last eve, how could she be in doubt as to the reason why. She missed the teasing and longing looks that she was growing accustomed to. This was her doing and she would bear the brunt of it. Until she could voice her feelings she would have to endure what she had wrought. The space between them gave pause to her earlier resolution to confess her heart to him.

There was no poetry nor words of love. They finally ceased with topics to discuss and lapsed into a heavy silence. There had been other silences before, but this was one that injured her the most. Gathering strength, Isabelle rose from before the fire.

"I believe that I shall retire, lord husband. These late evenings of ours are tiring, are they not?" She smiled down at him.

He joined her in standing. "Indeed. I shall see you in the morning. Rest well."

"Will you not seek your own rest?"

"Nay. I shall see that all is ready for our departure in the morning." He took her hand and kissed the back of it.

Isabelle smiled at him and then turned away. She tread into the hallway and reached the stairs. Pausing a moment with her hand upon the banister, she almost returned to the drawing room. The words that would correct everything were not on the tip of her tongue, so she really saw no point in prolonging the evening. Despite her earlier words to her father, she needed to sort through her feelings. *The last thing I desire is to create more of a muddle.*

That night Isabelle fell into a troubled sleep. She tossed and turned. Not being used to sleeping alone sans FiFi, she had never felt so alone before.

Daybreak brought relief in the thought of seeing her cousin and his lovely wife. Isabelle was waiting for George to join her in the breakfast room. She had already placed eggs and toast upon her plate. Fredrek was stationed by the doorway, his posture erect. She found it difficult to discuss things not directly related to the household with the servants. *I wonder if George sees it as a failing of mine?*

George entered the breakfast room and bowed before his wife. He then walked over to the side table and proceeded to fill his plate. "How is my lady wife this fine morning?"

"Well, thank you, my lord husband. And you?"

"Quite well and ready to set off on an adventure. Too bad I can think of none at present." He joined her at the rounded table and sat.

"How horrible. I am grieved for you." Isabelle smiled fondly at him.

"Just as well. I have business that needs to be attended to and a wife to woo." He began eating.

"You do not need to woo me, my lord. I am sufficiently wooed. All I could ask for resides within my reach." She meant to tease him but at his lack of humor, she understood that she had entirely missed the mark.

"I am pleased to have succeeded," he said, not looking up from his plate.

Isabelle felt her heart constrict. She ate her meal and did not bother to fill the silence that was lingering between them. She was in a dismal mood. The uncommunicativeness was a heavy presence that weighed upon her heart.

The carriage ride was spent by herself as George wanted to exercise his horse, London. Isabelle was no great horsewoman, but she vowed that if he would teach her, she would endeavor to learn. *That might be something that could draw us closer together,* she hoped.

Isabelle drew in her sketchbook to pass the time, though the road was bumpy. Emma had joined her in the carriage and read aloud from a book that was some sordid tale of gothic lore. *My own love life has become rather tragic.*

When the carriage took a turn, Isabelle blew out a breath. They had reached the long lane that led to Bramley Hall. Harrison and Mariah would be wonderful hosts and she meant to discuss matters of marital bliss with the lady of the Hall. Isabelle sat forward to peer out of the carriage door's window.

Now that she had had quiet time to reflect upon her union with George, she realized that there was a softening within her heart toward him. She desired to open herself to the possibility that more was attainable in their life together. Her husband had shown her kindness in every address he paid to her. He was patient and never sought to cause heartache. His words and actions were sincere. Isabelle wanted to show him that she could return his regard. The only issue she found was that she did not know how to begin to turn the tide that she felt swept up in. 'Twas far easier to remain distant and aloof with her cool exterior left to greet the world. In her heart, she knew that George deserved more from her than she had given to him previously.

The greenery surrounding Bramley Hall had woken up and was a vibrant engagement of color. The birds chirped and the rabbits could be seen in the fields among the wildflowers. This was beautiful country that always delighted Isabelle. She had painted the scenery many times before and still never tired from the view. When her gaze met Bramley Hall, she smiled. Its high walls and clematis archways led to the gurgling fountain. That had been a favorite picnic spot for her family.

After the tragic death of her aunt and uncle, her heart had always ached when she had parted from Harrison after their visits concluded. Of course, he had the Morten children as playmates, with Mariah never far from his sight.

"Welcome, my family!" Harrison's voice bellowed out in greeting.

"Thank you," George replied.

The carriage came to a stop and there was Harrison ready to help Isabelle descend. He grabbed her into a hug and swung her around to which she swatted him.

"Put me down, you big brute. George, come and rescue me!" Isabelle laughingly implored. Harrison set her upon her feet before any rescuing was necessary.

"Come inside! We have been counting the hours waiting for your arrival. Mariah is overflowing with excitement to share with you the plans for the nursery. She thought that with your attention to color and detail, you would be an asset," Harrison told her as she enfolded her arm with his.

"I shall be happy to lend my talents where they are needed." Isabelle smiled up at him as he led her into the Hall.

George was following closely behind. "How is the father-to-be handling these events?"

"As well as any new father, I expect. Mariah walks the estate too much for my liking. She still becomes ill in the mornings and tires easily in the evenings, but the in-between times, are wonderful." Harrison's face held a bemused look upon it.

Isabelle removed her cloak and bonnet, handing them to Billingsley. She made her way to the drawing room, not much caring if her hair was in disarray. There were none in residence to be scandalized and she knew that Mariah would set her to rights if there was a need. She did not want to waste time by seeking her bedchamber to refreshen as they had stopped at an inn not too far from Bramley. Mariah padded over to embrace Isabelle.

"You look lovely! This babe seems to agree with you." Isabelle said as she sat down with Mariah on the gold padded settee.

"I am well and so is our little lordling." Mariah's smile was filled with happiness.

"Lordling? How do you suppose it's a boy and not a beautiful girl?"

"'Tis only a guess. But he is very persistent in keeping time. I wake ill each morning at precisely seven o'clock. It seems he has a penchant for being on time. Just like his Papa!" Mariah chortled.

Isabelle smiled and said, "'Tis a very good basis in which to hypothesize."

Mariah nodded at her and then gained her feet to welcome George, who placed a kiss upon her cheek. "How wonderful to welcome you both back. I have missed you immensely."

"'Tis always good to be with one's relations," George replied.

Mariah directed them to comfortable seats and rang for tea. The men sat and enjoyed the tea and cake while they conversed about business. Mariah ate little and when Isabelle set her plate down Mariah grasped her hand.

"Will you lend me your expertise, dear cousin?" Mariah's sparkling sapphire eyes shone with excitement.

"Of course, I shall," Isabelle said as she rose next to Mariah.

The gentleman quickly gained their booted feet and walked to meet their ladies. Harrison wound his arm around Mariah, and leaned down to kiss her forehead. Isabelle sighed to see such tender regard as exemplified before her. George came to Isabelle's side and took her hand in his. He gave it a squeeze which she returned.

"I know that you are impatient to make your way to the stables. Isabelle and I shall repair to the nursery. We shall meet at dinner," Mariah addressed Harrison.

"The nursery is rather far from here, let us escort you there." Harrison brought his wife's arm and placed it in the crook of his own arm.

"'Tis not that far. Besides, Isabelle will walk with me. I shall be fine," Mariah replied.

"Indeed, dear cousin, no harm shall befall her. We're not leaving the house, only venturing above," Isabelle teased Harrison, who sighed as she disentangled them.

George looked amused and Isabelle smiled at him.

"Yes, but stairs, carpets, and creaky floorboards await. Harrison is my personal knight who cannot stand to leave my side," Mariah told them. "I had hoped that the addition of visitors would curb his worry. Attend to your business, dear husband." Mariah sent an imploring look at George who raised his hands as he stepped back.

"Harrison, go with George. All will be well. However, it may not be if you do not let your wife have her own time away from you. You are overreacting! The only threat to her safety is her sanity in dealing with an over-doting spouse. Now shoo." Isabelle folded her arms and stared Harrison down, who looked first at his wife and then at her.

"As you wish, but at the first sign that she is overtired-" Harrison began but Isabelle cut him off.

"I am not negligent. Furthermore, I have more knowledge of the female body than you ever could. I will look after our dear Mariah, never you fear. Now out with you." Isabelle stamped her booted foot impatiently.

Harrison nodded his head as Mariah covered her mouth with the back of her hand. Isabelle could see that she was trying to hide her mirth. Harrison gave a long last entreating look and then left the drawing room with George in tow. Smart man, her husband, to remain silent.

Mariah bit her lip and then chortled. "My poor darling's face. You have wounded his pride."

"He shall recover. Now, let us away to the nursery." Isabelle wrapped Mariah's arm in her own as they left the room.

Making their way up the staircase, Isabelle inquired, "Is his fear founded? Have you suffered complications?" The thought sent panic rushing through her. After all Harrison had lost, to lose another, or perchance even two, would cripple him. And her own heart would suffer as she considered Mariah her greatest friend now that they were grown.

"Not at all. I am perfectly well. The growth of a human being is more tiring than I had expected, but the joys far outweigh the complaints. You shall understand once George has fathered your child."

"I hope so," Isabelle said with sorrow lacing her voice.

"Is all still not right between you two?" Mariah's expressive eyes bore into her.

"It seems as if we make massive strides toward each other, only to be tossed back a few steps. He is the kindest husband, and heaven help me, I am trying my best to forget how our marriage came to be. But I find that it still pains my heart. I expect at any moment for him to come to the realization that he loathes me. Do you know how many suitors I drove away?"

They reached the nursery but Mariah halted their steps before they could enter. She looked at Isabelle with kindness.

"George is honorable, kind, and loving. He has met with such adversity in his life. You are his opposite in personality. But, I see him watching you and there is a great feeling reflected within his eyes toward you. His loyalty to you is unquestionable. Take this marriage and make it what you desire it to be. Woo him, spend time with him. You are all he needs." Mariah gave her a watery smile.

"Oh, I did not mean to upset you. Harrison will bar me from Bramley Hall." Isabelle bit her bottom lip.

"I shall not allow it. He has to abide by my wishes, I am carrying his babe," Mariah teased. "I am weepy because I so desire for this match to take well for you. For each of you to fall so helplessly in love that nothing could ever keep you apart. You are ideal for each other. Allow him into your heart, dearest. You shall not regret it."

The ladies stepped over the threshold into the nursery and Isabelle sighed. The room already held the family cradle and the rocking horse that generations of Pembrokes had made use of. This would be a welcoming room for the new addition as soon as Isabelle was allowed her paints.

Mariah was such a wonderful friend. Her advice was sound. She would endeavor to do as Mariah advised. George was worth a broken heart. True love was worth the beautiful disaster that might be on the horizon.

Chapter Twenty-Three

Sound Advice

U pon discussing the breeding of horses and examining the new stock that Harrison had purchased, they both retired to the study to allow the women more time in the nursery. How the ladies even had the ability to discuss the topic of children for hours on end astounded him. By the pleading look on Mariah's face and the sharp rebuke of his own wife, George did his best to steer Harrison away from them both; not only to make them happy but he also did not wish to cause any more irreparable damage to his own marriage. Displeasing his wife by not abiding to her wishes would do him no good.

George ran a hand over his face, trying to swipe away the stormy sea of a relationship he and Isabelle were having. One moment they were happy, harmonious, the next it seemed they were distant and cold. George couldn't figure out if it was of his own making or not. He didn't think so. He thought he had done well by her, but his wife still didn't care for his affection so he must have done something terrible. He gave her the space she first desired when they wed.

And upon his honor, he hadn't had a drink in nigh on a week. The sweats were easier to bear now. He believed in a few days time, everything would be set to rights. *Perhaps that is why she refuses me*, he thought, *because I am still recovering. Or 'tis just everything about me she rejects.* George sipped his beverage, setting it down on a coaster.

"Mr. and Mrs. Morten are to join us for dinner," Harrison said, breaking the companionable silence.

"Wonderful," George replied.

He loved the long conversations he had with wise Mr. Morten. The man gave the most ample and sound advice he ever heard. Perchance, he could shed some light on the subject of his wife and what to do. He was at his wit's end.

"How is he faring?" George asked.

Harrison grew dismal. "Not well, though the physician can find nothing regarding his ailments other than age."

George considered for a moment before inquiring, "Would it be possible for a second or third opinion? Just to be sure?"

Harrison shook his head. "Nay. Both he and my lovely wife are adamant that this physician knows the absolute best course of action."

"Well then, I shall pray for him to be well."

"My friend, how is your marriage coming along, if I may ask? Both of you do not seem joyous."

George leaned over, cradling his head in his hands. "I honestly cannot say. I don't quite know what I've done to earn her rebuke of me. I've given up drink, gambling, and endeavoring to further the line of Hathwell horseflesh to secure our family even more financially for years to come. I even bought a stud from Lord Taggart. I've given her space, given companionship, a private painting room, and I love her little dog *Francois*–"

"*Francois*? I thought it was FiFi."

"I gave him his masculinity back and now she wants to breed him."

Harrison guffawed.

George grinned dismally. "I don't have an inkling on what to do next."

"My dear boy," Mr. Morten said, being helped into the room by Mrs. Morten. "There is always something to do - pray. And even when you're done praying, do so again. If you feel like your prayers have gone in your favor, pray again," he said, sitting down with a heavy sigh. Harrison's butler brought in a brown lap blanket for Mr. Morten which Mrs. Morten draped across his lap. "Thank you, dearest. I believe Mariah is in need of you."

Mrs. Morten grumbled. "Are you that eager to be rid of me already?"

Mr. Morten smiled, a twinkle alighting in his keen blue eyes. "I wouldn't dream of it, my dearest Mrs. Morten. Mariah is actually calling your name."

Everyone took pause to listen and indeed, Mrs. Morten was being summoned.

"Oh you!" Mrs. Morten smiled, taking her leave. "Harrison, it is my understanding that you'll keep him calm and comfortable?"

"Anything for you, my beloved mother-in-law."

"A most excellent answer," Mrs. Morten beamed, exiting the study to attend to her beckoning daughter.

Once the door clicked shut, Mr. Morten turned to George, his face drawn yet thoughtful. "Have you asked her why she is rebuking you?"

He shook his head. "I have not. I don't think I could bear her answer."

Mr. Morten nodded. "Dear boy, you are trying to force her to love you. You're trying to earn her affection to make worth in yourself. This is not a war. Her heart doesn't need a stake through it to claim it's been conquered. From what I've overheard, you've given plenty and love is not a one-way lane. Take a step back, and allow her to see *you*."

"Thank you, Mr. Morten," he said softly, emotion hanging at the back of his throat. "I'm coming to find that I sincerely love her. I want to tell her but I don't wish to chase her away. I-"

He cut himself off. Through his experiences with women, he had come to find that they never cared much for him. He didn't understand it. He was kind, attentive, and pampered those he took interest in. Yet continually he was spurned in some manner. Now 'twas by his own wife and he could not fathom what he had done to earn her displeasure.

"You cannot keep pulling water from a well which is empty," Mr. Morten said, leaning back in his seat.

"Ask her tonight when you are alone in your bedchamber," Harrison offered.

"Our bedchamber?"

"Do you not share a room with your wife?"

"Nay," George replied, shaking his head. "She was enraged after our marriage, I let her be alone. We haven't shared a room hence."

Mr. Morten grinned. "Well, dear boy, it appears to me that tonight you are, which will benefit you in talking things out."

George didn't know what to say. He did not believe tonight would benefit him whatsoever in any manner with how modest Isabelle was. But he supposed at some point they would have to sleep, and they would have to converse about their issues. And tonight he would lay it all out for her. No longer did he wish to earn her rebuke, but if it was to continue, he assumed having a lengthy conversation about it would be imperative to them both.

Dinner was announced and George helped Mr. Morten to rise. The kindly man did so on shaky legs and with the aid of a cane. George and Harrison walked on either side of him toward the dining hall. The intimacy of the dinner was cause for the lack of societal propriety, and knowing his wife, it would be another nail in his coffin. Would she take her dissatisfaction out upon him? George refused to cringe thinking upon it, as he helped Mr. Morten to the nearest chair. Besides, it was her relations that they dined with. If fault was to be found, it lay at their host's feet and not his. After Mr. Morten was seated, George strode back to collect his wife. Even though she was already in the dining room, he helped her to her seat and pushed her chair in, taking his own seat on her left.

The butler directed the footmen to serve. First came soup followed by dishes of chicken, potatoes, and a cream sauce; the cream sauce over his potatoes was one of George's most favorite dishes. He couldn't help but eat gluttonously while the conversation to be had was about the impending child for the Earl and

Countess of Bramley. His wife, glowing and merry, was asked to paint a mural on one wall of the nursery.

"Please do so," Mariah begged.

Isabelle grinned demurely, choking back on words she was having difficulty finding. George turned in his seat to look at his wife. Her icy blue eyes appeared on the edge of tears. She looked at him with a softened expression he had not before seen. He wondered at what it meant. All he could do was to reach for her ungloved hand and run his thumb over the back of her knuckles.

"If you're concerned regarding my approval, then please put it from your mind. I would love nothing more than your happiness," George offered.

"But what about Hathwell? The new staff are coming, along with the new horse," Isabelle whispered though it echoed in the dining room.

George patted the top of her hand. "I shall go to Hathwell tomorrow and return for you in a few days so that you may paint. I would never seek to take an opportunity such as this from you."

Her mouth opened slightly. Her long lashes fluttered, kissing the tops of her cheeks. He swore he saw warmth reflected within those luminous eyes.

"May I accompany you, George?" Harrison asked. "I would love to gaze at the legendary horses of the Taggart holding."

"I would love your company."

"'Tis settled then," Harrison beamed. "We can fine-tune the details later. Though I must implore you all to save room for dessert. The chef has whipped up something sumptuous."

George grinned, loving the feeling of home, of camaraderie and friendship. It was a feeling he thought he would never feel again with the passing of his parents and then his brother. This night endeared itself into his heart. Having friends such as these meant everything to him. He was coming to realize that home was where you felt welcomed and your heart was refreshed.

He glanced at his wife and lovingly squeezed her hand under the table, letting it gently drop back into her lap. He wanted to confess his feelings for her. Perhaps the right moment would come eventually. For now, he was content just being near her even knowing he may never have her heart like she held his.

Chapter Twenty-Four

Pure Bliss

T he evening was spent in familiar company and it made Isabelle's heart swell with happiness. She was surrounded by loving couples and by her own husband who was doting upon her, much as Harrison was with his wife. When George agreed to let her stay for a few days to paint the nursery, despite their former plans and with an accepting and easy manner, she was nearly breathless. While she longed to paint and create something beautiful for the new life to come, she knew that she would miss George. If he had insisted that altering their plans was impossible, she would have been wounded. He was her husband and therefore she was to acquiesce to his decrees no matter how her own heart felt. Gratitude and something deeper had flooded her veins. *My wishes matter to him,* she realized with stunning clarity.

"The hour is late for these old bones," announced Mr. Morten from the comfortable chair in which he had been reclining. Harrison instantly was at his side to assist the man with gaining his own feet.

After they had dined, they had repaired to the drawing room. The men had declined taking port in favor of remaining with their spouses. George was never far from her side. Isabelle found that she rather liked his nearness and his warmth.

Mrs. Morten came forth to attend to her husband and directed her gaze at Isabelle. "When shall we have the pleasure of seeing you increase? My grandchild deserves exceptional company and you can provide that."

Isabelle felt her skin heat and yet she met the woman's gaze. "I supposed when the Lord sees fit." She wanted a babe, especially since seeing the joy that radiated between her cousin and his wife. *What would it be like to carry George's child? Would he be attentive and overbearing as Harrison, or would he grant me space? Would he be pleased?*

Mr. Morten patted his wife's hand and said, "Let us not pester the young; there will come time for new life to spring forth."

"Yes, but what is wrong with giving encouragement? Times are changing and I do not understand these women who perceive anything of more import than the gaining of children," Mrs. Morten addressed her audience. "My own dear Mariah took to the matter with an enthusiastic vigor and glee."

"Mama!" Mariah exclaimed while covering her cheeks.

Harrison's own color was high as he directed the couple from the room and to their bedchamber.

"I apologize," Mariah said as she came toward Isabelle to embrace her.

"Please do not. I believe we have all been on the receiving end of Mrs. Morten's attention to detail. She seems to have forgotten about Bernard. He will make an excellent playmate." Isabelle attempted to choose her words carefully.

"How right you are." Mariah kissed her cheek and they chortled together, sharing in their joint mortification.

Once the couples retired, Isabelle found herself in the same bedchamber with her husband. George followed her into the chamber and closed the door. Isabelle turned to study him and watched as his hand reached to the back of his neck in an anxious gesture. Then he walked to the bellpull and summoned Emma.

"I shall leave you to ready for bed and enter into the adjoining dressing area to see myself readied. This was not my idea, I hope that you understand that." George looked earnestly at her. Worry and something akin to fear were shimmering in his beautiful brown eyes.

Isabelle closed the distance between them and reached onto her tiptoes, giving him a kiss upon the cheek. "All shall be well. I cannot find fault in this with you. 'Tis normal when visiting that couples share a bedchamber. I had not given it thought. We can certainly share a bed, can we not?"

The relief that crossed over his masculine features made her heart stutter. He swallowed and nodded his head with his eyes gazing deeply into hers. Then his eyes roamed her face and he brought his large hand up to cup her cheek. Isabelle felt herself lean into his gentle touch. The butterflies returned to her stomach full force and she forgot how to breathe. George leaned his head down to her and when she did not pull away, he brought his warm lips to hers in a delicate whisper of a kiss. It was brief, and when he began to pull away, Isabelle encircled his neck and pulled him closer. Upon the tips of her toes she brought his forehead against hers and simply basked in his nearness. She was not ready for the meaningful moment to end.

The door opened and a voice exclaimed, "Excuse me, my lord, my lady."

Isabelle let George go and stepped away from him. "All is well, Emma. Shall we ready for bed?" Isabelle asked her maid.

"I shall let you alone," George said as he looked at Isabelle for a moment longer and made his way to the dressing area. There was a screen that separated the chamber for functional purposes and he quickly hid behind it. Though they would be able to hear each other, their sight would be blocked.

Isabelle looked at Emma and put a finger to her lips, letting her know that silence was her wish. She was embarrassed to be in this situation with her ladies maid attending upon her. But there was nothing to be done about it, and Isabelle supposed that at some point her maid would have witnessed a display of affection between her husband and herself.

Emma followed Isabelle to the rosewood changing table and helped her to disrobe. Once her nightgown and dressing robe were donned she sat upon the cream padded bench. She watched as her maid deftly unpinned her hair, and then began to brush it. Isabelle was conscious of the fact that all the rustling from behind the screen had ceased and she supposed that George was patiently waiting for her to be finished. Her nerves began to riot and she twisted her hands in her lap. When her hair was braided and tied at its end with a white ribbon, Emma bowed to her and she nodded her approval and gratitude. She watched as Emma padded over to the door and opened and closed it behind her.

Rising, she peered at the screen and rushed over to the bed where she hurriedly threw off her dressing robe as she kicked the slippers from her feet. Then she climbed into the massive four-poster bed. She settled herself and pulled the coverlet up to her chin.

"I am decent now, lord husband," she called.

George came from behind the screen in his own dressing robe and slippers. When he reached the bed he disrobed and threw it on top of where hers had landed on the foot of the bed. He sat down and the mattress creaked at his weight. When he had left his slippers to lay on the floor beside hers, he swung his legs and body under the covers. Why had she not ever noticed how massive he was? He took up substantial room within the bed, but there was still plenty of space separating them.

"Good night, lady wife," he softly said. He left the beside candle glowing, she supposed for a modicum of propriety. It was near its end and would soon extinguish itself; they were in no danger.

"Good night, lord husband." Isabelle was chilled and the warmth of his body called to her own. She watched as he threw an arm over his face and she ever so slightly moved closer to him. When he neither spoke nor moved, she slowly inched her own body closer again. There was barely a hand's space between them. Her body began to warm and she let out a contented sigh.

"Are you cold?" George inquired as he brought his arm away from his face and turned his head to look at her.

Isabelle nodded to him and he grasped the covers in his large hand, bunching them up and over them as he beckoned her closer. Isabelle took a moment to consider her next action. She could warm faster within his arms. But what would he make of her accepting his invitation? She chewed on her bottom lip while George patiently met her gaze. Deciding that there was no shame in cuddling up next to her husband, she moved into his side. Isabelle laid her head against his chest as her slender arm laid across his waist. They were touching from head to toe as her body perfectly fit into his side.

George tucked the cover around her and kissed her forehead, bringing a smile to her lips. Her heart was hammering in her chest and it seemed to be in tandem with his. She was very near to tears, vowing to not let them fall. But she did wonder if this was what it was like to be loved by another. The warmth, the feelings of safety, and something more: a desire to please him.

She felt and heard the sigh that escaped from her husband's body. His arm tightened around her. He seemed to be content with their present embrace and so she closed her eyes as her nose breathed in the scent of leather, the out of doors, and something wholly unique to George. She had never known what contentment was before, this was bliss. *Why have I been denying us this? When he returns for me, I shall never let another night pass without him by my side, hang society's constraints and dictates. I only have to convince him of the idea. But how I shall miss this until he returns.*

Chapter Twenty-Five

Three Days Time

He was surprised she sought solace in his embrace and even more astounded that she lay cuddled up beside him the entirety of the night. He had no objections, as if he would ever disagree with laying beside his beautiful wife. The petite woman fit perfectly against him. Being beside her felt euphoric. It was the best night of sleep he had ever gotten in his life. He recalled that as he felt sleep begin to claim him, he knew that it would be a peaceful night free from his night terrors. The memories that plagued his mind from the war whenever he had laid his head upon the pillow had been blessedly absent.

George kissed the top of her head and untangled himself from her, going softly to the dressing area in the chamber. Since he was traveling back today to Hathwell House, he forewent his choking cravat and anything purposefully showing off his title. He loved to dress simply. But if there was anyone untoward on the road, they would perchance bypass him altogether, thinking him an unkempt cad or even a highwayman and let him be. As far as those currently residing within the Hall, he did not worry either. Only Mrs. Morten would be taken aback and if she was, mayhap it would give her a new topic to ruminate about.

Once dressed, he tucked his wife in, pulling the coverlet up and around her, kissing her softly upon her head. He ensured that the fire was set to burn for a few hours longer. Creeping out of the room, George headed down the stairs toward Harrison's study. They were similar in manner and so if Harrison happened to be awake, he assumed he could find the man there. His reasoning did not disappoint.

Harrison sat behind his desk, his head in his hands.

"Good morning," George greeted, taking a seat at his friend's desk. "How are you faring?"

"Exhausted, my friend," Harrison groaned. "I love my dearest wife, however, she now snores. I do not know if it is because she is with child, but it is quite the sound to endure all night long."

George attempted to stem the chuckle but could not. "Well, if the babe is as broad and tall as you, I can only imagine her snoring is living proof of her exhaustion of carrying another Bramley lordling."

Harrison grinned broadly. "How was your night beside your wife?"

"Warm."

Harrison chuckled. "Did she press her icy feet upon your leg?"

"Nay, she did not," George replied with a slight glower.

Harrison nodded. "Then I shan't ruin it for you."

George chortled, crossing an ankle over his knee. Together, he and Harrison planned out the three days away from home. George had to get back to Hathwell to oversee and accommodate the new employees for the stables; also to ensure that the addition to the stables was incorporated seamlessly into the existing building. After a day at Hathwell, Harrison had some business in Town to handle. George was set to accompany him, then pay a visit to Harrison's uncle, who was also George's wife's parents, and invite them out to Bramley; whereupon the last day, they would ride back to Bramley Hall and have a merry reunion with all their loved ones.

They were set to depart once their wives had awakened and they had all broken their fasts. George sat in the study contentedly for the moment. This was the first time he would be without his wife. He wasn't sure how to aptly feel about it. He was certain he would miss her, but would she miss him? Was last night, wrapped in each other's arms, just out of a need to stay warm or was she coming around to him considerably? Again, he didn't want to read too much into it. Isabelle was more than likely seeking warmth.

George excused himself for a stroll around Bramley Hall. He greatly admired Bramley's open landscapes and lush fields. Hathwell was somewhat open but there were large trees to provide shade, and around its back it was like a gateway to an enchanted world with all the trees and vibrant flowers.

His mind wandered to different subjects like how many mares he wanted to have the stud breed with, what remodeling he thought would be good for a nursery, or if anything would ever blossom between himself and Isabelle. George gave her space. It seemed to him she liked it.

Mr. Morten suggested talking it out. Perhaps it would be best if he did so upon his return. He did not want to leave his wife in foul spirits and neither of them in an unhappy state. He would tread lightly in order to understand her better.

He raked his fingers through his hair and sighed. He did as Mr. Morten suggested and took a step back. The wise man was correct - his wife was not something to be conquered. He had already stopped with the flattery and stopped doting upon her hand and foot to see her smile. He needed to be seen as he was, as Mr. Morten suggested. Mayhap then she may come around. He truly didn't know. He was willing to try anything, most especially if more nights spent with her in his arms was to be the reward.

George shoved his hands into his pockets. He walked the property thrice before his stomach rumbled. He hadn't even noticed the sun was almost well into the sky and there was a long ride back to Hathwell before them.

He turned his feet toward the manor house and walked inside. The scent of food wafted under his nose, leading him to the dining hall. His wife sat at the table, well into her meal. Her head popped up from her food; concern lacing her brow as she took in his appearance.

Mr. Morten grinned at him knowingly. "How was your walk, dear boy?"

"Very fine," George said, filling up his plate from the selection along the back wall. "Before I knew it, I had walked the property thrice. 'Tis a splendid morning."

"I was concerned about you," Isabelle said softly.

George took his seat beside her and patted her hand. "I apologize. I shall inform you of my activities in the future, even if only in the written word. Please forgive me for my absence."

Isabelle smiled prettily, turning her attention back to her food.

"So," Mrs. Morten began chipperly. "How was your first night sleeping together?"

Mariah audibly sighed. George choked on his drink, staring at his wife for some sort of answer that eluded him entirely.

"My dearest Mrs. Morten," Mr. Morten grinned. "The look upon their faces suggests nothing happened."

Mrs. Morten rolled her eyes. "This babe needs a friend, a lifelong playmate and confidant. How else is this supposed to happen if I cannot offer a maternal push in the matter?"

"The Lord's time, dearest," Mr. Morten said.

"And sometimes, Mr. Morten, they need a push to see what is right before them," Mrs. Morten huffed as she drank from her teacup.

George ate his food, trying to not pay attention to anything being said. His cheeks heated and he knew without looking at his wife that she too was embarrassed. He shoveled the food into his mouth, wanting to be done with this conversation.

Mrs. Morten harrumphed. "Then I shall be this child's confidant. We would make a splendid pair."

Mr. Morten steepled his fingers together and grinned cooly. "A very unwise choice for the babe, dear. Perhaps better luck could be found with Simon and Alicia."

"Posh! Those two could not discover the setting sun before them, let alone raise a child. Any little ones they have would be upon our doorstep 'ere long."

George sputtered his drink. "Thank you, Harrison," he choked out, "for the lovely meal." He really must stop taking so many sips from his cup, he was likely to meet his doom at this rate.

Harrison nodded, staring at his plate of food with his head well bent over it. It seemed as if his host was not going to engage with his mother-in-law. George could not say that he blamed the man. He said a quick prayer of thanksgiving that his own in-laws were level-headed individuals.

"Mother," Mariah said softly. "Mayhap you have a moment to discuss with me, in the other room, the softest fabric for the babe?"

"But of course, my sweet girl," Mrs. Morten complied, helping Mariah from her seat.

Mother and daughter left the room. Mariah glanced over her shoulder, mouthing apologies. Isabelle rose from her seat and George hurriedly rose to join her. He made excuses for departing to go pack to leave now that bellies were full. He led Isabelle up the stairs and to their bedchamber, desiring to kiss her lips before leaving Bramley Hall for a few days.

George opened the door and ushered her inside. Already the bed was made and his clothes were packed and set upon the cushioned bench at the end of the bed due to the expert care of his valet, Seth. Not that he would be taking a chest of clothes with him upon horseback, but he would be returning for his wife as well as his things in a few days time.

"Would it bother you if I start on painting the nursery, lord husband?" Isabelle said, heading to her chest of supplies.

George met her at her painting chest, took her hand, and placed a kiss upon it. "Not at all. I can only imagine the excitement you must feel."

Isabelle nodded. "I am rather excited," she pursed her lips and frowned. "I shall see you off first."

George patted her hand. "Very well."

He took her to the door, standing on the threshold. He cupped her face, one hand behind the back of her head and the other on her cheek, drawing her close to him. Her soft lips upon his made his knees weak. Her scent of vanilla and lemon enchanted him and he committed it to memory. George adjusted his stance, holding her close in his arms as his kisses deepened. Her soft lips were yielding under his and the taste of her was like nothing he had ever encountered before. Her mouth allowed him entry and he enthusiastically caressed her tongue with his own. He had not drank in over a week, but now he was drunk off his glorious wife. This was an addiction that he hoped she would not find fault in, heaven help him if she did. He drew his head back from hers and gazed into her icy blue eyes. He would stop this now before he embarrassed them both with the force of his longing for her.

"I shall return here to you in a few days time," he said softly.

"I shall miss you and count the minutes until you return."

"Lady wife, I shall endeavor to return to your side as swiftly as I am able."

"I shall look forward to having you back with me." Isabelle lowered her lashes demurely.

George kissed her sweet lips again and went down the hallway. Harrison was already saying goodbye to Mariah at the end of the stairs. The earl appeared contrite and worried, while his wife wished him well, safe travels, and to have a splendid time.

"Do not tax yourself. Send Edmund if you need me right away," Harrison stated.

"I shall. My parents will be here with me until you return," Mariah consoled. "Look, here is George now," she stated, smiling. "And Isabelle will be here with me too. All will be well."

Harrison kissed his wife soundly. "I shall return in a few days."

George kissed his wife on the forehead, leaving her beside Mariah. Clapping Harrison on the shoulder, he steered the doting and worried man toward the door.

"Come, Harrison," George beckoned, "the sooner we depart, the sooner we arrive."

Harrison looked over his shoulder as they reached the door. "Stay safe beloved!"

"I shall!" Mariah replied, her voice echoing from down the hall.

"Lo, I am set to depart and she doesn't care," Harrison pouted as they descended the steps to their mounts.

"I have never met a woman more in love with her husband than Mariah," George replied, squeezing his friend's shoulder briefly before walking the few steps it took to reach his mount.

Harrison mounted deftly. "I love her entirely," Harrison admitted. "I know this time with Isabelle shall be beneficial to her, but it still concerns me."

George nodded, mounting his steed. "Let's make our business quick then, shall we?" He signaled to Seth to follow them. They would be traveling with only one valet, as Harrison had directed his to remain within the Hall should the man need to be dispatched to bring him back.

Harrison nodded, galloping down the drive. George followed, hoping this time apart from Isabelle would prove fruitful.

Chapter Twenty-Six

The Longest Days

I sabelle did not waste a moment in creating the perfect nursery for her newest cousin-to-be. It gave her great joy to see her work progressing and to have the time to visit with Mariah. They had never had so many hours to just themselves before and their friendship was growing more sisterly in nature. Isabelle was pleased to see that Mariah was delighted with the tree, clouds, and landscape of wildflowers that she had spread out along the walls. She had even retouched the peeling paint upon the cradle and other pieces of furniture.

Keeping herself busy was helpful in directing her thoughts away from missing George. She did not want to give voice to her feelings and only thought about them at night while alone in her bed. There she was free to ponder their future together and mourn for what could have been made of their earlier days. She was more resolved than ever to breach this gap between them, and her heart told her that he would be amenable to her desires. The man had clearly stated what he wished and now she was to make her own wishes known. Isabelle would gladly welcome George into every corner and crevice of her life. They were meant to be one and she was going to lovingly display her feelings to him. If only time had wings that she could make a move to bring him back to her. There were mere hours until he and Harrison would return and she was both anxious and excited. She could only hope that her exuberance would not sway his mind nor heart away from her. He had a solid constitution and should fare quite well after she told him her heart was making itself known to her.

Glancing out the window, Isabelle frowned. Rain was pelting the earth and the Hall. Fat raindrops rolled down the windows as the gray clouds hid the sun. It was difficult to have the proper lighting by which to paint, but not impossible. They had directed a few of the footmen to light candles and place them in various spaces throughout the room. As her fingers guided her brush-strokes, she worried for George and Harrison. Weather such as this was not ideal to travel in and could even be dangerous. She was keeping these thoughts to herself so as not to upset Mariah.

"Isabelle, do you think it would be terrible of me to propose that Mama visit Alicia at the time of my bringing forth this babe?" Mariah was gingerly chewing on a cookie.

Isabelle put down her paintbrush and turned to face her. "I think wild horses could not make her move from your side."

Grimacing, Mariah set the cookie down and brushed the crumbs from her dress. "I know. But I am in very real danger of her frightening me with the stories of her own experiences. And then it would make the ordeal seem nearly impossible."

"You have a valid concern."

"Would you mind coming to stay with me in those few weeks of confinement? Mayhap just a week prior? I have no sisters and my sister-in-law is not one to offer comfort. The idea of the two of them attending to me makes me ill. Please understand that I adore them both, but with Harrison constantly at my side suffering in quiet embarrassment, and receiving unwanted advice, I may be persuaded to run away. I doubt I would get far, but it sounds pleasing to me. I am quite nervous."

Isabelle knelt down before the rocking chair in which Mariah sat and took her hands into her own. "I would be honored to attend to you. I can well understand your grievances. I feel certain that when the time comes, we can manage to distract your mama with other things. I shall make it my mission to be of service to you."

Mariah smiled and gave a sigh. "Thank you. I am feeling so much better now. I wish that Harrison would be allowed to attend to me, he has shown that when in the thick of things he can be a steadying presence. I know 'tis not done, but how I long for him to be with me. He has seen me through every ordeal my entire life." She sniffed as a tear made its way down her cheek.

"I think you should do just as you please. If you want him there and he can handle the sight of your pain, then why not? It is *you* who has to do all of the hard work. Besides, who has to know he is in attendance?"

"I think seeing me in pain would be difficult for him. I know it would be for me." Mariah blew out a breath as her eyes scanned the nursery. "You have made this into something special."

"I am glad you think so. I am rather proud that we could accomplish this in such a short time. Let me get back to it, so that I may be finished when our gentlemen return to us." Isabelle smiled at Mariah and padded over to her paints as she chose her next color. Her hand stilled, thinking of whether she would wish for George to attend their child's birth and was staunchly against it. Having him view her in such disarray would not do. Besides, men were not easily built for such things, war and babes were complete opposites. The mortification alone would forever scar her and she did not know if she could look him in the eye were he to witness such an intimate event. No, he was not welcomed into the chamber should she ever bear his child.

They chatted on about odds and ends and then it was time to take tea. Afternoon tea was always a refreshing time for Isabelle when she had spent the better part of her day lost in creating. She assisted Mariah from the nursery and down the stairs. When they reached the parlor, Mr. and Mrs. Morten were already present.

"My, what a dreary day it is. The rain is falling from the heavens in bucketfuls," Mrs. Morten observed looking out the window. Isabelle noted the thick drops which were striking against the windowpane. It looked like a violent downpour.

"Indeed, I hope the men delay their journey if the roads become too muddy." Mariah padded over to the fire. "Billingsley, would you be so kind as to provide us with our refreshments?"

"Yes, my lady," the butler bowed before her and walked from the room, closing the door after himself.

Isabelle waited for Mariah to be seated and then sat next to her upon the settee. The elder couple had taken the wingback chairs nearest to the roaring fire.

"How are you progressing with painting the nursery?" Mr. Morten's kind eyes sought out Isabelle's.

"Very well. I am pleased with it and just have to add a few minor details once the light is better and it shall be deemed a success." Isabelle smiled at him.

"Well, well. Very good. And how are you this afternoon, dear daughter?" He turned to Mariah.

"Well, and I am missing my husband. I have become used to his constant presence and I will never shoo him from my side again." Mariah's sapphire eyes were twinkling within the firelight.

"You poor dear. Husbands are free to do as they please and it's us wives that keep everything running. I wonder that he has not sent word to you. I must say, I expected better from him. George is an excellent letter writer. He wrote to Mariah sheets and sheets. What an attentive suitor he was," Mrs. Morten remarked.

"He is a very good man, to be sure. But now that he has found his perfect match in Isabelle, and I have Harrison, everything is as it should be." Mariah looked at Isabelle and smiled encouragingly at her.

Mrs. Morten had not meant to be indelicate. Isabelle knew not to take the woman's words to her heart. She was often given to expressing things that went against the grain, and never was it accomplished with malicious intent.

"George is an excellent man. He has written me a note before and I saved it," Isabelle admitted. It had not been of a romantic nature, but none needed to understand that fact.

"How wonderful! I expect that at any moment they will come barging through the doors!" Mrs. Morten reached over and patted Isabelle upon the knee.

Billingsley brought the tea tray into the drawing room and placed it upon the mahogany table before the settee.

"Thank you," Mariah told him.

He bowed and departed the parlor. Mariah began to serve without needing to be directed as to what each of her guests would like. She had an intelligent mind that retained names and preferences. She was the perfect hostess and well-liked because of her attentiveness.

"Oh, the hopefulness of waiting when one's loved ones are set to soon arrive. It does us no good. But wait we must and let the longed-for gentlemen return when they shall," Mr. Morten sighed. He looked at his wife and said, "It seems we wait a good amount of time for those that are missed to return to us."

Mrs. Morten nodded at him. "Indeed we do. Mayhap someday soon we shall be the ones parting from them."

Mr. Morten chuckled and replied, "Yes, yes indeed." Isabelle caught the quick look of anguish that passed upon his face before he masked it away. The beloved man was not well and there would come a day when he departed from them all. The thought tore her heart. Though they were not related, she would mourn him. He was a king among men.

Taking a bite of her sandwich, Isabelle directed her thoughts to George. Now that his return was so close at hand, she felt her stomach tightening. She hoped that these long days apart had not diminished her within his eyes. The time apart had only strengthened her regard for him. Indeed, she came to discover that he held her heart entirely. She did not want to think about not being his wife. Thinking about the wager, she blew out her breath. The horrid affair had brought her to George, and regardless of the beginning, she could make this marriage a success. Her husband was right in the marking of his words - *our marriage can begin however it may, though it doesn't have to end before it even begins.* Isabelle was eager to express her newfound feelings to her husband and wished that he would soon arrive.

Chapter Twenty-Seven

Horses, Mud & Ruin

George had never seen a dog more excited to see him in all his days as was *Francois* when he walked through the doors of Hathwell House. The little fluffy thing barked excitedly. Without a doubt, he would have to find some way to take *Francois* with him when he returned back to Bramley Hall. His wife would be enthralled to see her beloved pet.

Harrison retired to a guest bedroom for a bath to be drawn, making himself comfortable in George's house. George didn't rightly care what liberties Harrison took and the man knew it. He directed Seth to see to his guest's needs. It was interesting, the stark contrast between men and women. How females had such attention to detail, superb articulating skills, and whatever they put their hand to turned to silver and pearls. His own wife took over his household and whipped it into shape in a matter of hours.

How she'd done so was entirely beyond him, but the feeling of being home, knowing her hand was in some way playing into the feeling, he loved her all the more for it.

George went straight to his study and began settling details on prices of items such as lumber and workers to accomplish the task of expanding the stables. His loyal butler, Linden, filled him in on all the accounts he had missed out on in the two days of absence. The latest horse purchased from Lord Taggart was already in a paddock with his finest broodmare.

Quickly, George handled the accounts, and the monthly pay-roll for all his existing employees and the new ones as well. The eight hired hands had yet to show but he gathered it would take them some time to get moving since all had families with children. George left explicit instructions with his land steward Mr. Barlow, to have them all accommodated in small cottages dotting his land, or in the small town just east of his estate. He knew of several dwellings that were available for renters in town.

George also sent missives to the men he hired to inquire whether they would require accommodations to make the tran-sition easier. He didn't want them to be lacking necessities, espe-cially after all they had done for their home and country.

Satisfied with the progress of all the happenings at Hathwell, George ordered himself a bath. While waiting for the hot water, he pondered something he remembered Isabelle asking of him: if he happened to like poetry or find any such musings delightful. Their one evening of reading Shakespeare's sonnets was firmly fixed upon his mind. His wife had enjoyed hearing the bard's words in his own voice.

Smiling softly to himself, he took out a sheet of paper to pen Isabelle a letter with a poem of adoration. He was no such poet, nor much in the way of writing. To be honest, he hadn't written a single letter of sincerity in a long time, but he felt he owed it to his wife to do his best. The missives he had sent to Mariah were really just notes.

In his letter to Isabelle, he described how much he came to adore her, that his heart found its breath to sing of her, for her, forevermore if she would allow him the chance to be the husband she deserved. He found that in writing to her, he was quickly consuming the sheets of parchment. So far, he had at least three sheets and was on his fourth and final piece. His heart constricted at the finish when he signed his name, torn between leaving the lengthy letter on the bed of her chamber, her painting easel, or even taking the letter with him. He couldn't decide so he took the letter to his bedchamber.

His bath was readied and he went upstairs, putting his wife's missive upon his bed. He would give it to her when he saw her next. He honestly couldn't wait to be reunited with her. Blast, he found that he was missing her greatly, but she was more than likely enjoying Mariah's company and that of Mr. and Mrs. Morten. *Does she mourn my absence?*

He quickly bathed and donned fresh clothes, feeling like an entirely new man. He had Seth shave his beard and cut his hair. Isabelle often remarked it was getting a little long and a bit scruffy to her liking. He hoped this improved look would satisfy her.

Walking out of his chamber, fresh and feeling good, he went to his study assuming Harrison would be there. The man didn't disappoint. He sat, leaned back on the softly cushioned divan, petting *Francois*.

"I feel remiss," Harrison began, a frown pulling down at his lips. "I long to be with Mariah."

George grinned. "Dear man, we have only been gone several hours."

"I know. I cannot help myself. I love her wholeheartedly," he said with a great sigh. "Do you think we can leave here first thing in the morning, and get business in Town handled and leave early the next day, for this is tearing me asunder, being this far from her side."

He nodded. He couldn't begin to understand the great weight Harrison must feel in regards to being apart from Mariah and her being with child. George acknowledged it was a great distraction for Harrison. He hoped to one day have children of his own with Isabelle. He hoped to be in attendance at the birth of his child as well. It wasn't the more proper thing to do, but curse the man who would try and stop him. He was not one to let the dictates of society step into his forged path.

"George," Harrison said after a long pause, "when the time nears for Mariah, do you think Isabelle could attend my wife?"

"Absolutely," George replied, taking a seat opposite his friend and rang for refreshments. "I wouldn't dream of having Isabelle away for the matter knowing how much she adores Mariah."

"Thank you, my friend," he said, sighing audibly like the great weight was lifted from him entirely. "You have no idea the great relief I feel. I love Mariah's family but they are a bit too much at times, especially Simon and Alicia," Harrison closed his eyes and cringed. "To have them there as Mariah wonderfully brings life into this world, would be a," he paused, "well, it just would not do."

George laughed uproariously. He liked Simon, he even appreciated his candor even at times, but the man was a doormat for bad form, and coupled with a female so forthright as Alicia was disastrous at all the wrong moments. George felt himself cringe and thanked the good Lord for having been married to Isabelle. In fact, next time he saw Mr. Pembroke, he was going to thank him personally.

Linden brought in tea and finger sandwiches to ease their hunger until dinner. They lulled in comfortable silence in his study as the warmth of the fire caressed their minds to take a nap.

George did not feel the need to nap so he rose from the cushioned chair and went out to see the studhorse he bought from Lord Taggart. The horse was incredible. Broad and muscular and as dark as ebony. He was proud to have purchased such an incredible beast to breed his mares with, that would further the line he already possessed. For generations to come, it would progress the Hathwell name and grace their home with prosperity. All he wanted was to secure the future of his children and future generations. His holdings were sound, but he longed to bring funds of his own making to line his coffers. *What man does not want to make his mark upon his lineage?*

He took another stroll about the estate, unable to keep his mind from last night. He was certain there was more to the cuddling in bed than he was noticing. There had to have been. George pursed his lips, heading to his favorite spot to ponder upon it.

She had, in the past several days, gazed at him more, noticed him, and whenever she glanced in his direction, her expressive blue eyes were not creased by a scowl nor harsh opinion. She had situated herself nearer to him as her alluring scent permeated his senses. She was almost agreeable in all matters and he found that both soothing and vastly confusing.

George ran a hand over his face, taking a turn around the pond, then went back inside for dinner. Harrison was still napping. George nudged his shoe and announced the evening meal. Together the friends partook of their dinner in silence, noting how odd it was to take a meal alone. They agreed to adjourn early in hopes of resting to be on the road early in the morning to head back to their wives more quickly.

He attempted to sleep but found it entirely too difficult. After one night, it was as if the whole of his body was used to laying beside his wife. George rose from his bed and was dressing as he asked Seth to pack a couple outfits for his saddlebag. Once dawn broke across the sky, he had their horses readied for the ride to Town.

George took the stairs down softly so as not to wake Harrison as he went to his study. Before even fully entering the room, he found himself face to face with his friend.

"Good morning," George greeted.

"Morning," Harrison replied.

"Are you ready to be off? I have directed our horses to be readied."

"Yes, thank you."

Linden came in with a tray of tea and fruit-filled pastries to tide them over until they made it to Town. They ate rapidly, eager to be on the road and to their wives as quickly as they could. The yipping bark of *Francois* echoed down the hall. George smiled, calling for the small dog to enter into his study. The dog came dashing inside, wiggling profusely, and took a seat right at his feet, eager to earn a scrap of something. George fed him a smidgen of a strawberry-filled pastry.

"Are you fond of the dog?" Harrison asked.

George nodded. "Yes. I am surprised I have grown attached to the little pup."

"Bring him to Bramley Hall. I know Mariah would love to see him. She often speaks of FiFi."

George glowered, wondering how he was going to take the happy and rambunctious little thing with him. He glanced at the corner of the study where his greatcoat sometimes hung on the coat stand. There he found a dark green sack and glanced at the little dog. FiFi took another pastry from the tray and proceeded to roll over it.

George fetched the sack, beckoning Francois to it with the stolen pastry thrown inside. The small dog barked, charging toward the sack. Quickly, George closed it and swung it over his shoulder. *I do hope that the strawberry filling won't stick to his fur. If he makes a mess, which I believe he shall, we shall simply have to address that later.*

Harrison burst into laughter. "That's one way to do it, I suppose. You could have carried him betwixt your arms."

George shook his head. "With my blasted luck, the dog would escape and I would suffer the wrath of my wife. I am not daring for divorce this day."

Harrison chortled. "Let us be off then. We can stop at the Pembroke residency first to drop off the wriggly thing."

George led the way out of doors, descending the steps to his mount. Already, his saddlebag was attached to his horse. He mounted deftly, waiting for Harrison to situate himself before they galloped down the lane with a mounted Seth riding behind.

It would take a few hours until they reached Town, but the sky was clear for the most part, save for a biting wind whipping past them. George rode, keeping his eyes narrowed most of the time to save them from becoming dry. It felt like the ride went quicker as he chatted with Harrison regarding business, their homes, and the differences in their wives.

George was absolutely smitten by Isabelle. He hoped she felt the same. The ever-present niggling feeling that something was growing pestered itself at the back of his head. Something was forging and he hoped to get back to her to determine what it was.

The trees on the road lined the way to Town. Before he could think of pulling the sack with Francois around to keep it hidden from view, they were already deep in the city. George felt like a ninny as he rode to town with his wife's silly dog strapped to a sack on his back. Francois poked his head out of the hole provided for air, tongue lolling out the side, as George's ever-loyal horse, London, trotted to the Pembroke townhouse of his wife's parents. Women stopped and smiled, pointing at him riding with the fluffy creature; the men, though, shook their heads disapprovingly. He was setting a bad precedent, and he felt their censure.

George turned his head to see if *Francois* had his head out of the sack, or if he huddled below from the wind. The clouds overhead did not look promising. He was met with a wet tongue to the face. He swiped off the slobber with a gloved hand, focusing on the road ahead. They didn't have much more distance to travel now.

I would do anything for my beloved wife. Even take her Francois just to see her beautiful smile and her alluring blue eyes, he thought, patting the inside of the coat pocket to ensure the letter he wrote her was still there. Come to think of it, he was no longer embarrassed by having *Francois* with him, but now a proud husband to know this would be special for her.

He knew Isabelle would love to see *Francois*, so he figured out a way to take the canine with him to Town, to then stop at her familial residence, and beckon her parents to Bramley Hall. Harrison was adamant they come to Bramley to see Mariah, share in the good news of his growing stable, and see their daughter's artful masterpiece of the nursery. George, too, was excited to see her and the beauty she had created.

George rode up the street to the Pembroke townhouse with Harrison on his left. Upon reaching the steps, they deftly dismounted. A stable hand was summoned from the mews situated behind the townhouse and he rushed out to take their mounts and tend to them. Side by side, Harrison and George ascended the steps and were announced just inside the foyer. George let down the little dog to greet his father-in-law.

"George, Harrison!" William Pembroke exclaimed, arms wide open to embrace them. "To what do I owe the pleasure?" He stepped away from them to look over their persons.

Francois jumped up on his familiar person, tail wagging profusely. William picked him up, enthusiastically loving the little dog within his arms. George cringed when he recalled the possibility of a strawberry mess, but there was nothing to be done about that at present.

Harrison beamed, clapping William on the back. "George and I have business here in town. Our ladies are at Bramley Hall. We came to invite you and Aunt Beatrice out to Bramley to stay with us for a jaunt about Town. You would not want to miss visiting with us all at the same time."

George nodded, confirming Harrison's words. "Indeed. And I was wondering if you would mind taking *Francois* to my beloved since having him on horseback is quite dismal."

William laughed. "Most assuredly! We are always more than pleased to visit with all of you. Beatrice and I shall leave first thing in the morning with our little Bernard and nanny in tow. Please stay the night here with us. I must insist."

George followed William into the house. The man spoke animatedly about how pleased he was to receive the most loving of people he ever did know. It warmed his heart profoundly to marry into a family who so readily accepted him as their own son.

William took Harrison into his study to chat privately about a country seat held within the family name, leaving George alone to wander the abode since Beatrice was asleep trying to cure a headache. He did not feel slighted at all. George wandered through the rooms, gazing at all the artwork that adorned the walls. Most of the portraits were, of some form or another, ones his wife painted. He had learned the flourish that she signed her portraits with. George made sure to stop and make time to admire every single one.

In their time together, he hadn't ever recalled her commenting about any of her work. He found it abysmal. His wife was utterly talented, so much so that he believed she should be famous. Hathwell House was devoid of color. He would love to see it vibrant and joyful, starting with his wife's art. Their townhouse was little better as Robert had not cared to have frills and lace surround him once his wife had died. *I shall let it be known to my wife that the residences are hers to decorate however she wishes to.*

George informed the Pembroke butler, Randolph, that he was going out for a spell. Inspired by his beloved's kind soul and creative side, he rode his horse to the nearest place that sold the supplies he sought, which was located on Bond Street. After locating a lad to watch over London, he ventured forth to make his purchases. Already his wife was well equipped with the necessary items, but since he desired to have Hathwell filled with paintings, he must insist that she need more.

He had the purchases made to be sent to Hathwell House. He then went down to another shop and bought her several hair combs since he noticed she only had two for her beautiful straw-berry blonde tresses. He bought her ribbons, lace, and anything of interest that he couldn't recall her ever having adorned herself with. Granted, Isabelle hadn't made a motion for being spoiled or needy, and never at all greedy in any form, but as her husband, he wanted to dote on her profusely. Her trousseau had been modest and he meant to spoil her.

Ever since the night they cuddled, he couldn't stop himself from thinking about it. He vowed to not read into it, but how could he not? There was something blooming now. Building toward af-fection, mayhap even love. Isabelle hadn't rebuked his offer. She stayed locked within his arms the entirety of the night, a smile edging at her lips, even in her slumber. In her own, quiet way, she was opening up to him and giving him her heart. He would be daft to spoil it, to not act upon it. If something ill were to ever happen, then he could look back with a peaceful heart, and declare that he had tried.

Shopping took him well into the evening when he made his way back to the Pembroke residence. He hadn't meant to be out so entirely late though he would be apt to do it all again. The Pembroke butler saw him inside and directed him to the bed-chamber in which he would be staying. 'Twas a good thing he had visited a tea shop earlier when his stomach had begun to make its displeasure known, so there was no need to disturb the kitchen staff.

Once inside, George shucked his clothes, donning his more comfortable nightwear. *Francois* was curled up on his own bed placed next to the four-poster bed. George tilted his head to the side, glancing around the room to find it still had a feminine touch to it. There were many portraits of FiFi that lined the walls and George smiled to himself. He walked over to the bed and pulled the coverlet back. Sinking his nose to the pillow, he happily inhaled the scent of his wife and grinned. Tomorrow couldn't come too soon.

Despite George and Harrison leaving early, the weather found them and rained relentlessly upon their heads. Their mounts were soaked. Everything about them was so thoroughly wet. At the first raindrop, George passed his lengthy letter to Beatrice for safe-keeping inside the dry carriage. The kindly mother-in-law smiled profusely while taking the missive, commenting that he was so loving toward her daughter. George took the moment to inform them both that he loved Isabelle unconditionally. He also took the time to express his gratitude to his father-in-law for matching them together, even if the way in which it was done had caused them all heartache. Those regrets could all be tossed into the wind, because better things were upon the horizon. Mr. Pembroke had teared up at his words. The carriage containing Mr. and Mrs. Pembroke and *Francois* remained parked at an inn in the last town they came to in order to wait out the storm, but would be headed to Bramley Hall shortly.

"Why does it seem as if I am forever returning to my wife while it pours rain?" Harrison miserably grumbled as he tilted his head to the side, allowing the collected water to fall from his topper. It just as quickly filled back up again as he righted his head.

Having no reply, George thought it wise to keep his mouth closed so as not to drown in this downpour. 'Twas a thought that did not surprise him, the weather was most foul. Other men had fallen from their horses in such weather and drowned in a muddied puddle; 'twas no laughing matter. At least the lightning had kept at bay.

George and Harrison continued on, wanting more than anything to be with their wives. They were still an hour from home, not too far away, yet not close enough to anything to seek shelter. George wiped his brow, trotting on the sodden path toward Bramley Hall.

Harrison came closer to his mount. "How are you faring?" He shouted over the din of thundering rain.

"Ready to be with my wife and have a hot bath."

Harrison nodded, "Then let's quicken the pace."

George followed Harrison's lead since he and his horse knew the way to Bramley better than he and his mount. The sopping road splashed upon his boots and face. George squinted, trying to see through the sheets of rain.

His thoughts focused on his wife, and how, when he returned to her, he would tell her just how much he loved her. In the beginning their marriage was one that Isabelle, he was sure, would've considered a scandal; to him, it was the best decision of his life to have gambled that night. Whether or not she wanted to hear it, he would tell her. Meeting William and placing that bet, rewarded him with the love of his life. He was certain the good Lord bestowed him the greatest blessing of his life in that hand.

The road took a bend to the left. The town came into view yet they were still a ways from the manor home of Harrison. A lightness crept across his chest. In a matter of a few moments, he would be ensconced up in his chamber room with his lovely wife and he would tell her exactly everything upon his heart.

George grinned, not caring about the rain falling upon his face. His horse wavered underneath him. London had his ears back, sidestepping, while Harrison's horse tried to bolt. George reigned in the beast, moving him in a circle to calm him. London reared. A giant gray wolf leapt out of a bush and snapped at London's foreleg.

Eyes widened in terror, George tried his best to stay seated upon the animal while drawing his pistol. He couldn't. The water upon his body made establishing a grip difficult. London reared again, kicking at the animal. The water made everything too slick; George couldn't stay on. He fell off of London, smashing his head upon a roadside boulder. It hurt so astoundingly, he was dazed and unable to make a sound. A gunshot echoed from somewhere. A yelp from the wolf announced its death. London whinnied shrilly, snorting and prancing so acutely George heard it over the rain. He tried to rise to his feet, finally wobbling to a standing position. His vision was hazy but made more disturbed by the pelting rain.

"George!" Harrison called though his voice was distant.

London faltered against him, knocking him to the ground. George tried to catch himself yet a stomping weight found his left hand. George cried out in pain. London whickered, nuzzling him.

"George," Harrison called again.

George glanced around, his vision blurred and unfocused. The rain against his face did not help. For a terrifying moment, he thought he was once again on the battlefield fighting for his life. He distractedly looked around for his men who were calling his name. He dreaded seeing the fallen bodies of his men when there was naught he could do to aid them in his current condition. Blinking the water drops from his eyes he spied Harrison who encircled his right arm, helping him to gain his feet and lead him away from the dead wolf. A cloud of confusion laced with pain clung to his mind. It felt like they had walked for many miles. He couldn't tell. The pain in his head and left hand was so alarming, George felt like he may vomit.

"Can you mount?" Harrison asked, thrusting reins into his right hand.

George swallowed, his throat thick, "Aye, I can. Though I am in need of a physician."

"I know," Harrison said. "We need to reach Bramley and I shall summon one. Can you make it?"

"I must," he said, wincing as he mounted London with one hand.

The rain ceased pelting and became a trickle. His head pounded relentlessly. Warmth rolled down his head and he refrained from touching it, knowing his head was bleeding profusely. He shut his right eye to curb the flow of blood mixed with the rain. He gritted his teeth, trying to keep his left hand still, yet finding it impossible. George closed his eyes, focusing on not moving nor falling from his saddle.

Harrison called out to him the entire way, to be heard over the heavy downpour, trying to keep him awake. George appreciated his friend's effort, responding intermittently to let Harrison know he was awake and with him. George crumpled over the neck of his horse, inhaling the scent of wet mane and dirt. Opening his eyes, he found himself much closer to Bramley Hall than he anticipated being.

The manor came into view and George spurred London onward. The road to Bramley Hall felt like it went on forever. Even trotting up the lane seemed to take a very long time, having to maneuver around so many muddy holes. Harrison led the way, but

George was unable to focus. All he could picture was the residence where his most treasured possession happened to be.

Like a beacon on the most disturbing of days, the front steps of Bramley Hall reached his eager gaze. George fell from his mount, unable to stay upon him any longer. George sucked in a breath at the pain.

Large hands encircled his upper arms on either side of his body.

"Come on friend," Harrison encouraged.

George wobbled his way to his feet, using the support of Harrison and one of the stable hands to make it up the front steps and into the foyer of the house. The walk felt as if it went on forever. His body ached. Everything in him wanted to rest, to close his eyes and let slumber claim him. George forced his eyes open, wanting to see the beaming smile of his Isabelle.

No longer capable of standing due to a pounding ache in his head and the intense pain coming from his left arm, he crumpled to the floor.

Harrison followed, descending to the floor with the weight of George, calling alarmingly for his valet, Edmund, and his butler, Billingsley, to assist. A high-pitched shriek reached his ears. George looked up. He smiled at the emotional blue eyes of his wife.

"George!" she exclaimed, coming to his side.

The warmth of her hands felt soothing on his icy cold skin. George exhaled contentedly, more than happy to be back in her arms.

"George!" she cried. "Oh my, George. What happened?"

"We were attacked upon the road by a wolf. George's horse startled and threw him against a rock, then accidentally stomped upon his hand. I have the physician being called for now," Harrison explained.

George closed his eyes and breathed peacefully. He had made it back to his wife. And she was here with him, happy to see him despite the circumstances of his arrival. He reached up and cupped her cheek, committing to memory the softness of her skin.

"Isabelle," he whispered. "I love you."

Having spoken the words his heart longed to say to her forever, he succumbed to his head wound and closed his eyes.

Chapter Twenty-Eight

Confessions From The Heart

T he entire world stopped turning and then suddenly sped up. Seeing him a haggard mess with blood trailing all over his face, and his left arm swollen, and facing the wrong direction, was near enough to upset Isabelle's stomach and make her feel faint. She had just finished cleaning her paintbrushes when she had heard the commotion and decided to investigate what was occurring. In all her days, she never expected to find her husband a bloody, sorrowful mess.

Isabelle's words were choppy and filled with panic. "George... Oh, George. You must recover." Tears fell down her face. "You must, so that I may tell you how very much I love you." Her gaze settled upon his head wound and she stifled a gasp. George groaned, lolling his head to the side where even more of the wound was exposed.

"All right friend," Harrison said, beckoning Edmund over, "let's get you upstairs." Together the men hoisted George, with Harrison ascending backward up the staircase.

They quickly carried him to the bedchamber as Isabelle proceeded ahead of them, opening the chamber's door, and then helping to remove his cloak and boots once he was upon the bed. She was fighting to keep her composure, but in truth, she had never been more frightened in her entire life. If he never got to hear her words of love, and if she never got to beg for his forgiveness, she would mourn her choices into her own grave. Head wounds were a serious business and not to be dismissed lightly.

Isabelle leaned over his prostrate form and cradled his unbroken hand to her chest. "George, you must return to me. Please, please try." Her whispered words were an entreaty just for his ears.

Harrison thanked his servants as he handed off his outerwear to Billingsley. Mariah frantically entered the chamber with her eyes grown large. She came to a stop beside Harrison and clung to his soaking arm.

"Dearest, mayhap you should depart from the room. George is not well and I will not have you upset," Harrison told his wife.

Mariah tilted her head up to look at him with a glare. "How dare you, my lord! He is my guest and family. Besides, I will not depart and allow Isabelle to suffer this alone." She moved a few steps to stand at Isabelle's side.

Harrison opened and closed his mouth.

"Is there anything I can offer you? Assist in any way?" Mariah inquired of Isabelle.

Isabelle shook her head nay, her curls dancing as her face scrunched up. Mariah reached for her and encircled her within her arms while Isabelle still clung to George. Mr. Morten made his way into the bedchamber and removed his handkerchief from a pocket and offered it to Isabelle who gladly took it, but did not make use of it.

Laying a hand upon George's head, Mr. Morten started praying silently as the ladies wept and stood looking on. All Isabelle could think about was how guilty she felt for how she mistreated him their entire marriage. She burned his heart without him ever giving her any credence. She was closed off, reserved to the point it hurt her. It took her father, Mariah, and now this terrible accident for her to realize just how poorly she had behaved to such a chivalrous and loving man.

It was some time before the physician, Dr. Carrow, entered the bedchamber. He was dripping wet, dressed in shades of black that matched his doctor's bag. Water drops fell from his blond head of hair. "My apologies, my lord and ladies, Mr. Morten. The roads have become quite muddy and almost untraversable." He laid his black medical bag down on the foot of the bed, opened one of George's eyes, and then the next. He took the hand that Isabelle was gripping and checked his pulse. "He has a strong heartbeat and looks healthy enough. I suspect his mangled hand shall heal well, but it will need to be set at once. I shall clean his head wound first and dress it appropriately; I believe that a few stitches would not be remiss. I can then tend to his hand."

Dr. Carrow reached into his black bag and began to pull items from within. With expert hands and gentle ministrations, he soon had George's head injury tended to and wrapped. Isabelle had ceased her tears and was calmly sitting on the edge of the bed. They had removed his sodden clothing in order to attend to him better.

"Lady Bramley, would it be careless of me to beg you for tea? I think those in this room could do with a cup." Dr. Carrow's kind gray eyes locked upon Mariah.

"Of course." Mariah rose from the wingback chair by the fire and walked to the bellpull, pulling upon it.

When Billingsley entered, and Mariah requested tea, Dr. Carrow brought his head toward Isabelle's ears and whispered, "If all goes as it should, your husband shall recover. We must be certain to keep the fever away. He is still in danger, my lady."

Isabelle nodded her head, understanding that he did not want Mariah to be distressed with the information since she was with child.

"Harrison, there is naught to be accomplished at present. Mayhap Mariah and yourself should rest. We cannot have you catching a chill," Isabelle said with resolve in her voice.

"That is sound advice. I shall check in on you soon. Come along, dearest." Harrison held out his hand to his wife who took it but looked conflicted.

"Mariah, please take care. Your health is of supreme importance. You have missed your husband, go spend the evening with him. We shall be fine," Isabelle told her with a gentle smile.

Mariah bowed her head and allowed Harrison to escort her from the chamber. When the door closed, Isabelle felt her smile wobble. She was terrified. She had greatly relied upon Mariah to assist in keeping her composure but with Mariah in such a delicate state, her own health must be paramount.

"Mayhap you too, Mr. Morten, should retire to another room as well," Dr. Carrow suggested.

"Nay, I shall not leave this dear boy's side for all the jewels in the treasury. I shall sit here quietly and calmly with tea once it arrives." Mr. Morten's firm voice broke no argument and Isabelle was relieved. She did not want to be without a friend in the bedchamber with her. There was no better steadying influence than that of Mr. Morten.

Once the door to the room clicked shut, and Mr. Morten's declaration of not leaving her side was stated, the doctor directed her to look out the window. He asked her to peer to see whether his assistant had arrived. Hearing a man grunting in excruciating pain, she immediately flew back to George's side. Dr. Carrow was splinting and wrapping George's broken hand. He then turned to creating a sling for it to reside in and elevated it to reduce the swelling.

Isabelle was dismayed that she had been directed to part from her husband's side when such a painful procedure was being undertaken. However, she understood the physician's reasoning in having diverted her attention elsewhere.

Billingsley brought in the tea tray and Isabelle rose to play hostess to the men in the room. She first served Mr. Morten and then inquired how the physician took his tea. When the quiet breaths of George and the sipping of tea were the only sounds within the chamber, Isabelle let herself have a moment of quiet reflection. She could still hear her husband's words: *Isabelle, I love you.* And she wanted to weep. It was not how she had envisioned their declarations to each other and she wished that he had heard her say the same words to him. *I cannot help but wonder if I shall ever have the chance to look into his eyes and say the words that my heart most longs to express.*

Isabelle bowed her head and closed her eyes. She had not prayed in days, she was a horrible wife. So embittered had she been that she could not bring her troubled heart before the Lord in prayer. She had made peace with her father and was soon to do the same with her husband. She must also do the same with her heavenly father.

Dear Lord, please forgive me, my spitefulness, and bitter ways. I shall endeavor to do better. I ask that you please heal my husband so that I may make amends with him. I do not deserve him. But if you would bring him back to me, I shall make it my mission to shower him with affection every moment of every day. Please let me have the opportunity to return his love, to tell him how I feel. Amen

Isabelle straightened herself and opened her eyes. Her prayer was simple, but heartfelt. She sat on the end of the bed, waiting for George to open his loving brown eyes.

"He understands your heart." Mr. Morten kindly said as he smiled sadly at Isabelle.

She smiled back at him and sipped her tea. She was uncertain whether Mr. Morten meant the Lord, or her husband, understood her heart, but could not summon the energy to inquire which he had meant. It would be a long evening and she must not let her mind nor her heart mourn before she even lost George. It was premature and a waste of her fortitude. Instead, she would monitor George to ensure that any change was duly noted and addressed.

Dinner was brought in on a tray and she hardly touched it. When Mr. and Mrs. Pembroke entered the room a little before eleven, they each embraced her and expressed their concern for George. Her father informed her of the visit Harrison and George had paid to them entreating them to come and stay. She bade them to seek their rest and returned to her husband's side. It did her heart good to know that they were in residence. FiFi was also with them, but it was deemed appropriate to keep the dog away from the sickroom as his rambunctious manner was not needed. Though she missed him, she felt secure knowing that he was being well-cared for.

It was well into the night when Isabelle could not keep her eyes open any longer. The physician was asleep in the adjoining chamber and Mr. Morten softly snored from the chair by the fire.

Dr. Carrow had located a stool upon which to place the parson's feet, seeing to the care of another of his patients. Isabelle had pulled a blanket from the back of a chair and draped it over Mr. Morten. Mrs. Morten had come in intermittently to see how things progressed; she broke up her time between visiting with them and seeing to Mariah.

Isabelle woke up with a start. She felt a heavy hand resting upon her head. Reaching up, she clasped the warm hand and then brought her head away from the mattress where it had been laying. Chocolate eyes met her gaze and she had to stifle the gasp that threatened to wake Mr. Morten.

Tears of thankfulness gathered within her eyes. "My dearest lord husband, you are with me again."

"Hear me now, I shall never leave you." He went to move toward her, but grimaced as he let her go to touch the bandage wrapped around his head.

"Stay still. You have serious injuries to your body."

"I am noticing that just at the moment. Ahhh. Yes, an accident upon the road. Harrison was there and we rode through the rain," George said quietly. Isabelle suspected it was due to the pain within his head. She was immeasurably relieved that he could recall the accident, as that meant that there must not be any serious injury to his keen mind.

"That is correct. You must remain still and not tax yourself. I shall wake the physician to attend to you." Isabelle made to rise, but she stilled with his hand coming to rest against her arm.

"All I thought of these past few days was returning to you. I cannot abide the distance between us. You must understand that I-"

Isabelle spoke over him, "You love me. Yes, I know, you told me that just as you were passing out. How very unkind of you lord husband to say such things to me-"

George was quick to interject, "I will not apologize." He peered into her eyes, searching them.

"I should hope not. For you see, I have found myself lost to you, lost in the feeling of a love so deep, so pure, that all I have wished for was the chance to tell you." Isabelle laughed as tears of happiness spread to her eyes.

"You love me?" George looked at her incredulously. "You love me," he said again, as the most loving smile overtook his handsome face.

"I, Isabelle, love you, George. Will you love me in return for all of your days, as I cannot be without you ever again? And I mean to make you understand the depth of my love every moment from here ever after."

George extended his uninjured hand to her which she took. He pulled her toward him. Isabelle moved carefully next to him and laid her head upon his chest. She felt his lips upon her head, kissing her and whispering prayers of thanksgiving. Her heart was full. This was all she had ever wanted, a husband who returned her affection in equal measure, one that would never want to let her go. If only she had not fought against this, against him, they could have had days of joy together instead of just these last precious moments. He was worth falling in love with; he was worth any scandal. The chance to love him, to be by his side, was all-encompassing.

Isabelle sighed. All was right in her world, or would soon be, once George was healed. *How soon is too soon to begin our family? I long to carry his babe and forever cherish our days together. I would love to gift the family with another little one, so that Harrison's babe as well as my darling little brother, have a playmate and confidant.* Isabelle lay next to George as plans for their future together blossomed in her heart.

Epilogue

Love That Lasts

I sabelle rolled her eyes at her husband's silly jests. He had been making them all morning just to see how she would react to his ruses.

"Darling," George began, "did you see that flash of lightning?"

"Yes."

"Indeed, it was very striking."

The spring storm was beating rain against the windowpanes and allowing very little light into the room. Candles had been lit and arranged throughout while Isabelle applied her brush to the canvas to create shadow and light upon the portrait before her.

Isabelle chortled, finding herself rolling her eyes again. He was indeed healed and whole as ever. She had finally talked him into sitting in the drawing room for a portrait. She had longed to paint him and now she was happily directing her brush to take in all of the supreme male perfection in her dear husband; from his chocolate eyes to his fine nose and the dark hair that refused to stay away from his eyes - he was perfect in every way.

They still had disagreements, but they were easily resolved as each was more than patient with the other. They had not spent a single night from the other's side since their reunion at Bramley Hall. The room she once occupied all alone at Hathwell House was the chamber in which her husband spent his nights alongside her now. Marriage was bliss and every day brought a new discovery to Isabelle's heart of how to make it even more wonderful. She delighted in surprising George with little trinkets or his favorite things. He appreciated the attention and never failed to reciprocate. He admitted once that giving up drinking was not the easiest endeavor he had ever undertaken. It had its challenges, but when the moments came crashing down upon him, he would think of Isabelle, or seek her out to spend time in her presence, and that gave him the fortitude to carry on. George had prayed to the Lord for forbearance and He had seen him through. This gladdened her heart and proved to Isabelle that no matter what, He had held them within His hands the entire journey that their marriage had taken.

Her thoughts turned to the days following the accident. They had remained at Bramley Hall for a fortnight before returning home. Mariah was a gracious hostess and was sad to see them depart. Together they had shared the nursery with their husbands who made the appropriate remarks and then in turn pointed out all the details to Mr. and Mrs. Pembroke.

The letter, which she had located with Mrs. Pembroke upon George's demand, told of his depth of feelings for her. She had read it seated beside him that next morning after his incident and the letter still bore the stains of her tear tracks. It was one of her favorite treasures and she tucked it into her reticule next to the other missive she had received from him.

Once George was well enough to go about the town, they visited with the parson, Mr. Ridley, and his sister. They stayed to take tea and planned the Spring Bazaar. The list that Mr. Ridley had presented to them was indeed quite extensive. They were to have their hands on many of the day's activities. The one that had pleased George the most was the rowing competition across the lake. He was eager to put himself and his men to the task. Isabelle was thankful that there would be some weeks more for George's hand to continue to mend. It was agreed upon to push the festivities back by a few weeks in order to accomplish all that was set before them with Mr. Ridley heartedly accepting the change. The additions and inclusion of the lord and his lady greatly pleased the man of God.

There was an evening that Isabelle expressed why her heart had been set so firmly against George. She had spent years guarding her heart, building walls around it while finding faults in others. It was bad form, but she could not be disappointed in herself for driving her other suitors away, for the Lord had seen fit to give her to George. When she began to feel deeper emotion for him, she was so frightened that he would scorn her; it was what she had believed she deserved. But no matter what she did or said, he remained steadfast and constant. When she understood why she was so harsh with him, as well as her actions in her past relationships, she began to heal her heart. In loving him, she was learning to love herself, faults and all. *You marvelous woman, how could you doubt my affection for you?* George had asked to which she had just shrugged.

Standing back from her easel, she sighed. George's portrait was almost finished. Though he kept smiling and patting FiFi upon the head, mirth was missing from his face. Mayhap then she would need to gift him with information that she was certain would keep a grin upon his face.

"Lord husband, I have a confession," Isabelle told him, attempting to keep her face in a neutral manner.

"Indeed, lady wife. Pray, tell me what that is."

"I have very good reason to believe that our family is increasing." She smiled at him.

George looked down at FiFi and cheered, "Huzzah! You little rapscallion, are you about to be a father?" They had located two female poodles of excellent pedigree to breed FiFi with, so his guess was not too far off the mark.

"Not to my knowledge."

Drawing his brows together, he frowned. Then she spied a light enter into his gaze as he brought his eyes to rest upon her midsection. Isabelle chortled as he leaped from his seat upon the bench and raced to her. He sunk down onto his knees, and with his large hands, held onto her hips. George looked up at her.

Isabelle nodded her head and said, "Congratulations, my lord husband, you are to be a father."

George's eyes began to fill with tears. He placed a gentle kiss upon her stomach and rested his forehead against her. "I am so very pleased to meet you, little one. Grow healthy and happily as I spoil your Mama. You cannot know what your presence means to me." He looked up at Isabelle again and said, "Thank you. This is all I ever wanted, ever needed. To create this life, to make our own family, this is the desire of my heart."

Isabelle could not reply, her own tears clogging her throat. Despite their dismal beginning, they had found a love that lasts.

Love Ever Lasting

Chapter One

Last Moments

The September autumn air was brisk as Matthew Morten, the eldest son of Mr. and Mrs. Morten, rode pell-mell through the countryside. The colors were changing to warm browns, vibrant oranges, and reds as he sped by on his horse, Minnow. His gaze took in none of the splendor, his focus solely on reaching Bramley Parsonage in time. He tightened his hold on the reins and breathed easier: Bramley Hall was rising up in the far distance. He would soon be home. Just this morning, he had received a letter from his sister, Mariah Pembroke, the Countess of Bramley. She wrote to implore him to drop all and attend to their father, who was not expected to see the next sunrise. His heart was breaking and there was naught he could do to repair it; it would soon shatter into even more shards. So he did the only thing he could; he rode on.

MICHELLE HELEN FRITZ, E.A. SHANNIAK

'Ere long he knew it, he was approaching the parsonage. There was a stable hand with Bramley Hall livery that awaited his arrival in the yard. He leaped from the saddle and strode to the front door as it opened. Mariah was standing on the threshold with tears in her luminous sapphire eyes. When he stopped before his sister, she threw her arms around him and held him tightly. He embraced her back and buried his nose in her hair.

"You have come home at long last. We have missed you, but most especially dear Papa." She let him go and then took his hand as she pulled him into the house. She took his greatcoat from him and he handed her his topper. Mariah placed them upon a chair and she took notice of the mud and muck. His boots as well were coated and were leaving muddy boot prints behind him. They would need to be cleaned, and he found that he could not care less.

"I believe he has been waiting for you before he leaves us all," Mariah tearfully admitted. "Mama is with him. This will be difficult for us all, but she will suffer the most."

Matthew stood before her having no words of comfort. He was failing before he had even begun. It was his calling to minister to the sick and dying and to have words or comfort at the ready. But how does one prepare for the loss of a father? *The best man that I have ever known is about to leave this earth and I am not ready. How can this be?* He felt numb.

"Pray, do not keep him waiting." Mariah nudged him toward the staircase.

Harrison Pembroke, the Seventh Earl of Bramley, came to wrap his arms around his wife. There was pain swirling within his teal gaze. A babe gave a wail and Mariah rushed into the parlor to attend to her newborn son.

Matthew took the stairs two at a time, his thoughts on what scene would next greet his wearied eyes. All he could think of was his dear father clinging to his last moments upon the earth. This was not how things should have been. Old age should have whisked him away upon angel's wings. *Too soon, this is much too soon.*

His mother's muffled cries reached his ears upon entering his parents' bedchamber. He wanted to comfort his Mama who sat in a wooden chair beside the bed, hunched over its side. But no, he'd have time for that later, after his papa was laid to rest. If he took a moment to address her now, he knew that his task would become that much harder to bear. He felt his throat thickening with unshed tears and felt as if he were still a boy. He was not ready for this parting and doubted if he ever would be. *Lord, grant me strength!*

He stood before the other side of the four-poster bed. In the gloomy darkness of the room, he could just make out the slim, sickly features of the one man who meant the world to him. He noted how small and frail his blanket-covered father looked. The candlelight only infused the sorrow threatening to overtake him. The fire in the grate made menacing shadows appear on the ceiling and walls, adding to the somber mood.

He leaned down and grasped his father's dry hand, saying, "I'm here, dear Papa. I'm so sorry I wasn't sooner."

Mr. Morten opened his eyes the slightest amount and nodded at his eldest child. "You've come, that's all that matters." He took a breath and began again, "Take care of your Mama, the parish..." Mr. Morten began great, wracking coughs that lead to wheezing.

Mrs. Morten gave an alarmed cry and reached for her husband's other hand as she brought her lace handkerchief to her mouth.

Matthew looked toward the bedside table and noticed the cup filled with water. He helped his father take a drink. When his father only drank a tiny sip, Matthew gathered all of his resolve to get through this night. He said a quick prayer to the Lord to take him swiftly and without further undue pain.

"Papa, you needn't worry about a thing," Matthew tried to reassure him.

Shaking his head ever so slightly, Mr. Morten whispered, "Promise you'll stay. They'll need you here. I need you here. I'm so proud of..." He grabbed at his night-gown clad chest and twisted his face. He died in the next breath, in his home where he had served the parish and where he most wished to be. He had never been a rich man, he had never taken holidays nor lived above his station. But he had always firmly insisted that he had the wealth of family and friends, and in his faith, he was the wealthiest of men. He never longed for more than he had been given. And he truly demonstrated his love for his fellow man daily. If only all men were as good as he.

Matthew's whole world was forever changed by his beloved father's passing. The insurmountable grief clutched his insides savagely, but he managed to offer up a prayer to his creator for strength and wisdom to see his family through this terrible tragedy. Heaven had just gained the most genuine and loving soul. 'Twas the greatest loss he had ever endured, and he promised that he would stay in Bramley to see that his family made it through this together. He would honor his father and make him proud, even from the promised land.

The loud sobs of Mrs. Morten shook the bed. Matthew was in no doubt that the entire household knew that their patriarch had just taken his last breath. Matthew crossed over to the other side of the bed and took his mother away from her prostate pose next to his father and held her within his arms. His waistcoat quickly soaked up her tears. He felt wetness meet his own cheeks, but he could not be bothered to care about that unmanly trait. He would grieve this loss and then be strong for those who needed him most. He would have to bury his father and lead his parish, should Harrison allow it. Either way, he had come home at long last. He only wished that it had been sooner. The following days ahead would be a trial for them all.

Matthew stared at his younger brother, Simon, who was dressed in his scarlet regimental uniform across the dinner table in the parsonage. Harrison sat at the head, immaculately clothed in a dark blue tailcoat and black armband in respect for his father-in-law, while Mama sat dressed all in the black of widow's weeds across from him. Mariah looked drawn out, but lovely nonetheless, in a black-colored day dress and was seated next to her husband, as was Alicia, who had chosen to wear pink. They were not standing upon ceremony, none cared to observe the societal rules at present. They had not dressed in dinner attire. *It should mayhaps bother me more,* Matthew mused. *But I cannot bring myself to be proper when I am so completely numb. At the very least, Harrison sits at the head.* They were all somber, attempting to make it through another meal without the shedding of tears.

Not much conversation was had as the dinnerware was cleared of its foodstuffs and the clinking of utensils was heard against the plates. The gaiety of the dining room was lost to all. No one so much as glanced at the dining room walls decorated in pale stripes with a floral pattern. The lit chandelier cast long shadows along the walls, which matched the mood of the room at present. Matthew was lost in thoughts of the past.

He had found the idea of his younger sister marrying so high above their station an anomaly, and certainly, he had reservations that his sister would have the knowledge to be a proper wife to an earl. He had difficulty in addressing his childhood friend as simply Harrison since he had inherited the title. It was something he would, in time, become used to now that family bonds joined them. There was no denying the great affection that Mariah and Harrison held for each other, and he was pleased for them. He most assuredly would never seek to rise above his humble station.

As for Simon, he seemed to be well suited to his wife. They shared a zest for life and were both at times senseless to the feelings of others, though 'twas not intentionally done. Supposing that another matched to each might have smoothed out their edges, it was not to be so. Matthew would try to overlook the absurdity that was inherent at times. The Lord required his servants to love one another, no matter their follies. *I had the best teacher in all the world to guide me. I shall not disappoint him in this world nor the next.*

"This does not honor our Papa. I shall not sit here another moment and take part in these ill humors," Simon began. "We shall reminisce about Papa and we shall be merry in celebrating the extraordinary man who walked this earth not nearly long enough."

Matthew looked around the table to the differing reactions upon his family's faces. He observed shock, grief, and delight at his brother's statement. *His wife seems quite pleased with him,* Matthew noted.

"Now, I shall take my turn first. I remember when I was but six, and I had just been covered in flour. The kitchen was coated as well. Papa entered just as Mrs. Kurly, bless her sweet soul, was screeching with her hands up to her face as she passed by him on her way to who-knows-where. Papa took one look at me, then at the mess, and sternly asked me what in heaven's name had I been up to. I was very afraid to answer, you see, and so I stayed quietly looking down at my shoes. Papa stepped forward, heedless of the flour, and sat down next to me on the floor. It must not have been very long before I blurted out that I had wanted to hide my treasure in a place where no one would ever be able to find it. Papa nodded thoughtfully, then asked what exactly my treasure happened to be." Simon chuckled, seeming to be lost away in the past. "I uncurled my chubby fist and held up my rock to him. It was only an ordinary rock, nothing so special to an adult. Indeed, there was nothing remarkable about the gray thing whatsoever. But Papa took it from me and it was as if he saw the beauty that I did as he turned it this way and that. He again nodded his head and told me that it was indeed a precious thing to want to preserve. It was something that the Lord had fashioned much as I was. We were each created with a grand purpose in mind and we just had to discover what mine was. In that moment, as a boy, he understood me as no one ever had before." Simon paused to rub a large hand over his face. "In the meantime, he begged me to please keep from the kitchen and to forevermore refrain from creating messes that would take days to clean. He rose then and pulled me to my feet and then he looked down at me. He told me how much he loved me and how proud he was of my tender heart. I remember thinking how humorous it was to see his lower half coated in the white dust, but now, as I recall this to all of you, I feel the pride he felt for me and the love that was ever-present within himself."

Mama began to weep. Matthew went to rise to offer her comfort and his handkerchief when Mariah spoke and the room's attention shifted to her.

"You should have seen Papa in the days that lead up to Daniel's birth. He could not be kept away from us. I thought we should have to permanently move him to Bramley Hall." A fond smile graced Mariah's face. "Then when the evening arrived, and I knew our babe was ready, Harrison sent a carriage for Mama and Papa. Papa came straight in to see me once he arrived and placed a kiss upon my forehead. He prayed for us and then, as he was leaving the room, he looked back at me lying on the bed and smiled. I shall always treasure that." Mariah wiped at her tears. "When Isabelle brought Papa back into the room and Harrison placed Daniel into his arms, he cried. Our dear father shed tears of happiness and

I suspect relief that he had held on long enough to meet his grandson. We all knew his body was tired, and he suffered, but he would not allow himself to miss this meeting. I am half in agony that we could not keep him with us for longer and also joyful that he made another memory for me to forevermore cherish." Harrison leaned over to his wife and clasped her ungloved hand in his. He brought it to his mouth and kissed the back of it.

There were so many memories created at his father's knee and then, as Matthew became older, at his side. He could not fix on a single one. His father had taught him so much and it was not in him to part with the teachings just yet. He felt as if half of his heart had been cleaved in two. It was his task now to see his family, and especially his mother, through this. He would take time to process his feelings later. He was not given to public displays and 'twas a wonder that he could even stand before a crowd to give a sermon. But he knew that in serving his Creator lay his purpose.

Matthew rose from the table and announced that they should retire. Come the morrow, the men had to see to the graveside while the women stayed behind. Mama had wept over Papa's body as the ladies had prepared him to be laid to rest. He had been present to offer aid as they bathed and dressed Papa. His mother was delicate as was his sister, therefore he would never subject them to seeing the wooden casket lowered into the ground. The sound of the dirt hitting the thin wooden lid would be haunting.

Chapter Two

Farewell To What She Knew

T he rain poured heavily upon her brunette head, soaking through her simple straw bonnet. Grace poked her head around the corner of where she was hiding. It was highly improper for women to attend or even view a burial, but she simply didn't care, she was not one easily given into superstition. Nothing evil would befall her if she were to step foot into the cemetery. Hang the consequences of it to boot. Mr. Morten was the staple of the entire town, and losing him had cast a dark shadow over the town, for he would not be easily replaced. *There was none like Mr. Morten.* Her heart grieved fiercely.

Men stood on either side of the wooden pine casket, holding ropes to lower the beloved man into the soil. Matthew Morten, the eldest son of Mr. Morten, stood at the head of the burial, praying. His voice rang true despite the soaking, bone-chilling drizzle.

Though she caught hints of his emotions upon declarations of certain words, she could not understand every word he said. While it wasn't customary to linger, the man was sending his father off with prayers and devotion.

Glancing around in fear of being discovered, she was certain none were there besides her siblings. For now, she could continue watching, but she dared not tarry much longer.

"Gracie," Adalie whispered, pulling at her brown dress.

Grace bent down and picked up her youngest sister, holding her close. It had been six years since she'd last seen the cemetery. The sole reason she was here now was due to Mr. Morten and his great love of people, including her family. *He has lifted us up many times and now I honor him.*

"I'm hungry, Gracie," Adalie whined softly.

"Once this is over, we shall return home."

Adalie nodded, kicking her feet to be set back down.

Grace set her down but held firmly onto her hand. Six years ago her mother perished bringing Adalie into this world, leaving her at three and ten to care for her three younger siblings and a newborn as her father, the only blacksmith from here to Town, was left to be the sole provider for the six of them. Mr. Morten had given assistance when the burden of difficult times struck their household. The kind parson was a beacon within the community. To have him gone filled the world with less light and great sorrow. *Though I am glad he is not left to suffer, I shall miss him dreadfully.*

She wiped a tear from her eye, feeling immense guilt wash over her for not even daring to visit her own mother here, proper or not. It was extremely improper for her to watch, linger, or be near here, but blast it all. She snuck to be here when her mother was buried and she snuck to be here now. She once expressed her guilt regarding her mother, about not being there, to Mr. Morten who then had taken her hand and given it a squeeze stating–*The Lord knows the loving heart and the deep sorrow at missing her. Simply pray, let your words be heard and your mother will hear them too.* Grace wiped her cheeks with her right hand, rolling her shoulders back to show strong character for her sister.

Grace brushed the drizzle from her face, that her poke bonnet had not kept away. She wanted to view Matthew through the downpour. She couldn't catch a proper glimpse from the odd angles in which the men were gathered. Grace smiled softly at the small peeks she did manage to spy. Matthew was still handsome, with a strong jaw and expressive brown eyes. Something about his kind manner had always drawn her notice.

The family male members began to disperse, heading away from the cemetery. One man continued to throw dirt onto the coffin. Grace took Adalie's smaller hand in hers and left as well, with her three younger siblings in tow. They took a short reprieve from their chores and work to sneak out to be here. Now that it was over, it was time to get back to it; and quickly, before their father arrived home for luncheon.

Grace led her family on foot through the country lane, staying well away from sight in case someone saw them, and reprimanded them for being too near the cemetery. They passed by tall trees and a pond with ducks gathered in it. Grace guided them back to their side of the village, where Bramley Hall oversaw them. Their small home was set in the midst of the town and had smoke pluming from the chimney. The pounding of her father's hammer on the anvil broke the silence of the dreary day. Grace felt relieved that her absence had not been noticed.

"Inside with you all," Grace ushered. "Quickly, before someone sees." It was impossible that no one had noticed their departure and return, such was the way of small-town life. Mayhap her comings and goings would not reach her father's ears, as she doubted that there were many who were not in mourning for the parson.

Christopher, the eldest boy and younger than her nine and ten years by two, took the hand of the twin boys, Fraser and Thayer, and led them inside to get changed out of their wet clothes.

"Hang them on the drying rack by the fire," Grace instructed. "I'll tell Papa I did laundry today." She did not like to fib, but she had learned that in some instances it saved her a great deal of trouble where her father was concerned. Her untruth pricked at her heart, but she swallowed it down in order to go about her chores.

Christopher waved his understanding, taking the boys up-stairs. Grace watched them go with a drawn smile. Their mother had the twins when Grace was one and ten. Hearing her mother wail and cry out still tortured her ears sometimes late at night; for it was those same screams that brought Adalie into the world and ended their mother's life shortly thereafter. Grace shook her head, taking Adalie up the stairs to the room they shared together.

"What's for luncheon?" Adalie asked.

Somehow, the six year old was in a constant state of hunger. Grace struggled to keep them all fed as their father's money went to the loan upon the cottage, his shop, and necessities. Whatever she made from darning clothes and selling candles went to food.

"Chicken chowder with rolls," Grace replied, helping the child out of her wet dress.

"Again!" she cried.

"Yes again. No complaints either. I won't have it. We are to be thankful of our blessings, and full bellies are always something to be thankful for."

Adalie's lip wobbled, but she kept quiet as Grace helped her into a fresh brown-colored dress and dried her mouse-brown locks. Grace felt her heart constrict. She was the elder sister, acting as a mother to her younger siblings. Even the twins sometimes slipped, calling her mother instead of sister. It pained her heart and made her father irate.

With Adalie taken care of, Grace addressed herself, changing her dress and allowing her hair down to dry somewhat before braiding it from her face and twisting it to make a bun that rested at the back of her head. Taking their sopping wet clothes, she descended the stairs two at a time to the kitchen. Grace hung their clothes quickly and began to get their meal plated before their papa strode into the house for the brief moments he spent with them.

"Grace!" Papa bellowed from the dining room.

"Here Papa," Grace said, slipping into the room warily.

"Where is luncheon?"

"'Tis ready Papa."

She scrambled to get her Papa fed first, plating a bowl of the chowder she made and several rolls. Her papa, Mr. Hagan Buchanan, was the only blacksmith in the entire small village near Bramley Hall. He was also not the same since their mother passed, sometimes taking to drink, but was at least responsible enough to pay his creditors first. *That was certainly a blessing*, she thought.

Grace glanced over her shoulder, spying her three younger siblings poke their heads around the wall that separated the kitchen and the dining room. She put her right hand behind her back, wriggling three fingers to signal them to wait until Papa was done eating. These signals had been necessary, as Papa was often in a foul mood.

"Is there anything else you might make?" Papa demanded over his spoon.

Grace's jaw slackened for a moment before she was able to reply aptly with a, "Yes Papa," as to not provoke his ire. The man ate ravenously, forgoing his spoon to practically drink the meal straight from the bowl as he stuffed rolls into his mouth intermittently. *His behavior was revolting.*

Papa hurriedly rose from his chair so abruptly it screeched across the floor. He wiped his mouth with his sleeve, exiting the dining room, and the house, abruptly. Papa slammed the door shut, making the dishes in the kitchen rattle. Grace let out a breath. It was one of the more tender moments with their father. Grace had everyone on a strict schedule to be awake and doing chores before her Papa went to work to be out of his way, and abed with the house clean when he came home. It was strict of her to be so with her siblings, but it proved to be a necessity for their wellbeing.

"You can come out now," Grace called, shaking the shivers from her spine.

Quietly, she dished up the meal for her siblings, setting a roll or two by their plates, and served them water to drink. Adalie dug into hers with gusto. The twins, mostly identical except that Fraser had an angel kiss on the left cheekbone, swapped bowls and ate.

Christopher stood in the entryway, clenching and relaxing his hands. The young man scowled at the floor. His long dirty blond hair hung in his eyes. Grace took the clothes in his fisted hands from him, hanging them promptly over the drying rack.

"Gracie," his baritone voice said as quietly as he could.

Grace went over to her brother, enclosing him in an embrace, and kissed the side of his head. "Everything is going to work out."

Christopher unhooked himself from her, taking her hands and patting the top of them. "I've come to a decision, dear sister, so please don't take this bitterly."

Grace tilted her head to the side, hazel eyes narrowing on her brother. "I could never carry bitterness toward you."

Christopher smiled softly. "I've decided to join the regiment–"

Grace gasped.

He silenced her with a finger to her lips. "Any monetary gains I get, I will send to you and our siblings. Papa has increased his habits as of late, and I cannot bear to leave you destitute. Already men do not vie for your hand. I want you to have a future too."

"But Chris, must you join?"

He sorrowfully nodded. "'Tis the only way to send you monthly security. That way you never have to worry for food. Besides, Papa does not allow me to attend to the work with him, so my skills have not improved enough to provide a living for us elsewhere."

Grace embraced her brother, holding him close. "When do you leave?"

"Tonight. There are several others signing up and we are departing within a few hours' time."

Grace wrapped her brother tightly within an embrace. Even though the war was over with the French and people began to see some semblance of normalcy, military units were still seeking able-bodied men. It worried her to see her brother's desire to enlist, not knowing where he would be sent to. His wish to see her future secured warmed her heart, yet it wasn't fair to him to have to undertake this. She had no doubt that he had earned enough from the odd chores he had undertaken for those in the town that needed an extra hand to procure his way into the regiment.

And he was correct that none here readily vied for her hand. It was difficult, as she could not leave her younger siblings behind. She turned a would-be suitor away when he made a remark about leaving her younger siblings, as they were no longer her responsibility to care for. She had slapped him across the face, hurt that he could be so cavalier to her desires and feelings. It was all of them or nothing. Grace couldn't bear the thought of separating from them. No man was willing to take on so many mouths to feed just to marry her. It was a fault of their station in life that providing for little ones that were not their own was indeed a hardship.

"I understand. I love you for it. Please write to me whenever you get a chance."

Christopher kissed her cheek, "I love you too. You've been taking care of us for so long, please, allow me to do my part while I'm able."

Grace nodded, wiping a tear from her eye. Christopher patted her hand, then went past her toward the dining table where the other siblings were all eating. Grace took a deep breath, composing herself to face her family with a brave smile. *Farewell to what I thought I knew*, she thought. *Dear Lord, please protect and watch over my brother.*

Grace shook out her hands, walking into the dining room with a smile upon her face. She sat across from her brother, soaking up the moments that would be her last for a very long time. This would be a memory that she would have to tuck carefully away and bring out when she missed him unbearably.

Chapter Three

The New Parson

T oday, Matthew had buried his father. He was still feeling numb and finding it hard to believe what he knew to be true: his father was never going to walk into the study to join him, nor take tea with the family in the afternoon. There would be no future advice given to him and no one whom he could confide in as he had his beloved Papa. Things in his world would never work in quite the same manner. They had exchanged weekly letters and those were almost as good as sitting beside his father. They had warmed his heart and given him purpose. *I shall never heal this rift within my heart*, Matthew thought as he rubbed his hand across his chest.

He sought not to begin to regret his time in Sussex. There, he had taken his first post as parson after his seminary studies had concluded. It was a smaller parish than Bramley's but the parishioners had been kind. They had included him within their society and he had never felt neglected, much to his consternation. Matthew liked his solitude, it was the time for reflection and seeking the Lord's will. But he had been called upon and dined almost every night at some cottage or grand manor house. His father would have been suited to it quite well, but Matthew, who always reserved himself, was made happier to observe than to be the acting party.

Now, his life was becoming re-fashioned again and he was powerless to stop its flow. Harrison had implored him to take over his father's role in the town and Matthew, being of the same mind, was most agreeable to the idea. Indeed, he had been waiting for it to be addressed. He did not dislike the town, nor its inhabitants. Matthew felt at home here. But it was that he had prior relationships here and acquaintances. Would they welcome his return? He used to be most stuffy, more inclined to reading and his studies than actually being among the residents. He socialized only when he absolutely must. Despite his father's good sense and advice given that one who is called by the Lord to serve Him and to minister to His people, should in fact, like to be amongst them. There were vices aplenty to be sure, but a man who holds his head too high missed the smallest among the masses, and 'twas the masses that needed a helping hand the most. *Papa was forever encouraging me to pull my nose from the sermons and to live their examples. If only he had seen how I have changed and how I did so in Sussex.*

Matthew peered out the study window without truly seeing what lay before him. He had never thought that a day would arrive when he sat in his father's chair, and not be expecting the man to soon reclaim it. Matthew was in his study now, all of the writing instruments, paper, the desk, the books, everything that was once his father's was now his. He felt relief in knowing that there was no one waiting to displace his mother nor take over the house. *It should always remain within the Morten family. I pray that if I should ever have sons, one would take up the family mantle and carry on our legacy.* Bramley was brewed into their blood even though his own dear father was the first to make his home here.

There was a knock upon the door and Simon peered into the room. "What are you doing, dear brother? You do not look busy."

He came to situate himself into the wingback chair on the other side of the desk.

"Why must one be bodily active to be busy in your opinion?" Matthew asked with a wry smile.

"To be in movement means to be getting things accomplished."

"Is that so? Pray tell, what have you accomplished this afternoon?" Matthew awaited the answer that was sure to amuse him, or make him want to run screaming from the room.

"I have calmed Mama several times and have eaten the last of the cake. I have read The Times twice over, at least the gossip bits, and have entered in here to beg of you to accompany me out for a walk."

"You are aware that it still rains?" Matthew deadpanned.

"Yes, but adventures can be had in weather too. Besides, I have bribed my bride to see to my amusement, but she is convinced that she is catching a cold."

"Poor creature. You could mayhap dote upon her?"

Simon grimaced and said, "To be sure. But even I am growing tired of her complaints. I miss our schedule. I have decided that we shall away on the morrow. I am missing the regiment."

"Then that is where you should be. Papa would not want you to linger here overlong. I can handle our mother well enough, and our dear Mariah is not so far removed that we cannot involve her."

"True. Tell me, when shall you be bringing a bride home of your own?"

"Why does my matrimonial state matter to you?" Matthew inquired as he furrowed his dark brows.

"We should all do our duty and marry. If a man can provide for a family, 'tis in his best interest to take a bride. Besides, just as I told Harrison before he set his cap at Mariah, 'tis such fun to take a bride. You may wink and engage in all manner of intrigues behind closed doors." Simon wiggled his eyebrows and then winked. The man was emasculating both Harrison and himself with the feminine phrase of setting his cap.

"You did not say that to him. I can barely believe that you are saying it to me. Have you no shame? No honor for the sanctity of your marriage?"

Simon tipped his dark head back and brought his large hand to rove from his forehead to his mouth. "You are so boring, brother."

"Better to be that than to burn."

"One marries in order to keep the hellfires at bay. You, and I must say your potential bride, would never, I suppose, act inappropriately. How ever will you beget children if all things carnal are beneath you? I can see you now, all manners and proprietary, 'Now my dear, I apologize in advance for my improper behavior but we must–'"

"Enough Simon," Matthew said as he pinched the bridge of his nose. He was in danger of acquiring a headache.

"You must admit that I do have a point. I shall leave you alone now. There are some things that I have more wisdom in than *you*. You are older than me, yet you lack my experience." Simon rose to stand.

"Your experience as a rogue?"

Smirking, Simon saluted him as he turned and opened the study's door. When he closed it after him, Matthew let out a sigh. He hoped that his brother was being faithful to his wife, but it was not his place to inquire and he had had enough of the man for one afternoon. His heart told him that Simon might be impetuous and at times verging upon vulgarity, but he did love his wife. It was evident in the sparkle that lit within his gray eyes whenever his attention was focused upon her.

Was he too staid and restrained? He did not think he was. Yes, he was proper and since that was the complete opposite of his brother he would always strive to be so. *Mayhap I just need to find the perfect lady to lure my more boisterous side to life? Though, I pray that whoever she may be will be of a more quiet nature and kind-hearted enough to put up with my relations.* He did not envy any lady who had to converse with his family.

After a few more hours it was time for dinner. Mariah and Harrison had retired to the Hall last eve. His sister had been with Mama while they had placed his Papa into the cold muddy ground. After, she had returned home to be with her husband and son. With Simon and Alicia to embark on the morrow, the house would be quiet and he would have to allow more time for Mama. *Mayhap I should hire her a companion*, he thought as he made his way up the staircase and into his former bedchamber. For as long as Mama lived, he would not ask her to part from the room that she had shared with his father. *My own bedchamber is adequate enough*, he thought as he freshened up. They were in mourning, so they need not bother with dressing for dinner, especially since no company was expected.

There was a rap upon the front door and Mr. Trawley was welcoming the person into the entryway as Matthew stepped from the last stair. Dr. Carrow took his topper from his blond head and looked straight at him.

"My apologies. I have need of you, if you can spare the time?" The doctor inquired as he turned over his hat within his hands.

Nodding, Matthew reached for his own outerwear. "Shall we be gone long?" He worked into his greatcoat and placed his top hat upon his brunette head of hair. He was thankful that he did not rely on waxed products to style his hair. This rain would soon see it dripping down into any man's eyes.

"Aye, 'tis a sickness in the village. Many cannot pay for my services and will turn me away. However, they will not do so to a man of God. Through you, I may gain entry into each home and ascertain just how serious this sickness is. I trust that you are in excellent health?"

They had made their way to the buggy where they would both fit, but not comfortably. The brown and white horse whickered at them as if to wonder why they were out in such foul weather. The sky was beginning to darken as the cloud cover was overshadowing all it reached. It would soon be dark with no moonlight in sight. The buggy had a slight overhang, but in the torrential spring storm, it offered no protection. They were both soaked before the horse even began to trot away.

"I am well enough. I do not fear the sick. I am your servant, you but have to direct me and I shall do as instructed." Matthew told him while he gripped the side of the conveyance.

Matthew's first act as the new parson might prove even more foreboding than he had previously feared. *I pray to you dear Father that we do not send any little ones into your loving arms this eve.* He had prayed a few young ones into the heavenly home before and it always tore into his heart.

Chapter Four

Midnight Knocks

G race sighed with relief that her father had yet to return home. After luncheon, he had stayed away. Where he happened to be, she knew not, nor did she care. Her father was getting angrier as of late, more harsh and more cruel toward her younger siblings. She could only pray that the good Lord looked after her father and was able to cure whatever ailed his heart.

She hung her head, sitting by the fire, unable to take to her own bed for slumber. Dishes and laundry had been attended to. Their clothes from sneaking to the burial of the late parson earlier today were dried and the entire town was none the wiser to her sneakiness. She was extremely blessed there. While part of her felt guilty over the naughtiness and wanted to pray for forgiveness, the other part of her felt honored she had been able to witness the event. *I needed to say my own farewells to a man that I highly esteemed.*

Grace had finished tucking her younger siblings into their beds, and assisted her brother, Christopher, in sneaking from the house to make his way to Town and the regiment. She broke down briefly once, watching Christopher disappear into the rainy night. Though she would miss her brother dearly, she understood his desire to be able to do this and get his life started before it was ended—much like hers felt— as if she had no hope for her future happiness.

Being nine and ten years old, caring for her younger siblings didn't afford her many options in the way of suitors. In fact, she was pretty certain that anyone who saw her with Adalie already assumed she was married since her younger sister was petite and appeared younger than she actually was. Thayer and Fraser often helped Papa in the smithy, cleaning stalls or apprenticing, leaving her and Adalie to run the errands and attend to the household tasks.

The front door burst open, revealing her Papa. The glow of the fire cast a mottled hue over his face from the drink he most likely had been consuming the entirety of the evening. He had yet to discover her presence. Grace crept softly from the living room area, down a small hallway that led past the kitchen to the dining room from the backside of the cottage. Creeping her way toward the staircase, she cringed when the floorboard creaked to give her away. *Wretched wood!*

"Grace!" her father's voice boomed, rattling the dishes within the cupboard.

"Yes, Papa?" she answered softly.

"Make my supper."

Internally Grace flinched. The supper they had was leftovers from their midday meal. Grace went to the pot over the fire, hoping there would be enough of a portion left inside to serve her Papa with and then be able to scurry away from him altogether.

"Gracie," Fraser said, coming down the stairs. "I don't feel well."

"Grace!" Papa bellowed. "My supper!"

"Coming, Papa. Fraser isn't feeling well."

Papa groaned. "Nothing sleep cannot cure."

Grace glared through the walls at her father and his inability to show compassion. Ever since their dear mother's passing, life had taken a sharp turn and made everything a little more bleak and dreary. It had taken its worst toll on their father, Christopher, and finally herself. Though she was so busy caring for those younger than her, she never gave herself a pause to grieve. It had been six years since she had wept at the loss of her mother. She felt like crying now at the stress of it all. But she had to be strong, keeping it all inside until she was able to retire and shut her bedchamber door. Mayhap then she could shed some tears. *'Twould be a world of good. If only I could do so without waking poor Adalie.*

"Sit here," Grace instructed softly to Fraser. "I will make you some tea after I serve Papa his supper."

"Gracie," Fraser whined, his face flush and sweat peppering his brow.

Grace gently rubbed his back for a brief moment. Turning around, she withdrew a plain bowl down and filled the contents with the remnants of what they had consumed for supper. She would need to get more foodstuffs tomorrow and be mindful of what she bought with her meager funds. Somehow she was able to stretch her currency but she didn't know for how much longer she would be able to perform such a feat. Mending clothes and odd jobs gave her the added funds she needed but with her father pestering her about what she was up to, she didn't know how to continually curb her father's inquiries.

She softly padded out into the area her father was in. He leaned back in his chair, feet kicked up on a stool, and was snoring worse than an old dog outside in the sun. Grace set his food down on the table beside his chair, knowing he would question her when he woke up about where his meal was, to which she would reply she had brought it to him; he would grumble and go about his day, effectively leaving her and her siblings alone.

There came a knock upon the door, pulling her from her next task of taking care of Fraser. She quickly went to answer before the person rapped again and woke her miserable father.

Dr. Carrow and the new parson, the younger Mr. Morten, stood before her, soaking wet while a tempest blew outside. She invited them in, taking their sodden cloaks from them. She quickly set them before the fireplace to dry, then turned her attention promptly to the gentlemen. The gentlemen had removed their toppers which they had placed down onto a wooden bench.

"My sincerest apologies, Miss Buchanan, for an unannounced visit," Dr. Carrow said softly, taking notice of her father sleeping in the chair.

"Quite all right, Dr. Carrow," Grace replied, clasping her hands in front of her.

"The reason for our visit concerns a sickness passing amongst children and since you have several younger siblings, I came to check on them to see if they have come down with it as well. Have any of them played recently with the Calder or Lowell children?"

She nodded, worry lacing her brow. "Fraser and Ian Lowell are the best of friends. Fraser is just in the kitchen complaining of not feeling well."

"Not to alarm you, but this sickness passing around amongst the children is quite serious. I am hoping to be able to treat the children early to prevent dire consequences."

Grace swallowed, feeling her heart plummet and shatter onto the cold, gray worn wooden floorboards. What would she do if she lost her sibling? How would she handle the loss of any of her siblings? What would her Papa do? *Sink further into drunken despair?*

Grace arranged her face with a soft smile and grateful eyes. "Thank you so much for coming by then. Allow me to take you to Fraser."

She led the way quietly through the house. Her father's snoring echoed in the narrow cottage. Fraser had his head laid atop the table, eyes closed and his face was even more reddened and sweaty. Grace fetched a clean cloth, dipping it in water for the back of Fraser's neck. Dr. Carrow assessed the young boy, stealing worried glances with Mr. Morten. Grace acted as if she had never seen the glances and kept making herself appear busy. *To try to understand their meaning would drive me mad.*

Mr. Morten took a seat at the table, opening his Book of Prayer to read scripture and pray over her brother. She watched his dark brows pinch over chocolate eyes and long lashes. Even in her childhood, viewing Matthew, he was always a reserved being, observing but not often participating; even still, he was always a handsome boy and now grown into a fine man. *His sincerity shines through his entire person.*

Dr. Carrow spoke low to Fraser, asking him questions and wanting to take him into the other room to properly assess him. Fraser stood, wobbling unsteadily to his feet. Grace watched her brother, her heart catching in her throat.

"We shall not tarry," Dr. Carrow assured as he gently held onto the smaller lad.

"Get out of my house!" Her papa stumbled into the room and bellowed.

"There is a sickness going around town, Papa," Grace interjected. "Fraser is ill."

"How dare you!" Papa roared at her. "I ought to spank you something fierce, Grace Lyn! As I've told you, this *sickness* is nothing sleep cannot cure!"

"My sincerest apologies, Mr. Buchanan," Mr. Morten interfered as he rose from the chair. "Miss Buchanan was being superbly accommodating to my wishes to ensure the children of this town were prayed over during this troubling sickness. We will be on our way. I am sorry for disturbing you."

Papa rubbed his face. Bloodshot eyes roved from her to the men standing around the kitchen table. Grace kept her eyes on the floor, though out of her peripheral vision she spied Matthew's hardened eyes directed upon her father and the square of his jaw ticked upward.

"Pray then leave posthaste," Papa growled, moving from the room and down the hall.

Dr. Carrow snapped his bag closed. "Keep Fraser cool, liquids only. Contact me immediately if his condition worsen and blotches appear to color his skin."

Grace nodded, smiling gratefully. "Thank you for your visit with my family, Dr. Carrow and Mr. Morten. 'Tis much appreciated."

"My pleasure, Miss Buchanan. Take care of yourself," Dr. Carrow replied.

Grace walked them to the front door and fetched the men their somewhat dried-out greatcoats "Safe travels. Keep well and God bless." They obtained their top hats and placed them upon their heads.

Mr. Morten glanced back at her as he took his leave, tipping his head to her. Grace smiled wearily and closed the door. For a moment, her breath caught in her throat. All these years apart hadn't curbed her opinion of Matthew Morten being one of the most handsomest men she'd ever seen. But as her life would have it, she would be a spinster before she became blessed enough to marry. She was already nine and ten, unmarried, and with her father the way in which he was, it would be a godsent miracle if she was to have a life beyond this cottage.

Grace went back to where Fraser was left resting at the kitchen table. Struggling, she gathered Fraser into her arms and carried him up the stairs to his room. She removed his trousers and shirt, doing as Dr. Carrow directed- to keep him cool.

She lit a candle by his bed, aiming to stay up all night. If the sickness passing around was as terrible as it was to bring the town doctor and a man of God to her house at midnight, then vigilance and prayer would see her through the night. Grace could only pray it would be enough.

Chapter Five

A Squalid Eve

T he rain was relentless as the doctor and parson made their rounds upon the town. Sickness had indeed come to pay its call upon Bramley and Matthew feared for his parishioners. The children were afflicted at the moment, but it usually followed that the elders were never far behind. He feared for the safety of his mother and his nephew, so he said more prayers. It was just after midnight when he pulled a man, around his own age, from the side of his mother. Matthew inquired whether the man would carry word to the parsonage and to Bramley Hall, instructing all to stay tucked away into their residences to stave off infection. Dr. Carrow approved of his request but cautioned that the man was not to enter another household, to prevent the spread of infection. The man set off on horseback to do as bid.

When Matthew had a moment to catch his breath, he remembered how Miss Buchanan seemed to tiptoe around the wishes of her father, who in his opinion was a blaggard. The man had been drunk and his appearance was lacking, as were his manners. How anyone could mistreat their own offspring was beyond him. It struck him as especially odd as Mr. Buchanan had always seemed to be well put together and pleasant. Not overly friendly, but not rude to the point of vulgarity. He found that he feared for the welfare of all who resided under the man's roof. If he had been physically volatile to his children, Matthew meant to step in and counsel the man, whether he desired the assistance or not. He would not stand by and let those under his parish be abused. Miss Buchanan's kind eyes had shone with hurt and embarrassment by her father's deeds. She was rather a pretty creature and had always been so, however her face was looking drawn. Life had not treated her kindly, it would seem. How she remained unattached was a complete puzzle to him. She was as graceful as his memory could recall. The more he let his thoughts wander to her situation, the more his temper flared. He would put a stop to her father's evil ways, or he was not worthy of his post as the parson of Bramley.

Matthew brought his attention back to the present as he realized that the doctor was addressing him.

"I fear there is nothing more to be done. I believe I can assuredly conclude that Scarlatina is the culprit of this. It has three variants, all worse than its predecessor. We are blessed that so far I have seen no sign of ulcers, but once we do, I fear, the grave will be the next step for those that worsen. 'Tis quite painful and heartbreaking to witness. Pray, Mr. Morten, because there is no treatment that I can offer at present."

Matthew held his head down low. He did not know how to offer comfort and peace to those that would forevermore be separated from their loved ones. His heart was already battered, and the night was set to be long and squalid. He was continually becoming wet through and leaving watermarks wherever he entered.

"Make more practical use of me. Direct me to assist in a more hands-on manner." Matthew requested of the doctor.

"I dislike to suggest it, but clean buckets of water would be an excellent aid. There will be those who will not wish to leave their children's sides to do that task. I wish morning was closer." Dr. Carrow said as he ran a hand through his blond hair. "The darkness always seems to be more aggressive and threatening."

"I agree and accept your chore. I shall attend to it at present. I am already water-logged. What should more raindrops upon my person matter?" Matthew picked up the lantern and proceeded to the well that was located within the center of the town. It was not too far away. The blustery wind was directing the rain to fall in sheets that were slanted. There was no chance of simply setting the buckets out in the weather to fill on their own in a timely manner, as the wind would direct the drops errantly. Upon reaching the first cottage near the well, he took note of the candlelight within and softly knocked on the door.

The man who opened the door to him was burly with un-kempt, graying hair. He was still dressed in his trade clothes and looked weary as he waited to hear what it was that Matthew wanted.

"I am sorry to disturb you. I would like to offer my assistance by drawing fresh water for your household. May I make use of your wooden bucket?" Matthew gave a slight curve of his lips.

"Aye, that 'tis mighty kind of you, Mr. Morten. I shall fetch it." The older man ambled away and returned within a few moments' time carrying the requested item.

"I thank you," said Matthew as he took the bucket's handle and turned around to leave.

"I was sorry to hear about your father," said the man.

Halting his steps and taking a deep breath to quiet the hot lance of pain that tore through his chest, Matthew said, "He shall be missed." He neither turned his head nor his body toward the man, but continued on to the well.

The well had a wooden ceiling covering the well's circle that extended out by a few inches on each side. While the ceiling did not shield him entirely, it did keep the rain from pelting his face and upper body. Matthew swallowed and tried to regain his composure. He was sorrowful and tired of heart, mind, and body, but he was well. He had many things to praise the Lord for. But the loss of his father was a shadow that was following in every footstep he took. Matthew reached for the rope to draw the bucket attached to its other end up from the water within the well. When he could get a firmer hold of the bucket, he poured its contents into the bucket that he had brought with him.

When Matthew returned the now filled bucket to the elderly man, he visited the next cottage and all the ones after it. It took him hours. The work helped to numb his mind, and he was thankful for that. He didn't have to overthink the chore, simply accomplish it. Once he was finished, he sought out the doctor again.

There were other homes set farther about in the country areas and it was arranged with Dr. Carrow that they would set out to visit those once daylight broke. That gave Matthew three hours to return to his own home and bathe himself. Dr. Carrow wanted to return to his own home to change and take what rest he could before they set out again.

"I am hopeful that those living farther away will not be infected. We shall not enter into their homes if no one is ill." Dr. Carrow told Matthew as he climbed into his buggy.

Matthew followed suit, and they made their way silently to the parsonage through the blinding rain and muck. When they reached the gate to the parsonage, Matthew alighted and turned to the doctor. "Thank you for allowing me to assist you."

"I am thankful that you were able to. Your prayers comforted many souls tonight and gave peace. I do not envy you in the days to come, but know that you are not alone. I too feel a great burden upon my heart for this town." Dr. Carrow's gaze bored into him.

Matthew nodded his head and made his way to the parsonage door. He entered the hallway and removed his greatcoat and topper, and hung them on the peg nearest to him. He bent down and removed his boots, holding one in each hand. Running a hand over his hairy chin and letting out a deep sigh, he let his head roll back to rest against the wooden wall. *Have I ever been so bone-weary before?*

"Is that you, Matthew? Or are you a thief who has departed the comfort of your bed to rob us blind in our time of mourning?" Called the voice of Mrs. Morten from the sitting room.

Huffing out an amused breath and then feeling repentant about his reaction to his mother's fright, he strode into the sitting room to greet her. He walked over to the fireplace where the flames were merrily burning and deposited his boot before it. They might not be dried out by the time he would need to make use of them again, but anything would be an improvement.

"I am sorry to cause you to worry, Mama." He said as he came to take the armchair that was situated across from her.

"'Tis a mother's most important occupation. That of worrying and sending up prayers to the Father about keeping her children safe. You have not greeted me properly, no kiss upon my cheek?" Mrs. Morten pouted at him.

"I am remiss. I do not believe though that you would welcome myself just at present. I am in quite a ruined state. Why are you not slumbering in your bed?"

"I cannot sleep. I find it difficult to be by myself. I have had years to become accustomed to the snores of your dear Papa, and now I find that I miss even that most annoying trait of his."

Matthew nodded at her words. *What can I say to console her?*

"You need not wrack your mind for anything to respond to me with. I know we are all feeling his loss deeply. But I find that I keep expecting him to reach over and take my hand, or surprise me with a gentle kiss upon my neck. And now there is none who will ever take over those affections again. 'Tis a very unsettling thing to be a widow. I find that I am now set apart from everyone else. My children, excepting you, have wed and they have no need of me." Mrs. Morten brought her embroidered handkerchief up to her eyes.

"We all have need of you. That will never cease to be so. This is an adjustment for us all. But in the quiet moments when no one is present, I still feel his presence. Memories of his words come to my mind, and I am as contented as I can be. He would not desire us to mourn him in every minute nor in everything we undertake." Matthew gazed into the fire, which was beginning to blur before his eyes. He blinked, but that did not help.

"But then when I do not think of him, the grief surprises me seemingly out of nowhere and I am ready to sink to the floor with great, wracking sobs. It is harder in those moments to remember he would not want me in such a dismal state." Mrs. Morten admitted as she twisted the handkerchief in her grasp.

"I well understand you, Mama. I need to change from my wet clothing and attempt to let myself rest. Dr. Carrow and I are set to visit the surrounding country homes in but a few hours. I shall not be of any use if fatigue keeps me from standing up." Matthew rose from his chair, picked up the lit candle, and held out his hand for his mother to take, being mindful of his wet state. He assisted her in gaining her feet and held onto her hand as he guided her up the staircase and into her bedchamber. She handed him her dressing robe, which he laid across the foot of her bed for her use in the morning. He helped her into bed and blew out the candle.

"Rest well, Mama." He leaned over and kissed her upon her forehead.

"You too, my special boy," said Mrs. Morten.

Matthew walked to the open door and exited it, softly closing it behind him. Finding his own chamber, he entered in and disrobed. The cold water alarmed his nerve endings as he scrubbed his skin clean. He pulled on his nightshirt and climbed into his four-poster bed. Closing his bleary eyes, he processed his day as well as the changes to his life. *I can recall when it was Mama reaching for my hand to tuck me into bed each night. How things have changed. I miss you, Papa. Look after us all from time to time. I pray that we, your family, are making you proud.*

Please, Lord, look after the Buchanan family. Guide me in my steps so that I do not falter where they are concerned.

Chapter Six

Not Nearly As Painful

T he night was long and relentless. It felt as though the sun would never rise in the sky. Even still, the rain was a continuous force against the lead-paned window. Grace kept vigilance over her dear brother Fraser, waiting to see if he happened to worsen throughout the night. By God's Grace, he did not.

Grace peeked out the window. She couldn't make out what time it happened to be, but by her estimation, it was still at some point during the nighttime hours. She settled back into her chair, glancing at the door to ensure her father wasn't lurking nearby. What he had done earlier still rankled her. More than anything it embarrassed her in front of the parson. *Why must he endeavor to be so cruel? And what must Matthew Morten think of it all? Of us?*

Handsome Matthew Morten had always caught her eye as a younger girl, but now as a grown woman, she found him even more attractive and she struggled to hide the blush that nearly crept to her cheeks. He had grown into his cleft chin and strong jawline peppered with a smattering of brown stubble. She closed her eyes, picturing his face and how the faint light from the fire enhanced his masculinity and she swore she would have swooned at that moment. Alas, a man like him would not have a woman like her. She resigned herself to becoming an old maid, caring for her siblings until perhaps a widower took pity on her in that advanced age and married her solely for companionship. With her horrid father also eliminating her chances at marriage, her life would remain forever complicated. *I do so long for a home of my own.*

Grace leaned forward in her chair and sighed deeply, hanging her head only for her hands to catch her and the tears she silently wept. The feeling of being overwhelmed consumed her, as well as an ache in her breast from the possibility of never finding a suitor. She couldn't leave her siblings behind. And her father would make any suitor cringe at the prospect of being saddled with her. Heavens, even the parson and doctor were astonished at her father's ill manners and temper. *Everything my Papa does these days is shocking and fills me with vexation.*

Grace took another peek over her left shoulder at the door. Adalie brushed the hair from her face and drug the small blanket Grace had made her across the floor. Grace rose from her seat, meeting Adalie at the door.

"Dearest, Fraser is very ill so I need you to not come in here," Grace said softly.

"But you're in here," Adalie grumbled.

Grace smoothed her mussed head and placed a gentle kiss atop it. "I'm taking care of him."

"The rain woke me up. Why must it be so loud?"

Grace smiled, directing her sister from the sickroom and down the staircase. Grace wiped her weary eyes. Then she made her way to the kitchen to ensure the fire was still crackling. She attempted to keep it going throughout the night since the chill this year was quite penetrating. She went to the back door, ready to get some wood that was stacked on the back porch only to find her buckets for water had been filled. Grace smiled, figuring the kind parson or doctor were the ones to do the chore. Everyone else would have been much too busy caring for their ill ones.

She sighed gratefully, reflecting on the kindness they bestowed to her by checking on her dear brother and bringing them fresh water. Both of them were young, unattached gentlemen and both very well out of her range of marriage. Grace glowered, melancholy taking over her once grateful heart. *These thoughts do nothing good for you.*

She brought the bucket inside first, then ladened her arms with the wood. Grace turned around after shutting the door and yelped.

"Adalie!" Grace breathed raggedly. "Announce yourself. You gave me a fright."

"There's a man at the door."

Grace scowled, never having heard it knock. "What kind of man?"

Adalie shrugged, arms out at her sides as her dark brown hair swished to the side. "A constable mayhap... I don't rightly know. But he told me to get you specifically."

Grace dropped her load, heading to the front door. "Head to your room directly," she ordered, not knowing what might be there for her and not wanting her sister to witness anything untoward.

The front door was wide open, permitting all the cold air into the once richly warm house. The man was indeed a constable, dressed in all black. His large brimmed hat was in his hand. Grace met him at the door, guarding the safety of the children inside.

"I'm Miss Buchanan," Grace greeted. "What can I do for you?"

"Is there not a male residing within this household?" the man asked, fidgeting from foot to foot.

Grace narrowed her eyes. "I am the sole adult here if that is what you are inclining toward. I have younger siblings that are not suitable to hear whatever words you might speak."

"Miss," the man acknowledged, dipping his head politely. "Are you by chance related to Hagan Buchanan?"

Grace nodded. "Aye. He's my father." She felt terror at the uncertainty that was pulsing through her veins.

The man bowed his head, twirling his hat within his large hands. "Miss," he paused, finally meeting her gaze. "I regretfully inform you that your father has gone to be with the Lord."

Grace opened her mouth to say something and then snapped it shut. The man probably wouldn't tell her in what manner her father had perished from this world. For some unfathomable reason, men in this society deemed women fragile. If only men truly knew what women were capable of, and could endure. Like her.

He probably died from drinking himself three sheets to the wind, she surmised. *And this weather would not have helped his cause any either.* Grace sighed, staring at the floor. *Well... this is a lovely mess. How am I to tell my siblings and Christopher?*

She was numb. Part of her desired to spill tears for her deceased father. The other part cared not one wit. He was a cruel man since the death of her mother years ago. In her mind, he wasn't worth the effort of sorrow. Somehow losing her father wasn't as painful as she had imagined. Her heart wasn't plagued and that oddity disturbed her to a point. *How odd... 'Tis true that he was most unkind, but he was still my father. Am I in shock?*

She blinked rapidly. "What must be done?"

"We have your father at the church where he will be buried when the rain relents. You need not concern yourself with the cost."

Grace nodded, feeling relieved with that aspect. What minimal money they had would more than likely go towards food. And whatever money her father had upon his person at the time of his passing probably went to the cost of his burial or somehow vanished from his pockets. Bramley was not a town ripe with criminals, but the small crimes were committed now and then. She suspected that many a lad would not bat an eye at taking the coin from a dead man's pockets.

"May I see my father?" she finally inquired, though not for the sentimental reasons that most desired to say their farewells.

The man hissed, sucking in a breath as if uncertain of what to disclose to her. Since there was no male to collect anything from her father, surely she would be permitted? And if not, would she dare have the courage to approach Mr. Morten regarding the matter after being thoroughly embarrassed the night prior? She swallowed, assuring herself that she had to do something to get whatever little her father had upon his person to feed her siblings, if any remained. He had no fancy cravat, pins, or buttons. Grace was certain he had sold anything of value and spent it on his excessive drinking. He did have one signet ring with the family crest that supposedly came with him from Scotland, yet she put no stock in whatever he said. His words had been mostly farcical as far as she could discern.

"Sir?" Grace prompted.

"Miss Buchanan, I shall have Mr. Morten retrieve anything upon your father's person and deliver it to you. I do not wish to cause you undue distress."

Grace raised her brows, ready to offer him a distressing opinion yet kept her mouth shut. "Thank you for your time in coming here to relay the news," she promptly said and shut the door.

Already the house had significantly chilled from the door being wide open while she conversed with the constable. By her estimate, she had several days before the landlord came knocking requesting her to either vacate or pay the due rent. Then, she would be forced to relocate. She hadn't the coin to pay the man. Her job darning clothes only took her so far. *What are we to do? I cannot allow anything to separate me from my siblings!*

"Blast it all!" she cursed under her breath.

Three children and herself would soon find themselves homeless. She had to figure out something. Her heart convulsed at the thought of writing to her brother. He left two days ago for the regiment. Knowing Christopher, he would either beg to come home to help her or take it upon himself and return, not caring about the consequences of his actions. She refused to allow any harm to befall him. Mayhap she could write to him next week and speak of her father's passing.

I must do what I have to, to secure a better life for Christopher, she decided. *He is making a sacrifice for us. I must do the same and beget the consequences of an angry brother later.* She closed her eyes and let out a deep breath. *But what to do now?*

Grace brought her hands up to the side of her head and gently tugged upon her dark hair, which was still pinned up, as if to ignite a thought into her head. There was nothing that came forth to her overwrought mind. What mattered to her most was keeping the house warm, figuring out breakfast, and how best to get Fraser well. After that, could she then allow herself to tackle her father's death. His leaving them all destitute and near homeless angered her fiercely. She would figure something out. She always had for everyone. She took a moment to gather her resolve.

Grace strode into the kitchen and got the fire going. This was just a bump in the rocky road of her life. The Lord gave her strength to rise above it before when her mother had passed, so she would rely on that strength again to see her through this. There was naught much else above that. She had three children relying on her. Come the devil or death, she would see this through.

Chapter Seven

Light Beckons Through

T he rain had finally let up, becoming a faint odd drizzle as the sky lighted with blues and purples that welcomed the sun to shine down on the town of Bramley. Matthew gazed from his bedchamber window to view the lane that was muddied. The lawn was flooded in places. He yawned as he stretched his sore body. Having not had nearly enough sleep, 'twas time to be about, doing what he could for his parishioners. He quickly dressed in his black trousers and a white shirt and cravat. His waistcoat and tailcoat were both of a basic black, as was the armband he wore in remembrance of his father's passing. He donned his slippers and made his way down the staircase to the sitting room. Leaning over the fireplace, he inspected his boots. They were not dried and wearing them today would be a miserable feat, but what was he to do? He would consider himself very blessed if that was his largest complaint to come this evening. *One thing is certain, I shall purchase another pair and soon.*

Mama was still abed, but their cook, Mrs. Kurley, and manservant, Mr. Trawley, were beginning the household chores quietly. He could hear the faint sounds of movement coming from the kitchen area. Matthew picked up his boots and turned to sit down in one of the armchairs. Wiggling into his boots took some effort, but he was successful. He tried to ignore the uncomfortable squish between his toes.

Standing up and exiting the room, he strode to the kitchen and peered in.

"I have never been so glad as to see the sunrise. I thought for sure this was my last night upon the earth, what with all the dreadful racket the storm blew in. Was a right tantrum it was," said Mr. Trawley as he closed the iron door to the stove. Straightening he spied Matthew. "There is a dead fellow in the church, he was dropped off by the constable not too long ago."

"Oh?" Matthew stepped into the kitchen.

"Don't know his name, but it was written down and placed in the man's pocket. He was bruised, but I reckon that he would be easily identifiable nonetheless. He reeked of the drink and sick as the constable carried him into the church. I locked the door, which your Papa instructed never to do. But I don't think anyone wants to walk in on that." Mr. Trawley's kind hazel eyes met his. He ran a thick hand through his dark hair.

"Thank you for your aid and forethought. I would not wish anyone to seek peace and encounter such a macabre scene." Matthew inclined his head to the man and then turned toward the cook. "I am about to depart with the doctor this morning for rounds in the countryside. I wonder, Mrs. Kurley, would you mind preparing a basket of foodstuffs for us? Whatever you have readied?"

"Of course, my lad!" Mrs. Kurley's kind cinnamon-colored eyes locked onto him. Matthew chuckled at her address to him. *I suppose I shall always be a lad to her, so long has she worked for our family.*

Matthew watched as Mrs. Kurley bustled about the kitchen filling the basket with things taken from the larder and shelves.

Mr. Trawley nodded at him as he walked to the back door. When he closed it behind him, the cook softly spoke to him.

"'Tis not been easy on that man, losing your father. They were thick as thieves somedays, always hiding away in the study." Turning around to face him, Mrs. Kurley handed him the basket.

"I did not think about their odd friendship," he mused. "Sadly, I am no replacement for my Papa."

Cupping his cheek, she said, "No one expects you to be! Just be the same unspoiled, humble being you have always been. No one could ever find fault in that."

"Tell that to Simon."

"*Psh!* Two different brothers I have never known. But you each have wonderful traits and strengths."

Matthew warmly smiled at her. "Simon and his bride are to away today. I shall endeavor to return before they depart to see them off."

"Very good. I shall inform the imp as soon as I see him. He has always scampered into my domain to steal sweets and take the best bits for himself. Sometimes I have even allowed him to," she said. The smile that lit up her wrinkled face quickly erased the years.

"I have no doubt. I shall return soon," said Matthew as he turned to walk away.

His steps took him into his study, which he entered, closing the door behind him. He stood with the basket hanging from his arm as he let his gaze linger over the desk. He imagined his father sitting behind it and when the light coming from the window lit up the room, from the direction within the specks of falling dust, he thought he heard a voice say, "*Well done, my son.*"

Matthew's eyes scanned the room, but it was empty. He hung his head and closed his eyes. Would this pain never cease? He was clearly overtired. The sound of a horse and buggy slowly coming down the lane claimed his attention. He straightened up, turning to open the study's door. He closed it softly behind him and walked the short distance to the front door. Mr. Trawley was just reaching for Matthew's greatcoat and topper when he reached him. He set the basket down beside where he stood. Taking his outerwear he donned them and let the man open the door for him. They nodded to each other, then Matthew made his way to the buggy.

"Thank the Lord the rain relented!" Dr. Carrow greeted him with a smile.

Climbing into the buggy and seating himself, Matthew agreed. They set off at a brisk pace. The countryside was drenched, leaves littered the ground and no animals had bothered to venture forth yet that Matthew could view.

Matthew reached into the basket and withdrew a pastry which he handed to the physician. Dr. Carrow adjusted his hold of the reins and took the confection.

"What a treat this is. I ate some stale crackers and questionable cheese before heading out." Dr. Carrow told him.

"I did not even have that much. I am famished." Matthew reached into the basket and pulled from it his own pastry. When he bit into it, blueberry filling met his tongue and he moaned.

"'Tis manna from heaven. Tell me, are you ready to begin another day of uncertainty and illness?" inquired Dr. Carrow.

"I am as prepared as I can be."

The doctor nodded his head at him. They remained silent as they consumed their breakfast. There were a few pieces of sausages, which would make a mess of their gloves, so the gentlemen removed them to feast.

When they were finished, they had just reached the first house that they wished to call upon. A stablehand met them in the yard to see to the conveyance. Climbing down from the buggy, Matthew straightened his greatcoat. He waited for the doctor to grab his black bag and the two proceeded to the front door.

"Oh, my manservant informed me that there is a male who has perished in the church. Do you happen to have any knowledge as to who he was?" asked Matthew.

"I do not. We can discover who it may be once we are returned," said Dr. Carrow.

"The constable left a note in the man's pocket with his identity. I was merely curious as to whether you knew who it might be."

A butler answered the tap that Dr. Carrow gave the door and ushered the pair into the manor home. It was determined that no illness had yet taken root within the residence, so their visit was shortly concluded. They made several stops within the course of the next three hours and it was only the houses that had recently been into the town that had fallen sick to the Scarlatina. Within the poorer community the illness was making itself right at home, much to the doctor's consternation.

When all was done that could be accomplished, they made their last stop at a farmhouse that belonged to an older couple who had two grandchildren visiting them. Both the little girl and boy were enveloped in the fever and the glassy eyes of the grandfather caused alarm as well. No one was well and the animals were neglected. The chickens had been scratching in the mud and the cows could be heard mooing in the stable. When the older lady had greeted them at the door, Matthew knew instantly that nothing was as it should be inside. They greeted the older woman and saw to the loved ones' welfare. Dr. Carrow's face was drawn as he whispered to the little boy who laid so still upon his bed.

After praying over each of the children and their grandfather, Matthew left them in the care of the doctor. There was naught else he could do to gain their comfort. He made his way out of doors and to the pen that housed the errant chickens. When he went inside, they scattered from him even when he scattered feed for them, being mindful of the muddied spots. He promptly locked the wooden door behind him. Hearing the hungry and irate cows, he knew not what to do. He had never milked a cow before and worried that he would get kicked for his efforts. He hoped to find some assistance in town once he was able to return. Locating the buckets for the well, he went about filling troughs with water, at least he could do that and that eased his conscience. At the back of the barn was a dry pile of hay. Matthew gathered several armfuls, dropping them in the pen with the cattle. The satisfied animals munched contentedly. What was a little muck and sweat to a servant of the Lord? He would much rather be seen disheveled than to appear pristine when all were in the midst of such a trial.

Dr. Carrow approached him a few minutes later. His face looked haggard and he ran a hand down it. "The boy will not live to see another sunrise and I fear that the older gentleman will not be far behind." He kicked at a blade of grass.

"I am sorry. There is truly nothing to be done?" It was a stupid question, he knew the answer already.

Shaking his head and swallowing, Dr. Carrow said, "This is madness. I cannot help any of them. Just what is the point of medicine if it cannot cure this? I fear that tonight will bring many deaths upon us. Prepare yourself, as best you can." Then he walked over to the buggy and untied the reins.

Matthew ascended to his seat and stayed silent. He did not know how to help or prepare his people other than with prayers. *How many will turn away from the Lord once this was finished? It was his experience that anger and judgment often followed grief.*

Dr. Carrow climbed up to his seat and directed the horse to the parsonage. It was a quiet ride as each dealt with their thoughts and feelings alone.

Before long, they reached the church and Matthew used his own key to open the door. The smell of death, drink, and mayhap stomach bile met his senses. He nearly became sick himself as he stepped to the side to allow the doctor to precede him into the sanctuary. Withdrawing his handkerchief from his coat pocket, he covered his mouth and nose. Then he trekked within and stopped before the body that was laid in the aisle between the pews.

Dr. Carrow was hunched over the male and had already withdrawn the folded sheet of paper from the man's pocket that bore his name. But neither needed to read what was written as there was no mistaking that it was Mr. Buchanan who was before them. Matthew closed his eyes and tilted his head up to the ceiling. *Poor Miss Buchanan. And those poor children, now left unprotected. I shall not stand by and allow them to come to harm. There will be a way to set things to rights for them, or as right as could be accomplished. He was a horrid man. I don't even know if he will be mourned. Just the same, I am grieved for the passing of another life and for his family.*

"'Tis too muddied to bury him," Dr. Carrow said, muffled through his own handkerchief.

Matthew nodded. "I do not disagree," he said, looking at the dead man and making a mental note of anything upon his person that Grace might need. "Hopefully in two days' time, it will be dry enough to bury the body."

Dr. Carrow turned toward the door. "Please advise your men to wear a cloth covering over their nose and mouth when burying bodies. This sickness is contagious, despite this man dying of excessive inebriation. I do not wish for more to fall to this terrible pandemic."

"I will tell them to utilize that and exert caution."

Matthew noticed the signet ring upon Mr. Buchanan's hand, removing it from his person to give to his daughter. He recalled her having a slightly younger brother, but that was years ago and the boy he remembered may have died or joined the regiment, as so many men of his station had done. Either way, she was not to be permitted here to retrieve what was once her father's. He did not wish her to become ill since her young brother, Fraser, was already not faring well. He checked the man's pockets, gathering whatever was in them to entrust to Miss Buchanan.

"Do we have a moment for one stop?" Matthew asked.

Dr. Carrow nodded. "Indeed. I am hoping the young Buchanan lad is feeling well, or at least, not closer to death's door."

Matthew strode out from the church, locking the door behind them. Together they remounted the buggy, taking off up the lane for their final stop of the morning. Matthew could only pray that Miss Buchanan and her siblings were faring well and would weather this new course of their lives with God's grace.

Chapter Eight

Hope Is Lit

G race sat at the kitchen table with her head in her hands. Thayer was out collecting more fresh water, taking Adalie with him. She had told the children she needed it so she could boil the water and wash linen; to help keep the sickness contained and from further spreading. While they were gone, she had already been through her father's room, and his belongings, in search of money to at least pay the house rent for another month, and purchase much-needed items from the shops in town. She found enough money to last them a while with food but not enough to pay the rent. *Heaven help us.*

She wiped the tears that silently fell from her cheeks bitterly. The stress of this entire situation was taking its toll upon her heart. She worried over her siblings since she was all they had in this world to rely on.

Grace leaned back in her chair and sighed heavily. " All right Gracie... you must think," she whispered to herself.

She let out a long breath, shaking her hands out from the nerves and the stress of the entire new reality before her. *First things first, Fraser needs to get well. I need to do as Dr. Carrow suggested, heed his advice and get my brother better. Afterwards, I need to secure a position of employment somewhere and move out of this place since I cannot afford it. Mayhap I should speak with Mr. Morten regarding the matter, and seek counsel from a man of the cloth.*

Her siblings entered through the back door, arguing about who in the heavens knew what. Water spilled in the hall and echoed throughout the quiet home. Thayer angrily chastised his little sister. Grace rose from the table to settle the disagreement, yet knocking pulled her to the door.

Sighing deeply, she moved to answer the knock on the front door. The bright sun shone through the curtained windows, giving a faint glare off the shine of the floor as dust specks floated like fairy dust through the home. Grace wiped her hands off on the worn apron covering her coffee-colored dress before answering the door.

"Mr. Morten," she said, surprised, stepping to the side. "Please come in." She allowed the door to open wider.

The man removed his topper. His boots made a squelching sound as he stepped in. He appeared to her as if frozen to the bone. Bags were under his eyes, yet he offered her a warm smile and a comforting presence.

"Miss Buchanan, pardon my unannounced visit," Matthew began.

Grace smiled softly, directing him further into her home and to take a seat by the fireside. "May I get you some refreshment? Mayhap some tea or a bite to eat?"

"No thank you, though, I appreciate your offer. I came by to drop off items found upon your father's person. I am deeply grieved for your loss," he offered, setting the items on the table to the left of his chair.

"Thank you. I shall pass these on to Christopher when he visits next. He joined the regiment," she said candidly.

The last time she had seen Matthew as a youth was right before he left home to go to the seminary school at a young age. Matthew had always been adept in schooling, or so she had gathered from the town gossips. The late Earl of Bramley had recommended him to a college and had funded his study. She didn't doubt Matthew's intellect for a moment. Even as children, he was a brilliant boy. She hadn't attended school past learning the basics. In any sense, he probably did not remember much of her younger brother Christopher. They did not play together but she thought she recalled that he had often spent time with Simon.

Matthew nodded, sitting forward in his chair out of courtesy. "Of course, how is he doing?"

"Well, I suppose," she shrugged. "Christopher left the night prior to Fraser becoming ill."

"And how is Fraser's condition?"

"Stable. He is sleeping upstairs. No change at all. You're welcome to go see him should you like."

Matthew rose from his seat, "I would indeed. Even if 'tis just to pray over the lad. I assured Dr. Carrow that I would report the lad's health back to him."

Grace nodded, rising from her seat as well. She took him to the bottom of the staircase and instructed him that Fraser's was the first room at the top of the stairs with the closed door. She watched Matthew ascend the stairs with careful footsteps in an attempt to be quiet. She smiled, appreciating his care for the household.

Grace went back to the room where, moments before, Matthew had set down the previous belongings of her father. She sighed despondently. Even though the man was crass, cruel, often bordering on belligerent, he was still her father. She missed who he used to be, not who he became. She fiddled with his signet ring in her fingers, wondering when Christopher would be back so she may give it to him. Other than that, there were a few coins to see her and her siblings through a few days of food but naught else.

She sat in a chair, wondering what would become of the smithy her father had, if she would be able to sell it or if one of her brothers would take up the practice. Grace knew a touch about smithing, but it was frowned upon by society to have a woman practicing a trade. Already she was in a precarious situation in thanks to her father's excessive drinking. Most of the town knew of her, and her family, and not in a decent way. The sole reason they had any income was based purely upon her father's skills as a blacksmith and the fact no one desired to travel to town and pay their inflated prices.

Mayhap an opportunity will arise for us, she thought, tucking the coins inside the pocket sewn into her dress. She glanced over her shoulder to the hallway, picturing in her mind beyond it to the stairs, and the parson up in her brother's room praying. Footsteps coming down creaked the old wooden floorboards.

She rose from where she sat, striding to meet Matthew. His face was carefully set in an instant from the hard, worn lines she saw to what it was now, open and thoughtful.

"He seems to be holding a stable condition compared to those in other households," he commented softly. "Are there any other children in this house besides Fraser? It was so dreary that night I'm afraid my brain is a touch foggy."

Grace smiled sympathetically. "Yes. My youngest sister, Adalie, who is six, and Fraser's twin brother Thayer. Both lads are eight. I've been keeping them in separate rooms and am about to wash linen. I hope this sickness doesn't linger in Bramley nor in many households. I do not wish for any to suffer or succumb to death."

"Agreed. I am hoping it passes quickly and without the perishing of many more."

"I shall pray. I believe it is all we can do."

Matthew's brown eyes brightened slightly. A slight twitch pulled at his upper lip. "Indeed, 'tis all we can do. The strength of God alone will suffice us."

Grace walked him to the door, bidding him farewell and appreciation at his visiting her. Despite the circumstances, she was pleased to have him here with her even if it was just for a visit to inquire about the health of the household. There was something about him and his presence she found warm and calming. *He has a steadying presence.*

"Thank you for your concern and for calling upon us. I appreciate your thoughtfulness," Grace said, a hand on the knob.

"The pleasure is mine. What kind of parson, or man of the cloth, would I be if I was not of service to my flock?"

Grace smiled thoughtfully, "You are very much like your father and a great benefit to this community."

Though her comment was direct and the sting of mourning for the late parson Morten was still heavy within this community, she desired that Matthew should know he was as great a man as his father. Much like his father, Matthew was kind and attentive, making himself readily available to all. Her heart grieved greatly for the late parson more than her own father. *How very odd that is, but true nonetheless.*

Matthew dipped his head to her and strode out from the home into the bright sunlight. He moved into the streets deftly, going to a nearby horse and buggy.

Quietly, Grace closed the door behind him, heading back into the kitchen to get the washing items for linen. She grabbed the washboard, heading to the back door to do the task outside for some much-needed fresh air. Before she could even exit, Adalie and Thayer came bursting into the home carrying a chicken apiece in their arms.

"Gracie!" Adalie exclaimed, her broad smile splitting her face, displaying some missing teeth. "Mr. Morten brought us chickens! He said there are too many at their home and he needed us to care for them."

Grace put a hand to her chest and swallowed her emotions. How often had the late parson brought them a chicken when times were rough? And now his son was taking over the action as well? *We are blessed, indeed.*

"We shall butcher one tonight for supper and cook the bones for broth for Fraser."

Thayer frowned, holding onto his hen with a smile. "Don't *butcher* Kelly."

"Well don't *butcher* Oscar!" Adalie cried.

Thayer scoffed. "It is a girl chicken, not a boy chicken."

"Her name is Oscar and you cannot kill her!"

Thayer rolled his eyes. "*Fine,*" he sighed dramatically. "You can kill Kelly."

"NO!" Adalie cried. "They're sisters. You cannot kill sisters!"

Grace set down the washing and put a hand to her head. She reached into her pocket, withdrawing money enough to purchase a chicken from the neighbor to the north. "Head to Old Penny's house and ask to buy a chicken," she said, handing the coin to Thayer. "If there is extra, come straight home and we'll head to the shops soon thereafter."

"Aye, Gracie," Thayer said, directing Adalie out the back door with him. "Where should we put Kelly and Oscar?"

"In the woodshed for now I suppose," Gracie replied.

Adalie blew her lips. "Why not in my bed? Oscar likes warm things."

"There shall never be a chicken in your bed," she replied with a firm motherly tone.

Adalie sighed dramatically, following her brother outside. Once the door slammed shut, Grace put a hand to her head and shook it. Of all the things Adalie desired! She figured at least the child would not want a chicken in her bed. *The idea was ghastly and yet humorous as well. Filthy chickens have no place indoors.*

Grace chuckled softly to herself, heading out of doors. The bright sun struck her face, giving her some warmth. She sighed contently, turning to the left where a small bench awaited for putting the washing upon, which was free of any clutter at the moment.

Things are looking up already, she thought, getting the wash bucket ready. *Thank you, Lord, for sending us Mr. Morten.* She glanced over her shoulder at the long alleyway that led into the street. Matthew was still there, conversing with a worried older gentleman. Grace felt her lip turn upward. *Hope is lit in me thanks to him. I wish there was a way I could repay him. And Lord, if he is unattached, I swear I would do all in my power to make him a happy wife if that would be your will.*

Chapter Nine

Fare Thee Wells At Last

Matthew reached the bottom stair in the parsonage and listened to his younger brother, Simon, boast about some nonsensical thing or another. He was too tired to follow along with the prattle. Upon arriving home, he had taken to his bedchamber to change his attire and tame his hair, which was curling in odd directions given the excessive moisture within the air.

"Mark my words, our babe shall be the merriest of all of your grandchildren," Simon remarked merrily.

Matthew made his way into the parlor and sat down beside his mama upon the settee. He rubbed his hand over his chin and then inquired, "Are there to be more grandchildren?"

Turning to face him from his place before the mantle, Simon gave him a beaming smile. "Indeed! My own child is soon to make its way into our world."

"Congratulations," Matthew said as he tried to order his thoughts regarding this event. Was it a blessing? The idea of a little Simon or even an Alicia running amuck was enough to make him desire to hide away. *Dear Lord, in your wisdom, if you could see fit to gift this little one with less wit and more sincerity of heart, I should gladly praise you.* Inwardly he flinched and then amended, *Though, I shall praise you in all seasons and all trials.*

Mrs. Morten reached her hand over to grasp Matthew's hand and drew his attention to her. "'Tis excellent news. I only wish that your own dear Papa would have lived to hear this!"

Matthew refrained from either frowning or rolling his eyes as the thought, *'Tis a blessing he remained ignorant of this news. 'Twould have carried him off sooner.* Then he did frown. *I am being most unkind. Must be from the want of sleep.*

"Most exciting news I have had recently," Matthew drawled. "What with the deaths and the Scarlatina outbreak. Say, 'tis a very good thing that you are set to depart today."

"I could not agree more! We must ensure that both mother and child remain untouched by this." Simon nodded his dark head.

"I was ever so worried that I would never bear a child for poor Simon. After all, we have been wed the longest and yet are the last to welcome our first into the family. I do hope 'tis a girl. But a little boy with Simon's curls and wit would make me exceedingly happy. You are the first to know and once we return to Town, my parents shall rejoice. I cannot wait to share this with them!" Alicia was nearly bouncing in her seat.

"A babe is always such wonderful news! I cannot wait to cuddle your little one. We are very blessed," Mrs. Morten said as she began to cry. Matthew withdrew his handkerchief from his pocket and handed it to his mother. She took it with a teary smile that wobbled.

"We need to depart if we are to reach Town at the fashionable hour for dinner," Simon told them. "My dear, shall we take our leave?" He walked over to his wife and held out his hand to assist her to her feet.

Matthew rose as well and aided Mrs. Morten with gaining her own footing. He tucked his mother's hand into the crook of his arm and they followed the couple to the entryway. Mr. Trawley stood silently at attention and held out Alicia's bonnet to the young woman. Alicia took it with a smile and walked the few steps over to the mirror that hung next to the door. Once she was in order, Simon assisted her with her cloak and then donned his own. The couple linked arms again and walked out of doors to the awaiting Purcellville carriage. Simon turned them around to wait for Matthew and Mrs. Morten to meet them. Matthew ensured that his mother was secured in her shawl and then escorted her to the couple. He didn't stop to don any outerwear for himself, too exhausted to care.

"La, but I am beyond excited to return home! I shall miss you though, darling Mama," Alicia addressed Mrs. Morten.

"I shall count the days until you return to me. With being a lowly widow, I know that my society shall not be paramount in your mind, but mayhap you can design to visit again before too long has passed. I, myself, could never travel so far."

"We shall return, have no fear, Mama. Mayhap not until the little one has been born, but return we shall." Simon leaned forward and placed a kiss upon his mother's forehead.

The two women hugged and then it was Matthew's turn to bid them farewell. He reached for Simon's hand and they shook.

Simon leaned in to whisper into his ear, "I am exceedingly relieved that at long last I have sired a child. I feel as if I have scaled a mountain and reached the other side victoriously. Took me long enough."

Matthew only nodded. He wasn't sure how to address the confession. Then he smiled at his sister-in-law and brought her hand up to place a kiss upon the air above her gloved knuckles.

"My, you are one charming man! Simon should consider himself blessed that I first laid eyes upon him." Alicia said as she winked at him and then turned herself. She climbed the steps leading into the carriage.

Simon gave a great guffaw at his wife's words and followed her into the carriage, seating himself next to her, and removing her hand from her lap, he brought it up to his mouth. The carriage door was closed by the attendant and once he had found his footing, the carriage departed.

"They are well-matched, are they not?" Mrs. Morten turned worried eyes toward her son.

Matthew took her hand and guided her back into the parsonage saying, "'Twould seem so." The wink had made him uncomfortable.

There was barking coming from behind the parsonage and Mrs. Morten stopped in the middle of the entryway. "Poor Solomon, he's been tied up for ages. No walks by the pond nor visits from your father," she reached for Matthew's hand. "What if the poor beast believes that he isn't wanted anymore? How shall he understand that your Papa has been removed from this world?"

Squeezing her hand, he spoke gentle words, "I think in time he will come to understand. I have been remiss of his care. Mr. Trawley does not much care for him. I will see that he has ample exercise and endeavor to spend time with him, please trouble yourself no further with thoughts regarding him."

Mrs. Morten smiled at him and then patted his cheek. "You are such a good man. I count you among my greatest blessings. What, though, are we to do with such a quiet household?"

Matthew guided his Mama into the parlor and helped her to sit before the fire in the wingback chair. He took to the chair opposite her, which his papa had always claimed. "Would you welcome the addition of a companion into the household? She need not reside here with us if that is your preference, but mayhap, you will find the company soothing."

"'Tis not a horrible idea. Do you have a lady in mind? Better to employ a lady of the town than seek out one bred in London. We country-bred are most comfortable around those of the same ilk. And a lady with airs would only vex my poor nerves," Mrs. Morten said with conviction.

"To be sure, we would find one that suits you. I do have one in mind, but her circumstances are such that she may not be able to part from her younger siblings." He refrained from mentioning her hazel eyes which were stunning and kept resurfacing within his mind at the most inappropriate of times.

"I would not mind the addition of little ones, as long as it was understood that when I was unwell, they must maintain a quiet disposition. They must be made to see reason that my nerves are not always kind to me."

"Absolutely understood. I shall pay a call upon the young lady and see if I can persuade her to come under our employ.

Perchance her younger siblings could assist with the care of the chickens and even with Solomon. Sickness has invaded her cottage, so it needs to be ousted before we can mix our households. I will not invite danger unto our doorstep." Matthew reclined in his seat and brought one ankle to rest over his knee.

He leaned his head back and enjoyed the silence that embraced him. *I shall call upon Miss Buchanan on the morrow and inquire as to whether she would welcome the position. I do hope that she agrees, 'twould save me time in attempting to fill the post. And it has nothing whatsoever to do with her lovely eyes, nor her soft voice. Now is not the time to consider such things when we are both in the midst of mourning. I shall banish all such thoughts from my mind.*

Chapter Ten

An Enticing Offer

The morning dawned bright and cheerful with nary a cloud in the sky. Grace woke well before the household, ensuring that the house was warm and breakfast would soon be underway. She yawned, pressing the back of her hand to her mouth to stifle the action and the unladylike noise that accompanied it. Exhaustion was an understatement for her. She had been kept awake, keeping vigilant watch over her brother who was abed all day yesterday. She had slept little the day before, endeavoring to get the house as clean as she possibly could.

Sunlight streamed through the crack in the dark curtain in her brother's room. She patted Fraser softly upon the arm, ascending from her chair by his bedside. The rise of dawn brought her some hope that Fraser did not suffer too terribly from whatever the sickness was passing around. The rash Dr. Carrow had mentioned did not attack Fraser's small body. Praise be to the Lord for that small reprieve.

She crossed her arms over herself as she descended the staircase from checking on Fraser for a third time that morning. The home was warm. The scent of breakfast wafted under her nose and she checked the pot and stirred the porridge. Today, she would add some sugar to the meal. It felt like a special new day with the way the sun rose in the sky and with last night's wonderful gift of chickens.

Grace inhaled deeply, smiling softly to herself. Today, she would head out after luncheon and search for employment. As far as she knew, hearing a tidbit of news from Thayer, that Mrs. Marshall was searching for someone to do laundry for her inn. It would be a good job, close to home and the school.

The stomping of small feet pulled her from her thoughts of employment. She poked her head out of the kitchen a bit to find Adalie rushing down the stairs holding onto her chicken.

"Really, Adalie!" Grace scolded.

"Oscar excreted an egg on my bed!" the child cried as if the action of a chicken laying an egg was absolutely terrifying. "Oscar can stay outside."

Grace blinked, unsure of what to exactly say. They were never able to truly afford animals. So Adalie's description of what took place was the only logical thing for her. The chicken had defecated an egg. For a moment, Grace felt terrible for not being a better provider to her sibling and teaching her the way of animals and the world. However, Grace was a child herself, set to raise children, and in those years, she learned how to navigate it all as events unfolded. She was busy trying to survive herself and help her siblings thrive in adversity. She did the best she could, though. Hopefully, the good Lord knew that.

The back door slammed shut for the first time today though it would not be the last. Adalie came in beaming, dusting off her hands triumphantly.

"Oscar is not allowed in the house," Grace said firmly.

"What about Kelly?"

"No animals, insects, reptiles, or any of God's outdoor creations are allowed in the house," she amended.

Adalie nodded. "You covered everything! Now, what can I have as a pet?"

"A rock," Thayer said, coming down the stairs two at a time. "Morning Gracie."

"Morning Thayer. Is Fraser awake?"

Thayer shook his head. "He's asleep. Want me to keep an eye on him?"

Grace nodded, getting down bowls and spoons. "Yes, when I go speak to Mrs. Marshall later about employment. As of now, wash up and get ready to eat."

She began dishing up the breakfast and giving it a smattering of sugar. A knock came from the door. She groaned, not wanting to answer it. Whoever it was, they could either wait or come back. One thing that annoyed her was calls during breakfast and the only few people to pay a call were the landlord or someone her father owed money to. She had informed a few people yesterday that her father had passed on, hoping the news would ignite like gossip tended to do. Her desire was for people to hopefully leave her alone. Apparently, it had backfired as the knocking continued.

"Someone's at the door," Thayer scowled.

"Can you answer it please?" Grace asked, moving the pot from the flame.

She scooped more porridge into a bowl to take to Fraser after it cooled a bit. There was just enough left for herself and she set it aside for after whoever was here had left. Grace wiped her hands off on her dingy apron and fixed her hair which was arranged atop her head in a simple knot. A few wispy tendrils framed her face.

Glancing to the left, Mr. Morten stood at the threshold of the kitchen.

"Good morning Miss Buchanan. I hope the day finds you well," Matthew began.

Grace felt her cheeks flush. He was a dashing man, even more so with his beaver-skinned hat off so she could clearly see his alluring brown eyes.

She swallowed. "Good morning, Mr. Morten. I find myself having a splendid day now after having received your visit."

She internally chastised herself for being so candid. Her mother was just as forward with a sweet smile and kind eyes that allowed her mouth to utter whatever it may and not one person batted an eye at the matter. However, with her, it landed her in more of a barrel of pickles than anything else. *I must learn to curb the offending habit.*

Matthew's cheeks heated slightly. "I have come to offer you employment on something I think you might find agreeable."

Grace took the two bowls to the gaping children at the table and set them in front of them. She went back to collect the spoons that she had completely forgotten about since looking at Matthew.

"What would be this employment?"

"Since the passing of my father, my mother has been in dire need of company. I would like to pay you as a companion to my mother, to care for and tend to. In return, the guest lodgings would be yours to accommodate and food would be provided along with any monetary necessity you or your siblings may be in need of."

Grace forgot how to breathe. It was a generous offer, more than she ever thought of receiving. She had worried long into the night about what to do in regards to their current housing situation and here the Lord provided it in an unexpected manner.

Tears peppered her eyes and threatened to fall. She sniffed, feeling an extraordinary weight lift from her shoulders. Was she imagining this? Was this offer something solely for her and her family? Could she finally thrive above her meager means?

"Miss Buchanan?" Matthew prompted.

Grace inhaled sharply, patting her eyes on the hem of her apron. "Yes, I'm sorry. 'Tis so much to take in and such a generous offer. Are you certain you wish for me?"

Matthew twirled the brim of his hat in his hands as his cheeks pinkened. "I believe you would make an excellent companion to my mother. She asked specifically for someone local who I thought would match her demeanor."

"So does this mean I get to see God since we'd be living with you?" Adalie piped up over her bowl of porridge.

Matthew grinned warmly at her sister, displaying perfectly straight white teeth. He went to where she was sitting and knelt beside her chair. "Nay, little one. God is all around us, keeping loving vigilance over us all yet we do not get the opportunity to see Him."

"Well," Adalie swallowed another bite. "That makes for a sad day, but I'll be all right."

"Finish up Adalie and get to your chores," Grace commanded.

Thayer finished his breakfast, grabbing his bowl and coming around to stand in front of Matthew as the parson continued to kneel beside Adalie and talk. Thayer smiled mischievously at her. Grace rose an expectant brow.

"If you're finished, go begin your chores, too, please," Grace instructed, taking the bowl and spoon from her brother. She turned around and set it by the sink.

"If you take the job, you know you'd be getting married to him, right," Thayer boomed.

"Excuse you, young man," Grace seethed. "That's uncalled for."

"Mr. Morten and Gracie–"

Grace took the spoon from her hand and flung it at her brother. Thayer ducked and unfortunately, it struck Matthew right on the forehead. Grace sucked in a breath, putting both hands over her mouth, and willed the tears to keep at bay. *Merciful heaven! What have I done?*

Matthew rose to his full height, his brow darkening as he loomed over a quiet Thayer. "Let me make this clear," he began, his voice commanding, "I'm offering Miss Buchanan employment. Nothing else. You need to apologize to her at once or I will bend you over my knee myself."

Thayer, wide-eyed, turned to her and muttered a garbled apology.

"Excellent," Matthew's deep voice continued. "Now on to your chores this instant."

Thayer bolted from the room and Adalie laughed, hopping down from her seat.

"That sure was dumb," she chuckled. "You'll get married eventually."

"Thank you, Adalie, please attend to your chores as well."

Her little sister stuck her hands in her apron pockets and went outside to fetch wood. Grace sighed, feeling overwhelmed and embarrassed. She leaned against the counter with her head in her hands. She sighed and straightened herself, gazing apologetically at Matthew.

"I'm so sorry, Mr. Morten," she finally said, wiping an errant tear from her eye.

"You have very good aim," Matthew replied, wiping his face off with his handkerchief.

"Again, I apologize. My behavior was abhorrent."

"I find no fault in you. I can only imagine the strife put upon you through the years you've undertaken to raise your siblings. Please give my offer of employment serious consideration. You do not need to answer quickly, but please mull it over."

Grace smiled wanly, wringing her hands together in front of her. "I accept the offer, Mr. Morten, on one condition."

Matthew raised a confused brow. "Pray, tell me what it is."

"Would you consider calling me by my given name? I would feel very uncomfortable if I were to be constantly called Miss Buchanan at every instance."

"Very well, Grace," Matthew said, offering a kind smile in return and a light twinkle in his brown eyes. "Please call me Matthew. Once Fraser is well, your employment shall begin."

"Thank you very much for this generous offer you bestowed upon me. I shall endeavor greatly to make an excellent companion to your mother."

Matthew donned his top hat and made a motion to leave. "Of that, I have no doubt; I just have one request from you in return."

"Absolutely. What do you need of me?"

"Do not teach my mother to throw items with precision. One such lady who has perfect aim is all that I require."

Grace laughed, finding his dry humor and little twitch of his upper lip charming. She got the door for him, pulling it open. Vivid sunlight made his brown eyes sparkle even brighter. Matthew stepped out beyond the threshold of the door.

"I agree to your request," she said.

"Thank you. I hope Fraser feels better soon. If you have need of me, please don't hesitate to ask. Dr. Carrow will be making rounds later this afternoon and will be stopping by."

"I shall be here to await his arrival. Thank you for informing me. Take care and have a wonderful day, Matthew."

"You as well, Grace."

She gently shut the door and sighed. The way he said her name sent shivers up her spine and all the way down her arms. It wasn't proper for them to address each other by their Christian names, but he hadn't seemed to bat an eye at her request. All the worries she had now dissipated to nothing except one- she would have to learn to keep business and personal separated now that she was employed by the Morten household. The trouble was, with her growing attraction to Matthew, she didn't know if she *could*.

Lord help me, she prayed, *for Matthew Morten is generous and thoughtful, an exceptionally good man in this world. I'm going to need to keep my head clear and I pray for the tenacity to make it so.* Grace strode back into the kitchen, heaving a deep sigh. *I'm going to need a carriage full of tenacity.*

Chapter Eleven

An Unexpected Meeting

Matthew stood before the fireplace in the drawing room and sipped from his floral patterned teacup. On blustery evenings, tea was a balm to his body and helped to ease the strain upon his mind. A week had passed and the town was faring better than it had been. No new outbreaks within Bramley had taken place, for which he continually praised the Lord for, though there were reports that new cases were springing up in other towns. He had prayed many prayers and buried some of his parishioners. Both the grandfather and grandson that he and Dr. Carrow had visited out in the countryside had perished. He had hired two additional local men, with Harrison's gracious coin, to dig and bury bodies, and they had done the job efficiently. Mr. Buchanan's grave had been dug first as his body had not kept well. Matthew had said an extra prayer for his soul. It bothered him that his children did not seem to mourn the man. *What cruelty had he bestowed upon them?*

In just a few days Grace and her three siblings would be moving into the parsonage. The lady had accepted the position, and all of their lives were about to change indefinitely. He felt the weight and responsibility fall upon his shoulders of helping to raise the younger siblings. He did not doubt the boys, especially, would test him and his patience, but in the end, he hoped they would come to accept him and their role within the household. *I am thinking as if I am undertaking the role of a father, but since they had never had a good one, I mean to assist their sister in their upbringing. A firm male presence has been sorely needed.* Here he chuckled.

The comments about marriage to Grace had seemed to mortify the woman. He felt acute sympathy for her in those moments. *As if she would ever consent to wed me. No doubt she has her eyes upon another man of the town. And even though there is something there within the air while I am in her presence, it must be denied. I am a man of the cloth and we are both in mourning. If she so easily takes offense to that which her siblings utter, then my family would likely see her stick her spoon into the wall.*

Matthew smirked thinking about the spoon that she had chucked at her brother but had the good fortune to meet his head instead. Then he frowned. *I do hope that Mama can withstand such rambunctious events which will no doubt occur. Though she has survived Simon and myself, she is advanced in years. I shall give this up to you, dear Lord. If this is your will, which I strongly feel led to believe, it will all work out. For I cannot stand to see her nor her siblings suffering in any manner.*

Matthew had spent the last few nights laying in his bed thinking about the situation. He often took foodstuffs from his own kitchen to provide for the Buchanan family. When a letter had arrived from Harrison inquiring how he could best serve the town, Matthew had not hesitated in replying. He had itemized a list of needs for food, medicine, and other household goods that were lacking by each ailing family.

Matthew had been in town when the Bramley Hall footmen had arrived by carriage laden down with baskets filled to their brims. It had taken Matthew a moment to gather himself and refrain from the tear that wanted to escape unbidden. He was not a sentimental man, nor he had ever considered himself to be one. However, recent events had turned his world upside down and shown him new sides to his own character and he was man enough to admit that those changes were not so terrible. He had grown closer to the Lord, his family, and even those under his care as parson. It was with thanksgiving that he greeted the Bramley footmen and aided them in the deliveries. The town of Bramley was set to thrive again and he was glad to have been a part of that process.

He strode to his desk and placed his empty teacup upon it. Taking his seat, he considered the task ahead of him. With his quill in his right hand and his unshaved chin resting atop his left fist, he stared at the blank paper before him. It was Wednesday, and Sunday would soon be here. He needed to compose his thoughts so that his first sermon as Bramley's parson neither fell flat nor left his parishioners wanting. 'Twas not that he lacked topics to tackle, nay, 'twas more that there were many things he felt that he could address. It was difficult to know which one to put down upon the sheet before him. He re-situated himself into the leather chair and closed his eyes for a moment. The town was mourning. Children had been taken as had some of the elderly. The person that would be able to comfort them all had preceded each of those losses in death and Matthew had no doubt that he had stood before the pearly gates to greet each of the town members who had been so precious to him. *I shall forever miss you, dear Papa.*

While the weather was colder, a walk around the pond would do him well. He stood from the mahogany desk and closed the inkwell and laid the quill beside it. He left the writing instruments there and left the study. Making his way to the parlor, he looked in on his mother to see that she was napping before the fire. Feeling as if his presence would not be missed, he walked to the front door and reached for his greatcoat and topper. He noticed the walking cane that Harrison had gifted Papa and did not think twice about taking it with him. Fashionable men about Town seemed to prefer the item and while he did not seek to be among the *cream of the ton*, he did seek the comfort that came with the cane grasped in his hand. It had belonged to his father and that was reason enough to now carry it with him.

He made his way out of doors, and shutting the door behind him, breathed in the crisp autumn air which had a chilling breeze. The leaves upon the trees were shriveling up and falling to the ground. The rain had nearly stripped all life from nature in the surrounding areas. The brisk wind had seemed to magically dry the mud and the ground was once again solid. His gait soon saw him before the pond. He had almost taken a step from the lane when he spied a woman coming from a turn in the bend. She was dressed in drab browns with little embellishments upon the parts of her dress that he could see peeking out from beneath her faded burgundy cloak. Her straw poke bonnet was doing its best to remain atop her dark head, but the wind was testing its pins and the ties of the black ribbons. He waited a moment to see if he may offer aid or direction to the lady when he finally caught sight of her face. 'Twas Grace. *What was she doing, walking alone on such a brisk day?* Matthew hastened his steps to meet her and when she smiled at him, he felt his heart tumble over within his chest. He patted it as if to calm a wild creature and frowned.

Grace came to a stop before him and the smile vanished from her face. "Is all well, Matthew?"

"Of a certainty for me, but what sees you out of doors today?"

"I had mending to deliver to the widow Smith and her cottage rests just beyond the bend in the lane." She smiled shyly at him.

"I see. Shall I escort you back to your own home?" Matthew held out his right arm for her to place her hand into the crook of his arm.

"I do not wish to trouble you." Grace furrowed her dark brows.

Feeling as if he was left adrift at sea, he let his arm return to his side. Then he reached up and pulled the brim of his hat to her as he bowed at his waist. *Mayhap she is right to be leery. I hope 'tis not that she loathes me.* He was turning himself to make his way to the pond when she spoke.

"'Tis only that I know you must be busy. You do so much for all within Bramley. I do not wish to take up your valuable time." Grace said earnestly, with concern shining from her hazel eyes.

Facing her again, Matthew thoughtfully addressed her, "Just now I am avoiding what needs to be attended to. Mayhap you can assist me with my chore, even if only for the short journey back to your residence? I can assure you that you are in no way a burden or an unwanted interruption. Pray, save me from my aimless wanderings and give me purpose."

Grace chortled at him. "Indeed? Well, never let it be said that I neglected my Christian duty where a man of God was concerned. 'Twould seem that I am indeed in need of assistance in returning to my cottage. What wonderful aid you offer me, kind sir." Grace gave a curtsy with a beaming smile upon her face.

Matthew held out his arm to her and this time she gently placed her palm into the crook of it. Matthew felt a thrill overcome him at her nearness as well as the ready banter she countered. *She is utterly enchanting.*

They began the walk to town when a thought occurred to him which made his brows furrow with disappointment. "If you wish, I may leave you to yourself at the edge of town once we arrive. I do not desire to ruin your chances with any of your gentlemen callers."

"Oh?"

"Indeed, I am not so unfeeling as to press my wishes upon you, nor do I seek to tarnish your eligibility to your suitors."

"At present your worries are unfounded. I have no suitors. There were a few, but my circumstances were such that I could not wed and leave my siblings to themselves and my father. And now, well, I will never be free to leave them and I do not wish to, either. They are as my own children; so long have I cared for them." Grace looked to the lane in front of her and would not meet his gaze.

"Hmmm. I see that all of the men must be daft. I cannot fathom the refusal of such sweet but energetic children. Though, I realize the extra mouths to feed would cause concern to some, a gentleman of modest means would have no such qualms."

"Such gentlemen are few and far between in my limited experience. I am content to care for my siblings; do not think I am longing for that which is absent."

Matthew halted their pace and leaned his head down to hers. "I do not have any definite ideas as to what you desire. I meant no disrespect. Nor do I claim to be a mindreader. Truly, I only thought of your comfort. I would be honored to walk you every step it takes to reach your door."

Smiling at him, Grace nodded her head. "Thank you."

Matthew straightened, and they set off again. He racked his brain on what to converse about. He did not wish to see her unhappy and he feared that he might blunder any attempt he might make. *Why must I always be so awkward when it comes to a simple conversation?* He silently berated himself.

"We are almost packed and ready to take the rooms you have so generously offered to us. You are certain that we will not be a hindrance to your household?" Grace broke the silence and he was immensely relieved. This was a topic that he felt safe to discuss.

"Not at all. I only regret that you must share a room with your sister. The boys will like Simon's old bedchamber. We could, if Miss Adalie would like Mariah's bedchamber, offer it to her again, but she was most adamant about staying with you." He guided her around a rut in the lane. *I shall send word to Harrison to have that fixed. He has always been such an attentive steward of the town.*

"I believe that for now, she will want my company. She has endured so many changes in her young life, but I thank you once again for the generous offer. We shall be quite cozy and comfortable, have no fear for we have long shared a chamber." Grace adjusted the black ribbons attached to her bonnet that the wind was whipping into her face.

They reached the edge of town and did not speak again. It was a companionable silence. Within ten minutes they were in sight of Grace's cottage when a shout rang out. Their direction was immediately captured by a fleeing Thayer who was running toward them as Mrs. Youst was yelling at him and raising her fist into the air. *Just what has the lad gotten himself into now?*

Chapter Twelve

Hands Quite Full

Grace cringed as she watched Thayer sprint headlong to them. Her stomach clenched so hard that she swore she would be ill. She had left Adalie and Thayer together to help Mrs. Youst clean out her chicken coop and collect eggs. Now, that same woman was yelling and chasing after her brother, and Adalie was nowhere to be found.

She peeked at Matthew out of the corner of her eye, waiting to see the disapproval and embarrassment of being seen in her presence. There was nothing amiss nor otherwise to be gleaned as to his feelings. Grace's stomach unclenched slightly as Thayer reached her side and hid behind her.

"Miss Buchanan," Mrs. Youst huffed, waving a rolling pin in her brother's direction, "the urchin you call a brother killed my hen! I demand compensation."

"Thayer!" Grace inhaled sharply, rounding on her brother. "Is this true?"

"Of course 'tis true!" Mrs. Youst snarled. "Look at your sour lineage."

"Why, thank you ever so kindly, Mrs. Youst. I'm sure yours is just as pleasant, is it not?" Grace replied calmly, turning to her brother.

She had nearly forgotten Matthew was beside her until he cleared his throat. Her cheeks heated immeasurably. She never had trouble defending herself nor her family. However, she hadn't done so in front of Matthew and she could only pray he didn't find her insults unbecoming for a woman. Either way, she didn't regret what she had said to the older woman. Mrs. Youst wasn't exactly the cream of the crop, either, with her husband a sailor and having a known penchant for loose tavern women. The wife had become hardened and taken on many of her husband's excessive faults.

Thayer shook his head, tears brimming within his eyes. "Nay, the hen was dead when Adalie and I were cleaning the coop and gathering eggs as we were directed to. It was stiff and its eyes were the color of milk."

"Liar!" Mrs. Youst seethed.

Matthew cleared his throat and took a step between them. "Excuse me ladies, I am sure there is a logical explanation as to what happened. I would happily mediate to sort it out so that no ill feelings are to be had, but where is Adalie?" Matthew interjected.

"Here, Mr. Morten," Adalie sighed, throwing her head back as she inhaled lungfuls of air in her dramatic show. "Mrs. Youst, I have to say, you run very quickly. I'm highly impressed."

Grace sucked in her lips. The angry older woman blinked at the child before resuming her glare at Thayer. Knowing Adalie had a penchant for telling more than what was asked, Grace turned her attention to the one person that could sort out the chaos. Grace just prayed that Adalie wouldn't embellish whatever story she was about to hear too thoroughly. After saying her quick, hopeful prayer, she realized it was a lost cause. Adalie would never give a direct answer.

"Thank you, Mr. Morten," Mrs. Youst began, tilting her chin and side-eye glaring at her and her siblings. "This matter is all but closed. I demand compensation for my dead hen."

"Compensation may occur once we have the entirety of the story," Matthew assured. "There are numerous sides to each perspective. yours, the children's, and God's."

Before Mrs. Youst could interject again, Grace asked, "Adalie, how were the chickens when you first entered into their pen?"

The little girl tilted her head to the side, dark brown hairs poked out from her bonnet. "Well. Except for the dead one in the back of the nest... Robert was right mean and pecked my hand. I don't like Robert. But Lewis is a nice rooster. Lewis got married today to Veronica. I don't think their marriage lasted long because Lewis then married Charlotte."

Grace pressed the back of her hand to her mouth, trying to hide a giggle. *Have I ever heard something so hilarious before? Oh dear me, what will Matthew think of such a speech?* "Well, I'm sorry their marriage hadn't lasted as long as you hoped, Adalie. So, the chicken was dead when you went into the pen?"

Adalie nodded, "Yes. Its eyes were milk-colored. Thayer picked it up and it was as stiff as a board!"

Mrs. Youst straightened herself and tilted her chin. She sniffed, "I won't be needing you nor your siblings' assistance any longer, Miss Buchanan."

"Oh no, Mrs. Youst? Pray, let that not be the reason?" Grace replied menacingly. "Is it not slow to speak, slow to wrath? I do so quite forget myself, but I believe that is the correct verse for the situation which you may recall?"

Mrs. Youst stamped her foot and stormed off in the direction whence she came. Grace let out a breath, more relieved that Thayer hadn't done something to the chicken. That ornery woman loved her chickens more than her fellow man, it seemed, but Grace attributed it to her husband's lack of care and her thirst for control. Either way, Thayer hadn't done anything horrific and it was an overwhelming relief. Grace felt her body begin to relax from the strain it had been under.

She peeked at Matthew out of her peripheral vision, trying to gauge his opinion on the entirety of the matter. She felt embarrassed that her tongue had gotten the better of her once again. But she wasn't apologetic in what she'd said. She had done as needed to discover the truth and that was never something that she would regret.

"Thayer," Grace addressed.

"Yes, Gracie?" Thayer replied, his voice soft.

"Take Adalie home."

Thayer took his sister by the hand and together they took off sprinting for their cottage. After this ordeal, she thoroughly wondered where she stood with Matthew. They weren't even moved into the parsonage, she hadn't even begun her new position, yet chaos was running amuck. How was she to be employed now? *What shall become of us if he rescinds his offer?*

Before this, they were having such a wonderful conversation and it took everything in her to not stare into his warm, inviting eyes. She could lose herself within those eyes happily and swoon every time. Yet Matthew needed someone more fitting a parson than she could ever hope to be. She did hope. It was wanton of her to do so. She hoped to be that person despite the fact they were supposed to be in mourning. She put the appropriate black ribbon around her bonnet as a sign to all that she was in mourning, yet if she could forego it, she would. *I do not mourn for my father at all. My heart feels nothing.*

She turned to Matthew. The sting of embarrassment returned over what had just occurred. Even if her brother was found innocent, it still bothered her. She hoped it didn't alter Matthew's perspective of her or her family.

"I apologize," Grace began, "if you do not wish to-"

"You're still employed," Matthew interrupted. "I am just happy the accusations were of a falsehood."

"As am I," Grace exhaled.

"I would still walk you to your door," Matthew said, offering his arm.

Grace smiled softly, taking it. The zing bolting up her arm from his touch enticed her to shiver. Instead, she held it all in and made herself relish the moment as her cheeks heated. *Will he always affect me thusly?*

Matthew was such a kind person. He was thoughtful and attentive. Any woman would be lucky to have him. She eyed him thoughtfully.

Grace softly cleared her throat, "I'm surprised you don't have ladies lining up outside your door."

It was rather forward, but she wasn't one to care. She was mindful about how she inquired, though, since it was solely the two of them, and she strived to not offend his quiet manner. *And had he not said much the same thing to her earlier?*

"Well," Matthew replied, cheeks heating. "I suppose I may lay your worries to rest as well. There are no ladies at present vying for my attention, though that could be attributed to the time of mourning I am currently residing within."

"I am sorry for your loss. I believe that the entire town is in mourning and shall remain so for quite some time." *How fortunate,* she grinned softly. *That there are no ladies beating down the parsonage door to gain your notice. I shall not have to chase them away.* They arrived at her doorstep and she forced her arm to unlink from his. "Thank you for the delightful walk. I thoroughly enjoyed your company."

"'Twas a pleasure," he replied. "I shall come fetch you to the parsonage in just a few days from now before luncheon? Your arrival on Saturday shall give ample time to get settled before services on Sunday."

"Sounds wonderful. Thank you for the employment and the opportunity to be of assistance."

"Thank you for keeping my mother company. I'm sure she will enjoy your companionship. Until Saturday," he said as he tilted his topper toward her, then he turned and began to walk down the street.

Grace entered her home and sighed. Never in all her days had she been so blatantly forward with a man in regards to expressing her fondness. She regretted nothing in what she had said. However, she would endeavor to be mindful since she was employed now by that same man. He was still mourning his beloved father and she was just the daughter of a soiled blacksmith. Matthew deserved better than she.

Though, he did not take offense to my words... it is pleasant to hope, but I must stop, she chastised herself and headed back into the kitchen to pack.

Chapter Thirteen

And So It Begins

The days passed in quietude and peace. Matthew was soaking it up because he was sure that everything would change once the Buchanan siblings had made his home theirs. While he did not desire to rescind this offer, he did pray that he was keeping within the will of the Lord. Still, the desire to continue along this path was pressed upon his heart, so he would see this through. He had no regrets. He kept thinking back to his conversation with Grace, how could he not? Neither had the prospect of callers seeking their hands at the present and he found that a comfort. For he could not keep a certain set of hazel eyes far from his mind. Her laughter would appear within his thoughts at the oddest times and he would find his lips curling. 'Twas all odd to him as he had never been–what was the word–smitten, in his entire life. Nay, that was not true. There was a time of childhood feelings when he first noticed Grace. He had always known her but never had she been a source of entertainment within his thoughts before that day. When Emory Meenks had dipped her braid into an inkwell in the schoolhouse, and she had punched him in the nose, Matthew had taken her measure. He had liked her spirit which was so very different from his. There were five years that separated them in age, and at that time, it was a vast difference. Now, it was nothing.

Matthew had attended to his sermon in those intermittent days and his message was about loving thy neighbor as the Lord had commanded. Mayhap this would speak to several of his parishioners. It was always wonderful to remind others that kindness was a choice. He felt satisfied with this message and was ready to take to the pulpit on the morrow. When the dead chicken incident had arisen he was again proud of the way that Grace had stood up for her siblings. She was civil, if a bit brash, but Mrs. Youst had been completely in the wrong and sought to take advantage of a family already injured. He hoped that his message would strike true.

Today, he would hitch the horse, Obediah, to the carriage to make his way to the Buchanan cottage. Earlier, a basket of linens and foodstuffs had arrived from Bramley Hall with the wish that the entire household would dine with them after the Sunday service. Harrison would have a carriage readied for their use. He felt comforted in this invitation as Mariah had such a sweet manner and was able to set anyone at ease. He admired this trait his sister possessed and was thankful that she had understood what a change this would be for all parties involved. He had a suspicion that Mariah meant to offer advice on how to best handle their Mama, that was a gift that he could not bestow. Mama, more often than not, did as she pleased and said what she would, but Mariah had a way of tempering those moments and adding ease to any situation gone awry.

Rising from his desk, he strode to the study door and exited it. Matthew searched for his mother until he found her in the sitting room which was located at the back of the parsonage. This room was reserved for special occasions and visits from honored guests.

"Is all well, Mama?" he quietly inquired.

Mrs. Morten turned her head to look at him with a smile alighting upon her aging face. Her hazel eyes were shimmering with unshed tears. "Just reliving fond memories. I cannot help myself." She was seated in one of the rocking chairs near the fireplace.

Matthew came into the sitting room and knelt down on the Aubusson rug before her. "I am persuaded more than ever that new additions to our household will be a welcomed thing. You will have company and I daresay they will keep your mind active on all things present."

"Yes. I think you are right. I do hope that they are not too lively." Mrs. Morten dabbed at her eyes with her handkerchief.

"I am about to leave so that I can bring them back to you."

"All is ready. Amy has aired out the bedchambers and changed the linen to what was sent over by our Mariah. Mrs. Kurly has adjusted the pantry accordingly to feed growing children. What are your plans, my son?" Mrs. Morten gave him a curious look.

"Plans, dear Mama?"

"Yes, once they are ensconced within our home. Are you courting the young woman? 'Tis an odd choice, is it not? For seeking out a companion of one, then to introduce not one but four new beings into our household. And lest you forget, we are in mourning, and courting and wooing are not permitted. You have never thumbed your nose at decorum before. So, I ask, what are you planning?"

Matthew swallowed. "In truth, I do not know. However, I feel led by the Lord in doing this. I have not forgotten that we are in mourning; I feel the loss in every breath I take."

"Is she pretty? Is that the reason?"

"She is pretty, is she not? You have seen her and visited with her. Surely, you must have your *own* thoughts regarding the matter."

"I do. But I did not understand *yours*. She is lovely, a bit lively for you, though. But I think she would do well within our household. But I ask you this; what sane man takes in a woman that has little ones for any position within the household? One who has a motive!" Mrs. Morten blinked at him.

"I have no *motive* other than aiding them and us as well. Can that not be all there is to the matter? May we not leave it at that?"

"Though we are in mourning, I shall allow you time to woo her. It is not done and though we are country people, we still must observe the customs and dictates of *society*. I shall never move on from my grieved state, but I know that you must. So, I shall endeavor to push you two together." She nodded her head decisively.

Matthew held up a hand, "Now Mama, you shall do no such thing. You have the right of it, we are in mourning, as is she for the next six months. We shall take any actions slowly and proceed from there. You *must not* put any ideas into the young woman's head. Do I have your word that you will not take any rash actions in regards to my marital state?"

"I shall do exactly that which is in your best interest, Matthew. Mothers are always sensitive to the needs and wishes of their children. I shall not embarrass you nor undertake any underhandedness, unless the situation truly calls for it."

I am going to be ill. Matthew felt the color leech from his skin. "Now Mama, I beg of you to behave. I have no designs upon Miss Buchanan whatsoever. Leave my love life to myself and trust that when the time comes I shall take the steps to secure my own future happiness."

Patting his cheek, Mrs. Morten replied, "As you say, my son."

Why then do I not believe her? Was there time to call a halt to the whole situation? I could mayhap make other arrangements. Dear Lord, help me weather this storm.

Slowly he gained his feet and rubbed the stubble upon his chin. This had now become an impossible feat. Bringing a young unmarried lady into his household, however innocently done, was going to be a disaster. His mother would declare a match made and there was naught he could do. He was capable of wooing his own future wife with no need for his mother. Without saying another word to the lady, he departed the room and in a daze he donned his greatcoat, topper, and took hold of his walking cane when he found his way to the front door.

Seeing that the horse and the open carriage were already awaiting him, he nodded his thanks to Mr. Trawley and climbed up into the seat. He reached for the reins and directed the horse to town. His thoughts were a muddled mess. *What was I thinking? I should have guessed that Mama would have machinations.*

It was with surprise that he found himself outside of the Buchanan cottage. Matthew blinked his eyes and shook his head to clear his whirling thoughts. The actions did not help. Resignedly, he climbed down from the carriage and was tying the reins to a column when the cottage door flew open.

Adalie rushed to him and threw her arms around his legs and held on. "I am ever so glad to be leaving with you today!"

Matthew patted her upon her back and said, "Are you set to depart?"

"Oh yes. Gracie is ready as well. She has not sat still all morning." She let go of him to peer at the horse.

Grace came to the open front door and smiled at him. He returned the gesture, but worried that it might have appeared to be more of a grimace. She gave him a quizzical look and tilted her head.

"Have Harrison's men been about?" he asked.

"Yes, they just left a few minutes ago. I would have thought that you would have passed them on your way." Grace answered.

Feeling like a dolt he nodded his head. *Mayhap they did pass each other. The Lord could have come back and I would not have noticed.* Matthew cleared his throat. "Right, well should we embark upon this new adventure, Mistress Adalie?"

The little girl bounced atop the tips of her toes in excitement and shouted, "Yes!"

"Very good, please ask your brothers to join us." Matthew directed her into the cottage.

"Is all well?" Grace inquired. She wore a dark blue dress with a black ribbon accent under her modest bosom. He could spy black boots under the hem of her skirts. She had taken more care with her dark tresses which were arranged atop her head in the current Greek fashion with tendrils that curled alongside her exquisite face. *She is a vision. A siren, a goddess.*

"Quite," he rubbed his gloved hands together with his walking cane tucked into the crook of his elbow.

Grace took a moment to look at his face and Matthew did his best to meet her stare. He was not a coward and he was not afraid of this woman. The idea of leg shackling to her was not what brought terror to his heart. 'Twas the idea of his mother forcing himself upon this woman and he had a vision of his mother asking for her hand in his stead. He did not want to be forced upon anyone. He did not want a bride just to be wedded. *Nay, I desire the right woman who holds great affection for me. Not one who simply accepts because her circumstances make the marriage a must. How far would Mama go to force a match? What embarrassments might they both face?*

Matthew stood rooted to the ground outside of the cottage and waited for the family to ascend the conveyance. Thayer and Fraser came bustling out from the door first, shoving each other with loud words. When they reached his side he spoke gently to them. "Now that is not the way gentlemen behave. We do not run and shove. Carefully and with voices to a normal level, please find your seats." He pointed to the carriage benches which faced each other. The boys looked to each other before meeting his gaze and scrambling to do as bidded.

Adalie was next to exit from the cottage and she clutched a worn rag doll to her chest. Her eyes were bright and her cheeks were rosy. She was a very lovely child. Matthew bent down and scooped her up into his arms and deposited her into the carriage. She sat upon the bench that was forward-facing with the twin boys opposite her. *At least the boys knew which seats belonged to the gentlemen.* He smiled wryly.

Grace came to his side when his back was still turned to the cottage door. She was tying her black bonnet ribbons and looked nervous. The sight of her anxiety was like a blow to his chest. *I do not like it when she is ill at ease.*

Reaching for her hand, which she placed into his, Matthew assisted Grace up the carriage steps. When she was balanced, she let his hand go and sat beside Adalie. There was nothing more to be done, but to set off. There was a strange tingling sensation in his hand and he refused to believe that the brief contact of hand to hand with Grace was the cause of it. They had touched through two layers of gloves. *Pull yourself together, man!*

Matthew took the few steps needed to untie the horse and then he climbed to the driver's seat. He gave the command for the horse to walk on and they were off.

"What is the horse's name?" Adalie called to him.

"Obediah," Matthew answered.

"I like that name. Are there any other horses at home?"

He assumed she meant the parsonage and he felt a tug in his heart that her mind was already calling it home. "There is just

Minnow, which is my horse. He has not been trained to pull a carriage, so he stayed home today."

"Can I meet him?"

"I suppose. You will also meet Solomon if you have not yet." Matthew scanned the lane for any other traffic.

"He is that large hound that barks a lot? He did so last time I was here and he scared me." There was a quiver in Adalie's voice.

"Dearest, he will not harm you." Grace was quick to assure her.

"He is old. And slow because of that, I reckon we could outrun him." Thayer piped up.

"Bet *you* cannot!" Fraser countered.

"How about we wait and see?" Thayer boasted. "I can do anything you can but better!"

"Boys, must we commence with the challenges already?" Grace gave a sigh.

Matthew smiled and was glad that he was not facing them. They were a handful and a half.

After a moment of silence, Adalie broke it by asking, "Are the horses married?"

"Uhm, no," Matthew answered.

"Why not?"

"They are both friends and both male, so they prefer to remain bachelors." Matthew turned his head to the side to look at her from his peripheral vision. She was pouting at him.

"Is Solomon married?"

Turning back around to watch the road Matthew answered, "No."

Puffing out a breath Adalie said, "Well someone *has* to be married."

Matthew rubbed a gloved hand down his face. He now knew without a doubt who would be his mother's accomplice and confidant in matching him with Grace. *Dear Lord, give me strength.*

Chapter Fourteen

Finding Her Place

Grace felt her insides clench at the constant questioning of her little sister. Adalie was on a current kick of wanting everything to be happily married from trees, to frogs, to any sort of animal or person. Grace attributed that aspect of her sister to not knowing what a true home and family were like. Adalie had never known the loving kindness of a mother nor the doting care of a father and even for Grace, it felt like lifetimes ago when she was informed she was loved and valued. Adalie was ignorant of it all, so Grace tried to be mindful and understanding when it came to her sister. Her brothers, however, she figured acted out due to the poor behavior and no authority of her father.

She had done her best to let her siblings know of their value to her, as well as the love she bore for each of them. Now, being in this small carriage with Matthew on her way to her employment, and to be residing within the parsonage, she found herself feeling rather guilty for allowing her heart to take the position of companion. Rather than rationalizing with her head how her family could be she now wished that she had done more.

Poor Matthew, she paused to think, *this has to be an enormous adjustment for him. Adalie will talk his ear off and pepper him with endless questions. And the boys will have him gray before his thirties. Oh dear... mayhap I should look for another position just in case this is too much for him and his dear mother to bear.*

The carriage trundled down the lane to the parsonage. The old hound dog Solomon began barking, though the poor soul faced the opposite direction. The old dog was advancing in years and was either going blind or deaf, it seemed, based on what he was currently doing. She would set the boys to task to take care of the dog and chickens, and to stay away from the parson's horses lest they be kicked.

"So when do I get to meet God?" Adalie asked. "Is he in your study?"

"Nay, dear child," Matthew patiently replied. "God is all around us, watching over us to ensure we are well. We can talk to Him at any time however. He is not anywhere within the house."

"But you just said He's all around us and watching, so where is He? Is God playing a game?"

"Adalie, that's enough," Grace chastised.

The child pouted. "I just want to see where He is. I have a few questions for Him like, how does He make it rain and if my Mama is doing better enough to come back?"

Grace looked away, trying to hide the tears brimming under her long dark lashes. She hadn't thought of her mama in a long time. She'd been busy being a caretaker to everyone, ensuring they were fed, loved, and clothed. Part of her felt guilty and distraught over not thinking of her mama, or even her papa; how he was before her mother's untimely death. But there was naught she could do other than to take care of those younger than her. Prayer only took her so far, and she was not about to worry the Lord with her needless whining for a different outcome to it all. She was fortunate now that Matthew allowed her employment, a roof over her head, and food in her stomach that she needn't worry about where a meal came from next; especially for her younger siblings as well.

"Dear child," Matthew began, clearing his throat slightly. "When the Lord calls someone home, it is forever because their time here is finished. Those we love are no longer in pain or suffering, so with God, they must be."

"Oh," Adalie paused as the carriage halted just outside the front door. "So is God married?"

"Adalie, why don't you see to the chickens out back?"

The child leaped down before Matthew could even think to help her. The boys, as well, took off as Grace called after them to be mindful of their clothing and the animals. Matthew offered his hand to her to assist her descent from the carriage. Grace felt jittery, as if she were shaking so terribly on the inside that it surely must have reflected on the outside, yet it didn't.

"Are you all right Grace?" Matthew asked. "You look a touch pale."

"Matthew," she began, meeting his warm gaze evenly, "are you certain you want us to be here with you? I do not wish to impose on you nor your hospitality with my siblings."

"I would very much like you to stay and be a companion to my mother. You are not causing an imposition. I'm certain the children will settle down once they become accustomed to the new surroundings."

She nodded, swallowing with the uncertainty of the entire situation. "Please discipline as you deem necessary. I've tried, but 'tis a difficult line to walk between that of a sister and guardian, and not the actual authoritative directness of a parent."

"I can understand the predicament in which you found yourself as a parental figure and it must have been very trying for you. But allow me to allay any concerns you may have and know that until you desire to terminate your employment here, you're not a burden and neither are your siblings."

Grace felt her eyes begin to tear up and quickly blinked them away. "Thank you very kindly, Matthew."

"Shall we make our way inside and I can show you to your room?"

"Matthew!" Mrs. Morten called out from the doorway, "Bring her inside at once before she catches a deathly cold!"

"Mother," Matthew replied, "We are coming along presently. Grace and myself were holding a private conversation."

Grace noticed the twinkle in Mrs. Morten's eyes and wondered what it meant. Matthew however appeared stricken and for a moment, it made her wonder what had transpired between them. Then it dawned on her that perhaps what Thayer was joking with her and Matthew about had found its way to Mrs. Morten, and she suggested they would court? Would Mrs. Morten dare to try to pair them together? Goodness, she hoped not! Matthew, in his kindness, helped her get back upon her feet. She felt the need to not burden him with her troubles more so than she inadvertently was despite reassurance that she was welcome. Never in her days had she known such benevolence. It was taking some getting used to. However, in her mind, Matthew deserved more than herself. She liked him immensely, had since they were children, but had set the notion aside given their differences in societal standing and then her familial encumberment.

Hiding her emotions with a demure smile, she headed toward Mrs. Morten and the parsonage. "Good afternoon, Mrs. Morten. I hope you are faring well today."

"Better now that you're here, dear. Having a lady about to talk with is just what I need. Allow me to show you to your chamber."

"Mother," Matthew pleaded.

Mrs. Morten turned around and rolled her eyes. She looked at Grace and said, "Take my arm so Matthew can keep his head."

Grace tucked in her lips. She especially esteemed Mrs. Morten; she was kindly, albeit a touch direct. Already she knew being tasked with being a companion to Mrs. Morten would be delightfully entertaining.

Matthew shut the front door behind them but immediately opened it again, with a drawn smile, admitting Adalie. The little girl sighed, marching right up to Grace, who bent over at the waist a little so Adalie could address her.

"What's the matter, love?" Grace asked.

"Mother, this is Grace's little sister, Adalie, as I am sure you remember," Matthew introduced.

Adalie sighed again but curtsied to Mrs. Morten before turning back to Grace. "There's nothing but hens in that coop. So none of them can get married."

"Well," Mrs. Morten grinned, looking between Grace and Matthew. "We must endeavor to find a rooster somewhere, I suppose."

"Really?" Adalie chirped.

"Adalie, please go gather your bag from the carriage."

The little girl sprinted past Matthew and Mr. Trawley who were still standing by the front door. Grace let out a slow, careful breath that more questions were avoided for the time being. She dared a cautious glance at Mrs. Morten who only gleamed with a twinkle in her eye. Grace swallowed. She was not put off by the prospect of being courted by Matthew, though it appeared to her by the somewhat stricken look upon his face, that he may find it otherwise. But how could he when just a few days ago, he made a remark about her eligibility? Grace closed her eyes briefly, putting it all from her mind. Matthew was in mourning and so was she. Nothing could happen for months anyway and by then, she was certain, the feelings and desires would have moved on.

"Mother, allow me to take you to the sitting room, while Grace and Adalie get settled for a moment. Mr. Trawley, can you please bring tea and some cakes for Mrs. Morten?"

The older manservant dipped his head to his bidding while Matthew seamlessly came up beside Mrs. Morten, taking her down a short hallway to the right. Grace let out a long slow breath, turning around in time to catch Adalie rushing back into the house with her sack of clothes. Grace bit into her bottom lip. Now that she was hired on to care for such a woman of standing as Mrs. Morten, they would endeavor to keep their clothing as presentable as possible. Grace glanced at her own worn day dress, refraining from grimacing. *Mayhap in time, we can purchase fabric to sew new attire so as not to be so set apart from the household.*

The booted strides of Matthew reentering the area made her head pop up and her face masked into one of open consideration.

"My apologies," he said softly.

"You have no need to apologize," Grace replied.

Grace ushered Adalie in front of her as Matthew ascended the stairs. He stopped at a room, opening the door to a beautiful four-poster bed on the left by a window with a desk situated right under it. The room was beautiful, immaculate. She ended up gasping at the bed and everything in the room of opulence and wealth far above her own meager station. It all just enhanced the idea that Matthew needed someone more refined than herself. *His home is elegant as befitting his station within the town.*

"I hope you find the room to your satisfaction," he said softly.

Grace nodded, swallowing the lump in her throat. "'Tis magnificent. Thank you ever so kindly for this opportunity."

"A bed!" Adalie screeched. "Look Gracie! A big bed!"

Grace dared not to meet his gaze. She hadn't ever shown Matthew the state of the cottage home nor the state in which they lived, but the man had eyes and a very astute mind. No doubt he had formed his own opinion and he was most likely in the right of it. The cottage was meager but they made do. She tried her best to make their home feel cozy and warm. *True, he had entered into Fraser's sick room, so he must have seen more than I imagined. Surely, he had a clear idea as to how the rest of the cottage had been finished. He was not ignorant of how we lived after all.*

"Unpack your things nicely, Adalie," Grace instructed.

"Yes, Gracie."

Grace turned to her employer with a soft smile. She hadn't a fathomable idea of what to say. What could she say?

"I shall bring up your things," Matthew said after a moment.

"Thank you," Grace replied, heading into the room.

She left the door open, welcoming any, including Mrs. Morten, should someone decide to make their presence known. Already this whole affair was off to an interesting beginning. Being here was the best thing for her siblings and for her. Could there be too much of a good thing?

Whatever may come to pass, I shall do my absolute best by the Morten family and repay their generosity, Grace decided.

Chapter Fifteen

Sermons & Memorable Meals

M atthew stood within the church's threshold and bid his parishioners a good day as they exited. He delighted in conversing with them and made mental notes as to what he could do for each family in the coming week. The nerves that had entangled his innards had ceased once he'd begun his sermon. His listeners were quiet, but seemed to hang onto his every word. He had so much to give thanksgiving about that he felt joy. It had been so long since a feeling other than loss or sadness had taken hold of him. *Had it really been three weeks since we laid Papa to rest?* He expected guilt to assail him that he could allow feelings into his heart other than those of sorrow. But he knew that his papa would never have desired to be continually mourned. Though very practical-minded, he had been a lover of life. Letting joy flood him did none any harm, indeed his good mood seemed to lighten the faces of his flock. He had never been one to threaten with fire and brimstone for wicked ways, he had learned from his father to preach love and be the example of Christ's love. Though Matthew was not averse to calling out those that needed it, he would never do so publicly.

When the last individual had exited, Matthew walked back into the church. He made his way to the mahogany pulpit which was decorated with carved cherubs and rosettes. He picked up his Book of Prayer and his Bible and held them in his large hands. He looked to the side and took in the sunlight that was streaming through the glass windows that depicted the life of Christ. The rainbow-colored light touched the cobbled gray stones that lined the floor. Turning his body, his gaze traveled to the effigies hanging from the wall behind him. He remembered that they had always hung there but his favorite piece has always been the fifteenth-century suit of armor. In his youth, he had imagined it coming to life and ambling about the church. This old building was rich with history and he was honored to now be the overseer of it. *Is it wrong to feel pride in one's calling?*

His inner musings were interrupted by Thayer and Fraser who came back into the church to claim him for the ride to Bramley Hall. The growing boys expressed their hunger, and he was eager to not keep the entire party waiting for him. He had been astounded by how much food they had taken in at last night's dinner. The entire table had set down their utensils and still the boys had eaten. He had wondered if eating their fill was a new experience for them and had remained silent about their gluttony. Seeing them run around in their trousers allowed him to take notice that they were in need of larger-sized clothing. He would take a trip into town and purchase fabric enough for the purpose of allowing them to be comfortable and decently clothed.

The ride to Bramley Hall was pleasant enough as the children rattled on about this or that person who had attended the service. They did no harm, so he was content to let them prattle on. They filled the silence and entertained his mother. He looked before him to Grace who had a steady smile upon her face as she made the appropriate comments. She was dressed in an ordinary day dress that was the color white. White was an acceptable color to don once the worst of one's mourning period had concluded. Grace had no black within her wardrobe that he had spied, and the white was considered appropriate as she had donned black gloves and boots. Grace seemed to wear mostly browns but he could not find fault in the effect the color gave to her hazel eyes and brunette hair. *Though, she would look stunning in reds and golds.* Her faded burgundy cloak hid most of her dress from him, but he had viewed her as they donned their outerwear to embark on the short trek to the church. She had taken his breath away when she had looked up at him as he held the door open for her exit. The smile that she had gifted to him was heart arresting. Matthew rubbed his face as he recalled the morning. *I am soon to be in trouble if I cannot vanish these musings from my mind. We will daily be in contact and I must find a way to make my mind quiet.*

Adalie sat in the middle on the padded seat between Grace and his mama. Adalie wore a brown dress that matched her brown boots. Her hair was braided down her back. Mama wore a black mourning dress that had no embellishments upon it. Even her hair was similarly arranged. She looked like a woman in deep mourning.

He sat backward-facing, between the twins. The seats were comfortably padded in a burgundy color that matched the drapes hanging in the windows, which had been tied back so the view could be enjoyed. It had been a crisp morning and their breaths had created a fog against the windowpane.

When the carriage began to slow, he noted they were reaching the front steps of Bramley Hall. The clematis was withering in the colder weather trying to cling to the sides of the stone mansion home. The country seat of The Earl and Countess of Bramley Hall was one of the finest to be found in the whole of England. The garden, when thriving in spring, was a riot of color and nature. The Hall itself was a marking of history where kings and queens had laid their heads and where royalty had been born. Harrison spent a great deal on its upkeep, but he was happy to preserve his estate, and the careful attention to detail that his staff undertook was notable in every facet of Bramley Hall.

"Welcome!" Harrison greeted them. Before the footman could open the carriage door, there was their host accomplishing the task himself with a beaming smile upon his face.

Harrison poked his head into the carriage and reached for Mrs. Morten's gloved hand. He aided her in standing and then taking the few steps needed to alight from the carriage. Matthew watched as his mother reached up and kissed Harrison upon his cheek.

When Thayer and Fraser went to stand up, Matthew stayed their progress by clearing his throat and saying, "The ladies are to depart first. If you wish to be of service, you may exit and then extend your hand for them to take."

The boys exchanged a look and then said tandemly, "Yessir!" Fraser was the first to reach the carriage door. He turned back and bowed toward Adalie.

"If you would allow me to assist you in departing?" Fraser winked at Grace as Adalie stood and reached his side. Fraser carefully helped her down the carriage steps and then let her go.

Thayer made a face of disgust, which he quickly masked when he caught Matthew's raised eyebrow. He turned to Grace. "May I offer my assistance in getting to luncheon faster?" Grace giggled in surprise and covered her mouth with a gloved hand, the other took hold of her brother's hand as he pulled her from the carriage and down the wooden steps. He did not let her hand go, he walked with her up to meet Harrison who greeted them.

Matthew allowed himself a small smile and shook his head. Then he alighted from the carriage and stood beside his brother-in-law. Harrison shook his hand.

"What a wonderful service. Your father would be proud of you." Harrison said as he allowed Mrs. Morten to grasp his arm.

"Thank you. I am glad that you think so. I admit to being nervous," said Matthew.

Harrison indicated that they should follow Mrs. Morten and himself into the Hall. Thayer held tightly onto Grace's hand with Adalie clutching her other. Fraser followed after them with his hands tucked into his trouser pockets. Matthew was the last into the entryway and he handed over his topper, walking cane, and greatcoat to their ancient butler, Billingsley.

Mariah's gentle voice reached his ears as he walked into the drawing room to await the call to luncheon. Matthew made his way to his sister and she turned to face him. She demurely smiled up at him. Mariah was clothed in all black as she had ordered from her modiste to accommodate her mourning period. Since funds had been of no issue, she embodied her state of deep mourning.

Draped in the matte look that black bombazine silk created she was a vision of sorrow and loveliness.

"I cannot tell you how pleased I was to see you standing at the pulpit this morning. You looked so dashing." Mariah reached up on her tiptoes to kiss his cheek. He drew her to him for a hug which she returned. Mariah had always been the only female he felt that he could ever be himself around. She had a way of making one feel comfortable and cared for. She looked happy despite the shadow of grief lurking within her sapphire eyes and his heart swelled to see her so at home in the place that in their childhood had held so much joy for them. *How astounding that now her own son shall learn to walk these same floors. The Lord worked his wonders in mysterious ways.*

"I don't know that dashing is an appropriate word to describe me." Matthew stepped away from her.

Mariah furrowed her dark brows and beckoned over Grace. "Would you not agree with me that Matthew looked quite dashing this morning, as he gave his sermon?"

Grace blushed and Matthew felt heat infuse his own cheeks. When Mariah seemed to notice the awkwardness that she had brought about, her eyes widened. "Well, 'tis only the adoration of a sister's affection speaking. Miss Buchanan, have you seen the view of the countryside from the window over here?" Mariah linked her arm with Grace's and steered her toward the window at the end of the drawing room. She looked over her shoulder at Matthew and mouthed the words stating that she apologized. Matthew inclined his head to her and then blew out the breath that he had been holding.

Harrison came to his side next and as the ladies had all taken their seats, they sat as well. The rococo-style armchairs were resplendent with their curved feet and carved filigree. The golden cushions gave it added elegance and as he remembered them formerly being a cream color, he deduced that his sister had reupholstered them to her taste.

"How are things coming along with the new additions to the household?" Harrison inquired.

"We are off to an excellent beginning. Mama seems to be pleased with the company and she and Adalie are as thick as thieves." Matthew frowned. "It causes me to worry."

Harrison chuckled. "I can well understand your feelings." Harrison looked over the room as his gaze seemed to take in each of his guests. "If you find that things are not working out well for any of you, we would be happy to step in and offer your mama a home here with us."

"And you would not be content should that come to be. I thank you, truly I do. But we shall manage well enough. Mama's place is with me and I am content to keep her in her home."

Billingsley entered the drawing room and announced that luncheon was served. Harrison rose and escorted Mariah from the room and into the dining room. Matthew strode to Mrs. Morten and offered his arm to her. They followed the lord and lady. Grace came next with Fraser claiming her hand while Thayer took Adalie's hand and tugged her along. Since it was a familiar affair, they did not observe the rules of proper etiquette. Mariah had not wanted to separate the siblings from the adults so they all took their meal together. The liveried footmen placed an assortment of cold meats and dried fruits upon the table between the china plates and crystal goblets.

The boys had kept quiet as their eyes took in every corner and crevice of the opulent dining room. They ate heartily but let the adults converse. The paintings of past earls and countesses lining the walls held much interest to their curious eyes as did the crystal chandelier hanging from the ceiling.

Adalie seemed to be content with trying a bit of each of the dishes and finishing almost every bit upon her plate.

When a lemon icing cake was brought in last for their dessert Adalie finally spoke. "Are you married, my lord, to my lady?"

The adults chuckled as Grace rolled her eyes in an exasperated manner. It was unladylike behavior, especially at the table, but Matthew could hardly blame her. Adalie had not stopped with her questions about marriage.

"Indeed I am. Me marrying Mariah made her my lady." Harrison explained patiently to the child.

"I think that's wonderful! I cannot wait to get married. Though, I don't think that I'd like for my husband to keep jumping on top of me whenever he would like to, just to poke at me, like the horses and chickens do." Adalie said thoughtfully.

Matthew had just taken a sip of his wine and it spewed forth from his mouth, spraying the white tablecloth and dripping down his chin to stain his cravat. At the same time, Harrison began coughing as his face turned an alarming shade of red. Matthew quickly reached for his napkin to wipe his face as all eyes were either upon him or Harrison. He felt his cheeks heat. "My apologies."

"No need to, dear brother," stated Mariah as she sought to hide her own blush. She made to rise from the table to aid her husband, but he held up a hand to stay her.

"Well, horses and chickens are peculiar beings. You are an astute child. I have often seen their crass behavior and been appalled. I dislike that particular aspect of nature. Why, when the weather heats the countryside all manner of odd things happen. And marriage vows mean nothing." Mrs. Morten spoke to the room as if the topic was perfectly acceptable.

Matthew looked across the table to Grace and he did not think he had ever seen her eyes so large before. They were almost lost to the cherry color that stained her face. This, he felt, would be a memorable meal for the ages. His stained cravat would forevermore remain a testament.

Chapter Sixteen

Silent As The Grave

G race could not articulate any words whatsoever. She was just entirely thankful that this was not some sort of social gathering beyond that of the family present. Even still, it did not diminish to the fact she strongly desired to sequester away from the world with Adalie for the next decade and emerge when the child had more tact. *How utterly mortifying! How shall I look anyone in the eye after this?*

"Gracie isn't married," Adalie chimed. "I really cannot imagine why."

"*Thank you*, dear child," she finally blurted, putting emphasis on her words. Her voice rang out in the dining room and she cringed at the volume.

Adalie's eyes widened. "But–"

"Not. Another. Word!" Grace scolded.

The child appeared close to tears. At the moment, Grace could not bring herself to care. She was thoroughly embarrassed in front of His Lord and Ladyship, and it was their first meeting with her too. How will they find her character now? *This is why society dictates that children belong solely to the nursery.* Grace tucked in her lips and stared at her plate. *How I long to disappear...*

"'Tis a lovely day out, is it not?" Mariah finally said, her dulcet voice charming the very air in the room with a quiet happiness.

"For it being a late fall day, the sun giving us warmth is lovely indeed," Matthew agreed.

"And since it is such a lovely day, would the children care to go see some kittens in the stables?" Mariah smiled, motioning with her eyes to the children.

Grace nodded, appreciating the kindness of having the children away to themselves while the adults could speak privately. *With a civil topic to bring some comfort to the room.*

"Kittens!" Adalie bellowed happily. "May I please be excused?"

Grace acquiesced. The children practically bolted from the dining room. Grace let out a long slow breath, wiping off her palms discreetly under the table. She couldn't make eye contact with Matthew just yet. More and more she was feeling like being a companion to Mrs. Morten was more of a burden than it was a gift. *I wonder if I will survive long enough to be seen as useful?*

Mariah and Harrison rose from the table, granting everyone else the permission to do so. Grace went to assist Mrs. Morten who was having trouble with her knees as of late. Matthew came up on Mrs. Morten's other side while they retired back to the drawing room to chat.

Grace felt her insides flutter not knowing what manner of conversation would take place. She hoped it wasn't about her nor her family. And hopefully, it wasn't in regards to her attire. She wore the absolute best she had and was up most of the night darning her dress and the clothes of her siblings to look their best for today. *And still, we do not nearly measure up.*

She bit the inside of her cheek, wondering what to say but opting for silence. She entered the drawing room, assisting Mrs. Morten to take her seat beside Mariah, while she went off to sit by the window. She felt as if she were intruding on the familial moment with the talk of the upcoming holidays and the winter festival prior to the beginning of Twelfth Nights.

She was still reeling from all that Adalie had to say. In her busyness keeping the family fed with a roof over their heads, she hadn't the proper time to teach Adalie the many rules of society and being proper. It was a failing on her part and one she now immensely regretted. Now, being under the loving-kindness of Matthew, she would endeavor to teach Adalie better manners. Especially since Mariah and Harrison were insistent that they held the holidays here at Bramley Hall. *We shall need to curb Adalie's tongue and curiosity. But how much would that change the child? Yet, we cannot continue along in this manner.*

I shall correct her directness at once, she decided. *To see Matthew and Lord Bramley all flustered has shaken me to the core. What must these people think of my family now? What am I to do?* Grace glanced out the window, trying to hide the tears that threatened to fall. She stared out the window until she felt she had a proper handle upon herself, then refocused her gaze to her lap. *I must find a different means of employment. I cannot, in good conscience, keep laying my head at the parsonage when my siblings lack tact and propriety for it brings a shadow on the light which is Matthew and his dear family.* The thought made her heart squeeze painfully.

She caught herself slyly gazing at Matthew from her peripheral vision. He smiled, chatting with Harrison in the corner about whatever men spoke of. She hadn't the heart to truly eavesdrop and it mattered not to her. Though, he was such a handsome specimen of a man to gaze upon. Before she could redirect her eyes, Mariah addressed her. Grace whipped her head around to the women.

"Do you not agree, Grace?" Mariah prodded, a knowing smile gracing her face.

Grace straightened, "My sincerest apologies, Lady Bramley. I was pondering on how best to curb Adalie's outbursts and did not hear your conversation."

A twinkle in Mariah's eye gave way to her believing it was not what Grace was ruminating on. "Adalie is a doll. I was quite outspoken at her age. It shall pass."

The assurance from Lady Bramley did little to cull the clench in her stomach. "The directness of my sister still needs to be squelched a bit. I appreciate your understanding, though, I must endeavor to teach my siblings how to behave when in polite society."

Mariah slightly frowned. "You've been caring for them for quite some time?"

Grace nodded. Her insides buzzed with apprehension and unease. Should she tell them the truth of it all? It wasn't like the entire sleepy town didn't know of her family nor her situation.

Grace nodded. "Yes. My mother died giving birth to Adalie. So I was left to raise her at three and ten as well as my other siblings. Christopher just recently joined the regiment."

"I shall write to Lord Purcellville and have your brother stationed under his care. He is a most excellent man," Lord Bramley added as he took part in their conversation.

"I thank you eternally, my lord," Grace said, staring at her lap.

"You poor dear!" Mariah exclaimed, a hand to her chest. "To be so young and caring for your family. Your father is the town blacksmith, is he not?"

"He was, Lady Bramley. He recently passed on."

"Oh, you poor dear. And we are family now, so please call me Mariah. You taking care of my beloved Mama means so much to me."

Grace's cheeks heated. Oh, goodness gracious! She felt entirely displaced, the kindness from Mariah touched her in an unexpected way. Indeed, the care from each family member she had met with since yesterday was almost her undoing. Grace had become accustomed to handling things on her own, yet her siblings were thriving under the care and attention of the Mortens, being able to eat entire meals instead of meager bowls of porridge. *And it has been a mere day since we have had our lives so altered.*

"I appreciate it. I find myself thoroughly enjoying being a companion." Grace found herself saying once she realized that she had been silent for much too long.

"And so you shall remain, dear," Mrs. Morten added delightfully. "And 'tis wonderful you are unattached to boot. We shall have a merry time finding you a proper suitor."

"Mama!" Mariah scolded, a twinkle shining within her eye as she glanced from her to Matthew. "Save it for the festivities. Grace, will you be a dear and help me and Mama plan? And while we plan and set it all up, you can stay here at Bramley."

Mrs. Morten patted her daughter's hand affectionately. "My sweet daughter, how you dote upon us so. We shall arrive a week prior to the festivities. That should be sufficient time for Grace and myself to be of help."

Grace smiled demurely. "It would be an honor to be of service."

Mariah clapped. "Splendid. We held a festival here last year, leading up to our nuptials and I would love to do so again. Many eligible men come. And with your pretty face, you shall have no troubles at all."

Grace kept silent. As she had told Matthew, her hand came with children attached. Not many men courted women who came with extra responsibilities. It was a hopeless endeavor that would be taken upon her account, but if it proved in providing a distraction for Mrs. Morten from her first holiday season without her husband, then who was she to dissuade the undertaking?

"We shall leave to discover what the children have gotten themselves into," Harrison said, rising from his chair. He strode to his wife, and bending down before her, he placed a gentle kiss onto her temple. The tenderness of the act and the brilliant smile that alighted along Mariah's face lit a fire of sadness and longing within Grace's heart. She clutched at her chest without her noticing the action. *I shall never be so beloved. How can I not mourn for what shall never be?* Matthew nodded to Grace and Mrs. Morten as he followed Harrison from the drawing room.

Turning back to the women, Grace gave them her full attention. They soon began the topic of guests and foodstuffs that the holiday festivities would need to have addressed weeks before the event was to take place. So lost in the conversation and communal feeling of belonging and being valued, Grace was surprised when her attention was called to the window.

Shouting and a loud, droning buzz could be heard from the out of doors. Grace stood to gain a better view of what was taking place. Her hand quickly flew to her mouth as she saw Harrison running pell-mell across the manicured lawn, away from the stables.

"Good gracious!" Grace said with alarm.

"What is it?" Mariah inquired, taking the few steps to Grace's side. She, too, peered out of the window and let out a horrified sound.

Grace clutched her hands together as she witnessed Matthew come running from around the corner into their view with his topper in his right hand and his walking cane gripped in his left; the look of utter terror upon his face. Grace's eyes grew large. Following after the parson was an angry swarm of bees that were buzzing with an ear-deafening noise.

Harrison made a movement with his hand pointing in the direction of the fountain that was currently bubbling with the clear water cycling through it. Matthew seemed to immediately know what action Harrison meant for them to take because he nodded as he continued to run. They both threw their toppers and walking canes aside as they continued their sprint. It took a few moments for the pair to leap into the fountain and let the water surround them. Harrison had reached the fountain first and seemed to attempt to make room for Matthew, but it was a small space when two large men tried to fit into it. Still, it worked as they had reached safety from the swarm of bees that came as close to the water as they dared.

"Can they breathe?" Mrs. Morten's shrill voice inquired as she reached the window. Her hands flew to either side of her face in suspense.

"I do not think so, unless they have grown gills. Oh, merciful heavens." Mariah's soft voice had an edge of panic to it.

They waited at the window to see what would occur next. In the next few moments, the bees flew away and dispersed. Harrison was the first to bob his head up from the water and take the measure around him. Matthew followed suit, and they both breathed in great gulping lungfuls of air. Together they emerged wearily from their watery hideyhole with sodden clothing and scowls lining their handsome faces.

Mariah gathered her skirts and raced through the room with Grace fast on her heels.

"Am I to be left all alone here?" Mrs. Morten called out.

"We shall return presently, Mama," Mariah called as her voice rang through the corridor.

Chapter Seventeen

The Trouble With Bees

M atthew felt his face swelling, though he could not determine which feature bothered him the most. Though, from the blurry vision in his right eye, he suspected mayhap that was the worst sting he had endured. He was immensely thankful that his greatcoat and trousers saved the majority of his body from the accursed bees.

"Arugh," came Harrison's pained voice beside him.

Matthew turned his head and was surprised yet again at how much the simple action caused him pain. "How many times were we stung?"

Harrison looked at him and attempted to speak, but instead, he poked his tongue from his mouth and went cross-eyed to look at it. It took Matthew's addled brain a moment to understand that the man was not sticking his tongue out at him, but was rather inspecting it. Harrison's dark brows furrowed and Matthew's gaze immediately went to his ears, both of which were swelling to twice their size.

"*Dear Lord, man!*" Matthew bellowed.

Harrison's tongue was swelling and Matthew wondered if 'twould ever fit within his mouth again.

"Oh, my dear husband," came Mariah's voice as she came to a stop before them. She latched onto Harrison's hand and began to tug him toward the Hall. "Billingsley, please send for Dr. Carrow at once!"

Grace reached Matthew's side and took a long look at him. She touched his eyelid with a gentle finger that sent the fires of hell through him and he could not contain the shout that escaped from his mouth.

"Take care, Miss Buchanan. I cannot be held accountable for my temper at the moment and 'tis my wish to not pain you with my ire. But you must be informed that my current sorry state and that of his lordship is due to the poor behavior of your younger brothers. They seemed to think it a great deal of entertainment to kick about a fallen beehive, which I have no doubt that they loosened from a beam of the stable's exterior. Now, if you shall excuse me, I shall find a bedchamber to lie down in and a willing hand to remove these pesky stingers from my person." Matthew mustered what remaining dignity he had left, and with water dripping from every inch of himself, ambled his way into the Hall.

He knew that after a good rest and something for the pain, he would regret his behavior. Though, at the present, it was all he could do to not concentrate upon the pain in his face, neck, and hands. He was losing vision in his eye almost completely and his perspective was off. As he entered the front door, his shoulder did not clear the doorway, and the pain of the impact nearly threw him over the edge of sanity. He was very near to tears. The continual drip of water falling from his person enhanced his misery.

Matthew felt a gentle hand upon his back and then one at his side guiding him into the manor home. Grace came around to his side and wrapped her hands around him as she helped him with ascending the staircase. A footman followed them and directed them into a bedchamber. The man aided Grace in helping to remove Matthew's greatcoat and cravat. Matthew sat upon the bed and let himself fall back onto it with a groan.

"Do you have an instrument to aid in the removal of the stingers?" asked Grace.

The footman nodded and exited the chamber. Grace blew out a breath.

"I will remove your boots, which shall never dry if we do not. You must be so uncomfortable in them. And as you look utterly miserable, any kindness that I can offer you, I shall endeavor to undertake. I am so sorry, Matthew." Grace blinked back her tears when Matthew shifted his head to look up at her.

"Grace, enough. 'Tis not your fault. We were remiss in letting the boys to themselves for much too long in an unfamiliar place. The fault rests with all of us. I apologize for my earlier behavior." Matthew said as he sat up.

"The boys! And dear Adalie too. Are they all right?"

"Harrison and I ran away from them once we earned the bee's disdain in kicking the hive down the hill and away. They should be fine if they managed to abstain from any other mischief."

Grace nodded at him and then bent down to remove his sodden boots. It took some effort but she managed the chore and had Matthew resting against a pillow when the footman returned. He held out tweezers and some sort of salve in a silver tub along with a few cloths. Grace thanked him and then sat upon the bed next to Matthew. Matthew swallowed as he looked at Grace's worry-lined face. Grace directed the footman to next locate a dressing gown or a change of clothing for Matthew. The footman quickly left the chamber again.

"May I attend to you?" she softly inquired.

Matthew nodded at her and closed his eyes. Grace leaned over him and began her chore. Within a few minutes, she had removed the stingers and rubbed the salve into his wounds. Matthew sighed as her gentle fingers caressed his skin. The salve was cooling the fire of the poison and he felt himself begin to relax at last. He had never been stung so many times before. His thoughts flew to Harrison.

"Would you mind finding out how Harrison has fared? He looked in bad form." Matthew asked her.

"I shall. Again, I am so sorry, Matthew." Her voice was unsteady.

Matthew took her hand in his and rubbed the back of her ungloved knuckles. "All is forgiven. Think no more of my discomfort."

Grace nodded at him and looked at their joined hands. Matthew let her hand go, though he was loath to do so, and she rose to do as he bid. Matthew closed his eyes and listened to the gentle rustle of her skirts as she left the room.

Dear Lord, please see that we all recover well from this adventure and be with Harrison. Comfort the children who are, no doubt, filled with fear.

The footman returned to assist Matthew with removing his wet clothing and redressed him in clothing Matthew had last left behind from a prior visit last summer when Harrison had composed a hunting party. Then he climbed back into the bed and closed his eyes. Matthew felt sleep's grip claim him and he willingly succumbed to it.

Gentle shaking of his shoulder awakened him and while he could open his left eye, the right eyelid would not oblige his directive to join the other. Dr. Carrow leaned over him and took a candle over his form to view him. *It must be late as the room has grown dark.* Matthew observed his surroundings.

"Well, I am immeasurably relieved that you have fared better than his lordship." Dr. Carrow told him as he sat on the side of the bed. The mattress dipped and Matthew adjusted himself to face the physician.

"How has Harrison fared?" he asked.

"Poorly. I will not mince words. I was worried. Never have I seen such a case before that has not carried the person to the Lord. He is a very blessed man."

"Thank you for doing all you could to circumvent the worst scenario." Matthew slowly sat up.

"Who saw to you?"

"'Twas Miss Buchanan."

"Ah, a lady of many talents, I see. I am glad that she took great care of you. Made my job much easier." Dr. Carrow smiled at him.

"Indeed. And I was the worst libertine. I railed at her at first. I have never been in such pain before."

"I am certain a hearty apology will suffice. 'Twas her siblings that caused this incident, was it not?"

Matthew nodded his head. His stomach growled and he scowled down at it.

Dr. Carrow chuckled. "Mayhap we should attend to that need next. The family is enjoying a late repast in the drawing room." He rose and picked up his black medical bag from the foot of the bed.

Matthew scooted himself to the edge of the bed and then rose. He walked the few steps to the lit fireplace and reached for his boots. They were mostly dry and he took them to the bed and sat back down. He pulled them on and stood again. Dr. Carrow handed him his cravat, which he attempted to tie into some semblance of a knot. Then he took his greatcoat from his friend and donned it. Together, they exited the bedchamber and took the staircase to the main floor as Matthew ran his hands through his short hair to bring it to order.

"Those Buchanan boys are a handful and a half." Dr. Carrow said with a grimace upon his face.

"They are. But I do believe that after this, they shall be better behaved. I shall make it my mission to instruct them and to see that their leisure time is well scheduled," Matthew said as they reached the closed drawing room door.

"Excellent. I would hate to see such boys really be the cause of tragedy."

Matthew nodded his head and followed the physician into the room. He was ready to see the children and make them understand the consequences of their actions while ensuring that they knew that no one thought any less of them. He was more determined than ever to give them a stable home that was filled with acceptance and grace.

Chapter Eighteen

A Step Forward

Grace couldn't shake the shame from her body. Her younger siblings had escaped the ordeal unscathed by the swarming bees, though Lord Bramley was not faring well at all. Grace worried over him earnestly. She felt wholeheartedly responsible for what happened. And the exclamations from Mariah and Mrs. Morten that they enjoyed having her made it worse. Matthew's words toward her made her realize the grip she needed to get on her brothers and lay down the law more profoundly.

I must do something with them, Grace thought. *This nonsense has to end and it is completely unacceptable how they are acting. I must do what I must in regards to them.*

Matthew and Dr. Carrow joined them in the drawing room. She felt her cheeks heat immensely at their arrival, and was unable to meet the eyes of either man. After Matthew nearly took her head off, granted he was in immense pain, the scolding made her understand just how much of a headache her brothers were.

The gentlemen took their seat upon the settee, helping themselves to tea and some cold sandwiches. Mrs. Morten was upstairs with Mariah tending to the baby and also Harrison, so it was just her down here for now.

"How are you faring, Mr. Morten?" Grace asked, breaching the silence. She did not feel as if this was a situation in which she could address him with his Christian name.

Matthew and Dr. Carrow both startled.

"Forgive me, Miss Buchanan," Matthew replied. "I am an oblivious man. I am faring well, thank you."

Grace nodded, opting to stare out the window though the sun had set and there was nothing to see. The boys were currently helping clean and work in the kitchen as punishment, though she needed to think of more to keep their hands busy. Idle hands and minds with her brothers just proved how disastrous it has been.

She glanced over at the men eating and drinking tea. She wriggled in her seat, heart pounding at what she thought to say. All that came to mind was an apology and a reasoning behind what she believed were the boys' issues. Not only that, but a promise to find a different means of employment so as to not upset any more people, especially the kindly Lord Bramley after what he was currently enduring.

Grace stood, wiping her sweating palms off on the sides of her dress. "Excuse my candor gentlemen," she began, clearing her throat. Both the men turned their heads in her direction, eyes narrowed with scrunched brows. "I humbly apologize for the actions of my siblings. I take complete responsibility. They are being thoroughly punished with not one iota of their day unscheduled henceforth, but please punish them how you see fit."

"Grace," Matthew said, rising from his seat.

Grace held up a hand. "Allow me to offer a reason as to why I think the boys have misbehaved. I was so focused on survival, ensuring all were fed and clothed, that in my negligence, I allowed their terrible behavior to slide, making excuses for them. Now I'm bearing the brunt of their errors in full force. By no means am I excusing their behavior, this is just my opinion as to why such a thing may have occurred. Also, in the meantime, I will search for other means of employment, so as not to burden you, nor your lovely mother, with my brash family. I thank you most sincerely for the offer, support, and accommodations which you have undertaken with such care. I, however, cannot in good conscience continue allowing my family to hurt those I care deeply for."

With her thoughts well stated, Grace strode out from the drawing room just before Mrs. Morten, Mariah and Lord Bramley were making their entrance. Matthew called her name, but she opted to not respond. She didn't care to hear how she was welcome to stay, that she was no trouble at all, and that all would be put to rights. Just with suitors who spurned her, something delightful wasn't meant to happen. *It may eventually, in the Lord's time, though that isn't today.*

She breathed out deeply, wiping away the tears that dared ~dge her eyes. Already, she missed what could have been for them—the pletnora of food, perhaps ~ better attire, and the happiness of being in the presence of his family. However, the two days were blissful and ones she would greatly treasure.

I cannot permit my family to ruin this good family, she decided, straightening her back. *I shall forever cherish what I was so wonderfully given.*

No matter the time of day, she was leaving here. Quietly, she strode down to the kitchen to collect her siblings. Adalie was sitting on a stool while the head of the kitchen directed them with a firm tone to do as bid. Both her brothers appeared miserable. Each child had a few welts upon their person, save for Adalie.

"How is Lord Bramley, Gracie?" Fraser asked, tears welling in his eyes.

"I cannot say," Grace said, crossing her arms over herself. "I do not think he has fared well due to your abhorrent actions."

"Are you still mad?" Thayer asked, hanging his head.

"Absolutely. I'm livid. I'm embarrassed because of you both. I cannot, for one moment, turn my back on either of you, so, I have given my resignation to search for other means in which I can watch you both and ensure nothing witless can happen."

Thayer cried, sniffling. "We're so sorry, Gracie."

"Be sorry. I'm thrilled you're feeling remorse," she yelled, though she did not mean to raise her voice so much. It was just all tumbling forth. "For years I have cared and done the absolute best that I could," she cried. "And this is how you choose to act believing it to be wise. How dare you both!"

"You had your head shoved up your–"

"Adalie! That's enough out of you forevermore! Next time, I will wash your mouth out with lye and ensure 'tis even more cleansed with vinegar."

"I heard it from the stable," Adalie shrugged. "I think it fits the moment."

Grace closed her eyes and sighed. "Before you speak, ensure that your words are appropriate. *Think* before you utter another one! Or you shall not like the consequences."

"What now then, Gracie?" Fraser asked, wiping his eyes and nose along his sleeve.

Grace wiped her eyes, willing the anger in her breast to quell, though it felt as if it never would. What she believed was a step forward in a good direction turned out to be disastrous. And poor Lord Bramley and Matthew bore the brunt of her family's actions. How could she ever think this would be a good idea? Granted she felt hesitation prior to taking the employment. Now, she was embarrassed beyond all reason. *Mortification is not a strong enough word.*

"We go back to the cottage and we live how we were," she said sternly.

"NO!" Fraser cried. "I don't want to go back there."

"To bad. How can you expect me to continue to show my face after your reckless actions that nearly–"

She choked on her words. Grace didn't want them to know that they had almost killed Harrison, and by the grace of the Lord alone, he was breathing. She wiped her tears, taking in several shuddering breaths.

"Come," she beckoned. "'Tis time we depart."

"But it is dark out," Adalie whined.

"There is light from the moon and the road is clear." She turned to the chef. "Thank you for seeing to my siblings and giving them an ample punishment."

"Miss Buchanan," the older lady began with kindness shining from her green eyes. "Shall I pass along instructions to have the carriage readied?"

Grace shook her head. "Nay, thank you. As another punishment, they can walk the distance. It is warm enough out and the way is clear. Thank you for your care."

Grace ushered her siblings out the back door of the kitchen toward the moonlit walkway. The path went from cobblestone to the dirt road leading from Bramley Hall. For certain, someone would be awake to greet her at the door to the parsonage and if not, that was even better. Tonight, they would collect what little they had and head back to the cottage where rent was still paid for a while yet. The landlord even informed her he would have the place vacant for a spell in case circumstances didn't work out.

It certainly didn't take long for it all to fail miserably, she thought, taking Adalie by the hand. She wiped her eyes and inhaled deeply, holding it in for a moment. How could she ever think she could take a step forward in life?

"Gracie," Adalie asked, squeezing her hand.

"Yes?"

"If we go back, I promise I'll watch my mouth. I won't say bad things. I promise-promise," she sniffed. "I *promise-promise* Gracie."

Grace paused, kneeling down to the child. Already, they were a bit away from Bramley Hall. The boys stopped and turned around with hanging heads.

"We cannot go back. I'm embarrassed. And I cannot *trust* any of you to make righteous decisions. So I have to do what I must do for our family, but also to ensure you cannot harm others."

"And that means going back," Thayer cried.

"Yes, it means going back."

Grace picked up her sister, carrying her past the boys and down the lane. It was going to be a long night, but one where her brothers wouldn't be able to cause harm to befall anyone else, ever again.

Chapter Nineteen

Bringing Her Back

Matthew waited a solid five minutes before he excused himself from the drawing room in search of Grace. He suspected that she had made her way to her siblings. From the butler, Billingsley, he learned that the children had been sequestered in the kitchen area. Matthew took the back stairwell and soon found a kitchen that was quiet and dark. The head chef, Mrs. Holmes, turned the corner and almost collided with him.

"I beg your pardon, Mr. Morten," she said.

"No need, forgive me for intruding upon your inner sanctum. Have you any idea where the Buchanan family is?" Matthew inquired as he smiled at the older lady who was dressed in all black. Her silver capped hair had a few wispy tendrils hanging around her face.

"I dislike to talk out of turn, but I did hear that they planned to go back to their home, their cottage. Miss Buchanan led them through the back door and to gather their things from the parsonage."

Matthew's jaw ticked. He could hardly blame Grace for feeling the need to flee. Though he had expressed his sorrow for his first reaction after having been stung to her, he had still not behaved with grace. He had attempted to correct things between them. *It seems that I have failed. This will not do.*

"Thank you for your information," he said, as he inclined his head to her and walked away. Matthew retraced his steps and soon stood in front of Billingsley by the front entrance in the foyer. He requested his outerwear and that of the Buchanan family and promptly left the Hall. He knew that the walk back to the parsonage would be long and mayhap not the best idea, given the lateness of the hour. At the very least, they would be safe from highwaymen, but that did not mean that some other misfortune would not meet them. 'Twas not safe to be out on the country roads with darkness present.

I will soon discover them and all shall be set to rights. This is but a bump in the road to the future. I well understand that things may not progress smoothly, and true this was a very horrible event, but nothing that can not be addressed. I shall correct this. Nothing short of bringing them back... her back will suffice. I cannot bear the idea that she feels to blame for this, this was not her doing. Her eyes were nearly my undoing with the unshed tears that rimmed them. Matthew clutched at his chest as it grew even more taut with anxiety. Truly he would not be well until they were safe. *They could not be too far ahead.*

Matthew increased his pace and when he took one of the bends, he soon caught sight of them. Grace was carrying Adalie who had her head buried against Grace's neck. Thayer and Fraser walked behind their sisters with their heads down. *A more apt feeling of dejection I have never witnessed. And they are very remorseful and that speaks well of their character.*

"Lo, my friends, how odd that we should meet upon this lane. Shall I accompany you to your destination?" Matthew called out to them.

Grace ceased her steps but did not turn around. Adalie raised her head and offered him a tearful smile and a small wave. The boys' heads rose and they turned to look at him. They raced the small distance to meet him.

"We are so sorry, Mr. Morten!" Thayer said with remorse lining his face.

"We are," agreed Fraser. "But it had nothing to do with Grace!"

"We saw the bees and followed them to the hive. We worried for the kittens and so we devised a way to remove the hive, only it didn't work right," Thayer told him, choking on his tears.

"Throwing rocks and poking it with sticks was a bad idea. When it fell we didn't know what to do. They were so angry and then you were there as was his lordship and then everything went wrong." Fraser locked gazes with him.

"I see. Mayhap in future, you will leave that particular task to the stable master? He would have known precisely how to handle that situation." Matthew spoke firmly though with a tinge of gentleness to his words.

Grace turned in their direction and began to walk back toward them. Matthew waved his hand in her direction and the boys followed his suit of meeting her.

"I cannot apologize enough, Mr. Morten, but I can vow that no harm shall befall you or your family at our hands. This was an utter disaster and we shall return to the cottage," Grace told him, but would not meet his eyes.

Matthew leaned his head down and spoke softly to her, imploring her to lift her gaze to his. "We, none of us, desire to see your parting from your position. As I stated earlier, this was not your doing and we all bore responsibility. There are bound to be issues that arise, Grace, but you do not need to meet them head-on nor alone any longer. We consider you a part of our household, in truth, you are home now. Mama would not be comfortable if you were to abandon your post. Though your employment has been short with us, she has come to rely heavily upon you. I beg of you to reconsider." He refrained from mentioning how he would feel if she were to leave.

"'Tis not your responsibility to raise my siblings and bear the brunt of their mischief," Grace said as she delicately sniffed. She set Adalie down beside her.

When Grace was seated next to Mariah and his Mama near the fireplace, the children became involved in a game. He sat next to Harrison in a quiet corner of the room.

"You have the look of a man with much upon his mind," Harrison said as he took a sip of his brandy.

"Do I?" mused Matthew.

"Indeed, I remember that look well enough. I used to view it any time that I looked into the mirror."

Scrunching his brows, Matthew inquired, "What?"

"You look like a man who is falling in love and cannot begin to slow his descent. 'Tis thrilling and frightening. Seeing it upon *your* face is entertaining."

"You are mistaken. I am in mourning and such thoughts would be entirely misplaced," said Matthew.

"And yet, here *you* are, and here *she* is. And here I am to witness it all. Good luck, my brother. Those Buchanans are quite the handful."

Turning to look at Harrison, Matthew inquired, "How are you?"

"I am well. I am blessed in truth. I was in the midst of leaving all that I love behind but then the pain seemed to lessen. I cannot express how blessed I feel. Know that I harbor no ill feelings. It was a terrible incident, but in the end, we are all safe and well."

"Praise the Lord," said Matthew and he smiled for the first time in what felt like hours. He could catch his breath. Everything was almost as it should be.

Chapter Twenty

Settling In, Again

G race sat by the window as she mended a hole in the knee of one of Fraser's trousers. The light was waning outside faster now with the changing of seasons. Soon, candles would need to be lit. Mrs. Morten and Adalie sat on the settee in the parlor as rain pelted the countryside. The two had been busy all morning as the older woman instructed the child in the delicate art of embroidery. Adalie was patiently heeding all of the directions with a skillful hand. It seemed that this was a skill that would keep her hands busy and her person out from underfoot. There was the added benefit that it aided in keeping Mrs. Morten's attention focused upon the task. The two enjoyed the companionship.

Grace bit the thread as she had misplaced the scissors and tied a careful knot. This task was finished and she was glad of that. Putting the clothing back into the basket that sat by her side, she arched her back. *Whoever had said that ladies lacked fortitude had never spent hours bent over needlework.*

She let her thoughts wander over the past week. Since settling in again into the parsonage, the boys had been well behaved and she was constantly thankful for that fact. Mr. Trawley kept them busy with chores out in the two-horse stable, or with the care of either Solomon or the chickens. The tasks left them dirty afterwards but what was dirt when they were employed honestly and without the risk of inventing their own brand of trouble? Matthew had also been keeping a careful eye on them, but with his own time being caught up in the needs of the town, and his parishioners, he had little leisure time. His patience with her siblings was not singular, he demonstrated it with his mother and herself. The bee stings were healing and none had suffered long-standing except Lord Bramley and even he was much improved. *Thank the Lord!*

She wriggled in her seat and smiled. She forced herself to focus on another hole to sew closed, yet her mind kept thinking about her siblings and their new routine. The children had kept attending the town school and that filled a few hours of their day, giving Grace the time needed to grow closer to Mrs. Morten. She was coming to understand the lady more by the day and she had attached herself to Grace's heart. Mrs. Morten spent her mornings writing letters to her friends and distant relations. When that was finished the two usually read. In moments of quiet, when the men of the house were absent, Mrs. Morten was instructing Grace upon the pianoforte. Grace did not care if it was a skill she could ever master, but Mrs. Morten loved music and with her fingers swelling with age, she found that it was not an easy feat to play the instrument herself any longer. Matthew had caught them yesterday during practice and Grace had turned several shades of red. It was mortifying that she was so advanced in age and lacked the skill. Yet, it was not a skill of common people. Laborers and those not gently bred had no need for such useless endeavors. But Grace found that she did enjoy it and was not very terrible at it. She was improving. She had missed a few of the pianoforte's keys when Matthew had popped his head into the parlor.

Grace smiled at the memory, picturing Matthew's kind chocolate eyes alight at the sight of her and his mother. In that moment, her heart skipped several beats and she thought she might be dead; not from embarrassment at being caught playing very poorly, but from the butterflies swelling within her breast whenever Matthew was near. By the heavens, Grace adored the man so. She let out a small breath, inspecting another pair of Fraser's trousers as another memory of the week flitted across her mind.

Mrs. Morten and herself had taken luncheon at Bramley Hall with Mariah twice that week. Both times were an intimate affair where they ate cold sandwiches and dried fruit. One of the Bramley carriages had collected them and brought them home upon each visit. One of Grace's favorite things to do when calling on Bramley Hall was the cuddling of Daniel. When Adalie had been a babe, there had not been much time for cuddles. The chores were neverending. But now, Grace could enjoy the fresh scent of the babe and play with him. Mariah was an excellent hostess and delighted in others' attention to her infant. While Grace had dreamed of a future with a house of her own and children had featured in those dreams, she had never understood how much she longed to hold her own child within her arms. *Mayhap that day shall never come. But if it should, I shall never want for a thing.*

Mr. Trawley kindly brought in tea for Mrs. Morten, Adalie, and herself before heading into the study. Grace smiled, getting up to pour everyone some refreshments since Mrs. Morten's fingers were giving her trouble as of late. Tea was an ever-engaging event. It flowed freely within the parsonage and there was never a moment that it seemed to be missed. But when it came to the taking of tea time, the children as well as Matthew were always a part of it. This was Grace's favorite time of the day, when everyone caught up on each other's day and what was happening in the town and beyond. Matthew would share local events and Mrs. Morten would read from her letters what was occurring elsewhere. The children would recite lessons and Matthew would take to quizzing them and oftentimes what he asked of them, they had no answer for, so they would go in search of the knowledge from the many books lining the bookcases in Matthew's study. These hours every day made everything right in Grace's world and made her heart sing with joy.

Grace glanced out of the room toward the stairs where Matthew and the boys were sequestered away. She couldn't help the grin on her face. She adored Matthew, basking in his presence even for a mere moment before he had to ensconce himself away in some other task.

Mrs. Morten sipped her tea, making a satisfied noise. "We are to have Dr. Carrow to dine with us tonight. He is such a fine young man who always is polite and thinks of all in his addresses," said Mrs. Morten.

"I like him! He made Fraser better," Adalie beamed up at the lady.

"Indeed, we are very thankful for him," said Grace.

"The poor dear is a second son, you know. He needs a wife. But not one from our little town. He needs an elegant lady by his side," mused Mrs. Morten.

"Has he stated that he wishes for a wife?" Grace inquired as she arranged her skirts.

"My dear, men will never admit to such things. 'Tis up to us matronly ones to set love into motion. I mean to ask my sister whom she thinks may be a fit, she has met him."

Grace only smiled softly in reply. When Mrs. Morten had decided on an action, she was hard-pressed to naysay her. Only Matthew seemed to be able to reason with her, and reason mayhap was too kind of a word to employ. There were instances when Matthew was firm with his mother, but she could tell that he was never pleased in those moments. *He possesses such a thoughtful and loving heart.*

As it was Sunday and with terrible weather, the parsonage household had kept itself indoors once they had returned from the church. The boys were in Matthew's study with him as was Mr. Trawley. Grace had thought it odd that Mr. Trawley had taken to visiting within the study when his duties were completed in those in-between times. Seeing her pondering the closed door one afternoon, Mrs. Morten had shared with her that the late Mr. Morten had always invited the company of Mr. Trawley within his study. Since Matthew did not yet need to compose the coming week's sermon, he did not mind the intrusion in his private room. Grace had no need to worry for her mischief-makers when they were within the study or under the watchful gazes of Matthew and the manservant.

Mrs. Morten hid a delicate yawn behind her hand.

"Oh, the hour is late. You must be in need of a rest," said Grace as she rose and went to Mrs. Morten's side. She helped the lady gain her feet and then with an arm to support her, guided her from the parlor and up the staircase to her bedchamber. It took but a few minutes to soon have Mrs. Morten tucked within her bed. When she was satisfied that the lady was close to slumber, she exited the room and softly closed the door behind her. Adalie greeted her with a smile and held out her hand for her.

"What shall we do now, little one?" asked Grace.

"Let's bake some bread!" Adalie had always enjoyed baking alongside Grace and since 'twas a useful skill to impart upon her, Grace had always readily welcomed her help.

"I don't know about that. Mrs. Kurly likes her kitchen to remain hers alone. Perhaps we can read a storybook?"

Adalie enthusiastically nodded her head and tugged Grace in the direction of their bedchamber.

Chapter Twenty-One

Dining With The Doctor

T he rapping on the door brought Matthew from his study. Mr. Trawley was ushering Dr. Carrow in and taking his outerwear from him. The doctor nodded his thanks to the man and upon spying Matthew walked to meet him.

"Well met, Mr. Morten. What a dismal day. I trust you and yours are all well?" Dr. Carrow's kind gray eyes met his, and they exchanged handshakes.

"In exceedingly good health. Have you fared well?" Matthew inquired as he led his guest into the parlor. They reached the room and sat as no one else was in the room.

"I have. I wanted to express my sincere gratitude for inviting me to dine with you this evening. I find that I really enjoy any time spent within this parsonage. And as you are in mourning, we can skirt the rules and socialize by simply saying that the doctor was needed," Dr. Carrow chuckled.

"Indeed."

"How are you, my friend? This past month has been a trial by fire, I daresay."

Has it really been a month? He blinked, scowling slightly in remembrance. *Yes, it had been. Time was flying by.* Matthew rubbed at the familiar ache within his chest. *A month has passed since Papa breathed his last.*

"And yet we have demonstrated resilience in the face of sorrow and here we are," said Matthew.

They were interrupted by the appearance of Mrs. Morten and Grace. The children followed in their wake. The gentlemen rose and greeted the newcomers. Before they could take their seats again, Mr. Trawley announced that dinner was served. Matthew stepped to his mother's side and took her arm, guiding her the few steps needed to reach the dining room. Dr. Carrow was quick to offer his arm to Grace, Matthew noted as his attention was taken away from his mother. Grace was laughing at the physician and the man was smirking at her. *What the Devil? I have never had Grace laugh in quite that manner before. What had the man said?*

Matthew scooted his mother's chair in. He walked the length of the table to the opposite side and took to his own chair at the head of the table. He was curious to learn what had been said to Grace. She sat upon his right and Adalie upon his left. The physician sat on his mama's right side and Thayer on her left. That left Fraser to sit beside Grace. Their number was off, but he had never given superstition of odd numbers any credit at all.

When the soup was before each who sat at the table, Matthew addressed Dr. Carrow. "I could not help but notice the earlier mirth you shared with Miss Buchanan."

"Ah yes. I reminded her about a prior incident." The doctor's eyes were twinkling.

"And what incident was that?"

"None that you need to concern yourself about, Mr. Morten," said Grace with a pointed widening of her eyes to the doctor.

"I see," Matthew stated. His appetite was disappearing at the familiarity that the two were engaged in. It made him want to land a facer upon his friend and further darkened his own mood. Which was surprising to him. *What is wrong with me?*

"If you must know, the good doctor performed a favor for me that turned into a mishap that I should like to forget ever took place," Grace said as she dipped her spoon into her soup bowl.

Matthew nodded his head at her and then turned to his friend. "What has you busy these days?"

"The usual complaints and I am thankful for that. Fortunately no more incidents with stinging insects," said Dr. Carrow.

"Do you think that the weather will hold as it is?" asked Adalie. Grace smiled at her and that lightened Matthew's mood a bit.

"I hope not. 'Tis bad for many of my patients," answered the doctor.

"Have you ever killed anyone with bad medicine?" Thayer asked as he set his spoon down.

"No, not yet. I pray that I never do."

"Even a really bad man?" inquired Fraser.

"Even then."

"Is poison medicine?" asked Adalie.

"I would think not, dearest. Let us talk of something else shall we?" Grace raised her dark brows at each of her brothers.

"Animals are not appropriate to mention at the table," said Adalie quietly to herself, but all heard her.

"Mayhap we shall talk about our favorite winter traditions," Mrs. Morten spoke.

"Excellent idea. What is your favorite thing, Adalie?" asked Matthew.

"Sledding! But I also like to drink hot chocolate," Adalie readily answered.

"You don't know what it tastes like!" accused Fraser.

"I do too! I had a sip once and it was divine. 'Tis my favorite treat," Adalie solemnly told him.

"What is your favorite tradition, Thayer?" asked Matthew.

"That's easy, I like the cookies and the food," said Thayer. "Grace always worked more hours to save up to do the special treats just for one holiday."

Ham was placed down onto the table and Matthew rose to carve it for his guests. Once his chore was completed and each plate had the meat upon it, he took to his chair again.

"And you Fraser? What do you like to do?" Matthew addressed him.

"I like to play with the small gifts that the other children receive," Fraser smiled at Matthew and then ducked his head.

And this year, you shall receive your own gifts, I vow that now. Matthew worked to clear his throat before saying, "Is that so? Well, all are excellent things. And you Dr. Carrow, what traditions do you enjoy?"

"Father Christmas has always been my favorite. But I also enjoy the sprigs of holly that hang from the eaves and doorways. Mayhap this year I shall find myself under some with a beautiful lady who possesses the most extraordinary hazel eyes," Dr. Carrow beamed at Matthew and then winked at Grace.

Matthew watched as Grace's face blushed and her gaze lingered upon her plate. Well, what was he to do now? Was a romance forming under his roof, or was it rekindling? He felt his heart squeeze painfully but his face managed to smile and nod at his friend.

"You can not mean me?" Mrs. Morten's hazel eyes had grown large in her face.

"Alas, I confess that I know better than to ever desire to displace your husband. Such men as he are rare indeed and I could never seek to fill his boots." Dr. Carrow told her with a tender smile.

The candlelight cast a glow over the doctor that made his blond head appear golden, giving him an angelic appearance. Matthew wanted to pluck every golden hair from his head.

Chapter Twenty-Two

Flirtations Afoot

Grace wriggled slightly in her seat, pondering on what to do with Dr. Carrow's attention. True, though he was extremely handsome and the forest-green fitted tailcoat and black breeches made him an excellent male specimen, her heart would not be swayed in his direction. It made her delighted that someone was interested in her, but also cautious since any suitor she engaged with did not like the fact she couldn't leave her siblings behind. Even more so now with the death of her father, she couldn't ever leave them. The saving grace to all of this was the fact that she was in mourning and had been for three weeks. The Lord save her soul, but she did not miss her father at all and found being in mourning for a wicked man repulsing.

The only man who did not seem to bat an eye to taking her and her siblings on sat across from her in the parlor. In the weeks of coming to know Matthew better, her opinion of his good character had been reaffirmed. He was gentle, patient, and kind. If she could ever merit to be married to such a man, she would ensure his life was blissfully happy. Silently, she wished it to be him. She couldn't help the smile that graced her face whenever he was around. *He makes my heart long to flee to his side and bask within his warmth.*

She glanced at Matthew again, wondering at what to say. She gave him a pleading look, though it constantly escaped him as he hadn't met her eyes since dinner. The children, after a long day, excused themselves and went to bed. Grace longed to do as the children to escape the flirtations, yet it would be unforgivably rude.

"I see the children are doing better," Dr. Carrow carefully commented. "And Fraser's welts have all vanished."

Grace nodded. "'Tis Mr. Morten's doing and attentive care. I am forever grateful."

She stared at her lap, feeling a touch out of sorts. Taking a long, deep breath, she raised her head to finally catch Matthew's eye. She smiled gently at him, pouring her emotions into her gaze and hoping that mayhap he would know how she felt. Surely he had to know with their previous candid flirtations? Though, with her candor, it might be prudent next time they were alone for a moment to make her feelings known? She wasn't one to mince her words and perhaps some direct conversation may help. *He seems to be the soul of discretion and while being direct in some things, he is not so much in others.*

"Miss Buchanan," Dr. Carrow began leaning forward in his chair. "I understand you are in mourning, though perchance afterward, would you allow me to see you more? Not to court, unless that is your desire, but to get to know each other better for the time being until you wish for more?"

Grace was sure to keep her face impassive, so as to not disturb the man with the actions of her expressions. *What am I to do? He is a kind and thoughtful man, but my heart cannot bear to fix itself upon another.* As carefully as she could, she began, "Dr. Carrow, any woman would be remiss to not get to know you. But I must make you understand that my duties to my siblings and Mrs. Morten come before anything else. I've had suitors place a call upon my hand, and then spurn it decidedly, once they realize my attention is forever divided."

"I understand your caution, Miss Buchanan," Dr. Carrow replied. "There is all the time in the world for you to make decisions of your choosing. I would not ask you to leave your siblings behind in any manner."

"I appreciate the sentiment, for no man nor God would make me leave them," she said firmly.

"But Dr. Carrow," Mrs. Morten cried, "if you take my dear Miss Buchanan away, then whom shall my companion be? Nay, we must find you someone else to court."

"Mama!" Matthew interjected.

Grace glanced in his direction, taking note of the lump in his throat he took care to swallow. *Was he jealous? Could it be?* Grace blinked, tilting her head to the side to gaze at Matthew and wonder at what she saw.

"Mrs. Morten," Dr. Carrow smiled, "if you know of any suitable woman with a likeness to yourself, please send her immediately in my direction," he rose from his seat, still grinning broadly with his eyes twinkling as he looked about the room. "I shall take my leave. Have a pleasant evening everyone."

Matthew saw to Dr. Carrow's departure. Grace sighed, exasperated once the men were out of earshot. She leaned her head back, softly groaning. The light chuckle of Mrs. Morten brought her back to the present.

"My apologies, Mrs. Morten," Grace said, embarrassment infusing her cheeks.

Mrs. Morten waved her off. "What do you make of Dr. Carrow, dear?"

"He is nice, pleasant, and *very* charming."

"But?"

"I have too much on my plate to think of a suitor," she said hurriedly, hoping it was enough to deter the meddling woman. "I enjoy my position here and raising my siblings. I am far too busy."

Mrs. Morten gave her a disbelieving look. A glimmer caught in her eye, coupled with a knowing smile that made Grace's heart twitter.

"Well, my dear girl," Mrs. Morten said, rising from her wingback chair. "I am rather tired. Please escort me to my room, for on the morrow, we shall pay a call upon Mariah to plan the festivities and her guest list. I have an inkling you shall have plenty of suitors to choose from."

Grace linked her arm with Mrs. Morten, helping her up the steps to her chamber. "I have a feeling I will be much too busy assisting Lady Bramley to worry about such men."

"Oh?" Mrs. Morten grinned mischievously. "And what if a man, let us say Matthew, happens to ask to court you?"

"Then I shall give serious consideration to his question. But since we are all in mourning I shall stick to the rules and wishes of society for now."

Mrs. Morten chuckled. "Be sure to give Matthew hope that once the mourning period has concluded, you will entertain his pursuit."

Grace didn't know how to respond, so she smiled shyly and then helped Mrs. Morten disrobe and get readied for bed. She found that she liked these moments with Mrs. Morten. The woman was wise, straightforward, and full of love; something she imagined a wonderful mother being, one she wished would be a likeness to hers. Grace reflected on her own mother a moment, just long enough to deduce the same likeness to Mrs. Morten. *She only desires that those around her make good matches. And there is nothing wrong with a mother's heart seeking out the one meant for her son.*

"Thank you, dear Grace," Mrs. Morten said, happily tucked within her bed. "Pleasant dreams."

"Pleasant dreams, Mrs. Morten."

Grace shut the door softly behind her and made her way downstairs. She had left her sewing basket in the parlor and meant to retrieve it. Spying Matthew's study door part way opened she quietly padded over to investigate. A candle was lit within the room. Curious, Grace poked her head inside. Matthew's large hands held his hanging head.

Grace stepped inside. "Are you all right?" she softly asked.

Matthew's head jerked up. "I'm perfectly fine. How was my mother?"

"Fine. She seems to tire a touch more quickly as of late. Though she is always in excellent spirits."

Matthew nodded. "That's all well and good. I think she is rather fond of teaching Adalie how to embroider," he finished, clearing his throat. "Grace, there is something I must ask."

"I'm listening."

Matthew worked his jaw and steepled his fingers. Finally, he sighed, not meeting her steady gaze. "Are you and your siblings in need of attire?"

Grace blinked, not believing that was the real question he wanted to ask. He had to have been thinking of how Dr. Carrow had her laughing earlier. It was a very embarrassing moment, one that found her covered in muck and a promise to never speak of the innocent incident.

He must think I hold affection for the kind doctor, she noted. She made a mental note earlier to be candid with him. Now seemed as perfect a chance as any since on the morrow, they would be at Bramley Hall and Matthew would be out with his parishioners.

"I am fond of *you*, Matthew," she stated. "Which is why I gave Dr. Carrow a circumvented answer."

Matthew blanched, opening his mouth and snapping it closed. "Miss Buchanan, Grace, I–"

"I thought you should know that I hold affection for you. I value you, your forthright yet patient conversations, and your kindness to me and all you meet with. Do with the information whatever you will. 'Twas my desire to let it be known to you," she stated, taking her leave from the study.

The creak of the chair gave way to his bulk rising. But Grace was already fleeing. She didn't mean to practically run from him. The shocked expression coupled with an open-hanging mouth gave her all the answers she needed to know. She had no regrets in telling him yet she couldn't bear the possibility of his rejection and ran like a coward.

She let out a long breath, hanging her head as she leaned against her bedchamber door. Grace had ascended the stairs two at a time. *Mother used to tell me that my candor would land me into dilemmas,* she thought, heading toward her bed. *Oh well, what has been said is done. Perhaps the morrow would be more delightful since we are to plan festivities. Mayhap Matthew will seek me out once we've returned. Though it is dangerous to my heart to hope after witnessing his reaction earlier.*

Chapter Twenty-Three

Thoughts & Winking

To say that Matthew was in shock still, the morning after Grace's declaration, would be a monumental understatement. Was it not the place of a gentleman to make his feelings known first? And yet he had been reserved and distancing his regard for her. The young woman was spirited and full of surprises at almost every turn. *Here I have been denying my feelings and setting them aside as I built a solid wall around my heart, and with just a few words, she has completely turned me topsy-turvy.*

Matthew had barely slept a wink the prior eve. He could not make his mind quiet nor his heart forget her words. Her beautiful face had been in his thoughts and the anguish that had appeared moments after making her feelings known tore at him. He was responsible for that. He had tried to follow after her, yet she had fled the room from him. He was in new territory caught up in the heady rush and not sure how best to proceed. She would welcome his addresses. But was he ready to make his heart known to her? It was too soon. They would have to hide their feelings from view as there was still a respective five months before they could begin to properly court. Could one woo another in the midst of mourning? There would be no dances, nor carriage rides, no walks. They could not be seen to be in each other's company as it would ruin both of their reputations. Would she be happy to be courted under such limitations? Would that he could make the coming months flee in the span of just a few minutes.

He took his breakfast in his study and remained, even when he heard the others rising and going about their day. When it was time for his mother and Grace to depart in the Bramley carriage he finally ventured from his study. He made his way to the front door where Mr. Trawley was handing over their cloaks. When the ladies were appropriately attired for the out of doors, he offered his arm to his mother. He escorted her to the awaiting carriage and helped her climb into it. Then he turned to assist Grace. She would not meet his gaze. He took her gloved hand in his and halted her progress. He leaned toward her.

"I would like to converse with you this evening, if you would be so kind as to lend me your company," he stated.

Grace rose her gaze to his with surprise expressed upon her features. She nodded at him and then began to mount the wooden steps that led her into the carriage. Once she was seated and facing in his direction again, her face held a small smile for him; she appeared nervous as to what it was that he wanted to converse about. He didn't want her spending her entire day worrying and so before he closed the carriage door he leaned his head in and winked at her as he gave her a slow smile. He suspected that the dimple in his right cheek was making an appearance. Grace smiled with more radiance and it made his heart stutter. *She is breathtaking!* He caught his mother's eye as he closed the door and she winked back at him. He was in no doubt that his mother had seen his wink as she had returned his expression. She could make of it what she so desired. He meant to lay his heart bare and see what came of it.

Matthew watched the carriage travel down the lane and then, when he could view it no more, he strode back into the parsonage.

He grabbed his greatcoat from the peg by the front door and put it on. Then he donned his top hat and took up his walking cane, and set out for his day. He made his way to the small stable where he saddled Minnow. It was quick work and once it had been accomplished, Matthew mounted his steed and directed the mahogany horse toward the town.

Within minutes he had tied Minnow to a pole and was making his calls upon his parishioners. He never stayed longer than fifteen minutes and never took refreshment either. He was not visiting to seek entertainment nor sustenance. His calling was to see how everyone was faring and what was needed to ensure that they made it through the winter weather, which was soon to arrive. He had given his word to Harrison to comprise a detailed list. Before noon, he learned that wood, blankets, and non-perishable foodstuffs would be welcomed by several of the elderly. There were some children in need of new boots and coats. His father had had the knack for instantly taking in a room and knowing what was amiss or what need was persistent and acted accordingly. Matthew had yet to master such a skill and so he had to be diligent in his attentions.

When his stomach rumbled, he knew he should soon return home, but had one more stop to make. He entered the establishment and located bolts of fabrics in blacks and browns. He was at a loss as to how he was to calculate how much was needed of each, but he figured if he overbought, he could always find a use for the material. So, he purchased it along with buttons and lace. He reckoned that he had enough to make up several pairs of trousers as well as a dress or two for Grace and Adalie. He wanted to give these items to Grace this evening to show he was sensitive to her needs. With arms laden down, he wished he'd thought to bring the buggy to town with him. But he shrugged his shoulders. 'Twas too late to lament about it now. He would just have to make do. He exited the shoppe and was walking toward Minnow when he heard a familiar voice that made his blood boil.

"Ho there, friend. May I assist you in returning to the parsonage?" Dr. Carrow's strong masculine voice rang out from within his buggy.

Matthew looked up and saw the smile that lit up the physician's face. He wanted to frown thoroughly and mayhap stomp his feet the few steps that it would take to reach Minnow, but he refrained. He looked to Minnow, wondering just how he was to mount the animal when his arms were so filled. Feeling like an imbecile, he greeted the doctor.

"That would be most appreciated." Matthew walked to the buggy and began to lighten his load. When every parcel was deposited, he retrieved Minnow and tied him to the back of the buggy. He patted Minnow's dark neck and walked to the front of the buggy and climbed into it.

"I wanted to thank you again for the invitation to dine last night," said Dr. Carrow as he led the buggy down through town.

"We were happy to have your company," Matthew cringed at the small lie. *Forgive me, Father.*

"Pray, please tell me if I was out of line in being so direct with Miss Buchanan."

"That is not for me to say. You are sensible to the fact that she is still in mourning."

"Aye, but she is quite pretty and since you have lifted her from her dire situation, I thought it prudent to make my wishes known before some other chap did." Dr. Carrow adjusted his topper.

"Do you mean to imply that if she were still living as she were that you would not have singled her out?" Matthew tried to keep the dark cloud that was hovering over him at bay.

"Not at all what I meant. You have simply made the option of calling on her more accommodating."

"Ah, I see." Matthew did not desire to have this conversation any longer. He had great respect for the man beside him and he really did not want to lose him as a friend. *Have I made it easier for another man to court her?* The thought soured his stomach and his hunger went away.

"Is Miss Buchanan presently within the parsonage, or has she ventured out?"

"She and Mama are currently paying a call upon my sister. They mean to stay until the children return from school." Matthew turned his head to look at him. He spied the quickly masked look of dismay.

"Another time then, mayhap." Dr. Carrow fell into silence and Matthew was happy to leave him alone to his thoughts. *I do not desire to hear him prattle on about Grace.*

The parsonage came into view and it was mere moments before the doctor stopped the horse. Mr. Trawley came from his place inside the house, stationed by the front door. The kind servant proceeded to take the parcels that Matthew directed him to. When Matthew alighted from the buggy, he turned to his friend.

"Thank you for your assistance," Matthew's address was stiff and formal.

Drawing his golden brows together, Dr. Carrow looked him over. "Is everything all right?"

"Splendidly. I apologize if I appear curt. There is a lot on my mind presently. Shall we see you for afternoon tea this week?" Matthew waited patiently for his reply. He wanted to be anywhere but standing where he was.

"I shall take you up on that! I plan to call upon Mrs. Morten on Thursday to see how she is feeling. I can certainly make the time to take tea with your household. It will put me in close proximity to begin my wooing of Miss Buchanan."

Matthew was thankful that he had not taken his topper from his head, or his clenched fist would have ruined it. As it was, the head upon his walking cane made a popping sound. 'Twould not surprise Matthew if it completely crumbled within his gloved hand. His grip was so tight upon it. Recalling that this had been his father's cane, he loosened his hold.

"Indeed. Are you certain that she welcomes your attention?"

"I am. She has always been so enthusiastic within my presence and last night she did not shy away from me." Dr. Carrow said thoughtfully.

Matthew didn't know how to reply to that. Yet, her words of "*I am fond of you Matthew*" kept repeating within his mind. He felt sure that she was sincere in her words and that she was not the sort to court attention from one when she was interested in another. But how to tell his friend that information? *I don't dare share a thing until I have spoken with Grace. I have no qualms about setting the doctor straight, but 'tis not my place at present.* What if after getting to know either man, she came to care for one more than the other? And the other was not he?

Chapter Twenty-Four

Time Ticks Slowly

G race couldn't seem to focus at all while at Bramley Hall. She added her input in regards to menu planning since Mariah wanted all who came to be comfortable and well impressed with the fare presented before them for the Yule Ball that was to take place on the eve following Boxing Day. They discussed which of the latest dances would do and from whence to hire the musicians. As the entire family was still in mourning, the idea to invite from the social set of the Earl and Countess of Bramley was set aside. Instead, they would invite the town of Bramley to partake of their good cheer and only meet with the townspeople in greeting. The servants could see to the rest. Anyone who wished to censure them for that was welcome to do so. Other than those menial tasks, she was at a loss. Her mind was elsewhere. In fact, her mind was on the moment Matthew winked at her. Mariah and Mrs.

Morten took it upon themselves to plan the guest list as she cared for Daniel.

Grace rocked Daniel in her arms while thinking about last night. When Matthew openly gazed at her like a deer caught in a foot trap, she realized then her mistake of being so bold. Granted, she wanted to tell him she esteemed him and only him, and was hopeful for a pleasant response. When he had said nothing, she left. Though today, when he winked at her, she felt assured all would be set to right once they were able to speak. How she wished it were now, just to know where she stood in the midst of it all. *This worrying and wondering is doing me no good.*

And after last night with Dr. Carrow asking to call upon her, she wasn't sure what to make of it all at present. If Matthew made his intentions known tonight, she would happily tell the doctor to all but take his leave of her. And if Matthew said nothing, what would she do then? Dr. Carrow never cared to speak so candidly with her prior to her position at the parsonage. *'Tis a curious development to be sure.*

Grace grimaced slightly. *Fickle men,* she decided. *The only genuine one is Matthew. Goodness, how I wish he esteems me in the same manner as I do him. I don't think I could bear his rejection. And if he does so happen to spurn me, I sure as the sunrise won't go for Dr. Carrow and his well-practiced grin.* She refrained from blowing her lips in an unladylike fashion that she was known to do when annoyed. *I must endure this slow passage of time until tonight when we can talk. I swear I may die first from waiting.*

Daniel cooed in her arms and she adjusted him. The little one passed gas and then closed his sapphire colored-eyes. Grace giggled.

"Dear Grace," Mrs. Morten smiled demurely, taking a sip of tea, "tell me, what was the wink Matthew gave you about?"

"Mama!" Mariah chided, casting her a knowing look as well. "Let them decide for themselves what to make of it all."

"Tosh! The last time a man of the family decided for themselves, it got him saddled with a ninny! And think of just how long that discovery took to make. Granted, I do love the sweet side of my daughter-in-law but one cannot be in public with her for an extended period."

Grace drew in her lips. She had an inkling to whom Mrs. Morten was referring to being the middle child of the Morten family. As there was only one other son it was not a difficult conclusion to reach. 'Twas more a kindness that she acted as if she was in the dark as to whom they could mean.

Mariah choked on her tea, setting it down and into the saucer. "Mama, Grace and I shall return in a moment. I need her assistance to put Daniel down for his afternoon nap."

"Hurry back, dear."

Grace rose from her seat, rocking Daniel in her arms. The little cherub was almost asleep. Grace followed Mariah up the stairs and into the nursery that a cousin of Mariah's had beautifully painted. The nanny waited patiently off to the side to take charge of the wee one. She was remiss to set the child down, but she did so with practiced ease since having to care for Adalie so young had given her the skills. Daniel didn't even squirm or make a fuss as Grace gently rolled him onto his back.

"Thank you for coaxing him to slumber," Mariah sighed exhaustedly. "I am at a loss at what to do at moments when he gets so fussy. Nanny would rather that he cry it out, but I cannot bring myself to follow her directions, nor can his Papa."

Grace nodded. "Adalie was much like Daniel as a babe. I found holding Adalie on her stomach in my arms, as you saw me do with Daniel, makes them content. They also release a bit of flatulence in that position," she smiled softly.

Mariah returned the smile. "Well, at least 'tis a trait not inherited by us."

"Indeed! Always best to put the blame where it rightfully belongs."

Mariah chortled, leading her out of the room with Daniel asleep in the crib. "May I ask you something? And please, do not feel inclined to answer if you do not wish to, as it is a bit forward."

Grace's brows furrowed. "You may ask me anything."

" All right then," Mariah softly cleared her throat and paused. "How do you find Matthew? And by that I mean, do you fancy him?"

Grace couldn't stop the blush from infusing her cheeks even if she were in her grave. "I do. I told Matthew so last eve, after Dr. Carrow left and made his intentions in desiring to know me better." Grace pursed her lips and met Mariah's widened gaze. "How would

I go about refusing Dr. Carrow? I believe I can be a touch direct for the soft doctor and I would not wish to injure his feelings for all the world."

Mariah linked her arm with Grace's as they descended the staircase. "I think you being your direct self is just what both of those men need," she grinned broadly. "I am delighted that you fancy Matthew. Not many women find his dry sense of humor charming. He has always been strict even as a child. But I do remember, even as children, how he was never that way with you."

Grace giggled. "My humor is pretty dry. I think it blends well. In truth, I've always fancied him. I'm surprised he returned and was also unattached."

Mariah tucked in her lips, giving credence that she did not believe he would have been taken. Grace considered herself a lucky woman. Matthew was strict as Mariah had pointed out. She figured, in part, it was due to his upbringing, but even the late Mr. Morten had a soft side with the same dry wit. Mayhap she could help Matthew discover it as well?

They landed on the bottom of the stairs where Billingsley announced luncheon. Together, the ladies collected Mrs. Morten and went to dine on a light lunch. Lord Bramley was out settling business with the neighboring Earl of Hathwell, so it was more talk of planning the upcoming festivities. Already every detail was described and noted for preparations to begin shortly. Grace wasn't absolutely certain of the time, but she believed, per Mariah's meticulous care, that the festivities would begin in three weeks' time. Mariah had promised Harrison's cousin that when it came time for her to take to her childbed, that she would be in attendance upon her. The same cousin was also her dear friend and had attended the birth of Daniel. If this should come to pass at the time nearing the festivities, then Mrs. Morten and herself would oversee the preparations and have them completed not on the eve of Christmas as was custom, but a day or two before. Family guests were to begin arriving and Mariah did not wish to waste time nor energy in completing the decorating while they were set to entertain, especially if Mariah herself had been traveling.

Grace glanced outside briefly, noting the time and how it ticked ever so sluggishly. She wished to be able to speak to Matthew now to discern his feelings. She disliked the anxiousness in her stomach and the never-ending butterflies swirling within her breast. Grace desired him to like her, though it was a selfish thing.

She let out a long sigh, forcing her mind to not ponder upon his deep chocolate eyes nor how the stubble lined his masculine jaw. She wriggled in her seat to further not think upon Matthew's lips descending onto hers in a salacious kiss that she craved and would forever dream about. To be held within his arms, even for a mere moment, she swore would sustain her forevermore. *What would his lips feel like pressed against mine? Would they be timid or would Matthew take control of the situation? Would he be patient or demand that I engage fully with him?*

However, the demands of society that they not court nor partake in socializing due to being in mourning was something she did not understand. Why must one grieve so long? Not only that, but why must she grieve for a man who did nothing but cause harm to her and her siblings? She understood grieving for a man like Mr. Morten, but to grieve a man like her Papa was a foolish waste of time.

Grace sighed, thinking upon Matthew. *If I could steal a kiss from Matthew, I happily would,* she decided. *Burn society. 'Tis nothing but a gossiping gaggle of ninnies to sully and bring down the name of another. Just one kiss would be the fire to keep me going. Even if nothing ever became of us, I would forever treasure that moment.*

"Grace dear," Mrs. Morten addressed.

Grace snapped from her thoughts regarding Matthew. "Yes, Mrs. Morten?"

"I never did obtain the answer as to why Matthew winked at you earlier this morning," she smiled slyly.

Grace dipped her head, feeling heat rise to her cheeks. "Though 'tis not proper, may I be so bold as to state my feelings?"

"Please do. I am rather fond of your candor. Alicia, the ninny-headed woman she is, could learn from you. I must say, only in front of you ladies, I am absolutely terrified of the life Simon and Alicia are about to bring forth into this world. Perhaps it was a decent thing the Lord took my Mr. Morten when he did so as to spare him the wrath of another Simon."

Mariah sputtered her drink.

Grace blinked, not knowing what to say. "Pardon?" she asked.

Mariah cleared her throat softly, "Alicia is my sister-in-law. Our brother Simon's wife. I feel sure that you have met her at church on several of the occasions that they have attended upon us. She is rather... tactlessly forward and says the most improper things. But she is a dear person who would do anything for someone she cares for."

Grace nodded. "Well," she paused, not knowing where to begin after that rather candid moment. "I am rather fond of Matthew. Though I cannot state how he feels about me, he wishes to speak to me this evening."

Mrs. Morten clapped her hands. "Most excellent! You are a good match for Matthew."

"I agree," Mariah said, wiping her hands on a cloth napkin. "And this upcoming holiday season will be wonderful. I shall have a dress made for you to be sure to catch Matthew's attention."

Mrs. Morten sighed and rolled her eyes. "I love my son dearly. Lord knows I do. But he can be such a stick. Please, dearest daughter, find Grace a bold, appropriate color to catch his strict eye. I care not for the wagging tongues of society from which here in the country we can safely be sheltered."

Grace heated, looking out the window again to find the passage of time forever stuck. She longed to disappear from the room and to finally be in Matthew's company. Hopefully, he would make her feel comfortable again. *And what would a bold-colored dress do anyway?*

Chapter Twenty-Five

Heart To Heart

The day was dragging. *Has any day ever been so long before?* Matthew paced his study floor so many times that he lost count. Afternoon shadows began to descend when he heard the sound of the children running up the lane from town. He drew a deep breath and then let it out. 'Twas best to greet them at the door to keep a watchful gaze upon them.

Making his way from his study and to the front door, his hand found the knob and twisted it, giving him a full view of the children. They had come to a stop and Adalie was breathless. She gave him a beaming smile and ran to him. Her little arms encircled his legs as she hugged him. Matthew patted her upon the back.

"How were your studies today?" he asked.

"Long and arduous," said Thayer to which Fraser heartily agreed.

"Well, how about we change your clothing and get ready for afternoon tea?" Matthew suggested.

Adalie let him go and ran up the staircase with her brothers following closely behind her. He shook his head at their energy. He went to close the door when the Bramley carriage came into view. When it had stopped, he walked from the parsonage and waved away the Bramley servant in order to open the carriage door himself. Grace met his view first and she smiled at him, but he took note of the fact that her face seemed taut. She helped Mrs. Morten to rise and then Matthew was assisting her down the wooden steps and to the ground. His mother looked up at him and patted him upon his arm.

"You're a good boy, my son," Mrs. Morten winked at him.

He frowned down at her. "Er, thank you," he said, wondering if he was asking a question.

Mrs. Morten let his arm go and stood to the side, allowing Matthew to turn back toward the carriage, but Grace was climbing down from it, unaided. By the time he held his hand aloft to her, she had gained the ground and so he let his hand drop back down to his side. Grace ducked her head without meeting his eyes. Her bonnet kept her face from his view. He felt an acute sense of disappointment by that.

Matthew turned back to his mother and offered her his arm which she took. He led her into the parsonage where Mr. Trawley stood awaiting their cloaks. The ladies handed them over and removed their bonnets, which Grace took to their bedchambers along with their reticules. Matthew watched her ascend the staircase and when she was removed from his view he turned to his mother.

"You need not fear, Mariah and I have all well in hand," Mrs. Morten stated as she patted his cheek.

"What are you in the mix of, Mama?" he wearily inquired as he guided her into the parlor. He took her to the fireplace and waited for her to sit in the wingback chair before he sat across from her. He leaned forward in his seat awaiting her reply.

"Just matters."

"If you are endeavoring any matters that pertain to me, I beg of you to please refrain at once. I am not in need of your particular brand of help." Matthew regarded her with a frown.

"*Tsk.* A mother knows when to push and when to pull back. I have your best interest at heart. Speaking of hearts, what is it that you mean to discuss privately with Grace?" She met his gaze with a challenging look alight within her hazel eyes.

Matthew could not contain the groan that escaped him. Could he not undertake anything and not have to explain himself? "'Tis not your place to question me, Mama."

Spluttering, Mrs. Morten sat forward and pointed a finger at him. "Not my place! She is *my* companion, or has that escaped your mind?"

"Indeed, I am well aware of the fact."

"You are a kind gentleman, I know this, but if you plan to toy with her emotions, I shall make you regret it."

"I am sorry, I have not had the pleasure of understanding you. Do you mean to suggest that I harbor ill-intentions where Miss Buchanan is concerned? Do you know me at all, Mama?"

"I thought I did. But you have always been so difficult for me to discern. I know you are honor itself, but I fear for Grace. Especially now that our dear Dr. Carrow is sniffing about her skirts." She tilted her head to the side.

"Mama! Where have you learned such brash language?"

"Have you met my youngest son?"

"I shall seriously consider before I let him enter the house next." Matthew raised his dark brows. "See here, Mama. Can you not let me handle things, if there is anything to handle, between Miss Buchanan and myself?"

Mrs. Morten nodded. "I fear it might be too late."

"What? What have you done, Mama?"

Before Mrs. Morten could answer, the steps were creaking letting them know that their private conversation was at an end and that they would soon have guests. The boys were talking as they entered the room. They each came forward and placed a kiss upon Mrs. Morten's cheek. Then, they quietly sat in their chairs and awaited the presence of Grace and Adalie.

Grace held onto Adalie's small hand and together they came into the parlor. They sat down upon the settee and arranged their skirts. Mr. Trawley peeked his head into the room and then disappeared. There was no need to ask him to see that the tea items were brought, as he knew the routine.

Matthew would not look at Grace. His thoughts were filled with dismay. What was his mother planning and was Grace knowledgeable of it? Or was she simply caught up in the midst of an older woman's schemes? He did not think that Grace was actually capable of scheming and that thought gave him some measure of comfort.

Dinner was as tame as it could be with three children present wanting to have their share of the conversation. Matthew did not care, it saved him from having to participate. His mouth was growing more dry as the seconds ticked by. *Were the ticking clock hands particularly loud this evening?* The day was finally winding down, but Matthew was feeling more wound up. His conversation with Grace was soon to take place. How was he to begin such an intimate subject?

When his mother indicated that she was finished, he rose to pull out her chair and assist her to the parlor where Thayer was to read to them this evening from one of his favorite books. He had a keen mind, and when applied properly, he was a master at solving difficult riddles. Grace and her siblings soon followed and they were all happily situated in their respective places. The fire was roaring and the room was toasty. The familiar setting pulled upon his heart. He longed to always have this scene enacted out before his eyes.

Matthew tried to listen to Thayer, but his mind was wandering. He cast his gaze over to Grace and finally allowed himself to drink in her beauty. She was ethereal. She was beautiful to behold and when she met his gaze and smiled, he felt as if he beheld the most precious treasure he would ever meet. Her expressive hazel eyes, set in a heart-shaped face, was a permanent fixture within his mind. He knew that were he to spend every minute of every day locked upon her face, he would never tire of her. Her smiles delighted him and when he was the cause of one, it was as if he had been gifted the riches of heaven. She was glorious and he hoped to tell her that presently. And when she was out of sorts, he felt the pain within his own chest. He was a besotted fool and none the worse for it that he could tell unless he counted his wandering thoughts.

Mrs. Morten began to yawn behind her hand and Grace rose to assist her to her bedchamber. Matthew immediately rose as well and bid his mother a pleasant slumber. He watched as Grace and Adalie escorted his mother up the stairs and then indicated that it was time for the boys to retire as well. He followed after them and once they were readied for bed, he heard their bedtime prayers.

"Thank you, God, for allowing us another day. Thank you for your blessings and your forgiveness when we are naughty," Thayer began.

"And help us not to be naughty, I would especially be thankful for that," added Fraser.

"Bless our family and friends and give us all a pleasant sleep."

"And one more thing. God, if you could please see that we have found our permanent home soon, we would appreciate that. Grace needs a husband and we need to know that no matter what mischief we wreak, that we will not be tossed out. Amen." Fraser let out a small sigh and climbed into bed, followed by Thayer.

Matthew wanted to simultaneously chuckle and rub and hand over his aching chest. *These precious boys,* he thought. He bid them a good night as he tucked them in.

Exiting their bedchamber, he met Grace at her bedchamber door. She softly closed it and smiled up at him. With a finger to her lips, she turned and made her way down the staircase and he followed. When they reached his study, he opened the door and let her pass into the room before him. He entered and lit the candles on his desk.

"Please, make yourself comfortable," he said.

Once Grace was seated, he went around to his desk and started placing the parcels he had earlier purchased upon his mahogany desk. He saw the puzzled look upon Grace's face and kept his mirth at bay. When the last brown paper package was set down he rounded his desk and came to take the chair beside Grace. He indicted the loaded desk.

"I did some shopping today. I have noticed how the boys are rapidly growing and it was my wish to provide fabric and the trimming for new clothing, not only for the twins, but for yourself and Adalie as well. Please understand that no matter how our conversation concludes this eve, these are happily gifted to you and I am glad to be of service." Matthew finished and watched as Grace's gaze flittered from him to the packages and back again.

"I cannot thank you enough, Matthew. You didn't have to go out of your way for us. I had plans to modify the clothing situation." Grace twisted her fingers in her lap.

"I've no doubt that you did. But I saw the need and had already made up my mind to act when you spoke to me last evening. This brings me joy. Allow me to do this for you, for them." Matthew earnestly held her gaze.

Grace smiled through her tears. "Matthew, no one has ever treated us as you have, as your family has. We are so blessed to be under your roof and this is," she waved her hand at the desk, "above and beyond."

"Nothing is above nor beyond where you and those dear children are concerned. Grace, this is your home now. 'Tis my greatest hope that this shall forevermore be your home. For, I could not abide it if you took another's hand in marriage when I feel the way I do about you. I am wholly invested in your happiness and that of your siblings. If you would consider waiting out this mourning period, I shall properly court you. You deserve to be courted as any young woman would be. I know that your position within the household is a new development, but 'tis my wish that we would grow closer together as we seek the Lord's will in our relationship. Though you have given your consent to Dr. Carrow to pay his addresses, will you allow me to do the same to see what a wonderous future we could build together?" Matthew ceased his words, which rambled around a bit, and held his breath. He felt certain she would not refuse him, but there were no absolute certainties in life. *Lord, this is in your hands now. Please let her speak her heart and mind with no fear for my own heart.*

Chapter Twenty-Six

Spoken From The Heart

Grace felt her throat thicken. Matthew's strong gaze holding hers made her feel pinned to the moment. She forgot what it was like to breathe. Thankfully her heart kept beating, pounding so much within her chest that she was certain Matthew could see it. Surely, he had just said that he was enamored of her. She was hearing correctly, wasn't she?

His deep chocolate eyes roved hers for an answer she had yet to give. How could she answer him when her mouth refused to work as her heart was overflowing with joy. Tears sprang into her eyes of their own accord. If she dared kiss him now, would he allow it? She seriously doubted a man of the cloth such as he would permit such a bold statement. *I barely know what to do with myself, I long to express my joy.*

"Matthew," she began, earnestly begging for his heart to understand hers.

Dejectedly, the man rose from his seat, his head hanging down. Her tears had been misconstrued by him, and it panged her heart for the briefest second, as she forced herself to snap from the moment to reply with her assurance.

Grace reached out and grasped his hand. "Forgive me. I find my heart pounding and my breath catching for I cannot fathom my same sentiments toward you being returned. Whether in mourning or not, I welcome you to court me," she sniffed, wiping her eyes. "I find it difficult that a man such as you would be desiring me and all that I bring with me. I adore you, Matthew. Wholeheartedly so. And it is my deepest desire to see you happy."

"Grace," he said, leaning over the arm of the chair as he wiped her tears away. "Having you near me, with me, brings me such joy. I cannot imagine a day without you in it, nor do I care to. To have you by my side, 'tis all I could wish for. These feelings came upon me so fiercely that I am unable to deny them any longer, nor do I wish to."

"Oh, Matthew," she cried into her hands for she could not meet his eyes any longer, such were the overwhelming feelings that consumed her.

"Dearest, tell me why you're crying. Is it something I've said?"

Grace shook her head. The endearment he had just addressed her by took her by surprise and it was a moment for her to treasure. "No. I am just deliriously happy. I do not know what to do with myself. You are all I have ever wanted. Since we were children it was you that I measured all other men against. And despite the circumstances of your returning back here to Bramley, I find myself selfishly happy you're not taken. For I desire to call you mine, forevermore."

Matthew picked up her hand, placing a gentle, warm kiss upon the back of it, the stubble of his jaw poked her hand and its texture thrilled her being. She loved it. Her entire body erupted with fire as it filled every void she had ever felt. All of her life, since her mother's passing, she desired to have a forever love, a love everlasting in its promise that not even darkness or harrowed times could break. Could she attain that dream with Matthew?

Was she surely dreaming as she had all those years ago as a young girl, turned woman?

"I never knew what I was missing in my life until I saw you again that night at your cottage. Your resilience and love outshone the darkness in that oppressive dwelling. And in that moment, I swore to myself that if I were ever blessed to merit such a woman, it must be you. But I did not let myself hope in earnest until you came to stay with us. And 'twas firmly fixed within my mind when Dr. Carrow sought your company, that I was a greater fool than even I knew, as you might be lost to me forevermore."

Not giving a single care, Grace leaned forward in her seat and claimed his warm lips. She held him against herself there a moment with a hand on the side of his face, deepening her kiss. His hot, soft lips sent a shiver up her spine. His warm breath tingled her nose as she inhaled all that he was. She committed this moment, his tenderness to heart; for as long as she lived, she would never forget this. Carefully, she disconnected her lips from his, already remiss that she had so boldly forced herself upon him. *Please let him not think that ill of me, not now.*

"I hope that will allay any concerns you may have had. And as far as Dr. Carrow is concerned, I shall refuse him most adamantly. You are all I desire."

"There is no mistaking that," Matthew smiled, cupping her cheek with his warm large hand. His chocolate gaze locked with her own.

"I would hope not," she replied, matching his dry humor. "I feel as though I should apologize for being so forward, and yet, I find myself without apology for what I've done."

Matthew grinned broadly. "Well, I find myself desiring to not hear one pass from your sweet lips. But may I ask that you allow me to properly court you and bestow affection in the future?"

Grace nodded, understanding what he meant. "As you wish. Thank you and thank you for the fabric and odds and ends."

"'Tis my pleasure. Pray, let me know if you require anything else. I confess that I have never needed to shop for such items before."

Grace rose from her chair and Matthew rose with her. She felt a tinge of embarrassment creep into her being. Though, from the open expression on Matthew's face, he bore no ill-feeling toward her. *Indeed, he looks like a besotted man.*

Softly she cleared her throat, "I shall retire now. Adalie will be wondering what has become of me. On the morrow, your mama is going to have me gathering, sorting, and seeing to many other tasks now that the festivities are not long at hand."

Matthew nodded, taking her hand and placing a gentle kiss upon the back of it. "I'm certain Mama will keep you busy. She loves the winter season. May I walk you to your chamber door?"

"Please do."

Grace linked her arm in with Matthew as he led her up the staircase and to her bedchamber door. The warmth of his person at her side seeped into her body. She closed her eyes at it, relishing the moment and the touch shared with someone that held her heart and returned her regard.

"What do you have planned for the morrow?" Grace asked.

"I have a sermon to write and I need to finalize a list for Harrison for the village."

"May I be of assistance?"

Matthew smiled, patting her hand. "I would not want to take you away from your duties."

Grace took the hint. Though she wanted to not feel the pang in her chest from being rebuked, she would allow him his space. She believed having someone so forward with one's feelings was making him uncomfortable. She would allow him space so he could do what he pleased in terms of their budding relationship. In all, she was just pleased he liked her as well and accepted her feelings toward him. *Time is what he needs and I shall endeavor to be patient as this new thing between us blossoms. I shall let him take the lead as that is what he wishes.*

"I bid you a pleasant slumber, Matthew."

"And I, you, Grace," he returned, bowing over her hand with a delicate whisper of a kiss as he left her at her chamber door.

She tilted her head to the side and watched him descend the staircase. Was it her kiss that affected him so, making him seem almost bashful? She was not sorry for what she'd done. Though now, she would take more caution into what she would say or do. Matthew was a strict man, desiring to follow the rules of the world. She was not like that at all. If anything, she hoped she could get him to let go a little bit of the tight reins of control he had, but she doubted her efforts would do much good. He was a good man, set in his ways, and she was the woman who adored him. *I do not seek to change him so much as help him to bend my way a bit here and there.*

Grace shrugged it off, heading inside her bedchamber. She let her hair down and finger-combed it, then she braided it tying its end with a black ribbon. Quietly, she disrobed and donned her nightgown. Grace climbed into the cold sheets beside Adalie who was fast asleep. Tomorrow would be a busy day sewing clothes for her siblings and preparing for the festivities.

And mayhap tomorrow, I can steal another quiet moment with Matthew and get to know him more, she thought, turning on her side to stare at the door. *I would love to see him smile more and hear him laugh. I don't think I've ever heard it.* Grace wriggled, laying on her back. *Whatever is to become of us, all I desire is his happiness. After all he has done for me, I shall do all I can for him.*

Chapter Twenty-Seven

A Grumpy Man

A fortnight had passed since Matthew had declared himself to Grace and things had been running smoothly ever since, somewhat. He delighted in seeing the new clothing Grace and his mother had sewn for the Buchanan siblings. They were all looking healthier with balanced meals and praise where 'twas due. He was never short on patience no matter the vast quantity of questions nor the reminders he gave out to ensure that they were growing into proper individuals. He discovered qualities to foster in each child and delighted in seeing them thrive where their interests lie.

He had yet to spend any alone time with Grace, and at first, that was his desire. He feared what another kiss would do to his sense of honor. He rather longed to be the one doing the wooing and yet, he did not know how to go about it. For the first time in his existence, he found that he wished for Simon's company. The man would have had an abundant amount of advice and he was in sore need of it. *Must it be so complicated? If it were Spring, and we were out of mourning, I could take her on a picnic, or for a ride in the buggy. I could present her with a bouquet.* Those were simple things many couples had done ever since time began. But this was not an ordinary situation and she was no ordinary woman. He desired to spoil her and make her understand that he would do anything for her. He found that he was missing her even when they were in the same room; he wanted her by his side. He was growing irritated as time passed. This constant longing would not do. He was getting easily distracted and all morning he had been in a grumpy state.

Mama had taken to bed with the megrims and Amy was attending to her. The children were seeing to their outside chores under the watchful gaze of Mr. Trawley. Matthew blew out a breath, 'twas now or never he reasoned. He went in search of Grace.

Grace was sitting quietly in the parlor bent over sewing. The sunlight from the window lit her brunette curls that hung on either side of her face. She seemed to glow. The sight made him catch his breath and rub a hand over his aching chest. How could such an enchantress have chosen him?

"Are you busy?" he asked as he entered the parlor.

Grace looked up at him with a beaming smile upon her face. "Not at all. I was merely seeing to a mundane task, but I would much rather be of service to you."

"May I sit with you? 'Tis not proper, but I find that I don't care." Matthew smirked.

"Neither do I. By all means, please do." Grace slid over a few inches upon the settee to give his larger frame space.

Matthew knew he should seat himself as far from her side as the room would allow, but he could not keep from claiming the spot beside her. Grace was putting the sewing into a basket and he took it from her once she was finished and set it down to the side of them. He gently lifted her hand and turning it over, he placed a gentle kiss upon her palm. Then he put her hand upon his chest over his heart and sighed. Grace was smiling at him with delight and he felt like he could gather stardust from the heavens.

"I am remiss. I should have sought you out earlier, but we have both been busy. I mean to rectify that today. Even if only for a few minutes." He brought her hand to rest on the settee between them as he caressed her delicate skin. Her hands were not as work-rough as they had been, and he enjoyed the contrast of her skin against his. The softness of her skin was a testament that she no longer had to toil away to greet each new day.

"You are here with me now, and I am thrilled to have you all to myself."

"We have no chaperone," he reminded her.

"Right you are. We do not, but as we are neither too young, I think we shall fare well enough. What made you seek me out?"

Swallowing he met her hazel gaze. "I couldn't stand my own company any longer. I have made myself most miserable with missing you and there is no reason why I cannot spend this time with you while the house is blessedly quiet."

"You missed me? But, dear man, I have been here under your eaves the entire time."

"Aye, that you have," he admitted.

"I am glad you sought me out. I was missing you dreadfully. 'Tis horrid to sit across the dinner table or take tea with you and not be by your side." She leaned her head against his shoulder.

Matthew leaned his own head down to place a chaste kiss atop her head. He nuzzled his nose within her pinned curls and breathed in her scent of roses and some spice that eluded him. "Have you any idea how one goes about courting without actually courting? I cannot pay a call upon you, nor bring you sweets. I cannot drive about the countryside with you nor walk with you as we shop through town. I have been wracking my brain for ways to spend time with you."

"This is much preferred to walking through town."

"But there is nothing remarkable occurring save my being next to you."

"Must there be? Our situation is very odd, you must allow that our courtship would be the same? I don't require much, just to talk with me, to sit with me. I was worried you would never seek me out." She looked up at him and pouted.

"I tried. A few times, but you are always in the midst of things. I have no wish to take you away from your priorities."

"Matthew, you are my priority. We must learn to make time."

"You are right. I will do better, I promise, dearest." He smiled at her and then squeezed her hand gently.

The sound of a buggy's wheels and the clip-clop of horse hooves could be heard coming down the lane. Matthew scowled at the window wondering who that could be. Then realization hit him and he cringed.

"Who is it?" Gace asked.

"Your would-be suitor, the aloof Dr. Carrow. I took his absence while tending to his patients as a sign of divine intervention, but now I see that 'tis time we dealt with his wishes to call upon you. I forgot that I sent him a missive this morning about Mama." Matthew rose from the settee and peered out the window. "Indeed, 'tis he."

"Mayhap we can just continue on as we were and let him make the conclusions he wishes to, with me cozying up to you." Grace batted her long dark lashes at him.

Matthew chuckled and said, "Minx." Then he walked from the parlor to the front door. He opened it and welcomed the doctor in. "Thank you for visiting. Mama has taken to her bed."

"I am sorry to hear it. No doubt we shall soon see her up and about." Dr. Carrow removed his topper and handed that and his greatcoat to Matthew who turned to hang them on the wall peg. He turned back around in time to witness the physician walking toward Grace.

"I am sorry to have disappeared on you, fair lady," Dr. Carrow said as he took Grace's hand and bowing over it, kissed her bare knuckles. Matthew wanted to lay the man out.

"You are too kind. Shall I take you above stairs to meet with Mrs. Morten?" Grace took her hand back and stepped away from him.

"Aye, that is part of my reason for calling," he winked at her.

Grace's eyes met Matthew's and he silently heeded her call. He closed the distance between them and came to stand beside her, mayhap a little too close, as he took note of the physician's eyebrows raising.

"What's this?" Dr. Carrow inquired. He waved his hand in their direction as he removed his gloves.

"Miss Buchanan and I are in an understanding," said Matthew.

"I see. And that means?"

"We are reserving time to court once our mourning period has passed," answered Grace.

A slow smile spread across Dr. Carrows' face as he rapped upon Matthew's back. "Huzzah! I am sure your mother is most pleased."

Matthew looked down at Grace who met his gaze. She shrugged one delicate shoulder at him.

"I see no harm in my admitting to humoring Mrs. Morten. For you see, 'twas her suggestion that I call upon the lovely Miss Buchanan. I see her reason why now. I never suspected you to harbor feelings for her, Mr. Morten. I never would have stepped upon your toes." Dr. Carrow shook his head and chuckled. "Your mother is a sly creature, well done! No harm done, my friend?" He held his hand out for Matthew to take.

Matthew met his handshake and smiled. "None. Though I can now understand that I did not credit my mother's ability to scheme to quite an extreme."

"You have no idea of what she's capable of," Grace admitted.

Matthew frowned and wondered what surprises were in store for him next.

Chapter Twenty-Eight

Compassionate Mischief

Grace went back to her sewing as Matthew sat beside her reading the newsprint. Grace smiled, loving the proximity in which they were and the lack of care of social decorum. She couldn't keep the grin from her face. *Surely, I must be rubbing off on him, she mused. His comfort with me thrills me endlessly!*

Dr. Carrow had finally departed after giving Mrs. Morten a tonic to help aid in relieving her of the megrims. She was peacefully sleeping above stairs since the house was still pleasantly quiet. The children, after completing their chores, went off to go play with other children in town while the weather was still beautiful outside. It was a nice reprieve from the rain they experienced last week and goodness knows the children needed to run around. Keeping them indoors had taxed them all.

Grace scooted closer to Matthew, resting her head upon his shoulder as she continued to sew in a delicate line. The cloth he provided had been perfect for them all. Dark colors would easily hide the wear and tear for the boys and hide all the stains for Adalie. And the lace and buttons would be great accents to her dress and a nicer one for Adalie. The clothing was coming along with the expert stitches provided by Mrs. Morten, indeed some items had already been finished.

Matthew leaned over, putting a delicate kiss atop her head. She smiled, righting herself as he went to move away from her and rose from his seat.

"I should get my next sermon written. What do you think it should be about?"

Grace pursed her lips to the side. "What about the Lord's timing? How not to worry as things will come in His superb timing?" she suggested.

Matthew beamed at her, "Most excellent," he agreed. "I shall see you at dinner."

"Happy writing," she finished with a wink.

He snorted, shaking his head as he smiled broadly. "Minx."

Grace giggled, going back to her sewing. She was hoping to have this dress done for Adalie in time for the festivities that were to be held at Bramley Hall. The last time she had spoken with Mariah, her kind friend was having a dress made for her for the occasion. It was entirely sweet of her and something that Grace really appreciated. Never had she had a dress made for her specifically nor something as fancy as Mariah had described. Currently, Mariah and her family were at Hathwell, spending time with Harrison's cousin Isabelle as she came closer to the time of welcoming the new Hathwell babe. Grace thought it was sweet that Mariah was so helpful and kind in attending to her friend. *Mayhap the little one has already made its appearance.*

Grace sighed, tying off the knot of the thread for the dress. It needed trimmings but she needed a break from this particular activity. Grace rose from her seat and stretched her back as much as her corset would allow. The back door to the house slammed closed, surprising her. Booted steps hustled up the staircase trying to drown an interesting noise between the children's steps. Frowning, Grace went to the staircase.

She spied Adalie climbing the stairs and called out to her. "Adalie, what is happening?"

"We've just returned, Gracie," the child beamed, heading up the staircase further. "We're going to get changed for dinner."

Grace nodded, heading toward the kitchen to help out and set the table. She understood the various chores it took to keep the parsonage running and had informed the maid, Amy, that she would always set the table for dinner. It was a small thing to do and she felt that contributing to that small task made life a little easier on the maid. And since Amy had been attending to Mrs. Morten most of the day, she knew this chore being accomplished would be appreciated. Mrs. Morten had been most insistent that Amy was the one to stay at her side as she wished for Grace to finish with the sewing.

Recalling the suspiciousness of the children who had returned none to stealthily, she assumed it was to rid themselves of the clothes they no doubt soiled to the point of utter destruction. Grace set out the dining ware and picked out a nice wine to be served with dessert for after. Lord Bramley was forever sending over treats for them from his own pantry. Earlier today, Grace had baked one of her mother's desserts at the insistence of Mrs. Morten to help alleviate her megrims. How a dessert was capable of accomplishing such a feat, Grace couldn't understand. However, she attributed the request to Mrs. Morten trying to push her and Matthew closer together in some way. Mayhap she desired for Matthew to learn that Grace was a superb baker?

"THAYER!" Adalie shrieked and began crying. "How could you!"

Grace bustled from the dining room, taking the stairs up two at a time. Matthew emerged from his study, scowling and meeting her worried gaze as he followed after her. Adalie was not one to cry out over a little matter, yet she stood in the hallway, in between their rooms, sobbing.

"I'm so sorry, Adalie. I needed it and did not think you would mind," Thayer replied downcast.

"Need what?" Grace inquired as she came to stand before them.

Thayer blanched. "Something... for a project," he stammered.

Adalie turned pale as she dried her tears on the back of her sleeve. The boys were indeed, as she predicted, muddy from head to toe. Even their stockings were caked in mud, but fortunately, they had the good sense to remove their boots and not track as much mud through the house. *But still what a sight they are!*

A sound caught her attention and she glanced at the boys. "What was that?" she asked.

"My stomach!" Fraser replied hastily. "I'm so hungry I could eat a horse."

"Or a cow," Adalie said, hanging her head.

"So what did you need of Adalie's, Thayer?" Matthew sternly inquired.

The noise came again, ending on a wail.

Grace perked a brow. "What was that?" she pointedly asked Fraser.

"Flatulence?" he squeaked.

Matthew snorted, turning his head to find Mrs. Morten emerging from her bedchamber.

"Is everything all right?" Mrs. Morten inquired.

The poor woman had dark circles under her eyes and her eyes themselves were red and bloodshot. The megrims must have hit her harder than they all expected. *Poor woman and all this fuss!*

"Do you want to lay back down?" Grace asked, coming to her side.

Mrs. Morten waved her off. "Nay, I am feeling better and ready for some tea. However, what was that horrid shrieking about?"

"We are trying to discover the meaning of it presently, Mama," Matthew replied. "Now children, what was that noise?"

"Flatulence," the boys replied unanimously.

The door nudged itself open, revealing a small, black calf. Grace put a hand to her mouth, shocked and trying not to laugh at the wide-eyed gaze of both Matthew and Mrs. Morten. *'Tis a certainty that the parsonage has never had a guest quite like this before.*

"How on earth did you get a calf?"

"He was abandoned by Mr. Wallace down the road. Mr. Wallace said we could keep him since we mucked out his stalls because the calf might not make it and we want to take care of him."

"But why the house?" Mrs. Morten sputtered, tucking in her lips.

"He was chilled!" Adalie cried. "And he's my best friend. And *Thayer*," she bit out his name, "wanted to keep Mervin in his room and use *my bonnet* to keep his head warm!"

Grace gave a delicate cough, attempting to hold back her laughter. Mrs. Morten sputtered, trying to contain her own mirth. It earned them both a pointed look from Matthew. Grace didn't care. This was too adorable. In all her days, she had never expected this. Usually their mischief was something idiotic without either of them thinking anything through, like the incident with the bees. This time, they had gone through the trouble of earning to have an animal. *And 'tis quite an adorable little dear, too.*

"Mr. Wallace said that you may keep this calf?" Matthew asked pointedly.

"Yessir," Adalie said, pouting and crossing her arms over herself. "We all earned Mervin. I cleaned out the chicken coop by myself," she stated proudly. "Mervin is going to get bigger and then he's going to get married."

"Mervin is never marrying, Adalie," Fraser scoffed. "Mervin is going to be a bachelor forever."

"Not so! Mervin is going to marry a beautiful cow and have a happy life."

Thayer rolled his eyes. "Well, hopefully, Mervin's wife is better than a whiny sister."

"Now children, that is quite enough," Matthew said, stepping between them. "I am very proud of you all for working together. I shall be contacting Mr. Wallace here shortly to inquire about this trade. Not that I don't believe you have earned... *Mervin*... but also to see if I can get milk to feed him. For he cannot eat from our table."

Adalie poked her head around Matthew and stuck out her tongue. The boys reciprocated.

Grace cleared her throat. "Why don't you take him outside and put him in the stable?"

"But Gracie," Adalie began, crying anew. "It is too cold out there for Mervin."

"Mervin will be fine," Matthew assured. "Stick the little calf in with Minnow. He is a gentle horse and won't mind the company."

The boys hung their heads. Together, they went on either side of Mervin and lifted him up, going in tandem down the stairs.

Thayer set the calf down, holding onto it while Fraser went to the door for his boots.

"Can Mervin have my bonnet?" Adalie asked.

"But of course," Mrs. Morten allowed. "We don't want the darling catching a cold."

Adalie beamed, wrapping her small arms around Mrs. Morten briefly before bolting down the stairs. "Wait for me!"

Once the door slammed, Grace erupted into laughter. Never had she ever thought they would bring a giant creature into the house. She could only pray it wasn't inside long enough to make a terrible mess.

Mrs. Morten chuckled beside her, waving her hand at her son. "Do not be so cross, Matthew," she scolded. "The children were expressing compassion."

"With a cow!" Matthew shook his head. "Of all the things."

"You brought home Solomon, did you not?" Mrs. Morten pointedly asked. "I do so recall you *saving* him, much to your Papa's consternation, and look how attached he became to the hound."

Grace smiled up at Matthew. Her eyes locked with his and for a moment, she too saw the mirth that was hidden. Slowly, he cracked a smile and chuckled, causing her to grin broader. His laugh was heartwarming. It was loud but not thundering and matched the deep tone of his rich voice. It made her shiver in delight and she vowed to make him laugh many more times in their long years together.

"Those children are besotted over a calf," he grinned.

Mrs. Morten turned, still chortling softly. Grace linked her arm with Mrs. Morten and they descended the stairs together. She took the woman into the parlor and settled her, then called Mr. Trawley for tea. Matthew followed them in, shaking his head and grinning.

"Compassionate mischief," he mused.

Grace draped a blanket over Mrs. Morten's lap. "You know, nothing can ever become of Mervin now."

Matthew scowled. "Whatever do you mean? Mervin is a male calf who will be raised and slaughtered."

Grace shook her head. "Nay, Mervin will be raised and married."

"Can I go find him a wife?" Adalie asked. She had silently followed them into the parlor.

"No you may not!" Matthew said sternly.

Adalie crossed her arms. " All right, but he's going to get married someday, then you'll have two happy cows."

Grace openly gestured with her hand toward her sister. "That is why you may not allow anything to happen to Mervin."

"Am I outnumbered in this?" Matthew asked, staring at Mrs. Morten.

The elderly lady chuckled. "You are, my son. Though I hope you take a wife before the cow."

Chapter Twenty-Nine

A Mouse, A Cat & A Parson

M atthew shook his head and chuckled again quietly to himself. As it was not yet time for dinner, he departed for Mr. Wallace's farm which was not more than a few miles removed from his own home. He briskly walked the lane as the crisp air filled his lungs. He enjoyed the exercise and the scenery. The trees were bare and the grass was dry. There were no clouds in the darkening sky, so ample moonlight was his guide. *What am I to do with a cow that I cannot even milk? If he's not to be butchered, he will be a great unnecessary expense upon my finances. And yet, I am loath to part with him, for the children's sake.* Having already added to his grocer's bill with additional needs, Matthew needed to reflect and seek what the Lord would have him do. *Mayhap Harrison has need of a cow?*

When the Wallace farm came into view he made his way to the farm where he could hear voices. He entered and was met by Mr. Wallace. Matthew nodded at him.

"Mr. Wallace, good day to you," he said.

"Mr. Morten, good day to you as well. I am guessing that you are here due to the calf?" Mr. Wallace inquired as he scratched his balding head.

"Indeed, you are quite right. I am given to understand that you have gifted it to the Buchanan siblings?"

"Right you are. They did some chores and I was happy to see the little one into their care."

"But, will he be all right removed from his mother?" Mr. Morten furrowed his brow.

"Well, that's the thing, I cannot say."

"Do you have any milk we can offer it? Or any idea how to encourage it to take nourishment? The children would be distraught if it doesn't live." *And I shall be exceedingly vexed if your gift proves to be a heartbreaker. I would have liked to be included in the decision-making.*

"I can gather some for you. I'll have my boy drop it 'round in a bit. We have more work to do before we settle for the night."

"Thank you. I trust all are well within your house?"

"Aye, well except my father-in-law, he has the gout you know. Terrible stuff." Mr. Wallace rubbed his grimy forehead with his dirty sleeve.

"Such a shame. Shall I pray with him?"

"He would like that. Just help yourself into the house, my wife will be busy in the kitchen, but her father will be resting in the front room." Mr. Wallace put his cap onto his head and turned away.

Matthew walked the short distance from the farm to the house and when he reached the door, he quietly opened it. He peered inside, but the dim lighting took his eyes a moment to adjust to. He entered the house and softly closed the door behind him. His ears picked up the distant sounds in what he thought must be the kitchen. He turned to his left and saw a small room with a lit fire and made his way into it. Before the fire sat a rocking chair and in it lounged Mr. Brently, the father-in-law of Mr. Wallace. The older man was sleeping and so Matthew reached his side as soundlessly as he could. He was completely covered in a brown blanket which was in stark contrast to the gray hair that surrounded his bald patch.

He heard growling issuing forth from the corner of the room and turned his head to see what creature was making the noise. He spied a brown and gray tabby cat with its back to him as its tail waved frantically back and forth from side to side. Matthew's attention was redirected toward the sleeping man when a snore began to fill the room. He leaned his head down to view the man's face. *Have I ever heard someone snore so loudly before? How does he not wake himself up?*

Hearing a clatter and more growls, he once again turned his head to the corner of the room. But the tabby was not there any longer, it was running straight for Matthew. He looked down at his boots in time to see a small brown mouse run across them and under the rocking chair. He didn't have time to straighten up as the cat flew at his leg and dug its claws into his skin, through his trousers, in an attempt to stop its momentum. Pain exploded in his leg. The weight of the thick cat threw him off balance and he fell to the side, landing in the lap of Mr. Brently. The tabby was nonplussed and continued along with its mission. The man startled awake in pain and it took Matthew a few moments to right himself so that he could remove himself from Mr. Brently's lap. When Matthew was standing before the man who had not stopped hollering, he tried to apologize. His pride and his person were greatly wounded.

"My abject apologies, Mr. Brently," he said.

"What is happening?" cried Mrs. Wallace as she came running into the room. The cap holding her dark hair in place was falling from its spot and to the side of her head. Her brown dress and spotted apron were covered in flour.

"I lost my balance when the cat attacked me. I am so sorry. I trust that your father is unharmed." *Please, dear Lord, let that be so!*

"Papa, are you well?" she inquired as she leaned over him.

"What has happened? I woke up to the parson perched upon my lap!" bellowed Mr. Brently in between grunts and cries of anguish.

Matthew didn't know how to handle the situation as the man was clearly irate and mayhap injured to boot. "Again, I offer my humblest apologies. The cat threw me to the side when its claw met my flesh. I trust that you are unharmed?"

"I am harmed. What has become of the world when an old man cannot peacefully sleep in his own home without being attacked. By a man of the cloth, no less!" Mr. Brently had fat tears that were coursing down his papery-thin face.

"There, there, Papa," said Mrs. Wallace. She had taken her father's hand into her own and was patting the back of it. She let it go and then turned to Matthew.

"How dare you come into my home unannounced and accost my father!"

"Your husband directed me to enter in as I wished to pray over the man."

"And a right fine job you did of it! Get out!" She stamped her foot and when Matthew did not immediately flee, she reached for a book that sat atop the nearest table.

Mrs. Wallace raised it in her hands as Matthew's eyes widened. She threw it with all of her might and it crashed into his face as it knocked his topper from his head. Matthew was stunned for a moment by the blinding pain and white light that filled his vision, but then quickly bent down to grab his topper. He left the room with the woman shouting curses at him. *Where has she learned such foul language?* It was enough to make the heartiest of men blush.

He walked briskly, just short of running through the front door. He didn't slow his pace until he was clear from sight of the Wallace residence. When he took a breath to settle his nerves he touched his forehead where a knot was forming. The simple touch sent pain ricocheting throughout his body that inflamed the fire overtaking his leg. He gingerly bent himself to take stock of his leg and torn trousers. There was blood that was still seeping from the claw marks that seemed to be very deep. How he was to walk the remaining distance to the parsonage, he could not say. But he had little choice in the matter. He was very glad that he had his father's walking cane so that it may aid him along his journey.

Shall I always be maimed when dealing with the fallout of the children's actions? Though, I can admit that my present health has no bearing upon them directly. 'Twas an accident. But how to hide my present state upon my arrival so that none are the wiser? My pride is just as wounded as my person. I don't wish to be pitied nor laughed at. And poor Mr. Brently... how had everything gone so wrong?

At long last, the parsonage came into view. Matthew blew out a pained breath and continued along. He reached the door after many pain-filled steps and quietly opened it. He stuck his head in first and when he saw no one, he opened it further and walked in. Taking as great a care as he could, he closed the door and endeavored to evade any of the known squeaky floorboards. He felt successful when he reached the staircase. But once he set his fist leg upon the step and brought his injured one up he almost gave a shout. It seemed as if his pain tolerance was waning. He had to gather himself and all of his will to climb the staircase. After what seemed to be an eternity had passed, Matthew was leaning against his closed bedchamber door. He wiped the sweat from his brow gingerly with his handkerchief. *All clear, so far.*

Matthew undressed himself and peered down at his leg. He would not need stitches, though some salve and bandages would not be amiss. He was a bloody mess. Though, how he was to gather those items, he didn't know. For now, he found an old shirt and tore it into shreds after bathing his leg. He wrapped the pieces of material around his leg and tied each one. Feeling like he could easily bear his weight, he went over to his washbasin and used the cloth beside it to scrub his skin. He pulled out fresh clothing and re-dressed. It was not the norm to change clothing for dinner in his home, but this was a must.

Looking into the mirror that hung along the wall over his washbasin, he took in his forehead for the first time. The bruise was already purple and blue and he wondered how to hide it from view. He combed his hair over the right side of his head and used his fingers to tug a few pieces over the knot located along his eyebrow. It was not a stylish choice and he cringed. He would never have styled his hair thusly and he knew that this change was sure to be taken notice of. Mayhap at the dinner table he could avoid questions, though he dared to hope. *I don't wish to cause concern to anyone present.* Though looking at himself in the mirror, he knew that his work was a vain attempt. *I look ridiculous. My head aches appallingly. This is going to be a very long evening.*

Now to descend the staircase and make his way to the dinner table without the aid of the walking cane.

Chapter Thirty

'Tis No Laughing Matter

When dinner was announced, Grace rose from the settee and made her way to Mrs. Morten's side to assist her into the dining room. They had been happily chatting in the parlor while the children put together a puzzle upon the floor in front of the fire. When they reached the table, they saw Matthew enter the room. Grace helped to scoot Mrs. Morten in and walked to her own chair. She paused a moment expecting Matthew to reach her side and pull her chair out. Such had been his practice for days. But he walked to his own chair and stopped. He carefully pulled it from under the table and gingerly sat. *Had he been limping? What was going on?*

Grace pulled her own chair out and sat to the right of Matthew. She shook out her napkin and laid it over her lap. She took a look at Matthew and inclined her head to him.

"Is all well?" she inquired.

"Perfectly," he curtly answered her.

What have I done? Has it taken all of this time for his humors to be ill-affected with the calf? Mayhap his meeting with Mr. Wallace had not gone well? Grace frowned down at her empty soup bowl. *But what would cause him to limp?*

Mr. Trawley entered the room and brought the soup tureen with him. He began filling the bowls. When he had walked out again Mrs. Morten spoke.

"What have you done with your hair, my son?" Mrs. Morten picked up her soup spoon and looked at him.

"It looks funny," Adalie commented.

"Adalie, shush," directed Grace.

Matthew would not look up. He said, "Nothing. I am trying a new fashion." He kept his head ducked down. Grace thought she spied blue skin underneath the dark locks that clung to his forehead.

"'Tis not a style that I shall try," pipped Thayer.

"Nor I," added Fraser.

Matthew set his soup spoon down and rubbed at his temples.

"Does the new style make your head ache?" asked Adalie.

"No." Matthew sighed as he took note that no one was eating, they were all actively engaged in staring at him. He wearily sighed. "I see that none of you will let this alone. If you must know, I had a slight altercation."

Mrs. Morten gasped and brought her hand up to cover her heart. "By highwaymen? Are they afoot? Oh dear, Matthew! Are we to be murdered in our beds? Oh, my poor nerves!"

Adalie jumped up from her chair and rushed to Grace as she cried. She buried her head into Grace's chest. Grace tried to soothe her, making soft noises with her head bent over her sister.

"Don't worry Adalie! We'll brandish weapons to keep you safe," said Thayer.

"Aye, right fine ones too!" Fraser agreed. He leaned over to Thayer and quietly asked him, "Where do we find any?"

"Boys," began Matthew as he looked up to address them. "There are no highwaymen. There is no need for concern. Please stop crying, Adalie. All is well."

Grace looked up at him and gasped. "Matthew! What is wrong with your head?" She patted Adalie upon the back and instructed her to re-take her seat.

There was a rapping on the front door and then they could hear Mr. Trawley's footsteps making his way to answer it. Mumbled words made their way into the room. In a few moments, Mr. Trawley was ushering Mr. Wallace into the room. Through her peripheral vision, Grace saw Matthew cringe, though she still had no idea why.

When Mr. Wallace stood before the table, he gave a great heaving guffaw as he looked at Matthew. He grabbed his portly stomach as his laughter continued on. The other members in the room sat in transfixed surprise at his behavior. Grace turned her head to look at Matthew, who she saw was glowering at the man.

She wondered if she should invite the lunatic to take dinner with them, or if she should insist that Mr. Trawley escort him from the house at once. Something was havey-cavey and she couldn't begin to understand what was happening before her eyes. *'Tis no laughing matter!*

"You are a sight, man! I heard the screeching of my Mae all the way to the barn. The bellows of my father-in-law were very loud, too. I saw you all but running from my house." Mr. Wallace continued with his laughter.

"What happened?" demanded Mrs. Morten.

"The man was attacked by the cat, who I suppose was chasing a mouse. Mr. Morten tumbled into my father-in-law's lap! That's what happened. Took my Mae forever to calm him down."

"I did apologize, profusely," said Matthew.

"You were attacked by a cat?" Grace rose from her chair and came over to brush the hair from his forehead. She brought her other hand up to her mouth and she gasped. "A cat couldn't have done that to you!" Matthew had a knot that was discoloring his skin, turning it to hues of blacks and blues. *No doubt he is suffering.* "My poor darling," she crooned to him as she observed his injury.

"I wish I could've seen it all!" Mr. Wallace tried to cease with his laughs, but he could not make himself, it seemed. Now, he had tears running down from his eyes. "My wife did that! She threw a book at his head when he refused to leave. Knocked his top hat clear off."

"I did not refuse. I simply took a moment to consider what the best course of action was. I was, and continue to be, worried for the health of Mr. Brently." Matthew told the man with indignation coloring his voice.

"Where did the cat attack you?" inquired Adalie with wide eyes.

"My missus said that his trouser leg was torn and a fair bit of blood could be seen. My guess 'tis his leg that got the claws." Mr. Wallace said as he snickered again.

"Are you going to call out Mr. Morten for your father-in-law's honor?" asked Thayer.

"No one is calling anyone out," interjected Grace and then quietly said, "I hope not." Which made Mr. Wallace double over again in laughter. *The rat-faced man!* Grace was livid that he could be enjoying the situation so immensely.

Matthew rose from his chair, wincing as he did so, but he stood straight and Grace felt a thrill go through her. *He is glorious!*

"May I inquire as to why you have called upon us at the dinner hour?" he asked.

"Right, I almost forgot. I brought the milk with me. My boy is seeing it to the stable. The boys should be able to get the calf to drink it. And I wanted to check in on you. That was a long way home to walk in your condition." Mr. Wallace had managed to take himself in hand.

"'Twas indeed, but I am well as you can see."

The man began to laugh again but was able to say, "That I can see."

Grace bristled and looked at Mrs. Morten. "Pray, do we have a rolling pin handy?"

Mrs. Morten blinked at her and then a slow smile alighted her face, "Indeed we do! Mr. Trawley, would you be so kind as to ask Mrs. Kurly for the item and bring it back to us?"

Mr. Wallace stopped his laughter to inquire, "What need of that have you? You're all set down to dinner."

"'Tis for me to throw at your head!" Grace seethed. "Mayhap we can share the humiliation and pain of such an act upon your person. You seem to take great delight in the plight of Mr. Morten, so shall we see how it affects you?" *I shall not back down! I shall hold my ground against this overgrown bully.*

"Now that is not showing true Christian charity, Miss."

"Nay?" she asked, defying him with her unwavering stare.

"She possesses quite the perfect aim; I would take my leave if I were you. I am but a simple man of the cloth, but Miss Buchanan suffers no such hesitation." Matthew smirked at the brute.

Grace was taken back to the time she had thrown the spoon at Matthew's head while they still resided within the cottage. *His poor head always seems to be injured.* However, Grace's smile increased ten-fold at how Matthew spoke of her. He was not mortified to have her support and that thrilled her to no end.

He nodded at Mr. Trawley, giving him the instruction to do as the ladies bid. Mr. Trawley left the room and Mr. Wallace paled.

"Now, there is no need to go and do that. I shall go. I am sorry if I caused offense." Mr. Wallace held up his hands, palms out.

"We accept your apology under one condition. Tell me how your father-in-law has fared?" Matthew folded his arms across his chest.

"He is fine. The old man now has something valid to complain about. I've no doubt that gout plagues him. He incessantly whines about it."

"The poor man. I shall make up some salve for him. It will bring him some measure of comfort," Grace offered.

"That's right kind of you," Mr. Wallace said as Mr. Trawley re-entered the dining room with the rolling pin in hand. Mr. Wallace's eyes rounded. "'Tis time for me to depart." With that, he turned and walked from the room. Mr. Trawley followed him while still clutching the rolling pin.

Before the two men reached the door, Matthew sat heavily down into this chair and laughed. It was a hearty laugh and made Grace join in. Mrs. Morten gave a chuckle and then the children giggled. It was due to half relief and half mirth.

"Would you have really thrown that at him?" asked Adalie.

"No dearest! Violence is never a good solution. I only wanted him to question whether I would." Grace assured her.

"He deserved a facer! His laughter was obnoxious!" Fraser stated as he frowned.

Matthew cleared his throat and then said, "True, but as your sister has said, violence is never a good idea. We are to turn the other cheek."

"How many cheeks do you have?" asked Thayer.

Matthew ignored him and when Mr. Trawley came back into the room, he directed him to remove the soup bowls. The soup had long since grown cold. Mr. Trawley did as bid and then set the meat down atop the table.

"Is anyone else going to address the fact that you, Miss Buchanan, addressed my Matthew 'as *my poor darling*'?" Mrs. Morten asked the room.

Grace looked over at Matthew and saw his face redden. If he could ignore a question, she was happy to follow his lead.

Chapter Thirty-One

Velvety Kisses

With the morning came a sense of peace. Dawn brought beautiful colors of oranges and pinks to light the sky. All was quiet within the parsonage as none had yet to rise, excepting for Mrs. Kurly and Mr. Trawley. They attended to the business of preparing breakfast while Matthew sat rigidly within his study in his leather chair.

Matthew was stiff. His leg was bothering him with any movement that he made. Mrs. Kurly had handed him salve and bandages after dinner was concluded and he had thanked her. He retired early to dress his wounds appropriately. His head was still aching this morning and if expected to pretend that any noise was not a great nuisance, he was sure to disappoint. He hoped that the house could refrain from being too boisterous this day. *One can hope, however unlikely it may be.*

He had finished composing his sermon which was a blessing. He had no will to put quill to paper and try to organize his disordered thoughts. He simply wasn't up to the task. He leaned his head back to rest upon the top of his leather chair. It brought some measure of comfort. He understood that he was days away from being pain-free, and while not one to complain, nor dwell upon how miserable he felt, he took comfort in the fact that he was utterly and completely miserable. Matthew closed his eyes and let his thoughts wander. He knew that there could be no doubt that his mother was well aware of what lay between Grace and himself. She had addressed him in such a way that one could not excuse away upon the mere slip of the tongue. He discovered that he couldn't care less. Let the world know that he sought to make Grace his.

A little later in the morning, there came a soft tap on his study door. Matthew wearily opened his eyes and looked in the direction of the door. There was only one being who he would readily welcome into his domain. The door opened a crack and Grace poked her head in. He smiled at her and waved his hand signaling that she was free to enter. Her hazel eyes were alight with affection as she padded over to stand beside him. She leaned down and examined the knot upon his forehead.

"My, it looks like it hurts. Are you all right?" Grace placed a gentle kiss along the uninjured part of his brow.

"I should say that it looks far worse than it feels, but that would be one monumental lie," he admitted as he wanly smiled at her.

Grace pouted and then said, "I am so sorry. I'm beginning to wonder if you shall survive my siblings or if they will put you into an early grave."

"I would not trade a single second by your side for anything. Besides, they have to grow up at some point, do they not? I shall wait them out. You can visit me here in the safety of my study. I think we shall be quite happy here, don't you?" He tried to wiggle his eyebrows at her and ended up grimacing instead. *Dear Lord, how that hurts!*

"Do not injure yourself further. Are you certain you still desire to court me? I simply could not hold you to a promise when your health suffers because of us. I would understand if you even wanted to fill my position with another." Grace wouldn't meet his gaze. She looked off toward the door while she chewed upon her bottom lip.

The idea of her parting from him filled him with devastation. He could not fathom the day when he was forever separated from her. If it were to ever happen, it would not be due to his actions and he would move heaven and earth to avoid any such occurrence. *I must put all thoughts from her mind forevermore. By my side is her place and I shall not be long for this world were our circumstances to alter.*

Matthew straightened in his chair and gently grasped her by her sides as he brought her to sit upon his lap. He had never been in this position before and it did things to his pulse, which in turn sent pain to his head. But, he would not remove her. He would focus on the pain to keep other unnecessary thoughts at bay. *Like how the weight of her body against mine is delicious. And how... no, stop now, old boy.*

Clearing his throat he tilted her chin with his index finger so that he could meet her hazel gaze. "My darling, dearest Grace. How could you question my regard for you? I never wish to be separated from you by ill-tidings. I look to you, to be by my side until my dying breath. 'Tis you that I want, you that I need, you that I desire above all others and that is a fact that nothing shall ever change. My world, my entire being, would cease to work without you. Indeed, ever since my heart fixed itself upon you, it ceased to beat for me, it only beats for you and every beat whispers your name. Yours alone and no other. I am a ruined man and it could not be more glorious. I beg of you to never question my feelings. I know that I am not always well-spoken and my humor can be dry. All of my many faults aside, I ask that you cease the idea to ever part from me. I would be a broken shell of a man of no use at all and with no will to continue on."

Matthew brought his head down to hers and used the slightest pressure of his lips against hers. Her delicate, full lips were warm and enticing. She tasted of honey and ripe strawberries. When a soft moan came from her mouth, Matthew seized the moment and slid his tongue against her lips. When she didn't shy away from him, he allowed his tongue to enter her mouth. His tongue brushed against hers and Grace returned the action which caused him to groan this time. Velvet to velvet they dueled, learning the feel of each other as they came to know the contours of each other's mouths. *She is divine and soft and yet she is capable of banishing the breath from my body. What wondrous enchantments she weaves upon me.*

They only parted when Grace pushed against his chest. He leaned his head back against his chair as his lungs worked industriously to take in much needed air. Grace leaned her head against his chest, situating herself under his chin. The top of her pinned hair became caught in the stubble along his chin. He tried to keep from dislodging it further, but with both of them breathing so heavily, it was a lost cause. *So what if she looks in disarray, the sight would no doubt fill my mother with unending glee.*

"I am to depart from you, you do remember?" Grace said not moving from her position.

"To my sister's? I well remember that. A week apart will not do, look for me to attend upon you every afternoon." Matthew grumbled. "Can you not simply go over every day and return for dinner and to your bed each evening?"

"I suppose, though, will the constant back and forth wear your mother down?"

"Mayhap. I would not wish to put Mama's health in jeopardy just to be comfortable myself."

Grace hummed in agreement. "Speaking of your Mama, I should be getting back to the parlor. I've been gone much too long. She has been giving me secret looks all morning and when I inquire if all is well, she tells me that everything is perfect. I think she knows we mean more to each other than we are presently showing. I do not wish to hurt her feelings, but I feel as if I were a bug under her inspection. She was giggling with Adalie at the breakfast table and neither would disclose what was amusing them. She had no qualms about talking about us right in front of me before, I am not sure why she will not confide in me now."

"I'm not certain who is the worst influence upon the other."

Grace pulled herself forward and stood. Matthew immediately felt the loss and wanted to tug her back to him. This thing that was between them was likely to be his undoing. Grace reached up and fixed her hair, how she was able to do so without a mirror and unaided by any tool was a wonder to him. A minute's time saw her hair as perfectly arranged as it had been when she entered the study. Though the slight red irritation that lined her mouth from his stubble was likely to be noticed. *Hopefully, that will disappear shortly. But again, that would only please Mama in letting her know that her scheming was proving fruitful.*

"How is Mervin?" he asked after a moment.

"He seems to be well. He took to the bottle straight away and the boys have been excellent caretakers. I think that we are going to be stuck with the beast."

"What would the ramifications be if Mervin would move to Bramley Hall? I am uncertain whether we can afford the expense to keep him." Matthew looked at her and hoped that she would not dislike this truth.

"If he is too great an expense and Bramley Hall will welcome him, I see no reason why the children would be upset. I heard the boys grumbling this morning at having to wake so early to feed him. I estimate that by tomorrow the newness of him will wear away and the boys will welcome their freedom. No harm done, Matthew. Besides, they may visit with him from time to time if Lord Bramley is agreeable." She came toward him and leaned down to place a kiss upon his nose. When she straightened, he reached for her hand and kissed the back of it, which earned him another beaming smile from his lady.

"I shall see you 'ere long to take tea with us." With that, Grace padded over to the door and opened it. She closed it softly behind her.

Matthew blew out a breath and leaned his head back to rest against his chair again. He closed his eyes and let sleep claim him. He dreamed of kisses and oddly of baby cows.

Chapter Thirty-Two

Preparations & Loneliness

Grace made her way back to the parlor where Mrs. Morten was still sitting before the toasty fireplace, working on a fair bit of knitting. Adalie sat beside her, adamantly watching and remarking upon how the item was growing so quickly. Grace smiled, retaking her seat. She wanted to add the finishing touches to Adalie's dress in time for the festivities.

Today, they were to depart after luncheon for Bramley Hall. They needed to create and set up the decorations while overseeing the other various preparations, since Mariah and Harrison were still at Hathwell House. They had three days to complete most of everything before the Lord and Lady returned. It was going to be quite daunting but Grace was up to the task as she wished to make a good impression upon Mariah.

"Your dress should be completed by tomorrow," Mrs. Morten remarked. "I do hope you love vivid colors."

Grace smiled demurely. "I love all colorful things."

"Splendid," the elderly woman replied. "And how fares Matthew?"

Her cheeks heated. "He is fine though his head still aches, but he shall live," she paused. "It was a good thing Mr. Trawley kept hold of the rolling pin. I would have used it."

Mrs. Morten chuckled softly. "Of that, I have no doubt. Adalie, please go check to ensure Mervin is still warm."

The child bolted from the room excitedly, heading outside.

Mrs. Morten held up what she was knitting. "A scarf for the calf. The child insists that he is chilled," she sighed, smiling at Grace maternally. "'Tis a beautiful thing to see compassion, especially in one so young."

Grace nodded. Her siblings were quite the raucous handful. As of late, they were better behaved and dare she say it, good. Not one had gotten into a physical altercation, none were lying, and everything one could take exception to about them and their last name was changing. It was a relief, to say the least. No doubt, she owed the beautiful changes to Matthew and his family for she had never been able to produce such upstanding behavior in them herself.

"Tell me, are you smitten with my Matthew?" Mrs. Morten inquired as a knowing smile graced her face. "Your lips appear a bit pink, my dear."

She cleared her throat. Heat crept to her cheeks. She was certain she appeared akin to a summer cherry. Grace floundered for an answer. *What am I to say?*

"Mervin seems warm enough," Adalie replied, bursting back into the parlor.

"Aye, he's still extremely hungry though," Fraser added, sitting on the floor with a thud.

Grace exhaled, thankful for the rowdy intrusion interrupting Mrs. Morten's questioning.

"Grace," Mrs. Morten began, "would you be a dear and help me to my bedchamber to pack?"

She tried to control her face from going slack. She set down what she was working on, having finished sewing a bit of lace onto a hem, and helped the woman to rise. Grace cursed herself a fool to think the keen Mrs. Morten would allow something like that to drop. *She is ever persistent.*

Grace escorted her up the staircase and to her bedchamber where the lady began instructing her on how she wanted her things packed. The maid that would have handled the packing was given time off from her post in order to visit with her family in London for the upcoming festivities; Grace was more than happy to see to the task, but leery, wondering what Mrs. Morten would say.

"The dress Mariah picked out for you will have many a man drooling over you," she remarked, grinning mischievously.

"I shall happily wear whatever is given to me. Though I doubt many men will seek me out simply because of a new dress. And if they do, I have no issues with beating them all away."

"Oh?" The kind older woman questioned. "And pray tell, why is that?"

Grace didn't answer. She kept packing. Matthew hadn't remarked upon if and when they wanted to announce that there was anything afoot between them since they were both supposed to be in mourning. And since he hadn't mentioned to her when would be the proper time, she didn't want to sour the budding relationship between them by being discourteous.

Mrs. Morten guffawed. "For heaven's sake!" She grumped. "I am not so incompetent as to not notice what's happening between you both, now I'll have the truth of it."

Grace ducked, setting the first trunk onto the ground. "Matthew and I have an understanding."

Mrs. Morten's brows practically reached her hairline. "Indeed? Well... it is high time. And I'm most pleased he's chosen you. Do you have an idea on the length of courtship?"

Grace shook her head. "However long it takes is fine with me. I just long for his happiness."

The older woman leaned back in her chair, rolling her eyes as she snorted. "You'll both be married before that blasted cow is, or I shall tan both your hides with a rolling pin! And box your ears to boot."

Grace's lips thinned knowing full well what the lady was capable of; she wasn't kidding. She hoped to be married to Matthew whenever he deemed it suitable for them both. She had not a single care to uphold the structure of society, but with Matthew being a man of the church, it made things more complicated. She would happily wed Matthew however it came to be, though she, too, hoped it was before the cow. *Based upon the kiss of earlier, I would think sooner rather than later. Matthew possesses more depth of passion than even I would have guessed possible.* Recollections of the feelings his lips had awoken in her made her shiver in delight. *Our marriage bed should not be a cold nor lonely place.*

She readily packed Mrs. Morten's trunks, setting them by the door one by one. She helped the woman into bed for a light rest prior to luncheon and then they'd be off for Bramley Hall.

Grace scooted quietly from the room and toward the study where, no doubt, her love was locked away inside. It was an excellent hideaway for him as he was still in pain. Peeking in, she found Matthew, a light snore emitting from his mouth with his head tilted back against the headrest of the chair. Grace smiled softly, heading further inside to place a gentle kiss upon his temple. Having done so, she began to tiptoe from the study.

"Goddess of mine," Matthew's sleepy voice called out. "Come back to this lonely mortal."

Grace smiled, returning to his side as requested. She carefully crawled in his lap, arranging her skirts, and then rested her head upon his broad chest. She delighted in the sound of his heartbeat.

"I wish there could be many days spent like this," she remarked.

Matthew kissed the top of her head. "I should hope so too. I cannot think I shall live much longer if I cannot call you mine by next summer."

"I was thinking springtime would be a wonderful season."

"I was trying to give us ample time."

Grace blew her lips. "I have a lack of care for the timing, nor opinions of others. If you want to be married soon, then I see no issues with it being as soon as possible."

"Is that your wish?"

"If it is yours then it is also mine."

I do not want to press him if he is not yet ready. His honor must be satisfied as he could never rest with a hasty decision.

Matthew wrapped his arms around her, holding her close as his lips lingered upon her head. "Then spring it is."

Grace smiled. "Splendid. Your Mama forced me into admitting that we have an understanding. She threatened to beat us with a rolling pin should we not marry before the cow. She even went so far as to mention boxing of the ears as well."

"Dear Lord, she said that?"

"Indeed, and I'm fully inclined to believe her. Though she often speaks rashly, I am inclined to believe this is not a matter that her mind shall easily be swayed from."

"I shall save both our bottoms and ears. We shall be wed as soon as 'tis proper."

Grace lifted her head from off of his chest and kissed his lips. "Sounds wonderful, dearest."

She was thrilled to no end that things were settling down and that soon, she too would possess the last name of Morten. *'Tis like some dream, so long have I wished for this to be so. Soon, I shall be able to say that he is my Mr. Morten to one and all forevermore.*

Chapter Thirty-Three

A Heart At Unrest

It had only been one day since Matthew's mother and Grace had left the parsonage for Bramley Hall. He was lost as he ambled about their home. His thoughts would not rest and his heart would not stop longing for its other half. How had this happened to him so quickly? Being unable to walk into a room to locate Grace, to tease her, to smile at, or be smiled at by her, was a sore subject and made him grumpy and irate. He suspected he was irritating Mr. Trawley when the man huffed loudly as Matthew made his fifth round within the hallway from his study. What could he do? He was a man thoroughly and completely ruined and undone. It had only taken one woman to turn his entire schedule and well-being into chaos. Spring could not arrive quickly enough. He was thankful that within a matter of days she would be returned to his care. He could suffer through the days until their respective mourning periods were over, but only if she was by his side, under his roof. *And an occasional kiss...*

Though it was not yet the afternoon, he made a decision. Walking into the parlor where the boys were engaged in a game of Spillikins arranged upon a mahogany side table, he watched as each carefully took their turn picking up the ivory sticks. Thayer drew his stick and the entire structure crumbled to which Fraser jumped to his feet to give a cheer. Thayer stuck his tongue out at his brother.

"Now boys, sportsmanship is a very important tool to master. No one likes to be made to feel terrible for losing," said Matthew as he leaned against the doorframe.

"Sorry," the boys said to each other at the exact same time.

Matthew nodded his head at them. "Who is ready to hitch up the buggy to Obediah and make their way to Bramley Hall? Are you missing Mervin?"

The calf had been removed to the Bramley stables the evening before. The stablehands at Bramley were more than happy to take on a bull calf. One hand remarked upon Mervin being a giant of an old boy once he was grown. Matthew hadn't the slightest idea how large cattle grew, so he only replied with his gratitude in caring for the calf.

"I guess so. I would like to see how he is faring. He must miss his home," said Fraser sullenly.

"His new home is with the other Bramley Hall animals, and I believe that you will find that he is one happy calf once you see him. That is, if you agree to behave. You may not cause nor be the cause of another ruckus. Do I make myself perfectly clear?" Matthew arched his brows awaiting their response.

"Yessir," they both assured him.

"I shall hold you to that." Matthew looked at each of them with his best no-nonsense look. Then he said, "Gather yourselves and meet me in three minutes. We shall depart after getting the buggy and horse readied."

He strode with purpose up the staircase and to his bedchamber. He opened the door and went in to stop before his mirror where he inspected his hair and face to be sure that all was right. He heard the wind begin to moan from his window and frowned. *That shall not make a pleasant journey and we shall all appear windblown. But what is such a matter when I shall be standing before Grace again? Braving wind, rain, or snow is but a little thing to get to feast my eyes upon her, and the chance to hold her hand.* Aye, he was clearly a man lost in the throes of another.

He returned belowstairs and grasped his greatcoat from the peg it hung from by the front door. Once it was donned, he placed his topper atop his head and nearly shouted as the action had the lump upon his forehead smarting again. He gingerly tilted the top hat so that where it rested was not against the knot. That he could bare. He took a deep breath and let it out, then leaned over to fetch his walking cane.

Fraser and Thayer came to meet him and he helped them to bundle themselves in their outerwear. They would need new coats and he was vexed he hadn't noticed that fact before now. The wind would be relentless as they traversed the lane to Bramley Hall. He opened the door and motioned for the boys to exit. They quickly gained the stable and began the chore of attaching Obediah to the buggy.

When they set off, both boys were covered with a blanket and Matthew was satisfied that they would not catch a chill from this adventure. The Scarlatina scare had remained with him and he never wanted to witness either boy in the throes of fever again. He glanced up to the heavens and noted the clouds looked as if snow was imminent. Matthew hoped it would hold off at least until they had safely returned to the parsonage. The buggy would not do well in such weather.

With a gusty wind pushing against him and the conveyance, he held the reins with one hand and his topper with the other. The miles eventually were gained as the Hall came into view. He felt elated that soon he would be seeing his lady again. *Happy thoughts indeed!*

Matthew stopped the buggy before the steps at the front entry to Bramley Hall. He helped the boys unwrap themselves from the heavy wool blanket and descend from the buggy. A footman came to promptly take the buggy and Obediah to the stables. When they had reached the heavy door of the Hall, Billingsley opened it and greeted them. After handing over their outerwear to the butler, Matthew inquired where Grace and his mother were. He was informed they were currently making up kissing boughs in the drawing room. Then Billingsley offered to bring tea and hot chocolate for them, to which the boys heartily agreed. 'Twas too cold to venture to see Mervin just then, and it saved Matthew from having to brave the wind again, so he also readily agreed. They walked to the drawing room while the butler fetched the refreshments.

"What's a kissing bough? And why would anyone desire to have one?" Thayer asked.

Chuckling, Matthew answered. "Tis greenery of evergreens and mistletoe. Sometimes ribbons or apples adorn it as well. Various bows can also be added."

"But what do you do with them?" Fraser's brows furrowed.

"You decorate with them. And sometimes couples may kiss under them."

"Sounds like a lot of work," said Thayer as they let themselves into the drawing room.

A large wooden table had been placed in the middle of the room. Grace, Adalie, Mrs. Morten, and a few maids were busily twisting the greenery together to fashion them into circles or clumps to hang. They were chatting amongst themselves, oblivious to the newcomers who had entered the room.

Adalie looked up first and gave a shout of glee. She left her chair and ran to throw her arms around her brothers. Grace was looking in Matthew's direction while Mrs. Morten addressed them.

"Here at long last! I daresay I suspected you would have paid a call upon us sooner." She continued on with her hands busy.

"We came with the wind in our faces!" said Thayer.

"Indeed?" inquired Grace as she rose from her spot. She elegantly crossed the space separating them. *Everything she does is with a grace of manner, her name suits her beautifully.*

"Indeed, but 'twas well worth it to visit with you." Matthew smiled at her and took her ungloved hand. He brought it to his warm lips and locked his gaze with her as he kissed her delicate knuckles. Quietly, for her ears only he said, "Am I remiss to say how dreadfully you were missed?"

The beaming smile that overtook Grace's face was all the answer he needed. He made himself let go of her hand and then walked over to his mother. He leaned over the back of her chair and placed a kiss upon her cheek. Mrs. Morten cupped his cheek tenderly and then let him go. He straightened and then took in the array of greenery before him.

"You have all been very busy, I see. They look wonderful. Mariah will be pleased."

Grace padded over to him after hugging her brothers and kissing their foreheads. They stood a mere few inches away from each other and the close proximity was not a proper distance. Matthew was loath to take a step away. *I shan't*, he decided.

Mrs. Morten was listening to the boys recount their hours away from Mervin as she continued on with her work. Grace and Matthew both listened as did Adalie.

"I've been to visit with our Mervin and he looks happy. There is even another calf in his stall. I'm certain that they will soon be married. Isn't that wonderful?" Adalie enthused.

Grace's eyes widened as she looked at Matthew and he had to hold in his laugh. He tried to let her know with assurance shining from his eyes that he would not let his Mama take them to task.

"The calf still has to grow more before he can properly take a wife," he told the room.

"Is that why you aren't married yet? You haven't stopped growing?" Adalie's confused expression had mirth and warmth growing within him.

"I think Mr. Morten has adequately grown enough. You remember me telling you that we are in mourning? Do you remember what that means, dearest? That when in mourning, you cannot socialize and most certainly cannot wed to another?" Grace took Adalie's hand and led her over to sit beside her upon the gold padded settee.

"I think that is the stupidest thing that ever was." declared Adalie as she pouted. "Does that mean that I cannot get married?" Her voice held a hint of alarm.

"No dearest, the mourning time shall be long over before 'tis time for you to worry about such things," Grace assured her. There were soft laughs throughout the drawing room.

Billingsley entered the room and placed the refreshments upon the side table. Grace served the room and then sat down beside Matthew upon the settee. They had made space at the long table for the children to drink their hot chocolate and eat the sweet sugary treats provided. There was less of a chance for mess-making if they were situated in that way. Grace insisted that the maids stay and enjoy the break with them.

"I am glad to see you," Grace told Matthew in a low tone that she hoped couldn't be heard by the others who were currently involved in their own conversations.

"I could not make myself stay away. I do hope that you are ready to put up with me for the remainder of the day," Matthew told her with a twinkle in his eyes.

"That sounds wonderful. As long as you let me attend to my duties, that is," she teased.

"I am happiness itself just to sit in the same room as you."

He moved his hand to rest next to Grace's hand that was settled upon the settee in the middle of them. He extended his pinky to brush it against the side of her hand. She looked down at the movement and then sought his gaze. She smiled demurely at him, neither of them even pretending to drink their tea. They locked their gazes and let all of their hopes and dreams mingle in the air between them.

Chapter Thirty-Four

Kissing Boughs

After tea, Grace was a flutter directing footmen and maids on where best to put decorations throughout Bramley Hall. The grand banister was wrapped in greenery and the sight was spectacular. Sprigs of mistletoe hung from doorways. She was in the ballroom where the dancing and most of the celebrations would be taking place. Already tables were decorated and awaiting the elegant dining wear that Mariah had purchased upon her union to Lord Bramley. Placements for bowls of punch and hors d'oeuvres were properly noted and marked with labels that Mrs. Morten's perfect penmanship had written. In all, it would be magnificent. Grace knew that the townspeople likely had never seen such a sight before and she was delighted in having a hand in creating such grandeur. The family would spend the evening of the ball within the drawing room being merry in whatever games they playcd, as the footmen assured that the guests remained in the rooms solely marked for the night. Those who attended the ball would be mostly laborers and men of business and would be more comfortable without the presence of the lord and lady of the Hall.

Grace made her way back to the drawing room, putting together the final touches upon the kissing boughs. Matthew sat by the fire with her brother's playing some kind of game since the wind was whipping too much outside to go visit with Mervin. Already her little sister named the other calf in the stall Melody. What gender the calf happened to be, Grace couldn't say, but she cringed each time her sister asked what date the calves would be grown enough to marry. She smiled whenever she caught herself staring at Matthew. He was so patient and paternal with her siblings. *A better man I have never known.*

She peeked out of her peripheral vision. The mischievous eye she kept catching from Mrs. Morten made her skin prickle. *We better marry before those cattle*, she thought. *Would it be prudent to tell Mrs. Morten their plans to allay any concerns?* She hadn't an inkling what would be best, but from the way the woman kept eyeing her, Grace was certain she would blurt it out for all the world to hear soon. Grace went back to the final kissing bough, adding some white ribbon. She peeked at Matthew in between thinking about the day they would marry and where.

The thought was dashed when an interruption occurred. She glanced over her shoulder, spying Mrs. Morten waving at her. It seemed as if she had been calling her name.

"Yes, Mrs. Morten?"

"Please come here, there is something I must tell you."

"Yes ma'am. One moment if you please."

Grace tied the final bow to the kissing bough. Finally, the piece was done. It was her most favorite, with the bright red apples in contrast to the green boughs, the mistletoe, and the white lace ribbon. Grace announced it was finished, directing the awaiting footmen to hang it above the archway leading out into the gardens from the ballroom.

Promptly leaving her spot after the direction was given, Grace moved to sit beside the woman and near her siblings and Matthew. The tempest outside was blowing ferociously. It seemed as if 'twas increasing in its force. She did not think Matthew nor the boys would be able to head back to the parsonage this evening. Grace turned in her seat, ready to aptly listen to whatever Mrs. Morten had to say, but also internally cringed at what it might be regarding.

"Children," Mrs. Morten beckoned. "Please go to the kitchen and tell the head chef that I said you may have a treat for good behavior."

"Yes ma'am," the boys said in unison, snagging Adalie on their way out of the drawing room.

Oh no, Grace swallowed. *Whatever could this mean? Surely she intends to do or say something regarding the matter of our scandalous secret courting.* She dared a glance at Matthew who stoically stared at his mother. Grace slowly turned back and gave the woman her whole attention.

"Yes, Mama?" Matthew prompted.

Mrs. Morten crossed her arms. "Dearest son, when did you plan on telling me that you are courting Grace?"

"When was proper. We are both in mourning. We cannot engage in such activities," he replied. "Once our mourning period has ceased, we planned to announce it."

The woman narrowed her eyes. "Posh. I want you both married this spring. I demand it, Matthew Jarison Morten!"

Matthew's jaw dropped slightly. "Mama, we were already discussing a spring wedding."

Mrs. Morten's mouth formed a perfect O, then a radiant smile lit up her face. "How you vex my nerves. Here I thought I was to die an old woman never having seen her oldest son wed. I was given to think I was to attend a wedding of a silly cow over my own son."

Grace chortled at the woman's dramatics while Matthew rolled his eyes.

"Mama, you shall live long and will indeed see us wed."

"And I do not think a parson could marry cattle," Grace added, her brow furrowing.

"I shall never officiate over any animal," Matthew retorted pointedly.

Mrs. Morten beamed. "I am most thrilled. Come the start of the year, we shall have the banns read."

"Mama!" Matthew cried. "'Tis not proper. Though we reside within the country, we must maintain some semblance of civility."

Mrs. Morten waved him off. "I do not care what is proper. Blame it on an old woman coming near the end of her days," she sighed dramatically.

"You're not expiring any time soon, Mama."

Again, she sighed, "One never knows. I just hope to see the day my oldest gets married to our wonderful Grace."

Grace let out a small laugh, earning her a chastising look from Matthew. "Come now, dearest," she calmly added, batting her lashes. "Allow your Mama this moment. We did desire a spring wedding after all."

"Oh, my good girl. Please call me Amanda since we are soon to be family," she said, grabbing onto Grace's hand. "I adore you for giving Matthew sense enough to see you married soon. I mean, what would be the harm on the first nice day in spring. On perhaps a Friday in February."

"February is not spring, Mama."

"'Tis close enough, my child."

Grace giggled. "I must agree, Amanda. A Friday in February is most agreeable."

"Perfect. The banns shall be read in January."

Matthew pinched the bridge of his nose. "Grace, would you accompany me to the kitchen to check on the children?"

"I shan't be long. Will you be all right?"

Mrs. Morten sighed, leaning back in her seat. "I shall be most content now that my poor nerves are laid to rest. I shall continue to rest most easily now. Take your time. I shall remain here, planning your dress my dear Grace."

Matthew helped Grace to rise from her seat. He tucked her hand into the crook of his arm, leading her from the drawing room. Mrs. Morten dramatically sighed again, resting further into the divan. Grace giggled, fixing her gaze ahead. *What theatrics she possesses! She would have done very well upon the stage. She is striking enough now, though touched by age, she must have been spectacular in her youth.*

Servants bustled about, arranging garlands, bows, and whatever else needed to be hung. Placements were decided upon and the feeling of the season was quickly taking over the Hall. She smiled at them all, thankful for their prompt assistance and eagerness for the coming holidays. Grace had but two days left to get the Hall in ship shape before the Lord and Lady returned and guests began arriving just in time to celebrate Christmastide.

Matthew led her to the ballroom, taking the long way to the kitchen. The door was open in the ballroom. The large glass windows facing south afforded her a beautiful view of the garden area but also the ugly tempest raging outside.

"Please, tell me you are not leaving me this eve in that horrid storm," Grace whispered.

"Nay good lady, here I shall remain. But on the morrow, I will take my leave with the boys. We must gather our attire or we'll be sorely out of place. The wind must break at some point."

Grace nodded, resting her head on his shoulder. "Are you all right? Your Mama was most adamant about what she desired."

Matthew gave a breathy laugh. "I'm fine, my darling. I was more concerned her antics would frighten you away from me. Does what my mother suggested sound agreeable to you?"

"It is," she replied, sighing contentedly, "I would marry you any day should you desire it."

"Temptress."

Grace grabbed his hand, leading him over to the kissing bough, though she feigned to look outside. Whether or not Matthew caught onto her antics, he hadn't voiced. They stood side by side, watching the wind howl and the tree limbs shake from the violence. Grace grinned, watching the storm swell in the sky.

She paused to give her mother remembrance, thinking of all the holidays she had spent helping her Mama in the kitchen or listening to her melodic voice as it filled the cottage with beauty. The fond memories brought a tear to her eye that she quickly swatted away before Matthew could see. Grace got closer to the glass, peeking up at the clouds and wondering if her Mama could see her now. And if she could, would her yearly superstition prove fruitful for her.

Grace smiled wanly at the sky and sighed. "My Mama used to tell me that snow during the first and last days of the holidays were signs of good luck."

"Is that so?"

Grace nodded. "I believe it is so. If you recall, the last several years it has snowed on every day but those days during the holidays."

"I hadn't noticed. If it were to snow on the first and last day, what do you suppose this luck would bring?" he asked, turning toward her.

Grace leaned up, claiming his lips with hers. She slid in her tongue boldly, softly, as she wrapped her lithe arms around the back of his neck. Matthew held her against him with one hand while the other cupped the side of her face. Grace melted into his touch, loving the powerful yet tender caress as their tongues slid against each other. There was a peculiar feeling down below in Grace's abdomen as the butterflies assaulted her. Matthew broke the trance, pulling apart from her.

"I have no inkling what the luck would bring," Grace whispered breathily. "So long as I have you, I haven't a need for the fickle thing."

Matthew snorted. "I feel the same, my dove. Though, I suppose if there is such a thing, it brings everyone in Bramley a prosperous year."

Grace leaned up on her toes, kissing him again. "I'm already rich."

"As am I, in having you."

All was right in her world. Grace never knew that such contentment and joy would be hers. *I have all that I could ever desire right here with me.*

Chapter Thirty-Five

Let the Festivities Commence

Christmastide was upon them. Matthew's morose thoughts were filled with his Papa. This was to be the first holiday season without him. The ache within his chest was abating, slowly. He suspected that it would never really go away, he'd only learn to live with it, much as he had already been doing. Things were changing so drastically that he longed to hear his father's counsel. *Gone too soon and forevermore missed. How he would have loved to witness these new beginnings. I cannot help wondering what he would have thought about my courting Grace.* He suspected his Papa would have had a merry twinkle within his eyes as he congratulated him and approved of his choice of bride. It made his heart swell to know that while Matthew had been away, his father had been doing what he could to offer care and kindness to the Buchanan family. *The Lord guides us in wondrous ways.*

After an afternoon and day separated from Grace, whom he could not stand the thought of missing anymore, 'twas finally time for Matthew and the boys to enter the carriage that had been sent from Bramley Hall to collect them. His missing Grace was something that he could remedy and he meant to ease some of his heartache.

Matthew brought himself back to the present and took note of his surroundings. Though the wicked wind had abated, the weather had plummeted into freezing conditions. Snow would not be long off.

Dear Heavenly Father, please grant safe travels to all who are set to reach Bramley Hall this day. Let each soul be enriched and each heart gladdened as we celebrate the meaning of the season. Amen.

Matthew was feeling a prickling within his heart that neither Mrs. Kurly nor Mr. Trawley would be leaving the parsonage. The manservant had no family and was a bit of a recluse; he was happy to stay behind and care for the home and animals. He would ensure that the church would be ready to greet its parishioners come Christmas morning. The cook had a niece some distance away who had been married and the dear lady did not wish to interfere with the happy couple's plans to visit with his family. She rather disliked the idea of traveling, much preferring the warmth of her familiar kitchen.

After seeing that the trunk was ready, which would house his and the boys' clothing, he directed the liveried Bramley servant to load it. He donned his greatcoat and his topper. Mr. Trawley handed over his walking cane, to which Matthew nodded his appreciation. The boys were adorned in their outerwear and stood beside the carriage waiting for Matthew to direct them to enter it. He turned his attention to his employees.

"I wish to express my gratitude to you both for your many years of service to my family. You are each an integral part of our family." Then Matthew handed each of them a small money bag. Enclosed were a few extra coins. It was customary to give gifts to the servants on Boxing Day, but as the family would be absent, he wanted them to have a token before his departure.

"I thank you kindly, sir," said Mr. Trawley. He bowed his head to Matthew. Matthew smiled at him and inclined his head as well.

"'Tis most kind of you. I remember when you were but a small boy. To get to see you now as you are, grown and the very image of grace and godliness, well it brings me joy," Mrs. Kurly said as she wiped her eyes with her handkerchief.

"I am the blessed one. Thank you both," Matthew told them and then he took his leave. When he closed the distance to the carriage, he indicated that the boys should enter. He followed them as the man of Bramley closed the wooden door behind them. There were heated bricks placed upon the floor and Matthew watched as the boys situated their booted feet near them. The carriage blinds were drawn closed and none of them bothered to open them. The twins were practically bouncing upon the padded seat across from him and he smiled. He could not find fault in their exuberance when he too was feeling the magic in the air. The festivities would be commencing with his new family by his side. *What could be more glorious?*

The distance to Bramley Hall was gained much quicker than any within the carriage thought it would be. The merry chatter had seen the time pass them by. When the carriage came to a halt, the boys jumped from their seats and waited for the door to be opened, then they bolted for the Hall's front door. When Matthew alighted he spied Billingsley standing ready to receive them.

Matthew followed after the boys and helped them remove their outerwear and then he followed suit. Grace came from the corridor to welcome them with hugs to her brothers.

"Happy almost Christmas!" Grace said as she let them go. She turned to Matthew and he stepped forward to place a gentle kiss upon her cheek. The open sign of affection took her by surprise as she gave a little sound of shock. Matthew noted how brilliantly her eyes were shining and felt a jolt of thrill go through his entire being. He had given her that extra bit of pink that was presently coloring her skin.

"Eww," said Thayer who was making a face of disgust.

Fraser stepped forward with his hand upon his hips and inquired in his best formal tone, "And what is this? You are much too ungentleman like, sir!"

Matthew tried to contain his mirth as he replied. "You are quite right, my good man. It shan't happen again, my apologies." Here he bowed to both of the brothers.

Fraser gave him an unbelieving stare, Matthew felt like he had been called out and cleared his throat.

"Let us make our way into the drawing room. Mariah and Harrison should be returning within an hour or two, I should think." Grace waved her hand in the direction of the room.

"I want to go visit with Mervin!" Thayer countered.

"Oh, me too!" Fraser nodded his agreement.

Grace looked at Matthew and then toward the drawing room. "Mayhap Adalie would like to go as well."

"The weather might not hold off for too much longer, if they are set to go, it should be now," Matthew said as he met her eyes.

"And before we begin our lookout for the lord and lady," Grace said as she began to pad in the direction of the drawing room. She addressed them from over her shoulder.

Matthew directed the boys to follow Grace with a wiggle of his finger. "We must say hello to Mama first before we leave her all alone."

The boys groaned but did as instructed. When they entered the drawing room and made their way to Mrs. Morten, they each kissed her cheek and bid her their greetings in which she took pleasure in. They explained their intention to visit with the calves and Mrs. Morten thought it an excellent idea, provided that they did not get themselves dirty. The children solemnly promised to stay pristine and tidy. Grace decided to stay with her, so the men on their mission, along with Adalie, returned to the front door where Billingsley handed out their outerwear. It was a chilly few minutes walk to the stable where the calves were.

Entering the stable, they were greeted by the head groom, Winslow, who was happy to let them visit with the calves. He waved them to the correct stall as he went about overseeing the stable lads and their chores. Fraser reached the stall first and opened the door. The others followed his lead and Matthew closed the door behind himself.

"Aren't they just adorable?" cooed Adalie.

"They are," agreed Matthew. He gingerly stepped toward the other calf and leaned over it. He peered at its nether region and smiled. "Lo, my small ones, but I must tell you that this is *another* boy. They'll both remain bachelors."

"Aww. I was so looking forward to a wedding," said Adalie dejectedly.

"No matter, they can grow up to be first-rate mates! Think of all the cow entertainments that can be embarked upon," soothed Fraser.

"'Tis not the same," she pouted.

They remained watching the cows chew their food for another ten minutes when Matthew insisted that they return to the drawing room. With merely a few grumbles, they acquiesced and trudged back up to the Hall.

Once they were situated with hot chocolate and tea to begin the lookout for the return of the lord and lady, Matthew addressed the room. "I must inform one and all, the other calf residing with our Mervin is in fact a male. There shall be no further talk of a wedding for them."

"Oh?" questioned Mrs. Morten. "How fortunate for those that remain to keep secrets such as courtships to themselves. Now, there is no race to be had to the altar, how sad."

"I am exceptionally relieved to know that that is the case," Grace said with a small smile before taking a dainty sip of her tea.

"As am I," said Matthew as he winked at her. Then he leaned toward her ear and whispered, "There is no need of rushing our nuptials."

Grace gave him a slight smile and he thought that he might have erred in his words. Truly he desired to marry her, but having the banns read three weeks before their wedding was the correct course of action, and having it held in the springtime with the promise of new life, and the beauty returning to the earth, was what he sought. He only hoped that his female relations would agree with him. Given time, he felt sure that they would accept his decision on the matter, but since a proper proposal and the event itself was so far away, he felt certain that he had ample time to address his wishes. He could not in good conscience rush their beginning. He would never cause Grace to fall under scrutiny, and should they find themselves with a babe on the way shortly after their vows, he felt that they both would come under censure. *What would our children look like? Will they take after my line or hers? Perhaps a good combination.* He had once worried about taking on the role of father, but now that he was placed much into the role of one with the younger Buchanan siblings, he knew that he had nothing to fear.

Luncheon was addressed shortly thereafter. With a light fare of cold meats and some dried fruit they supped. When they returned to the drawing room, Adalie was sketching in her book and the boys played a game of Charades with Mrs. Morten. The air was charged with the excitement of the upcoming festivities and even Matthew could say he was anxious to get the proceedings underway.

An hour later they heard a commotion in the Hall and Matthew rose from his seat and offered his arm for Grace to take as he assisted her to her slippered feet. They made their way to meet the newcomers while instructing the children to stay where they were.

Mariah and baby Daniel were being bustled through the front door by Harrison who looked happy to be home. The nanny followed them through and took the babe so that Mariah could discard her cobalt-colored traveling cloak and matching jockey hat. Harrison handed over his greatcoat, topper, and walking cane to Billingsley and then assisted his wife. Mariah took Daniel back into her arms and turned.

"How delightful to be back home and with such a wonderful greeting before us," Mariah exclaimed as she closed the distance between them. She gave Grace a kiss upon the cheek and hugged Matthew who took care not to crush the little bundle between them.

"We are glad to see you back," Matthew told them as Harrison slapped him upon the back in greeting,

"'Tis good to be home, my friend," Harrison gave them all a beaming smile.

"Do you wish to hold him, dear?" inquired Mariah who looked at Grace with a demure smile.

"I certainly would!" Grace stepped forward to carefully take the little one to whom she immediately began to cuddle and coo. The sight hit Matthew like a ton of bricks. A babe in Grace's delicate arms was nearly his undoing. *How I long for this to be made real, for it to be our babe that she holds with such love and tenderness.* Grace smiled up at him.

"Are you neglecting your elderly?" Called Mrs. Morten's voice from the drawing room.

The couples chuckled amongst themselves. Mariah came to gather Daniel and led the way toward the drawing room with Harrison's arm wrapped protectively around her shoulders. He reached down and placed a kiss upon her nose to which she made a small sound. The smile upon her face radiated love and joy.

"They are perfect for each other, are they not?" Matthew took Grace's smaller hand and placed it in the crook of his arm.

Grace walked alongside him with a dreamy expression upon her beautiful face. "They are."

"I imagine that given a month or two of marriage, we too shall look as they do."

"Oh no. We shall look even more in love for I am certain that I have never been more in love with a person as I am you." Grace said the words but did not see the way that they affected him. She kept her gaze fixed upon the lord and lady.

Matthew lit up like a chandelier might with its many glowing candles. Of course he knew that Grace esteemed him, had chosen him, but still to hear those cherished words coming from her lips meant more to him than even he could have known. *What a cad! You have not returned the words to her,* he lamented.

He watched as his sister and brother-in-law entered the drawing room. He halted his own steps, and that of Grace's, just shy of reaching the doorway. They would remain undiscovered should no one seek them out.

"You love me?" he questioned, meeting her weary gaze.

"Of course, I do. I adore and love you. So much so, that at times, the force of it knocks the very breath from my lungs."

He bent his forehead down to rest against hers and closed his eyes. He took a deep breath. The scent of roses and an elusive spice filled his senses, yet it was everything he knew to be her. "Grace, you must know that I too love you. I feel so foolish that I have yet to say the words to you, when you deserve to know the depth of my feelings. My regard has long been secured to you, but 'tis just now that I realize that 'tis so much more. I do love you, Grace, with every breath I take and with every beat of my heart. Love for you is what has been driving my every action and thought for so long.

What a dolt to not have discovered that until this very moment. Will you forgive me?"

"For loving me?"

"For taking forever to say the word, forever to understand my own feelings upon the matter."

"What is there to forgive? You are all of my happiest joys and thoughts. To have your heart, whether yesterday, today, or on the morrow, is all that I could ever hope for. This, right here, is my Christmas gift and I absolutely adore it."

Matthew could not help himself, he could not contain his emotions any longer. He claimed her lips in a kiss that was passionate and filled with all of his longing. He poured everything he felt into the pressure and cadence of their kiss and she matched his ardor back, stroke for stroke. He could die from want of air and have not a care, and still, he would treasure this charged moment between them. He was loath to pull his lips from hers.

Chapter Thirty-Six

Oh Goodness

"Oh my..." Harrison's voice broke Matthew and Grace apart as blushes infused them both. Grace pulled away first. Harrison's face was a portrait of surprise, vexation, and then finally alarm as he colored a very vivid shade of red. *Poor man! We have thoroughly shocked him and earned his displeasure in the process. Though, I regret nothing.* Matthew had declared his love for her. It was the best gift she had ever received. To have earned his affection was more than she could have desired.

Matthew stepped away from Grace to put some distance between them. "Harrison–."

Harrison held up his hand to stay his explanations. "I trust that there is at the very least an understanding between you? I am surprised by *you*, Matthew."

"I beg of you, hear me out."

Harrison waved a hand for him to continue.

"I do have an understanding with Grace. We are to wed this Spring. I hope that I may count upon your discretion upon witnessing this indiscretion." Matthew told him calmly.

"I must request that you make your intentions publicly known. You have placed my honor and that of those under my care in this household in jeopardy. Such a scandal, should another have discovered you, would not do either party any good. If you cannot refrain, please do not do so in such a well traveled space." Harrison frowned at Matthew.

"I well understand your censure. I have earned it, but please do not think poorly of Miss Buchanan."

"I think poorly of *you*, my friend. You risked a great deal. With my other company set to arrive promptly, this could have ended very badly. You are lucky 'tis the holiday season, as I should have seen you mounted and departed for a special license. Take care, my friends, in the future." Harrison took his measure.

"My lord, 'twas not his fault. I was the one to accost him. He is a very honorable gentleman." Grace felt the need to speak her thoughts. This dressing down of her beloved would not do. Not when she felt that the responsibility rested upon her shoulders. True she was thrilled to soon be wed to a man who loved her in equal measure, but she could not remain silent. Her feelings were waxing between euphoria and despair.

"Indeed?" Harrison cleared his throat. "I hope to hear an announcement before Boxing Day concludes." He looked pointedly at Matthew and continued, "Believe me, I too well understand the allure of what a pair of fine eyes in a beautiful face can do to one. I do not wish any to question your match. You'll have my full backing and congratulations once you make your announcement."

"Matthew! Matthew! And where have you gotten to Grace?" Mrs. Morten's voice rose from within the drawing room, "Shall I have the banns read now?"

"That's enough, Mama," Matthew hollered back. He pinched the bridge of his nose. Grace could tell by the dropping of his shoulders that he was mortified to be raising his voice back to answer her

"She knows?" questioned Harrison.

Grace nodded. "She does. So I do not think she shall remain silent upon the manner, even once guests are in residence."

"I must have my share of what is happening out there!" Mrs. Morten shouted again. "You must come back to us, this is most unfair."

Harrison took a deep breath and then nodded his head toward the drawing room.

Grace linked her arm with Matthew and they made their way into the drawing room. Mrs. Morten was situated where they left her by the fire. The younger Buchanan siblings beamed up at them all when they entered. Grace beamed back, happy to be surrounded by those who loved her. Matthew saw her to the settee and took his place beside her.

Her nose stung and her eyes began to prickle with tears and it had nothing whatsoever to do with having been caught by Lord Bramley. For the first time in years, she was able to have a Christmastide season where she was in a loving home, where she wouldn't have to worry if there would be enough food or clothing to make it to spring. Grace wiped the tears from her eyes. *I have a home where not only am I loved, but my siblings too. I feel like I have grown in myself and my security to allow my heart to lay bare for my future husband.*

Mariah walked toward Mrs. Morten, handing over a happy Daniel to his grandmother. Now that their full audience was ensconced within the room, the children immediately began relaying the story of the calf to Mariah and Harrison, and how Adalie wanted the calves to marry prior to finding out the second calf was a boy.

"Could you please get Mervin and Alvin wives, sir Lord Bramley?" Adalie asked.

Harrison chuckled. "I'm certain that when they are old enough to entertain the idea of wives, we could procure some."

"Mr. Wallace did come over the following day to give us papers for the calf if he did survive. Mervin is thriving here," Matthew added. "I'm certain if you wish to do cattle and horses, it would prove well for you."

"If," Harrison chuckled, "Mervin does prove fruitful and a stocky breed, I see no reason why it wouldn't prove well. Though I am remiss, I do not know as much about cattle as I do horseflesh. What an exciting, spontaneous new adventure."

Grace smiled demurely. She was certain Harrison was being gracious with this newfound burden of raising a calf. Grace ducked her head, opting to stare at the crackling fire. She was embarrassed because, now, the toll of her siblings was affecting those around her more profusely. *Will there ever come a time when others do not have to leap to the rescue for an action caused by my siblings?*

"I think expanding our resources is a most pleasant enterprise," Mariah added. "'Tis best to have multiple avenues with these changing times and looming uncertainties. Thank you, Grace."

Grace dipped her head, thankful for the kind woman and her keen intuition regarding people. "Thank you for your generosity."

"In other news, Isabelle and George welcomed a little girl. They should be arriving later today as they were readying themselves for travel, despite George's hesitations regarding whether Isabelle could safely make the short journey. I believe they are awaiting Mr. and Mrs. Pembroke to arrive, then they shall depart altogether. Lord and Lady Purcellville will be on their way shortly with Simon and Alicia," Harrison informed the room. Grace understood that, usually, a month was the appropriate time for recovery from childbed. As far as she knew, it had only been three weeks since the new bundle had made its introduction.

"What is the little dear's name?" Mrs. Morten inquired.

"Celeste, and she is the prettiest little babe. Isabelle was so in love." Mariah sighed.

"George is more smitten with his daughter than with his wife," Harrison joked. "The little girl is quite darling with her mop of the same strawberry blonde hair that Isabelle possesses."

"I cannot wait to meet her," Mrs. Morten replied.

"Neither can I," Grace added.

Mariah rose from her seat, beaming broadly. "I cannot wait to see how you and my dear Mama decorated all of Bramley in a matter of three days time. I am most impressed. Would you mind greatly showing me what you have accomplished?"

Grace rose from her seat beside Matthew, heading to link arms with Mariah. They exited the drawing room, heading in the direction of the ballroom. Once out of earshot, Grace turned to Mariah and grinned.

"I do hope that you find everything as you hoped it would be," Grace told her.

"I am in no doubt that I shall. Pray tell, how are things progressing between my brother and yourself? I caught the shade of red that Harrison was trying to hide when you all entered the drawing room. Has my poor darling caught you two sharing your affections?"

"I adore your brother," Grace admitted.

Mariah giggled. "I honestly could not tell," she sighed happily, pausing in the hall to look at her. "I remember when we were children at school. One particular boy picked on Matthew and you came out of nowhere and landed quite the facer upon him. I believe Matthew was smitten with you from that day forward."

Grace laughed. "Where had you been? You were not attending the school at the time were you?"

Mariah shook her head. "Nay. It was a pleasant day so Papa took me on a walk to the school to pick up Simon and Matthew when we heard a raucous gathering. Papa took my hand, sprinting to the schoolyard where you hit a boy square on the nose, yelling at him to not pick on Matthew."

"Yes, that boy was quite the terror," Grace giggled profusely.

"Who was it? I cannot seem to recall."

"I cannot recall either, but I remember the look upon Mr. Morten's face and the stern lecture I received afterward about turning the other cheek."

Mariah's melodic laugh flitted through the halls as they began traversing to the ballroom. Grace grinned, feeling comfortable and content in Mariah's calm and accepting presence. Matthew often remarked upon his sister and how she had this uncanny ability to make all feel welcomed and comfortable. Grace thought naught of it until this day, not until she needed to be put at ease.

"You are so suitable for Matthew. He is like our dear Papa and our grandpapa as well—so stoic and serious yet thoughtful, giving, and kind," she breathed out as if recollecting a fond memory. "And you bring out the side long-hidden within him."

"And what is that?" Grace prodded.

Mariah swished her head to the side. "He has always been more aloof, reserved in a severe sense with often considered pointed yet judgmental opinions. You, dear Grace, have softened him. 'Tis like looking at a new man; a man, in the image of my father, that he was always meant to be."

Grace blushed from the high praise. "Well," she softly cleared her throat. "It seems I am destined to be your brother's forever champion."

Mariah tilted her head and Grace promptly relayed the incident at the Wallace's and the subsequent visit to the parsonage from Mr. Wallace. It had Mariah rolling with laughter.

"You are such a breath of fresh air! You do Matthew a world of good. You must inform me at once if he ever fails to deserve you, " she exclaimed as they entered the ballroom.

"I shall be so forward as to admit that I love Matthew, wholeheartedly."

"And I welcome you to the family, dear Grace," Mariah said, patting her hand. "By the stars! I love what you've done. You took my vision and exceeded it tenfold." Mariah's sapphire eyes were shining with undeniable excitement.

"You give me much-unneeded praise. Your servants helped most generously."

Mariah patted her hand, leaving her to inspect the rest of the decor Grace and her Mama had created and arranged. The kindly lady beamed the entire time, offering coos and praise for what Grace and Mrs. Morten had accomplished.

Grace stood near the entrance of the ballroom, feeling her cheeks heat from the esteemed praise and also from reminiscing about being caught in such a passion-filled kiss. *My mind keeps recalling those moments and I must rein myself in. This mooning will not do at all. Though, his warm breath against my... stop this,* Grace ordered herself.

"This is absolutely superb. People will remark upon it for years to come and we shall be woeful in trying to recreate the specialty of which you and my Mama executed perfectly."

"My lady, you praise me too generously. 'Tis the least I can do to be of assistance after all your family has done for mine."

"We are family, Grace. There is no owing back to another."

Again, they linked arms, heading off toward the kitchen to inspect the specialities their cook was creating. The scent of yeast and sugary goodness wafted through the air and Grace swore she could see the tendrils of warmth whisk through the air to her nose.

Her stomach rumbled, though thankfully not with any sound to accompany it.

Together, they entered the kitchen, seeing the beaming cook pull a sheet of chocolate cookies from the oven. Grace stood to the side while Mariah inquired what other delights the cook was planning on spoiling them with. Grace couldn't help but stare at some fudge. After a moment, she redirected her gaze, causing the cook and Mariah to giggle.

"Dear lady," Mariah beamed. "Have one. Mrs. Higgins made them this morning."

Not wanting to seem gluttonous, Grace took the smallest piece and popped it into her mouth. She closed her eyes, moaning at the deliciousness of the confection, and immediately regretted not taking a larger piece. The ladies giggled at her.

"I've never had something like this. 'Tis magnificent."

"Thank you, dearie," the kindly older lady grinned. "I've got more comin' out shortly."

"You spoil us completely, Mrs. Higgins," Mariah grinned.

"Oh dearie, Lady Bramley," Mrs. Higgins replied, patting her eyes. "'Tis so much a pleasure to serve you."

Grace smiled at the cook, whose graying hair was arranged in a loose bun that wobbled as she talked. Her kind eyes appeared mole-like and pinched together, but it did nothing to take away from her cheery and grandmotherly demeanor.

"Dearest," Harrison said, coming toward his wife. "I was informed some carriages are coming up the drive. It could be the Hathwells."

Mariah linked her arm with her husband, striding off toward the entrance to greet their guests. Grace made her way back to the drawing room where Matthew, the children, and Mrs. Morten were still sitting in their respective spots where she had left them. Grace glided into the room, taking a seat beside Mrs. Morten, and waited anxiously to see who else would be arriving soon. She avoided the questioning eye of Matthew as her mirth and joy grew.

Chapter Thirty-Seven

Welcoming The Relations

M atthew quickly gained his feet as the Lord and Lady Hathwell entered the drawing room. He had met the man while they had both attended the Bramley wedding. They'd even conversed, though since they had such differing personalities, they had not quite hit it off. Isabelle had been his childhood playmate as Harrison's cousin, so he was very happy to see her looking so well and content. Indeed, she was radiant. *Mayhap she has found love with her husband? The addition of their daughter seems to do them both good,* he mused. Mr. and Mrs. Pembroke entered after them with their young son Bernard held within his father's arm.

Matthew closed the distance between Lord Hathwell and himself as the ladies converged upon Isabelle to view the sleeping bundle she cradled to her chest. He could hear their various sounds of rapture and was happy to leave them to it. Matthew grasped the outstretched hand of his lordship and shook it.

"Well met, Lord Hathwell, your family is stunning," Matthew told him.

"Well met, Mr. Morten. Thank you. I was sorry to hear of your father's passing. His death has reached far and wide since his presence was so far-reaching. A better man, I have never met." Lord Hathwell told him with a sincere smile that reached his chocolate gaze.

Matthew felt the familiar tightening within his chest at the remembrance of his father. The praise from the man standing before him helped to ease the sting a bit. "He is much mourned. Thank you for your kind words."

"Indeed. I owe him much. Please, we are among family here. You must call me George; the title still doesn't sit quite well with me."

"Then you must address me as Matthew."

"Darling, your daughter misses you," Isabelle's voice said from beside them. She smiled at her husband and handed over their wailing babe.

George took his daughter immediately and began to croon to her. His soothing voice did the trick as the babe quieted down.

"As you can see, my husband has quite the way with our little Celeste. For he is constantly at my side and forever inquiring whether we are well. She has grown used to his endless prattle." Isabelle's amused voice addressed the room.

"Hush you. My darling lady wife has quite the sharp tongue and regardless of my attempts to curb it, it remains ever sharp. But, I would not change her for all the world." George reached over to place a delicate kiss upon her brow.

"'Tis just as well, because you cannot give her back now," chortled Mr. Pembroke. He came up beside Matthew and squeezed his shoulder in greeting.

"You are looking well, Matthew. How have you been?" Mr. Pembroke's kind blue eyes held his gaze.

"I am well, thank you. You seem to be in top form."

"Indeed, I am. It seems as if a granddaughter was just what I needed," Mr. Pembroke enthused.

Matthew smiled at the older gentleman and then closed the distance to reach Mrs. Pembroke. He bowed over her hand. "How wonderful to see you again."

"Matthew, you charmer," Mrs. Pembroke said with delight.

"Only stating the truth ma'am." Matthew backed away from her and turned to Isabelle who was close by.

"My Lady Hathwell, how wonderful to meet with you again. How are you faring?" He bent over her hand to place a kiss upon its back.

"Very wonderful, Matthew. Thank you for inquiring. You, I trust, are in good health?" Isabelle's icy blue eyes were filled with mirth.

"Exceptionally. Has Mariah introduced you to Miss Buchanan yet?"

"Indeed, she is a very striking woman, is she not? I notice her gaze seeking your movements. Is there romance afoot?"

Matthew did his best to stifle the blush that wanted to overtake his complexion. He bowed his head and then met her intense gaze. Isabelle had always been able to read him like a book. "Mayhap." He winked at her, to which she chortled.

"You rogue! How very sneaky of you, Matthew Morten."

"You realize that I am in mourning? Miss Buchanan is also in mourning for her father. We are sensible of the fact."

"*Psh!* What does that matter when compared to true love? 'Tis the most powerful all-consuming force there is." Isabelle winked at him.

My, how she has changed, he thought. "I remember a time, very recently too, when you would have rather expired upon the spot than flout the rules and dictates of *society.*"

"Love comes first, Matthew. Remember that. Love *comes first* in all things. Don't let anything come between you and what you love. Life is so tragically short, why waste a second of it in fear of going against the grain. Be the spark that ignites a firestorm! Choose love. Always." Isabelle took his hand in hers and squeezed it. Then she let it go and padded away from him.

He stood watching the room's inhabitants. He was stunned that he had been on the receiving end of such a statement from Isabelle. Isabelle was the darling champion of what was proper and what was not. To hear these thoughts from her lips threw him for a loop. He was still trying to wrap his mind around her words when Grace came to stand next to him. She was holding a blanketed Celeste in her arms. When Grace looked up and smiled at him, he felt the power of Isabelle's word to his soul. He wanted to say something to Grace, but Billingsley entered the drawing room to announce the presence of Lord and Lady Purcellville, Mr. and Mrs. Morten, and a Mr. Buchanan.

Mariah and Harrison were immediately standing before Lord and Lady Purcellville and greeting them. His attention was focused on his brother Simon, who was directing his wife to a chair near the fireplace. When Matthew looked over at Grace her face was a mask of shock and then it registered with him, that alongside Lord Purcellville was Christopher, Grace's brother. Mariah was leading the introduction. Grace passed the sleeping babe off to Mrs. Morten.

Matthew and Grace exchanged greetings with Lord and Lady Purcellville and when they walked away, Grace threw herself into her brother's waiting arms. Matthew was happy to witness their reunion and he found that surprise was again within his being. How wonderfully kind of the lord and lady to bring the lad home for this visit.

Chapter Thirty-Eight

A Tearful Reunion

G race felt her breath catch within her throat. She had never expected to see her brother Christopher so soon. In fact, she didn't expect to see him until the end of January when it had been hinted that he would be allowed to come home. Grace threw her arms around his neck and held him close as tears coursed down her face. *What a surprising blessing, so very much needed. I did not realize how much his absence has injured my heart. How very dashing he looks in his regimental uniform.*

She hiccuped, not having cried like that in forever; not since the death of their Mama. Grace pulled back, wiping away her tears. What she thought would be a lonely road by herself with her siblings turned out to be heartwarming and filled with the unending aid and guidance of Matthew Morten. She was grateful to such a kind man, soon to be her husband, but also proud of her brother. *The two could not be more different in personality.*

Christopher took her to the side, away from the giddy chatting and laughs consuming the drawing room where all were gathered. Grace settled herself in a small chair while he took one near her as he continued to relay his experiences and admiration for his commander. Christopher began detailing his time in the regiment under the command of the excellent Lord Purcellville. Grace listened intently, marveling at the small changes that his time and experience had given him. *He is becoming quite confident and a man to be much admired.*

"Oh, before I forget," Christopher said quickly. He pulled an envelope from his pocket, shoving it into her hands. "'Tis my first payment from the regiment," he said, beaming proudly. "I wanted to hand it to you in person."

"Oh, Christopher. Thank you ever so kindly. But you need not fuss anymore, I–"

"Whatever do you mean?" he asked loudly, a scowl deepening on his brow. "I left to provide for you and our siblings now that Papa is blessedly in the ground."

"Lower your voice," Grace admonished.

"You had no faith in me, did you?" His eyes shone with hurt.

Grace shook her head. "That isn't the reason at all. I found a position and a better roof to lay our heads under."

Christopher snorted derisively, shaking his head. "You sought the parson to take care of you because you didn't believe I could! You were always searching and grabbing at any better opportunity to flit past your eye," he seethed. "And now you've meddled yourself in that!"

"'Tis nothing of the sort, Christopher Buchanan," Grace barked back tersely. "How dare you think so poorly of me! I did the best I could do for our family while taking Papa's ire so you wouldn't bear the burden of it," she said heartbrokenly, wiping the tears from her cheeks. "I was approached by Mr. Morten to be a companion for his mother and I was reluctant to take it because of our siblings and you. Do not approach me again this day unless you mean to make amends for your accusations."

The room went deadly silent save for the soft, small coos of Celeste. *Have I spoken too loudly?* Matthew caught her eye, unspokenly inquiring if she was all right. Grace felt her cheeks flame. Rising promptly to her feet, she strode from the room they were all in. She cared not to show her face anytime soon. Nothing could coerce her to rejoin the drawing room at least for the next little while. She was heart-sore and sick that her own brother should think so vilely of her. *How have I earned his disrespect?*

Grace went down the hallway toward the ballroom where she felt was ample space enough to try and walk off some of her own ire. She was thoroughly embarrassed, more embarrassed to think her own brother thought so ill of her that she would seek the companionship of another to make ends meet. She was no dockside harlot, though she understood the reasons for those ladies being what they were; she, however, would rather stick her spoon into the wall first. Death would be preferable. *As if I could bear to be degraded in such a manner.*

She wiped at her eyes again, her tears of frustration and hurt could not be calmed. She continued to walk the perimeter of the room. Arms crossed over herself did little to block the outside world from intruding upon her. Standing in front of the long glass window afforded her a view of the sky threatening to snow. She breathed out, closing her eyes. *Mayhap my luck is to change again*, she thought with a slight scowl upon her brow. *Whatever is to come, I hope it spares the Morten family and their relatives.*

"Grace?" Matthew said, coming toward her. "Are you all right? You all but fled from the room."

"Did everyone hear the conversation?" she asked painfully.

Matthew nodded, opting to stare at the ground instead of meeting her eyes. "They caught the tail end with Christopher's remark."

"I was three and ten when my mama died, leaving me to care for Christopher who was one and ten, the twins who were two and then a newborn. My papa raised his hand to me whenever he was too drunk and sometimes when not," she turned, meeting the hard, stoic gaze of Matthew whose features were growing dark with displeasure. "I did all I could for them," she paused, biting her bottom lip as she wiped the fresh tears away. "I did not take this job to take advantage of you. I cannot bear that anyone, let alone my brother, should think me to be so opportunistic."

Matthew held her close as she cried. Even with all the guests in the house, she cared not if there were pistols drawn at dawn or a declaration to obtain a special marriage license, and clearly, her lack of care was rubbing off upon Matthew, too. She needed Matthew's comforting warmth more than words could ever express. Matthew forced himself from her clinging embrace, and she felt the cold, stinging slap of his departure through her skin. She was being selfish; pistols or even a special license would only cause injury to the one man that she sought to treasure. No *harm shall befall him upon my account. I could never wish that.*

He stepped toward her again and then tenderly wiped away her tears with a gentle stroke of his thumb. "Dearest," he crooned. "You are my everything. And I know, as does everyone in that room, that you are far above that in character and in my esteem. Indeed you and your actions are far above reproach."

Grace let her head fall into the warmth of his palm. "You're too kind to me."

"Nay, sweet lady," he said, placing a gentle kiss atop her head. He let his lips linger for just a moment more. "When my thoughts turn to what you have endured by the one who was to protect you above all others, my blood boils in my veins."

Grace stiffened as she gazed beyond Matthew, spying her brother who cleared his throat. He loomed in the doorway with George and Harrison standing a short distance behind him.

"Mr. Morten," Christopher said firmly. "Unhand my sister."

Grace stepped past Matthew, hands upon her hips. "You've done enough in the past half hour, Christopher Buchanan. Let me alone. You're being irrational."

"Are you with this man?"

Harrison moved through the doorway. "I'm sure there is an explanation." He was calm in manner, but she could tell by the ticking of his jaw that he was not pleased.

She folded her arms over herself protectively. "There is, Lord Bramley," she replied though she wished she had kept the anger of her voice from the kind man. "I repaired here to be alone. I wished to cry and be at peace. I see now that I was remiss to not have sought out my bedchamber. Matthew found me and offered a comforting ear to listen. There was nothing improper that occurred."

George shrugged, coming to stand by Harrison. "Let's allow the family to sort out this matter, my friend. Our wives are probably already scheming on what to buy next for the babes. How they delight in spending our inheritance. "

"Matthew," Harrison addressed him, "come join us in preventing the women from scheming. I'm sure Mrs. Morten already has plans. You hold more sway over her."

Grace nodded to Matthew, ensuring with a reassuring look that she would be all right. Matthew nodded after a moment's hesitation, then joined the men ambling back in the direction of the drawing room where everyone was still visiting. She was certain that by the rigid set of his shoulders he wasn't pleased to be dismissed. But he had obliged her request nonetheless.

Once she was sure they were out of earshot, she rounded on her brother. "How dare you!" she seethed.

"Are you in love with him?" Christopher growled.

"So what if I am," Grace bit back. "'Tis my right. I am unattached."

Christopher rolled his eyes. "But I can take care of you and our siblings now. You don't need him. You don't need to settle. You can do so much better for yourself, Grace," he pleaded. "Allow me to send you as much as I can. I might be able to arrange for you to be married to a high-ranking officer."

Grace's jaw dropped and she swore it could touch the floor. "I am happy where I am, Christopher," she boomed, wiping the tears from her eyes. "Why must you seek to ruin the only happiness I've ever felt in my entire life? Are you trying to drive me to the grave?"

Christopher took her hand, patting the top of it. "Nay. I'm sorry. For a moment, I felt betrayed that you sought to seek help because your faith in me was lacking. I got angered and I apologize. I just desire to give back to you since you have always done so much for our little family. I want to give you the best. You deserve that."

"Oh, Christopher," Grace replied, embracing her brother. "You're a twit and I love you. Now, please make amends. I am perfectly happy with Matthew. He makes my heart whole."

"I'm glad to hear it. I shall apologize."

In tandem, they went back to the drawing room, taking their respective seats with Christopher next to Matthew and Grace situated beside Mrs. Morten. Simon and Alicia delighted all with music and song. It had been a tearful reunion, filled with the ever-present Buchanan drama. Hopefully, come the new year and the holidays, hcr luck would change forevermore. Grace took a deep breath and let herself enjoy the company and the feeling of belonging that claimed her. *This is right where I belong.*

Chapter Thirty-Nine

Gathering The Yule Log

M atthew stood before his bedchamber window and peered out at the winter wonderland before him. Fresh snow blanketed the world of Bramley making it appear white and pristine. He was excited about venturing forth into it today to gather the yule log that Mariah had tasked him and Grace with. While it was improper for them to be out together unchaperoned, this was a long-held Christmastide tradition that had been brought back once Harrison married Mariah, and they began to bring life and joy back to Bramley Hall. Every twenty-fourth of December, a couple was to embark into the surrounding forest to choose the yule log. Tying a burgundy ribbon upon the choice, a trio of Bramley footmen would then set out to cut and bring the offering home, where it would then be presented to Mariah as the Countess of Bramley. It would then be lit and burned until Epiphany which was the sixth of January. 'Twas an honor to be chosen for the task. Matthew figured Mariah had chosen him and the fair Grace for the task so that they could be unchaperoned within each other's company, and it made his chest burn eagerly to have a moment alone with Grace.

I must be sure to thank my sly sister when this is over, Matthew mused.

His thoughts turned to Grace's confession the eve prior, to the foul treatment her father had heaped upon her. He'd set aside his feelings of despair and helplessness in order to get through the night. He'd simply let his mind be consumed with the here and now. Grace had looked so broken when discussing it that he wanted to break something. His heart was wounded for her mistreatment and it only intensified his desire to protect her. Come what may, he would remain steadfast and loyal and endeavor to be the one man who would never let her down. This promise lightened his heart and returned him to the earlier excitement he had felt for the day ahead.

It was after breakfast and Grace was donning warmer clothing, as was Matthew. He had arranged for a sleigh to be pulled by two Suffolk Sorrel draught horses. The Earl of Bramley housed an impressive stable with several useful and beautiful equine breeds. The collection of all of the breeds was built with beauty in mind with the exception that a few were solely horses used for estate work. Lately, Harrison had been partnering with the Earl of Hathwell to build both of their lines. Each had stables that boasted of impressive breeds.

The thought of the horses brought back the memories of last night and how thoroughly he enjoyed himself. After the ladies had retired the prior eve, Matthew had joined the men in Harrison's study. They had lounged in chairs and sipped their brandy. When Christopher had taken a seat next to him after his conversation with Grace, Matthew had instantly gathered his wits, ready to rise to whatever the lad would throw his way. The apology had nearly dumbfounded him. Christopher's words, though hastily offered, had been sincere. As they were in the company of others, Matthew was not free to discuss all that he wished to, but he made a plan to seek out the young man before he departed with the Purcellvilles. He had been content being within the company of such fine gentlemen. He grew to like both the Lords Hathwell and Purcellville. They each had a ready wit and were quick to introduce topics of interest. Matthew had taken in the room at large and felt blessed to count such men among his family and friends. He was not used to partaking in pre-bedtime male companionship, and he found that to his surprise, he rather enjoyed it.

With a satisfied sigh, Matthew exited his bedchamber clothed in black trousers, boots, and a fitted tailcoat. The rest of his attire was white except his waistcoat, which was forest green with golden swirls decorating it. He quickly gained the distance to the drawing room. The adults of the party were currently partaking in a game of Charades. Simon was in front of the room using his hands to mime some action or another to cheers and shrieks from the room's other inhabitants. The children were enjoying games of their own in the nursery under the supervision of the nannies for Celeste and Daniel. Grace came into the drawing room after Matthew and he turned to greet her. He took her hand and brought it up to his mouth for a kiss. Grace's eyes lit with merriment and love. Grace's day dress was a shade of gray and the wide black ribbon under her bosom was her only statement of mourning. Her hair was arranged atop her head in the same fashion that both Mariah and Isabelle wore theirs: in the Greek fashion with loose curls and curled tendrils that hung along the sides of their faces.

"I am ready to embark upon an adventure with you today, my love. I have asked the cook for hot chocolate and warm bricks for our feet. There will be blankets to keep us warm as well," Matthew told Grace and then winked at her.

"How very prepared you are, Mr. Morten," she teased.

Matthew bent at the waist and swept his arm out. Grace giggled and gave him a curtsy. Taking her arm and entwining it within his own, Matthew escorted her from the drawing room and they sauntered to the front door, where Billingsley awaited them.

Billingsley bowed before them, "All of the preparations have been readied. Be sure to stick close by as there may be snowdrifts. And if the weather should threaten to endanger you, do make your way back as quickly as you can."

Matthew had never heard the older man speak so much in his entire life. He nodded his gratitude to the butler and assisted Grace into her burgundy cloak and black ribboned bonnet. Then he donned his black greatcoat and topper, opting to leave his walking cane behind. Billingsley opened the front door and a blustery gust met them. He felt the shiver rush through Grace and smiled gently at her.

"We shall endeavor to return as quickly as possible," he told her.

"Pray, do not rush upon my account. I am happy to be with you, solely." Grace reached up and placed a kiss upon his cheek to which they both heard a sharp cough from Billingsley behind them.

Smiling, Matthew led Grace from the Hall and out of doors. The sleigh was standing at the ready, not too far off. The two horses tossed their docile heads in greeting and Matthew helped Grace take her seat in the shiny hunter green sleigh. He walked around the back and seated himself into the sleigh. He arranged the blanket around them, ensuring that Grace was securely tucked in. Taking up the reins of the brown and black beasts, he gave the signal for the horses to walk on.

"'Tis so beautiful." Grace gave him a dazzling smile.

"The view is spectacular, to be sure," Matthew said as his eyes refused to leave her face for the span of a few moments. Grace colored prettily and it could have been attributed to the cold, but he chose to believe that he was the cause. *I love viewing her this carefree. I shall endeavor to make her blush at least once a day.*

They sat in the silence that only two who were truly comfortable with each other could reside in. They took in the white snow coating the trees and laid so peacefully upon the landscape. The horses expertly trotted through the snow and soon they came to meet the treeline. Matthew removed the blanket and exited the sleigh. He walked over to Grace's side and helped her from the conveyance by latching onto her waist with both of his hands and setting her down beside him. Grace reached up onto her tiptoes and before she could place a kiss upon his cheek, he turned his head and met her mouth. The kiss was an exposition of passion that stole his breath as he gave in to its fire. She tasted of honey and tea, and he swore he could easily get drunk off of her glorious kisses. He explored the corners where her mouth met her cheeks and they were equally as delicious. The little gasping noises that Grace made fueled him further. When his tongue met hers, he was the one to groan. Velvet met velvet in a soft caress. This was what passion was all about, the thrill of fire in the veins and the rush that heated him from inside out. He needed to break this kiss, needed to put distance between them. *Heaven me, I shall never tire of this.*

Matthew pulled himself up to his full height as he towered over Grace. She brought her gloved hand up to touch her mouth with a dazed look upon her features. Matthew couldn't help the smug feeling of pure male satisfaction that overtook him.

After a moment, Matthew cleared his throat and reached behind Grace for the basket that had been packed for them. He opened the lid and withdrew the wide burgundy ribbon that would be the marker for the yule log. Returning the basket to its place in the sleigh, he straightened and took Grace's hand in his. Together they began the trek into the trees.

"I have never been tasked to choose the yule log before. I have seen plenty of them burning within a fireplace, so I have an idea of what to look for. If you see any you think would be ideal, do point it out," said Matthew. He was watching where they were going, so that he could foresee any awaiting mishap.

"I have never seen one either, burning or not," Grace told him.

"This shall be a first for you then."

"A first of many in our long lives together."

They trudged through the snow which was tiring for one's limbs. Matthew made sure to assist Grace at any stumbling point and she was always ready to bestow a winning smile upon him.

Matthew let her hand go and took a few steps away from her to a fallen tree. He inspected it and nodded. He liked the idea of a downed tree, so as not to cut short the life of one that was thriving down. "I should think that this one looks promising." He continued to walk around it.

Grace made her way to the tree and shrugged her shoulders. She wasn't an expert and neither was he. But Matthew bent to tie the ribbon around a limb that was jutting away from the trunk.

This is neither too far in nor too large; the footmen are sure to make use of this one, he mused.

He held out his hand for Grace to retake once he was finished tying the knot. Grace readily joined his side and they began the trek back to the waiting sleigh. They had not taken more than a few steps when fat snowflakes began to fall from the sky. The tree's branches were catching most of the falling snow, but here and there some was alighting upon them. Grace held out her gloved hand to catch a snowflake. She tilted her head up to look at the sky. Matthew turned his head to watch her. *She is so very beautiful.*

Grace turned her head to look up at him and he was hit with a lightning bolt straight from his eyes to his heart. He nearly forgot to breathe. The look she gave him made him think that she knew what strange magic she wielded against him. *The minx!*

The snow began to fall in earnest and Matthew encircled Grace's shoulders with an arm as he guided her. The warmth of their bodies so close together was intoxicating.

"I hope we are able to safely get back to the Hall," she voiced.

"Do not worry, my love. We are not too far removed from it."

Grace stopped her progress and bent over. She tried to lean against a tree trunk so that she could bring her booted foot up to inspect. "Oh bother. My lace has broken."

Matthew bent over her foot and tried to repair the damage of the broken lace as best he could. He hoped that his fix would hold until they reached the sleigh. But in truth, if needed, he would gallantly carry Grace the distance in order to keep her warm and safe from the hazards of either falling or allowing snow to enter into her boot. Grace put her foot down and went to take a step and her boot stayed, stuck in the mound of snow before her. She stumbled and Matthew caught her but lost his balance. He had enough time to swing her around so that his back would take the brunt of their fall. Their descent into the snow was shocking. Matthew flung out his arm and knocked it into the tree. All of the collected snow upon the tree's branches abruptly dumped upon them. He blinked his unbelieving eyes as the weight of Grace rested upon him. He was on his back and she was laid out upon him, facing him. They were completely sunken into the powdery substance. When her shoulders began to shake he felt terror flood him. *She is injured, I failed to protect her.*

Musical laughter met his ears. It took his brain a moment to recognize the sound and the fact that Grace was laughing, not sobbing. The wetness of the snow was seeping into his clothing and no doubt Grace's as well. They were unhurt and so he moved to sit up, cradling Grace to his chest. She was so delicate, he took care not to hurt her.

She rose her head up and away from his chest as she continued to laugh. He brought his gloved hand up to brush the snow away from her eyes and only impacted it more as the collected snow from his glove addcd to it. He hastily used his sleeve and made it worse. *Dear Lord!*

"No," Grace paused his actions. "You are only making more of a mess." She slowed her laughter and then took a deep breath as she reached for her skirts and used an underskirt to wipe her face.

"I... my apologies. I did not mean to make it worse," he seriously told her.

"I know. But you should have seen your face. From the moment we began to fall to just now. I never knew one could have such animated reactions cross their face so quickly." She began to giggle again.

Matthew shivered and then stood up. He located her boot and picked it up by the knotted lace. Then he reached down behind Grace's knees and picked her up. She wrapped her arms around his neck and nestled her head under his chin. He instantly rejoiced in the small amount of warmth their bodies radiated together. His fingers were frozen and he was amazed that he had any feeling remaining within them.

"You are my hero. How very dashing, Mr. Morten." She smiled up at him.

Matthew kept his eyes on where they were traveling to avoid any more pitfalls. "I am entirely selfish. This is the fastest way in which to ensure that my frozen bottom and reproductive parts remain intact. So we must make haste if you ever desire your own little ones. I am thoroughly miserable."

Grace brought her hand to her mouth to stifle her laugh, but stopped quickly when she noticed the snow still attached to it. She tried to shake her hand to free it, but gave up. She tilted her head to kiss Matthew's chin. "Does that help to warm you?"

"My love, while I appreciate the sentiment, nothing could warm me. Indeed, I am convinced that I shall never be dry nor warm again."

The snow was fastly falling, but as they neared the sleigh, Matthew gave a sigh of relief. He closed the distance and then placed Grace carefully into the sleigh. He ambled over to his side and once he was seated, he directed the horses to return them to the Hall. Grace reached for the basket and withdrew the hot chocolate offering it first to Matthew. He took a sip and then she took one as well.

"Does that help?" she asked.

"Only a very little," he answered.

If there is one thing I hate it is being cold and wet. How this ethereal goddess can remain so cheerful is beyond me. I want to be grumpy and enjoy my misery, but how can I when she sits beside me? I am eternally enriched by her mere presence.

"How did you lift me as if I weighed nothing more than a mere feather? How sir, do you possess the ability to carry me so far?"

"I retain excellent shape. I learned some exercise and I walk a great deal."

Before more could be said, they were in front of Bramley Hall. A stable lad was walking briskly out to take the reins. Matthew assisted Grace from the sleigh. They rushed through the front door where Billingsley greeted them with an arched graying brow.

Chapter Forty

Joyous Family Moments

Grace quietly listened as Matthew related the events to Billingsley, then they both made their way to their bedchambers. The shivers were racking violently through them both, and Matthew feared that they would catch colds or a lung infection, so he was adamant that they properly attire themselves at once. *He takes such careful thought of my well-being showing me that I am truly close to his heart.* From the disapproving frown upon the butler's face, she didn't think that their explanation warranted his grace. But there was nothing to be done.

The thoroughly sodden lady giggled all the way up the staircase to her bedchamber, parting ways with Matthew. She was soaking wet and had shed her boots once she had entered within. All she had left were a pair of slippers and they would do so long as she didn't need to venture out of doors again. She would have to inquire if there were extra laces available from one of the maids because tomorrow was Christmas Day and she would be attending Church alongside everyone else. She promptly went to the closet, where she pulled her cream day dress from within and placed it upon the large four-poster bed. Then she began to change out of her wet things and dry off. She donned the appropriate underthings and then the dress. It was somewhat sheer, not able to keep heat well, but it could not be helped. It was the best dress she had. Finding her gray shawl, she draped it over her shoulders to help keep in the heat. Grace checked herself once over in the mirror, ensuring her lips were not swollen from all of Matthew's passionate and lovely kisses. *I wouldn't trade this day no matter what, for the time alone was a glorious gift.* Smiling, she strode out of her chamber and down the staircase to where all were gathered.

Quietly setting foot within the drawing room, Grace glanced over at Matthew who had been quicker in donning his new attire. He was currently informing the members within the room that they had returned safely and with success in choosing the perfect yule log. He sat in a wingback chair looking relaxed and at ease. She took a seat beside the fire, wanting to be warm. Isabelle scowled, and Grace suspected that she was taking notice of her change of attire. Isabelle and Mariah exchanged quick glances, though Mrs. Morten peeked around them both, grinning broadly.

"Are you well, my dear?" Mrs. Morten asked. "Matthew came to tell us you both had returned, though he did not give good enough descriptions of the yule log, nor the pretty scene you must have passed through with the falling snow. Men never do such justice, unless he's a poet, and I never bore any of those sorts."

Grace stifled a chortle. "Yes, we are fine. We picked out the yule log and were on our way back when the lace to my boot broke. Matthew attempted to help me re-tie it, only it failed. I stuck my foot back into the powdery snow to take another step when the boot completely failed," she began giggling. "I stumbled terribly and was about to fall upon my face. Matthew went to catch me when, he too, lost his own footing. He attempted to grab a branch and slipped. We fell to the ground in a sharp heap when the tree gave way to its bulk and snow fell on top of us. Poor Matthew had to carry me all the way back to the sleigh and now until I can locate new laces, I am without a pair of boots." She laughed. "His face was animated in so many different emotions that I am still finding humor in the entire situation."

Those in the drawing room chuckled lightly. Finding the humor within the situation had been the correct way in which to discuss it. Grace still felt a slight sting in the humiliation her brother presented her with yesterday, though she was striving to overcome it and make this day a better one.

"It was dreadful!" Matthew exclaimed. "Poor Grace's boot completely collapsed and I had snow in all of the wrong places. 'Tis not a moment I wish to replicate."

Grace pressed the back of her hand to her mouth, trying to stem the wave of giggles that desired to consume her person. She kept picturing his raised eyebrows and the shape of his mouth contorting between a perfect circle to shapes she didn't believe lips could move.

"Dear lady," Matthew addressed, "are you continuing to laugh at my expense?"

"Dear man," she teasingly retorted, "do not forget that, I too, was neck-deep in that same snow. But yes, I am laughing at the manner in which your lips moved at the oncoming torrent of snow. 'Tis something I shall never forget and continually reflect amusingly upon. Though, I shall endeavor to not cause you embarrassment nor irritate you."

Simon's thunderous laugh permeated the room. "Most excellent, Miss Buchanan! I am glad my stuffy brother is pairing himself with such a delight as you. I wish I was there to have witnessed his folly."

Alicia swatted her husband's arm. "Allow me to push you into the snowdrifts dear," she teased.

"Simon quite enjoys the bitterness of the chill," Mrs. Morten added. "He will go out and play in it like a child if you take your eyes off of him for too long. He has even rolled around in it, much like a dog would."

The people in the room nodded unanimously given the outrageous thrill of life Simon was quite known for. She rather liked the man and his wife for their unapologetic nature. They lived their lives how they desired without a woeful thought to society and often not propriety. If they were crass in language or manner, it was never done intentionally nor with malice.

Grace turned, smiling softly at Isabelle who was chatting with Mrs. Morten. She was becoming rather fond of Isabelle and her educated air. From what Matthew had told her, she was quite the accomplished painter, and her husband George, who she found quite humorous, supported his wife's painting endeavors.

Grace scooted a touch closer to the fire, still feeling a pinch of cold from earlier. Not that she would trade the moment nor the kisses for anything in the world, her feet were still quite chilled.

The guests partook in games and various amusements as the day progressed. Luncheon was served with cold meats and various breads and dried fruits. After which, Mrs. Morten retired to her bedchamber for a rest, as did the other ladies. Grace was happy to rest under her coverlet and finally felt warm. The men retired to the game room to play billiards.

Billingsley entered the drawing room, announcing that dinner was readied to be served. Grace rose after Mariah and Harrison had, since the care to formal dining seating etiquette was waived given the closeness of the family gathering. She found herself enjoying this time with everyone. It was certainly the most loving and fun she had ever had. *No wonder Mr. Morten had so loved his family and had spoken so lovingly of them.*

Matthew took the arm of Mrs. Morten while Christopher came to Grace's side to escort her into dinner.

"You do look rather in love, dear sister. Again, I apologize for yesterday and my outburst," Christopher said contritely. "I have since apologized to Matthew and everyone else for that matter. All is forgiven for me, though I feel undeserving if I may not have *your* forgiveness."

"Of course, I forgive you, Christopher," Grace replied softly, "Our family has been through much and I understand how you might have felt."

"You're too good to me, Gracie. I am happy that you have found Matthew and I have given him my blessing to have you."

Grace beamed up at her brother. When he had the chance to do such a thing, she knew not. It must have been when she was staring off into the fire. However it came to be, she was forever grateful her brother was happy for her and approved of the match. She was relieved that there were no ill-feelings between the two most important men in her life.

The children followed in behind her, escorted by the nannies of Celeste and Daniel. The nanny that had accompanied little Bernard had been given time off as her family was located not too far off. It was a family tradition to include the wee ones in the joys of the season and that included dining with them. Grace was seated toward the end of the long table by her family. Matthew came to sit on her left-hand side with Mrs. Morten on the other side of him. She beamed at everyone, thoroughly happy and blessed to be a part of these joyous family moments she knew that she would forever treasure.

Servants came in bustling with trays laden with a thick chowder to start. Conversation flowed happily from one and all about the coming new year, new ideas, desires, and the babe to be born of Simon and Alicia. Grace happily listened, content with still being a companion to Mrs. Morten. And if her luck would have it, a marriage to the man she loved.

The dinner feast was exquisite and Grace was sure she was certain to burst when she finally set down her fork. Billingsley came in, announcing dessert and tea would be served in the drawing room since most were sighing contentedly and boasting full bellies. She, too, felt as if she could not move much more than a few inches. The wholesome food was just what she needed to warm her body.

She glanced over at her siblings, seeing the food still piled upon their plates and the adults looked down the table at them and remarked at how much they were able to consume. It made her even more blessed and grateful to be able to share this with them. If it were just her providing, she would have given them plenty of porridge and not much of anything else. Many years had passed in that exact manner.

"My dear," Matthew leaned in and whispered, "shall we prepare our overstuffed selves to repair to the drawing room?"

"In a moment, my beloved man," she whispered back. "I fear I may not be able to move."

Matthew smiled, slyly sneaking his hand under the table to grasp hers. Ungloved flesh met ungloved flesh bringing butterflies to take flight within her stomach. Grace grinned, keeping a leery eye on the whole of her surroundings since Harrison had caught them both in several interesting predicaments. The man himself was busy, happily conversing with George and Lord Purcellville about the equine breeding for next year.

"I love you," Grace hastily murmured to Matthew. "And I love every sneaking moment I am able to steal away with you."

Matthew beamed at her. "And you, my dearest woman, have taught me to be sneaky. I am finding I quite enjoy the moments I snatch. I beholden them to my heart until I am able to thieve another."

"Together, we shall be very naughty. If we are not careful, we may get a special license thrown into our face; not that I would care," she willingly admitted.

Matthew raised his brows. "That information could be beneficial."

Grace shrugged. "Do with the information as you please," she finished with a smirk.

"Minx."

Harrison and Mariah were the first to rise now that the children had finished their hearty meal. It was the signal that all were welcomed by their hosts in rising from the table. The Buchanan children were entreated to join everyone in the drawing room for dessert and games. Excitedly, they rose, ready to burst through the door. A stern look from Matthew silenced their eager motions and they fell in step behind the adults.

Grace took a seat beside Isabelle, chatting with her about her favorite paintings and what else she planned to paint in Hathwell House. Grace had caught snippets of conversation about how her portraits were bringing a new flair to the country manor.

"You should see her artwork upon the staircase," George proudly remarked. "'Tis a magnificent mural of a valley of flowers and a tree that climbs up the riser on the stairs. I've not seen anything so beautiful or comparable."

"Dearest lord husband, you flatter me," Isabelle gushed.

"I speak only the truth, my darling lady wife. You are masterful and I love to sing your praises as they should be sung."

Grace smiled at the loving couple. She felt completely relaxed within their presence and relished in the ease and banter of conversation. Christopher was well into a game of chess with Thayer and was sorely losing. Matthew, trying as he might to help coach the losing elder brother, could not help him so much as to even win one game.

Harrison rose, procuring another chessboard, challenging Lord Purcellville to a rousing game. The elder man beamed broadly, expressing his notion that he would sweep the floor with Harrison merrily.

Grace peeked over at Matthew, smiling broadly. *How my heart is so happy. I long for many more years spent in company such as this. 'Tis a merry and wonderful holiday season.*

"Grace," Mariah beamed. "Would you care to be on my team for charades?"

"Absolutely, sweet lady," Grace said, taking a seat beside her.

Grace stole another glance at Matthew, unable to help the loving warmth that spread throughout her body just by viewing his person. This was the best part of the holidays: spending time in the loving, joyous company of family.

Chapter Forty-One

A Christmas Promise

After breaking of fasts, Christmas morning was spent in church with Matthew behind the pulpit. His message was upon the blessing of Christ and new life. He made the sermon short because he was as eager as any to partake in the festivities that awaited the parishioners within their own homes. He felt he could do this as long as he brought the reason for the holidays to the forefront.

When all were safely departed, as the snow was again falling from above, he entered into one of the awaiting Bramley carriages and found himself across from his brother and sister-in-law who were the ones tasked to await him, as the others had already taken their leave.

"I say, I thought I should have been bored to tears, but you really do have a certain spark of life that shines through when you give your sermon," Simon greeted him.

"Thank you?" Matthew couldn't keep the question from his voice as he tilted his head.

Simon guffawed merrily and Alicia smiled brightly at her husband.

"You are so stodgy, when not in the presence of Miss Buchanan. 'Tis a pity you are ever without her by your side," Simon remarked.

"She is a wonderfully, amusing individual to be sure," offered Alicia.

"Pray tell, big brother, when shall we be adding a new family member, or should I say new family *members* amongst our ranks?"

"Lest you forget, we are still in mourning for our father." Matthew frowned at Simon.

"Lo, that we are. Society has been so dull with no society at all. Though, we cannot help but mix with the company of my dear in-laws as we reside with them."

"Will you remain with them once your addition arrives?"

"I do believe so. I can think of no better option in which to satisfy us all than to reside all together. My father-in-law quite relies upon us both." Simon said good naturedly.

Matthew nodded his head. He could say that when viewing the family dynamics between the Purcellvilles and the two before him, there was a true accord of harmony that seemed to suit them all well. Not many could say the same.

Before long, the carriage stopped before the manor home that was Bramley Hall. Greenery was hung along the outside giving the snow the perfect backdrop in which to show off the regal setting. A footman met them and opened the door so that Simon could descend first and then turn to aid his wife to alight. Matthew watched as Simon exerted care and consideration for Alicia and to see his younger brother, who had always been so rough about the edges, acting the gentleman to his wife gladdened his heart. They were a couple destined to be together and he had no worries about how the trials of life would affect their union. *They are both so eagerly merry that nothing much could change that, I imagine.*

Taking to the wooden steps, Matthew also departed from the carriage and made his way following after them to be greeted by Billingsley. He handed over his outerwear when it was his turn, then sought out the drawing room where a light luncheon was being served. Christmas dinner was to commence at precisely four o'clock and none wished to be too full to enjoy what had been planned for the feast.

Matthew took a chair beside Grace soon after and held her hand. He cared not who viewed them, because it was almost time for presents to be handed out. Though it was customary that this day was reserved for gift giving to the children, he could not resist bestowing a small trinket to Grace and he also meant to announce their courtship. When he had first caught sight of her this morning his breath had rushed from his body in one long exhale. She had been wearing a day dress of cobalt blue that was trimmed with cream lace along the hem and the neckline. A golden ribbon spanned under her bosom. Grace had informed him in a whisper as she passed him on her way to the long breakfast table, that 'twas a gift from Mariah and his own mother. Her hazel eyes had been sparkling in excitement with her confession. He could find no fault in her attire if the lord and lady of the Hall had bestowed this upon her. Grace was spectacular no matter how she was dressed, but in this beautiful day dress, she was magnificent.

"Let us cease with this waiting at once, the smaller ones deserve to be amused and I mean to share in their enjoyment at once," announced Simon gleefully.

While it was not his place to direct the flow of the festivities, Harrison was not offended. His heart was too large to feel slighted. Though, Matthew shook his head at his brother's antics.

"Indeed," agreed Mariah who rose from the gold padded settee. She directed Billingsley to have the footmen bring in the brown packages wrapped with string in various sizes. The majority were for the Buchanan siblings as the Hathwells and Pembrokes had not traveled with gifts for Celeste nor Bernard in tow. Smaller gifts would be gifted to Daniel, Celeste, and Bernard who never lacked for what they needed. This was to be a day to shower the young Buchanan siblings with not only necessary items but also a few playthings. Mariah had taken notice of what was needed and Matthew had willingly contributed funds to aid her project.

Harrison took over and directed the footmen to place the pile of presents in various places throughout the drawing room. When all was arranged satisfactorily, the children were respectively directed to their section and the merriment commenced.

Grace gripped Matthew's hand tightly, then made her way to seat herself next to Adalie while Matthew settled himself between the twin boys. The paper was quickly removed with exclamations of excitement and surprise. Clothing and outer-wear was quickly piling up, as were new boots, slippers, and robes. Unpacked boxes were tossed to the side. When they had finished with the necessities, which the children were extreme-ly thankful for and expressed much gratitude, the playthings were revealed one by one.

"A doll! One of my very own. Oh, thank you. She is so lovely," enthused Adalie who withdrew the porcelain doll from the box to her little chest. The doll had long curled brunette hair and an adorable pink ball gown. Adalie removed other various forms of rainment from the same box and lovingly touched them all. The worn rag doll she had carried about within the parsonage had been made for Grace by their mother. Grace had lovingly gifted it to Adalie. Tears filled Grace's eyes as she watched her sister; and in watching his Grace, Matthew felt his own eyes sting. *This is more than I ever could have dreamed for them. What a blessing Harrison and Mariah continually are to us all. Thank you, Lord, for giving us such caring and loving family members.*

Next, Adalie unveiled a toy theater that was immediately of interest to Thayer and Fraser. They all proceeded to play for a few minutes until Simon came bounding over and joined in. The miniature stage was intriguing to all who had their own inspection of it. The cardboard characters were colorful and very cheerful.

The boys each were gifted sleds, a backgammon board to share, and the popular game Fox and Geese which was to be played with marbles across the cross-shaped lattice board. There were a few odds and ends for all three of the siblings, but these were the favored gifts.

Mrs. Morten's eyes were alight the entire time. She delighted in the gift-giving which she too had contributed ideas toward. When Adalie stood up and skipped over to her, she welcomed the child to share her chair as they took in all of the beautiful doll's attributes. Matthew had noticed that throughout the day, his Mama had had tears rimming within her eyes. When Adalie returned to her mountain of gifts, Matthew rose and made his way to seat himself in the wingback chair opposite Mrs. Morten who smiled at him.

"I have been terribly remiss, Mama. I apologize for not paying the proper attention to you," he began.

Mrs. Morten reached forward and held out her hand for him to take. "You are wooing your Grace, I have not been neglected. Still, I cannot set aside my longing for your dear Papa. How this scene before us would have brought him so much joy. I cannot help but miss him, especially at this time of the year. I am trying to think of him looking down at us from his place in Heaven. You know, at the oddest times, I still feel his presence and await his arms to enfold around me, and then my mind catches up with my memories, and grief overtakes me. But then, I remind myself of how blessed we have been and still are. I would not leave you behind, nor this world, but how I long to once again take my place within my Mr. Morten's arms." She withdrew her handkerchief and wiped her eyes.

Matthew felt a tear fall and brushed it away. "Dearest Mama, I cannot begin to imagine what you are feeling. I was only his son and the loss has been enough to severely wound me. You have me, and soon Grace, forever at your side. While that is not nearly the same, we shall endeavor to cherish you."

Mrs. Morten smiled through her tears. "Do you not have something else that you should be attending to at this moment? Mayhap a certain small box for a certain lady?"

Smiling and gathering himself, Matthew took a deep breath and nodded. He stood and then leaned down to place a gentle kiss upon his mother's forehead. He strode over to Grace and simply held out his hand for her to take. He didn't speak, only awaited her hand. He was in no doubt that they would be the center of attention, but he could not bring himself to care.

Grace took his hand and he assisted her to gain her feet. He walked her over to the window in the corner, affording them a little privacy. He knew that once he knelt before her, the occupants of the drawing room would likely hush. Engagements were meant to be a private affair just between the couple and if he held any doubt within his heart that he would be refused, he certainly would have asked her in private.

He settled her before the window and then took to bended knee. Grace brought her unclasped hand up to cover her mouth as tears began to fill her hazel eyes. Matthew was correct, all had taken to silence and they were the focus of interest.

"Miss Buchanan, would you do me the very great honor of accepting my hand in holy matrimony? I promise to love and adore you endlessly for all of my days." He cleared his throat, he could have said more to her, but his nerves were making themselves known as his heart began to pound.

"Of course, I shall, you dear man," exclaimed Grace. She attempted to wipe the falling tears from her face, but they were flowing too quickly to catch each one.

Matthew stood, withdrawing his handkerchief, and gently wiped her face. He kissed her upon the lips chastely to which the entire room applauded. The couple smiled at each other and Matthew brought the small blue box from his waistcoat's pocket. He opened it and showed its contents to Grace. Inside lay a ring with silver filigree along the band and it held three sapphires embedded into its center. The light from the window danced along the jewels making them shimmer.

A gasp left Grace's mouth before she ran a finger over it. "'Tis exquisite."

From across the room, Mrs. Morten spoke, "'Twas mine gifted to me by my mother upon my coming out."

"Mama, you had a season?" Mariah inquired incredulously.

"Indeed, I did. But that was before your dear Papa came along and my entire world changed. Some day, when I am not so tired, I shall recount the entirety of my love story to you."

The room was silent. Mrs. Morten had just changed their view of her. While Matthew's parents had not been of the mind to recount their pasts, he had never suspected that his mother's family possessed the funds for such a feat. They had never talked much about Mrs. Morten's family and he had always come to the conclusion that they were deceased. *How very wrong in that assumption I just might be! I always thought that their families had been equally matched.*

"Does this mean there's to be a wedding?" inquired Adalie.

"Indeed it does, poppet," Simon answered her.

"May the calves attend it?"

"Absolutely not." Matthew was quick to answer.

Adalie looked around herself as she frowned.

Matthew withdrew the heirloom and placed it onto Grace's third finger upon her left hand. He was overcome with emotion and had to swallow a few times to get himself under control. He didn't desire to be the brunt of Simon's wit. But his whole world had just forevermore changed. The weight of the responsibility of caring for a family, or caring for the one he would create with Grace, was a solemn vow. He was not an irresponsible man, but still, the weight of this decision was now upon him. And he was equal parts frightened and elated.

"I shall treasure this, always." Grace smiled at Matthew and then at Mrs. Morten who was beaming back at them.

Mrs. Morten inclined her head. "'Tis a perfect match and that ring belongs upon your finger, my dear. Mariah has many of the Bramley jewels to wear and pass down to her children. I wanted to give this to Matthew so that when he proposed, you would have a token of his esteem. I did not disclose where or how I had received it and Matthew being a man didn't think to question its worth. I figured to leave well enough alone." She shrugged.

Taking Grace's hand, he brought her to sit beside him near the fireplace. They were content to watch the others partaking in the games and general merriment. She and Matthew had already gone beyond what was considered acceptable with the engagement so why not let his love wear the token of his affection, even though the exchanging of gifts was just not done. Since they were within the realm of family, it was overlooked. Each of his siblings have found marital bliss and they would not deny him the same happiness. Matthew smiled at Grace gently every time their gazes held.

Billingsley came into the drawing room at exactly four o'clock to announce dinner was served. The couples paired off and made their way from the room and into the dining room, taking their places of choice. Harrison and Mariah took the head places and their guests filled in the empty seats. A feast was set before them in alternating courses of Christmas pies, goose with stuffing, brussel sprouts, carrots, and potatoes. Everyone ate heartily as the merry spirits and conversation flowed.

Epilogue

Love Ever Lasting

U pon the first morning of spring, among a small circle of family
and friends, Grace and Matthew exchanged their vows. It
was a joyous occasion and a touch bittersweet as it was the first
marriage where Mr. Winston Morten was not officiating. Mrs.
Morten was given to tears, as were several who attended, not only
for witnessing such a beautiful match being made, but also for the
sad loss that they continued to feel. It was a lavish affair held within
the grand garden of Bramley Hall where the scent of blooming
flowers and a riot of color greeted one and all. The bride carried
roses and gardenias in her bouquet and wore a pale yellow gown
accentuating her curves with golden flowers sewn along its hem
and neckline. The matching slippers that peeked from beneath her
hem were exquisite. Grace's hair had been arranged high upon
her head with cascading curls framing her lovely flushed face;

Matthew was seated beside his intended. "No matter how much you or Mama try to coax or torture me, I am still adamant about a spring wedding."

Grace rolled her eyes and replied, "Then there is only one thing to be done, my love."

"And pray tell, what is that?"

"I shall simply meet you at the altar upon the first day of Spring." She smiled at him beautifully.

Harrison rose from his place at the head of the table and said, "I would like to say that each of you are always welcome back to Bramley Hall at any time. We've become family and friends. Those whom I count as my favorite people are before me and my heart is full. I am truly a blessed man and it is my honor and privilege to know you."

Matthew smiled at Grace. He could not have expressed better sentiments himself. He was home and all that he desired was before him.

though the bonnet hid most of the effect. Babies' breath had been interwoven throughout her dark tresses and decorated the bonnet as well.

When Christopher, who was donned in his regimental colors, had escorted her down the ivory runner toward Matthew, her breath had been stolen away. Matthew was dressed in fitted black trousers and tailcoat. The fabric of his waistcoat perfectly matched that of her dress. Mariah had arranged this pairing beautifully. His black boots and carefully knotted cravat were just as fashionable. 'Twas the smile upon his face that stole her breath. Had she ever seen such joy upon his features? She felt sure that his expression was mirrored upon her own face.

A friend of Matthew's from a neighboring town had led the ceremony and when called upon, the bride and groom eloquently exchanged their vows. Matthew bestowed a simple band of gold onto Grace's finger. Those gathered cheered joyfully, decked out in their wedding finery.

The wedding breakfast was an equally grand affair, and for a fortnight after, the wedded couple resided in the dowager house upon the estate. They were loath to be separated from Mrs. Morten and the Buchanan siblings by the space of many miles. It had been arranged that while they took their time becoming intimately familiar with each other, Mrs. Morten and the children would extend their visit to the Hall.

With the exception of Simon and his wife, their near and dear had witnessed their promises to each other. Alicia was nearing her confinement and from what had been written, she was most uncomfortable and unable to travel the distance to attend the wedding. Simon had been adamant about staying beside his wife.

Despite some small antics from the children, none involving the harm of Matthew, the days since Christmastide had been pleasant. They had settled more into their lives together and grew to care for each other as a true family. Grace had still snuck into Matthew's study to steal kisses, much to the man's delight. But they used caution to never compromise the other.

On the last eve of their stay in the dowager house, Matthew took Grace into his muscular arms and laid his head atop of hers. He breathed deeply and she smiled. They were content and happy. All that they could have wished for was before them. They looked out at the garden, magnificently lit by the light of the moon. Everything was peaceful and still.

"I shall feel remiss to have to share you upon the morrow," Matthew admitted with a sigh.

"You have had me all to yourself for a fortnight."

"'Tis not enough. I have discovered something which I fear has forevermore changed me."

Grace turned to face him and inquired, "And what is that?"

"I cannot bear to leave your side. I have become some besotted pup. I thought that given time, my addiction to you would lessen and a comfortable existence would take root. I am sorry to say that I was wrong. For the more I have of you, the more I want. 'Tis quite the quandary."

"Indeed? Do you regret me?" she teased.

"Nay, my lovely wife, I only regret that I must share you. But I shall man up and carry on. Is not that what one must do?"

"I suppose, dear husband. But you are missing one very important thing."

"Am I?"

Nodding her head, she reached up to clasp her arms behind his head. "You have the entirety of myself at your disposal tonight. As you will each night of our lives together."

"Quite right you are. So I shall man up and take my bride back to our bed where I shall treasure you and give you every reason to seek me out through the daytime hours for more kisses." He waggled his dark brows at her.

Grace giggled. "Why not just kiss me now?"

"Excellent idea, my love, I believe that I shall."

He brought his warm, moist mouth to hers and nibbled her lips as he guided them backward away from the large bay window. This was how she desired to spend her last evening with her new husband. Within his arms and with the promise of a love everlasting.

Love That Blooms

T he day Christopher Buchanan's life changed had begun ordinarily enough. He'd been serving under the esteemed Lord Purcellville for the span of six years and found that the life of an officer greatly suited him. As no lady had ever gained his notice enough to intrigue his mind nor capture his heart, he remained a bachelor. Christopher was content to bid his time until love blossomed between himself and his undiscovered lady love.

Christopher found himself before the book shop, decorated in colors of olive and cream, situated in the center of Town. Lord Purcellville had given him the task of procuring a collection of military volumes that the proprietor had set aside for him. He entered the establishment and made his way to the wooden counter. Gingerly he rang the bell and waited.

From off to the side, he heard a muttered, distinctly feminine, voice. With raised brows, he set out to locate the source of trouble. His eyes rounded as they came to rest upon the scene before him. There stood a ladder, and perched precariously at its top was the most breathtakingly beautiful woman he had ever gazed upon. Her blonde hair was elegantly arranged atop her head with loose curls softly framing her heart-shaped face. Her full lips were pressed together in a determined line as she leaned to the side, trying to shelve the errant tome. Thinking her situation was dangerous, he silently stepped forward until he halted at the ladder's side. He dared not make a peep for fear of startling the lady. Ever so slightly he shifted his weight just as she finally set the book into its spot. The floorboard creaked, giving his presence away.

With a gasp, the goddess looked down from on high, shrieking frightfully as she threw her weight in the opposite direction. Christopher rushed to the ladder's other side and caught the petite lady as she tumbled down.

Her bright emerald eyes gazed at him with utter shock at the near mishap, then quickly changed to an expression of gratitude.

"Are you alright?" he inquired in a rich baritone.

She took a moment to answer him, and her delicate brows furrowed. Then she nodded.

"You really must take more care when lifted up so high."

"I wouldn't have nearly killed myself if *you* hadn't sneaked up on me!" the unnamed goddess bristled.

"I did ring the bell," he smirked at her.

She scoffed at him as she rolled her mesmerizing eyes. "Do you suppose that you could put me down now? This is highly improper."

What would she do were I to refuse? Though I realize the scandalous nature of cradling her in a public place, I'm loath to let her go. She's soft and delicate, though there's a delightful fire that simmers within. How may I feed the flames to see what passion she possesses?

"Now sir, if you'd be so kind." She brought her small hands up against his chest to push him away. But they rested there instead. Their gazes locked onto each other; searching for what he couldn't say. His focus shifted to her rosebud-shaped lips and he brought his face closer to hers.

"I say! What is happening here, Louisa?" demanded an older gentleman with graying hair and blazing emerald eyes that threw daggers at Christopher.

Now, she was quick to push against his chest. Reluctantly he set her upon her feet, not stepping away as propriety dictated. The situation was beyond that now.

"*Papa!* I fell from the ladder. This officer did us a great service in catching me. He bore my weight as if I was nothing more than a feather," she breathlessly confessed.

"Is that so?" The elder gentleman folded his arms, the glare intensifying.

Christopher wondered why she spared him the rightful wrath of her father when she'd been so irate at him just mere moments ago. She might have been correct; if not for him, she might not have fallen. But she might just as easily have broken her beautiful neck. He had been so close to tasting her sensuous lips. Did she too feel the pull between them?

Squaring his shoulders, Christopher stood to his full height. He might have been impetuous but he was not some green lad and he wouldn't stand for a dressing down. He'd vowed to never let another man rule over him as he'd suffered enough abuse at the hands of a drunken father. Nor would he allow this father to treat his daughter with disrespect. "'Tis just as your daughter has stated," he said, and cleared his throat. "Is the lady free upon closing time to discuss our courtship?"

"Aye, free she may be, but not for the likes of *you*," the proprietor hissed.

"Now, a moment if you please!" begged the young woman.

"*You will hold your tongue!*" bellowed her father.

Christopher closed the distance separating himself from the man, whom he towered over. "*Careful sir.* I am an officer in the regiment. My record is spotless and there are none that could naysay that. Your daughter is innocent. I humbly apologize for any lack of decorum I've demonstrated. Truth be told, I was dumbstruck when I spied your daughter. 'Twas my intention to see her to safety and I'll use the same care now with her reputation. Again, I mean to make amends and properly court your daughter. My intentions are honorable." Christopher stared the man down. The thought of parting from the beautiful woman's side sent a wave of crushing despair through him.

The elder man's jaw ticked. "I see you will not be swayed in this. If Louisa wishes it, I shall agree."

The gentlemen turned their attention to the young woman who spoke. "He has the kindest eyes I've ever beheld. I fear that if I were to let him go, I'd be making the greatest of errors. I very much wish to see if something extraordinary blooms between us."

The smile that lit Christopher's face swept into his heart. Surely, this was how love blooms.

Also by: E.A. Shanniak

Alien Prince Reverse Harem – Ubsolvyn District: 1. Stalking Death - *prequel* 2. Securing Freedom 3. Saving Home

Clean Fantasy Romantic Fantasy – Zerelon World Novella: 1. Aiding Azlyn 2. Killing Karlyn 3. Reviving Roslyn

Clean & Sweet Western Romance – Whitman Western Series: 1. To Find A Whitman 2. To Love A Thief 3. To Save A Life 4. To Lift A Darkness 5. To Veil A Fondness 6. To Bind A Heart 7. To Hide A Treasure 8. To Want A Change 9. To Form A Romance

Harlequin Fantasy Romance – Castre World Novel: 1. Piercing Jordie 2. Mitering Avalee 3. Forging Calida 4. Uplifting Irie 5. Braving Eavan 6. Warring Devan 7. Hunting Megan 8. Shifting Aramoren – *short story* 9. Anchoring Nola – *short story*

Slow Burn Enemies to Lovers Paranormal Romance – Dangerous Ties: 1. Opening Danger 2. Hunting Danger 3. Burning Danger

About E.A. Shanniak

E.A. (Ericka Ashlee) Shanniak is the author of several successful series – A Castre World Novel – Whitman Western Romances – Dangerous Ties. She's hobbit-sized, barely reaching over 5ft tall on a good day. When she wears her Ariat boots, not only does she gain an inch, she's then able to reach the kitchen cabinets to get all the snacks. When not in her fox den (writing cave), Ericka loves to spend time with her family – outside having firepits with wine, camping, fishing, or zooming in her jeep on another Midwest adventure. Ericka loves all the animals her kids bring home including numerous barn cats and their newfound kitten named Stormy. Ericka works in the Register of Deeds office residing in a small town in Comanche County with her supportive, wonderful husband, two amazingly compassionate kids, and all the animals (including those her husband knows nothing about yet).

Also by: Michelle Helen Fritz

A Bramley Hall Regency Romance
Love At Last
Love That Lasts
Love Ever Lasting

Shades of Bramley Hall Regency Romance
Love Holds True

Courts & Curses
A Court Of Broken Dreams and Curse
A Court of Broken Promises and Nightmares
A Court of Broken Hopes and Wishes

About Michelle Helen Fritz

Michelle Helen Fritz began her literary career as a personal assistant to Indie authors. She enjoys being immersed in the process of turning an idea into a complete and published book. Michelle loves to write about dashing heroes and the compelling women that tempt them with a bit of intrigue and an abundance of romance, creating swoon-worthy characters and stories for her readers to enjoy. Occasionally, her characters talk to her and change the entire plot. Maryland is where her humble abode resides, housing her four home-schooled children along with her jaunty hero-husband who makes all her dreams come true. Michelle fully believes in happily-ever-afters and wishing upon stars.